PENGUIN BOOKS

The Plumb Trilogy

Maurice Gee is one of New Zealand's best-known writers, for both adults and children. He has won a number of literary awards, including the Wattie Award, the Deutz Medal for Fiction, and the New Zealand Fiction Award. He has also won the New Zealand Children's Book of the Year Award. In 2003 he received an inaugural New Zealand Icon Award and in 2004 he received a Prime Minister's Award for Literary Achievement.

Maurice Gee's novels include the *Plumb* trilogy, *Going West*, *Prowlers*, *Live Bodies* and *The Scornful Moon*. He has also written a number of children's novels, the most recent being *The Fat Man*, *Orchard Street* and *Hostel Girl*.

Maurice lives in Wellington with his wife Margareta, and has two daughters and a son.

The
PLUMB
Trilogy

PLUMB • MEG • SOLE SURVIVOR

Maurice Gee

PENGUIN BOOKS

PENGUIN BOOKS
Published by the Penguin Group
Penguin Group (NZ), 67 Apollo Drive, Rosedale
North Shore 0632, New Zealand (a division of Pearson New Zealand Ltd)
Penguin Group (USA) Inc., 375 Hudson Street,
New York, New York 10014, USA
Penguin Group (Canada), 90 Eglinton Avenue East, Suite 700, Toronto,
Ontario, M4P 2Y3, Canada (a division of Pearson Penguin Canada Inc.)
Penguin Books Ltd, 80 Strand, London, WC2R 0RL, England
Penguin Ireland, 25 St Stephen's Green,
Dublin 2, Ireland (a division of Penguin Books Ltd)
Penguin Group (Australia), 250 Camberwell Road, Camberwell,
Victoria 3124, Australia (a division of Pearson Australia Group Pty Ltd)
Penguin Books India Pvt Ltd, 11, Community Centre,
Panchsheel Park, New Delhi – 110 017, India
Penguin Books (South Africa) (Pty) Ltd, 24 Sturdee Avenue,
Rosebank, Johannesburg 2196, South Africa

Penguin Books Ltd, Registered Offices: 80 Strand, London, WC2R 0RL, England

Plumb first published by Faber and Faber in 1978. First published in New Zealand by
Oxford University Press in 1979. Published in paperback by Penguin Books New Zealand
in 1991.

Meg first published by Faber and Faber in 1981 in association with Penguin Books.
Published in paperback by Penguin Books New Zealand in 1983.

Sole Survivor first published by Faber and Faber in 1983 in association with Penguin
Books. Published in paperback by Penguin Books New Zealand in 1984.

The Plumb Trilogy first published by Penguin Group (NZ), 1995
This edition published in 2007
1 3 5 7 9 10 8 6 4 2

Copyright © Maurice Gee, 1978, 1981, 1983

The right of Maurice Gee to be identified as the author of this work in terms of
section 96 of the Copyright Act 1994 is hereby asserted.

Printed in Australia by McPherson's Printing Group

ISBN 978 0 14 300756 2

A catalogue record for this book is available
from the National Library of New Zealand.

www.penguin.co.nz

In memory of
James and Florence Chapple
and
Lyndahl and Len Gee

PLUMB

1   On the morning of my departure I stood by the open window with my trumpet to my ear, hoping to hear the thrush in Edie's plum tree. That bird and its forebears have sung to me for thirty years. I remind myself that other families than mine have made their home in Peacehaven. On that morning though the bird was silent, so I put my trumpet aside and went along to breakfast. Although on festive or family occasions I carry the instrument with me, more to satisfy expectations than out of a wish to hear, in normal times I'm allowed my aural blackness. Indeed, I enjoy it. It sharpens my other senses, especially my sense of otherness.

    I had no sooner sat myself down than Meg was at my elbow, shouting something in my ear, of which I heard only the word "see". From her gestures I understood she wanted me to follow her to the kitchen, where I would find something I must admire. Her face was pink and her eyes held the expression of shy delight she takes from Edie. That expression, and her workworn hands, Edie's hands, are thorns of remembrance. They start in me a pleasurable pain. It prompts me to my journey, my gathering in of my children; prompts me to a searching of my past.

    I had the wish to please her and so followed the poor girl to the kitchen. Her pleasure, I saw, rose from the brand-new object in the corner: an electric stove. Contraptions, engines, have no interest for me, but they have the habitual effect of bringing Emerson to mind—my son, not the great transcendentalist for whom, laughably, he is named. The effect is so strong in fact that I looked about the room for him. Of all my children he is the strangest to me; although I recognize and hail in him enthusiasm, faith. He dropped me a letter one morning from his Gypsy Moth, flying not a hundred feet above my lawn. The blossoms fell from the plum tree in a fright.

    "Oven," Meg shouted, opening the door of the stove and

1

showing me its polished insides. "Elements," and she raised three fingers to show their number—on one of which a pot of porridge boiled glueily. The thing, I saw, was called Atlas. There was even a picture of the god kneeling under his burden. These are promiscuous days. Atlas, Vulcan, Milo, Thor. I expect before I die to see some contraption named Jehovah: a wireless perhaps.

"Scrimp and save," Meg pronounced, recounting the history of her purchase, and I nodded approvingly, for I was glad to see her brought to life. The things she had wanted had once been very different. She stirred the porridge and shifted the pot to the back of the stove. Then she turned a knob, cutting off the flow of electricity. I saw a further sign of approval was needed and as a tribute to the magical qualities of the machine I laid my hand on the element, expecting to find it cold. The pain was like being bitten by some fierce animal. I cried out and Meg shrieked and for five minutes the house was upside down. Raymond and Rebecca (come running at the noise) ferried me to the bathroom and sat me on the edge of the bath, into which, half fainting, I almost tumbled. They coated my burn with vaseline and wound a bandage round it. Outside the door Fergus gave poor Meg a dressing down. He's careful of my person. Knowing that Peacehaven comes to him and his wife when I die, he makes it a matter of principle to keep me alive.

We had cold porridge for breakfast. Meg lacked the confidence to re-heat it. I explained my belief that electric stoves cooked with electricity not with heat, and Bobby shouted down my trumpet (fetched by Rebecca, for this was a special occasion) that really I didn't belong in the nineteen-forties. I agreed. I agreed that one of the new hearing aids would serve me better than my antique trumpet. But they could not get me to agree to try one. My trumpet I see as companion to Edie's coal range, still in its place by Atlas in the kitchen. Neither will ever bite me.

After breakfast they were all away: Bobby to the teachers' training college, Rebecca to her job selling buttons, Raymond to school, and Fergus in his shining new van, with blowtorch, bag of tools, quantities of lead pipe and lavatory basins, off to some brand-new housing estate. *Fergus Sole, Plumber.* A good and useful man, enjoying his first taste of success, and dying a little to his wife and children daily. Meg, the most vulnerable of my girls, the most open in soul, married for love.

I have known much disappointment in my children, seeing so many of them disappoint themselves. Although they have moved on the margins of my life, each has known his path to the centre, and all have come, all have taken comfort in their need. They have brought little comfort to me, but that is no proper complaint. I have never wished for comfort, but for thorns, for battle in the soul's arena. I have had what I wished for. And the thorns that prick me now are the thorns of remembrance. Children, followers. Along that other way, where I found so few to accompany me, and for distances so short, I reached my goal. The striving is done. I turn at my end to other cares. Life on the margins has a pain the sharper for my knowledge that here those I love are in a state of exile.

2   After breakfast I walked in the orchard: Edie's orchard. She was always the planter, the one who wished to put down roots. For me movement and stillness are in the spirit, going forth and coming home for the soul. The most I can say of Peacehaven (the name Edie chose) is that it was pleasant to have my body lodged in this spot during thirty years of my journeying. If I love the place now it is because I loved Edie.

I crossed the little brick bridge beyond the plum tree, pausing to look at the eel-haunted creek where my younger children and my children's children swam. Meg had slipped some crusts into my pocket for the eels but with my burned hand I could not take them out. I do not know why I enjoy calling these creatures up from their deeps. Slimy and snake-like, they drive themselves through the water like thoughts better not admitted. Do I still have evil passions? No! I have conquered. My ideal was Wordsworth's, plain living and high thinking, and all I have ever known of lust or rage or envy or greed I have plucked from my heart and put from me and the very places where they had their life I have burned in the cleansing flame. It is not pride that speaks.

The eels that come for my crusts are God's creatures like the thrush in the plum tree. How foul this new symbology of the mind that sees a creature of darkness in every thought. Even the poets, the half-poets of this poor crippled time, creep about on all fours:

> I think we are in rats' alley
> Where the dead men lost their bones.

No! and again, no! Men must be fed with Angel's food. Only then will they arrive at God.

Enough. This is not to my purpose. I walked in Edie's orchard, among the ripening fruit. It has been my habit to walk there daily. Sheep graze among the trees in place of the house-cow Robert milked. Robert (for whom today's rough Bobby is named). The bravest of my sons, but the simplest too, not understanding his way but taking it from instinct. I walked by the apple tree from which he had fallen and broken his collar bone. A fearless climber after fruit, but always the ripest was for me or his sisters or Edie. He took the one part of my way his understanding made open to him and spent the war behind spiked wire as I spent part of that other war in Lyttelton jail. He rests now, on his community farm, among the "God-fearing" folk who have taken him in. He tends the sheep, milks the cows, prunes the fruit trees, gathers the honey. Quiet is all he desires. Robert, my son, bruised beyond his endurance. The rest of his life is a convalescence.

I walked along by the creek or stream—Edie in the Englishness imposed on her by her mother would have it stream, would have the paddock field, would even have the tea-tree picnic hut Robert built on the lawn a summer-house. She never adjusted to colonial ways, least of all the ways of her rough sons. Rough sons? Oliver, dry Oliver, rough? But Emerson, Willis, Robert, their edges caused her pain. My Edith was a lady—gentleness, fineness, were the air she breathed. Every act of hers was a spiritual act, an act of praise. In her weariness, in her pain, she praised; scouring pans, mopping floors. Giving birth, she praised. But a sense of their bodies was natural to my sons. How in this rough land could it be other? Their loudness struck Edie in the face, their language, their ugly vowel sounds, drove her out of the room. But she fought for them. I brought my sons to her by their ears; and then got out of the way into my study, or into my deafness. She set their hands on the ivory keys. Their fingers thumbed out tuneless sound. And Edie wept inside herself for their stillborn sensibilities. Oliver, though, tried hard. A mannerly lad. No pine-gum on his fingers. He is a good square pianist to this day. Edie, I do not criticize you. I would not have had one hair of your head different. I understand the approval you felt for him; as I understand your love for that other, the one I do not name. Who died to me on that morning long ago.

Let it stand.

I walked by the hollow where the stump of the quince tree rots. I neither looked nor turned my face away. Wife, I know to whom you were going on those mornings you pulled on your gloves, settled your hat, gave me your sad apologetic smile that set me at naught. I do not judge you. I understand your love for the person, your son. Alfred. My hand does the work. I pray that one day I may speak his name.

In the hollow past the quince stump bracken grows, young pine trees raise their heads. This is a lesson to me. Along these paths I may travel to the Light that shines in my life in every place but this.

3 My hand was causing me pain. I lifted the edge of the bandage. Great blisters had come up under the vaseline. A good thing, I thought, it isn't my writing hand; for being deprived of that activity would be as damaging to me as being deprived of food.

In fine weather I write in the summer-house. From the top of the orchard I saw its skeleton roof, and saw too Meg pegging out washing on the line. In this world, I thought, there are so few voices and so many echoes. Goethe; and I smiled at my quickness in turning him up. But I wanted my notebook under my hand and my pencil busy. I walked down the line of the stone wall, scattering the silly sheep, and along the path by the Butters's rose garden. Merle was kneeling on a cushion, snipping with her secateurs, and Graydon forking compost by the greenhouse. I stepped off the gravel and went along quietly. These two have been kind neighbours; and great robbers of my time. I hoped to get off on my trip without their goodbyes.

But once in the summer-house I found my thoughts no longer worth recording. I sat there remembering Edie. Her presence in this place is like the scent of a flower or rustle of a leaf. I see her beautiful hands on the worn yellow keys, see the wave of her hair, her gentle eyes; and see her lips parted breathlessly over the beauty of a Chopin nocturne—but not fully willing, as at some struggle in her puritan soul.

4 Mrs Hamer, a widow, was a teacher of pianoforte, and Edie, her younger daughter, assisted her. Florence, the older girl, was devoted to good works, and indeed a more selfless and patient creature I have never known. She was a doer of good and kindness, an angel of mercy. This is Edie's terminology, and I adopt it without hesitation. I am aware of modern "discoveries" that would see in Florence's long life of service—the sitting up with the sick and dying, the sewing of garments for the poor—a form of self-punishment, a species of religious hysteria. Cleverness passes for knowledge in these times. Florence was good and kind. What more needs to be said? She put self to one side and discovered her real self in loving others and in loving God.

As for her disappointment, it took place before I met the family. The story Edie knew was only part of it. Mrs Hamer, that sharp and clever woman, knew the rest. Florence was nineteen and engaged to a young Church of England curate; a promising young man from all accounts, and handsome, easy in his ways, attentive to his elders, jolly with the young. He was very popular, and she very much in love. One day this young man vanished, simply vanished. He took nothing from his rooms, no clothing, no books. Only his bicycle was gone. The police began enquiries. But at the end of two or three days his bishop received a letter. The young man explained that he had undergone a crisis of soul, had come to understand he had no calling for the church. He had thought it better in the circumstances simply to take himself off. He had left Christchurch and was leaving the country.

Florence's letter—it arrived in the same post—told another story. He had met a young lady, the curate said, and fallen in love with her, and he wished all arrangements for the coming wedding cancelled. He was leaving, he said, for Australia, where his wife-to-be would join him presently. A tale that need not have been so cruel. I doubt he was as gifted as people believed. The truth, never known to Florence or Edie, but told me in confidence by Mrs Hamer, who had not wished me to believe another young lady preferred to one of her girls, was this: the curate was bicycling in the country when he found it necessary to answer a call of nature. He retired behind some bushes, looked about to be sure of his privacy, made water, and turned, buttoning up, to find himself observed by a party of ladies out picking wild raspberries—wives and daughters of members of his church. In that time, the eighteen-eighties, in the place of his curacy, a suburb of well-to-do tradespeople and professional folk aping the genteel ways of Home, he took his only course. He mounted his bone-shaker, rode off down that country road, and through the town of Christchurch, and on again, and stopped somewhere to write two letters, and for all I know is riding still. And Florence, jilted, kept to her room, refused to go to church; but emerged at last to find a life that suited her very well.

Edie was deeply affected by her sister's disappointment. For several years she believed she would never marry. By the time I met her she was not so sure, but no young man had yet found the way to her heart. It was, in truth, a way that was strait, a daunting way to the frivolous and shallow. She was at that time troubled by

7

the rituals of her church. Something in them too much of the world had begun to repel her. At the very moment when I was finding myself attracted by the austerities of Presbyterian worship, she felt its simplicity making a deep call to her. So that when we came to speak—but I go too fast. There was first a different meeting: that first tremulous delighted touching across the gulfs of loneliness. Popular literature has debased the term "love at first sight". ("He's so handsome." "She's so glamorous.") I use it to describe a spiritual meeting. When I first saw Edie I knew I was looking at my Wife; and she at her Husband. The moment was sacramental. (Of course, we were too young and too immersed in the orthodoxies of the time to phrase it so then.)

I saw her first on a hot Saturday afternoon in Linwood, Christchurch. February 4, 1893. I was fielding on the long leg boundary in a cricket match. Let me say now, I have always been impatient of those who sneer at sport. Nothing better promotes deep and free breathing, which is the basis of health. And indeed a physical skill has its own beauty; and benefits the mind, which it exercises. Walking, cycling, fishing, cricket, bring a rare conjoining of our mental and physical being—but I preach; another of my sports. Let me just say, I loved my cricket. I was no batsman but a tireless bowler of what today is known as the in-swinger. My team-mates called me the steady little trundler. And there I was on the boundary, resting between overs, when Edie and Florence and Mrs Hamer walked by.

I saw a young woman fashionably dressed, in the full-sleeved and be-ribboned style of that day, but—I could not see how she managed it—quietly dressed. She carried a parasol that kept her face in shade. From that well of coolness there looked into me the finest hazel-brown eyes I had ever seen, eyes full of calmness and purity and determination and womanly modesty. How can I describe their quality? Beneath a brow both delicate and noble, the eyes of saint, nurse, mother, helpmeet. Wife. Companion of my soul.

And what did those eyes see? A young man in cricket flannels and cap, a rather sweaty young man (to you his sweat was perspiration, Edie); short in stature, red of hair, small in hand and foot. Grass stains on his whites, I believe, and an untidy belt holding his trousers up. An undistinguished young man (to whom Mrs Hamer gave no second glance). But in *his* eye the knowledge of a meeting.

5   I bowled another over, took a wicket. On the boundary, under the trees, one of the ladies softly clapped her hands. Her companions drew her on and out of the park.

I wasted no time in finding who she was, discovered in fact before the day's play was over by the simple means of questioning a legal acquaintance of mine, an international batsman, who had raised his cap to the ladies as they strolled by.

And so on Monday evening I presented myself at Mrs Hamer's house as a student of pianoforte. That clever lady was not long deceived. Before half the lesson was done I made the suggestion that a person of my poor abilities had best be left to an assistant. She understood, gave me such a sharp appraising look that it was all I could do not to describe my prospects on the spot; and rose with dignity, saying, "Very well, Mr Plumb. My daughter has a good way with beginners." She left me trembling by the piano in that little front parlour, and returned in a moment with Edie, whom she introduced and left with me. There was a good deal of nonsense about Mrs Hamer, but none in matters of real importance.

Edie trembled too. She sat down at the piano and asked me to sit beside her.

"Do you know the keyboard, Mr Plumb?"

My mother had taught me that much, so for the next few moments I answered her shy questions sensibly. But she stopped them soon. Her nature was too serious for pretence. Looking at me straight, she said, "I don't think you've come here to learn the piano, Mr Plumb."

"No, Miss Hamer. I've come to see you."

"Yes, that's what I thought."

"Do you want me to come again?"

"I think I would like that. But I shall have to tell mother."

"She knows already, Miss Hamer."

Edie smiled. "My mother is very clever." But she was not untroubled. "You are very good in your cricket, Mr Plumb. Do you care for it a great deal?"

"There are things I care for more." She thought games frivolous. "It's a diversion from my studies."

"What are you studying?"

"The law."

She was neutral about that. I think she wanted to ask me my church; but instead she said, "And do you like music? Or was that just a pretence?"

"I like it." And because, in spite of our knowledge of being joined, we laboured a little, I asked her to play something for me.

She chose a Chopin nocturne. I saw her lips open as I have described: the music enraptured her and yet she was disturbed that beauty should exist for itself. She was, I came to know, a person eminently practical, of that religious nature that finds its way to God through man and concerns itself with works ahead of faith. In this she was not a natural Presbyterian. She seemed so, as I did, for we were attempting to come before God less by strenuous labour, less by subjective faith, than through a form of worship. It took us many years to discover our error.

But our similarities we discovered at once, in that little front parlour, on the double stool. (Her mother was not in too much of a hurry and made us play the game out.) The nocturne done, we talked about our parents. She found my story sad. My mother reminded her of Mrs Hamer. Both had been widowed in middle life but had not let it get them down. Both were very much concerned with appearances.

6 Mr Hamer died when Edie was thirteen. He remained when I met her ten years later the man against whom all other men were tried. His chief quality, she said, was kindness; though its greatest measure, I suspect, was saved for his younger daughter. Because of his kindness she overlooked his failings (her mother did not), the worst of which, in any case, was simply bewilderment in the face of the world. He left his wife in what we called "straitened circumstances", although the house was secured to her. The garden, large and beautifully tended, supplied many of the family's needs and would have brought in money if the widow had not been too proud to sell its produce. Edie and I spent many happy hours in it in the summer and autumn of 1893. Our favourite place was a wooden seat under the quince tree in what Mr Hamer had called his fruit garden, a term Edie used too in preference to orchard. From there we looked down through the trees, cherry and white heart and pear, greengage plum and prune and almond, and over the patch of gooseberries and black and red currants, to the vegetable garden, the woodshed and potting shed, and the house, overgrown with scarlet japonica and jessamine and rambling roses.

"My father gave way to mother in everything," Edie said. "But he never would come in out of the garden, even when she grew angry. We sometimes had visitors and father would stay out here with his trees. He used to come round to the front gate as they were leaving with baskets of plums. One old lady thought he was the gardener. Poor mother."

Mrs Hamer possessed the most delicate of mechanisms for what I can only call the measurement of her due. But though no one would ever have judged her less than a lady there was a streak of coarseness running through her. It distressed Edie; for it was moral coarseness, and pride its manifestation. When some unfortunate soul came to the door and asked to buy fruit it was

11

pride not generosity that made Mrs Hamer say, "We don't sell fruit but I will give you some." And pride it was, not concern for them, that made her keep her daughters out of service in the days of her worst need before Mr Hamer's affairs were put in order. "No woman," she said, "shall be able to say that one of my daughters ever worked for *her*." The teaching of music was acceptable for a lady. I paid for the lessons I never took before Edie and I graduated from parlour to garden; but paid unknown to her, in a moment carefully engineered by her mother; paid with embarrassment, in a most thick-fingered way, into a performance quite beautiful of refusal by murmur along with acceptance by hand. Well, she had the need, just as she had need of her sense of her station; and, too, of her belief that in marrying Walter Hamer she had married beneath her.

This was the thing that hurt Edie most. Her father, her gentle loving father who had carried her through the garden teaching her flower names, who had built her a swing in a pear tree and bought her dolls to play with when her mother turned neighbour children away at the gate. Poor Edie, poor lonely girl, with her sister away at a "school for young ladies", she would sweep under her swing, put a clean sack on the ground, and with her dolls on her lap sit and swing for hours, until that ailing kindly man, already unable to face the world, came from among his vegetables and walked in the flower garden with her, saying, "Japonica, Edie. And this is jessamine, my mother's favourite flower. It has a beautiful scent, especially at night." He died, and she remembered him and loved him all her life.

She loved her mother too but was troubled by a suspicion that she did so out of duty. The nearest she came to rebellion was after her father's death when Mrs Hamer refused to let her work in his garden. That was no occupation for a lady. She might pick fruit from time to time, no more. But Edie wanted to do what he had done. She wanted to dig, she wanted to plant and weed and prune and spread manure. Gardening, she knew, was more than a matter of collecting ripe fruit in a basket. It was a moral act, a giving as much as a taking. It was a discipline and a duty and its rewards were not in harvesting alone. More than once in later years I heard her tell one of her sons that he could cure his boredom or discontent by getting out into the garden and doing some digging. But in her mother's house she obeyed her mother's rules. So for several years the gardens became a wilderness. When money was a little more plentiful Mrs Hamer hired a man but his best efforts never managed to restore them to the perfection they had known under Walter Hamer.

Edie inherited many of her mother's tastes and attitudes. She loathed common-ness, poor speech, expressions that were inexact or coarse. She disliked showiness in dress. Colours that were too bright or varied she called a peacock display. Her rings and brooches were always modest. She hated cheap lace, or jewellery that was not the real thing. She used to say, in her mother's voice, "Better none than imitation." I do not think she would have cared for my mother.

7 For that dear lady was a lover of bright things—she collected them like a magpie. Perfume, of which Edie was sparing, she spilled about her person in a most extravagant way. My mother's arrival was always heralded by an olfactory wave of the boldest, the most unsubtle and sugary kind. Her dresses were gay and her hats—I can do no better than Edie's term, a peacock display. And yet I believe it was love of life, a hunger for the beautiful, that drove her to these excesses. My father found no fault with her. To him she was everything that was feminine, she existed in a magical enclosure, a glittering and perfumed garden, from which the loud sounds and rude activities of the world of men (a world in which he was very much at home) were excluded. My father mentally took off his boots in mother's presence. He was always a little breathless, a little apologetic—and yet there showed through a fierceness, a pride in possession.

I never managed to explain my parents to Edie. Her pity for me was always too quick: to lose a father at seventeen in such a dreadful way (he choked on his food after taking too much to drink at what has come to be called a stag party) and then have my mother abandon me and fly back to her family in Kent! It was useless for me to explain that I was happy, that my mother was happy. I had been home the year before and found her most affectionate and generous. An American gentleman called Weedon, a follower of Mary Baker Eddy, was paying court to her. Little in this picture appealed to Edie. She had a grievance against my mother and held it till the day she died. There had been a failure in both duty and love; there had even been, I believe she suspected, cruelty, and this was the unforgivable sin. It was not so, of course, but my Edie, was, in some things, an obstinate woman.

8 "George," she said to me one day as we sat beneath the quince tree, "do you think a person should put off doing something he believes is right because he knows it will hurt somebody else?"

I was a little alarmed. But I knew her well enough to answer a serious question in a straight way, so I said, "I think as a general rule one must do what is right. And who is going to be hurt, my love?"

"Mother."

"How?"

"I think we should be married at St Andrews."

"I see."

"That is where we belong now. And so I feel we should be married there."

I agreed. I knew there could be no argument. For this was a serious matter, one that touched us in our profoundest feelings. We felt that to carry on as Anglicans, to take in that church the most precious of sacraments, simply to avoid hurting Mrs Hamer in feelings that after all were no more than social, would be to call into question the special, the religious quality of our union. Mrs Hamer, seeing us sit on that wooden seat with fingers intertwined through the long hot summer, had supposed us talking sweet nothings. But we were exploring our beliefs, we were mapping out our lives under God. Already we had attended Presbyterian services. We did not keep this from Mrs Hamer, she simply did not ask. (Florence had begun to move in that way too and so did not give us away.)

What did I believe in those days? The doctrinal part is remote from me and when I try to bring it back seems so trivial I find it hard to believe two earnest and intelligent people exercised their minds on it ardently, as on a matter of life and death. But it was so. I had told Edie I was happy—but I had been unhappy, sick with a malady of the spirit that caused me to see man as banished eternally from God. This was worse than the Manichean state, for I had no sense of the divine. *I know that my Redeemer liveth.* "I know it not," my answer would have been. My sense was of evil. I saw it in the lusts of the flesh, in the ambitions of the mind (both known to me, for I was my father's son). It fed in a way both hoggish and refined upon the spirit and substance of my life. The point of light on which somehow I managed to keep my eye was simply that, a point of light, without warmth, without content, and further off than I believed I could travel in a dozen lives. But I kept my eye on it: and slowly worked my way out of the darkness towards it by the practice of bodily and mental austerities that now make me shudder to think on. But this, this foretaste of a dark night of the soul, this devastation of spirit, marks the point of my beginning. And I do not find it in me to sneer at the step I put my foot on because it will no longer bear my weight. It was a rock. I said, "I enter in at the strait gate. I shall have to stoop, i.e. subdue my nature and my ambitions. There will be hard struggle and little company. There is no other way to God."

For a time I kept up a form of worship in the church of my fathers, but I no longer took communion for I had embarked on a harsher way and trod now the path between Bozez and Seneh. The time came when I found myself among a sterner sort of folk (the first thing I noticed was that this worshipping body smelled of soap and shoe leather, not confections and emollients and sachets). And soon Edie and I were both there. I had not found myself long without company.

Sitting under the quince tree, we prayed for guidance; prayed that the light of understanding would shine on Mrs Hamer.

We went inside to break the news to her.

9 A man called Matthew Willis, an importer of cotton goods, had come to take afternoon tea, and with him his schoolboy son. Mrs Hamer was at that time busily introducing me to influential men. Willis was self-made. He had come to New Zealand from Australia and worked on the West Coast diggings. After a few years, seeing no fortune was to be made, he had set up as a storekeeper, and done well enough at that to sell out and buy a half share of the Christchurch importing business he now controlled. He was a difficult man to talk with. His structure was geological: a stratum of self-importance, formed in the years of his success, with below that the shrewdness and tightness of a shopkeeper, and lower down again the miner's open-ness and practicality. The trick was to chip down deep, for there one found a man worth talking to. On that day he was all pomposity.

"So this is the young man," he said, in imitation of some lordly figment, and he studied me benignly, though with an air of not yet being fully satisfied. "And they give me to understand that you have carried off our fairest rose."

I could not take too much of this (nor could the boy, who blushed) and the shrewd shopkeeper part of Willis saw it. He turned the conversation to my prospects. I named the senior men in the firm I was articled to, and he recounted an anecdote about each to show his familiarity with them. Mrs Hamer watched with a mixture of edginess and approval. I sensed her longing to correct, to shape, Mr Matthew Willis, and a colour that came to her cheeks now and then set me wondering. It was not until Willis mentioned he was a widower that I understood. I looked at Edie for her response. But Edie was withdrawn, her mind still on our religious concerns.

"My son, John," Willis said, "has made up his mind to study for the law."

We looked at the boy, and he said in a tone of forced manliness that he hoped his studies wouldn't interfere too much with his cricket. He began to talk to me about the game. I understood before very long that he was a clever boy, and one troubled in some obscure way. Perhaps, I thought, the loss of his mother has put him off his balance. He spoke with too much emphasis, as though he believed force would disguise his unhappiness; and there was in his way of saying "my mother", which he did several times in the few minutes we talked, the suggestion of some inner compulsion, and a delicacy, a defensiveness, and indeed a flush of emotion, that hinted at a love still having part of its course to run. This, I thought, is close to a sick condition. And I saw that the boy did not want Mrs Hamer for stepmother, or any woman for that matter. I saw too, and drily stated, that he was not interested in cricket. He went pale and retired to a corner; and I was sorry.

Florence brought in tea and Mrs Hamer poured it. Edie too was brought into this play and Willis paid her one or two heavily roguish compliments. He grinned at me and winked—the miner now. Had we not both found the colour? I felt myself warming to him at the moment when Mrs Hamer went cold. It was her he must please: he pulled himself together. "And when are the banns to be proclaimed?"

I frowned at Edie, warning her that now was the wrong time to speak, but she had put her cup down.

"We hope to be married in the Spring. At St Andrews church, mother."

"But that," Willis said; and stopped.

"Yes, Mr Willis," Edie said, very pale, "it's the Presbyterian church. George and I are becoming Presbyterians."

"George," Mrs Hamer cried, so loudly Florence placed her hand on her arm, "this is your doing. I hold you responsible for this."

"No, mother," Edie said, "we've come to it together. We've talked about it and it's something we must do."

"I shall get Mr Willis"—forgetting for the moment he was there—"I shall get the vicar. He will put this straight."

"Please don't, mother. Don't distress yourself." And Florence added her voice.

"Mrs Hamer," I said, "there are some things that can't be altered. Edie and I haven't decided this lightly. It's a matter of how we can properly use our lives." And being young, I began to preach, saying that in these times men were too wise and that the early Christians had been babes and that we must return to that simplicity and freshness and cleanse ourselves in the Holy Spirit for our minds were corrupted from simplicity in Christ. "Be ye filled with the Spirit," I said, and, "Out of your inmost soul shall flow living waters." But Mrs Hamer broke in upon me, crying that spirit was all very well for those who go to China but we had to live in Linwood. And she cried, "I blame you, George Plumb. My Edie didn't have a religious thought in her head until she met you." It was her honest opinion. Proper observance was for ladies, intensity of faith was not. We could not calm her. That was the work of Matthew Willis.

"Mrs Hamer," he said (the shopkeeper speaking), "make the best of it. They mean what they say. And after all, it's no great tragedy. It's a perfectly respectable church. It could have been the Wesleyans. Or something in the Other Direction." And while she sat biting her lips, he said, "I've attended many churches in my time. And I've almost come to think the one round the nearest corner is the best." He shocked us all. Perhaps he meant to.

"Matthew," Mrs Hamer cried, "keep such opinions to yourself"—a cry that showed us plainly how things stood between them.

Willis smiled. He asked Florence politely for more tea. He was pleased with himself, for with two minutes' work he had had himself admitted into the family.

The talk went round and round, as it will on such occasions. We were called selfish, wilful, ridiculous, enthusiastic (a very hard word), and even thoughtless—but there was a good deal of forcing in the performance. For Mrs Hamer's life had changed its course. Willis knew it. I caught him once grinning like a Cheshire cat.

10 We were married in the Spring in St Andrews church; Mrs Hamer in the Autumn at St Bedes. My mother sent us fifty pounds along with the news that she too intended to marry, to Mr Weedon. Her home would be in Philadelphia. And so we all changed course. But the time for decision-making was not yet done.

The season changed. We sat by our winter fire in our cold little house. Edie knitted. Our child was growing within her. Booties, bonnets, tumbled from her needles. She was utterly familiar to me, utterly strange. I never knew from moment to moment whether our love was to be holy dread or pikelets and sweetened tea. On the night I speak of I said, "How shall we use our lives?" It was ground we had covered before. We had even seen what our decision would be. But it remained unspoken, waiting its sign. I said, "I can go into the firm when I graduate. Mr Barclay called me in today. And I didn't know what to say, my love."

Edie put down her knitting. She handed me our bible. I read aloud from St Paul's first Epistle to the Corinthians, whose key word is wisdom. I came to that chapter in which the apostle praises charity, "Though I speak with the tongues of men and of angels and have not charity, I am become as sounding brass, or a tinkling cymbal." Part way through I felt her touch on my arm, and fell silent a moment, and read again the verse at which she had stopped me: "When I was a child, I spake as a child, I understood as a child; but when I became a man, I put away childish things."

My career in the law (and I wanted it very much still) was a childish thing. We saw it plainly. And because our spirits were ready, our minds prepared, the call that came to us was neither obscure nor arbitrary.

I said, "They're liable to send us anywhere, you know. Even the Coast," mentioning it as though it were Brazil. For a door had clanged shut behind us, there was no turning back, and I wanted

19

her to know where it was we stood. "Rough people and no comforts, and probably the house will be tumbling down."

"Then," she said gaily, "we'll build it up again."

"It will mean more study. And loneliness for you."

"You forget." She laid her hand on the child to be born.

"Yes. But Edie, think how upset your mother will be."

"Bother my mother," said Edie.

And so we talked and laughed and were very excited and gay, and frightened too, for these were our lives, and this our love for each other, we dedicated to the service of God. It was a great and terrible thing we were doing and Edie's calm fled away and she wept on my shoulder. But nothing in this life could have made us change our minds.

"I'll get you some cocoa, my love."

"No, I'll get it," for she never would let me do a thing in the kitchen and in any case I would have been helpless there. When she was out of the room I prayed, placing my hand on her cushion for I wished to include her, and the child too: "Lord, accept our lives. Make us useful, Lord." It was best, I believed, to pray short and pray hot, and pray in confident expectation. I had not the least doubt I would be useful; and believed it sinful in any case to offer more than one could give.

11   I sat in the summer-house with climbing roses drooping about my head and thought of Edie's loving eyes and her cheeks wet with tears of happiness and fright. But I was troubled, as though by the buzzing of a mosquito or a fly. In a moment I became aware of Meg shouting at me on my left, which for some reason she believes my better side. She was trying to draw my attention to visitors.

I was not pleased to see Merle and Graydon Butters, smiling ingratiatingly and bobbing their heads in unison, but behind them, cutting herself off by a sideways stance and a half indignant look, was Wendy Philson. And Wendy I am always pleased to see.

I motioned them in and accepted my trumpet from Meg; placed it to my ear, and the world began to squeak.

"—do hope you're going to enjoy your trip," shouted Graydon.

"—enjoy your trip," echoed Merle.

"But what have you done to your hand?"

"—poor hand?"

"It looks so painful."

"—painful."

"Doesn't it, Merle?"

"Yes."

"Yes."

"It must have hurt so much."

I left it to Meg to explain, left them my hand to exclaim over and delicately prod, and beckoned Wendy to sit beside me. She too was concerned about my burn. I cut her off and asked what she had been doing.

"Nothing," she said.

"Nothing?"

"I've been learning German. Reading Jung."

But I did not want to hear about her reading, and she would not have talked about it with Merle and Graydon by. We could not, in fact, talk at all, so I sat and enjoyed her company, which has meant so much to me since Edie died, while Meg kept the Butterses entertained.

But soon they came back at me, like two puppets worked by the same set of strings. Edie and I met them in 1919 when we bought Peacehaven. The Butterses lived next door, and they were enchanted to meet the well-known jail-bird. Merle and Graydon are cultists; a pair of butterflies flitting from movement to movement, not in any frantic or driven way, but charmingly, intelligently, and always in perfect accord the one with the other. I am fascinated and repelled by the perfection of their dance: he turns, she turns—impossible to tell which was first; he executes a tricky step, oh so lightly, and there she is completing as he completes. Their flashes of understanding are in common, their

21

turns of phrase the same, even their dreams identical. If he had been Theosophist and she Steinerite, or she with the Oxford Group and he a Rosicrucian, I might be able to take them seriously; but no, they have gone hand in hand, in perfect step, through every movement of the last thirty years, safe and charming behind the glass wall of their money. Lately they profess themselves socialists, and pacifists to boot, and believers in the Higher Consciousness, and some extraordinary *mélange* of these, some politico/mystical porridge, they have the impertinence to call Plumbism. For they are followers of mine.

Graydon shouted that he and Merle had written an account of their most recent experience of illumination. It had taken place in the rose garden and in intensity it almost matched that experience of Wordsworth's at Tintern Abbey. Almost, not quite, they had known the Brahmic Bliss. Would I read it? Graydon asked.

I said no. I had not the time. But if he liked to read it I would listen; and I pointed my trumpet towards him and smiled benignly. (Meg went off to make tea.) Graydon read, a little flushed in the face, for loud speaking is a strain to him. Merle nodded emphasis. I heard a word here and there: "—that serene and all-pervading light . . . we stood in a state of perfect stillness, perfect harmony, etc." I was overcome with weariness. Half my life has been spent listening to nonsense. Why, I thought, can't these people look into their hearts? Why must they inflate what they feel? And I wrote in my notebook for Wendy to read: *How long does this go on?*

She took my pencil: *Are you tired?*

Knowing her capable of asking the Butterses to leave, I shook my head. She wrote: *They're fools.*

Merle was watching. I began to be alarmed. And having my trumpet by chance at the right angle and hearing the words, "We shall arrive," I said, "Bravo!"

The Butterses went pink with pleasure. Graydon read on. Merle reached out and held his hand. I was touched. I felt ashamed. For they love each other, these two. And have known sorrow in the death of their son.

When Graydon finished I said I felt they were close. I agreed they were still in the twilight but if they held themselves open one day perhaps the true light would shine. For this cowardice I do not blame myself. The truth is I needed my cup of tea; and I asked Merle to see what was keeping Meg. She went off, Graydon followed, and I was left alone with Wendy. At once she took my hand. Her touch was comforting. She put my notebook on her knee: *Are you well?*

"Yes," I said.

Truly?

"Yes." I raised my burned hand. "This is nothing."

Why are you going?

"To see my children."

Felicity?

"Yes. And Oliver and Robert."

But why at this time?

"It's summer. I don't want to catch cold."

She wrote nothing more for a while, then suddenly scrawled: *Why have you been avoiding me?*

"Me?"

You haven't written.

I sighed.

I'm sorry. I don't want to trouble you.

"You don't trouble me, my dear. You've never troubled me."

Do you mean that?

"You've been a great comfort to me."

And that was no more than the truth.

12 My daughters disapprove of my friendship with her. It is not that they dislike her. Meg and she have much in common. It is simply that they believe themselves looking after Edie's interests in chaperoning us. They do not understand. Edie was my wife, my life's companion. There is a coarseness in the girls, in Esther especially, that prevents them from understanding. One might say *Wife* and *Life's Companion* and still they would not see it. They measure things by the marriages they made. Edie is in no danger.

I do not forget though that Wendy made an effort to be my wife. And when I explained to her why it could not be, offered to bear my child. The time is long gone, the possibility faded, and something in Wendy faded too. She is not now even my pupil—just a woman I can sit with comfortably and tell my thoughts to. She is the only one I invite to a "paper chat"—Edie's term. It makes my poor Meg jealous.

13 Wendy heard voices approaching and let go my hand. She wrote: *Can I come and see you when you get back?*

"Of course. I'd like that."

How long will you be?

I did not know. I had not planned. "A month possibly. It depends on Felicity."

Meg came in with a tray of cups, Merle behind with sugar and milk, and Graydon with biscuits on a plate. Meg frowned when she saw Wendy writing in my notebook.

I read: *Look after yourself. Goodbye.*

"Stay for a cup of tea."

She shook her head and I watched her make her goodbyes to the Butterses and Meg. She kissed me quickly on the forehead. Then she walked across the lawn and down the path: a short squarish woman with swollen legs and a large bottom and a self-conscious set to her head. One would never look twice at her, except . . . Much of Edie's beauty had been in her eyes. All of Wendy's is there.

I drank my tea, and kept my trumpet at my feet. Merle and Graydon fretted. But when I leaned forward and tapped the manuscript in Graydon's pocket and smiled encouragingly they cheered up; and after fluttering about me for a while and wishing me *bon voyage* they took themselves off.

"Do you want anything else?" Meg asked.

I said no.

"How does your hand feel?"

"It hurts."

"—doctor?"

"No. I'll go in Wellington if it's still sore."

She gathered up the tea things and went to the house, walking a little dejectedly. She feels always there is something more she should be doing for me and so all our exchanges have an unsatisfactory ending.

14 The Revd Mr Geddes interviewed me in the vestry of St Andrews. He seemed not in the least surprised at my request, but showed no approval. He began to catechize me at once in a contemptuous manner. I thought it official and did not object, but decided later it rose from a disapproving nature.

"You came to us from another communion?"

"The Anglican." There was in this a whiff of Rome, even to my nostrils. I was not surprised to see a sour expression on his face.

"Your wife too?"

"Yes."

"It's unusual. An unusual direction."

"For a time," I said, "I attended no church."

"For how long?"

"A year or two."

"Exactly, please."

"Fifteen months."

"You made no religious observances? None at all?"

"I went to one or two Salvation Army meetings."

This did not impress him. "What was the nature of your doubt?"

I told him as clearly as I could, which was not very clearly. And he said, "You understand we must examine this fully. There's a self-indulgence in this—this terminology, that frankly I find distasteful." And he began to put to me those questions I had already answered on entering the church. He made no deviation from the form. I was offended, with the feeling of one who offers himself for matriculation and finds himself placed in an elementary class. But as we continued I began to experience a cleansing of spirit. My resentment, my pride, fell away from me, and I thought, I offer myself to a life of service and I must behave with humility. And I answered in a simple and childlike way, yes, that I acknowledged myself depraved and corrupt in nature; that I knew my salvation lay in Christ, etc. And I promised to contribute according to my ability (Mr Geddes put extra weight on this phrase) for the support and extension of the Gospel, and by a holy and active life of Christian usefulness to adorn the doctrine of God our Saviour.

Mr Geddes looked upon me with not a jot more favour when this was done. "You must understand, Mr Plumb, our first consideration must be not your willingness to this work but whether you have seen the Glory of God in the Person of Jesus Christ."

"Yes," I said.

"No other gifts you may possess can compensate for a deficiency in Christian conviction."

"I understand that."

"It is essential that you do. I'm disturbed by your lapse from worship, even in that communion. You have found your way to us by your own efforts—perhaps too much so. Independence can lead one into unsound doctrine."

"I hope I've avoided that."

"Or grievous heresy." And he examined me in the Statements of Faith. I saw that my perfect responses troubled him. But he had to give up, for how can a true test be made? If one is a parrot one is through. I was feeling clever again by the time he stopped. He saw it, and left me to pray. He was a man who knew his business. Again I had to face myself, and face my pride. I prayed in humbleness; prayed for the purging of my soul; offered nothing, asked for nothing except to be shown my place and to be made useful. After I had finished I remained on my knees, and in this attitude Mr Geddes found me when he returned. He was refreshed (had been, I believe, for a cup of tea). He sat down and motioned me into the chair before him.

"I can hardly think you a proper candidate, Mr Plumb. But then, I may be wrong. It is not for me to judge. I shall forward your application. I should like to say something about your educational suitability?"

I told him. He was, I think, impressed; and showed it by looking sour. "If the Presbytery accepts you it will want you to complete your degree."

"Yes, I want to complete."

"The law has much to offer an ambitious man."

"I have no ambitions. Except to be useful in Christ."

Mr Geddes was silent. "Who shall judge usefulness?" he muttered. We both knew the answer to that, but neither spoke, and presently Geddes dismissed me.

I walked home through the cold and windy night. I was disheartened. Yet I had learned much from this interview. I must not look for approval in others and must beware of approval in myself. I had not lost my belief in my calling; but it had been shown me (what before I had simply heard) that the gate was narrow and the way lonely. In my ministry I must learn to stand with Christ and with no other. I thought of Jeremiah, whose life was a prolonged martyrdom. He served forty years of ministry, this man so full of shrinkings, and prophesied with invincible perseverance. What cannot the weak do? I thought (who knew myself strong); and I said over several times, "For thou shalt go to all that I shall send thee, and whatsoever I command thee thou shalt speak."

15 The ordeal by Geddes was the worst. (His name became useful to us. "Now George, don't play Mr Geddes," Edie would say, when my severities threatened to run away with me.) Mr Timmins and Mr Stephenson, appointed by the Presbytery to examine me, were a pair of cheerful gentlemen, pleased to welcome a candidate so obviously suitable, and the Presbytery itself was full of encouragement. Early in the following year I was asked to proceed to the town of Kumara on the West Coast to take up the duties of a Home Missionary.

Willis and his son John helped us pack. Florence took the child Oliver off Edie's hands, and Mrs Hamer (I never could call her Willis) looked in once and sorted Edie's half-dozen pieces of jewellery. She was upset at our going. She refused to accept that I was called, regarding this as a delusion. Willis himself was disappointed. He had hoped, he said, to take me into his firm. But he became the miner soon enough and entertained us with stories of the Coast. He had once owned part of a sluicing claim in Kumara and still had an interest in a sawmill there. He had known Richard Seddon well, in his days as mayor of the town and publican of the Queen's Hotel. He had been a supporter of Seddon in the election of 1879 but changed sides in 1884 over some mining issues. His conversation became technical at this point, full of sluice-heads and sludge-channels. Willis had been a "back number man" and Seddon a "prior rights man". I never came to understand this. But I remember Willis's feeling as he declared it had been a black day for New Zealand when Seddon gave up serving beer and learned to spout.

Later in the day he told me of Sullivan, the Nelson murderer. And this tale had a profound and terrible effect on me. Sullivan and his henchmen were ticket-of-leave convicts from Australia. They preyed on miners bringing in their winnings to the towns. It will never be known how many men they killed before those five in 1866 on the Maungatapu mountain. Willis had been a young man then and had left the Coast for the Marlborough diggings. The news came back to Deep Creek of how Sullivan, Burgess, Kelly and Levy had waited on the track from Canvastown and ambushed first an old flax-cutter, Jimmy Battle, and later a party of three shopkeepers and a miner. They had robbed them and killed them all, by strangling or shooting. Several days later the murderers were arrested in Nelson. Sullivan turned Queen's evidence and saved his life. His companions were hanged.

Willis had seen Sullivan; come, he said, in spitting range of him. He was on the steamer that took the man to Hokitika after the trial, where he was wanted for questioning about the murder of Dobson, a surveyor. It was Willis who shouted out to the mob on the wharf that the police had taken Sullivan away by dinghy to another landing place. Sullivan was nearly lynched that night. But the police saved him; he gave his evidence; was imprisoned in Dunedin for a time; and pardoned. And vanished then from the knowledge of the Coast. Such was Willis's story.

It brought down on me a feeling of dread, a sense of things abominable. I experienced again that devastation of spirit, that dreadful knowledge of being lost in the darkest of nights, that I had known in my days of alienation from Christ. I smelled the stink of evil, felt its slimy touch. I believe I almost fainted for I felt Willis's grip on my shoulder and heard his voice crying to his son to bring me a chair. But I put their hands off. I wanted no touch upon me. I said I was all right, I had these turns now and then when I worked too hard. I let them bring me water. And I begged them not to worry, and above all not to tell Edie. And then Edie herself came into the room, carrying Oliver, whom Florence had just returned, cradling him in her arms and making to him those small cooing bird-like sounds women alone have the secret of, and everything was right with me again.

But when I was alone I prayed, and I gave thanks to God for the light that shone upon me, for I saw clearly that I was a soul lost and damned the moment my foot strayed an inch from His path. I thanked Him for the sight He had given me of the abyss, and the soul of the murderer Sullivan writhing therein. The slope was long and slippery and my foot not an inch from its edge. I was not saved beyond damnation. And I saw that I stood where I did by an act of will as much as by the grace of God. I said, "I must work. Or else I die."

So as I embarked on my career I fell into what our friend Geddes would have called a grievous heresy. In it I have remained until this day.

16 We came up from the junction in a horse-drawn van, a journey of some four miles. The town had the appearance of a thriving little community—shops of every kind, a newspaper office, a school, a police camp, a hospital, four churches, and, we saw with alarm, twenty hotels at least. It was though, as we discovered, a town in decline. While we were there five of the hotels closed and two or three of the shops. But even in our first drive through the main street I felt the rough vitality of the place and I told myself that here was a stony field and one that a young and active man could test himself in the tilling of. Home missionaries were sent to these hard and difficult places to see what they were made of and to find if they were really in earnest. I did not know then that my sternest battles were to be not for the souls of men but against wet bush, swollen streams, rough and muddy tracks.

We drew up at the Manse and began to unload, and soon I saw my joke about tumble-down houses had been a bad one. No door or window opened without a battle. The floor, covered with oil-cloth worn to its fibre, undulated like a sea and had several holes rotted in it, into which the dust and refuse of many years had been swept. We discovered that night that the roof leaked. "We'll never be short of water," Edie said.

While we were unloading, several ladies arrived to give us tea. They brought new-baked cakes and loaves of bread. Their pleasure in Edie's clothes was childlike. She told me later theirs were a good ten years behind the fashion. This did not put them out. They were pleased the wife of their minister should outshine those of the Wesleyan and Anglican. I did not pass muster so easily. One lady was troubled by my tan shoes. "You're not going to preach in those things, are you?"

"Why," I said, "what's wrong?"

"They look like circus boots. If you've no black ones my boy will lend you his." She was our strictest sabbatarian, but a kindly soul. She sent her boy, who turned out to be her husband, to mend the holes in our floor. He also made several of the windows work. But I preached in my tan shoes of course, beginning as I meant to go on.

The Kumara station had been empty for several months when I arrived, the congregation attending Wesleyan services, or none at all. The charge was a large one including the towns of Dillmans, Humphrey's Gully, Greenstone and Stafford and a number of scattered preaching stations. I began pastoral visiting at once, and services on our first Sunday in the town, but before really coming to grips with the district and, too, embarking on my studies, I knew I must put the house in order. So I worked with paint and hammer and saw for several weeks and the little house began to look brighter. Edie scrubbed the walls and floors, made new curtains, put out our few pictures and ornaments. ("The likes o' these are not seen in Kumara," our sabbatarian said.) Just as she had promised, we built the house up again. Watching her work about the place with her hair pinned up and an apron of sacking tied about her waist; listening to her sing or in her firm and friendly voice direct the girl Kate we had taken on to help with the household work; seeing her with our son Oliver, washing him in the tin bath, towelling him, dressing him, singing him to sleep; and feeling when I was worn out with my work, her loving hand upon my shoulder, on my brow, I knew that I had been blessed. We lay in our iron bed listening to the Coast rain thunder on the roof. With my body I thee worship. It was so. And in our spiritual journey we were side by side. I knew that with this woman I would never be lonely. She was my home, my rest.

Of physical rest I had little. I had chosen a faith whose traditions were evangelical. There was no time even for thought.

31

People flooded into my life and filled it to overflowing. The Wesleyan and Anglican ministers came to my door, axes on their shoulders, and took me off into the bush to chop a winter supply of firewood. The friendliness between the churches was something I came across in no other place. We had our socials and picnics together and even the Catholics joined in. Father O'Halloran would have come along on our wood-chopping trip if he had not had a burial to attend to. From a hillside over the town we watched the procession pass through the main street and climb up to the cemetery.

"A good chap, O'Halloran," said Montague, the Church of England man. "Takes a drop too much, of course. If you see him fall off his bicycle you must tell any children standing about he's had a heart attack. He has frequent heart attacks."

Brice, the Wesleyan, was not amused. But he was a great hand with an axe. Our pile of rata logs mounted up. Late in the afternoon we carried them down to the roadside, where a dray was waiting to take them to the Manse. The drayman had boiled a billy of tea. He was a Catholic and called us Father indiscriminately. He wanted to know if I played cricket and tried to enlist me in a team playing against Dillmans the following Saturday. It was a temptation, but I said no, I must study every Saturday. I saw he judged me a poor specimen. Father O'Halloran was a great cricketer and wrestler and player of billiards.

This drayman mended the bicycle I found in a shed behind the Manse and on that rickety machine I made my rounds. Sometimes my way was on roads, sometimes on tracks or paths in the bush, sometimes along the old horse tramway. But whichever the way it was muddy. I came to love the West Coast storms, they exhilarated me and I stood in them many a time laughing and shouting, and was taken for mad. But the electric rain, falling in sheets with an elemental roar, and the brilliant sunshine after: all other weather is tame after this. With my shoes in my pockets and my bicycle on my back, I waded across rivers and streams to visit old miners, relics of "the golden days", living in their shacks in the bush. Or I cycled down the road to Dillmans for the Sunday afternoon service, into a landscape that seemed of another world:

great craters and cliffs sluiced in the fields, water races on their spindly legs, and blind iron sheds. Or I took a rutted and pot-holed track out to a mill, and over the scream of the steam winch and breaking-down saw bellowed my way through Christian counsel to some stump-armed or three-fingered sinner. Then home to long evenings of Latin and Greek and Theology.

Edie protected me. "The minister is busy in his study." (Obstinately she called me minister.) And then, knowing her loneliness, I dug grimly into my books; into that dreadful work of Hodge, *Systematic Theology*, from which I took nothing but headaches and dust in my eyes. "The minister is busy in his study." But one night I heard her call "George" in an urgent way, and hurrying out saw that another time for joy had come. And leaving her with Kate, I cycled down the road to fetch Mrs Cornish, who advertised herself as Midwife and Lady's Nurse. We walked back, I pushing my bicycle with Mrs Cornish's bag strapped on the back, and failing to hurry her; she had a voice like Napoleon, this woman, and meant to be obeyed. Sensible Kate had Edie in bed; Oliver, who had woken, pacified; and everything ready. But Mrs Cornish put me to work, as a matter of principle I believe, and I could not, as I had meant to, get to my books. I was left holding Oliver, while Kate helped Mrs Cornish in the bedroom.

It was an easy birth. Edie cried out several times, but apologized later. At one o'clock in the morning I was allowed in to see my second child, a daughter. Edie was pale but happy and the child red. I placed my hand on her head, cupping her tiny damp brain-case in my palm, and as I had done for Oliver and was to do for each of my ten other children, prayed for her and pledged her soul to God. Mrs Cornish watched with approval. Edie cried and laughed. Kate made tea. And Oliver, again disturbed, set up a squawling.

We named the newcomer Felicity.

17 By the start of our second year I had visited everyone whose name was in the Blue Book except one couple, Edward and Mrs Gardner. They had not appeared in church and all I could discover was that he was a retired miner who lived in a bush clearing with his wife along a track off the Goldsborough road. Edie came with me on many of my visits and so one summer afternoon as I prepared to set off in search of the Gardners I heard her say that she would like to come with me. I warned her of the distance, but secretly I was pleased, for it gave me great satisfaction to have her with me when I spoke to plain honest folk (I was proud of her, she was so sensible and simple and beautiful), and too, it gave me delight to walk the roads with her as though we were courting. So we set off. But this is her story, which I take from a notebook she filled many years later in idle or pensive moments. As I copy it down I hear her voice:

G.O.P. said that perhaps this time I ought to stay home as it was a *long way*, but the day was lovely and I wanted to go. Kate could mind the babies quite well, I said. After a little argument I had my way. So we set out. But neither of us had known quite how far it was. Up hill and down dale we went, until our shoes were yellow with mud and the hem of my dress was heavy as lead. I became *very tired* indeed and so did my husband. But we felt it would be silly to turn back—and I enjoyed it so much when he carried me over streams, and so did he. We kept on *walking, walking, walking*. At long last, through trees and along a one track path, we came on a little tumble-down house, almost overgrown with weeds. An old woman answered our knock and looked astonished and almost frightened to see us. We told her we were the new Church minister and his wife and of course she asked us in. She called her husband from the back-room, a poor infirm old worn-out looking man, and my husband talked to him and I talked to the old woman. It was

34

nearly tea time and they asked us to stay for tea. The place was anything but *clean*, and as it was beginning to rain we thought perhaps we had better go. But it *poured* with rain, and the West Coast (or wet coast) is proverbial for heavy rain. So we had tea. Mrs Gardner put her hand in the teapot and pulled out the leaves and threw them out the front door. The bread looked dark in places, almost like marble cake. There was jam which she had made, and condensed milk mixed with hot water. It was not a very comfortable meal, but they were so pleased with the visit. Then as the rain had not stopped, there was the problem of our return, which seemed *impossible*, as we would be *drenched*, and it was getting *dark*. Mrs Gardner said we must *stay* the night. She had no proper accommodation, but there was another shed room and a sack bed, and of course we had *no choice*, and had to make the *best* of it. She took us into the room where we were to sleep, it had a bed made of sacks, filled with straw. She said a man who had worked there slept on it one time. The sacks looked clean, but we had to have a little ladder to get into it, it was raised up from the floor. There were pieces of bacon hanging up, and strings of onions hanging from the roof. One string was over our faces. We took things *humorously* and G.O.P. laughed as he pulled me up the ladder.

Mrs Gardner brought in a new pink flannelette nightdress, which she said she had *never worn*. I thanked her. Then she brought in a big white chamber, trying to hide it from my husband. She apologized for not being able to give him *night* clothes. My husband read the Bible to them before we went to bed. I kept on thinking, *whatever would they do* if *one* or the *other* was *suddenly* taken ill.

Next morning it was *breakfast* I *wished over*. My husband went outside. In front of the house was a plum tree with *ripe fruit* on it. When Mrs Gardner called him he said, "I've eaten so many plums that I *really* could not eat porridge." I had to manage to eat a little. The sun was shining and we started our long walk to Kumara. When we got home everything was *all right*. The baby had been *good*, and Oliver. My husband said, "Oh Kate, make us a good cup of tea, *as fast as* you can."

In the winter Mrs Gardner fell and broke her hip and her husband trying to walk the track into town to fetch help for her lay down at the side of a stream and did not get up. So they died. I was away in Christchurch and became weatherbound getting back. I telegrammed Edie that she must ask Brice the Wesleyan to take the service, or read it herself. She chose to read it herself.

These were our days on the Coast and this was my wife.

18 I put my suitcase in the hall; a small case, for these days I need very little. Meg had borrowed Graydon Butters's car and was driving me to Esther's for lunch. While she turned it round in the yard I walked about the house. I was an old man and it was quite on the cards I would not see it again. But I could not work up much feeling. Rather I found myself recalling small annoyances and triumphs. The bed for example, "the monster" as Meg's children call it; a huge four-poster, ugly I admit, but stately too, and speaking of birth, generation, death: this Meg has been at me to sell. The making of it breaks her back she says, and she tries to persuade me I would be more comfortable in a single bed. But Edie and I shared this and I mean to keep it. I have had my way so far. A triumph.

And in my study I found Browning's *Poems* on my desk. I had been reading it the night before, looking at *Paracelsus.—progress is the law of life—man's self is not yet Man!* As I picked it up it fell open at the fly leaf, and there were the smiling orange sun and purple birds and blue trees Raymond had drawn with his crayons twelve years before. My study was forbidden, but he had crept in and defaced half a dozen of my books. I cannot instil into these two generations a proper feeling for books. And I stood there and felt the blood beat in my temples.

Meg blew the horn; but then, remembering my hand, ran up the path and took my bag herself. We drove down to the gate.

"Stop at Bluey's, Meg. I want to see him."

"Do we have to?"—or something like that. She has Edie's dislike of Bluey Considine.

"He doesn't know I'm going." I had deliberately not told him. He would have been upset and pestered me with visits. (I had known the risk I took in renting him the cottage but he had been very good and not come to see me more than two or three times a week.) He was sunning himself in a wicker chair as we drew up, and his friend Sutton pottering in the garden.

"Reverend," he cried, heaving himself to his feet like a steer. He made me take his chair. Meg went off to wait in the garden and this drove Sutton, the woman-hater, out. He came to the front yard, but could not stay there, being a parson-hater too, so he went inside.

"Well Bluey, I'm off for a week or two."

"Eh?" he shouted. Our conversations are like this. He too is deaf but refuses to do anything about it. Once or twice, exasperated, I have tried to ram my trumpet in his ear but he pushes it away in a kind of terror. He thinks himself unworthy.

"I'm going away, Bluey."

"What's that?"

"To Wellington. To see my son and daughter."

Sutton, who must have been listening, came out with a grin, and set off for the creek, carrying a fishing line baited with a lump of rotten meat.

"Eels," Bluey shouted. "He's after the eels."

"Don't you let him catch those. They're my pets."

"Eh?"

"Don't try that with me."

He cupped a hand behind his ear, grinning.

"You can hear."

"No I can't, Reverend." And at this joke he wobbled with laughter. A clever one, Bluey. He had got past the eels all right.

"You can pay the rent to Meg while I'm gone."

"You're not going away, Reverend?"

I explained again. Shouting tires me and I found myself little moved by his distress.

"Reverend . . ."

"All right, Bluey."

"There's a little thing that's been troubling me."

So I ran through for him the anthropological view of the hell myth. For Bluey is bog-Irish and though he threw his religion off as soon as he was able to think for himself, it comes back now to claim him. He came to me as a political follower, but in these days, both of us over eighty, it's my rationalist hat he wants me to wear. As I talked—or shouted rather (and a cyclist on the road turned his head in amazement)—I saw from workings in his eye that this was a battle I would lose. The dread of hell is in his bones; was fed him with his potatoes; and I knew that on his deathbed he would call for a priest. I grew disheartened. I like Bluey Considine. I watch with a humble respect his kindness to the little cripple Sutton, whom he has taken care of for fifteen years. He washes the man's club foot and oils his hump. I have seen him chase jeering schoolboys with his stick. It saddened me on that morning to see fear brighten his eye.

"Bluey, there is no hell. God is kind." I shouted it to him as though he were a child.

"I know, Reverend. I know." He did not know.

Meg came from the garden and tapped her watch. I said, "I've got to go now, Bluey."

"You'll come and see me when you get back, Reverend?"

"Yes. Don't you let Mr Sutton catch my eels."

"Eh?"

"You're a rogue, Bluey."

He came to the gate with me, heavy as an old elephant. Even through my deafness I heard his wheezing.

"You look after yourself, Bluey."

"You too, Reverend. You give them politicos down there a bit of your old stuff."

As we drove away I saw Sutton limping up from the creek, a red carnivorous grin on his face, dragging an eel twice as long as himself.

19 "Impossible," Meg cried, and I told her to be precise. But she could not. My children are short of language.

"Bluey Considine is a good man."

She shrugged and her lips moved again, making some word I did not bother to hear.

"He was kind to you when you were a girl."

"—dirty and smelly. Mother—"

I suspect the rest was "hated him". But that was not true. Edie hated no one. She hated cruelty and selfishness. But while she could not hate Bluey Considine, she disliked almost everything about him; his coarse language and coarse manners, his greed, his way of calling her "Mum", his betting on race horses, his fatness and smell and smoking; and, especially, his way of taking me off to my study after dinner and closing the door. He had made off, she calculated, with years of my time. (A different matter if he had been worthy.) She stamped her foot when she saw him on the drive. But I reminded her Bluey was a good man, an intelligent man. Brought up on prayers and "spuds", Bluey Considine. Brought up under Rome. And look, he had won free. And he was kind to the children. He brought them chocolate fish.

I reminded Meg of it. But she cried, "Oh, I couldn't eat those dirty things. They had bits of tobacco stuck on them. Robert and I used to throw them in the creek."

I was shocked—although I did not believe what she said about Robert. I could not see a hungry boy throwing good chocolate fish in the creek. But I could see a girl brought up by Edie, with her notions of cleanliness. And I thought, gentility is the enemy of life, it gets in the way of natural responses, it's like trying to eat your food with gloves on or drink tea from a thimble. Gentility had been Edie's vice. Not puritanism. Nothing wrong with that, it's maligned by the ignorant and self-indulgent. I have been a puritan all of my life. Meg on the other hand is not. She

39

has not sufficient intelligence for that, she has too much hunger. She's a modern woman and is not going to deny herself. Genteel is what she is. She gets her share of cake, but eats it in the manner Edie taught her.

She saw she had upset me and she took one hand from the steering wheel and patted my face. This is a female trick I hate. They take on this nursery manner, try to overcome us with their specialism. I don't deny there's some good feeling in it, with Meg at least. But there's more of looking down. They can't manage us as men so they make us babies.

I said rashly, "I'm going to let Bluey have the cottage rent-free." And having gone that far, told her something else: "I'm leaving it to him in my will." I almost believed it. But not quite. The cottage will go to Robert, of course.

20 When we arrived at Esther's the two girls retired to a bedroom to discuss my latest delinquency. I prowled about the house. I can never rest there. It has the air of camp, not home. It has taken nothing from the people who live in it. Fred and Esther come back here to eat, sleep, drink wine, and listen to the races. Their real lives are lived in some other place. And the house shows it. It has a depressed and temporary air for all its expensive furniture and glossy ornaments.

Fred Meggett is more to blame. Fred is busy accumulating wealth (which Esther, to be fair, finds to her taste). He left his father's butcher shop to become a land agent, and bookmaker on the side. And money began to find its way to him like tacks to a magnet. He missed the war (for which I do not blame him): he dealt in some obscure way in American army surplus; he quit bookmaking; and now he's in land again, in a big way as the saying goes. He saw before anyone else that our town must change its centre and he bought up the land where he thought it must go. And it goes there, of course. The shops are starting to spring up now, all owned by Meggett or on sections bought from him.

Esther jokingly calls the place Meggettsville. It doesn't seem to be a joke to Fred. I admire him, in the way one can admire a weasel or stoat. I enjoy reminding him I'm a socialist.

"Dad," Esther yelled, coming up on me with a glass of some purple drink in her fist, "what's this about the cottage?"

I did not want to argue. My hand was hurting and I wanted my lunch. "That was just a joke."

"It'd better be. Old Bluey'd sell the place and blow it all on the races." But she's a good-hearted girl in her clownish way, and she put down her glass and unwrapped the bandage on my hand almost without my feeling it. "As soon as you've had lunch you're seeing a doctor."

"No—"

"Yes. Don't argue." The smell on her breath was wine. "And don't turn up your nose. Mum liked her little drop."

"She did not. That was invalid port."

"You stick to that story. Come on, let's eat. I've made a bacon and egg pie."

After lunch she took me to see a young man with oiled hair who bandaged my hand again and tried to talk me out of going to Wellington. He turned my trumpet over in his hands like some Hippocratian relic. I was short with him. And when we were back at the house I told the girls I was going to take a nap. Esther led me into David's room, took off my shoes, laid my burned hand on my chest. She tiptoed out. And there, on my grandson's bed, I dozed the afternoon away, surrounded by photographs of football teams and film stars.

21 The time for my ordination arrived. Edie and the children returned to Christchurch, taking Kate with them (she was part of our family now). I went down to the function to see them off. I was to stay on a week to welcome the new Home Missionary.

Many people from my flock travelled down. Edie was much loved. There were tears; and a passing of goodies and cakes—the largest from our sabbatarian (kind and spiteful lady), who assured Edie it was full of butter and not "reekin' wi' grease" like all the rest. And so my dear ones left and I went back to Kumara and prayed in my church for guidance on my way, which I knew would be hard. I was going to a world less simple than this, and to folk whose needs were less plain to them. I did not expect to be liked as I had been liked. But I had the clearest knowledge of my duty.

I preached one more time in the church, reading the lesson from Isaiah 61: "The Spirit of the Lord God is upon me; because the Lord hath anointed me to preach good tidings unto the meek: he hath sent me to bind up the broken-hearted." And I read on through words I would hear again at my ordination but would not recognize even then as prophetic, as laying on me an injunction, "to proclaim liberty to the captives, and an opening of the prison to them that are bound". It was the first part of the verse that spoke to me and I would have declared then, if asked, that my special care was for those it named, the meek and broken-hearted. The rest I took for underlining. I spoke that day on Christian kindliness and the counsel one man may bring to another; on the sense in which all may be the Lord's anointed. Geddes would have seen error in this but to the simple folk listening that day it was no more than common sense.

On Monday morning I set out to make some visits. There were many old miners living in shacks round the town; old-timers

who had come to the Kumara rush in the eighteen-seventies and
stayed to work on sluicing claims or in the mills, and built their
little huts to see out their days in. I took special pleasure in visiting
these independent old men. They asked for nothing, many rejected
counsel, but they enjoyed a yarn and I had fallen into the habit of
calling on them for the pleasure of hearing them talk. Johnny
Potter was my special friend. He had been a forty-niner, and
worked on every Victorian and Otago and West Coast field. Gold
was his life, the "colour" his *ignis fatuus*. When the fields died,
when all that was left was sluicing or dredging, Johnny took his
shovel and pan and headed for the mountains. He was bent like
a bow, his fingers were set in a hook, before he came down to
Kumara and built his shack.

With Johnny I did talk religion. He was a free-thinker
(beautiful word, much to be preferred to Huxley's agnostic). He
could not read or write but from somewhere, perhaps from half a
century of camp-fire talk, he had picked up many of the rationalist
arguments. To him they were simply natural sense and I found
myself more than once stopped in my flow of scriptural exposition
by some simple, some practical contradiction, some "fact" as plain
to Johnny as that wet kindling won't take fire. He came down
especially hard on the First Cause argument, enjoying
tremendously his picture of endless Creators, each bigger and
better than the last, stretching on into infinity. Darwinism he had
not fully grasped: and one of my tasks was to explain it to him. So
I, a Christian missionary, sat in his little tin shack on many a wet
afternoon, with my bible on my lap (for he let me read now and
then), taking him through the arguments he would use to attack
my faith. I refuted them of course as I went along, but this gave
Johnny special delight and he would cackle in his high cracked
voice, "Wriggle, Reverend, wriggle. This is one hook you won't get
off." He made me tea, a painful business. Wet camps and icy rivers
had locked his joints. But he made no complaint. He had enjoyed
his life and had no quarrel with the way it was ending.

But on that Monday I had no talk with Johnny. As soon as I
came to his door he told me his "mate" Tom Clarke was "cashing
in" and wanted a preacher. I had no Tom Clarke on my book, and

told him so. Perhaps, I said, he wanted Mr Brice or Mr Montague.

"One preacher's as good as another," Johnny said, "so save your gab." He took me along the road and up the tramway, a walk that took us an hour or more, and would not talk as we went along. I could not help improving on the occasion, saying that in the face of death the way to Christ became broad and open. Johnny had a simple answer: he spat.

We turned into a track in the bush and found at the end of it a small wooden shack. Johnny sat down on the step. "Tell him I'll be in when you've finished your gab." I went inside and saw an old old man, whiskery and filthy and jutting with bones, lying on a sack bed in a corner. The room was full of unclean smells all magnified horribly. I had to push my way through them like a fog. There was no chair or stool so I knelt on the floor. The man scratched at his bedding with hands dry and horny as a turkey's claws. He had true *facies Hippocratica*: pinched nose, sunken eyes, pendent lips, but had a kind of residual redness in him, a flicker of life. He hung on to complete something.

I leaned forward. "Tom Clarke." I held my bible up so he might understand a "preacher" had come. "Tom Clarke, I've come to pray with you."

His eyes reached the Book, and came on to my own. He made a sound with his mouth—a magpie gabble. I thought for a moment it was the rattle of death; but he had not spoken for many days and his tongue had the stiffness of wood. I caught the word "confess". It caused me to think he was a Catholic and I wondered if there were time to fetch O'Halloran. I had a strong desire to be out of the shack, and away from this mad filthy sinner on the bed; for it had come to me suddenly, through no sense I can name, that here was an antechamber to the Ultimate Darkness, and here, in this man, a being who had Commerce with the Devil. I held my bible tighter and said, "Are you a Catholic?" and when he made no reply, ashamed of myself, said, "I'm going to pray for you. Can you hear my voice?"

He nodded, and said more strongly, "Confess."

"What is it you want to confess?"

He replied with a word I thought was "Nothing"; but when

I repeated my question, spoke again; and I understood it was, "Murder."

"Yes?" I said, beginning to shake, for there were rustlings and shiftings in the place and I could not keep my eyes from straying to the corners. I lifted my bible. "Are you saying you have killed somebody?"

He made a choking sound: "Murder," again.

"Who?"

And then he spoke with clarity, like someone calling a list he had by heart, or checking off goods. The names came out. I did not record or count them, but there were a dozen or more, and several amongst them I knew: Battle, Kempthorne, Pontius, Mathieu, Dudley. I was looking at the Maungatapu murderer, Joseph Sullivan.

I went to the door. "Johnny, wasn't it a priest this man asked to see?"

"Preacher, priest, they're all one to me," Johnny said.

"Go and get Father O'Halloran."

"It's a long walk, Reverend."

"Then I'll go."

"I reckon old Tom'll be dead by the time you get back."

"That can't be helped."

Johnny said, "What's the matter, Reverend? Doesn't your bible tell you what to do?"

I went back to the bed. "Are you Joseph Sullivan?"

"Joe Sullivan."

"Tell me about the men you killed."

I kept the Book between us. And I listened while the middle of the day passed, and the afternoon, and night began to come on. Once, late, I looked for Johnny but he had gone. I lit a lamp against the darkness of the place.

He had been a prize-fighter, a baker, a thief; a transported convict, a ticket-of-leave man; then a storekeeper and publican, and proprietor of a sparring-ring. He was a man with great strength in his hands. When he killed he preferred to stab or strangle. He killed George Dobson by strangling, or "burking" as he called it. He looked on as Burgess choked the old flaxcutter Battle with his

45

hands, and the next day showed him a better way, strangling Dudley with a sash taken from the victim's waist. He shot Pontius, stabbed or "chivved" Mathieu. And the others . . . Why go on?

His remorse was greatest for his killing of Dobson. He had mistaken the young man for a banker, but once he had stopped him could not let him go. He wept. "He was joking with me." And then, and many times, scratching with his hands and clutching my coat with a sinewy strength, "I am deeply dyed with the blood of my fellow creatures."

He had lived many years without remorse. Greed had drawn him back to New Zealand. As Tom Clarke, ten years older than Sullivan, he had gone to Nelson, meaning to dig up the gold buried after the murders. But there superstition caught him. He crept up on the place, he circled it, but the closer he came the more dreadful it seemed. He heard voices, heard the sounds of dying men. Several times he had come within yards of the spot, and once got his shovel into the ground, but had known if he lifted the sod the ghosts of the murdered men would spring on him and devour him. So he crept away, and crept away, and each time he tried to go back found himself stopped shorter. For a while he haunted Nelson, but there on a hill was the jail where Burgess, Kelly, Levy had been hanged. Kelly, whom he called Noon, preyed on him specially. Kelly, it seems, wept as the judge passed sentence and cried, "I don't want to be hanged," and Sullivan counted him as one of the men he had murdered. At length he came to rest in Kumara, and there he lived fifteen years in greed and fear—and in the end remorse.

I asked him the proper questions and heard his replies, and prayed for him, and so guided him into the Church Universal. I was not happy about it. It seemed too easy. I told myself the judgement was not mine. I let him hold my bible on his chest.

Johnny came back with some bread and a billy. He lit a fire in the yard and boiled up tea. I asked him why he did not use the shack. He replied that he had never been able to touch any of Tom's things.

"So you know who he is?"

"He's Tom Clarke."

"Did he ever ask you to get his gold?"

"It don't be gold." He looked angry, as though I had tried to mark a stain on his life. We drank the tea and ate the bread. Johnny told me he had known Sullivan as soon as he'd set eyes on him. He had fought him once in Ballarat for two pounds.

When we looked at the man next he was dead. I closed his eyes. I was glad Johnny was with me for I could not be sure evil was out of the place. I had no sense of having won this man's soul to Christ. I had felt evil but not its defeat, I had known as though by putting my hand on it and feeling its texture the corruption that can feed and flourish in a human heart, but I had not felt the redeeming Blood of Christ. Why? I asked myself in a kind of torture. Had I not carried the offer to him? Had we not, between us, put the abomination out, and had he not freely and gladly come into the arms of the Redeemer?

Why did I not know it?

The question was troubling me still on the morning we buried Tom Clarke or Joseph Sullivan. Scroggie, my replacement, had arrived. We followed the undertaker's cart with a dozen old miners, Johnny amongst them. The old men dropped out at the bottom of the hill and left their *crêpe* hatbands hanging in a tree for the undertaker to pick up as he came down. They went back into town to a hotel. Scroggie and I walked to the cemetery. He took the grave-side service; and I saw my congregation was in good hands. The remains of Joseph Sullivan sank into the ground. ". . . earth to earth, ashes to ashes, dust to dust; in sure and certain hope of the resurrection to eternal life, through our Lord Jesus Christ . . ."

And indeed I began to have some knowledge of it.

We went back to the Manse and I packed my bag. After that for many months I had no time for thought.

47

22 Fred Meggett hums like an electric motor. It's a fearful energy that possesses him, driving him on to what he calls success and I damnation. (He means of course power and possessions and I the lost possibility of becoming a Man.)

When he came home late in the afternoon the smell of the world of gaining and getting was on him; the reek of money. He tried to relax with a glass of beer and a racing guide, but as he sat in his over-stuffed chair he was shaken by small mental explosions that made him clench his face up like a walnut. He tried to talk to me. (He's one person who doesn't need to shout.)

"Well George, they tell me you're off."

"Yes, tonight."

"That's a hell of a trip, that *Limited*. You'd do better to fly."

"If God," I said, "had meant us—"

"Sure, we'd have wings. And wheels if He'd meant us to ride."

A point to him. In spite of my disapproval of Fred, and hatred of what he stands for, I find myself liking him at times. He's a boy.

"How many widows and orphans have you put on the streets today, Fred?"

He enjoys this game. "None. But I fired a girl."

"What did she do?"

"It's what she didn't. She forgot to write an appointment in my book."

"Was that serious?"

"Not much. I wanted to get rid of her, that's all. She was too dumb."

"Will she be able to get another job?"

"Sure. Plenty of jobs. She can go and work in the jam factory. That's about what she's good for."

"Fred, when the revolution comes you'll be first up against the brick wall."

"Not likely," he said. "I'll probably have the contract building them."

We exchanged a grin, pleased with ourselves and each other. I had, in fact, switched off a part of myself, otherwise I would have been angry. Fred Meggett is dangerous—Fred and his kind. Other people are not real to him. He's surprised to see them move and speak, and outraged if they show feelings. They must be pushed here, pushed there, and fitted into the places made for them even if arms and legs get knocked off in the process. Fred is a dictator, a brother under the skin to Hitler and Stalin. I've told him this frequently, demonstrated it, but it drives him into a pious rage; so I did not try that afternoon. I had a sore hand and a long journey ahead of me.

Meg looked in to say goodbye. Fred pounced on her. "You tell Fergie I want him down at those shops first thing tomorrow. Sure—" he waved her quiet—"I know he's got other jobs, but I got that contract for him and now I want some action. O.K.?" He grinned. "You're looking well, Meg. Esther been feeding you wine, has she? Esther love, when's tea?" You could almost hear the switches clicking on and off under his skin.

Meg kissed me and left. I joined the Meggetts at table. These small families seem unnatural to me. Esther has David, seventeen, and Adrian the late child, five. Where are the others that should have come between? What chemicals, what techniques, prevented them? My life and Edie's together was a tree that bore fruit in its season. In every sense what came from it was natural and blessed. I look at David, I look at Adrian, greedily gobbling his food, and I think, Why not those others, the poisoned ones? I find it hard at these moments to put food in my mouth.

"Is your hand sore, dad?"

"No."

"I don't think you should go."

"I'm all right."

"Can't you put it off a week?"

"Felicity's expecting me."

"We can send a telegram."

"They cost too much."

49

"Oh, dad."

They think I'm mean. I turn them aside from all sorts of other ground by pretending it.

23 Edie never complained at the shortage of money. Not only our early days were hard, but all our days. There were many mouths to feed and bodies to clothe. We managed. I have never had much satisfaction from it. But minds— that's another matter. There were young minds to feed and clothe.

Oliver was born in Christchurch. Felicity and Edith in Kumara. Willis, Florence and Agnes in the town of Emslie, where I was called on my ordination. Emerson, Esther, Rebecca (who died at thirteen), Alfred (who died to me one day at Peacehaven), Margaret and Robert, in Thorpe. After 1910 there were no more babies. Edie was not strong enough.

Some of my children have told me I cut myself off from them. But those years, 1895–1910, were years of hard work for me, and bitter struggle. They were years of growth and self-education. I left day-to-day matters to my wife, and never heard her complain. And if at the end of her child-bearing she was bone-tired and aged beyond her years, if her face was lined and her eyes weary, and her hands, her beautiful hands, were those of washerwoman rather than pianist, she would have said it was no more than proper; her eyes and hands and hard-used body were those of wife and mother, no more; she had done her duty in the eyes of God, in the service of her loved ones. There's a modern piece of cant about happiness being our due; and those who utter it do so with a greedy look on their faces. Happiness equals self-gratification! There's a truer sort that can only be found in service.

She came to me one day with a piece of paper on which a child had written: *Our father which art in his study writing a sermon.* She was shocked, and amused a little. I was neither (though pleased at what I took to be the beginnings of literary skill).

"Is this Felicity?"

"Yes."

"She's got a good hand."

"I don't think she meant any harm."

"Send her in to see me."

The child came in pale and quaking. They were used to coming to my study for punishment. (I beat the girls, but only with my hand.)

"Did you write this, Felicity?"

"Yes, father."

"What did you mean by it?"

"Nothing."

"Come now, child. You can't write a sentence and mean nothing."

"I only meant you were in your study writing a sermon."

"'Our father which are in his study.' Some people would say that was blasphemous."

She began to cry. She was only eight.

"It's all right, my dear. I'm not going to beat you."

"You only come here to read," she sniffed.

"Only!" I was shocked. "You mustn't speak to your father like that Felicity. Otherwise I *will* have to punish you."

"I'm sorry."

"Come here, child." I took her on my knee. "I come to my study to read, and to write, and to think. I can't think with children running round me, can I?"

"No," she said.

"That's why your mother brings my meals in here. Now, look. Can you read that?"

She read, hesitatingly, from my notes. "The wider bible of literature."

"This is an essay I'm writing for the paper. I'll be paid for it, just a little bit, and that will buy us food. But that's not important. The Wider Bible of Literature. Do you know what that means?"

"No."

"It means we can learn about God from other places than the bible. From books men have written. When I became a minister Felicity I had not read much. Mostly the bible and books about the bible. But now I'm reading other things. And I'm learning more about God. That's my job. Do you see? So I can help other people learn about Him."

She said she saw. I read her a little poem of Ella Wheeler Wilcox:

> Let there be many windows to your soul,
> That all the glory of the universe
> May beautify it. Not the narrow pane
> Of one poor creed can catch the radiant rays
> That shine from countless sources. Tear away
> The blinds of superstition; let the light
> Pour through fair windows broad as Truth itself
> And high as God.

"Now, you take this book away and learn that poem and come back and recite it to me tomorrow night."

After that I made it my practice to have one of the children in for half an hour each evening after tea. It should have been longer. I should have given them more. They crept in so pale, with such a hunger in them. Yet I did much. I have seen Oliver sitting quietly in the corner reading *Sartor Resartus*; heard Felicity read me her first poems; seen the shine in Willis's eyes as I read him Emerson's great words, "God will not make himself manifest to cowards"; and in Emerson's as I read him *Locksley Hall*. Oliver had the sharpest mind, but alas, a narrow pricking thing; Felicity the bravest; and Willis or Theo the strongest sympathies. (I had discovered Browning shortly before the child's birth, and through Browning Theophrastus Bombastus von Hohenheim, or Paracelsus. So Willis got his useful second name.) Emerson was a practical lad, not easily taught, but easily moved. A good boy. Edith, Florence, Agnes; intelligent children, eager for knowledge, eager for the blossoming of spirit that, had I known it then, creates from man *Man*. I gave them much but should have given them more. I was a child myself and did not know.

The later ones—well, there were other books and other evenings. Only let me say that of all of them, all of my children, it was Margaret or Meg who pleased me most. Her soul sparkled like water; and when she lifted her tender eyes to me, Edie's eyes, my heart grew full of joy in my love for her. Margaret, who grew up to marry a plumber and smoke cigarettes and worry about the colour of her lipstick.

Edie looked after their bodies; their food, clothing, schoolgoing, household duties. The girls as well as the boys worked in her garden. From her they had their lesson that idleness is a sin. And their reverence for growing and living things. Their everyday morality (the higher from me). And of course their manners and habits. Meg showed me a letter given her by Edie on her wedding day:

Teach your children to be *good, clean, honest* and *truthful*. A child is an *unwritten* page, a "bundle of possibilities". Teach them to have clean habits, clean teeth, clean fingernails, and never to spit before people, or blow their noses *violently* as that is a habit that assaults the nerves of the eyes, ears and throat. Teach them to value their *eyes* and their *teeth* because one set of permanent teeth and one pair of eyes are to last them *all* their lives and they are *precious* possessions. Teach them to have nice manners. They should not pick their *teeth* or their *noses*, or *scratch* their heads. These things if they *must* be done should be done when they are *alone*. Teach them not to sneeze loudly in company. I once lived near a woman who used to come to her back door and sneeze so that all the neighbours could hear her. That is a *vulgar* thing to do. Make them respectful to elderly people. I hate to hear a young boy address an elderly man as Tom or Jack. It makes life more pleasant to be with *good-mannered* people. Watch their speech, don't let them fall into the habit of *bad grammar*, like [oh my dear good Edie!] children often do. It does not take more than a minute to correct them. Also teach them good manners at the table. I have seen many a meal *spoiled* by a naughty child. *Punish* them for *swearing*. Make them *abhor* it. *Good strong* men *don't* need this filthiness to make their words *tell*.

Remember your father's prayer for his children, "Let them be *original*."

Never call your children "kids".

53

24 My time in Emslie was a time for gaining strength. The little town of tradespeople and farmers was a stonier field than Kumara. I met with kindness there, and with many good people, but I met too complacency and selfishness and greed—what I came to call, and plainly, from my pulpit, a fatness of the soul.

It did not take me long to discover that I was in a town of haves and have-nots, and that the distinction was carried into my church. And I would not have it. I made it known in Session that I would allow no renting of pews, and at once a storm broke about my head. One would have thought I proposed some new theological doctrine. They were elderly and in the main prosperous men, and I was young and poor. But I stood my ground. I reminded them I was their pastor; that not a month before they had attended my induction and promised me (and I spoke the words) "due honour and support in the Lord". They wagged their ignorant heads. It was not that sort of argument, they said. This was a financial matter, a matter of organization, and my duty lay elsewhere, in the care of souls. And Cheeseman, who had seen ministers "come and go", reminded me that a part of *my* promise had been to promote unity and peace within the Church. I grew angry. I would not be told my job by these satisfied men. Unity and peace, I said, were not promoted by the sale of favours. I told them I was disappointed to see such an appetite for precedence in my congregation, such a concern for worldly things. "Beware of the scribes," I said, "which desire to walk in long robes, and love greetings in the markets, and the highest seats in the synagogues." And I said renting would stop at once. If recompense must be made then we would run a sale of some sort to raise the money. Or, I said, it could come out of my stipend. One or two looked ashamed. But not Cheeseman. He gave in, of course. He was politician enough to know battles are not won or lost round a table.

When I told the congregation on the next Sunday that renting was finished, they murmured a little—at least those in the front—but I saw no rebellion. The matter was left quiet. But on the next Sunday the same people were in the front pews. And the next. I was stumped. I could not scourge them out.

Cheeseman said to me in Session, "It's all very well laying down the law, but people are used to their seats and the ones up the back won't come down the front simply because you say so. They like it where they are. Some of them have been sitting there for twenty years. You wouldn't shift Mrs Carter with a block and tackle."

"Very well," I said, knowing I had lost. "They may sit where they please. But from now on we won't take rent."

"Then how will you pay for a roof?"

"We'll manage."

The roof began to leak. And soon I was having to use my handkerchief to wipe water drops from my bible. (It kept the little boys amused.) I had to set about organizing galas and jumble sales and cake stalls to raise money for repairs; and all this was a great strain on Edie, whose job it was to see them properly run.

25 Cheeseman: dangerous as a jersey bull. I can still hear him bellow, still see him paw the ground.

One day I took as my text Matthew 26:40: *Inasmuch as ye have done it unto one of the least of these my brethren, ye have done it unto me.* I said a teacher in the town had told me her children were falling asleep at their books. One small boy had toppled out of his desk and curled up on the floor and not stirred for an hour. Others had been found in the playground, sleeping under the trees. Their health and their work were suffering, I said. And why was this? A good half of the children in the school came from farms. And most of them were called from their beds at 4 a.m. to work in the milking sheds. When they arrived at school they had already been labouring four or five hours. (Some even came unfed.) Whatever their parents might call it, I said, this to me was sweating: and sweating was evil.

I told them of child labour in factories and mines, and how in all civilized countries it had been stopped by enlightened legislation. I told them of the work of Rutherford Waddell—a Presbyterian, I emphasized, a minister of their church—who, almost single-handedly, had wiped out the practice of sweating in New Zealand. But some classes were less fortunate than the girls who had sewed moleskin trousers for fourteen hours a day at twopence halfpenny a pair. And these were children, whose parents could do with them practically as they chose. Drag them from their beds, I said, these eight- and ten-year-old mites. Send them out into the mud and sleet, work them till their fingers froze and their bodies trembled with fatigue and hunger. Then send them off to school unfed, or with only a gulped plate of porridge; and complain as you did so at the loss of wage-free labour. And when they came home work them again. Then come to church on the Lord's Day, into the presence of Christ, into His very house, and ask, nay demand, His blessing? Never, I said. Never while I was pastor of this flock. I would have, I said, no sweaters in my church. And I led them in prayer: Almighty God, most merciful Father, forgive us thy servants who have fallen into evil ways, purge us of our greed and hardness of heart—and so on.

During my sermon several people left the church. There was much stirring and grumbling. But I saw that some were moved and as I led them in the singing of the hymn—I had a fine clear tenor that put a few choir noses out of joint—I had a feeling I had not yet known in the pulpit: a sense of good work done, of a burden shouldered with joy and ease, and of the long hard way I must carry it. And I told myself that at last I had begun my ministry.

Cheeseman was of the opinion I had ended it. He was a farmer, his son was a farmer. It was his grandson who had fallen out of his desk; a fact I had known. Cheeseman read me a lesson in the economics of farming. He complained that my sermon had been no sermon at all but a piece of socialist rabble-rousing.

Where, he asked, was the doctrinal content? The Presbyterians of Emslie went to their church for religious reasons, not to be told how to conduct their lives.

I could not believe what I had heard. "Would you say that again, Mr Cheeseman."

He had the good sense not to. But he cried: "I challenge you, show me the Christian doctrine in that sermon."

"As ye do it unto the least of these," I said. "That should be doctrine enough for anyone."

"The way you twisted it," he cried, "it was socialism."

"Socialism not to want children exploited? To want them to get their education?"

"Book-learning. Where does that get anyone? Work is what children need. Hard work—that's the way to the Lord. Not fancy ideas. I worked. We all work in Emslie. And we won't have any city preacher coming out here and telling us how to live. You think these children are hard-used. They'd be into mischief if they weren't kept busy. I know. My father made me work and I thank him for it. I was out in the sheds from the time I could walk. I was milking a dozen cows a morning, and afternoon too, by the time I was ten. And look at me now."

I looked at him, at his meaty face and swollen eye, and I thought, This is the enemy. I was shaken. "Mr Cheeseman," I said, "it's my business to look after the spiritual welfare of the Presbyterians of Emslie. I'm surprised I have to remind you conduct is a spiritual matter. Unless you do good—"

"Faith in the Lord is all we need. No more. *I* remind *you* that we are among the elect. The grace of God is upon us."

"Unless you do good how can you come into the Lord's house—"

"Works," he roared from his bull's throat. "You ask us to seek salvation through our works." And from some Calvinist hole in his mind dug out the tag:

> Doing is deadly thing.
> Doing ends in death.

The enemy, I thought. But doctrinally he was on safe ground. It was mine that was shaky. I contented myself with saying, "Good works are good works, Mr Cheeseman. They're no road to salvation, as we know. I would hope we do them not to be saved but because we are saved."

He did not let the matter lie, but raised it in Session. He wanted authority to report my sermon to Presbytery. He had some support in this, most noisily from a storekeeper called Hay who thought too much schooling bad for children and hard work and beatings a way to the Lord. I learned, without surprise, that he had been raised in that way. "I was beaten every morning," he said, "for the good of my soul. And taken away from school at ten. I've no complaint. I learnt enough reading and writing to do my accounts—and read my bible." This, of course, was back-blocks Presbyterianism. I reminded them of the church's work in education, that its ministers were university graduates. A mistake— it enraged Hay and Cheeseman. I was claiming superiority now, they would not put up with it. But one or two of the others were uncertain. And I took the opportunity to produce my strongest argument. They beat me about the ears with Presbytery; I beat them in turn with the Southern Synod (soon to be joined with our own Assembly). Simply, I took from my pocket and read: "The Synod deplores the existence of the sweating system in the Colony, and instructs the ministers and the office-bearers to discourage it by every means in their power, and enjoins all to bear each others' burdens and so fulfil the law of Christ."

It silenced them quicker than a biblical text. They came on to the attack again—Cheeseman and Hay, at least—but cautiously. Was not this an historical document? Twenty years old at least? Ten, I replied; the principle as sound now as then, and the instruction as clear. But sweating, they said, was an industrial matter, and we were talking of children in milking sheds.

So the argument went round, and Cheeseman and Hay warmed to their task again. My concern, they declared, must be for the spiritual welfare of my parishioners. I must keep my socialist rabble-rousing out of the pulpit, etc. We fought a war of texts. I began moderately, "But whoso hath this world's good, and seeth his brother in need . . ." They bombarded me with fundamentalist nonsense—hellfire and damnation and worms that dieth not. I lost my temper and cried, "I have seen the wicked in great power and spreading himself like a green bay tree"; which I suspect they had meant to use themselves. We were like schoolboys throwing stones at each other. I saw it and was ashamed, and going to my wider bible, said, "In Religion What damned error but some sober brow Will bless and approve it with a text?" They took it personally. Useless to explain I had aimed it at myself. So I apologized. They did not. They complained to Presbytery.

But they were complaining to educated men; narrow perhaps and limited in their religious understanding (as I was then), but men who knew the importance of book-learning. When they discovered that children were falling asleep at their desks they came down firmly on my side; advised me though to fight my battle discreetly. Which I did; and won some ground.

Cheeseman and Hay were a thorn in my side for the whole of my stay of Emslie. Edie called them "the Bullock" and "the Crab".

26 I see myself cycling home from a pastoral visit, a small red-headed man, hair a little thin, hearing a little dulled; hot in my suit of grey and turn-around collar. People smile at me and call, "Lovely weather, Mr Plumb." I come to my gate, unsnap my trouser clips, put my bicycle in the shed. Children run to meet me from the garden, their fingers stained with weeding. They hang about my knees, and one, Emerson, climbs me like a tree and perches on my shoulders. Through an open window I hear my wife playing the piano. She allows herself a quarter of an hour each day. It is *The Rustle of Spring*. She welcomes me home with a gay tune. Kate clatters dishes in the kitchen. (Dear Kate, plump and bossy, more mistress to Edie than servant.) I go into the parlour, kiss my wife, and drink a cup of tea. I tell her about my day. Kate looks in, demands her in the kitchen, and she goes off with a smile of apology. I walk in the garden, examine the children's weeding, put the boys to stacking firewood. I eat a plum, think about my sermon for the next Sunday. And some neat turn of phrase drives me to my study, where I begin to write.

An hour later Edie comes in with my dinner on a tray. I tell her the children have been very quiet and she grows pink at my compliment. I have got a lot done, I say, and I read her some of it. She approves; and goes out to eat her own meal. Later a child creeps in. They are always excited and nervous. This is Aladdin's cave. I hear her recite:

All wondering and eager-eyed, within her portico
I made my plea to Hostess Life, one morning long ago.

I praise her and sit her down on a stool to read; and feel her kiss on my cheek when after half an hour she creeps out. I do not look up. I have found a new argument.

Later I hear the sounds of children going to bed. There are tears, and I watch the door to see who will come in for punishment. It is Willis. He tells me he has been bad. He has drawn a moustache on Edith's doll. It is a small offence and I strike him only once with the cane. He says he is sorry and goes out smiling bravely. The house is quiet.

I write a letter to the paper. Some bigot in a religious column has said the Sabbath-breaker is as bad as the murderer. A sensible word is needed on this. I go out to the sitting-room and read Edie what I have written. She is darning socks, but she listens and approves. I see how tired she is and tell her to get an early night.

Then I read for two hours: Emerson on the Over-Soul, or Behmen or Swedenborg; or the new London Ethical Society pamphlet with its account of the debate between Joseph McCabe and the Revd Waldron. No doubt about the winner.

At eleven Edie brings me a cup of tea. She sits and talks to me. She tells me we must pay Kate more; that she has seen some cheap material that will do for dresses for Felicity and Esther. Oliver needs a new shirt and winter shoes. Willis's teacher says he is getting on well. I am pleased at that. She kisses me and goes to bed. After reading in my "bible" I follow her.

This is my life until 1910, in Emslie and Thorpe. I fish in the rivers, and walk in the hills, and play cricket. (I bowl leg breaks now but they still call me the steady little trundler.) People look sideways to see Edie expecting again. We smile and say, "The more the merrier." On Wednesday nights I lecture at the Literary Institute: Wordsworth's *Prelude*, the novels of George Eliot, the bible in literature, Dickens and the poor, Thoreau, Richard Jefferies' *The Story of my Heart*, Hardy and Meredith, Browning and Tennyson, Plotinus, Emerson as poet, Emily Brontë, the *Satires* of Juvenal, Socialist thought in the English poets. I am learning to speak, to spout. It shows in my sermons. I am told I declaim too much. Others say I am too insistent. Nobody yet has accused me of doctrinal error. They accuse me of socialism. In this they are right.

27 I joined the Socialist Party in 1902, shortly after I moved or, to use the ecclesiastical term, was translated to St Andrews, Thorpe. The move was a happy occasion. It brought us closer to Christchurch, which we thought of as home; closer to Edie's mother and sister; into a familiar landscape. I expected it to bring me in touch with like-minded men.

I was straining to break my bonds. Years of ministering to simple folk had made me familiar with much that is noble and generous in human nature, but it had also brought me close to the dark. There are holes and corners in the mind, lidded tight. I had prised loose some of the lids and seen spring out genie-like, and swell to giant size, things whose names are ordinary enough, greed, envy, cruelty, race hatred, class hatred, lust, sloth, hatred of man, of God, and of the self; but whose shapes can shrivel the mind. An example: I was called to a house where the police had found a four-year-old child tied to the leg of a table. It had not been freed since it had learned to crawl. It was filthy, emaciated, clothed in rags, and it made its wants known in grunts and whimpers, like an animal. We had it taken away to an institution but it never recovered human shape or mind. Another: a young boy, given for the first time his body's evidence that generation requires a physical act, hanged himself from a rafter in his father's barn. Another: the behaviour of "the Bullock" and "the Crab", whose belief was a tightly closed door; who saw with naked glee those outside consumed by eternal fires.

In Thorpe, and even in my church, I expected to meet men and women whose minds were open to the light.

I joined the Socialist Party, the Eugenics Education Society, and became a subscribing member of the Rationalist Press Association of London. For several years I had been reading widely in socialist literature. I was master of the doctrines of communal Utopians and Marxians alike; and if as a Christian I found myself settling at first somewhere near the former, as the years went by I travelled leftwards and became a root-and-branch man. My key text in those days was the one I had used against Cheeseman and Hay: But whoso hath this world's good, and seeth his brother have need, and shutteth up his bowels of compassion from him, how dwelleth the love of God in him? A good question, and not to be answered by donations to charity.

I could not say from my pulpit that socialism was the answer. But I said it on week nights, in halls about the town. I spoke on the need for a eugenic programme. For it seemed to me socialism and eugenics travelled hand in hand. The socialist state must be the eugenic state, where men and women could be healthy in mind and body and morals.

These were days of intense mental labour for me, of wide reading and wider enquiry, and the beating out of ideas to a fine gold leaf; and it gave me joy to walk in the country with friends, to talk and joke and dispute with them and try upon their intellect and spirit the ideas working within me and drawing me with an inexorable force, elated mostly, uplifted, but sometimes, I admit, shrinking and nervous, into my life of rebellion. They came about me, a band of brave and open-hearted men: Edward Cryer, John Jepson, Andrew Collie, John Findlater. And there was too the young John Willis, a lawyer now, who came down frequently from Christchurch. These were men on whom I leaned, who gave me comfort and support in the cold times that slowly crept upon me.

Later there was Bluey Considine. But at first it was Edward Cryer and John Jepson who were important.

Edward was a member of my church; at least his name was in the Blue Book, but I seldom saw him at a service. I saw him at my Literary Institute talks and my Trades Hall talks (and later at the Unitarian Hall). He was shy. He was ugly and inarticulate, and full of pain at unregenerate man. He approached me after a talk I gave on William Morris, working his way up like a yacht tacking against a breeze. He asked me if I knew the writings of Robert Blatchford. "Of course," I replied haughtily; offended that anyone should suppose I did not know of *Merrie England*, know of the *Clarion*. Edward drew back as though I had struck him. It was an instinctive animal-shrinking from danger. He mumbled something and turned to make his escape. But I took him by the shoulder. I apologized. We walked home together and drank a cup of tea and talked (at least I talked); and we became friends. I drew him slowly into a closer intimacy than I was ever to know with another man; into comradeship. And in that state he lost his halting manner of speech and talked as well as I, and often to greater point. His mind was more sensitive than mine, and he had a greater purity of ambition. Self played no part in it.

Edie grew fond of him and my children called him Uncle. He never came to see us without flowers for my wife (he was a florist), sweets for the younger ones, and a book for Felicity and Oliver. I whipped Willis severely one day for aping Edward: pushing out his ears like flags, beetling his brows, and thrusting out his jaw prognathously. And stopped Felicity's puddings for a month when I learned she called him "Old Hairy Ears". Edward brought her bags of cakes to make up for it.

John Jepson was different. A bluff and hearty man. No nonsense about solid John. He was well-to-do, the owner of an aerated-water factory. His library was the best I have ever seen privately owned. He too came to me after one of my talks. He offered me the use of his library. I went along expecting the usual half-dozen shelves of books, expecting perhaps no more than one or two titles unfamiliar to me; and came, like my children, into Aladdin's cave. Infinite riches in a little room. It took my breath away, I almost fainted. It took the ordinary—a glass paper-weight, a chair, John himself, a glow of honest pride on his face, moving to stack green pine-cones on the fire—to bring me to myself.

"You may borrow what you like, Mr Plumb. Except my prize birds here." And he showed me a glass case of eighteenth-century first editions—a set of *The Rambler* I remember, *The Deserted Village*, the *Poems* of Ossian. I made polite noises; but was drawn, even as I spoke, to the other shelves. For here, without doubt, was the wisdom of the ages. And here, especially, was modern thought, modern heresy. Here was the future if I could only hammer it out from these shelves.

We must have talked, although in my memory I simply sat down and started reading. His wife came in with tea; a disapproving Presbyterian lady—yes, one of mine. She sniffed at the book-leather smell, the pipe-tobacco smell, the smell of male clothes (I was wet with rain), as though she detected something going off; but John dismissed her with a wave of his hand.

"Women and books don't mix. Now, have you seen these?" He placed on the arm of my chair a dozen brand-new titles, just out of their wrappings. We fell to dipping, and talk, and quoting, and the reading of passages aloud; and our tea went cold on the table. (Mrs Jepson removed it without a word.)

So John Jepson became one of the group about me. He made me careful. He made me think before I spoke. He would not be carried away. I can hear his voice: "Yes George, but these are just fine phrases. What exactly do you mean when you say 'higher ethical altitudes'?" (Or, "sublime democracy", "world-wide communal soul", "eugenic knowledge", "one-man humanity".) I came to value him for more than his library.

I remember those afternoons when we strolled along the byways and over the hills. John and Edward became friends, though not as close to each other as each was to me. They had a competition to see who could provide me with the funniest joke for my next week's talk. Edward's were innocent, boyish, and often, I thought, without point. John's leaned towards earthiness. I made it a condition of telling that each man should demonstrate the usefulness of his joke to my argument. Those were vigorous and manly afternoons. We walked hard—John at fifty and Edward at forty-five perhaps a little less hard than I: they sometimes sat down to rest while I went ahead or off to one side to get some quicker or wider view. John had the habit of whacking stones with his stick, using it like a golf club. Edward gave us the name of each flower and bird. I hear his voice (a little less free than if he and I had been alone): "George, I came across a beautiful phrase the other day. The understanding silence of a long married life."

"Is that your joke?" cried John. "It's easy to see you've not had a wife."

"I think it describes my marriage very well," I said. "At least the part of it I've had so far."

"Then you're a fortunate man. But tell me how you can work it into your talk." (For my subject was marriage.)

"Well," I said, "I'd have to give it some thought. Perhaps Edward can tell us."

"That," he said, "is how I imagine marriage. And one of you has told me I'm not wrong."

"I'll tell you you're wrong," John cried. "Haven't you heard the Chinese proverb: A woman with a tongue six inches long can kill a man six feet high?"

Edward and I both found this improper. He was married, and we knew his wife.

We were, I remember, a full company that day. Andrew Collie, John Findlater, John Willis, had joined the band; and we made an unusual sight—six men of varying ages and varying dress (John Findlater was casual, and John Willis coloured, and I of course in my dog-collar), inclined very much to laughter and declamation, and the scribbling of notes in pocket books, and the spouting of poetry. John Willis said, "There's another proverb, John. God could not be everywhere and so he made mothers."

"And what of the dying man?" Edward asked. "He caught sight of the Other Side and said, 'That is my mother's land.'"

"That could mean the opposite of what you think," John Jepson said; and we roared with laughter. "In any case, we were talking of wives. And George, I offer you this. Women are good for making butter and trouble."

Andrew chimed in in his uncompromising Scots. He could recite the poems of Burns from front page to back; and now he gave us:

> John Anderson my jo, John,
> We clamb the hill thegither,
> And monie a cantie day, John,
> We've had wi' ane anither;
> Now we maun totter down, John,
> And hand in hand we'll go,
> And sleep thegither at the foot,
> John Anderson my jo!

"There's your answer, John," Willis said.

"*An* answer," John replied. Like Edward and me he was impressed by Andrew's courage in reciting the poem. We three knew his story. He had been engaged to a young woman in Aberdeen and had come to New Zealand to establish himself in business. He would send for his girl as soon as he was able. The story is common enough. He met another, and fell in love with her; and wrote the painful letter home; and prepared himself for marriage. And then came the horror—I choose the word with care. His *fiancée* would not release him. She wrote that he was pledged to her. She loved him and would keep him to his contract, which he must honour as an honest and God-fearing man. She would be on the next ship out. Well, Andrew was God-fearing no longer, but he remained "honest". So he gave up his dream of happiness, and lived in the nightmare. He cut himself off from the girl he loved—her agony was something he could not bring himself to speak of—and married the one he did not. They had been together now for fifteen years, in bitterness and hostility. There were never any children. The marriage—if I can call it such—was, he told me, never consummated.

We walked along, talking of women and morals. John Findlater, a cricketing acquaintance, flicked a ball from hand to hand, or practised his strokes. He was a lover of poetry, and would-be poet himself. His verses, which he read without shyness on these walks, were full of lark-song and breaking bud, pretty enough, but for men of our belief almost without content. He was, too, politically ignorant. He believed the government of the day—Seddon had just died and Ward was running things—a benevolent institution. We had undertaken to educate him. Indeed, he was often in a state of shock by the time we finished our walks. But he came along nicely and was one of my great supports in my times of trouble.

"I would have all marriages as happy as my own," I said. "And," I said, "I would have all marriages cease to exist that are less happy than mine. For happiness is the end of marriage—that is the divine purpose of it. Happiness and children are the fruit. And a barren tree should be chopped out at the root. The law and religion drag behind this truth. I would have divorce made easy, and the immorality of marriage without love put an end to. It cannot be called marriage, in the sight of God or man. It is prostitution." I did not spare my friends in the pursuit of an idea.

"Now George, now George," John Jepson said, "what do you mean by divine purpose?"

"And what," Andrew asked (an atheist), "what do you mean by God?"

"Look here," John Findlater cried, "that's going too far."

Young Willis was on another line. "Just think of the women in bondage to cruel men. Think of them—delicate creatures, forced to yield to the embraces of drunken tyrants."

None of us cared much for his tone, or his choice of words. He was still harbouring, it seemed to me, a too personal view of things; thought I could not see how drunken embraces fitted in. His father had long been a total abstainer (from strong drink, I mean). But John was a generous and cheerful boy, and sharp-minded enough when his filial emotions were not in play. So I welcomed him to the group when he came down and hoped long walks and country air and the company of my friends would freshen that part of his mind where he kept his obsession.

"What we must aim for John is to prevent unhappiness in marriage. There are many sorts of unhappiness besides the one you mention. I don't advocate, John"—and I turned to Findlater here—"free unions and free divorces. What I do say is that the higher ethic is to ease the way for the separating of unhappy couples."

"What do you mean by higher ethic?" John Jepson asked.

"What God does not hold together by love, let not the Church paste together by texts and laws," I quoted.

"Very fine," Edward said.

"And all very well, but how do we go about changing the church's mind?"

"There's too much talk of the church here. And God," Andrew cried. "You don't change their minds, you sweep them away. They're part of the rubble of the past. Sweep away God and the church, I say."

"But good heavens," John Findlater said, "what would become of morality? Why, there would be nothing to restrain us."

"Morality is not the property of the church. Morality has its home in the free mind. All else is superstition. The free mind needs no restraint. The free mind," I said, "is God."

"Hear, hear," Edward said.

And we marched along.

28 But how was I to reconcile all this with my position as minister of St Andrews? A murmur had begun and it grew with the passing years and at last even my children began to hear. For people shrewdly guessed that my political and social beliefs must have as their companion an unorthodoxy in religious doctrine. If challenged I would not have been able to deny it. But it did not enter my church. I married people, and baptized and buried them; I gave the Lord's Supper. Sunday had become an annexe to my real life; one I found it harder and harder to enter. Only when I had pulled the door shut behind me, closed the shades, so that no light from the wider place should enter; only then could I remind my flock that they were corrupt and depraved, call them to repentance, speak of the passion of Christ, and declare that faith in Him was the single pathway to salvation.

I was in a curious state; for in that little room I was a believer. My years of intellectual acceptance and emotional need had placed a part of me in thrall, and this my rebellious self, the new man, failed to win over. It was a Dark Tower, the old need and superstition, and I came to it like Childe Rolande many times, and set my slug-horn to my lips and blew; but the beast did not emerge and the tower stood. And while it stood I remained in my ministry.

This is high-flown language. Yet I believe it accurate. Those were painful and emotional days as well as being full of intellectual striving; as well, that is to say, as being joyous. I preached and prayed, and remained doctrinally sound in those activities—though less heavy than most of my flock must have wished. I administered the sacraments according to form. In my visiting I gave comfort and counsel. And socially I was very good, very good indeed. Mr Plumb at a picnic was a wonder to behold. He sang and joked and blessed the food (and did not forget to praise the cooking). He jollied old ladies and little children; he sat on the greasy pole, drove nails in the nail-driving contest; shied the cricket ball; he judged the children's races, strolled in the shade with the ladies, talked plumbing with plumbers and law with lawyers and the Good Book with a pious elder. He climbed a tree to rescue a trapped child. Spanked his naughty son. Gave his arm to a faint young bride. All beautifully done and much approved. At the end of the day he stood by his pretty wife and called his healthy children close about him. An ideal Christian family. He saw them into their trap—a squeeze. He made a joke. His parishioners laughed. Just for this occasion they were pleased with Mr Plumb.

And Mr Plumb waved, dignified now, and drove off to his home; where he unwrapped the mail he had turned his mind on all through the afternoon—the latest copy of the *Hibbert Journal* and the latest reprint from the R.P.A.

I have forgiven this man his duplicity. But I will never make him my close friend.

29 I was sorry we had no workman in our group (sorry too we had no woman, but found only Edward agreed with me in that). We went on a good deal, I said, about our faith in the working class to sweep away capitalism and imperialism and establish a world of peace and plenty, but which of us had as friend a man who worked with his hands? It was a challenge. And one that Edward answered with Bluey Considine.

He was not sure about Bluey. The young man (an aging young man) had come into his shop to buy roses for his girl. But, they discovered, he had left his money at home. "Now how did I manage that?" He turned his pockets out like a stage comedian. Then they talked about progressive literature. Bluey had read books Edward had never heard of (he invented some of them). Edward was impressed; and let him walk out in the end with a dozen of his best dark reds, sprinkled with water and done up in coloured paper. The following week Bluey was back, and did it again, this time with a grin; paying in talk. But on his third visit wanted no roses, except perhaps one for remembrance: his girl had found a young man she liked better. Edward brought "Mr Considine" to meet us; and whispered that he would not vouch for him.

I discovered fairly soon this talkative County Corkite was more vagabond than workman. But at first I was delighted with him. He was not only a wharf labourer and union man but a fugitive from Rome as well. Early in our acquaintance he turned up at my home unasked just as we were sitting down to dinner. It was Sunday. We were back from morning service. I was not pleased to see him; but soon recollected my claims for myself—I was a Christian and a Socialist. And here was a brother in Christ, and one of the exploited. So I asked him inside and introduced him to Edie and sat him down at table with my family.

And Bluey began to gobble—there is no other word for it. He

carried great loads of food to his mouth and chewed them noisily.
We saw half potatoes, lumps of meat, travelling down his throat
like fish down a seagull's. He stretched his arm half the length of
the table to snatch bread or butter or salt from under Edie's nose.
"Push that gravy along, Reverend." He forked a piece of fat from
Oliver's plate and an uneaten potato from Agnes's. The younger
children were delighted with him. Edie became excessively polite.

"Do you find the meat to your taste, Mr Considine?"

"I was brought up on prayers and spuds, mum, so a good
piece of beef is a treat to me. I'll have a slice more if you don't
mind. I don't like to see good food going to waste. Here youngster,
don't you want them beans? I'll eat them for you. Push your plate
over here."

Edie saw a roast she had meant to last two meals vanish in
one. Bluey sat at the table sucking skewers and string. "You're a
good cook, mum. You don't mind me sayin'? But the Reverend
here, he eats like an old maid with lockjaw. Too much going on
up top, eh? Got to fuel the engine, Reverend. Don't want to get
top heavy. Now mum, you make him eat. You ask me here again,
I'll show him how to eat. And if you don't mind me sayin', a bit
of hot mustard with that gravy would improve it."

"You are not married, Mr Considine?"

"I nearly got married once. That was in Australia. Half my life
I'd been wandering, and I said to myself, It's time you settled
down. So I found me a girl—a little slip of an Irish colleen she
was, and a refined wee thing. Why you'll never believe it, she wore
scent. It's the truth now, and I don't know how she could put up
with me." He gave a grin: he was not blind to himself. "But," he
said, "her mother died, and me being broke she gave me some
money to buy a wreath. Well you know, I put it on a horse, and
I'll give you a guess where that horse ran. Dead last, Reverend.
Dead last, mum. It's a way all my horses have, of running last."

Edie was shocked.

I said, "It must have been in Australia you got your name."

"Bluey. Because of my hair." (It was redder than mine.) "I was
glad to get rid of the other. Francis is what I was christened. Now
there's a good Catholic name, and it's no wonder. The town was

crawling with priests where I grew up. Like beetles in a log, they were—and always telling me I'd burn. I got out of there Reverend, I got out on my feet, as soon as I knew which was the way to Dublin. I only had my uppers left when I got there."

I took him to my study. We talked about books and religion and the labour movement. I respected him. He was his own rough-and-ready creation; dishonest only in things that did not matter. (Edie told me he had slipped a baked potato into his pocket.) From Dublin he had gone to Liverpool, from Liverpool to London; from there to the world, as stoker on a series of broken-down freighters. In San Francisco he had jumped his ship. He bummed his way (his term) back and forth across the continent. At one camp somewhere in the Mid-west he had shared his frying pan with Jack London. Later he had been a "mate" of Pat Hickey; witnessed the birth of the I.W.W. He had seen the strike-breaking tactics of the American company police—had his head broken in one encounter by a brawny Mick from his home town of Clonakilty. Lately he had come across Hickey again; been with him in Blackball in the miners' strike, where the workers had won a great victory, half an hour for lunch instead of a quarter. "And," Bluey said, "there's trouble brewing here."

"Where?"

"On the wharves, Reverend. It's not long now and we'll be coming out."

30 Two weeks later the Thorpe waterside workers went on strike. They had been encouraged by the miners' success. It wasn't more time for lunch they wanted but a fair day's pay. And though the strike petered out after several weeks for a while it seemed we were in for a long bitter fight. The union was fined for breach of its award; refused to pay; saw distress warrants issued against its members (Bluey one of them, but he had nothing), and property carted into the streets for auction. It organized the bidding and so spiked that gun. (Chairs were bought for a penny ha'penny that day.) Garnishee orders were served and the fine collected. But meanwhile more serious events took place. The employers got together a team of farmers to load the ships. Scuffles, blood, arrests, much bitterness; and the first signs of hardship in the strikers' homes. At that point a message came across from the employers that certain concessions might be made providing matters went through the proper channels. So the strikers went back to work, against the wishes of Bluey and his committee, and the grind of the Court began. The watersiders got little in the end, but by then the spirit had gone out of them.

A small strike; but the first of several events that turned my life upside down.

At first I felt helpless. I was a talking not a doing man. I felt uncomfortable with Bluey; and even more with the strikers and their wives in my congregation. I drew my fat stipend (relatively fat) and fed my children, while they had nothing and saw theirs begin to go hungry. I made a number of speeches in the town, in halls here and there. This was my usual activity—gab. But at last I could not hide from myself a way in which talking might be changed into doing. I had turned my steps away from it too long.

Edward was in church that day, John Jepson too, and John Findlater. (Not Andrew. Nothing would bring *him* past the door.) I chose as my text James 5:4: *Behold, the hire of the labourers who have reaped down your fields, which is by you kept back by fraud, crieth: and the cries of them which have reaped are entered into the ears of the Lord of saboath.* It was the first piece of text-hunting I had enjoyed in years.

I began moderately, telling my congregation of the obligations of honesty that lay on men in their dealings with one another. I said the relationship between man and man reflected that between man and God. Very much one of my bread-and-butter sermons. But then I was launched. There was, I said, an event taking place in our town that touched every one of us. We were fortunate, I said, that we in Thorpe had been given the opportunity of taking part in a skirmish, a frontier skirmish, in a war that was being waged throughout the world, and right to the gates of Heaven. The Lord of saboath, who was the Lord of hosts, of armies, had heard the cries of them which have reaped and had gathered His armies about Him, the armies of the workers of the world, and was marching on the citadels of privilege. He was battering at the gates and the walls would tumble down and the labourers enter in to claim their hire. I kept on in this vein for a good long time, and saw Edward restrain himself with effort from crying, "Hear, hear."

Then I paused, climbed down from my soapbox; and asked very reasonably, had not Moses led a strike, and at the Lord's command? Were not the twelve Apostles, the chosen of our Lord, working men, labourers with their hands? Fishermen, not shipowners. And, I asked, was not Jesus himself a working man, a carpenter, with callouses on his palms? For almost twenty years he had earned his daily bread with hammer and saw. He had strained his muscles in the shaping of timber, in the lifting of beams. He knew the agony of labour, the aching bones, the sweat, the pittance for pay. Never forget, I said, those years of his life before he became a teacher. Never forget that in the figure of the saving Christ there lives another, the man with calloused palms, Nazarene Jesus, the Carpenter. He never forgot it. The labourer, He said, is worthy of his hire; a belief that informs His teaching. And more. For what, I asked, was his moral creed when it was boiled down? What was it? (And I made them wait.) Why, I said, it was simple. We must not be frightened of it. It was the creed behind whose banner the working men of the world had assembled themselves, the waterside workers of Thorpe amongst them. It was the creed of the future. It was the future. What was it, the teaching of Jesus? Why, I said (for I had wound them tight enough), it was socialism. Simply that.

Edward said, "Bravo!"

Here and there I saw a face that glowed. The rest were closed up tight.

We prayed. We prayed for the sick and suffering; for the hungry and exploited; for a softening of the hard-hearted. Afterwards we prayed the usual prayers, sang the usual hymns.

A strange and threatening stillness marked the going out of my flock. Their clothes seemed to rustle less and their shoes strike the floor more softly.

74

Our little band crossed the road to the Manse: Edie and I, the children, Edward and the two Johns. We sat in the sunshine on the wooden seats by Edie's conservatory. Andrew came round from the back garden where he had waited beyond the sound of hymns. I told him what I had said. He was elated. He was always one for large brave happenings; and he flapped his arms like a rooster and almost crowed. Kings, capitalists and priests were on the slippery slope. The age of the common man had dawned. All at a sermon from the Reverend Mr Plumb.

"Oh Andrew," Edie said, "they looked so angry."

"Angry? So they should be. We'll have a battle, never fear. We'll have a fine old battle on our hands. They'll fight to the last ditch, while there's still a penny they can get their greedy paws on."

"There'll be Session trouble, George?" John Jepson asked.

"It won't stop there, I think."

"Presbytery?"

Bluey Considine came through the gate, with a bag of sweets for the children (he was penniless and must have stolen them). They ran to him and soon he had them lolly-scrambling on the lawn—to Edie's anger and my disapproval. I had not told Bluey what I meant to do. He might have tried to pack the church and I wanted to speak only to my usual congregation. He came to us and Andrew told him the story.

"Aye Bluey, you should have been there. I had a wee look George, I admit it. It did my heart good to see all yon donsie faces comin' out o' the temple." (He called it temple, implying dark and bloody rituals.)

"Well Reverend, I wish I had been. But it'll do no good," Bluey said. His eyes had a beaten expression I had until that moment put down to hunger.

"Why Bluey, what's the matter?"

"We've lost, comrades. Our friends have lost their nerve. Their wives want them back to work. So we've agreed to arbitration. You'll read about it tomorrow in your newspapers."

"But," I cried, "it's the Arbitration Court we're trying to get rid of. We'll never get anywhere through arbitration."

"It's the tool of the profiteer," Andrew said.

"Of the master class." We used this language. We were not the hungry ones.

"And so we lose. Well, there'll be other battles," John Jepson said. The rest of us could not manage this larger view. We sat there a downcast band. The children, seeing their chance, ran and screeched about us in a way that had Kate frowning out from her kitchen.

"Don't think of your sermon as wasted, George," John said. "Whatever the outcome of this strike the struggle for minds goes on. You've struck a blow in that."

"Aye, the scoundrels have been set back on their heels. They'll be quaking tonight over their port and cigars," Andrew cried.

John laughed. "Andrew, you should have been a pamphleteer."

These two and John Findlater strolled down to the orchard to look at the blossoms.

"Is it really over, Bluey?" I asked.

"Over," he said. "The wives have won the day." He was more cheerful. He was looking forward to his dinner.

"I wish you had let us know, Mr Considine," Edie said. "Then George might not have had to preach his sermon."

"No Edie, that's not fair. I should have told Bluey what I meant to do. And anyway," I said, "the time had come. It would have been cowardly to behave in any other way. Edward, a church is not a lecture hall. You don't cry out Bravo."

Edward turned pale. "I was carried away, George."

I laughed. "So you were. And I was pleased to hear you. That was an awful silence."

"Mrs Porter cut me dead when we came out. Willis, come down from that tree," Edie said.

"Porter is one of your elders?"

"Oh yes. There'll be consequences. Willis, you heard your mother. Wait for me in my study."

"Ah now, don't beat the lad. That would be cruel," Bluey said.

"Willis is being disobedient, Mr Considine," Edie said.

"Why mum, he's probably hungry. Boys suffer in that way. I hope you've got a good piece of beef in the oven."

76

The others came back, with fallen petals decking their Sunday clothes. Andrew was in mid-poem:

> See yon birkie ca'ed a lord,
> Who struts and stares and a' that;
> Though hundreds worship at his word,
> He's but a coof for a' that.

I was heartened. I had friends. I had friends down through the ages. Men of sense and goodwill had always been on my side.

John Jepson, Andrew, John Findlater, went off to their homes. Edie and I, Edward and Bluey, went inside. Edie played the piano. The children made off to corners of the garden. I watched through the parlour window. Oliver read. Felicity brought the little girls their dolls. Willis, believing his punishment forgotten, made Emerson bend over and mimed a beating. Then he patted the smaller boy on his head in just my forgiving manner. I burst out laughing. I let him get away with it.

31 That was Sunday. On Monday Session called me to a meeting. I was dealing with civilized men—or so they seemed after Cheeseman and Hay. They acted with firmness rather than savagery. And at first they were inclined to charity. My error could be mended by a show of penitence. They wanted to keep the matter within St Andrews.

I sat and reasoned with them. We went through my sermon's argument step by step. Some of them had memories like rat traps. But I would not give way. It was my duty, I said, to indicate the course of Christian behaviour in any matter involving my congregation. The strike involved it, as I had made plain. And there was nothing doctrinally wrong in presenting Christ as a tradesman. The scriptures were clear on that point.

They replied that my error lay not in doctrine but in my use of my pulpit to preach a political creed. Socialism belonged on the street corners: the Lord's House to the Lord's business. And there we rested. I reminded them as I left that they had no right to exercise discipline on me. As a minister I was not subject to their court.

I cycled home. It was a fresh Spring day. A shower had left everything brightly coloured. Well, I thought, this little business is launched and it will end soon enough, one way or the other, but the seasons go on. It seemed, as such things do, an original discovery, and I wondered at the pettiness of men.

Edie met me at the front door. Her face was drawn, she looked in middle age. I smiled to give her courage and took her hand and we went inside, through the entrance hall she loved so much (an imposing place, with leaded windows and carved seats and a profusion of mirrors: in style quite unlike my Edie), and into the parlour.

I told her I thought this thing would soon blow over. "They're men who prefer private dealing. And they like to control things themselves. If it gets into the hands of Presbytery they'll find their importance shrunk."

"Oh yes, George," she said, "I see that. But this is only the beginning, isn't it?"

"Are you frightened, my dear?"

"A little."

"Would you have me stop?"

"No. But . ."

"But, my dear?"

"I love this house. And the children must be fed and clothed and educated. George, I will stand behind you in everything you decide. But before you decide, look at these things too."

"If we feed their minds we are doing our duty by them. And do you think I haven't considered these things?"

"I know you have, George. I didn't mean to doubt you. But we've been so happy here."

"Edie, I've had a hard morning. Bring me a cup of tea. I'll be in my study."

And when she brought it I said, "Don't be afraid. I'll do nothing that harms you and the children. But I must follow my conscience. You would not have it any other way."

"No, George. I would not. I'm sorry."

"I'll do nothing without your knowing. You knew about my sermon. And my dear, I'll tell you this, I won't quarrel too deeply with my church over a matter of politics. If that were all our quarrel I'd have it out now. But there are things that go deeper. When we do face each other, Edie, it will be on other ground." I looked about the study. The books frowned down on me: a stern, not unfriendly frown, calling me to duty and honesty. "If they can show me anything I should apologize for then I'll apologize. I think that's all they want. I'm not guilty of heresy, Edie. It hasn't come to that." I implied, and she took my meaning, that soon it might.

"We may have a little time yet, my dear. But don't love the house too much. Or our comfort too much. There are more important things."

She came and kissed my brow. I took it to mean she would follow me where I led.

32 I was wrong in thinking Session would keep the matter to itself. Several of the members were men of substance. They were threatened in their purses.

I had a visit from the Revds Mr Downie and Mr Mitchell. They were, they explained, appointed by Presbytery to look into certain remarks I had made in my sermon; which, they were bound to say, had an unorthodox sound. But their inquiry was an informal one. They were anxious I should understand that.

I took them to my study, where I fed them tea and cake. Soon they began to feel very much at home. They were two courteous and gentle men, though each, I think, had some iron in him. The books soothed them (they were both short of sight and could not read the titles); my bible, open by chance on the desk, lent the room an air of piety. Mitchell approached it and marvelled at the wealth of annotation. "May I?" And he turned the pages with a decorous motion, reading aloud to Downie; first a text and then my comment on it.

"'I will be as the dew unto Israel: he shall grow as the lily, and cast forth his roots as Lebanon.' And of the lily Mr Plumb notes, 'No plant is more productive. One root often gets 50 bulbs. Pliny.' You are a scholar, Mr Plumb. Now what have we here? Amos 9:2 'Though they dig into hell, thence shall mine hand take them; though they climb up to heaven, thence will I bring them down.' And the commentary is 'Sinner leave yr sins & fly to yr Saviour's bosom; this is the only way to escape punishment.'"

It startled me that I had written this. It must go back to my days in Kumara. Could not Mitchell see the ink was faded?

"Do you mind if I turn to the Gospels, Mr Plumb? My word, there's not a free quarter-inch in the margins. Look at this, Mr Downie. Remarkable." He browsed for a good quarter-hour. I poured him more tea. "Thank you. Thank you. Listen, Mr Downie. 'For where two or three are gathered together in my name, there am I in the midst of them.' And Mr Plumb says, 'The advantages of social worship. I. It promotes spirituality of heart. II. It is a stimulus to secret worship. III. It affords a lesson to the household.' Very true, Mr Plumb. It's a practice that unfortunately is not as widespread as it used to be. Why in my day . . ."

And Downie came to the desk. He found: "'And some fell among thorns; and the thorns sprung up, and choked them.' The annotation says, 'Ground not thoroughly purged & cleansed! Strangled by secret sins!'"

This made them happy; and me depressed. Well, it was they who must be satisfied. And when we came to chat about "this other little matter" they wanted from me no more than the smallest nod at Mitchell's suggestion that perhaps my judgement had been a little astray. I gave them their nod, willingly. I undertook to keep politics out of my pulpit. For I saw my quarrel with them was of another sort.

Mitchell laid his hand on my bible. "The Scriptures are close to your heart, Mr Plumb." He was a kindly old man.

So ended the first of my battles with Presbytery. My sons would have called it a fizzer.

33 Willis 'phoned me before we left for the station. The stupid fellow had trudged a mile to the box, quite forgetting I cannot converse on the 'phone. Esther had to act as my voice and ears.

"He says to give his love to Felicity. Oliver too. That's an afterthought."

"I will."

"He will, Willis. And he says how are you getting on?" I hadn't said that, but no matter.

Esther yelled, "He's got rheumatism in his wooden leg."

"Tell him to rub it with alcohol. It'll stop him drinking the stuff."

"Dad says rub it with alcohol. It'll stop you boozing." Silence. "He says Mirth has drunk all the alcohol. It keeps her warm."

"She'd keep warm if she wore clothes. They all would. Ask him if he's taken any more wives."

"Have you taken any more wives?—Do you mean other people's, dad?—No, just beginners.—He's got his eye on a little filly up the ranges. He showed her his wooden leg last week."

"Tell him it's time he grew up."

"Dad says you're nearly fifty, it's time you grew up.—He's been up and it's more fun coming down."

"Tell him goodnight. We'll be late for the train. And give him my love. He's an idiot."

"Dad says you're an idiot."

I left them talking and went into the bathroom. I love Willis. He's a natural. Not in the old sense of that word, or the more recent one. He follows his nature, which is a pleasant enough thing, not an iota of mean-ness or cruelty in it; but it leaves him without reason or understanding.

Fred and Esther drove me to the station. There I found Meg had booked me a sleeper. I was angry. I do not like to waste

81

money. Nor do I like being treated as a child. The old are expected to put up with this. I never will. I told Fred to go along to the booking-office and change my ticket to a second-class one.

"It's too late now, dad. The train's nearly going," Esther said.

"We've got ten minutes. Go on, Fred. And don't forget my refund."

"Dad, you need a good sleep. Especially with that hand."

"Fred."

"O.K. George. Keep your shirt on. Here, give me the ticket." He went off, but I caught his wink at Esther. And now there was a bustle on the platform; porters and guards rushing about, children crying, and young people kissing in that open-mouthed way they've learned from Hollywood. No shame and no sense of cleanliness. Intimacy lies in another direction. I said, "Go and get him, Esther. I'll miss the train."

"Oh dad, make up your mind."

"You know as well as I do he's round the corner smoking a cigarette."

She burst out laughing. "There's no flies on you." She fetched him back and they got me into my compartment.

"Goodbye. Don't wait."

"You're not angry, dad?"

"Of course not. I like being treated like an imbecile."

"Cheer up. Don't lose your trumpet."

Off they went, grinning; a modern couple, not much love between them, but a lot of laughs to be had. I sat down and pulled myself together. I'm not really bad-tempered. I've got my temper well under control; always have had. Never for a moment in my mature life, and I date that from my Presbyterian days, have I been without a sense of the divine. How can one admit temper, lust, etc, these flurries of the ego, when one has had my experience, entered into the Light, that is into Manhood. When Fred and Esther had gone, when the beating of my heart had subsided a little, I sat in that musty narrow box and experienced a moment of deepest peace. "God comes to see us without bell." I heard Him calling my name, and felt a lifting, a lightening, under my heart and in my skull. I wondered if my earthly life were ending, whether

82

I would die on this worn red seat with the bustle of departure all about me. I was ready.

A young man came in. Ah well, the man from Porlock. I gave up dying and said Good evening to him. He looked a little taken aback to be sharing his compartment with an old codger like me, bald as a cricket ball, shining-eyed with the remnants of his vision, and armed with a weapon like a gramophone speaker. He was well brought up, however, and he offered me the choice of berths and the seat by the window. I smiled at him; touched my ears. I did not want to talk. He settled down to read his evening paper.

Later, as the train was rushing through the fields of south Auckland, I noticed something had excited him. His wandering eye had picked out my suitcase label.

"Plumb," he shouted. "Unusual name."

I agreed.

"—relation of Emerson Plumb?"

"He's my son," I said. "Do you know him?"

"—saw him land—Takapuna beach—nineteen-thirty." Something like that. I grinned, inclined my head. I have lost the art of comporting myself in the light of my aviator son.

"What's he doing now?" the young man shouted.

"He's piloting flying boats across the Tasman."

"Fair go? What a bloke, eh? The Sundowner of the Skies."

The Australians called him that and it crossed the sea. It was many years since I had heard the name. It brought tears to my eyes. To hide my emotion I set about preparing for bed. The young man was helpful. He called the attendant and soon the seat was transformed into bunks and I was able to change. My companion found a reason to leave the cubicle. An octogenarian naked brings strong reminders of mortality—or perhaps he found my shanks a comic sight. Anyway, I was alone; and grateful. I climbed between the sheets, switched off my light, and turned my face to the wall. And although I had gone there to examine what it was that had moved me so, I soon passed into sleep. I slept for a good long time.

34 The small hours. A moon-rayed closet full of dead air and burnt coal. A swaying circular motion that set my stomach floating as though on oil. As I put my feet on the floor they knocked over a cup of cold tea. It was another kind thought of the man sleeping above my head. He must have bought it at Frankton or Taumarunui and left it by my bed in case I should wake. I thanked him; and paddled to the window to see where I was. No difficulty. Close at hand Mount Ruapehu was shining in the moonlight.

I have always looked at scenery in an eighteenth-century way—a Johnsonian way that is, not Wordsworthian. It is the grandeur of man that moves me, not mountains. Mystical experience for me is not set in motion as for that good gray man of the Lakes. And so when he says:

> I have felt
> A presence that disturbs me with the joy
> Of elevated thoughts, a sense sublime
> Of something far more deeply interfused,
> Whose dwelling is the light of setting suns,
> And the round ocean and the living air,
> And the blue sky, and in the mind of man—

I say, Yes, and give my intellectual assent to his catalogue, but am moved to joy only by its last item.

The flanks of the mountain were certainly beautiful. They were smooth and pale, like cold butter. I enjoyed their slow turn about the train. No stirring in my soul, to be sure, but a calm enjoyment of beauty. I have been accused of lack of enthusiasm. A cold intellectual fish. But it's not so. I've seen a good deal of "pure" response in my time, and seen what it leads to—fanaticism, self-indulgence, locked iron doors in the mind. I prefer the scalpel and microscope; and so have been accused of choosing them. It

84

may have been true at one time, but not any longer. Dissect, experiment, by all means. But sooner or later one comes to the dark or Light. And entry cannot be made until the laboratory smock has been put off.

But my children have accused me of coldness, of pedantry. Even Oliver. Astonishing. A mountain to him is something to mine; a tree to mill for timber; a stream to dam. He's the cleverest of my sons, and the most limited. Full of sharp little thoughts that scurry about, pricking here, pricking there; but none escape from the box of his prejudices. His mind, it seems to me, is like an ant nest under glass. The little creatures are so busy, so full of purpose and hive-importance; they're never aware of the eye looking in. Well, Oliver; he is what he is; and he has, as they say, climbed to the top of the heap. Many people have told me I should be proud of him.

The train turned away from the mountain. I struggled into my blankets. My hand was painful again and I nursed it across my chest and thought of my sons. It had been kind of Willis to stump a mile on his wooden leg to say goodbye to me. He was full of natural goodness. And underneath, I was sure, was a good brain. But Willis was a vagabond, like Bluey. Adventure not knowledge was the object of his quest. I remembered him hauled back home after his first escape; from Bluff, where he had joined an oyster boat. He took his beating like a man; and the next week was off again—to the Coast, the gold dredges. I had to let him go in the end. He signed on a freighter as cabin boy. And ten years later limped into Peacehaven on his wooden leg, grinning like a gargoyle. No letter for over a year; but in his seaman's bag a Finnish doll for Edie and a brass buddha for me. What could we do but cry over him and shake him by the hand?

Yes, my sons. Oliver the success, and Willis the failure. And Emerson, the Sundowner of the Skies. Plodding, courageous Robert. And Alfred. What was Alfred? On that night in the train I thought of him as Chatterton, dead at seventeen. Marvellous boy. But dead. And then became aware of my self-deception. I have noticed many times that I turn to some example or case from literature when I want to evade a clear sight of my behaviour. It will not do. And for the first time in twenty years I saw that Alfred's life had carried on. I felt the pain of his loss. Somewhere in the world Alfred was living; journeying as I was journeying. He would be forty-two: middle-aged. I could no longer feel that he was evil. I felt tears on my cheeks for the brilliant boy.

So in the witching hours I dozed and dreamed. The train murmured on. From time to time my hand dragged me to the surface and I felt the motion of rushing ahead. Dawn came. The young man climbed down from his bunk and fetched me tea and sandwiches. He took himself off again while I dressed. And soon we were in a long tunnel; then bursting on to the harbourside.

"—pleasure meeting you, Mr Plumb."

We went through shunting yards, side-stepping over points; and rolled slowly at the side of a crowded platform. Smiling faces, hair blown by the wind.

And there was Felicity. My daughters are more reliable than my sons.

35 "Daddy," she said, "have you really stopped believing in God?"

"No, my dear, I have not. And never will. Who told you that?"

"Helen Brockie," naming the daughter of one of my elders. "She said she heard her father telling her mother. They said it was a disgrace and you'd have to be stopped." At fourteen she is easily hurt by the bad opinion of her schoolfellows. "I've been reading about Shelley. Was he really an atheist?"

"Yes."

"But you're not?"

"No. Did Helen say I was?"

"She asked me what it meant, that's all."

"Did you tell her?"

"I told her to go and look in the dictionary."

"Good girl."

"Dad?"

"Yes, Felicity?"

"If *you* believe in something it must be right."

I was alarmed. I hid it. Now was not the time to disturb her faith. I took her hand and asked her to recite me the *Ode to the West Wind*. I told her the man who wrote that need not fear the judgement of the Brockies.

This took place in the garden behind the Manse. It was autumn 1910.

36 My children were growing up. Oliver, the oldest, was sixteen. Only three, Alfred, Margaret, Robert (new-born, red-headed, the last of our children) were not at school. They were handsome and lively, the Plumbs. We were complimented on their good looks and cleverness; but never on their piety. It was a scandal in my parish that my children were not regular at church and Sunday school.

I do not think I influenced Edie against her judgement. She followed where I led but tested every step of the way herself. She was an open-souled creature, yet robust, hungry in her religious nature as a new-born babe for milk. And she was no longer nourished by a penitential religion. That, I think, is why she loved our house so extravagantly. It was a cloak she drew about her so she might know warmth in her bodily life at a time when spiritually she wandered in the dark. We had not been so close in our Thorpe days as in Kumara and Emslie. I had thrown myself too much into my search for a political way and religious truth. But in the cold winter of 1909 we came together. I discovered that while I had been questing she had been taking her first wary steps, brave steps. *Audax et cautus*. I would like to say those words described my way. But I was less honest. I still kept Sunday in its box and entered it with the better part of my being held in check. I marvel that it went on for so long.

Edie was more in my study at the end. We spent long evenings together, talking and reading. One thing we never questioned: our vision of life was religious. What we sought was a form of worship that would not cripple us as rational beings. And more and more it grew plain that what we must do was put aside Christ, sweep Him into the past, those dark and superstitious times in which He had his genesis, and turn to the real person, Jesus the man. And go on through him, as an example of goodness, to God, to the One, of whom we were a part.

This brings into small compass ten years of searching, two years of it in the company of my wife. I will say nothing of our reading, or of that stretching of mind and spirit that set the air in my study trembling as at a charge of some force like electricity. Rather, I remember our companionship.

Her hand takes mine, signalling support of some new intention. I feel its roughness and have in that instant a knowledge of part of her life that has escaped me: the scrubbing, the sewing, the labour of her days as I drink tea and scribble in the margins of my books. We read again. We talk. She laughs with excitement. Later she cries. The cure is hard, often we are in pain—she more than I. I have been ten years on this way, my coming to health no longer requires cuts and dislocations.

We sit by the fire. Midnight chimes on the hall clock. Kate is asleep, the children asleep. The embers are taking on a coat of grey.

"And so it's decided," she says.

"If you will stand beside me." (I mean this metaphorically—there is no place for wives on the platform I have agreed to mount.)

"I will, George. You know that. I can even lose this house now."

"We'll find another house."

"Yes." She is quiet. "Oliver's going to be upset."

"Oliver must learn courage. He cares too much about what people think."

"He's very good at school, George."

"He's clever."

She sighs. "The others won't mind so much. We'll be able to feed and clothe them."

"Educate them. Feed their minds. They won't suffer. Not in any way that matters."

"We'll have to let Kate go. She'd stay without wages but we can't ask that."

"Can you manage?"

"I can manage, George. Felicity's a help now."

We are quiet for a moment. Windows rattle in a gust of wind.

"George?"

"Yes, my dear?"

"Will you be able to buy the books you need?"

"I may have to cut down. John will let me use his library."

"You must buy what you need, George. The rest of us will get by."

Again we are quiet. She smiles.

"What is it, my dear?"

"I was thinking of Rebecca. She was at a birthday party yesterday and they asked her to say grace. The minister's daughter."

"Had she forgotten?"

"Listen. 'God in heaven, thank you for the party, which looks very nice, especially the jelly.'"

We laugh delightedly. "Were they scandalized?"

"I don't know. At least, Rebecca doesn't. She was too busy eyeing the jelly."

We laugh again. We are very pleased with our children.

37 All except Oliver. I am not pleased with him. Worship for our eldest son was an act of conformity. He had a saintly style, or should I say monkish? and a jesuitical manner of argument. Legalism was his vice, even at that early age. There was no spirit, no emotion, in his religious behaviour; but a narrow-eyed concern for proper observance. For some time he had been unhappy with us.

"Oliver," I said, "your mother and I have been doing a lot of thinking."

"What about?"

"About our faith. Our souls. And about our future. I mean," I said, for he provoked me to exactness, "our condition in eternity."

"I thought all that was taken care of."

"How?"

"We're Presbyterians aren't we?"

"Yes, we are. And I hope to remain one. If I can change one or two parts of the doctrine." Hearing my voice say it, I became breathless, I felt myself shrink. There was no hope. I knew it. "Oliver," I said, "I'd like you to share what your mother and I are finding. You and Felicity. And Edith, perhaps. The others are not ready yet. But you three could come to my study after tea—"

"No."

"Why not?"

"I don't want to hear what you're saying. I know what I believe."

"At sixteen?"

"I believe what I was taught. I'm not leaving the church. Not for you or anyone. People would .   "

"People, Oliver?"

"You want to throw everything away."

"No son. All I want to do is follow my reason and conscience. Your mother too."

"Reason? Why? You've got your bible. You're a minister."

"Has your reading taught you nothing, Oliver?"

"You made me do it. I never wanted to read half the stuff you gave me."

"Stuff?"

"Emerson. Theodore Parker. All that bilge."

"Listen, Oliver." I clutched him as though he were drowning. "You come with me next week. There's a lecture I want you to hear. There's so much for you to learn—"

"If it's McCabe I'm not going."

"Why, Oliver?"

"Because he's Anti-Christ, that's why. And you should be getting up and preaching against him."

"Is that what people are saying?"

90

"It's what I'm saying. And now can I go? I've got to get to school."

"Oliver—"

"I'm a Presbyterian now and I'll be a Presbyterian when I die. And I'll go to heaven. And you and mother will go to hell and burn."

All of this he said quite calmly; and kept a clear straight eye. He says it to this day.

38 Let them be original, I used to pray. A late prayer. Earlier I had planted in my son the doctrines of a narrow creed.

There was no weeding them out. The certain torment of his parents in hell caused Oliver less pain than his own condition as child of heretics. This may be seen as original.

Felicity came to hear Joseph McCabe. So did Edie. Oliver went to his Christian Endeavour meeting. And I?

Well, some months earlier John Jepson had come to me with the news that McCabe was visiting New Zealand, and Thorpe, on a lecture tour for the R.P.A. of London. Spreading the word, John called it; a missionary visit. He was giving two lectures at the Choral Hall: "The Evolution of Man" and "The Present Conflict between Science and Theology". John was chairman of the lecture committee.

I was excited. I knew all about McCabe: his Catholic upbringing, his twelve years in a Franciscan monastery—Father Antony—his struggle to shake superstition off: and then the books, the pamphlets, the lectures, the life lived with a purpose; the crusade, if you like, against the forces of religious obscurantism. I had read every word he had written. He was one of the shapers of my mind. And this man was coming to Thorpe. Yes, I was excited. When John offered me the chair at the second lecture I accepted without a moment's hesitation. I even brought forward a long-planned visit to Auckland so that I might be in Thorpe on the date.

McCabe arrived on the Christchurch express one Monday evening. A large party met him at the station. John introduced him to Mr Bridewell, the Deputy Mayor; and many of us saw the humour of the situation as this High Anglican gentleman cautiously explained that it was the custom in our town to extend an official welcome to well-known persons from the Old Country. However, we rescued McCabe, John took him off to his home; and later in the evening Edward and Andrew and I called there to take a cup of tea with him. What a glorious evening! The book-lined walls, the glowing fire, the company of like-minded men, the talk that threw a beam of whitest light down the road of the future. From time to time a wordless Mrs Jepson brought in pots of tea and plates of rich plum cake, which I must say was delicious.

"Mr Plumb," McCabe said, "I've had many fine chairmen on my tour but I can't remember that any of them have been men of the cloth. Now tell me, what are the consequences to be? Does the breadth of mind of your fellow ministers extend to having you stand on a public platform with an heretic like me?"

"No," I said, "it does not. Though one or two will support me privately."

"I know them. Closet free-thinkers. Ah, what a place to be free in. You're expecting trouble, then?"

"I am."

"The Presbyterian *Statement of Faith* is a tightly written document."

"Very much so."

"And the disciplinary powers?"

"All laid down in the *Book of Order*. Neat and tidy."

"So, Mr Plumb, I've come at a high point in your life, I see. I'm pleased my talk will be your vehicle."

"I'll not say much," I said.

"But enough," Andrew cried, who would have seen me hauled to the gallows and my children starve for a principle.

"Oh yes, enough."

"Our careers are not dissimilar," McCabe said. "Will you write and let me know what happens?"

But our talk was mostly of a general future. I look upon the evening as among the happiest of my life.

McCabe's mind was an instrument of strength and delicacy. He had the reasoning powers of a John Stuart Mill and the wit of an Oscar Wilde, if one can imagine a marriage between those minds. His breadth of reference amazed us poor colonials; and his history caused us to look on him with awe, as on one who has spent a season in hell. He was a being of power. This though was not all. This, so to speak, was the then and now of the man. It was as seer, as prophet, that he impressed us most. The future was brought into John Jepson's library on that cold winter night.

"Our work is to lift the Christian dogmas from the human mind. What is good and true in men and women does not need this foundation to rest upon. Only when it is gone will we know that we act in a selfless way and not out of self-interest. The after-life is a mirage, an *ignis fatuus*—a glorious term I came across recently, the celestial honeypot. (Laughter.) Only when we fix our whole attention on this life, this life here, among men and women, our brothers and sisters not in Christ but in humanity, only then will we discover this life's possibilities and enter our golden age."

"Hear, hear. The future is with us," Andrew cried.

Mrs Jepson came in, very still of face. She put tea and cake on the table.

"Thank you, ma'am. This is a very fine cake." And when she had gone, "A fine lady, Mr Jepson."

None of us answered that. Edward and I smiled sadly at each other. We had a better knowledge of the lady. And Edward, skilled with his pencil, slipped me a little sketch of her (I have it among my papers) mouse-like in the half-light by the door, with one of her ears extended like a hearing-trumpet. Underneath he had written *The Ear of the Past*.

39 The lecture "The Present Conflict between Science and Theology" was the second of the two. The hall had been packed for "The Evolution of Man"; but there were not to be lantern slides in the second. And the weather was bad. Only a hundred people came along.

Joseph McCabe and I were alone on the stage. We chatted while the audience settled itself. The Choral Hall was built like a barn and we shivered as we spoke.

"Not nerves, I hope, Mr Plumb."

"No. It's the cold that troubles me. I've had plenty of practice in speaking. Remember George Jacob Holyoake?" (McCabe had written his life.) "No man who has studied Holyoake's method can be nervous at facing an audience."

"Now there's a man who suffered for his convictions. They tried George for blasphemy, you know. And threw him in a dungeon. Poor stammering George."

The example gave me courage. I had a quick look at my notes. McCabe touched my arm to wish me luck. I rose, had quiet (that quiet that always seems both slow and sudden and turns one's stomach once, like a falling lift) and began to talk. McCabe had agreed I should state my position. So I said, "Many of you will be surprised to see me on this platform. And for those amongst you who can see only my collar but don't know my face, I'm George Plumb, Presbyterian minister of St Andrews. You will want to know what I'm doing here. Well, the answer is simple. I'm introducing Mr Joseph McCabe, a great scientist, writer, and Haeckelian philosopher, whose words to you tonight will, I believe, send you out of this hall far better and wiser people than ever you are likely to be on coming out of a church—my church or any other. That's the truth of my presence here. And yet it's an evasion. So I'll speak plainly. I stand here as chairman of this meeting in protest against the absurdities of the orthodox teaching of the present day."

"Hear, hear!" Edward cried; and Andrew echoed him.

I held up my hand. "You are not in church, Mr Cryer." A joke that won some laughter, though it puzzled a good many, including McCabe. Edie smiled faintly. She was sitting towards the back so her nervousness would not distress me. Beside her was Felicity, her face white and brave. I spoke to another quarter, hoping to turn inquisitive glances from them.

"As a Protestant I can understand the position of the Catholic authorities." ("No!" Andrew shouted: a hot-head.) "It is logical and consistent." ("No!") "But I remember that Protestantism began as a rationalizing movement and I cannot understand any Protestant person or body objecting to the teachings of science—of evolution, for instance. I look forward with hope to the complete rationalizing and liberalizing of religion as the work of Protestantism in its best sense. I hope that Mr McCabe's visit will have as one result the setting up in Thorpe of some sort of society for the study of the views which Mr McCabe will present to you tonight." ("Hear, hear!") "He will leave behind him the seed of his thought in all our minds, and our duty as thinking men and women will be to bring that seed to its full growth. There is a task for us that will test our strength and courage. We must show in intellectual things that same 'nerveless proficiency' that a London paper gives us credit for in athletic pursuits." I went on a little longer. I have made better speeches, but none in which I have felt so plainly my strength and nakedness. Then I introduced McCabe, and sat down.

I was astonished at my calmness, my enjoyment of my dislocated life. Here I had thrown away the easy future and laid on my back and on my family's back a burden that might break us all. And I felt like laughing. For the first time in many years I was my own man.

McCabe, in his plain polished way, said friendly things: he was happy in having such a chairman, my church in having such a minister. He said he had found much breadth of thought in our town—such as could not have been gained by the listening to sectarian pulpits. (One would have thought he wished me hanged for a sheep.) Then he spoke for an hour and a half on science and theology.

I heard very little of it. I was in a daze of happiness and optimism. From time to time I heard bursts of applause and Scottish shouts. But I watched a star of light winking on the rim of the water jug; and lengthening my sight, saw the pale blur of two faces dear to me; and I required no arguments to convince me of the rightness of my way or of my strength to travel it. McCabe wound up. Theology was demolished; but true religion left intact. For, he said, he knew many scientists who were deeply religious. As honest men they believed the evidence of their senses, of their researches, yet they must believe too in a great controlling Power. "I respect such men," said McCabe. "They prove that science has not lost spiritual vision. Yet how different spiritual vision is from the creeds of the Christian churches. Indeed those creeds are dying. As the torch of science moves onwards through the world the lanterns of theology are fading out before it. We have evidence tonight of how far the cause of science is advanced. We have it in our chairman, Mr Plumb, who has moved from a position of orthodoxy, from the religion of the churches, to a new and noble ground from which he can utter his brave challenge to superstition. He is the man of the future, Scientific man. And yet I would ask you to remember that he remains deeply religious. That is not my way; but I respect it. To those of you in intellectual or in spiritual doubt I recommend it as a stepping stone."

There was much applause; some of it for me. McCabe sat down with a happy look on his face. Even in such little halls as ours these moments were the high points of his life. I rose and invited questions. For a moment the hall was quiet. Then a man stood up in the shadows at the back. I saw the immaculate band of a collar like mine, and only then a face I recognized. Mr Mitchell, who believed in my love for the scriptures, had died, and the call of his congregation at Trinity had gone to Morrison Macauley, the type of coldly burning young fanatic who would have gladdened the heart of John Knox. He it was who said now, "I have listened. I have come here against every inclination of my being, impelled by my Christian duty to face the Enemy of Life. I have heard filth and smelled the stink of the Pit. But even here I bring a message: That to sinners of the blackest dye the way remains open—"

There were cries of "Shame", and "Quiet", and "Put him out" And I called loudly that I had asked for questions not for speeches. Macauley was not to be stopped. "The Christians of Thorpe are outraged by the presence among them of the Anti-Christ. We have met together today and formed the Thorpe Christian Evidence League. It will meet at my house on Thursday evenings, and for your salvation I implore you to seek us out and listen to the truth that we have for you. For the worst of sins is to deny the Lord—"

A pack of young men like a rugby scrum heaved Macauley down the aisle and into the street. As he went he chanted the 97th Psalm. And such was the power of the words that I felt my spirit shrink.

> His lightnings enlightened the world: the earth saw and trembled.
> The hills melted like wax at the presence of the Lord, at the presence of the Lord of the whole earth.

"These fanatics are interesting cases," McCabe said.

We walked home in a group. For a time I felt threatened, wary of doorways and shadows. But the good company restored me to cheerfulness, and I made them laugh with tales of Macauley's zeal. A young man who had helped put him from the hall said, "He's out for your blood, Mr Plumb. He said you'll be called to account for your words tonight."

"I know I will. But Macauley has already been judged by a better band of men." They applauded that.

We dropped them off one by one (McCabe with a quick handshake, for I would be at the station in the morning). At last only Edward was left. He lived on the other side of town but asked if he might walk as far as our gate. Macauley's psalm had taken him on a raw part of his mind—he had not rid himself of superstition any more easily than I. Edie saw his need for company. She took his arm. I walked with Felicity.

"Well my dear, did you enjoy Mr McCabe?"

"I liked you better."

"Now Felicity, that's not being sensible."

"Mr McCabe had said all his things before. Yours were for the first time."

"That's true."

We walked in silence. She came close to my side, under my umbrella.

"Dad?"

"Yes?"

"I'm going into full communion next month."

"Well, my dear?"

"I don't want to any more."

"Are you sure of that?"

"I couldn't belong to the same church as Mr Macauley. He looked like a murderer. With his eyes."

"He's the sort of man who used to burn people at the stake."

"Yes, horrible."

"Don't let him trouble you. He's a man of the past. But tell me Felicity, what will you believe?"

"What you believe."

"No, child. You must work out your path for yourself."

"But dad—"

"My days of telling people what to think are over. What are you smiling about?"

"Nothing, dad."

At the gate Edward shook my hand.

"Well, Edward?"

"You've crossed your Rubicon, George."

"And a better man for it."

"You've friends who'll stand by you."

He strode away down the wet street, his shoes making a lonely sound—back to his room above his florist shop. Edie and I and Felicity went inside.

40 The weeks that followed were a trial to our patience. For nothing happened. The town simmered like a pot but did not boil over. Our lives appeared to keep their even flow. We read reports of McCabe's Dunedin lectures. Edie, I believe, began to hope we would be able to stay on in the Manse. I found her walking in the frozen garden, and from her eye knew she could see the seedlings of the Spring. But I knew my fellow ministers too well. Somewhere they had come together. This time there would be no fraternal visit.

I stayed away from the next Presbytery meeting. In the afternoon the clerk brought me a letter, explaining that the members had not wanted me to discover its contents from the morning paper. I thanked him; offered him tea, which he refused; saw him on his way; and retired to my study. There I read that at the meeting the Revd Mr Macauley had moved that "in view of Mr Plumb's having appeared and presided at a lecture delivered by Mr McCabe, the Rationalist, and in view of the statements made by Mr Plumb at the meeting, and of other disquieting utterances, the Presbytery ask him to meet them in conference at Trinity Hall, Thorpe, on August 16 at 11.15 a.m." The Revd Mr Oddie seconded the motion, which was put and carried without dissent. Mr Plumb was therefore asked to present himself at the appointed time and place.

As the young man had said, they were out for my blood. I called in Edie and showed her the letter. And saw a light die from her eyes; and another take its place. She said, "You had better work on your defence, George."

"It will not be a defence, my dear. It will be an attack."

Yet we were both in pain. In spite of everything I had kept a hope that I might be able to stay on in the church. I was attacked from several quarters in the weeks that followed—once in a newspaper editorial—for not resigning when it became clear to me that my beliefs were no longer those of the church. But I was not a destroyer, I was a reformer—honourable profession (Luther, Calvin, John Knox—a trio I no longer care to stand with!). And I refused to admit that a statement of faith is set for all time. *Tempori parendum*, was my cry. (I had not, I see now, an institutional nature. But a religious nature, yes.) I suffered at being struck in the face by men at whose side I had worked for fifteen years. I had grown and wanted to make them grow along with me.

Edie's concern was more for the children. She was sure of her way. But for Oliver she had a mother's pain at seeing him go off down his blind narrow street. She blamed herself. And she saw how the others must suffer at their schools, at the hands of other children. I believe she exaggerated their trials. Felicity, and her sisters in her train, Edith, Florence, Agnes, little Esther, became my ardent supporters. There were enough of them to keep out the cold. Willis saw the whole thing as a sporting event. I was David taking on Goliath. He would have liked nothing better than to keep me supplied with stones. Emerson was so busy building a trolley he did not know anything unusual was going on. The rest were too young to know.

It was Kate, our broad kind Kate, who dealt them their hardest blow. She came to us in the study and said she was giving notice. She wished to leave at once.

"But why, Kate? What's happened?" We thought some piece of naughtiness had been too much for her.

"I can't watch the children brought up without religion."

"Oh Kate, oh Kate," Edie cried. And I said, "But they won't be, Kate. They'll be brought up without superstition, that's all."

"I won't listen," she said. "I won't listen to that."

"But Kate," Edie said, "we'll be giving them a new religion. A better one. They'll still believe in God."

"I won't," Kate said. "I won't. Oh those dear little things"— and she began to cry—"denied their eternal comfort."

Where had she learned such phrases? But I knew. And I shook my head in a rage at my blindness—at the damage I had done. I had thought faith and worship were simple for Kate, like the taking of food; and in a sense I was right. A bitter gruel was her nourishment and she could not live without it. This was the food I had brought her and told her to like. And brought to how many others? Poisoned how many others in this way?

"I'll say goodbye to them in the morning," Kate said. "Will you say I'm going home to nurse my mother?"

"Oh, Kate."

"It's true. She's very old. She can't walk any more."

"Stay with us, Kate. At least for a little while."

"I can't, Mrs Plumb. I can't." Tears dripped into her bosom. She raised her hands to ward us off. Edie followed her to her little room, but Kate would not allow her past the door. She came back to me.

"Oh George, she thinks I'm bad." And she wept. We loved Kate. She had been with us fifteen years.

She left the next day. All the children cried. Oliver cried.

41 But now there were other things for me to think of. Two more Sundays I presided in my church—a packed church now. I preached careful sermons that raised not a single eyebrow. At home I worked in my defence/attack—let me call it statement. I wrote to the Presbytery clerk saying I would be present at the meeting, but that it must be open to the press. I would not, I said, suffer the fate of Mr Bridges of Templemore, who some years earlier had been rebuked by his Presbytery for unspecified misconduct, and not been allowed to defend himself in public. I would have full publication of both charges and defence or I would leave the meeting.

The morning came. We sat around the table, chatting politely, until the Moderator, Dr Green, called us to devotions. These done, he told us the meeting would be private, in accordance with the *Book of Order*. He asked the reporters to leave.

I protested. But Green would not hear me until the two young men, one from the *Herald*, one from the *Post*, had left.

Then he said, "Mr Plumb, this is a fraternal conference and the *Book of Order* provides that conferences of this sort be private. If you like I'll read you the section."

"I know it," I said. "It's a rule made to be broken. I won't be bound by meaningless rules." I looked at these men gathered at the table—nine ministers and five elders—at kindly, bumbling, ordinary Green, trying for authority like a bad actor, and granite-souled Oddie, and troubled, sad McGregor, and puzzled Downie, who remembered my bible and Mitchell's approval of it, and angry Gates, and angry Matheson, and smooth smiling Graham, who wanted a quiet recantation, and the rest; especially Macauley, who had me speared like an infidel on his eye; and I said, "I ask you to behave as Christian charity dictateth. At the moment you're hiding behind a book. You're carrying on as if you have something to hide. I have nothing to hide. Let's have the press in. Let's have some light in the dark places."

"You can move to have the press in, Mr Plumb. You have that right," Dr Green said.

"Very well, I move that the press be invited back."

"A seconder?" Green asked.

There was none.

"So, Mr Plumb. We remain a private meeting."

"I can't agree to it. I wrote to Mr McGregor telling him I wouldn't discuss the matter unless in open meeting. And I won't go back on that."

"But Mr Plumb"—Green was puzzled—"I think you misunderstand what we're about. We've made no charges against you. We're asking you to explain your behaviour, that's all. Fraternally. Who knows, we may be satisfied?"

I laughed. "You may be, Dr Green. But not Mr Macauley. He won't be satisfied until he carries out my head on a platter."

"I protest at this language," Macauley cried.

"And I," Oddie said. "I think we should put an end to this bickering and get on with our business. Mr Plumb has been called here to explain certain things—called not invited. So let him get on with it. Or let him leave. We can do quite well without him."

I looked at Green. "We're a private meeting?"

102

"We are. That is my ruling."

"Then good day, gentlemen. And good day Mr Oddie and Mr Macauley." I walked out.

In the street the reporters came at me with their pencils drawn. I told them why I had left.

"What happens now, Mr Plumb?" the *Herald* man asked.

"You'll have to ask Dr Green. But you may say that I won't discuss anything unless in open meeting. I have my defence, my statement. And if they refuse to hear it publicly then I'll give it to you gentlemen. And you can publish it. They can shelter behind the *Book of Order* if they wish. I'll come out in the open."

"Will they suspend you, Mr Plumb?"

"I don't know. They'll no doubt frame some sort of Libel against me. That's the procedure. But you'll have to ask them."

"What will you do if you are expelled?"

"Continue telling the truth. They have the power to take away my living but they can't take away my principles." I remember saying too that the most pathetic being in the world is a minister cut adrift, but I meant that in no self-pitying way, as some accused me of.

While I was talking out there and, being no politician, saying too much, the Presbytery was deliberating inside. They produced the following resolution (a copy to me, a copy to the press):

"Whereas the Revd George Oliver Henry Plumb, of St Andrews, presided at a meeting held in the Choral Hall, Thorpe, on 13 July, 1910, when the well-known Rationalist, Joseph McCabe, spoke on 'The Present Conflict between Science and Theology', and

"Whereas Mr Plumb stated that he took the chair in protest against the absurdities of the orthodox teaching of the present day and hoped that a result of the meeting would be the setting up in Thorpe of a society to study Rationalist views, and

"Whereas it appears that the Revd Mr Plumb is a member of the Rationalist Press Association, of London, recognized as one of the leading infidel organizations in Britain, and

"Whereas Mr Plumb has publicly recommended some of the Rationalist publications of this Association, and

"Whereas Mr Plumb, while a Presbyterian minister professing the Christian faith as held by this Church, preached on 3 July, 1910, in the Unitarian Church at Auckland, which church was about to become vacant, and

"Whereas such conduct is totally at variance with the principles of this church and inconsistent with the solemn vows which every minister makes at his ordination, and contrary to the principles of conduct expected from a minister of a Christian church, and

"Whereas Mr Plumb has refused to meet the Presbytery in private to have a brotherly and frank disclosure of his opinions,

"The Presbytery hereby requires Mr Plumb to furnish the Presbytery with a written explanation of his conduct, and the Presbytery resolves to adjourn for a fortnight to receive this explanation and further deal with the case."

42 "Five charges now." And Edward, more innocent than I, scratched his head.

"It seems your errors are breeding, George," John Jepson said.

"Aye, and if we didn't live in a civilized age yon priests would be at you with the thumbscrew and the rack," Andrew said.

"You'll not go to a private meeting, George?"

"No. I'll write to them." I was tired. As soon as I laid down my pen, which was not often, I became oppressed with a sense of having mismanaged the affair. This country walk, promoted by Edie, was meant to cheer me up. But I was not easily cheered. John Findlater read us his latest poem and I offended him by saying, "There are no poets in this country. Apart from one thing of Bracken's there hasn't been a single true poem yet."

Bluey was gobbling licorice straps. He offered me one. "Reverend," he said, "I'm sorry I missed that McCabe. Now there's a good Mick name. And a rebel priest, you say? I'm sorry I missed him. But those Dunedin pubs are hard to get out of." He had gone south to a Saturday race meeting and stayed for a week. Jobless, he came to the Manse for two or three meals a week. He was a disappointment to me, yet I could not dislike him—as the others did, thoroughly, by now. I had him placed as vagabond, a class not without its uses. His place as workman in our group was filled by Dan Peabody, a young railway stoker I had found in the town library one night asking for Marx's *Kapital*. I had taken him home and loaned him my copy and he had declared political ambitions so extravagant that at first I thought he was making fun of me. He meant to be New Zealand's first Socialist Prime Minister. He was impatient of our religious concerns; and thought poetry and rambling on the hills a waste of time. He thought Bluey a waste of time.

"Ah Reverend," Bluey said, "I wish I'd been there to help throw out that priest. I'd have had my little shillelah in my coat." By coming after me on one of my side-jaunts he managed to get me alone. "Is it true you're having to leave the Manse?"

"If they expel me, Bluey. And I think they will."

"Now you couldn't reach some agreement with them, could you?"

"Let them buy me, Bluey?"

"Ah now, I don't mean that. But it's such a cosy place. I'll miss coming there." This though was not his real concern.

"Now, Reverend."

"What is it Bluey?"

"You tell me about this rationalist business. Does it mean you don't believe in an after-life?"

"I'm not an atheist, Bluey, if that's what you mean."

"So you think there's a God?"

"A power of some sort. Call it what you will. A Supreme Being."

"But if there's that you need priests."

"No, Bluey. No. That doesn't follow at all. There's just man and his Maker. Man facing God. Nobody in between. No priests. No Christ."

He found the idea un-nerving. "No hell, Reverend? No torments?"

"None, Bluey."

"No?"

"None. That's superstition."

"Aye, Reverend. That's what I think too." He did not. Even at that age, far he believed from his death, he was a man in terror. They had had him from birth to young manhood and though he had escaped they crept back to haunt him in the night.

"Come Bluey," I said, "let your mind work. You're a man now. You don't believe in fairies any more. Or Father Christmas. So let this other stuff go. Just turn your mind on it and it withers up."

"Aye Reverend, that's so. That's all I have to do." And he grinned and ate some licorice. But fear was not quite gone from the back of his eye. "I'm ashamed of meself. I really am. I don't believe that stuff. Not in a beautiful world like this. Look at those clouds, Reverend. Lovely, aren't they? How can you believe in eternal punishment in a world like this?"

"True, Bluey."

"But Reverend, if you could have heard those boyos spouting. Real artists, they were. Sparks crackin' from their lips and us poor little b——— curling up. Aye, telling how the red-hot worms would wriggle up our a—holes."

"Now, Bluey." (I can no more write down ugly words than say them.)

"Well, Reverend, it wasn't quite like that. But it was near."

The others were stamping up and down to keep warm. We went back to them and the seven of us walked down to the town—a quieter group than usual.

"This whispering campaign, George. Who do you think's behind it?"

"Just my good God-fearing co-religionists."

"Macauley?"

"Macauley doesn't whisper, Macauley shouts."

"They'll have you taking black mass in the cemetery next."

"Aye," said Andrew. "What haven't they accused you of? Atheism, Pantheism, Monism, Arianism."

"They could make Arianism stick," John Jepson said.

"Dictionary words," Dan Peabody grumbled.

"They all have meanings, Dan. Arianism was Milton's heresy."

"But still, I don't like isms," I said. "I'm a free-thinker, no more."

"It's a grand title," Edward said.

"And did you know," said John, "Nietzsche wanted a monastery for free-thinkers? Would you go there, George?"

"To an institution? No. They'd all end up believers soon enough."

"But in what?"

"That's not the point. Belief closes the mind. Thought knows no final decision. It looks forward always to new evidence. And speaking of Nietzsche, remember his terrible phrase 'the castration of the intellect'. That's the end of belief. I'll keep a free mind."

Edie's stratagem worked. I was happier when I came down.

43 I sat in my study and wrote Presbytery a letter telling them I had their resolution and would come to a meeting with them and read my statement but leave if the press were kept out. Then I wrote a letter to the *Herald* and the *Post*:

"Sir, In your issue of Wednesday last I note the resolution of the Presbytery in regard to myself and remarks made when presiding at Mr J. McCabe's meeting. Does it not cause food for thought that two of the finest words in the English language, *freethought* and *rationalism* should have a kind of stigma attached to them by orthodox clergymen! That which is rational is sane and falls in line with common sense. My protest was a protest against the orthodox teachings of the day relating to the creation of man, and suggested by the teaching of evolution, which is now an accepted scientific truth. Outside of this I attacked no doctrine, and will answer no questions on any doctrine whatever, outside or inside the Presbytery. My worthy Scotch friends (and they dearly love a heresy case) who think that they are coming together for a good two hours enjoyment at my expense must be disillusioned.

Trippings, trappings and pitfalls after the old inquisitional style will be useless. Samson with his eyes gouged out does not intend to make sport for the Philistines. Here is my reply to their charges:

"Yes I am a member of the R.P.A.—proud of the fact. It is not an infidel organization, but exists for the purpose of educating the ordinary people out of their superstitions by putting into their hands in a cheap form the results and verified conclusions of modern science. It is resulting in a loud clamour the world over for a liberal religious view. Ultimately it will save people from the materialistic and atheistic drift. Man must and will worship, but he must do so in a rational and sane way. I have faith in the religious instincts of man, and know he will return to a sensible shrine when the message is modernized and brought into line with reason and fact. No sir, the publishing of the R.P.A. literature does not mean the destruction of the Christian religion, but only of the obsolete and useless parts of it, and the building up of a newer and brighter faith. The list of subscribers to the R.P.A. is fairly well sprinkled with the names of clergymen, so I do not stand alone, excepting that I am the only minister in New Zealand. But this Dominion is conservative in religious matters, and about fifty years behind the rest of the world. Even so, I know of Presbyterians who believe as I do, and ministers amongst them. Let the Revds Oddie and Macauley go round the Presbyteries of New Zealand with the hot pincers, they will find more than one who will give a good healthy squeak.

"Yes again, I procured a student to conduct my services, and went for a holiday to Hamilton and Auckland. At Hamilton my kind host asked me to preach in the Wesleyan Church, which I did. At Auckland I stayed with Unitarian friends, and again was asked to preach. I did not go as a candidate to a charge becoming vacant. But yes, I stood in that pulpit, unashamed. My query to the minister, Mr Jellie, as to what line I was to go on, brought forth a reply that clings to me yet with a peculiar fascination. 'Mr Plumb, when you stand in my pulpit, bring your religious message into line with the latest scientific knowledge and the latest and most scholarly results of the historical criticism of the Bible. In fact, take off the muzzle and be free.'

"Blessed thought—it refreshes the mind like the scent of the spring violets coming through my window. Much of the orthodox teaching affects my mind like the smell of mildew and fungus. See, I would gladly give my right hand to hear the Presbytery say to me what the Revd Mr Jellie said. I preached in the Unitarian Church to one of the finest congregations of young people I ever saw, and on the Monday was asked to become a candidate. Yes, there is no denying it. I feel a strong, strong pull that way. Still I must await events. The Presbyterian Church will reach that point in time. It is a weary waiting. This reminds me of a southern minister, an M.A., holding a Presbyterian charge, telling me some time ago that he moulded all his sermons from Unitarian literature, and especially the *Hibbert Journal*. Now this journal is the leading philosophical journal in the world, and is edited by Mr Jacks, a Unitarian, and filled with articles written by Unitarian ministers, and those in orthodox churches holding Unitarian views. So the poor old world wags on.

"While I say all this, let me add that although I have dropped many old views overboard I still hold to the great moral verities of the Christian belief, and would not have introduced the subject of Unitarianism only for the Presbytery mentioning it. A word more, and I finish. All kinds of rumours are abroad, and some members of Presbytery seem to have a greedy ear for gossip, which they even whisper to the papers. The *Book of Order* I do not know well. If given the choice whether to read a page of that book or take a dose of castor oil, I would take the oil gladly. There is one sentence in the *Book of Order* that clings to my memory. It is this: 'Hearsay evidence is not admissible.'

"I am etc.

"George O. H. Plumb."

44 Felicity brought in my tea.
"Where's your mother?"
"Sewing a dress for Rebecca."

"Oh yes." I was seeing less of her now Kate was gone. "Ask her to come in a minute. You come too."

When they were standing before me I read my letter. It moved us all. I looked up from time to time and saw Edie's careful attention; and the face of my daughter. Her eyes grew bright at the smell of violets, moistened and shone at the loss of my right hand, sparkled with humour (an emphatic, dogmatic humour) at my mention of castor oil and the *Book of Order*.

"It's wonderful, dad."

"Yes George, you've said it beautifully."

These two, these women, were a pair of Aeolian harps through which the winds of my history whispered and roared. I heard their harmonies, which I took into my being like a food.

45 On the morning of my "trial" I had a visit from McIlwraith, one of the St Andrews' managers. We talked of the painting of the belfry, but when this was done he came to his real business.

"Many of us support you, Mr Plumb. Mr Kydd and I will be at the meeting to say so."

I shook him by the hand and told him I regretted not paying more attention to the good people of my congregation: in my pride I had thought myself alone. I apologized. And I said I was sure I had spoken no heresy from my pulpit.

"We know that, Mr Plumb. I won't say we're happy about what you've done—or said for that matter. But we think you're impetuous, not that you're unChristian. And if there's any disagreement it's for us as a congregation to iron out. We won't be told what to do by Mr Macauley. I've come to tell you that. And I'll tell Presbytery this morning."

"If they'll let you speak."

"They'll let me speak." I heard the swish of the claymore.

So I went along heartened and ready, knowing I was not to stand alone. Edie, holding Robert in her arms, saw me off at the gate. I rode my bicycle.

46 The faces were the same: Green, Oddie, Macauley, Graham, etc. In addition there were a dozen members of the public: McIlwraith, Kydd, Brockie, from St Andrews; Scroggie, who had followed me at Kumara; Geddes, observing for the Christchurch Presbytery, and looking as lemonish as ever; Buttle, a visiting Wesleyan; and three or four I did not know. No women. No Edward or John Jepson. I had told them to stay away. There were six reporters.

The meeting opened with devotions; and how weary I found that. I uttered a silent prayer for strength and patience. This, as it came at the end, was noticed. Macauley took it for hypocrisy. I looked around the faces of my peers, who were judging me, and noted those that were closed, those that were open, those that hungered for the fight, and those that wanted no trouble. They were practical men, and men of intelligence—albeit intelligence strictly set within bounds. By their lights they would be fair with me. By their lights. How dim those were. The bare room, the hard seats, seemed chosen with a strict propriety. And I had a premonition of defeat. So that as sad McGregor read the minutes I spent the time steeling myself. I was here to fight, and if I must go down would go down with my sword weaving a band of light about me. They would find my body by the wall. It helped to dramatize things so. I was smiling by the time McGregor finished.

Green cleared his throat. The man was a soft and woolly bear;

and like a bear must not be enraged. I had always treated with him formally. He fixed me with a reddish eye and I saw that he had missed his breakfast honey.

"I wish to underline a point made in the minutes, and that is that the Presbytery has offered to meet Mr Plumb and talk this matter over with him in a friendly way. Mr Plumb has declined that, although it would have been in his own interests and the interests of his congregation and indeed of the whole Presbyterian community of Thorpe. We did not wish for a public enquiry, but a public enquiry has been forced upon us. It is Mr Plumb's doing, and if news of today's proceedings is blown abroad and takes other shapes as it travels, and I know it will do that, knowing the world, then Mr Plumb must bear the responsibility. That, Mr Plumb, is something I felt I must say."

We inclined our heads at each other, like a pair of ancient clubmen over brandy. Green then moved that the meeting be held in public. Macauley seconded, saying the Presbytery had nothing to fear. It was carried without dissent.

Then Macauley's voice—a sharp voice, a cutting instrument—came again, and I saw it was to be very much his day. He waved some newspapers about. "I have here some copies of the Thorpe *Herald* and the Thorpe *Post*, and two Christchurch papers. They contain statements made by Mr Plumb, and I move that they be held *in retentis* as documents in this case."

So the field of possible charges against me widened. I could have challenged the correctness of this, but I did not. I was here to attack, not quibble, to strike with a sword not prick with an inky nib. The motion was carried and McGregor shuffled the papers nervously.

"Now," Green said, "I must raise another question about the nature of this meeting. And that is simply, whether we now begin a formal enquiry? If we do this then Mr Plumb has the right to decide whether he wishes to be tried by libel. And I would remind you—remind you too, Mr Plumb—that in that case he's suspended *ipso facto*. And that of course takes us into deep waters. My feeling is that a formal enquiry should not begin until we've heard Mr Plumb's explanations." As he warmed up on that cold morning, as his position and the flavour of formal language comforted him, he began to mellow. Benevolence was his habit of mind. So alas was the desire to please. Now and then he became aware of it. His kindly smiles were interspersed with anger and hard judgements.

Oddie said, "I must disagree. We could go on having meetings endlessly while Mr Plumb examines his beliefs. The charges are laid. Let's hear them answered. Now. And an end to the talk. I move that this meeting be the first step in a formal enquiry."

Macauley seconded it; and it was carried.

"I disagree," Green said. "But as chairman I'll carry it out. Perhaps you won't object if I give Mr Plumb the option of saying whether he wishes to be tried by libel."

I was impatient by now, and growing angry. I was a little drunk with my cause, and these words, these procedures, were brambles and bushes, preventing me from coming at it again. "I don't mind. Try me how you will. Just let's get it done with. I have an explanation and I'd like to read it."

So trial by libel it became—I saw Macauley's eye glisten at that—and Green gave me leave to read my statement. I stood up. From behind me came a clapping of hands.

At once Macauley cried, "I protest. I protest at this behaviour."

Oddie said, "Mr Plumb's supporters are turning this into a circus."

"Throw them out," Macauley said.

"Gentlemen," Green interrupted, "I remind you I'm in charge of this meeting." He turned to the clappers (Kydd and McIlwraith) and said, "This is not the occasion for applause. Public or not, it's a meeting of the Thorpe Presbytery, and I'll have it conducted in a seemly manner. Any more clapping and I'll have to ask you to leave. You'll not though be thrown out."

It did me good to see Macauley go pink. I'd forgotten he was human. I had made up my mind not to leave him unscarred, and now I said, "Before beginning, I wish to have my protest recorded against the attitude of one member of this Presbytery, the Revd Mr Macauley. Mr Macauley has prejudged my case. He'll deny it, of course. Yes, I hear you Mr Macauley, but please allow me to finish. I ask him to examine his conscience, and if that won't do examine his memory, and he'll find there evidence that he's prejudged me. He's said on the streets of this town, and I can prove it sir, I can call unimpeachable witnesses if you wish, he has said that I'm as guilty as the devil and that he'll not name the place I should go to preach in. No, it's true sir"—for Macauley was shouting by now—"it's true, the words were spoken, and similar words at other times, and I'm placing them before this meeting and I ask to have them written into the records of this meeting."

The clamour that rose was like that of a children's party, for I had placed on the table a most exciting toy, and they played with it for a while with enjoyment. Green had trouble getting order; and he turned an unfriendly eye on me when he had managed. All the same, it went down in McGregor's nervous hand that Mr Plumb had accused Mr Macauley of prejudging him, and Mr Macauley denied it. A victory, I suppose, and a shabby one I take no pride in now. But then it was important. It gave me a foothold in their camp, and I stood firmly there to read my message. I'll not record it here (in 1927 I printed it as an appendix to my book *The Growing Point of Truth*), but say how they received it.

The argument is a simple one: that a false theology, and in particular the false dogmas of creation and fall, stand in the way of scientific truth: that the Christian churches lose ground because they hold to a foolish theology and so close their doors to rational men and women; that our Christian duty is to open our minds and admit the truth and so stop the drift to atheism and materialism. To this end, I said, I had stood with McCabe, and made my famous "utterances" To this end I read and recommended the publications of the R.P.A. of London. To this end spoke freely from whatever pulpit was handy. We must rescue, I said, the great word "faith" from degradations, separate it from outgrown and outworn dogmas. Our cowardice, our hypocrisy, prolong the discord and confusion of religious thought, the anguish of religious doubt. Let us be true and brave, I said, and in time we shall "know the truth and the truth shall make us free" To know, to love, to serve—these are the ends of life; these are alone what makes life worth living, and better far to sacrifice life itself than profane it to the conscious and deliberate slavery of error.

It took me half an hour to read. It fell on deaf ears. I am not surprised today. But on that day I believed, believed increasingly as I went along, that I might find a path into their minds. Their silence when I finished, their cold closed faces, struck me like an iron fist. I was stunned by the sight of them. Presbyterian clergymen. I am not being cruel. I am not being unfair. Or if so, to myself. Naïvety, enthusiasm, are not to be sneered at. I honestly believed I could reach them, these men in their iron cage. And my head, when I saw them there, rang with the weight of their blows, and I almost lost my senses.

Green said, "Thank you, Mr Plumb." The rest said nothing. Until at last Macauley moved that my statement be held *in retentis* by the clerk. And Oddie moved that the Presbytery meet in private to consider it. I was too stunned to object.

The public began to move out. I stood up to follow them.

"No Mr Plumb, no. You're still a member of the Presbytery." So I sat down again.

47 And then came an interruption. McIlwraith and Kydd approached the table. McIlwraith asked permission to speak. "Who are you?" Green asked, though he knew.

"My name is McIlwraith. And this is Mr Kydd. We're two of the managers of St Andrews Church. We'd like to put some evidence before you."

"We've called for no evidence. We need no evidence, do we?" Green asked round.

"It's a simple matter of fact I want to state. It can be done very quickly."

"Simple or no sir, that is not the point. We're a private meeting. You have no status here. I must ask you to leave."

"I move that we hear Mr McIlwraith's evidence," I said.

"If you hear his you'll hear mine," a voice cried from the door. Brockie came forward. But now everyone had something to say, and the most persistent voice was that of Macauley, saying that we had met for a certain purpose and no other business could be introduced. If parishioners of Mr Plumb wished to make statements they could do so after the meeting.

"Exactly," Green said. "Now I must ask you to leave. At once. Without a further word."

"The matter concerns us. Mr Plumb is our minister."

"At once," Green, going the colour of port.

"We're used to him. He's unorthodox but he's honest. We want to keep him."

"We do not," Brockie cried. "The man's an atheist. A tool of Satan."

"Mr Kydd and I have canvassed the entire congregation—"

"Out, sir, out!" Green bellowed.

"Every name in the communion book. Fifty-eight want Mr Plumb to go and a hundred and fifty-six want to keep him."

"Not me. Never," Brockie cried.

"That is our evidence. And I ask this committee to receive it."

"No, sir, we will not. We will not receive it."

"Then I think you'll have to obtain two new managers for St Andrews as well as a new minister." And with that McIlwraith left, Kydd along with him; and Brockie in the rear, looking as if he meant to strike at their backs.

Two courageous men. How had I overlooked them? Their support gave me no help, damaged my case in fact, but I was grateful for it.

"Mr McGregor, have you noted that? A hundred and fifty-six for, fifty-eight against." But that only brought another bellow from Green, and McGregor dropped his pen and had to crawl under the table to retrieve it. "A circus," Oddie said. "You are responsible for this, Mr Plumb. You seem to have a congregation entirely without discipline."

"A congregation of free men, Mr Oddie. They think for themselves."

"Not so," Macauley cried. "A divided house. For. Against. What sort of language is this? We're a church sir, not a debating society. Your congregation is in tatters. In rags. This is the greatest shame that has fallen on our church since it was founded."

"Mr Macauley, Mr Macauley," Green was calling out. But Macauley was not to be stopped. "I move that we abandon formalities. We have a soul here to be saved. We must pray, we must mend our house. The fire of Heaven rains down. The sinner is taken. But there is time. That is the joy of it. There is always time. A second will suffice. The barest word. Ours is the duty to bring his salvation before him. We must—" etc, etc. He went on for quite a long time. His was the old apocalyptic style: fire in the eye, froth on the lips, and rivers of blood everywhere. As McCabe had said, these fanatics are interesting cases. But at last he was quiet; and looking spent, drank a glass of water. And Green, in some embarrassment, got the meeting under way again.

48 "Mr Plumb's statement," Oddie said, "makes it clear that he is no longer a Presbyterian. He is not in fact a Christian. Surely this is clear to you, Mr Plumb. I am at a loss to understand your desire to continue in your charge. Is it simply that you need the money? We know you have twelve children. No, I am not being offensive. I am simply trying to reach the truth of the matter." In his way, he was. The truth for him was like something hooked out with his little finger from a narrow hole.

"The Presbyterian Church is my spiritual home," I said. "Not a comfortable home, I admit. But I've no desire to leave it simply because I'm no longer happy there. That would be cowardly. I wish to improve it, sir. To alter it. Not run away somewhere else."

"This is sheer arrogance," Oddie said.

"Perhaps. But Luther was arrogant. And Calvin. And John Knox. Every reformer has some arrogance in him. If it wasn't for this you gentlemen wouldn't have wives. You'd be sunk in Mariolatry. You'd be turning your faces to Rome instead of burying them in the *Book of Order*." An unworthy jibe; and so good Downie made me feel by saying, "We turn our faces to our Saviour, Mr Plumb, and in no other direction." And he went on, "I honour your desire to improve the Church. It can do with improvement.

We all see that." (Oddie did not, his expression made it plain.)
"But improving a church and altering the basic tenets of its faith
are two different things. Our doctrines are unchangeable and
eternal. They come from the scriptures, and with the scriptures
there can not be any quarrel. There can not be any quarrel within
the Church. Outside, well sir, that's for you to say. But inside, no.
Now, Mr Plumb, already you've denied two of our doctrines. The
doctrines of the Fall and of the Creation. And what I want to
know is, does it stop there? Are there any other doctrines you
deny? I think we've a right to know. Could I ask you simply
perhaps, do you still hold to the doctrines of Incarnation and
Atonement. Are you a Christian, in fact?"

A good question. I could not answer it. I had simply to say I
did not know; my beliefs were something I examined daily. They
were living things, they changed their shape. I told Downie the
doctrines of the Incarnation and the Atonement were open to
more than one interpretation. But, I reminded them all, they lay
outside the charges brought against me. I would not discuss them,
I said.

Downie sighed and shook his head. "Mr Plumb, I think
you're an honest man. And I don't think that honestly you can stay
inside the Church."

49 And Macauley came to life. The fellow was like a battery.
He shot out electrical charges, and ran down, and
slumbered while his strength built up again. He was ready
now. He asked for the papers he had given McGregor and spread
them on the table. "These are part of our business. And with the
chairman's permission I'll read from them. Now, we've heard Mr
Plumb's statement—and I must have my opinion recorded that
it's a thoroughly impertinent document. Arrogant and outrageous.
But for Mr Plumb it's expressed in moderate terms. Let me give
you the true man. Let me show you what he really thinks of his
church. I have a letter of Mr Plumb's written to the Lyttelton

Times. And in it he declares that the Christian Church at the present time is one of the most immoral institutions in the world. And as if that's not enough, he goes on to characterize the Presbyterian Church, and I quote, as 'that great lying Church'. Yes, gentlemen. Most of you have read these letters. But they're new to some of you, I see. And I ask you to forgive me. There's more. From the Christchurch *Post*. Listen. 'If the Presbyterian book were before me now with my signature beneath the vows I would with my broad-nosed J pen put a mighty stroke through it that could not be mistaken. I would not on any consideration put my name to anything of the kind again. It would not be true and sincere.' Now gentlemen, these are Mr Plumb's opinions. He may wish to deny them now—"

"No," I said.

"—but they stand here, in public newspapers, over his name, and he cannot. And I submit that they constitute a resignation from the Church. 'I would put a mighty stroke through it that could not be mistaken.' Very well Mr Plumb, we make no mistake. The action is clear. But as for mighty, dear me no, never mighty. Childish rather, I think. The action of a naughty little boy, wishing to shock the adults. You may come to manhood one day, Mr Plumb, but at the moment you're simply pulling wings off flies."

"I protest," Downie said. "We're not here to bandy insults about."

"I think it's improper language too," Oddie said. "Mr Plumb is not playing with flies. He's putting his immortal soul in peril. And worse, the souls of the people in his charge."

"I agree, and withdraw my words," Macauley said. "But I wish to move now that we take this letter as Mr Plumb's effective resignation from the church."

They turned that over for a while. I kept silent. I was trembling with anger and would not trust myself to speak. That terrible phrase came back to me, "the castration of the intellect"; and I looked at these men, leafing through their rules, knew them for what they were, a tribe of eunuchs. I grew sorry for them. I came to pity them. And that I did not want. I was tempted to offer them comfort, but knew my real task was to lead them into the cold light of their reason. I had not strength for it. But resolved to try again.

In spite of Macauley's insistence, they decided my letter was no resignation. At that point I said, "Gentlemen, can we go back now to my statement? It hasn't been properly considered yet. It's not my business to run this meeting but it seems to me charges have been made and charges answered, and we should be keeping to those." Green agreed. He was tired and needed his lunch. He had learned his procedures thoroughly and saw the way to the end was to stick to them. So we looked at my statement. But no good came of it. It might as well have been written in Sanskrit. My hope that I might persuade even one of these men to my view I saw to be a piece of wild optimism. They had not the language. But no— that they had. And they had my frame of reference all right. It was as if two universes existed side by side, and in mine the inhabitants had an extra sense; could see the monsters in the thickets, the supernatural beings, God and the devil, for what they really were. They shone a torch where the others hid their eyes. This I tried to explain. But they saw my cloven hoof and made signs against me.

"Have none of you," I cried, "done any reading? Look at Darwin. Look at Huxley and Haeckel and Romanes. Gentlemen, I beg of you, open up your minds. These dogmas that you live by are dangerous. They poison the souls of men. I don't exaggerate. They kill." (I was thinking of Oliver, who on the last two Sundays had cycled over the hill to Macauley's church.) "Why, I'd rather face a doctor, a drunken doctor with a rusty lancet, than a Presbyterian parson armed with dogmas." I sank my boat (but could not have saved it). And several of them, seeing it, became quite gentle with me.

Green was first. "It's foolish of you, Mr Plumb, to suppose we haven't read these books you mention. It's simply that we read them from a different point of view. We see them on the one hand, and on the other Christ. He made certain claims. He promised certain things. And we believe Him. Our ways are very different, Mr Plumb. Do you really wish to stay with us?"

And Matheson said, "Romanes died a Christian, Mr Plumb. He died in full communion. It's a history full of instruction. And

I think I speak for all of us when I say that our hope for you will never be lost."

He did not speak for Macauley. Macauley had not finished with me yet. He had sat there trying the words "drunken doctor" on his lips. Now he cried, "Enough argument. Haven't we had enough? There are some of us here who wish to get out in the air. I'll not try to describe the smell in here. And I wish to move that Plumb, the apostate Plumb, be deposed from his charge of St Andrews, and have his name struck from the books of this church."

"Mr Macauley," Green said, "the *Book of Order* makes no provision for this. Deposition, yes. But it says nothing about striking names from books. No, sir. I will not accept that motion. Not until you phrase it in a moderate way. And you will refer to Mr Plumb—a member of this Presbytery still—as Mr Plumb. Apostate indeed!"

"We are not an inquisition," Downie said.

"We're a court," Macauley cried. "An ecclesiastical court. And this man is the accused. He's charged with heresy."

"I don't see it here. Five charges. But no mention of heresy," Downie said.

"Heresy, Mr Macauley, translates in your Greek lexicon as choice," Green said. "And before we hear any talk about deposition I suggest we offer Mr Plumb a choice. I think we've considered everything now, Mr Plumb. And we want to act towards you in as brotherly a spirit as possible. (One moment, Mr Macauley.) I'm sure you see this church is no longer the place for you. Therefore, I advise you as strongly as I can to withdraw from it. And I think it's fair if we adjourn now for a further fortnight to give you time to think it over. (A moment Mr Macauley, if you please.) Now I'll ask the clerk to phrase that as a motion and if we can find a seconder we'll put it to a vote. Now Mr Macauley, you had something to say?"

"Evidence, Dr Green. I have further evidence. We must not let him have more time. We must not let him sneak out of here today. Or else he's made a joke of us. Listen." He snatched a piece of paper from his pocket. "Mr Plumb, did you say this? Do you deny you said this? 'My brethren of the church are men who mince and prance, equivocate, cough, sneeze, amble, sophisticate, and lie like troopers to save themselves and their livings.' You said that. Do you deny it?"

"No," I said, looking about me. Forewarned of a dreadful anger in myself, I was, in this moment, sad: sad at the ending Macauley had brought on us. I was ringed by a group of hurt and decent men—and the one or two charlatans I had meant my words for, and one or two bigots. Their eyes were fixed gloweringly upon me, their silence had the threat of a back-drawn fist. "No, I don't deny. it. But she must have a very good memory. Or perhaps she just writes fast."

"What do you mean, sir?"

"You had that scrap of paper from a lady who was listening at a keyhole." For I had spoken the words to Joseph McCabe, a little drunk with talk and company. And outside the door pious Mrs Jepson had written them down.

Poor Downie looked as if he had been struck. Green was the colour of port again, and Oddie the colour of tin. I had not had them in mind. Not had Macauley in mind. But Graham, smiling Graham. I hardly knew the man—yet he existed in my mind as arch-equivocator (ambler, prancer, sneezer, liar yes); Graham, closet free-thinker, coward. There were a good many of him in the church. I do not misjudge him. He came to me in the street the day before my trial and told me insistence such as mine was ungentlemanly, that no one would think the worse of me if I quietly crossed my fingers and said I was sorry. Looking at him— he gazed at his finger nails—I had no regret for my words. I regretted hurting Downie though, and Green and McGregor— and said so. But said that as Macauley had tabled the words I would let them stand. They had been spoken privately. Men say such things and laugh and enjoy themselves. It is a part of good-fellowship. The crime, I said, was in the posting of spies, in the creeping about of people with long ears. I would remove myself from that, I said.

McGregor had some paper in front of him. I shot out my hand and took a sheet. (The poor man jumped a foot into the air.) Angry talk went on all about me. I dated the paper (with my broad-nosed J pen), addressed it to Green, and wrote: "I herewith tender my resignation of the St Andrews charge and withdraw from the Ministry of the Presbyterian Church of New Zealand."

I signed it; pushed it in front of Green; and left.

I went out of the Church into the air. Into fresh air.

50 The wind blew down the bare street and through the naked trees, bringing an icy drizzle. The little group of people standing under black umbrellas appeared like arctic birds on a shelf of ice. Half a dozen peeled away: reporters, rushing at me, shouting questions. I told them my statement said all I wanted to say, and asked them to print as much of it as they could. I had resigned, I said, but they must have the rest of the story from Dr Green. I went to McIlwraith and Kydd and thanked them. I told them I hoped they would stay on at St Andrews to help the new minister. Then I turned to Geddes. He surprised me by coming forward to shake hands. "Aye laddie, it's Robert Elsmere over again."

"You tried to warn me," I said.

"You get a nose for these things. What are you going to do now?"

"I don't know. I've a message. And if God wills I'll deliver it."

"Aye, I see that. Good luck, then." Life had changed him. "We're all toilers in the same field." He went away to sit in the church.

Scroggie approached me next. He had a charge in Hokitika but visited Kumara still. The people there sent their good wishes. Our talk was inconsequential. He wanted to show kindness, that was all. We did not know it then, but he was to be my successor at St Andrews.

I fetched my bicycle and rode home. And there were Edward and John Jepson, keeping Edie company. Edward had closed his shop. They took my news well; managed to see a victory in it. Edie remained calm. She spoke of our future with some lightness, even gaiety. Over lunch we began to see our way clear. John and Edward had a plan. I listened; and soon agreed.

In the late afternoon I walked over the road to my church—mine no longer. So, I thought, the easy living is gone, the Manse and glebe. And this is gone too. I had pain, but no regret. For a greater agony was gone from me—a soul agony. No more tossing up of theological balls, no more of the spiritual three-card trick. Now I had the task of knowing God. But I would make one last sentimental journey into the building that had seen so much of my life. When I wrote to McCabe I described the moment to him. I can do no better now than quote from my letter:

"It was evening, the sun had found a gap in the clouds, and its rays were striking through the coloured-glass windows as I opened the door of the church. I walked up the aisle slowly and stepped into the pulpit. I looked at the old bible, the bars of red and blue and yellow light falling on the empty seats. I saw the patch on the carpet where the nap was worn off by my standing on the spot for so many years. There I had dispensed Communion to the people who had trusted me and believed in me. To this spot and the messages from this spot, I had consecrated my life. This was the end of it and the last visit. I had never really knelt there before but I did so now. And I re-consecrated my life to God and Social Service and Truth at all costs. With these vows I rose to my feet, and since then I have not been on my knees! There is something better than that—it is never getting out of touch with the unseen forces—continuing instant in prayer. God is real to me now in a wonderful sense. To find God I had to leave the Church!"

Felicity was waiting in the porch. I took her hand and we crossed the road to the Manse.

I threw away my collars and called myself "Reverend" no more.

51 Others kept it up. Bluey for one. And many years later Felicity's husband Max Waring adopted the term. He even came to say Rev, as one says Ken for Kenneth or Tom for Thomas. "How are you this morning, Rev?" He is a man of ironic temperament. It amuses him that he, an atheist, should be married to the Catholic daughter of an "unfrocked" Presbyterian parson. He has too that fascination with religious behaviour one finds so often in unbelievers; and being a man who never in his life will rock the boat, he judges me a rogue. If I had not been unfrocked (his term) he would not have abbreviated my title.

Max is my favourite son-in-law. He's a gentle creature; caught somewhere on the middle of the public service ladder, unable to move up, or to fall off. He suffers from paralysis of the ambition, perhaps of the will; but it has not led him into spite or cynicism or self-pity. Nose like the beak of a flesh-eating bird; cruel mouth; small red eye. But how kindly in his nature. I have found the physiognomical method of judging character misleading nine times out of ten—and think of Edward Cryer, who was called by the sharp-tongued girls of our town Dr Crippen, but who in his nature was saintly. Max reminds me of Edward. Both men loved Felicity. The strange thing is that Edward who knew her as a child came to love her as a woman; and Max, who married her, who married this strong and emotional and opinionated creature, loved her for the child he saw in her, and never knew what to do with the grown-up person.

They met in 1922 when Felicity came to Wellington to teach, and married in 1928. Max was her faithful attendant all through those years. I have no way of knowing how many men entered and left her life (apart from the one who dominated it); but Max waited, concealing his unhappiness, and won her in the end by a combination of persistence and hard circumstance. The latter they have never confessed—not to me. But I have some detective ability. Their son Peter was born four months after their (registry office) wedding—an only child. I look at him and see who his real father is. He's a good-looking boy.

52 "What are you writing, dad?"
"Oh, nothing. Just putting my thoughts in order."
But her sharp eyes had covered a couple of lines. As I closed the notebook she thrust her hand inside. "What is it? A family history?"

"No, no. Reminiscences that's all."

"'They measure things by the marriages they made.' Who, Esther and Meg? They won't like that."

"They won't see it." I managed to get the book closed again.

"What have you said about me?"

"Nothing yet."

"Probably that I fell into superstition."

"No my dear, your spiritual life is your own affair."

"I don't like the way you say that. Like something illicit. Out in the lupins at the end of the beach."

"Don't talk like that, Felicity." I put down my trumpet so I would hear no more. It pains me that life has coarsened my daughters. Life should refine, should burn away the dross. Felicity feels it too. But her delicacy, her refinements, are selective. She keeps her life in compartments. The spiritual one is closed to me; a mystery. There, for better or worse (worse, I believe), the white flame burns, behind doors locked to me, and Max, and indeed all other humans (except for one or two celibates clad in black). There her soul meets its maker—both in a form I do not recognize. And because her energies are employed so strenuously there, the social, the family mask she wears is a rough-and-ready thing. She sees it herself and becomes girlish in apology—and for me almost the old Felicity. But soon goes back and is lost. She is the sort of Catholic, ardent and secretive, who must cause embarrassment in her church. It is frequently so with converts, I am told.

"Sorry, dad. Didn't mean to shock you. Come on now. Come into the lounge. We've got a fire going." She took my hand. I was unwilling. For fifty years I have sat alone at night and read or written. But print and solitude, Felicity says, are drugs I am "hooked on". She is going to break me of the habit. People are more important than books. Besides, she said, pulling me to my feet, Max wanted to change my dressing.

In the lounge Max was stacking pine cones on the fire. He collects them in coal sacks from the Tinakori hills. His Sunday outing, while Felicity goes to Mass and Peter sleeps off his Saturday night. They are not a sharing family. But they like each other and give each other licence.

"Now Rev, I'll just get my kit." When he was back he made me get up from the plain chair I had chosen and sit in a great winged affair like a throne. He lifted my legs and slid an upholstered footrest under my feet.

"Now." He would have made a good doctor. He had that rare combination of passionate interest and unsentimental concern.

I said, "Did you ever think of being a doctor, Max?"

"Yes." He was kneeling by the chair, unwinding the old bandage. He threw it on the fire and began smearing ointment on my raw palm.

"Sorry."

"It's all right. What stopped you?"

"Money. My father was a railwayman. Railwaymen don't put their sons through medical school." His predator's beak and ferine mouth were poised above my flesh; but he said mildly, "Of course if I'd had any gumption I would have put myself through. Plenty did."

"Everyone should have an equal chance." I spoke without force. My hand was throbbing painfully.

"I had my chance. I just couldn't face the hardship. Besides Rev, I wanted to be other things as well. A lawyer for one, and a poet, and a concert pianist, even though I can't play a note. And an All Black, believe it or not. I was going every which way, you see. Dreaming it all and not doing a thing. So I ended up a civil servant. In the great rubbish bin."

127

I did not like that. It was a humorous statement, but I saw the pain that escaped its cover. He understood he had wasted his gifts.

"Why don't you resign? It's not too late to do something you want."

"Ha ha!"

"How old are you? Fifty? You're a boy."

Felicity said, "That's my meal ticket you're trying to subvert."

"He can do it. I did it. And nobody suffered."

"That was because you had wealthy friends. We would have starved without them."

"Nonsense. I could have gone back to the law. But I had a message and my friends thought it was important. And Edward wasn't wealthy. Edward was poor."

"John Jepson had plenty."

"John Jepson built the hall. But his interest stopped there. Rich men don't understand hunger. It was Edward who kept us in food. And John Findlater and Andrew Collie."

But the strain of catching their wispy shouts had tired me. I had endured three days and nights of it. I put down my trumpet, saying I wanted to rest, and as Max finished bandaging my hand stared into the fire and remembered those hard joyous days. Memory with me is an active thing, not an undisciplined dreaming. It can be, and was now, an acceptable substitute for reading and writing. I get a hold on acts, words, gestures, worry them out of the corners they've got themselves lost in, and brush the dust away. And yet because they come from far away, from lost realms, and because their shapes are refined and mysterious, they have a visionary force. The processes of memory are religious. Each image I contemplate is an answered prayer.

I see a stage in a draughty hall and a small balding man passionately speaking of the True, the Good, the Beautiful. His clothes are well-worn grey, a minister's clothes; but his collar secular. The audience responds. This is the Litany of the Universal:

"It is the will of our Mother/Father God, that the people of Fellowship 'stagger not back to the mummeries of the dark ages, but rather that they found a New Church of men to come, having heaven and earth for beams and rafters, science for symbol and illustration' . .

"Our Mother/Father God, help us to do Thy will on the earth.

"Immanent Spirit of Universal Oneness, may we loyally cooperate with Thee to create Thy Kingdom on the earth for 'We doubt not through the ages One increasing purpose runs, and the thoughts of men are widened with the process of the suns.' Amen!"

The years pass. The hall is the same, the man a little balder. Now the emphasis falls less on theology:

"It is the will of God that the eyes of the people be opened to the anti-social spirit of modern Capitalism, Militarism, and Imperialism—a trinity of evil—resulting in the folly of fraternal slaughter; so that the reign of reason and love may appear, and the dominance of hate and bitterness be ended; that swords be turned into ploughshares and spears into pruning hooks, and that nations learn war no more."

Oliver's troopship has sailed out of Lyttelton harbour. Men are dying at Gallipoli.

"It is the will of God that his children of the Spirit, extend their horizons and cultivate the true Patriotism—Loyalty to Humanity—and the Communal Consciousness of the New Age . ."

Now there is a small house in the country, children four to a bedroom, two to a bed. Out the back a fruit garden grows, and at the side cauliflowers, cabbages, corn. Fowls scratch among the trees. A boy milks the house-cow and dreams of flying-machines. Another has gone to sea and will not come home. The girls go barefoot, breaking ice on the puddles with their red toes. Heavy plaits hang down to their waists. Their father wheels home a bolt of striped cloth. It lies on his bicycle like a roll of lead. One of his friends has had it cheap at a fire sale. Their mother sews, treadling into the night. And they wear identical dresses, like butchers' aprons. Children hiss at them. The word is, "Passifisst."

A chain appears on the iron gate of the Unitarian Hall. A policeman with a key unlocks it for Sunday services, but Thursday lectures are not allowed—not when they are called "Militarism—

the assassin of Demos". The speaker brings a stool with him—a nursery stool, painted pink. He mounts it in the street. And stones fly. He tastes his own blood on his lips. The Unitarians do not care for this. Half a dozen stones, two or three shouts of "Judas", "Traitor", two or three threats of death: the movement in Thorpe lies down and will not get up.

At home the speaker broods, thinks of new lands. He must preach or die—so it seems to him. Over the seas is America, the great Democracy. He does not see it as the New Jerusalem. But Woodrow Wilson sits in the President's chair, and Wilson has said there is such a thing as a nation being too proud to fight. The man does not fully believe him. He has been watching politicians for half of his life. But Wilson has the sort of face he trusts.

So they talk into the night. His daughter says, "You'll be able to say what you want there, without being put in prison." And his wife thinks of her budding trees and the blossoms she will not see. She weeps a little, then dries her eyes and smiles. "Another shake of the kaleidoscope."

53 I spoke of these things with Felicity. She leaned forward and touched me on the mouth. "You've still got the scar."

"It broke one of my teeth." And our going—I did not say it— broke Edward Cryer's heart. He had told me of his love for Felicity; deluded in so far as it had its beginnings in his love for me. But it was a pure passion when one considers the impurity of most, that begin in self. I told him he might speak to her, and could not tell him what the end must be. It took place on a country walk. I saw from his dead look when it was over, and Felicity's pallor and a kind of shame in her eyes, how it had gone.

Our train pulled out. Edward and John Jepson ran along the platform crying, "Good luck", "God bless you", "Come back when it's over". And behind them a man cursing us and waving a Union Jack. John Findlater tripped him up. Andrew Collie tore his flag in two. Tears ran down Edward's cheeks. "God bless you, God bless you all."

He died while we were at sea, suffocated by smoke when his shop burned down. His will left all he owned to Felicity. It was less than a hundred pounds.

54 In California I preached again. I was looked on neither as evil, nor as an oddity. That place is the land of a thousand creeds, a thousand contending voices. Weird beliefs, distorted truths, the verities in costume prancing madly; and plain lies of course. But my own simple message was broadly Unitarian, acceptable to various congregations. In my anti-war activities I was sponsored by groups whose beliefs ranged from the altruistic to the crudely isolationist. Sometimes I spoke seven nights a week. So I was active, and believed myself useful. But I never felt at home. I missed the cold of Thorpe; the climate of Calvinism; missed the flag-waving, the jingoist hatreds; Empire Day, the Steinway piano axed in the street. Missed, that is, my known enemy. I missed the plains and the mountains, the trout rivers, the shingle beach and grey cold sea. I sorely missed my friends. We knew very soon that we would not stay in California. But for two years we pretended we were settled.

We rented a timbered house in a suburb of Berkeley called Thousand Oaks. The boys dug up a lawn and Edie planted vegetable seeds. We were in a well-to-do neighbourhood but were poor. In the hot summers the neighbours splashed in their swimming pools. Our children listened over the garden wall. But soon our pretty daughters found their way in. They were happy. At school they concealed their lunches of home-baked bread.

Edith and Florence left school and took jobs in a clothing store. That was a sad day for me. They were clever girls. I had thought they would be teachers at the least. But a fever flushed their cheeks in this rich noisy land. A kind of infection struck them. They laughed more loudly, made their eyes glitter and their hair take unnatural shapes. Their voices quickly had a nasal twang. They spoke words strange to me—a language of possessions, pleasure, clothes, romance, and dancing. Edie was troubled by it too. But we quarrelled, for she said it was simply that they were growing up. "Yes," I cried, "and in the land of Baal." She agreed with that.

So a year went by—two years. A dreadful loneliness came on us. Clouds of greed and hatred enveloped the land—and my voice was like a plaintive bell in a sea-mist, warning of danger. It seemed to reach no ears. I sank to making a noise like a sparrow-squeak. And the land of Baal rushed into the war—a great river of foulness swept us away. (In everyday terms—and unmixed: the police closed my lectures. I was an alien, they said, a charge against me would be more serious than a charge of sedition.)

Again we talked into the night. We sat like conspirators in my little study, we hunched at the desk with paper and pen, counting our cents, while in our creaking house the children slept. We plotted to betray them. California was theirs. They had grown into it. (All except Meg: she pined, she failed to grow.) They slept unsuspecting; while a gladness fell on Edie and me. We scraped our money together. Enough, and some dollars to spare. We could go home. In the instant I knew it an image of grey streets came to me, and cold crashing waves, and humourless faces. It made me happy. There—that was mine. It was like one's knowledge of Effectual Calling. I said, "If I'm going to prison let it be a New Zealand prison." Edie only smiled. She saw Linwood and her father's fruit garden.

The next day she told me I must go to Philadelphia to see my mother. "Yes," I said. "We won't be coming to this country again."

I travelled by train. In a brownstone house in a quiet neighbourhood I faced a woman who let me kiss her cheek but then sat me down and kept me at a distance of many years. The lady of the peacock hats was gone. The widow Mrs Weedon and I found a great chasm between us. It was distressing to me, but did not appear to give her any distress. I saw my own face before me, my round features, softened by femininity and hardened by belief. We spoke of religion. I could not get a word in. And I wondered if I affected others the way she affected me. I grew resentful. With my fluency but without my weight, her voice ran on, persistent as a stream on pebbles. "Sin is in the mind, George. Sickness is in the mind. All cause and effect is mental. Even death is mental. Death can be healed. All the great fevers that infect our minds—all can be healed by a proper understanding of the Scriptures. Jesus was a healer and a teacher. His divinity lies in his teaching. Now, let me tell you of my good friend Hannah Brown. She discovered a lump in her groin that grew and grew . . ." And so on. For the five days of my visit. Except that on the final afternoon she discovered my hardness of hearing. It warmed her to me. "George, this is no deafness, this is Error. We can banish it, we can put it out. All that you must do is know the Truth . . ." For the whole of that afternoon she dragged me about Philadelphia, showing me to her friends and testing my hearing. They planned assaults on my unbelief. I did not mind. It made a change.

In the morning I said goodbye. Weedon had left her well off. "George, I feel bound to warn you, you can expect nothing from me. Everything I have will go to the church. That is where my heart lies." A frank disclosure. Perhaps my visit had not been without pain for her. "But George, if you'll send me your address when you get to New Zealand I'll post you some books explaining the Christian Science teaching. Your hearing can be cured. Remember that." I took my cab to the station. And never saw her again.

She had not once asked about Edie and my children.

55 I said to Felicity, "Do you remember Wolfie Rendt?"
"Oh yes," she cried. "How could I forget him? He was the love of my life."
"No, not really?"
"I was wild about him. I nearly fainted when we said goodbye."
Wolfie came often to our house in Thousand Oaks. He was

not the only one. An underwear salesman, Phil Critch, came to see Edith. A high school boy whose name I forget came to see Florence. Even Agnes, Esther, and little Rebecca, had their "boyfriends". I flushed them out from corners of the garden and drove them away. But Phil Critch was "serious"; and Wolfie Rendt was serious. He was not a boyfriend. He was Felicity's young man. They shared intellectual interests. They wrote poetry, they read Thoreau and Emerson aloud. I liked Wolfie. I liked his immigrant parents, who ran a small ironmongery shop and struggled to put their son through college. I would have been happy to see Felicity marry this German boy. But she did not. She chose to come back to New Zealand. And, it seems, nearly fainted on saying goodbye. Wolfie went to the war and was killed.

Edith was the one who married. Edith married Phil Critch. I wept as I gave her away to this bullet-headed, loud and stupid man. He slapped my back and called me Pops. He told his friends I was in the God-business. He spoke of wops and kikes and niggers. He spoke of doing his bit to preserve democracy. And Edith loved him madly. She stroked his wiry hair and squeezed the muscles in his arms with a rapt expression. Like Felicity, she nearly fainted. My arguments made no ground with her. So I left this daughter in the land of Baal, married to one of the natives. She writes and tells me how happy she has been.

The S.S. *Ventura* sailed out of San Francisco with ten Plumbs on board. It steamed through dangerous warm seas into the south. I felt cold spray on my cheeks and knew I was going home, and going to battle.

We rented a house in the suburb of Shirley, Christchurch. I began to lecture at once.

56 Peter came home early in the afternoon, bringing a young woman with him. She was wearing the new style of dress, the "new-look", and with her pink cheeks and curly brown hair I thought her very attractive. Nick Carter was her name. "Nicola, Nicola," the girl shouted into my trumpet, laughing at Peter. They were, Peter said, going to "swot" together, and they went to his bedroom. That was too bare-faced. Straining with my dead ears, I could hear nothing. But when I put my trumpet to the door there was a sound of laughter. The place for me, I thought, was out of the house.

I sat in the garden, enjoying the autumn warmth and the scent of roses. Gardens I find calming to the mind; and calmness of mind a necessary condition for the quickening of the spiritual faculties; the stirring in its slumber of the soul; the sense of mystical union with the One. I have read that this is brought on by a change in body chemistry. But we penetrate *terra incognita*, we plumb the human deeps, search for the self, the soul, the Light within the dark, by means other than the scientific. Mystical experience is the chief. Science is busy in the margins. Or, to put it another way, science works on the vehicle but knows not the rider or his destination. Curious that I set such store by it in the old days. I was a limited fellow.

Such thoughts as these are not conducive to calm. Nor was my old man's curiosity about the two young people in the house. I went inside, wrote a note to Felicity, and set off for town and my meeting with Oliver. I walked down the neat suburban street and came to a little station called Simla Crescent. Soon a unit swayed up to the platform. I got inside and was carried down the gorge into the city.

I knew where to find Oliver's court. But as I went towards it I saw Parliament Buildings off to the right, on top of their low green hill. Up there were half a dozen men I knew. I grew curious to see them at their work—curious especially to see Dan Peabody.

I went through the shadow of Dick Seddon's statue (the sculptor had him spouting, just as I had seen him once outside the Queen's Hotel in Kumara); up the steps, through the Grecian columns; and found my way into the public gallery. And there they were, in their rimu-panelled, padded-leather pit. I looked at them with emotion. A sense of the years came down on me and a grey oppression of spirit. So much left undone, so much that will never be done. I knew these important men must feel the same when they were out of this chamber, when they stood alone, facing their young selves. Fraser was there, Nash was there. I had seen them last in the flesh at an unemployed meeting in an Auckland hall in 1933. Savage had been there too (dead Savage, the "hero", the "saint": I still met people who believed in him). And Lee, not yet "traitor". I had made my mark on that meeting. I had given those men trouble. There had been too much oil on their tongues.

I found a seat and stared at them. I heard no words. My trumpet was on my lap. Bill Parry was speaking. I had heard Parry before. And the bitter-faced man beside him, the man with the Calvinist eyes and bar-room vocabulary. Semple. I had missed him by less than a year in Lyttelton jail.

Dan Peabody was in the second row, leaning back with his arm on the rest, and a patient expression on his face. A meaty face, Dan had, and the face of a disappointed man. It seemed to me only half alive. It had not the lightness, the inner life, one sees in the faces, however gross, of men who still have ambitions to realize. Dan was going nowhere. He had never made it to the front bench; had entered Cabinet all right; but his portfolio was minor. Even now, I had trouble remembering it. Mines? Broadcasting? It did not matter. He could not have been further from the post he had told me so confidently he would fill one day. Even his seat had become marginal. And he had an election to face in less than a year. It seemed his life in politics was over. It was the only life he had.

Felicity had loved Dan Peabody. She had borne him a son. And I thought with a painful amusement of my old faith in the "science" of eugenics. Eugenic betterment, eugenic sense, the eugenic ideal: I had bristled with weapons, carrying these phrases. "The higher sense of marriage." "The Divine right of maternity." "What God cannot do the child can." Well, I would have said that Felicity, my daughter, intelligent girl, and Dan Peabody, Socialist, man of courage, would have a child who must carry on God's work. And I thought of that child: ordinary-minded, pleasure-seeking Peter, blank in the eye at the great old causes, but lighting up at news of a football score.

Dan had stumped the country in the First War, talking against conscription. They had put him in jail for sedition. But in the Second he changed his tune and helped pass the law that gathered the conscripts in. There is no science that can measure behaviour. It is even less easy to understand than inheritance.

I looked at the other side. Holland. Now there was a name. Once it had belonged to honest Harry—a politician who rose above his trade. I was pleased this cramped man in the Leader's seat was not related: Sidney Holland. He had a cunning clever face. Ambition, the expectation of power, had set a gleam on his eye that was not on Dan's. In his ugly cheek was a bunching up that strained against the now. I watched him with fascination, with a prickling on the spine, as one watches a stoat. Beside him was the man I recognized as Holyoake. A pleasant enough looking fellow. But I felt a little sick, felt the blow. For I had been told this man (well-fed, well-dressed, on the Tory side) had a blood connection with George Jacob Holyoake, of the English nineteenth-century radicals perhaps the greatest—certainly the man of greatest courage. How the line had twisted.

Bill Parry finished speaking and sat down. Dan leaned forward and spoke into his ear. Then, as he sat back, he saw me watching. For a moment his face was naked. I knew what he felt. Time rushed away from me too, the years made a hollow boom, and all was loss. Then Dan grinned at me, and winked elaborately.

I stood up. I made him a nod of farewell, and went out into the bright still afternoon.

57 My 1918 lecture tour took me to the Coast, to Westport, Hokitika, Greymouth. Back in Christchurch, I picked up Felicity, and we set off for Dunedin and Invercargill. On the way home I gave two talks in Thorpe. Mrs Jepson was dead. Felicity and I stayed with John.

Our meeting was sad, for we remembered Edward. But in the evening, back from the hall—my old Unitarian Hall, without a name—we gathered in the library, almost the old group: John and I, Andrew Collie, John Findlater, Dan Peabody; and the ghost of Edward became a companion presence, one that I turned to from time to time when I grew tired of words. I was close to tears that night, and cannot tell even now if they would have been of acceptance or of pain.

I was proud of Felicity. In the old days I had wanted a woman in the group. And here she was, my daughter. She held her own. She had passion, fire, and the prophetic mind; but an impatience of high-sounding talk, a practical good sense, an earthiness of expression (where had she got that? the single thing I was unhappy with) that pulled us up short many a time and made us think again.

At first we talked of the great exciting event of those days, the Russian revolution. The news had come late in the previous year. I had been sitting in my garden in the Spring sunshine. On my knee was the paper, a great sore, with its four pages of New Zealand's dead and wounded. (One of those names, one day, would be Oliver's.) I sat in that sunny green place as though in a pit of ash and mud. Then my eye fell on the special headline: *Russia Has Turned Red, Troops in Revolt*. It was like a spiritual revelation—in quality, in intensity, like a first sighting of the One. I came alive in an instant, that which I had thought dead in me began to move. And I saw burning in the sky those words of Ezekiel, "I will overturn, overturn, overturn it; and it shall be no

138

more, until he comes whose right it is; and I will give it him." But soon I set my vengefulness aside; and I thought, Mankind is out of his trap, the blind turning is over, the hatred and greed. Glory, glory, glory. I breathed deeply of the fresh Spring air. And soon I hurried inside to my study, for I had work to do.

Four months later our enthusiasm was running even higher. The war went on, but so did the revolution. Imperialism, Militarism, Capitalism, were the past, and the war their last convulsion. The Red Flag (the red blood of humanity) was the future.

We spoke of it that night in John Jepson's library; many ringing (and alas unprophetic) words. But my second talk was "The Glorious Bolsheviks of Russia" and I did not want to give too much away. So after a while we talked of other things: progressive religion, marriage and morality, poetry and love, law, justice, poverty and wealth, education, control of the mind— talked until the sky began to lighten, *de omnibus rebus et quibusdem aliis*. It reminded me of our evening with McCabe. Except that there was no plum cake, and no Mrs Jepson listening at the keyhole.

Dan Peabody was a month out of Lyttelton jail, where he had been put for sedition. Paddy Webb was out recently too and Webb's account of the horrors of the place was, Dan said, a good deal short of the truth. I liked Dan better on that night than I had before—or have liked him since. For a time he was without his political skin. His voice shook with emotion as he told us of the mad or haunted eyes of men released from solitary confinement, the "dummy" as it was called. He told us he had worked alongside a rapist, a sodomite, a murderer. He was a damaged man, and I wonder now if he ever fully regained what Lyttelton jail crushed out of him. He discovered the terrible fact of human cruelty and was not coarse-fibred enough to let it pass through him and out; or, I must add, firm enough in mind, clear in mind and spirit, to hold himself steady, get a sight of the foe, and enter the battle. Felicity's eyes filled with tears as she listened to him.

"You must go into Parliament," she said. "You can do something about it."

"Parliament," cried Andrew. "There is no hope left in Parliament. The ballot box is dead, lassie. It's gone the way of the horse and cart. And a good thing too. What has it got us? Men like Bill Massey. No, my friends, this is the age of the armed uprising. Revolution. And the ballot box goes into the dustbin of history."

"You must work to get into Parliament." She was alone with Dan Peabody. Andrew was only a bit of Scotch comedy on another part of the stage. The rest of us did not exist. I saw the girl give herself to this man. It could not be other. She was young, passionate, idealistic—and recently in love. And he, well, he was handsome, he thought as she did, he had suffered. He was too lost in himself to know what was happening, but the rest of us saw, even Andrew; and sanctioned her in her feeling. We were children in our view of love; romantics, idealists. Even I. Had not Edie and I understood in a flash? Besides, we were tested in our beliefs. These two were the "fit". And had not woman been bound for hundreds of years by scriptural texts? Now she was free. This was her century. I had declared it earlier in the night. She might select her man and have her babe and know that her act served the true morality. If God held the partners together in love what need of churching, what need of the sanctions of law? And speaking generally—for this was Felicity's moment—I said from Ecclesiasticus: "If thou findest a good man, rise up early in the morning and go with him, and let thy feet wear the steps of his door." That was not, after all, fully scriptural.

Dan had a wife at home, but she was a silly woman. She was one of the "unfit".

58 John came to me privately in the morning. "George, I don't want to worry you, but there were two men in the hall last night taking notes. I don't think they were from the newspapers."

"Policemen, you think?"

"They had the look of it."

"Ah well, I've been expecting them. We'll see if they're there tonight."

They were, one on each side of the hall. They scribbled industriously in their little books. I remembered George Jacob Holyoake. When the police came into his lecture and ranged themselves round the walls in their shining hats he spoke an hour longer, not having foreseen, he said, such a chance of extending liberal views in official quarters. Well, I thought, I'll take him as example. And I let myself go. I spoke for an hour and three-quarters without drawing breath.

Felicity sat in the front row. Dan was beside her that night. Her face was calm and happy. I thought how like Edie she looked.

59 It took the police two weeks to prepare their charges. I had time for lectures in Nelson and Blenheim. But when I came back I was summonsed. There were two charges, both of seditious utterance. I appeared in the Christchurch Magistrates Court at the beginning of March.

On the morning of my trial I dressed in my warmest clothes and stoutest shoes. Edie put half a dozen handkerchiefs and a pair of woollen gloves in my pockets and I chose a small volume of Emerson's essays. I said goodbye to the children and told them they must work hard at school. Then I set out. Felicity came with me. Edie was not well enough.

I had wished to defend myself, but when I showed my friends the statement I meant to read they were horrified. John Jepson and Andrew had hurried up from Thorpe. Even Andrew was horrified. They might have airy notions about love, but about the justice of courts they were realistic. What I needed was a smart lawyer. They made me retain John Willis. And John would not even let me on the stand.

That was a wrong decision. I see it now. My statement had been carefully thought out. I speak very well. In speaking I'm a professional. I would not have moved the magistrate—a little

Oliver—but there was an audience in court that day and it went to waste. I might have planted a seed. And a seed can grow into a forest tree. I look at the statement today: Appendix 2 in *The Growing Point of Truth*. It begins with a short history of sedition, from Jesus to Mazzini and Kossuth. Today's seditionmonger, I said, is tomorrow's political hero. And I showed how the lawbreaker may be more important to society than the lawmaker. Then I went on to the charges, and spoke of "the patriotic poison" in our schools and the need to teach loyalty towards the whole human family. I explained why I wished for no victor in the war and why praying for victory is a blasphemy. I tabulated New Zealand's war profits and showed who is the real victor. I explained my attitude towards war loans. And I described the sort of revolution I wished to see in my country. Then I made a more personal statement (or would have made it). I explained my decision to come back to New Zealand. New Zealand had a destiny, this destiny drew me back, for it was bound inextricably to my own. I made my "utterances" at the command of God and my conscience. My conscience would not let me hate seventy million Germans at the State command. Nor would it let me be silent. I spoke for myself but I did not stand alone. For "God standeth in the shadow keeping watch above his own," (Lowell). And although my lectures had cost me this agony—public trial—I regretted nothing. I had simply obeyed a call to duty, duty to my country and to mankind. "The truth," I said, "is my burden and not sedition."

But all this sat in my pocket, unused. John Willis conducted my defence on technicalities.

The case was brought under the War Regulations, section 4, which defined what was seditious or had a seditious tendency. The first charge stated that on February 14, in a lecture entitled "Julius Caesar or Jesus Christ", I said:

"You are under the heels of the War Lords. We have not enough population in our country, yet we are lusting after the annexation of Samoa. The patriotic poison is in our schools. The children are taught to salute the flag and sing the National Anthem. I am hoping with a fervent hope that in this war there will be no victor. To pray about a war is blasphemy. A woman goes down the valley of death to bring a child into the world; she nurses it, sends it to school, sees it through the sixth standard; then comes a call to arms, and it goes away to war. What for? To die for its country? No! To die for the profiteer."

The second charge stated that on February 15, in a lecture entitled "The Glorious Bolsheviks of Russia", I said:

"Russia wanted war, England wanted war, the upper class in New Zealand wanted war. Never has there been such a wonderful five days as the five days of the Russian Revolution. The old Russia has gone and the new Russia has come in. I hope before I die to see a similar movement in New Zealand. I hope the day will come in New Zealand when these war loans will be repudiated. I hope not a penny of the war loan will be repaid. You do not authorize them."

These were my seditious utterances. I pleaded not guilty.

60 The prosecutor was a man called Malcolm. He was a matter-of-fact, a dry-as-dust sort of man, but I heard a detestation in his voice once or twice in the morning. We anti-war folk were looked on as worse than murderers.

The clerk read the first charge. Then Malcolm set the scene: hall, chairman, sponsoring body (the Labour Representation Council), the audience of one hundred and fifty persons. Dry stuff. But then he showed some passion. "There can be no question that these words uttered by the accused are seditious. The only question can be, were they used? They were. That we shall prove. And we shall claim they were uttered not under momentary excitement, not in the heat of argument, but coolly and deliberately by an educated man brought to the town of Thorpe and speaking in a public lecture designed as part of an organized propaganda."

He called a Senior-Sergeant of Police, Sampson by name: one of the men who had taken notes at the meeting. He was a burly man, slow-speaking, slow-moving, and even I could see an excellent witness. If in those rites of Justice we can look on the magistrate as the Godhead, then Sampson and Malcolm had the role of serving priests. And Sampson was the senior. Malcolm handed neutral objects to him and Sampson sanctified them. Thus:

"How long did the accused speak?"

"I timed the speech. He spoke for an hour and twenty-two minutes."

"Was there any response from the audience?"

"There was frequent applause. There were shouts of 'Bravo' and 'Hear, hear'."

"Did you take notes of the words of the accused?"

"I did."

"Now Sergeant, are you a shorthand writer?"

"No, sir. I take a fast longhand note."

"Are the words charged in the information the only notes you took?"

"No, sir. Prior to those words I took the following." (He opened his notebook.) "'If Jesus Christ was now on earth he would be tried for sedition. The churches are the recruiting agent for the world's greatest tragedies. Some of the clergy are now known as the black militia. We are weeding out the best of our manhood and leaving the weeds. Where is this going to land us?'"

I leaned across to John Willis and told him the Sergeant was not being strictly truthful. These words were not consecutive. They came from different parts of my talk, like the words in the charges. John nodded. He had seen it. And when he rose to question Sampson he began on that line. I saw very soon it made up the substance of our defence. I was unhappy at that. I persisted in thinking this trial was part of an argument and my job was to persuade. There was the box. I should be in it, delivering my message. John kept stolidly on, though he must have felt my disapproval pressing on his spine. In court he dropped his uncertainties, hid the dark side of his nature, and came out the honest legal tradesman. It was a good piece of acting. But I was too angry to admire him for it.

"Do you agree, Sergeant," he asked, "that Mr Plumb is a fairly rapid speaker?"

"Yes, sir. Fairly rapid."

"And you are not a shorthand writer?"

"No, sir."

"But you managed to take a lengthy note?"

"Yes, sir."

"Did you copy down all his words or just some?"

"Some, sir. There was no time to take them all."

"No time? Then there are gaps in your record?"

"The notes are not consecutive, sir."

"How long are they spread over?"

"The whole lecture. An hour and twenty-two minutes."

"You will admit then that there are many words left out from the body of your note that might moderate or qualify its meaning?"

"No sir, I will not admit that. There are words left out. But those words do not change the meaning. The note gives the general trend of the lecture. Each sentence is a complete consecutive rendering."

"Sergeant, when Mr Plumb said that he taught his children not to sing the National Anthem, did he add nothing to that?"

"Not that I remember, sir."

"Did he not go on to say that he taught them to sing 'God save the people'?"

At once a shout of "Bravo!" came from behind me (Scotch, of course) and a short burst of clapping, like a pattering of rain. The magistrate nodded sharply, and the orderly was on his feet, threatening to put the offenders out. John was cross. He looked sternly at Andrew. Then he put his question again. The Sergeant remembered my words, but the magistrate, still frowning down the court, seemed to make no note of them. John glared at Andrew. But it all struck me as a piece of comedy; and Andrew's cry as a good honest response. Sooner that than the legal splitting of hairs.

John went on for a while; he produced qualifying remarks; had Sampson remember some; and sat down at last well pleased with himself.

Malcolm called the second policeman, Wood. He was not a shorthand writer either. He had less control of himself than Sampson and spent his time on the stand glaring at me in a cold

and weighty manner I found upsetting. He was, I should guess, a
good hater. Wood gave nothing to John. He admitted taking
down only the words he thought seditious, but declared roundly
that my other words had not altered their meaning. He had no
memory of "God save the people".

John made one good point. He asked Wood if he did not
think it strange that he and Sampson had noted the same words.

"No sir, not strange at all."

"But the words you took down and the words the Sergeant
took down are identical. Down to the last full stop."

"I didn't see what the Sergeant took down. We were on
opposite sides of the hall."

"You didn't copy from him later on?"

"No, I did not."

"It's odd then that you should have what he has."

"No sir, not odd at all. We took down the words we thought
seditious."

"From a talk that lasted an hour and twenty minutes—some
eighteen thousand words—you both took down the same fifty.
And you say it's not odd?"

"I do."

"Coincidental, then?"

Wood made no reply, and John left it at that. Then, as
Malcolm closed his case, he stood up again to defend me. He
called no witnesses, but addressed the court. He did so in a stodgy
manner. Eloquence would not have been acceptable to the robed
individual on the bench; a man loose-lipped, dewlapped like a
bulldog, and suffering a red collapse of his lower eyelids. His voice
was like the creaking of a door. Appropriate, I thought, to the kind
of justice that locked free speech away.

John began by admitting that the words in the information
would be seditious if used consecutively. But, he said, they were
not so used. The policemen had admitted it. And he submitted to
the court that he had shown beyond any doubt—beyond the
shadow of a doubt, he said—that they had taken their notes
haphazardly and ignored the qualifying phrases I had used.

"This case," he said, "is very different from a case of indecent language. The words in a sedition case should not be taken out of their context. What the accused said should have been rendered in full. I could of course put him on the witness stand and ask him to render it in full. But that would take up too much of the court's time. I have shown already how all the remarks in the information were qualified. And I suggest to the court—and to my learned friend" (a lawyerly nod at Malcolm) "that the summons should have been drawn up to show where the intervals occurred between the sentences."

The magistrate interrupted. "There should have been a row of points between the sentences. That is the proper manner."

John was encouraged by this. He droned on like a great black bee, but it was plain to me he was trapped in the bottle of his legalistic mind. How I longed to jump to my feet and tell him and Malcolm and the magistrate what this case was all about. Words, words. A point here, a point there. "It is manifestly impossible for anyone to take down in longhand any sentence such as the one submitted by Mr Sampson. That contains fifty words and would have been uttered in less than twenty-five seconds." The magistrate scratched with his pen. Sampson folded his hands. Somebody coughed in the body of the court. I looked round and Felicity smiled at me. Dan Peabody sat beside her. I had not known he was coming up.

The magistrate—Bradley was his name—kept his nose down. He scratched on with his noisy pen, sucking in his newborn baby's lip. Malcolm yawned and studied his thumb-nails. Wood kept his deadly eye on me as though I were his prey. John whispered encouragement—all of it nonsense. To cut him off I took out my Emerson and started to read. "No, no," John said, "that'll make a bad impression on the court."

Finally Bradley laid down his pen and folded his liver-marked hands. I had thought we would be in for some legal knitting but he surprised me by coming straight to the point. "I have no doubt these words were used or that they are seditious. Naturally they are only part of what was said, but I accept the evidence of the police that there were no other remarks that modify to any serious extent what is reported here. The only modifying clause is the reference

147

to 'God save the people', and that, it seems to me, could very well be sung as well as the National Anthem. The two are not contradictory. However, we are not concerned with that here. We are concerned with the reported utterance. And it is plainly seditious to say that children should not sing 'God save the King'. We shall confine ourselves to that, and to the whole tendency of the words in the information. That tendency is to excite disaffection against His Majesty's Government. I find the charge of seditious utterance proven and I direct the court to record a conviction against the defendant. However, I shall defer sentence until the hearing of the second charge."

He nodded at the clerk. And so we went through the solemn farce again. John enlivened it a little by reading a sentence from the charge to Sampson and having him write it down. Sampson did it perfectly.

"Yes," John said, "well you probably know it by heart." And he read two short paragraphs from a newspaper. Sampson got down only the opening words.

"Well, sir," he explained, "what Mr Plumb said impressed itself more forcibly on my mind." I was pleased to hear it.

In his final speech John said it was beyond human probability that two witnesses should have noted the same few words in speeches lasting an hour and twenty minutes and an hour and three-quarters. This was the only point he had to make but he looked at it back, front, sideways, and from underneath. The magistrate played with his lip and wiped his damp fingertips on his robe. When it was his turn to speak he wasted no time. I saw he wanted to purge his court of me. He could not understand any suggestion that New Zealand should repudiate its war loans. He could hardly imagine that New Zealand should have a revolution such as was still going on in Russia. Anyone who wished such a thing must be mad. To see his infantile, his stupid eye fix itself on me, and hear his grating voice declare me mad, was more than I could bear. He spoke for greed, stupidity, cruelty, death. I tried to get my statement from my pocket, tried to climb to my feet, but John held me down by my arm and hissed at me. He was saying, I believe, that if I sat still I might get away with a fine. "Nonsense,"

I said, "this man wants me locked up."

"George, be still, be still." And on my other side the court orderly restrained me too. So I let Bradley get on with it.

"I find the defendant guilty on both charges. And because in these troubled times a man holding beliefs such as his is too dangerous to be at large, I sentence the defendant to fourteen months' imprisonment on each charge. The sentences will run concurrently."

61

Felicity cried, "You cannot do this. Shame!" Her clear light voice was the first sound in the room as the door closed behind waddling Bradley. There was pain as well as anger in her cry. This was the point at which games stopped for her. Like Dan in Lyttelton jail, she looked into the dark. We had been until then, she and I, engaged in crusading. White chargers, gleaming swords, cannot have been far from her mind. Now she knew the truth. I leaned over the rail and held her hand. She kissed me and burst into tears. I asked Dan to take her home to Edie. He put his arms about her and led her away.

Because I was not a desperate criminal I was given time to say goodbye to my friends. They filed past and shook me by the hand. John Jepson. Andrew. Bluey Considine, who had come over from the Coast. Then men and women I did not know began to walk by. I felt the touch of many hands. Last came old Matthew Willis. "You should have got yourself a good lawyer, boy." He told me not to worry about Edie and the children. "I'll see they come to no harm."

Then I was taken out and put in a van, and delivered to Lyttelton jail.

62 I rested in the sun outside Oliver's court. People going by looked at me curiously. Perhaps they took me for a beggar and my trumpet for a novel collection bowl. It struck me after a while that the ones who grinned were not grinning at me but at something written on the wall above my head. I stood up and looked at it. *Goodlad rides again.* And above that an obscene drawing. I remembered that Oliver was hearing a divorce case that had roused much disapproval and delight. Goodlad was a racing journalist who had committed adultery with the wife of a well-known brewer. The papers were full of the case, printing details I thought most improper. The whole thing stank to me of lucre and lust and hypocrisy. On the other hand, I was not sorry to see the bourgeois world held under a light.

The sun went behind a tall building and at once a wind sprang up. I remembered this was Wellington. The stillness of the day had been a rare thing. A coldness began to play about my head and down my back. It drove me inside—this and a curiosity about the Goodlad case and my son Oliver's distinguished part in it. (Its only other distinctions were of a low sort.) Because it was late in the day I managed to find a place at the back of the court. The room was full of people, all leaning forward breathlessly. A good nine-tenths were women. The hats there would have stocked a milliner's shop. I could not make out the parties in the case.

Oliver, set on a ledge, had the look of an eagle. His beaky nose, his wig and steel-rimmed glasses, added to it. He looked capable of spreading wings and swooping down on some squealing victim, some plump and hatted woman—a tasty bite. But, I reflected, the simile was too bold for him. He had a meaner nature. Everything about Oliver was clipped, controlled. His mind especially. In that garden with square beds and gravel paths, no proscribed plant, no interdicted insect, lived for long. Oliver had a well-stocked shelf of poisons.

PLUMB

I felt easier in his court after thinking this. It was necessary for me to get Oliver set, get him square, before facing him. My exaggerations were not malicious. They rose from disappointment. I had had high hopes for Oliver, my first son.

He made no sign of having seen me, but I knew he had. Oliver misses nothing. I lifted my trumpet to hear. At this the woman next to me shifted away, rolling her posterior like a ball. She probably took me for a tramp. (Meg can never get me to buy new clothes. If the cloth remains warm, I say, what does a frayed cuff matter? Waste is immoral.) I was pleased to have the space. I laid my book there—a Browning selection I had borrowed from Max. The woman looked at it suspiciously, and moved off another inch. I smiled with delight. Perhaps Browning and I could clear the whole bench. Then I began to hear words. "Bedroom." "Bed." "Naked." Was this what held these women spellbound? This squalid event? Two foolish people satisfying an urge—the hired room, the hired bed? How had Browning put it?—"the unlit lamp and the ungirt loin." The words were too good.

The man in the box was an investigator, one who spied on guilty couples for money. He was saying, as far as I could make out, that he had shone his torch into the room. A strong torch. An orderly held it up as evidence. And then had the naked pair, blinded like possums, tried to hide from this light that murdered their joy? If joy it was. I began to be more troubled than I liked, and I put my trumpet down.

Oliver wrote; as Bradley had, so many years before. I wondered how he enjoyed doing this job. A scrubbed and Lysolled man, Oliver. He must feel dirtied by what he was forced to hear. He wrote; looked up severely; gave a ruling. He was at the top of his profession. Perhaps his sense of this served him like a doctor's rubber gloves. He could handle sores and take no infection. Down there on the floor, Goodlad and Mrs Mottram, taken in their carnal act: up here, Oliver Plumb, Supreme Court judge. I could see how the two need never meet.

Court rose until the next day. I turned sideways to let the women out. Several stayed in their places to watch the actors go by. And here they came. Goodlad, bold and smiling; a whisky

151

face, broken veins high on his cheeks, blue jovial eyes; and was that pain, bewilderment in them, moving like shadowy fish, deep down? Now Mrs Mottram, heavily befurred; perhaps on this mild day so dressed to keep up her morale. Pale, dark-eyed, queenly. Lips set in a small manufactured smile. The women beside me gave a little, "Ooh". They would, I think, have curtseyed if they'd had room. And they came by me in a great hurry to follow the lady out, but drew in their skirts not to touch me, this shabby ancient.

I waited in my seat and presently an orderly in a black gown took me to Oliver's room.

"Dad."

"Oliver."

We shook hands.

"What have you done?" It was more complaint than enquiry. Sickness, injury, affront Oliver's sense of propriety. He believes in solitary confinement for the sick.

"It's a burn. Nothing to worry about."

"That bandage doesn't look too clean."

"It's all right. Max put it on."

Oliver made a sour expression. "And you've still got that?" He tapped my trumpet with the edge of his nails. It sent painful vibrations into my ear.

"Don't do that."

"Isn't it time you got rid of it?"

"No." But I took it down as it offended him, and that cut me off. I sat and waited for him to get ready. First he washed his hands. Then he took off his wig and put it in a cupboard. From the way he handled it I saw it was a sacred object. He put his gown on a hanger and hung it against the wall. Then he put some papers in a satchel. He snapped it shut. Every move was quick and bare. I remembered his skill in weeding carrots, his manner of eating his porridge. He had spooned his way round it clockwise; made an island of it with scalloped cliffs; then eaten round it again, and again, keeping it perfect all the way. He kept milk and porridge in exact proportion so that the last of each came together in his final spoonful. A beautiful performance. Edie had become aware of it first, and made me watch. It worried her. And in fact if it was interrupted he screamed in an hysterical frenzy, and subsided at last into a trancelike state. A ritual disturbed, a certainty lost, the structure of his infant world came down like a cardhouse. Edie had to take him in her arms and warm him back to life. What warmed him now? He put on a tweed overcoat; drew on leather gloves; picked up a cane, his satchel, a homburg hat. I was impressed. He looked ready to issue from 10 Downing Street. But he looked too a plaster man, ready to be broken. And how then could he be fixed. To stay whole in his artificial shape, in this rude Dominion, he must walk on paths unknown to the rest of us. If I had to choose, I thought, I would choose to be with Goodlad and Mrs Mottram.

In Oliver's quiet car we drove to Wadestown.

63 Dante says, "A lady appeared to me robed with the colour of living flame." And in another place, "I knew an angel visibly . . . Blessed are they who meet her on the earth." Oliver's Beatrice rose from her seat and approached me. I felt her large cold hand in mine; saw her bitter mouth make sounds of welcome and her eyes simulate warmth. The joke is really too cruel. Beatrice Plumb is barren, or Oliver sterile. They adopted a girl but the child went to the bad: ran away from home, lived with a Maori; then came home one day blind in one eye from a punch and demanding money. Oliver had seen her last in 1944, drunk on the streets of the town, held on her feet by black American sailors. (I had this from Felicity.) He and Beatrice spoke of her no more. It's no use now asking who was to blame. But Beatrice is a woman three parts dead. Love is dead, pity is dead, the desiring part of her nature, that is dead. Alive in her is a sense of what is owed her. But this is not simple: it has a positive and a negative side. The world she inhabits is, in a sense, religious.

We sat by a small electric heater in the living-room. Beatrice too frowned at my bandage and trumpet. I gave her news of Meg

and the children. She was too well-bred to shout. She leaned close
to my trumpet and closing her eyes as though she might see wax
in it, spoke in the voice Esther calls la-di-da. The sounds that
came to me were distant.

"—Emerson?"

Yes, Emerson was well. Still in love with flying machines.

"—Fergus?"

Fergus was all right. Starting to make money.

"—Esther?—husband, Fred?"

Oh Fred was well. Making money too. Barrels of it.

Oliver nodded approval. They did not ask after Willis. They
did not approve of him.

In the dining room we ate a frugal meal, blessed by the head
of the house. We had boiled potatoes, boiled cabbage, boiled neck
of mutton chops with parsley sauce. It suited me well. I prefer
plain food. We drank tonic water sweetened with orangeade. After
the meal Oliver took me to his study. I wondered which of his
brothers and sisters he meant to talk about. Willis and Alfred were
blotted from his mind. Felicity, a Catholic, lived beyond the pale.
We had covered Esther and Meg and Emerson. That left Robert.
As I had seen him so often in his youth, Oliver sat down and
folded his fingers—like a magistrate, I thought. And that of course
was what he was. Better: a judge. This sudden rushing of past and
present to fill one space confused me. The intervening years were
thrown aside. All that time, all that human life, vanishing as
though into a void, filled me with horror. Significance? Where was
significance? It seemed to me I was gazing into emptiness: Oliver's
life.

"Now. Robert." His voice was sharp as scissors; excellent for
my trumpet.

"No, I won't discuss him."

"Why not?"

"Robert has made his choice."

"Some choice."

"It's his to make. He's nearly forty."

"Robert's a child. We all know that. And he's fallen under an
evil influence. This Parminter. The man's a lunatic."

"As far as I can make out he's a fundamentalist Christian. Same as you."

"I'm a Presbyterian. And we're talking about Robert. He's fallen in with a den of communists."

"Wrong again, Oliver. There isn't any doctrine. They just hold things in common."

"Including their women."

"Is that so? I hadn't heard that. But it shouldn't upset you. Free love can be perfectly moral. And can you imagine Robert taking part in orgies?"

"I can. Under certain influences. Have you seen *Truth* this week?"

"No."

"They sent a reporter out. And now it looks as if the police are going to investigate the place."

"They won't find anything."

"They'll find a man called Plumb. And where do you think that will leave me?"

"Ah, now I see."

"It's all your doing. You have to take responsibility for this. Blasphemy, heresy, sedition. What chance did he have?"

"I don't think I was ever guilty of blasphemy."

But Oliver was in a rage. His voice remained steady, his face still, but a trembling in his fingers gave him away. I wondered if he sentenced in this state. What an asset to a judge: to appear under control while in a moral frenzy. I was thinking on this, on the grotesque shapes the cramped mind takes, on my visionary knowledge, my consciousness of the One; and my love for poor pharisaical Oliver, whom I would have share my certainties, if a way of sharing could be found, if a path into his darkness could be found: thinking all this, in a state of sadness and confusion, when I heard half a dozen words, a sharp little cracker-burst: "—the miserable life you led mother."

"What?"

"She had a miserable life. No money. Never any proper food. Did you know she used to eat our left-overs? You were in your study. You didn't have the slightest idea what went on. Meat and potatoes for you. The rest of us had porridge, even for tea. And all mother got was the scrapings out of the pot."

"Nonsense."

"It's true."

"We had one or two hard years—"

"And clothes. Mother liked beautiful clothes. You dressed her in rags. And everybody stared at her. She couldn't stand that. She stopped going out. And the girls in bare feet."

"Two years, Oliver. Three perhaps. It did nobody any harm."

"And then you had to go to prison. To prison. My father. How do you think I felt in France, half of the calf of my leg shot off, and my father in prison for sedition?"

"Quiet, Oliver, quiet. You should be over it now."

"I'll never be over it."

That was true. I looked at him sadly, but from a great distance. Poor crippled boy. Edie came close to me. She stood by my side and put her hand in mind. Edie in her worn clothes, Edie with her troubled face. Yes, Oliver was right, her life had been hard—perhaps at times even miserable. But he did not understand: Edie knew love, she knew joy.

64 "Now Felicity, tell me, did your mother ever give you porridge for tea?"

"Who's been telling you that?"

"Oliver."

"Trust him."

"Did she?"

"It happened once or twice."

"And what did I have?"

"Oh, meat. A chop perhaps. I can't remember."

"Eggs?"

"You were doing brain work."

"I see."

"You're not going to worry about it now?"

The car was parked in a resting bay on the Rimutaka hill. The engine had become overheated and Felicity was letting it cool down. A stony gully dropped away from the roadside. Beyond it hills went rolling off to the north.

"And when I was in prison what did you eat?"

"Oh dad, fancy worrying now. It's thirty years ago. It's dead and gone."

"I want to know how the rest of you got on. I had other things on my mind."

"We did all right. Grandpa Willis looked after us."

"Did you get enough to eat—"

She moved impatiently. "Why worry about food? I said we did all right. It was the talking that was hardest to bear. The way people treated us."

"Yes?"

"Did you know they threw stones through our windows? And left white feathers in the letter-box?"

"Your mother didn't tell me."

"She didn't want to 'worry you. And then there was the morning we found muck smeared all over the front door."

"What? What was that?"

"Faeces. Excrement."

"Good God."

"They'd tried to print a word with it. 'Judas.' Oh, don't worry, mother didn't have to wash it off. Emerson did that."

"Your mother—"

"She was all right. She was no wilting violet. It made her more determined, that was all. Florence and Agnes were the ones who got upset. Florence didn't get out of bed for three days after it happened. And she went off to the States as soon as she could. To get away from the shame of it all."

"Florence never forgave me."

"'I was born to be a lady.' I've got no patience with her."

"A girl at that age feels things very deeply."

"You don't have to tell me."

"Were you unhappy too?"

"I was all right. I never let the flag-waggers worry me. My worries were something else."

"What?"

"Nothing you'd be interested in.—The engine should be cool enough by now."

"Religion?"

"I won't talk about religion with you, dad. You can stop right now."

"But I want to talk. You believed the same way I did then."

"I did not. I pretended to. I even fooled myself."

"But—"

"Poor dad. You thought I was something special. Woman of the twentieth century. Mother of the new race. And all I really wanted was poor silly Dan. A house and babies."

"I don't believe that."

"I wanted him to divorce his wife and make an honest woman out of me. So much for the New Woman."

"Dan's your own affair. I don't want to talk about Dan."

"What then? God? The Oversoul? Don't you see dad, it was all too intellectual. Not an ounce of feeling in it. All that Unitarian stuff. Mother/Father God. It meant nothing to me. I didn't feel it. I needed something else. Anything. The old gentleman with the white beard. So long as it wasn't just a light shining in the sky."

"It was more than that."

"To you. But not to me. I needed something I could understand. Father and Son and Holy Ghost. I was getting all dried up. I was dying. And because of all your silly terminology, all your Nirvanas and Cosmic Souls, I couldn't find out what it was. But now I know. I wanted something I could hold. Something I could get inside my body."

"I'm not sure your priests would approve of that."

"Bother my priests."

"And Felicity, my religion is more than you think. I know God. I have seen him."

"Bully for you." She got out of the car and lifted the engine hood. In a moment a cloud of steam rose up. She went round to

158

the boot and came back with a jar of water. I thought, I don't know her any more.

Her conversion was by self-surrender. She must—such a strong-willed girl—have wanted it to be volitional. (See William James on conversion.) But she came to Christ by an act of yielding. Then, as far as I can make out, she asserted herself on the next step, made it a willed one, made it intellectually, into the One True Church. But that step, in her latter days, has the appearance of a sitting down. The first was the vital one. Curious. Ironical. Her conversion took her that extra distance to Rome just because she was my strong-minded daughter. There, having proved to herself she was herself, she relaxed; and today she sits enjoying her patch of sun like a frog on a rock. I look at her and I think: What a waste of mind and passion, what a dreadful defeat.

She slammed the hood shut. The car bounced. And bounced a second time as she closed the boot. She got back inside.

"Did I ever tell you," I said, "that I once heard the last confession of a Catholic?" I told her about Joseph Sullivan, the Maungatapu murderer.

"Did you get the priest afterwards?"

"No. We buried him. Scroggie and I."

"But a priest could have come. There was still time for extreme unction. As long as you got him there as soon as you could."

"The man was dead, Felicity. Already he was face to face with God. What need of priests?"

She looked at me, and I at her. Near the house where I grew up a long culvert ran under the road. My playmates and I would stand at either end and shout at the tiny beings far away, against the foliage of another world. I saw Felicity as such a being; and in some such way she must have seen me.

"What will you do?"

"I'll have a Mass said for him."

"For the repose of his soul?"

"Exactly. Now put your silly funnel down. I've finished talking to you."

65 In the week I arrived in Lyttelton jail a man called Eggers was hanged for murder. The morning I left on transfer to Paparua a rapist was flogged. I spent seven months of my sentence in that place, and everything that happened seems of a piece with that hanging and flogging. Locked in our cells we heard the trapdoor drop—heard the death of Eggers. But I did not hear the sound of the whip on the young man's back or hear him screaming. I went into Lyttelton jail hard of hearing. When I left I was stone deaf in one ear and could hear only faintly with the other. I told no one. The warders pushed me roughly or struck me between the shoulders to make me move.

They put me on light work: cleaning, painting, simple carpentry, much of it outside the prison walls. It was a great relief to come out of that building into the daylight. I might see women hanging out their washing or children playing hopscotch in the street. After the cold, the damp, the cells and iron doors and tasteless food, the shadow of the inhuman lying over everything, I had begun to doubt the world outside was real. Coming out, even under guard, was a visionary experience. I learned from Lyttelton jail that physical things, a sun-warmed stone, a flower, a human face, can be known spiritually; and Understanding be reached through the eyes and fingertips as well as through the mind.

But as winter came on most of my work was inside. We were put in our cells at half past four and kept there until morning. I read very little. Bob Semple told me he studied in Lyttelton jail. A warder brought him all the books he needed. The man must have been gone by the time I got there. The governor allowed me one book at a time. My Emerson was returned to me, but taken away before I could claim something else. Edie brought out books on her visits, but only the safe ones reached me—safe in someone's uncertain judgement. Le Bon's *The Psychology of Socialism* was

160

kept back. So was Laing's *Modern Science and Modern Thought*, published in 1885! They allowed me Dickens but not G. B. Shaw. I could follow their reasoning. But *Queen Mab* and not Amiel's *Journal*? Still, it was not important. I could not read in that place.

Nor could I think. Thinking cannot be done in darkness. And in Lyttelton jail I was afflicted by a dark oppression of mind. I could not hold myself steady. I heard in imagination the iron and wooden crash of the gallows trapdoor. I could not pray. I could not find God or Man. "Out of the way of darkness cometh the path of light." I held the words before me. But the path would not be found. I heard the trapdoor crash. I felt the noose choking me. And the bullets Eggers fired smashing into spine and heart. And bayonets cutting my flesh, gas burning my lungs. The hell and the despair of the world were in my cell. When I think of that winter I use the term "a dark night of the soul". And I think of Whitman's words, "Agonies are one of my changes of garments," and "I am the man, I suffer'd, I was there." Unlike Whitman I was not able to say, "All this I swallow, it tastes good, I like it well."

In the spring I was shifted to Paparua prison. Some of the weight lifted from me. Edie came to see me more often. I let her bring Felicity and Emerson, and once Rebecca and Esther. My friends came out. They gave me conversation for an hour or two a week, shouting their faint words into my ear. With my wife and children, they gave me love and warmth. So I came from my darkness into a kind of grey. It was neither dawn nor twilight, it did not promise day or threaten night. But in it I could think and I could live.

The war ended. Oliver limped home, but did not visit me. Felicity began her training as a teacher. Florence went off to America. (She came to see me before sailing—a sad little interview. She was caught between love and resentment and so could not do anything but cry.) Emerson left school. If I had been at home I would not have allowed it. He was too persistent for Edie. All he wanted was to drive motor cars or fly aeroplanes. He went down to Thorpe where John gave him work in his aerated-water factory.

Matthew Willis was true to his word. He paid my family's food and clothing bills and paid the rent. Edie's sister Florence helped if anyone was sick (there was much sickness in that bitter winter), and her mother had the girls go one by one to stay with her. She was a sharp old lady, very much against me, and she considered it her duty to talk good sense into my misled children. Late in the year she died. And at once old Matthew fell ill. It was plain he would not last long. He came to see me, very bent, very sunken in cheek and eye, and told me I need not worry about the future. He was leaving me more than enough to get by on.

Matthew lived through Christmas into the New Year. But in the summer a new grief hastened his death. He rented a cottage at New Brighton beach so that Edie and the children might be away from the city during the worst of the influenza epidemic. They spent two happy months there. On the last Sunday our daughter Rebecca was drowned.

66 The Governor called me to his office. There was Edie with white face and bruised eyes. I knew it was death, and I asked, "Who?" She could not shout, but I saw her lips say, "Rebecca—drowned." I put my arms about her and we wept. The Governor left us alone. For a long time we stood there, giving each other what comfort we could. It was not much. A part of us was dead. I was taken by a dreadful sense of waste and of cruelty, and a love for the dead child that became more pain than love. I found no help in God.

67 The day had been colder than usual. The sea was rough with small sharp waves, blown to spume on their tops.

Matthew and Edie and John Willis sat on the sand, watching the children swim. Rebecca did not swim well. She was a thin child and felt the cold. Usually she was first out of the water. But she was excitable and the broken waves exhilarated her. When the others ran in no one noticed she had stayed behind.

The cold must have caught her suddenly. She must have found herself too exhausted to swim. And she drowned silently, while her brothers and sisters, wrapped in their towels, were walking up to lunch.

Later everyone searched. John Willis found her, only a short way out. She was white and cold and dead. They tried for a long time but could not bring her back.

Rebecca. Thirteen. A quiet child. Her hair was the darkest in our family. Her eyes were brown. She was good at her schoolwork and wrote little stories about wizards and princesses. I did not know her well, but she came sometimes, saying no word, and put her cheek on my sleeve. That is the memory I keep of her.

68 The sea took one of our children. And the Spanish flu brought me near to my death. I lay in the prison infirmary for many weeks, as near to a corpse as it's possible to be while remaining alive. My hearing was gone, my hair was gone, and most of my physical substance wasted away. I was bone, and an unhuman kind of silken skin. Manikin. Homunculus. Shrunken in my spiritual being too. I had strength for neither pain nor rebellion. Or even for complaint. I lay there week after week; passive, dry, physical, as good as dead.

In April the prison van delivered me home; put me on the steps like a parcel of groceries. My family carried me in. They set about the task of breathing life into me. Edie, Felicity, Esther, took turns beside my bed; and Meg, my youngest daughter, sat with me after school and drew pictures for me (Phoenix, unicorn) and modelled dragon-killing knights out of plasticine. My friends came often. Some of them, I saw from their eyes, thought me finished as a man. They could not look at me straight. But I came back to health; amazed, perhaps dismayed them. (Dan had seen uses for me as martyr.) Andrew began to talk of a lecture tour. It would be a triumph. The returned men would be for me one hundred per cent. I said no. That book of my life was closed forever.

"Edie," I said, "we must think what we're going to do."

"Are you well enough, George?" (I had my trumpet now and she leaned forward and spoke into it clearly.)

"Matthew has left us well off. Well enough. I think we should leave this town."

"We've moved about a lot, George."

"This will be the last time. We'll find a house, a comfortable house, and never move again. I promise you that."

"Do you really promise, George?" She was firmer with me these days, nurse with invalid.

"There's nothing to keep us here, Edie. Whatever we need we can carry away in our minds. Florence and John will look after her grave."

"Yes."

"So, my dear?"

"I want to go somewhere warm."

In the spring we paid a visit to Auckland and hunted in the suburbs and the country round about. We found a little town out by the ranges; a house that seemed to have grown up like a tree. It was of the style known as villa, but pieces had been added to it. One stepped up, stepped down, into green dark places or sunny places. It stood on a slope beside a slow-running creek, with fifteen acres of land up a tributary stream. There were gardens on the flat land, well-grown pines and wattle trees by the road, and an orchard running back to a neighbouring farm. We bought it; and hurried to Christchurch for our children. We packed, we said goodbye, and we travelled north. (Oliver and Felicity stayed behind.)

"I'd like to call it Peacehaven," Edie said. I agreed, though secretly I had wanted Journey's End. Instead I put that name on the door of the room I had chosen for my study. From time to time people say it's morbid or defeatist. Then I explain it comes from John Davidson's poem:

> At the journey's end I see a new world
> Where men are healthy, women beautiful,
> Humanity tender, good and dutiful.

For this green place, this warm, garden-surrounded, bird-echoing house, made me optimistic. Just a little. It was to be many years before I freed myself from weight and pain. But in moving into Peacehaven I made a beginning.

The children loved it. They grew. They bloomed. I think of it especially as Meg's place, Robert's place. They were the youngest. They made the creek, the orchard, the paddocks, their magic land. Robert ran there like a pagan, setting up over the years a blood-bond with those fifteen acres. I have seen him sniff the soil and would not have been surprised to see him taste it. It would not have startled or worried me to come upon him embracing a hillock or praying to a tree. Meg leaned more to house and yard. But she too formed a bond with growing things. We came upon her sitting among ripe apples ten feet off the ground, singing a little song of her own composing—a tuneless song, Edie told me, of love for branch and leaf and fruit. But she had sophistication enough to be ashamed. She cried out, blushed, hid her face as though caught in some guilty act; and ran away among the trees and had to be hunted out at dusk and carried home in my arms.

Robert milked the cow and looked after the fowls. He would not let anyone share these tasks. There was though little danger of that. Emerson (he had left John Jepson's factory to come to Auckland with us) was an apprentice mechanic at a motor garage in the town. When home, which was seldom, he tinkered with his motorcycle, a filthy foul-smelling machine called Indian, decorated with a picture of a brave wearing a war feather. The sound of its engine as he tested it in the shed out the back penetrated even my deafness and gave Edie headaches. He came in to tea in greasy overalls; and ate dreaming. He did not see his brothers and sisters or hear what they said to him. He was blind and deaf. He dreamed his future: pistons and petrol, goggles and floating scarf. Already he was airborne.

And Alfred? Books were his passion. In a sense he was airborne too: in two senses. For he liked to sit in trees to read or write. From my study window I looked across the gardens and the stream and saw him high in a pine tree, up where the wind set it swaying. He wrapped his legs about its slender trunk and read with the needles pricking his throat and cheeks. Edie had a hard time washing gum from his clothes. She did not complain. Most of his poems were to her. But there were also odes to skylark, thrush, Ceres, Spirit of the Stream, and later hymns to Social Justice. At fourteen he looked like Shelley: small head round as a ball and cluster of auburn curls. I had great joy in him. He was the son who would carry on my work. And yet I never knew him well. I did not get close to him, as I got close to Robert, or even understood him, as I understood Emerson. He kept a part of himself hidden from me, and intuitively I did not try to uncover it. He admired me, came near to worshipping me, but I sensed he did not like me. I turned aside from this, and was pleased with his accomplishments. Yet I was afraid!

> Like one that on a lonesome road
> Doth walk in fear and dread,
> And having once turned round walks on,
> And turns no more his head;
> Because he knows, a frightful fiend
> Doth close behind him tread.

I had not had that glimpse and did not have that knowledge, but in the dark of the night, in my lonely times, I knew the dread.

But I was saying, Robert's preserves were in no danger from his brothers. With a startling lack of originality he christened the cow Daisy and the goat Nan. He knew which hens were laying well and which should be next for the pot. And it was Robert who got the tomahawk and chopped their heads off. He did it without regret or enjoyment. It was a job, and part of his life. He was patient with the Butters's boy Royce, who would come to watch, but turn his back, and peep over his shoulder, and squat to examine the entrails, and then run home and tell his mother how cruel Robert had been. But Robert was kind. He taught Royce to milk and to bait fish hooks, and during the Butters's Radiant Living phase fed him cold chops from our kitchen.

"Dad," he said to me, "I want to leave school." He had a way of making decisions I must call elemental. There was no quarrelling with them. I looked at his plain honest face. It was time for him to finish with book-learning. He knew it. I knew it. His next season had come.

So Robert settled down to digging and composting, to planting and pruning. He ran a small flock of sheep on our fifteen acres: wormed and dagged and sheared them, put the ram in at the right time, and brought us his fattest lamb for Christmas dinner. He learnt about bees and before long had half a dozen hives. In the summer and autumn he set up a stall at our gate and sold fruit and eggs and honey and vegetables. Edie and I rested on him. He was a piece of firm ground under our feet. We loved him, and took him for granted; we trod on him unthinkingly. In the depression when I lost my money it was Robert who saved Peacehaven. For three years we bought practically nothing: fruit, vegetables, milk, meat, all came from his labour. He sold eggs and honey to the grocer, and kept us in tea and flour and clothes. He even gave me money to buy books. And as much as he sold he gave away. Sundays he set out with a sugar bag of corn or pumpkins slung on his shoulder and came home for lunch with the sack empty and no money in his pockets. And again he was taken for granted. One old man attacked him with his walking stick when he showed up late, and another complained of Codling moth in his apples. But Robert only grinned and shrugged. He made no judgements on people. People were in nature. He did not question the shapes they had grown into.

He brought home several girls. One, Barbara, we thought he might marry. But she, like the others, made the mistake of thinking his end was his beginning. He took her on a tour of his land—I thought of it soon as his—showed her his hives and his sheep and his fruit trees and squirted a jet of Daisy's warm milk in her mouth. They walked hand in hand, and lay on a blanket under an apple tree. They kissed—and maybe did more. I do not know. But sadly we watched the girl's happiness fade. She was an honest homely girl. She and Robert should have been right for each other. But the times had infected her with ambition, the world had made its brassy call to her with ambition, and she betrayed herself. She wanted possessions, glamour, the twentieth century. Poor damaged thing, she had gone past the point of finding happiness with a man who needed no more than a piece of land, seeds to plant, sheep to tend, potatoes and mutton for food, and a pine fire in the evening.

Edie heard their final argument. Robert said, "I'll never change." And the girl called him hick, hayseed, worm, imbecile. And stormed away, weeping. I believe she loved him.

Robert said, "I don't think I'll ever get married, mum."

69 His letter had said he did not want to see Felicity. She dropped me at the gate and drove away to visit a friend in Carterton. If she was hurt she kept it hidden well.

The letter-box said simply *Parminter*. But on the cream-stand someone had painted *F— Farm*. Envy and hatred, I thought, even in this lovely place. For it was lovely. Over the fields mountains reared up like giants. Groves of native trees stood in the plain, sharp-edged as storybook islands. The red roofs of the barns and houses showed above orchard trees. Post-and-rail fences made geometrical patterns, bone-white, on the pastures. The cows were Jerseys, gleaming like bottle-glass. They chewed their cud placidly and watched me as I crunched along the shell-strewn drive to the settlement.

A child playing on a rope swing in a tree told me I would find Robert at the beehives. I went the way he pointed and found the hives on the far side of a row of guava trees. Robert was busy taking out frames of honey. Bees droned about him and crawled on his clothes. They seemed more bemused than angry. He banged a frame sharply on the edge of the hive and sent a small army of them tumbling back inside.

"Robert," I called.

He waved at me not to come close. I watched as he filled his handcart with trays of honey. The white wax and brimming cells had a quality both rich and virginal. And Robert had the right to handle them. He too was in nature. It was fanciful in me to think the bees understood. They did not sting him. One of them stung me. Robert knew at once. And I supposed, fancifully again, that he had felt the pain of its death. He closed the hive he was working on and came to me.

"Is that the sting? Don't squeeze it."

I could not for the fingers of my burned hand no longer worked. He took off a glove and scraped the sting out with his fingernail. Then he took a small tin of chalky powder from his pocket, wet a little with spit, and rubbed it in the hurt place. That done, he turned to my bandaged hand. He took off his other glove and unwrapped the bandage. Half my palm and my fingertips were raw and red and damp. They had an unhealthy look that alarmed me. Robert straightened out my fingers a little. He slanted my palm at the sun. "Let the sun get at it," he yelled. Then he went back to his hives.

I had not seen him for four years. I stood and watched him work, with the sun making my hand tingle, and a pleasant fading itch in my bee-stung wrist. Four years in a prison camp had damaged Robert badly, but he was a man who had found useful work to do and was doing it well. Oliver should envy him.

He pushed his cart to a shed and stored the honey.

"Well dad, how are you?"

I gave him Margaret's love.

"Meg, how is she?"

"Well."

"Meg's a good person."

"She talks about you a lot."

"We were together."

"She'd like you to come and see her."

"No, dad. Tell her I love her, that's all. What's Peacehaven like?"

"Much the same."

"Do you still have sheep?"

We strolled through a field of tomatoes, where half a dozen people were busy picking, and a worked-out strawberry field, and a field of cauliflowers. The pickers looked up as we went by with a simple or glittering curiosity that gave me the feeling of being in an institution for the moon-struck and possessed. But Robert saw nothing unusual. He told me about his work, his troubles with insects and weeds and with a soil that was not all he would like it to be. His words came to me almost independently of sound. I knew what he would say before he said it.

"You never told me much about the camps, son."

He had been in Strathmore, Whitenui, Hautu, and others whose names I forget; and in Mount Eden prison for a time. When I had gone to visit him he had smiled and said he was well. He had looked well. Nothing terrible had happened; nothing openly brutal or openly cruel. The camps were not as bad as Lyttelton jail. But a part of Robert died in them; died behind the wire; in the messes and dark icy huts; under contempt and restriction.

He said, "I don't want to talk about those places."

"I'd like to hear, Robert. I was in jail too."

"No, dad. I won't talk about them. Come to see the new tank I'm putting in."

Later we waited in the yard as people came up from the outbuildings and fields. They went into the dining-hall. An oldish man went by, bald like me, thick in his body and muscular in his face. He had cheerful and slightly mad eyes—the madness brought out by steel-rimmed glasses. Except for his working clothes he looked like a Californian evangelist. He nodded at me. Parminter, I guessed.

Presently a gumbooted woman came up. She approached

Robert shyly. She had wispy hair and a bulging brow, almost hydrocephalic, and a body shaped like a bran-sack. I thought perhaps she was mentally retarded. Robert patted her on the shoulder.

"This is Betty, dad. My wife."

The eugenicist in me was revolted. But I kept hold of the thought that Robert was happy. And I shook hands with the woman gravely and said I was pleased to meet her. We went into the hall. Robert gave me a chair beside his own. The table was a long planed board on trestles. There were fourteen adults and ten children. Parminter sat at the head with his sons (Robert's fellows in prison camp). This "family" was, I saw, hierarchical. Parminter said, "Our visitor is Bob's father. We welcome you to the Ark and to our meal."

Everyone said, "Welcome, Bob's father."

Parminter blessed the food.

Yes, I thought, mad. But happy. Robert is happy. I thank God for that. I supposed I must thank Parminter too.

As we ate a young woman with red scrubbed cheeks and her hair in a bun—a look I associate with fundamentalist sects: less wholesome than they suppose—sat in a chair by the window and read aloud from the bible. I had put down my trumpet and so could not hear. Now and then Parminter stopped his chewing and said something, perhaps "Hallelujah", and the table echoed him. Once he prayed, piercing the ceiling with his eyes. The others stopped their eating till he was done. Even I stopped. Then benignly he signalled us to carry on. The food was plain, home-grown, home-made: meal bread, butter, honey, sour cheese, apples, milk. Robert spread my bread to save my hand.

After lunch he said he had a job to finish in the carpentry shop. I watched him for a time; admired his skill with chisel and saw; but soon became restless and said I would wait in the gardens. I walked about until Parminter came out khaki-handed from the tomatoes and invited me to sit with him on a stile.

"How do you find Bob?"

"Very well. He seems to be happy here."

"You sound surprised."

"No. He's always been a simple person."

Parminter took it as a compliment. "One must be simple to come into the Ark. I'm sorry Mr Plumb, I can't ask you to stay."

"Because I belong in the world?"

"The world is Satan's world. Gehenna. And yes, you belong in it. One must speak the truth. Baal, Mammon, Satan and his angels. You come from that, and I smell their smell on you."

"It's good of you to let me visit."

Parminter shrugged. "Bob wanted it."

"He's unregenerate then?"

"You may joke, but none will joke on the Day of Wrath."

"Except those on the Ark."

"There will be rejoicing on the Ark. And weeping and wailing and a rain of fire outside. You will see."

"Will it be long?"

"Not long."

I saw why a dirty word or two on his cream-stand did not upset him. But looking at his mad good-humoured face, I felt pleased with him, almost fond of him. I would sooner spend an afternoon in his company than with Oliver, or for that matter with Sidney Holland or Peter Fraser. He saw behind the official face of things.

"I've heard you believe there'll be a Second Coming."

"He is amongst us now."

This was more than I had bargained for. I wondered if Parminter were about to reveal Himself. I admired him tremendously. To bring Ark and Second Coming together—what an achievement! But he still had surprises for me.

"He slumbers in one of our number. And on the Day a transformation will take place. The human skin will fall away and Christ will stand in His glory."

This was theologically preposterous. This was out at the far reaches of delusion. But I was moved by it, and made aware that possibilities lay in me—that the rock of my sanity might under some chance encounter be cleft, and the waters of a crazy joy well out; and that I could call the event revelation, and believe. I pulled myself together.

172

"And who is the one?"

Parminter looked up—speared Heaven on his eye. Put a question, had an answer. "I may tell you, Mr Plumb."

"Not Robert?"

Parminter nodded wisely. He looked at me with pity, and with a respect that must have had something to do with my role as Joseph. "Yes, Bob Plumb. Our Lord has entered the Ark by its lowliest gate and waits His time. And on the Day when the Vengeful Angels go forth Bob will be transformed. Bob will stand revealed as Christ and He will ride with His chosen ones over the fire."

"But," I said, "but, none of this is in the bible. How do you know it?"

"The Lord called me into the mountains. He revealed it to me."

"I see."

"You do not, Mr Plumb. But never mind."

"Does Robert know?"

"Only I know. And you. And I advise you to pray, Mr Plumb. There may still be salvation for you. You must have some special merit as father of the Vehicle."

"But Robert?—you've let him marry."

"That was his wish. Bob heals. He brings happiness. Betty has come out of her sleep. She seeks her salvation. This is a miracle."

"He works miracles?"

"He touches things and they heal. He is closing up the wound in Betty's mind."

"Well, well," I said. "Well, well."

"And I saw him touch your hand. That will heal too."

"In the natural course of things. There's no miracle there."

"Has it been getting better?"

"No, but—"

"You will see."

"Who married them?"

"They came together at the Lord's command."

"That's all very fine . . . What if they have children?"

"That would be a great joy." He stood up, a solid and

convincing man: he looked as if he belonged in a boardroom—except for those eyes, glittering with knowledge and craziness. "But I think there will be no time for children. The Day is soon." His eyes went red—the red of self-delight and righteousness and blood. I recorded through my sight the Voice booming in his skull. He turned and walked away from me, across his gardens, through the growing plants, towards the hills.

"Mr Parminter."

"The Lord is calling me."

"The police are going to raid you, Mr Parminter. I heard in Wellington."

"We have no fear. He has chosen us." He kept straight on. The others in the gardens knelt as he passed. And Parminter grew smaller, crossing paddocks, climbing fences. Cattle lumbered aside to give him passage. So might Moses have made his way up Mount Sinai.

Finding that thought in myself, I said, "Oh no. This is just a case of religious dementia. I've seen them before." And catching one of Parminter's followers grinning at another, I thought it unlikely they believed all he said. Wise of him to keep Robert's condition to himself. They might not be happy with it. Robert would be unhappy. But I watched Parminter out of sight with a feeling of regret. I liked the man.

Then I walked about the gardens and paddocks, seeing Robert's hand in everything: neatly carpentered kennels, firewood stacked in a special way, a compost bin built on the same design as the one at Peacehaven. Robert, I thought, might or might not be the lowliest gateway into the Ark, but he was plainly this farm's cornerstone. Parminter's saviour in the mundane sphere.

70 It was getting on for two-thirty when I went to the carpenter's shop. I came up on him quietly. He was sharpening chisels on an emery wheel. Cold sparks played on his hands. I touched him, "Robert," and pointed to my watch.

He switched off the wheel. "Time to go?"

"I'm glad you're happy here, Robert."

"It's a good place."

"Come and sit in the sun for a moment."

We found a seat at the head of the drive beside a grapefruit tree. Yellow fruit hung in the polished leaves. Over a trellis jasmine tumbled like water. But Robert himself denied the Arcadian setting. He smelled of sweat. Dry manure was caked on the soles of his boots. He wore a tartan shirt and an ancient grey silk waistcoat and a felt hat with its brim cut off. It sat on his head like a basin. He seemed to me neither a likely nor an unlikely vehicle for the time-marking Christ.

"How does your hand feel?"

"Better. Parminter says you heal people."

He grinned evasively. "I make them look after themselves."

"But you look after Betty?"

"The others were getting at her. So I told her to keep with me."

"And now you're married."

He shrugged. "It makes her happy."

"How long are you going to stay here, Robert?"

He did not answer.

"You can have the cottage at Peacehaven."

"Thanks dad, but I like it here."

"What do you think of this ark business?"

"I don't take much notice of that. That's just Tom Parminter."

"You don't believe the world's coming to an end?"

"I don't think about it."

"He's gone off into the hills. God called him."

"It happens all the time."

"But this time it's different. He's going to announce the end of the world."

"He's done that three times already."

"Well," I said, "what happens? When it doesn't end?"

Robert shrugged. "Tom just says God's testing him. He goes on a fast. And freezes himself in the trough. Or else he gets his wives to burn his feet with matches."

"Good God."

"Tom's mad. But he's not doing any harm."

"You know who he thinks you are?" I had a vision of Parminter crucifying Robert, but put it out of my mind. It was too crazy, even for this place.

"I've got a fair idea," Robert said. He touched my hand. "The sun's doing it good. Don't let Felicity put a bandage on it."

"But Robert, you know the police are coming out. They've heard about the free love going on here."

"I keep out of that. Betty's enough for me."

"They could close this place."

"Then I'll go somewhere else."

"With Betty?"

"She's my wife."

"But not to Peacehaven?"

He shook his head.

"Why, Robert?"

He would not answer. I think he saw Peacehaven as part of the world, and the world had hurt him. The world in a way was hell; and this place, the Ark, stood outside it. Parminter's craziness was necessary to Robert. If he left here it would be for some place lost, some place where no one would ever find him. I knew I was seeing Robert for the last time. I loved him most of my sons. I took his hand and said goodbye to him.

Felicity's car drew up at the gate.

"Will you come and say hello to her, Robert?"

He shook his head.

"Goodbye, son."

176

"Goodbye, dad." He understood what was happening. I took some pleasure from finding him less simple than Parminter supposed, less simple than I had supposed.

I walked down the drive and got in Felicity's car.

"Is that Robert standing there?"

"Yes, that's him."

"He looks like the village idiot."

71 I told her she was stupid and malicious. I told her Robert was the best of my children.

The car boiled again on the Rimutaka hill. She lost her temper with it and sat on a boulder beside the road, waiting for it to cool off. I was feeling a little sick with the motion and I opened the glovebox to see if there might be something inside to settle my stomach. But there was only a rosary and a mess of Catholic pamphlets. I shut it angrily. In my nauseated state I saw Felicity as crazy like Parminter.

The rest did us good. We apologized to each other. And as we drove along I reflected that my claim to have freed myself from the base emotions was a false one—and a good thing too. I was happy to be no longer a prey to my appetites; but the emotions? It had seemed to me once, after I had come into the Light, that I was about to be translated into a state of superhumanity. I could not feel as men feel. But, thank God, it did not last. Yes, I thank God. One does not live in the Light, one remembers it. That is the way. And remembering, one is both man and Man. Not always a comfortable state. For man may fall into anger, or rise into it (the healthy anger of the rational mind); and Man knows anger not, but only love; and a most unpleasant condition results, a kind of pins-and-needles in the mind.

We stopped for a cup of tea.

"Won't Max be worried?"

"He'll be all right."

I guessed he would set about cooking our meal. I could not

get used to that. To take my mind off it I told Felicity about Parminter. She gave a snorting Catholic laugh. "Does Robert swallow that stuff?"

I explained about Robert: as much as she needed to know. I did not tell her his touch had set my hand mending. For that was so, I accepted it without question. Something had passed from the boy to me and I thanked him for it. Part of his goodness? Why should that quality not be transmittable by touch? And meeting no unbelief, why should it not heal body as well as mind? It met no unbelief in me. No question. For I loved Robert.

Felicity did not need to know about this.

A week later she cancelled my rail booking and announced that she would drive me to Auckland. By that time my palm had grown a new skin.

72 When everything was in order at Peacehaven I began to write. I had tried the platform, now I would try the pen.

Today I look at my books. They sit on my shelves in their brown covers, a trio without distinction of style or content: sunk without a trace. (In 1934 I posted copies to G. B. Shaw when he visited Auckland, and had a note from him from Panama. He had donated my books to the ship's library!) Only *The Growing Point of Truth* found a publisher. The others I had to publish myself. That was a costly business.

But writing kept me busy. Through writing and my family I slowly came back to health. I won back the territories I had held before Lyttelton jail. I worked in a disciplined way. On weekdays only Edie and I were home. Edie was happy. Of all our houses she loved Peachaven best. I would sit in my study, find a new thought, express it well I believed. "We shall yet learn the healing effect of love! The world was full of hate when the post-war influenza epidemic swept over it. Hate prepares the body and mind for disease. But love heals literally!" Then I would look up and see Edie in the garden, weeding or planting, and, I could tell, humming a merry tune. I would think, what more does one need than useful work and a loving contented wife? I would write again. And then go out for lunch and find her playing the piano. It was in these years we began our "paper chats". I learned to read her lips a little too. She was the only one I could follow in that way.

In the weekends the view from my window changed. The landscape was filled with people. I would look out and see Alfred climbing to the top of his tree, Agnes picking plums with Meg, Robert building the summer-house, mowing the lawn, Esther in the shrubbery, hand in hand with butcher boy Fred Meggett, and Emerson setting out on his motorbike, with a sack of greasy parts strapped on the pillion seat. They did not always start me on a happy train of thought. I remembered Felicity. She was teaching in Wellington, for Dan Peabody had entered Parliament. She would find no happiness with Dan. I saw it now. And thought of Oliver, scratching away at the law, and Edith married to Critch, and Willis somewhere at sea. Having children is a stern course in reality. I looked out my window again. It was like a Breughel landscape: activity everywhere. Edie was cutting withered heads from the roses. Robert hammered on the summer-house roof. Down by the creek the goat nibbled blackberry leaves. Emerson broadsided home (and crashed into the rose garden once. Edie was digging thorns out of him for weeks). Fred Meggett went off with lipstick on his cheek. And here came Meg with a ripe plum for me. I knew a lot about these active beings (even the goat). Knew my children's discontents and dreams—Agnes fretting to get to California, Alfred to publish a poem, Emerson to fly. But they were not unhappy. And could I reasonably ask for more than that? My discontents were company for theirs. I would not admit to being unhappy either.

There was in any case no time for that. For here came Merle and Graydon Butters with news of their latest steps on their current Way. And look who was on the drive (Edie put her head down at her roses): my good friend Bluey Considine, puffing blue smoke in front of him; a broken-down steamer coming into port.

73 I had received a note from the Post Office asking me to call for a parcel. When I went along the Postmaster took me into his office. He was unfriendly.

"That's it, Mr Plumb. I think it's a bit of a cheek expecting us to deliver that." The parcel sat in an ooze of pinkish brine in a tin tray on his desk. A length of twine still circled it and scraps of paper clung wetly to its sides. On one of these the Post Office staff had deciphered the surname Plumb.

"It is for you, I suppose?"

"Corned beef?" Bluey had wrapped it in several thicknesses of newspaper and tied brown paper round that. The letter he had put inside was now a glob of *papier mâché* held in place by twine. "It's from my friend Mr Considine. I think he's coming to dinner."

The Postmaster would not see the funny side of it. "There's regulations governing perishable goods."

I borrowed more paper, wrapped the corned beef up, and took it home. On the way Bluey began to overwhelm me. Who but Bluey would do a thing like this? I found myself hoping he was in Auckland to stay.

Edie was scandalized. She refused to cook the meat. I gave it to Robert who fed it to his dog. But I made her buy the same sort—brisket: silverside was short on fat, Bluey said—for our Sunday dinner.

And here now on the drive was Bluey himself. I ran out and we pumped each other's hands.

"Reverend," he boomed, and the Butterses, approaching, stopped dead at the sound. Edie got in their way and side-tracked them into her roses.

"Now what's this, what's this contraption?" He took my trumpet and pretended to use it as a spy-glass, pointing it at Merle and Graydon, waist deep in greenery.

"Give me that, Bluey, or I won't hear a word you say."

"A cornucopia, Reverend. A horn of plenty. But isn't that your good wife in the roses? I must go and give her a kiss."

"She's got friends with her, Bluey. Come with me and I'll show you over the farm."

So we walked about for half an hour, until Bluey began to complain of hunger.

"That was a nice piece of meat you sent, Bluey."

"You got it then? I was worried. A friend of mine bet me it wouldn't go through."

"You won your bet. But the Post Office wasn't pleased. So don't do it again."

"I won't, Reverend. A nice roll of brisket, that was. I think I can smell it cooking."

"Tell me what you're doing, Bluey."

"Why Reverend, I'm working a system now. It's very demanding and I'm thinking of giving it up. There's too much paper work."

"I haven't heard of this. Is it on the wharves?"

"No, no, Reverend, the gee-gees, the horses. I go over the whole field and pick out the ones that came first to fourth at their last start. Then I take the newspaper tips and tie those in with the totalizator betting. It's working against time that I don't like. And the running around. Bad for my feet. The returns are disappointing too. Sometimes I have to cover half the field. It takes all the fun out of it. I'm thinking of selling out."

"Selling the system?"

"You can always find a buyer, Reverend. But my word, that corned beef smells good. Is she cooking it with carrots?"

He had no interest in union activities, or politics, or reading. His concerns were his next meal and his soul's destination. Yet because he was kind I loved him. And because he was strapped beyond hope of escape into the cruellest of his religion's torture machines I gave him my time and my arguments, and endured my wife's disapproval.

As we approached the house again she came from amongst her roses and gave Bluey a hand in a gardening glove. "Mr Considine, how nice to see you."

181

"Now mum, call me Bluey." He had meant to kiss her. But Edie, as lady, was unkissable. Bluey was a man of resources though. He robbed her of her secateurs and cut a fine late bud from the nearest rose bush. "Here, mum. Beauty to beauty calls." It was not pleasure reddened Edie's cheeks. In haste I brought Merle and Graydon forward, and Graydon's mother (wearing her muse-visited look that day, and so to be introduced as Ella Satterthwaite). Merle and Graydon had the finest of social noses. It took them only a minute to sniff Bluey out; and sniff out too the discord he unwittingly sowed between Edie and me.

We sat about a cloth Meg had spread on the lawn and drank tea and ate scones spread with gooseberry jam. The smell of corned beef boiling in onion-flavoured water drifted out from the kitchen and stimulated Bluey's appetite. He sent Meg up to the house for another plate of scones.

Ella Satterthwaite, an ethereal lady, clad in something gauzy, pre-Raphaelite, hid her pleasure in this by raising her eyes. Her hearty appetite compromised her in her role as finer spirit, and she disguised it by looking elsewhere whenever she reached for food. Many a time I had seen her fingers come down in sugar or jam. Looking skywards, securing a scone, she said, "You knew Mr Plumb in Thorpe, Mr Considine?"

"That's it, mum. When he was giving those bible-bashers what for."

"I understand John Findlater was one of your circle?"

"He was. Drove us barmy, John did, with his poetry. All about singing streams and talking hills. I never knew there was so much gab in nature."

"Mrs Butters—Miss Satterthwaite—is a leading poetess," Edie said.

"Is that so? You've got the look of it mum, if you don't mind me saying."

"You were privileged knowing John Findlater," Ella said. She bit a scone with delicate greed. "He is the best of our poets. He has the finest perceptions. One can forget the world in reading him and hear the voice that speaks from a leaf or stone."

This was very much in her poetic style. There is a magic in

naming. Ella had the beginnings of an understanding of it. John Findlater had it too. But only the beginnings. Their gaze was not clear enough, their understanding fell short in strength and sternness. Gentility and sentimentality spoiled them as poets. Leaf, stone. They could never leave it at that. It was too crude, it made them avert their eyes. So they added an adjective (and one led to two), a softening "thought", a humanizing fancy. They posed their troublesome children in pretty clothes.

Ella said, "John's most recent book is dedicated to Mr Plumb. It compares him with the kauri, the forest giant, standing above the common trees and speaking with winds and storms."

I blushed. And Bluey grinned. "Have another scone, mum. They'll fatten you up. Too much poetry is a thin diet."

"Thank you, Mr Considine. Delicious. Yes . . . 'trunk as hard as iron and stern as love' I find the image a little unpolished myself."

I was pleased to be twitched in their direction by Graydon and Merle—then alarmed. A kind of greed was on them to share their grief. They had not slept, they said; for they lived in the dreadful knowledge of having committed a crime against their son. They had damaged Royce, stunted the growth of his responses; they had allowed him to count, to read, to have black paint in his paintbox. All this before seven, before he had shed his milk teeth. The consequences were dreadful. A child's first seven years were years of natural response to his surroundings. The intellect must not intrude into that sacred time. Or notions of right and wrong. Why, Steiner said .

I understood. They had become Anthroposophists. Soon they would launch their campaign to convert me.

"Surely," I said, "Steiner has nothing against black paint?"

"Oh yes, it's not in nature," Merle cried.

Not more than thirty feet away a blackbird (*Merle!*) was scattering pine needles. I did not think it would help to point it out.

"You probably used black paint when you were a girl. And look, it hasn't affected you. You've come to Steiner."

"But my understanding is so misty. Our understanding. Isn't it, Graydon?"

"Yes. We're damaged beings. The trouble we have in perceiving the spiritual world."

"The dreadful trouble. So often we've wished to be children again."

"To begin again."

"Yes."

"Little children. Before the change of teeth."

"Before the time of moral-feeling judgement."

"And now poor Royce, we've done the same to him."

They suffered. I was sorry for them. "What is this spiritual world you talk about?"

"Reality. The substance behind the shadow."

"We must come back from our exile."

"To reality."

"A lifetime's work," I said.

"But we shall get there."

"Yes."

"Yes."

Nudging each other along, they began to be happy. If I had told them that inside a year they would be into Radiant Living, or Christian Science, or psycho-analysis, or automatic writing, or tapping on the lid of Joanna Southcott's box (well, no, not that), they would have recoiled from me as from the serpent in their Eden. It was true all the same. How happy they would have been in California.

I did what I could for them: advancing the proposition of child as tough guy, who would be himself in spite of his parents' intentions. It was as near as I could get to saying Royce was a dull boy. (His only liveliness was in avoiding the demands made on him by Merle and Graydon's shifting beliefs.)

At half past twelve the Butterses went home and I sent Robert to muster the family for lunch. Bluey lumbered round the table and put a chocolate fish on the children's side plates, even Agnes's. They were too old to be amused by him. I had to say, "Thank Mr Considine, please."

"Thank you Mr Considine."

"Gobble 'em up," Bluey said.

Robert's excepted, their faces were hard and still. An ugly expression. I was sorry for them, and angry with them too. I set myself the task of making sure my family caused Bluey no pain. I am still at it. But at that Sunday meal I did not begin. It turned into a party, a celebration, Bluey became simply part of the background. For as I began to carve the roll of brisket we heard a sound on the back verandah. The clump of a heavy step, then a wooden tap: clump tap, repeated. (Even I heard: a psychic hearing.) It advanced into the kitchen.

"Whatever's that?" Edie was pale.

Something heavy banged on the floor. She rose, pushing back her chair. "George?" I put down the carving implements. But we waited, we needed a sign. In a moment it came: a mouth organ playing a sailor's hornpipe. (He played it again later into my trumpet so I could share the moment fully.)

"Willis, oh Willis," Edie cried. She ran. And we ran after her, jamming in the doorway. Bluey was left at the table, open-mouthed, looking at the corned beef, which would not be served for another half-hour now.

74 It happened in Copenhagen. A hawser snapped and the mashed lower part of Willis's limb went skidding on the deck. Into his wooden leg he carves the names of women he has known. Lately, I believe, he has run out of space, even though it's his fourth replacement he's walking on. But when he came home in 1923 there were only half a dozen names.

"Lily. Now Lily really was a stunner. She worked in a bar in Havana. Don't look so shocked, mum. You would have liked her. One of nature's ladies. And very kind. Very kind to me. I should have married Lily."

All his stories ended in that way. "Brigid. Ah yes, I should have married Brigid." And Rosy and Dolores and Ingrid and Sue. The sea was not in his blood so much as adventure; and he had found his best adventures in women. He did not need to get on a ship again. The lovely creatures were everywhere. At first I took his talk of marriage for a piece of hypocrisy; but saw after a while that he expressed loyalty in this way. He did not exploit his women. They were true companions, loving and loved. And if he had to leave them in the end, well, there were plenty of songs to prove sadness was the lot of man. He sang them in the sunshine, in a tear-filled voice.

"What will you do now, Willis?"

"You're not going back to sea?" Edie said quickly.

"That little cottage down by the road? Is anyone living in that?"

"No. But it's tumbling down."

"I've seen worse. Tell you what—you buy the paint and timber and I'll do it up."

So Willis became our first tenant in the cottage. He relined the walls, put new iron on the roof, took out weather-boards feather-light with dry rot and replaced them with new. He painted the place red and white, put lino on the floor, sewed curtains, planted a garden. And soon I saw other men's wives entering or leaving the place at unrespectable hours.

"They're just friends, dad. They come to chat. They like my wooden leg."

"I'm not a fool, Willis."

"Dad, do you think I'd do anything wrong?"

"I don't know what that word means to you but I know what it means to other people."

He laughed. He looked at me in a way both mischievous and honest. "I make my girlfriends happy, dad. That's all. I help them enjoy themselves. You can't call that wrong."

"The road to hell . . ." I said.

"You don't believe in that place."

"All right, the road to trouble. To the law courts."

And trouble came soon enough. The mayor of our town, relaxing one afternoon in a Queen Street cinema, looked down from his seat in the circle and saw his wife cuddling in the stalls with a wooden-legged sailor. They were eating ice-cream and resting their foreheads together.

At midnight I found at my door that sad and comic figure, the wronged husband. He bounced with rage, he trembled with indignation; and, alas, tears of pain overflowed his eyes and ran down his cheeks. He dashed them away with a show of manly disgust. It took me a little time to understand what he was saying. Then I sent Edie in from the doorstep, ordered my craning daughters back to bed.

"Follow me." We marched down the drive and through Willis's garden. A light was burning through his bright red curtains. I was glad we would not get him out of bed. A man in pyjamas is at a disadvantage. I had no hope of his innocence, but wanted him to keep what dignity he could. I marched in without knocking. And of course the woman was with him—a pretty buxom thing with tumbling hair. She was bare-footed and, I'm sorry to say, in her petticoat. They were cosily drinking large mugs of Ovaltine. I had not time to appreciate the scene. The husband, Richards, darted past me, shouting "Slut!" I think, and aimed a slap at his wife. Willis came round the table, surprisingly quick for a peg-leg, and knocked him down. The rest is a mime. (I had not brought my trumpet.) I see the woman, Mirth, help her husband up and sit him at the table. I see Willis bring water in a basin. Together they bathe Richards' face. He cries, and pleads perhaps; and the woman weeps, but holds Willis tightly by the hand. Willis is kind and gentle. He is, I understand, something of a monster—a being of extreme simplicity, infinitely kind, moved to tears by his pain and the pain of others, but entirely without a moral sense. I wonder if this forty-year-old woman, Mirth, whose suitcase I now see through the open door, spilling undies and blouses on the bed, this apple-cheeked *bourgeoise*, understands the nature of the man she is leaving husband, car and bungalow for. I think not. Such simple people are never understood. But I see too she has caught a sight of happiness and is after it with both hands.

"Dad, you'd better get home. You'll catch a cold."

"I'm not happy about this, Willis."

"In the morning, dad. I'll see you in the morning."

We met in my study. He told me Mirth was coming to live with him. I gave him notice. I would not have a *liaison* of that sort close to the girls. It was not as if it were a true union, I said, not in the eyes of God. And that was what mattered. A man and a woman must be drawn together by more than the lusts of the flesh. Love in a higher sense, duty, the wish for children, these were the moral and eugenic and divine bases on which a "marriage" rests. Anything less was a piece of self-indulgence. I would not have it under my nose. I would not have Edie insulted and my girls led astray.

Willis laughed. "O.K. dad, O.K. I'll move out. As a matter of fact I was going to talk to you. I've got my eye on a piece of land up the valley. It's just right for grapefruit and lemons. Now if you could see your way to letting me have a couple of hundred pounds . . ."

75 I helped him buy the place. I could not be angry with him for long. He settled in with Mirth and lives there still. I'm told he and his wife and children and his other lady friends practise naturalism, which means apparently running round in the summer with no clothes on. Emerson told Esther, who repeated it to me, not without relish, that on a recent visit to Willis's orchard he had come upon the naked peg-leg chasing an equally naked Mirth among the grapefruit trees. "He caught her too."

He has, as he told me once, a talent for making his women happy. Mirth made a good choice. Nymph at sixty. Few woman can have known that.

76 Agnes and Emerson left Peacehaven in 1925. They took the same ship for California. Emerson was off to see the world. He would go on to England and the Continent. "When I come home," he joked, "I'll be flying my own aeroplane." Agnes though meant to stay with her sisters in San Francisco.

I did not believe I would see Agnes again. That land, that rich, noisy, blue and golden land, for me, for Edie, a dry and bitter place, was full of a sweetness my daughters learned the taste of. It drew them fatally and made of them people whose language I do not speak. Agnes too. I waved. I felt the streamers snap, and saw the smartly dressed pretty girl waving madly from her high rail as the ship turned heavily into the stream. No, she would not come back. No more than Rebecca. Hers was almost as surely the "undiscovered country from whose bourn . . "

We went home sadly to our house by the creek. Esther, Alfred, Robert, Meg. We had four children left.

More than I had before I passed my time with them. I wrote my books, I lectured in Trades' Halls and Mechanics' Institutes and in the Unitarian Hall. But I came home to Edie and my children with a sense of having come out of a monochrome world into a coloured. I gardened with Robert, or walked in the orchard with Meg. I listened to Alfred's poems. His clear thin voice came down my trumpet like water. Esther, a loud, happy girl, kissed me on top of my head and wiped the lipstick off with her handkerchief. Even in her vulgarity I took pleasure. I had the sense of living in my own and my family's history, but not in the world's. In that decade the feeling was widespread. The war had been more than we could grasp. Difficult now to apprehend Mankind. It took the depression to bring us back to that.

One day behind the summer-house I came on Fred Meggett kissing Esther in what I took to be an improper way.

"Young man," I said, "you get off my property. And

189

Esther, I'll see you in my study. At once, if you please."

She stood there five minutes later, grinning. "I'm going to marry him, dad," she yelled. "So you'd better cool off."

"What," I said, "marry a butcher?"

"Hey, where's your socialism? One man's as good as another, isn't he?"

"It's not his trade I object to—"

"Besides, Fred's not a butcher any more. He's a land agent now."

"I won't have him kissing you in that way. Not where Margaret might see."

"Meg knows what's what, dad. Don't you worry about that. Besides, I've got to give poor old Fred something. I've had him on the string for four years now. He'll go off the boil if I don't keep him stoked up a bit."

"I'm disappointed in you, Esther."

"I know. But I like you. I think you're a good old stick. Now dad, I want you to do something for me. You can still marry people can't you?"

"I can. But—"

"Here on the lawn. I don't want any churches."

"No Esther, I won't do it. I can't approve—"

"Come on, dad. For me. Now say you will." She stroked the top of my head. "I'd love to be married by you. By my own father. And Fred's not too bad. He's really quite human, you know."

So in the Spring, beside the blossoming plum tree, I married Esther to Fred Meggett. Everybody came. Oliver brought Beatrice up from Wellington. Felicity came with Dan Peabody. (Oliver was stuffy about that.) Willis and Mirth were there. The Butterses walked over the bridge, bringing Graydon's mother, who turned herself into Ella Satterthwaite the moment she understood that the man exclaiming over the plum blossoms was John Findlater himself. Edie could not prevent me from asking Bluey. I promised to set Andrew Collie to keep him out of mischief. For Andrew was there too, happy as a spaniel off its leash, and full of the songs of Burns for this happy day. John Willis, whom I had not quite forgiven for his bungling defence of me, and whom I associated with Rebecca's death, turned up in time to give the bride away. I found myself glad to see him. He was just on his feet again after yellow jaundice and had only decided to come at the last moment. These and a number of bright young girls, chattering like birds, were the guests from Esther's side. (There was too, I almost forgot, our new tenant in the cottage—a schoolteacher, Wendy Philson.)

Fred's people I did not see much of. They seemed to talk mainly about race horses.

I married Esther and Fred—the Unitarian service. Then we feasted. I kept away from that. I have never liked to see people gobbling food. I sat down on the lawn and talked with John Willis. And gradually my friends came about me. I felt like Socrates. There was though an elegiac note in our talk, not just for John Jepson, dead of a stroke, but for times that were gone. Our beliefs were not dead, far from it, but we found they no longer led us into actions. Still, we were happy. The bowl of the lawn was full to its brim with sunlight. Over by the plum tree Willis was playing merrily on his mouth organ. Pretty girls were everywhere, in white and blue and lavender frocks. We could smell their perfume and hear their happy talk. (My trumpet had a sharpened sense that day. I heard with a fine-ness that had not been mine for years.) Edie strolled about with Meg at her side. They drew my eye like the focal point in a painting. I saw their mother-and-daughter likeness—a liquid movement, a happy eye; and saw too their spiritual beauty. Self had its proper place in them. They were loving and charitable beings (always excepting their dislike of Bluey).

I saw them a second time, and a third. Then the currents of my life flowed together. I passed into the room of my own soul. I faced the Light, and knew the way to go, and entered it. "Behold I show you a mystery." Which was made plain. And though I had not strength to endure it long it did not matter. As I have said, one cannot live in that place. Memory is enough for one's daily living. I had my glimpse, my time. It was the vision splendid. A great light, a bliss, a splendour, a white radiance, streamed through me. The whole of my life had been a preparation for this moment. I rose from the tomb of my body and its inheritance and, as

Carpenter says, identified with the immortal Self of the world. "I, the imperfect, adore my own Perfect." These are better expressions of it than I can find. For myself I say, I knew with all my being, in every fibre, that love is Life. I had known it already. But this was more than intellectual knowing. All doctrines, all other beliefs, were blown away like dead leaves in a storm. "When I burn with pure love, what can Calvin or Swedenborg say?" I had seen God.

"Are you all right, George?"

"Fine. Never better."

John put his hand on my shoulder. (The others had wandered off.) "It's good to see you looking so well. After Christchurch."

"That was a bad time. It seems far away."

"George, I've sometimes thought, you must hold me partly responsible for . . . certain things."

"No."

"Rebecca . . . I should have been watching."

I comforted him. The jaundice weakens a man and makes him emotional. "Enough now, John. We've come to terms with that time."

"Yes, but—"

"No buts, John. Do you know, I think I could prescribe for you. Do you know what I'd prescribe?"

"No."

"A good woman. A wife. You need looking after."

He blushed. "They're hard to find, George."

"Nonsense. Look at my lawn. Full of them. Shall I find you one?"

"No, no." He looked alarmed.

Andrew came back; and John Findlater (Ella not far behind). Felicity sat down and put her hand on mine. Dan lay next to her, resting his head on a fold of her dress. At this time their love was at its strongest. We spoke of the old days again: of the Thorpe strike, and my heresy, and mad wild Morrison Macauley, and street-corner spouting, and draughty halls. We spoke of John Jepson and Edward Cryer. Bluey came up with a plate full of food. "Ah Reverend, that John Jepson. Many's the fine meal I've eaten in his house. There's a lot to be said for ill-gotten gains."

"Ill-gotten, Bluey? You can't use that word of John."

"A capitalist though," Andrew cried. "A man can earn so much with his own two hands. After that it's ill-gotten. John had more than his share. Someone went short, that's plain to see."

"Well Andrew, we won't go into that. Let's remember old friends kindly. Now give us a poem for my daughter's wedding day. Give us 'John Anderson'. I haven't heard that in years."

He obliged—that beautiful poem. And then gave us "The Rigs o' Barley". Ella, I could see, found them too rustic; and the latter improper. She asked John Findlater to recite us something of his. But John had too much sense. He knew real poetry when he heard it. Pressed though, he extemporized a couplet:

George Plumb, your name speaks true:
It tells of deeps and of the straight line too.

It pleased me, for it was kindly meant. I said, "Well, well, I hope it's true. It needs a bit of polishing."

Off to one side I saw Alfred smiling. I had not known he was close. I grinned at him. The boy was wild about T. S. Eliot, and if he could make anything of that stuff had earned his right to look down his nose a little at John Findlater. Seeing him there, and seeing into his mind, I had a sense of time, of generations. Beyond him, private, but not I thought unhappy, was the young woman, Wendy Philson: square of body and, I saw, with eyes that were beautiful. Now there was a girl for John Willis. Not too young, not frivolous. In fact, a woman, not a girl.

John said, "Your father tells me you write poetry, Alfred."

"Yes," said the boy, going red.

"I'd like to hear some."

"So would I," John Findlater said.

"No, I'm sorry. I don't read in public. Besides . . ."

"Besides?"

"I don't think you'd understand it."

"Ah, I see, it's in the modern manner."

John Willis persisted. "I'd like to read it though. Will you give me some?"

"All right," Alfred said ungraciously. "But it's a waste of time. You won't understand it."

His arrogance pleased me. Everything pleased me on that afternoon.

77 Alfred was nineteen, and full of scorn at the jollity and back-slapping of Esther's wedding. Walking about among Fred's racing acquaintances, listening to Meggett senior's ribald talk, and observing Fred's mother weeping like a rainstorm, he gave to his mouth a Byronic twist. Esther's chattering friends— and there were some pretty girls amongst them—might as well have been a tribe of monkeys. He silenced them with a down-slanting look. Esther herself had always been close to him, and he had an affection for her that he tried to make appear tolerant. It was in fact as strong as any of the multifarious loves that kept our domestic air humming with the noise of a giant top. He was angry with her for marrying Fred, a "peasant".

The couple came down from the house to set off on their honeymoon. People threw rice and confetti (Robert frowned to see it on his lawn) and two young men tied an old boot to the car. A girl wrote *Just married* with lipstick on the window. Earlier I would have turned my shoulder on this. (Oliver turned his shoulder.) But I took Edie's arm and we moved through the crush to kiss Esther goodbye. She was looking coarse and happy. "Goodbye, Esther," I said. "I wish you joy, my dear."

"Don't worry, I'll have plenty of that."

"I'll look after her, George," Fred Meggett said. I had not invited him to call me George.

They got in the car. "Dad," Fred called, and his father came to the window. Fred handed him a scrap of paper. "Will you get that on for me?" Meggett senior looked at the paper. "Pot Luck? It hasn't got a bolter's, son."

"You just get it on."

"Goodbye, goodbye," everyone called.

"Goodbye mum, goodbye dad. Alf, come and kiss me," Esther cried.

Alfred kissed her cheek through the open window. Rice rattled on the car like hail; and Fred drove his unblushing bride away.

78 Edie would have liked to see the guests go home after that. But they stayed for another two hours, drinking beer Fred's father brought out from his car. "Can't let me boy get married without having a snort or two, George," he explained. Soon the young ones were dancing to the sound of Willis's mouth organ.

I looked for Alfred. A sense of superiority can be a painful thing. Meg told me he had gone into the orchard. I found John Findlater strolling there with Ella Satterthwaite. John recited his verses; and listened to Ella's with only the faintest appearance of bending down. I left them to it. Alfred, they told me, was down by the creek with John Willis and Miss Philson; holding forth on a poem of Eliot's— "The most unmitigated tosh," John said. They had had to come away to avoid saying hurtful things.

The three by the creek were cooling their feet in the water. I came up on them and sat down to one side. John looked at me gravely. He gave a small nod I took to mean he found my son a remarkable boy. I angled my trumpet at Alfred long enough to hear him say, "We are the hollow men, we are the stuffed men, leaning together, headpiece filled with straw," and then put it down. Clever young people cannot help being taken in by the current nonsense, even when it has a death-smell about it. It would not help to condemn this stuff to him. I did not doubt, in my glowing state, that he would come through on his own. I was pleased to see him treating Wendy Philson as an equal, and pleased to see Wendy attending to him with an interest more than literary. Many a boy has been helped on to his path and given a push along it by a sensible older woman. Wendy was sensible, no doubt about that: sensible clothes, sensible manner, sensible opinions. But older? Not by more than a year or two. She wore graveness like a garment, covering her accidental youth. I was pleased she thought Alfred worth listening to. And I hoped if she meant to befriend one of these men it would be Alfred. John, I saw now, was too old for her. And alongside her would become conscious of his lightness of weight. While Alfred might take weight. I thought too that friendship with Wendy Philson was something *I* might try for.

"I wouldn't look on Eliot as a god," she said, "or even as a prophet. If he's anything he's a doctor. And not a healing one either. A diagnostician."

"He's a poet," Alfred said sensibly; and that was a point to him.

Wendy smiled. "Yes," she said, "and it seems to me a damaged one."

"How?"

"Damaged by the times he lives in. Oh I know, all poets and all people are that, although you can put it a different way. Shaped, I mean. But it seems to me these new poets have nothing to celebrate. True poetry is celebration."

"What is there left to celebrate? After the war?"

"Why, God. He still exists, doesn't He? Poetry is an attempt to find God."

"No. Not for me."

"What is it then?"

"An attempt to understand man."

"Isn't that more or less the same thing?"

John Willis smiled at me. He felt left out. I plucked him by the sleeve. I wanted to stay and listen, but wanted more to leave Alfred and Wendy to themselves. John dried his feet with his handkerchief and when he had his shoes on we took ourselves off. We strolled down through the orchard. Angling my trumpet cunningly, I heard Ella say:

> The sparkling thrush, the sparkling thrush,
> Upon the orchard bough,
> He sings of past and future,
> But never of the now.

"I would have thought the opposite," I said.

"I like it better though," John said, "than headpieces stuffed with straw."

79 John was ill again that night. He should not have travelled. We put him in Esther's bedroom; and kept him with us through the Spring.

Edie enjoyed looking after him. For her he meant the old times: her mother, Florence, the house in Linwood. He made her face Rebecca's death again. It strengthened her and brought her peace. She never lost her belief in a personal survival for the soul.

It was a happy season. Alfred sat his university exams and said they were laughable (meaning easy). In his holidays he worked on farms about the district, making hay, cutting scrub. I did not worry about him. I no longer had the sense of secret places in his mind. He was open, glowing with happiness and expectations of fame. He did not read me his poetry, knowing I did not care for its new direction; but read it to Wendy Philson. Good. She had a better understanding than I of modern verse, would indicate to him more acceptably, though no less plainly I hoped, that it was muddy stuff, diseased—"rats' feet over broken glass"—and that Alfred must raise his eyes and study Man.

He and Wendy spent much of their time together. I saw no more than a friendly affection between them. That was exactly what I had wished for. I thought of Alfred as setting off on a long journey on which he would make himself. And Wendy I saw as a rock, herself already. He might come back to her when he was a man, but now it was enough that they should put their heads together and talk about poetry; and laugh more freely than they laughed with other people. John, I thought, was jealous of that. Wendy was formal with him.

My own explorations continued. My experience of the Light lay in me like a seed. It was the business of the rest of my life to make it grow. I do not mean I abandoned my work for social justice. But my larger work was to reach understanding of my revelation. I was swollen a little with pride, but sufficiently aware of it not to be damaged. And as I read through that Spring it burned away and dropped from me as a kind of ash. Spiritual excitement burned it away. I read everything I could get my hands on about the great cases of illumination from God. I read the Gospels in a new light. And studied the lives and teachings of Mohammed, and Paul, and Gautama the Buddha, and Plotinus and Jacob Behmen. I looked into Dante again, Pascal, Blake, Spinoza, Edward Carpenter, my old friend Ralph Waldo Emerson. I had not read so intensely before, and have not again. And I came to believe I was candidate for a second illumination, a more glorious one. I had only stood in the margins. It was enough, more than enough, for the rest of my days. But I saw I might be one of the few called to the Heart of things. Earthly, domestic, mortal cares became a black and troublesome weight, but could not hold me back. Man's dual nature was shown me clearly; soon I would be free of the lower part. I kept before me Edward Carpenter's lines: *That day—the day of deliverance—shall come to you in what place you know not; it shall come but you know not the time.*

The time would be soon.

One Saturday morning I set off to walk into town. I kept up my habit of walking and often covered five or six miles at a time. Edie and Meg were visiting Esther, Alfred was working on a neighbour's farm, and Robert helping Willis in his orchard. John had said he would keep me company but cried off at the last moment to write letters. He was in his last week with us. I joked with him, saying perhaps he meant to slip down to Wendy's. He blushed again. He was a man for black-blushing and for pallors.

I walked along the road at a good brisk pace. The creek ran on my left, a chain of deep slow pools of a muddy green linked by yellow-white rapids. On my right a clay bank rose from the side of the road, which swam a little in the bright Spring sun. I thought of Lyttelton jail and the darkness that had fallen on me there; and of my present quest. I had come to think of the goal as "cosmic consciousness"—R. M. Bucke's term—a consciousness of the life and order of the universe, an intellectual enlightenment, a state of moral exaltation and quickening of the moral sense, and a knowledge of immortality. All this, Bucke said, comes to one in an instant, as a fire within the self, and it may never come again. But one remembers; and possesses a new sense or faculty. It has had many names. Jesus called it the Kingdom of Heaven; Paul called it Christ or the Spirit of God. For Buddhists it is Nirvana; while Mohammed called it Gabriel. Dante: Beatrice. Whitman: My Soul. I thought if it came fully to me I would call it Love. I remembered too, as I walked along, that Bucke who had had the faculty himself had never lost it, even in periods of black depression. I found that a comforting thought, both in its upward and downward looking directions. I did not think I would care to be entirely without troubles.

My thoughts were broken by the distant cry of "Reverend", coming, it seemed, from the most unilluminated times of my past. When I had shaken myself back into the world I saw, and was glad to see, Bluey hoisting himself to his feet from his resting place in the shade of a tree. I shook hands with him and indicated my ears.

"It's lucky I heard you at all, Bluey. I haven't got my trumpet."

He shouted something about finding himself barred from the Avondale race-course. (I never discovered why.) So he had got on the bus and come to see me. He also said something about lunch.

We walked back together. Bluey talked but I heard only a word or two. It was, I think, all about horses and hellfire. I told him there was no such thing as hellfire.

When we arrived at the house I sat him down in a cane chair on the veranda and went to fetch John. I felt I would like help with Bluey that day. But John was nowhere in the house. I took Bluey a plate of biscuits and told him I would not be long.

"No hurry, Reverend," he said, munching.

I went out into the orchard to look for John. I did not hurry. Bluey was happy and the morning beautiful. I crossed the brick bridge and turned into the apple trees, where the green fruit was taking a blush of pink. Far away in the Butters's garden Ella in something gauzy and blue was walking in the roses. The white of

Wendy's cottage shone through the trees. I hoped I would not find Wendy in John's company. I was jealous for Alfred's sake. I told myself that was unworthy. Wendy was free to do as she chose. I reminded myself she seemed not to care for John. I went through the pear trees and the peach and climbed a little hill overlooking the corner where our quince tree grew. There I stood. To the couple in the grass I must have risen like some frightful beast from their most hideous dreams.

I saw what it was inevitable I see. It stunned me. I had a moment of utter blackness. I almost fell. When I came to my senses I found I had gripped the branch of a tree to hold myself on my feet. And my mind became full of a clamorous boiling rush, full of Old Testament bloodiness. I cried that they were unclean, that they were filth. And I called down death upon them, I called down brimstone, fire; I smote them so they died. It is true. I saw life go out of their eyes. I saw a death come on them. Their flushed men-faces grew white and bestial. They croaked like toads. And I fled from them, I fled back through the orchard, but it was an orchard no longer, I ran through the slimepits of Siddim, where the kings of Sodom and Gomorrah fled and fell. I ran on the plain and did not turn my eyes, for behind me the smoke of the evil cities went up as the smoke of a furnace.

So my early training kept a kind of doubtful sanity in me. It held me on a course. I remember thinking Edie would become a pillar of salt.

When I came to the house I ran to my study. But there was no refuge there. My books had turned to ashes. And in a moment I was scrabbling in my drawer, bringing out the little tin box in which I kept a store of golden sovereigns. I did not count them. I took a handful and ran out of the house.

Alfred and John were coming over the bridge. I met them, raised my palm to ward them off.

"Don't come into my house. You are dead. You are dead to me, Alfred. Never come here, again." And I flung the sovereigns on the bricks in front of him. "Your name isn't Plumb. There's money to change your name." And I fled again, for I saw the danger of his face becoming human.

I shut myself in our bedroom. I lay trembling on the bed in which Alfred had been conceived and borne. It was my right to kill him, kill the beast, as God had killed those creatures of filth long ago.

So in my mind I killed him; and killed him again.

Bluey found me there when he came searching. He covered me with a blanket. Somehow or other he made a cup of tea. And he sat with me until Edie came home.

80 It is not surprising I behaved as I did. I had believed my spiritual strength, my certainty of my self, gave me the power to gaze steadily on human depravity. Gaze; and forgive. It was not so. More than I knew, I was a man of my times. I might question religious doctrine, or struggle to alter a political system, even smile on a daughter's irregular union; but my location was fixed in the matter of sex between men. I had never made a study of it, had prevented it from even crossing my mind. It was there all the same, a black invisible planet in a sky of stars. Many years later I opened my bible at Genesis, chapter 19, and read of the sins of Sodom and Gomorrah, and of those cities' destruction. The margins are blank. Mitchell had said there was not an empty square inch. He had not looked there. But how had I understood what was spoken of, what that "knowing" was the men of Sodom planned? Someone must have whispered it to me. (The commentary I used kept a decent silence.) Did something in myself whisper it? In any case, I knew. For the language of that chapter boiled from my mouth when I discovered Alfred and John Willis under the quince tree.

I told Edie I had sent Alfred away. I had found him sinning. And when she pressed me, said his sin was the sin of Sodom. Her calmness was extraordinary. I guessed she had known, below full consciousness certainly; but known the truth of his nature, and forgiven him. Now it was out in the open she was calm. Her love was deeper than mine. It gave her the means to forgive him fully.

I said, "You're not to see him, Edie. I forbid it."

"You don't have that power, George."

"You're my wife, and I forbid it."

"George, you must listen to me. We have the rest of our lives to spend together. And so we must never talk of this again."

And we never did. But Alfred lay between us for the rest of our days. I saw her on Saturday afternoons put on her hat and gloves and walk off to visit him. She smiled at me like a stranger. And I thought, Edie has become a pillar of salt. There was no understanding of what she was doing—not for me—and the biblical words gave me a painful comfort. They pointed to mysteries; and where mysteries were there was hope of miracle. But I could not come to her. We reached out our hands but only our fingers touched.

She met him, I think, at Esther's place. (I wonder how Fred liked that.) Esther never spoke of Alfred to me. Nor did Robert or Meg. Willis was the only one who dared. I had made up my mind to call him Theo, but he refused to answer to the name.

"You chose Willis dad and you're stuck with it. Now tell me what this nonsense is all about."

I told him to mind his business; and that I would call him what I pleased.

"Did you catch them in the act?"

"Willis," I cried, "be quiet."

"Look dad, I've been on the ships. I've seen it all. You can talk about it with me."

I put down my trumpet. But he simply bent close and raised his voice. "What were they doing? Kissing? Holding hands?"

"Will you get out of my study."

"A little bit of ——, eh?" (Even today I'm ignorant of whether the word is slang or clinical.) "It happens quite a lot, dad. In the best of circles." (And today I see he meant this as a joke.)

"Will you go away?"

"And you turned him out for it? You old parsons really take the cake."

"I won't have you talk to me like that."

"O.K., dad, O.K. I guess it's time he got out in the world. He'll manage without your blessing."

"I won't have him mentioned, Willis. *Theo*. Not in my house."

"Banished to outer darkness, eh? Well, if that's how you want it. But ———." (The word again.) He laughed. "Poor old dad. You've got a lot to learn."

A few months later he told me John Willis had come to Auckland. He and Alfred were sharing a flat. And Alfred, though he had left my sovereigns lying, had changed his name.

I said I was not interested.

For more than twenty years no one spoke his name to me again.

81 Meg must have wished to many times. For a girl of her affectionate nature and sentimental habit of mind it must have been agony to have a brother banished. She thought love could heal all wounds and bridge all gulfs. The affair was a lesson in reality for her. She was wounded by it in her courage and faith. Hardened by it, I think, and checked in her growth. But through the joyless Christmas that came on us soon she gave Edie and me the loving company we could not give each other.

She left school at the end of that year and enrolled at the Teachers' College. I had wished her to go to university. She said she was not clever enough. That was true. Her mind was receptive of "thoughts" not ideas. Her reading had already disappointed me. She was moved to tears by the novels of Mary Webb. She kept by her bed a shelf of favourite books: *Precious Bane*, *The Constant Nymph*, *The Forest Lovers*, *The Small Dark Man*. They were there for many years—are still there, I think.

Sentimentality was her vice, as gentility was Edie's. She was in touch with the springs of the religious life, in a sense one of the elect. Goodness was natural to her. Love was natural. But between response and understanding her feelings were spoiled; between conception and expression they passed through a falsifying element. It took her many years, our loss of Alfred, marriage, motherhood, to come to terms with the real. By that time she was a diminished being.

But Christmas, 1926. She gave us love. We were not critical. I took to eating alone again. Meg brought my evening meal to me in the study. Sometimes she stayed to talk. I tried to explain to her my belief in man's spiritual destiny. She could not grasp the logic of it, but found the idea beautiful. I talked in large optimistic terms—because I had lost my path. I was in darkness again and felt I might never come out of it, and so I made loud noises to persuade back my memories. For unlike Bucke I had not retained them in my deep depression.

Meg sat with me, listened; now and then made a response— that she thought something I said was true or beautiful. And when she really thought so tears came into her eyes. As I came to think of my own cares less I saw I had done a great wrong to her in letting her get that way. I did not see how I could go about undoing it.

82 Edie came to me in my study. "Will you have tea with us tonight, George? Meg's young man is coming."

"I didn't know she had a young man. Is it serious?"

"Everything Meg does is serious. He's a plumber's apprentice."

"A plumber's apprentice? What's his name?"

"Fergus Sole."

"Can't she do better than a plumber's apprentice? There must be young men at the Training College."

"She likes his dirty hands, George. She thinks they're honest." She tried to joke, but I saw she was troubled.

"Have you met him, Edie?"

"Once. In the street."

"What's he like?"

"Very polite. He behaved very well."

"Is that all?"

"He's good looking. At least Meg thinks so. And he dances well. She said to tell you he plays cricket too."

"I don't like the sound of this."

"He's a pleasant boy, George. Be nice to him. It mightn't go any further."

Fergus Sole was late. And when he came he beamed at me in a way I thought idiotic. I could not see that he was good-looking. His face was flushed and his eyes, I thought, slightly crossed. He gave me a handshake that made my finger bones creak. Meg was the colour of a tomato. She looked as if she might be going to punch him.

We sat down to eat our meal. With the first thrust of his fork Fergus Sole scattered peas over the table cloth. He looked at them stupidly. Then he began to spear them one by one. He worked with a fearful concentration. It took several minutes. One elusive pea he trapped under his water glass. "'Scuse fingers." He popped it in his mouth. "'Licious peas, Mrs Plumb." Then he scattered his second forkful.

"Oh Fergus," Meg screamed. She jumped up and dragged him from the table and out of the room.

"What's wrong with that young man?" I said. "Is he sick?"

Robert grinned.

"Well, what is it? Tell me."

"He'll be all right, George," Edie said. "He needs a little sleep, that's all."

"Why should he need a sleep?"

Edie made no reply. I pointed my trumpet at Robert.

"He's blotto, dad. Pickled up to the eyeballs."

"Robert, I won't have that language," Edie said.

"Well anyhow, he's drunk."

I could not believe it. I had never had a drunk man at my table, or in my house. I could not believe Meg would introduce one.

In a moment she came back, very still in the face.

Edie said, "Where have you put him, dear?"

"On the sunporch."

"Will he be warm enough?"

"I don't care if he freezes to death." She began to cry. Edie took her away. That left Robert and me.

"Do you know anything about this fellow, Robert?"

"He was in the first cricket eleven at school."

"And?"

"The girls all liked him."

"Anything else?"

"I think he's a good bloke."

"A good bloke. I must look up my dictionary."

"A nice person, then."

"Nice can't be used in that way."

Robert shrugged. "You'd better get used to him, dad. Meg's going to marry him."

"But why, for heaven's sake?"

"She's in love."

"Love, love. She hasn't the faintest idea what the word means. And I'll say whether or not she gets married. Your mother and I." Robert just grinned at that.

Later Meg came to me in the study. She crept in in her old way and sat on my footstool.

"He's not usually like that, dad."

"I should hope not . . . I hope you're finished with him now, Meg."

"Oh no. Oh no. I love him."

"Nonsense, my dear. Love is for grown up people."

"I'm eighteen."

To me she seemed no more than eleven or twelve. She was open, eager, silly. She saw things that were not there. I shuddered when I thought of this creature thrust into an adult world. At thirty, I thought, she would become a woman. She would be fully grown. And worth knowing. And ready to love and be loved by some adult man. But the world would not leave her alone to grow. Fergus, or whoever replaced him, would not leave her alone. She was not to have time. I saw it plainly. I saw how life would break her.

"He's a drunkard, Meg. He'll make your life a misery, my dear."

"No, dad. He doesn't drink. He hardly ever drinks. He was nervous about meeting you, that's all."

"Am I an ogre?"

"No. But you do frighten people."

"Me?"

"You're clever. And Fergus is not."

"I wouldn't have expected him to be. A plumber's apprentice."

She looked at me reproachfully.

"All right, my dear. I'm sorry. That was unworthy. But tell me, has he any interests? What do you talk about?"

"Oh, everything."

"Does he read?"

"No, but . . ."

"Meg, it just won't work. You're a clever girl. Well, you've got some imagination. You want to write books, don't you?" Even, I added to myself, if they are just romantic twaddle. "He won't understand that. He won't understand any more than a Hottentot. My dear, you're in different worlds. And if you get married he'll never be able to come into yours. You'll have to go into his. And you'll be unhappy there."

"But we love each other."

Always it came back to that. I became angry to hear her use the word. She had not earned the right. Children speak of God, and think of a kind old man with a long white beard. We allow it. And Meg spoke of love, and thought of what? . . a cloud of pink cotton-wool on which she and Fergus would float away into the future. That I would not allow. So I forbade her to think of marriage, I forbade her to think even of an engagement. She was eighteen. I told her to come and see me again when she was twenty.

She said, "All right, dad. He wants to finish his apprenticeship anyway. We can wait."

"You'll get over him. You wait and see."

She touched me on the cheek as though I were the child. "I love him, dad. And I know you'll love him too."

So Fergus became a fixture. He learned to sit at table with me without the aid of strong drink. He brought me gifts: a pineapple, a jar of Chinese ginger. And because he was a generous person, because he played draughts with me in the summer-house, and because Meg did not seem to be getting over him, I began to take trouble with him. I gave him books; which he thanked me for and carried away and did not read. I tested him. He looked embarrassed and mumbled something about being short of time. (It also embarrassed him to talk down my trumpet.) "To tell you the truth Mr Plumb, I haven't read it. But I will. I've put it aside to read. It looks like a good one." He did not even know what a bolshevik was. Come to think of it, he did not know the name of our own Prime Minister. But the ginger was tasty. I beat him at draughts. And he took me to cricket matches. So I told Meg he might come again, or that she could go with him to a ball or a movie in town; but she must not think of an engagement yet. I watched for signs that she was getting over him. I watched. But they strolled hand in hand and her face glowed, her eyes looked into that sparkling unreal future. Or he hit a six and she clapped as though he had made a speech to the nation. I saw I was going to lose. My pity for her increased. I began to be sorry for Fergus too. Some of the pain would be his.

What little there was to him I came to like.

83 I have never got used to riding in motor cars. It is a method of getting about that flies in the face of nature. As we hurtle along at forty miles an hour missing by no more than a foot or two cars that hurtle towards us at the same speed I expect to be punished. I grieve for man, who has travelled so far from himself. The twentieth is not my century. Nor, I fear, is it mankind's. He took a wrong turning, is on a wrong road. As technological man he has entered the time of his death. The signs are plain to see. Unless he turns aside and passes through the Door he will stay mere man, the thinking brute, until he dies—which is soon—and never be Man.

Meditations of this sort shorten my journeys in motor cars. I derive no pleasure from them—but take them like the pills that prevent car sickness.

We spent two days driving home from Wellington. Many times I wondered if I would see Peacehaven again. And when we reached it, at last, at last, thank God, I climbed out of the car with the speed of a boy and stood by the gate trembling. This was land under my feet. I was back in nature. Thank God.

I swung the gate open. Felicity drove through.

"You go on. I'll walk up."

"Are you all right?" she mouthed.

"Perfectly." I turned away from her and looked at the name on the weather-warped board: Peacehaven. Edie's choice, and Edie's work with the brush. The white paint of the background was flaking away and the letters themselves were gone. I read them in bare grey wood. (Fergus wants to repaint the sign. No, I say, when I'm dead. I can beat him in argument any time with my death.) Peacehaven. I remembered her painting those plain shapes on a piece of wood as yellow as butter.

Her presence reached out to me. Patience my dear, I thought, I'll be with you soon. Of course, I attributed impatience to her wrongly. There can be nothing of that on the Other Side. But the mortal Edie was my real listener. I walked up the drive and turned away from the house towards the creek. She became less a presence than a memory. And this made her less easy to face. For those last eight years were a dark sad time. The shadow of Alfred lay over them. We never spoke his name but he was there—in the smallest of our exchanges, in kitchen, garden, bedroom, he was there. Her love for us was perfect—painful to her. It struck her with a mortal wound, her life bled away. She saw both of us as outside nature. Alfred because of his practices—equally with me she believed them unnatural—and me because my love had proved insufficient. Hers was sufficient. It began to kill her. (The doctors said the trouble was her heart. They were right, though they did not know it.)

I tried. I tried with the whole strength of my mind and will. *Homo sum; humani nihil ad me alienum puto.* I tried to make it true. But I was preacher, teacher, moralist. I could not do it.

But now, I thought, resting in the summer-house, now I can do it. I can love Alfred. I can forgive myself. I am a man. Nothing human is alien to me.

I had Robert to thank for this. This had only been possible since his touch on my hand. I said, "Edie you would be pleased with him."

"Dad, dad," a voice cried at my ear. And there was Meg waiting to kiss and hug me. "Talking to yourself?" she cried. I saw her eyes wet with emotion at having me back, and her cheeks pink with happiness, and felt her strong plump arms about my body, and I returned her kiss, thinking, "This is a good girl too."

We went inside. Felicity was buttering pikelets and wanting to shuffle me off to my bedroom so she could gossip with Meg. She had had me for three weeks: I did not blame her. But Meg made me sit down. She poured me tea and gave me pikelets and shouted all her news into my trumpet: Fergus and Fred had quarrelled over the plumbing in the new shops and Fred had been forced to back down; Rebecca had won the mixed doubles title at her tennis club; Emerson's flying-boat had turned back on its Sydney flight with engine trouble. The last affected me. I did not like my children to be in danger. And only half an hour ago I had been reflecting on the petrol engine. How much more presumptuous the aeroplane than the car. And a son of mine entered the great tin belly of the machine and pulled the knobs that made it fly, and mounted close to the sun. I feared he would be punished like Icarus.

"I'd like to see Emerson," I said.

"He's coming on Saturday."

"And Willis."

"We can drive up there."

"And Alfred."

Meg dropped her cup. Then there was a great to-do: mopping out, sweeping up. I waited till it was over. "Alfred Plumb, or whatever his name is now."

Felicity was less agitated than Meg. Meg believed the journey had made me delirious. She wanted to put me to bed. But I said, "Stop fussing Meg. Felicity's got something she wants to say."

"I just want to ask if you're sure you know what you're doing."

"I think so. Why shouldn't I?"

"For twenty-five years you pretend he doesn't exist. And now you think you can snap your fingers and have him come running to see you."

"I don't think that. I'll be surprised if he comes."

"So will I."

"But I'll go to him if he won't come to me. And now Meg dear, I think I'd like to lie down." For I was very weak suddenly. I felt as if I might topple off my chair. But Felicity said, "His name's Hamer, you know. Alfred Hamer. He didn't take your money but he took your advice."

"Stop it, Felix," Meg said. She helped me to my feet.

"And while we're on the subject," Felicity cried, "you might as well know John Willis is dead."

"Is he?" I said. "I'm sorry."

"He and Alfred lived together. Like any old married couple. They made each other happy."

"Felicity, stop it. Come on, dad. You don't have to listen to this."

"When did he die?"

"Three years ago. Another attack of yellow jaundice. His liver wouldn't stand it. Alfred's a widow now."

"Felix," Meg shrieked.

"My dear, I've been cruel," I said to Felicity, "but is there any need for you to be?" I let Meg take me to my bedroom.

"Is it true his name is Hamer?"

"Yes."

"That must have pleased your mother."

"I don't know."

"She didn't talk to you?"

"Not about that."

We were quiet for a moment.

"I'm glad you want to see him," she said, "but . . ."

"You think he won't want to see me?"

"No. Not that. What I was going to say was, why now, after all these years?"

"It was Robert, I think."

"Robert?"

"Not anything he said. Or did either . . . He healed my hand Meg, see. But it's more than that. I've been possessed. For twenty-five years. And after seeing Robert the madness has gone. Nothing human is strange to me any more. He showed me love."

I could say no more than that, and understand no more. Meg placed her palm on my healing one. She kissed me.

"Go back to your sister, dear," I said.

But she stayed with me. Presently I went to sleep.

84 Meg and Fergus were married in a Presbyterian church. The Presbyterian was Fergus's communion—though, he said, he hadn't been to a service for two or three years. He meant to please me.

I went along in a state of sorrow for Meg. I did not believe in this marriage. But for myself I was excited. I had not entered a Presbyterian church since my last visit to St Andrews eighteen years before. I sniffed the air of the place like a retired surgeon returning to the wards. The stained-glass windows, the bars of light striking through the gloom, the architecture of the place— even in this country box there was a lovely soaring—set me quivering with recognition and filled my throat with the pain of loss. I shook myself out of it. Used the old arguments. They were true after all. But the place set up echoes, a haunting moan, inside me. From some things there is no escape. Remembrance of this kind is another sense. I had not read Proust in 1928. But that day I stood for a time in one of his "true paradises".

The young man who married Meg and Fergus might have been Scroggie or my young self. He did well. He allowed the words to do their own speaking. Hearing them, I began to have hope for Meg. Love and a sense of duty might help her put unreality off.

There was no reception. Meg and Fergus drove away. We said

goodbye to his parents. Fred and Esther drove us back to Peacehaven. And there we lived with Robert for six more years, and loved each other through the dark that had come down on our joy.

85 Six years. How much happened in that time. Felicity married, had her child. Esther, Meg, Mirth had children too. I published my third book, my last. I wrote for the radical papers, lectured sometimes three nights a week, supported Labour candidates for parliament. My friendship with Wendy began. Ella Satterthwaite died. My mother died and left her money to her church. Emerson came home—the Sundowner of the Skies—and went away again. In America Agnes married a car salesman. And we all lived through the depression.

But there is a deeper level in my experience. There only one thing happened. Edie died.

She was not afraid. Perfect love casteth out fear. But I was afraid. I was afraid to be without her. I was afraid to see her go before I had knowledge of the thing she knew. She had perfect love. And I did not. I believe she made herself live as long as she did in the hope I might find it. Her hope for me prolonged her life while her love for Alfred and me was killing her.

86 The new babies brought her much delight. And Emerson's triumph made her blush with pride while she laughed at the craziness of it.

Emerson learned to fly in England. He had a natural aptitude for it. It is almost as if he feels wings attached to his shoulders the way Willis feels his amputated leg. People liked to believe the first time he flew was solo. It caused the kind of sensation in flying circles a new immaculate conception would cause in religious.

Emerson saved and bought himself a Gypsy Moth, for which he gave his car in part exchange. For a year or two he flew it about Britain. It kept him poor. Then one day in 1930 he walked into the Croydon airfield carrying a few clothes tied in a bundle and a packet of sandwiches wrapped in a brown paper bag.

From a British newspaper:

Mystery Airman
    A light aeroplane landed at Croydon yesterday and from it stepped a young man who announced his intention of starting at 4 a.m. today on a flight to Australia.
    This morning he reappeared and after stating that his name was Emerson Plumb and that his home was in Auckland, New Zealand, he climbed into his machine and flew away.
    Aerodrome officials have no idea where he came from.

Legends are made in this way. A pity it could not go on. I like to think of him chugging over the Arabian desert, munching sandwiches, singing a tuneless song; or speeding south from Timor over the shark-infested sea, with his silk scarf flying behind him and his bundle of dirty clothes perched on his knee. He lands at Wyndham in Northern Territory, and is found there in the dusk tinkering with the engine of his plane. Eighteen days out from Croydon. The Australians name him the Sundowner of the Skies.

But soon we had too many details; the magic went out of Emerson. For me it was as if Theseus, arriving from the north, had recounted his adventures in Frazerian terms. Still, he was a hero. The right hero for his times. His plane came on a ship from Australia and he flew in triumph about the country, from Whangarei to Stewart Island. He was welcomed by mayors and mobbed by little boys. People began to say he should be knighted. And soon *Kia Ora* disappeared from the fuselage of his plane and the name of an oil company took its place. I thought it a great pity.

But when we had Emerson home we found him unchanged. He was gay and dreamy by turns, as he had been in his motorcycling days. In the midst of a conversation he would go off somewhere; would take to the skies and fly into the sunset. He

214

had an inviolable self. Fame could not alter him. He looked ahead to his freedom—Emerson Plumb soaring in his machine above wind and weather. The mayors, the little boys, were no more than a bit of fun.

And faced with him I began to recapture some of the magic of his flight. There was more than daring in it, there was spirit.

Croydon: *Only one or two people were out to see him as he taxied his tiny blue and silver machine across the aerodrome in the grey light of the morning, and with a wave of his hand started on the first lap of his eleven thousand mile journey.*

Lympne: *The weather conditions were only fair when the lone flyer took off on the six-hundred-mile hop to Munich. A southerly breeze was blowing banks of fog in from the sea; and the hills were shrouded in mist, although over the Channel the sun was breaking through.*

At Munich he swung the propeller while the throttle was open and the plane came alive like a bucking horse. He threw himself flat; then chased it, caught its wing, and climbed aboard.

At Aleppo he ran out of petrol and made a forced landing. And another at Baghdad after flying through a sandstorm. From Jask to Karachi he flew in company with the Hon. Mrs Victor Bruce, who had been lost in the desert. Then on to Jodhpur, and through a strong headwind to Jhansi, where in the dark he could not find the airfield. After circling for half an hour he came down in a ploughed field. The plane turned over and broke its propeller. And during the night the monsoon rains began. But with his little money Emerson hired some villagers to turn the plane on its wheels. He unstrapped his spare propeller from the fuselage and fitted it. Then he had the villagers haul the plane two miles to the only dry ground in the district and took off between trees that almost clipped his wings on either side. Calcutta. Rangoon. Singapore. Batavia. Bima—where he stayed overnight with a tribe of Malay headhunters. Koepang. And then the shark-infested seas; and Wyndham, where three hours after his arrival someone found him overhauling his machine.

I felt a ridiculous pride. It needed Emerson's presence to keep it alive. Edie's delight was girlish. She escaped into her aviator son.

215

She had no fear for him. It seemed she thought of him as a being under some other dispensation. I thank him for the happiness he brought into her last years.

Soon he went back to England. And from there to South Africa, where he formed a flying circus. He sent us a photograph of himself wing-walking. Edie laughed with joy.

87 Joy. In those years it was in short supply. The dream of a Utopia in the southern seas, of God's Own Country, had never been more than that: a dream. Holes had been shot in it before the depression. But in the depression it rusted like an old tin can, it fell to pieces. All we had left was human kindness. Without it we would have become a nation of beasts.

On the level of simple survival the Plumbs survived. My few invested pounds fell down a great hole. But Robert saved Peacehaven with his hands. Willis struggled on, copying him. Felicity was all right: Max kept his job. And Esther's husband was a bookmaker. The parasite class keeps food in its belly. Meg suffered most. Fergus lost his job early and was on relief through most of that time. Their third child was born in 1932.

They lived in a three-roomed shack a mile down the creek from us. One Saturday morning I shouldered a sack of vegetables and walked round to see them. I found the two older children playing in the front yard, while the baby slept in a butter-box under a tree. Meg was boiling the copper to wash napkins. She lugged water from the rain-water tank to a leanto that served as a wash-house, using an old kerosene tin as a bucket. Fergus had fitted a wire handle to it. It cut Meg's fingers cruelly, but she would not let me help. When she had the copper full she dropped the napkins in, trying to hide the stains from me. Poor Meg. Genteel even in this extremity. She took me inside for a cup of tea. The children ran in and she gave them baked crusts of bread—Edie's *zwieback*. The baby cried. With her back to me she fed it from her breast. Now and then she turned her head and shouted something into my trumpet.

216

Fergus was out on his bicycle. He was off relief for a time, finding his own work. He had managed to put together a toolkit that would do for plumbing and carpentry. Each morning he rode off to the local timber yard with his kit over the handlebars. Whenever a loaded truck came out he pedalled after it. Often he fell too far behind, and cycled back exhausted to wait for the next truck. But when he managed to follow all the way (one of the drivers helped him by slowing down) there was sometimes work for him stacking the timber; and now and then a day's plumbing or carpentry. He preferred this to relief. He was his own man.

But that morning he had gone out on other business. I was close to Meg's shoulder watching the baby's peaceful greedy sucking. (Edie had fed our children locked in the bedroom.) I saw its eyes jerk open with shock as a tear from Meg's eye splashed on its forehead. At once she was contrite. She cooed. She wiped the tear away. She helped the tiny pursed mouth find her nipple again.

"What's the matter, my dear?"

"Nothing."

"Is it Fergus?"

She made a movement of her head. I took it for a nod.

"What's he done?"

"It's not his fault."

"Of course not."

"He's so proud."

She told me the story. She spoke quietly and I held my trumpet almost to her mouth. The baby became still as a bird, watching this strange black object hovering over it.

Last night the nightman had come. (Meg blushed.) He was a young man who had been at school with Fergus. And of course he was in steady work. (Her colour deepened.) Fergus made a joke of him, but liked him: a friendly young man and very kind. Well, last night was his night. She had heard him rattling his cans at two o'clock while she fed the baby. And heard something soft land on the step. After the baby was asleep again she had gone out to look. And there it was, lying on the doorstep: a sack of old clothes and shoes. She pulled them out gingerly, with great fastidiousness, but

217

saw that after a boil the shirts and dresses would be all right. The underclothes, no. One had to draw the line. And the shoes—one could not boil shoes. She would pass those on—although a pair of walking brogues looked her size. She washed her hands and went back to bed. Two dresses she could wear; and a shirt Bobby's size; and a dress for Rebecca. It was like discovering buried treasure. But she lay awake worrying: Fergus would not be pleased.

She got no further for Fergus himself came in. He was flushed from riding his bicycle. Meg laid the baby down. She poured him a cup of tea.

"Well," he said, "it's done."

"I suppose you punched him on the jaw?" This was sharp for Meg. I looked at her with sorrow and respect. She would come through. I did not like to think of the cost.

"I told him to keep his cast-offs," Fergus said.

"What did he say?"

"Nothing. He was in his pyjamas, the lazy b———."

"Fergus! Dad's here."

"Sorry, Mr Plumb. But still, at ten o'clock in the morning."

"He was working all night," Meg said.

"You call that work?"

Fergus had stood in the front yard and called the nightman out. And when he had appeared, pyjama-ed and rubbing his eyes, Fergus had thrown the sack of clothes at his feet. The man had said nothing; picked up his sack, gone inside and closed the door. And Fergus, back home and drinking tea, was ashamed of himself. He blustered. "I don't need any man's charity. I can look after my family," etc.

"One of the dresses was just right for Rebecca. We've got nothing for her. And winter's coming."

"We'll be all right."

"But Fergus—"

"We'll be all right, I said."

"Yes, Fergus." After a moment, she said, "Dad brought us some vegetables."

"Thanks, Mr Plumb. But I can grow my own." As if to prove it he went out to his garden.

"He's so touchy," Meg said. "He hates taking things from other people."

"Shall I take the vegetables back?"

"Oh no. He didn't mean it. As soon as you've gone he'll come in and say he's sorry." And very soon she said, "Listen, he's whistling. Just like a boy."

"Your mother wants you to come round for dinner on Sunday. Robert's killing a sheep."

"Oh, the poor thing. Why does he have to be so cruel?" This was my Meg. I smiled at her. But in a moment I saw she was crying again.

"What is it, my dear?"

"I don't know. I don't know. Something seems to have gone out of things."

I tried to cheer her up by giving her the book I had brought: a little volume called *The Kingdom of Love*, by Ella Wheeler Wilcox. She had read it as a girl.

"Thanks, dad." She laid it on the table. "I don't get much time for reading. I'll put it away for the children."

"Do you still write?"

"I told you," she cried angrily, "there's no time. Besides, Fergus wouldn't understand." We both thought of the warning I had given her. She jumped to her feet. "And anyway, I don't want to. That was a silly game. I'm married now. And Fergus is a wonderful man . . . Oh, my copper. The fire will be out." She ran to the wash-house. She sent Fergus rushing for wood.

I did not know who to be sorrier for. But I find today that when I think of the depression I think most often of Meg crying at her kitchen table; and of the nightman, dressed in his pyjamas, turning back into his darkened house with his sugarbag of used clothing in his hand.

That was the depression. It was not a simple thing.

219

88 I played little part in the politics of it. My failure to find a course of action confused and disappointed me. I understand now I'm not a political man. My eye has always been fixed on ends, I've not had a clear view of means. Politically I am a child. Always the action I have wished to take has been impossibly direct or wildly idiosyncratic. I am not a Communist, though I was often accused of it. I was a member of no party—had been free of them all since the U.L.P. swallowed the old Socialist Party. What I wanted was a workers' revolution. I wanted spontaneous uprisings all through the country. Though with the rational part of my mind I saw that Savage and Nash and Fraser were the men of the future, the political idealist in me would not accept them. They were too mundane, men not Men. As the swell mounted behind them I watched them set their feet on the rocks of tradition. They would not be carried away. Someone has said that political parties are a breed. When new they have some marks of individuality, but they revert to type. And for the radical that means they become conservative. It is true. Under a Labour Government there would be, I guessed, two or three years of reform of a half-baked kind, and then would come the old cry that economic realities must be faced. And the new order would change its shape to the old. What I wanted was not a new order but new realities.

I sat one evening with Bluey in an Auckland hall. It was full of hungry men. Savage and Fraser and Nash were on the stage. Lee with his empty sleeve. Semple. Dan Peabody. They were all there. I did not hear what they said. Deafness can be a blessing. Now and then Bluey scribbled something on a piece of paper and handed it to me. I saw the politicians were at their old game of buying votes with promises. But Bluey wrote too: *They don't like it.* And I heard a murmur about me and saw angry faces. These men were not to be fed with words. They had suffered enough. I rose to my

220

feet. Nash was speaking: scattering his handfuls of tin tacks about the hall. My voice has a wider range. The pulpit trains more thoroughly than the soap-box. For a moment or two we fought in single combat. He scratched my surface like a rasp, I beat on him like a hammer. The men in the hall enjoyed it—egged me on. But when Nash sat down and the chairman threatened to have me turned out they began to bellow with rage—a frightening sound (made hollow and other-worldly by my deafness). For a moment I thought I had unleashed revolution. The weight of the noise beat the chairman back to his seat. I saw him put up his hand to ward it off; and I thought, This is honest anger, this is the voice of the people. And at once said so, and told the politicians they were right to be frightened, that unless they obeyed the people's will they would be swept into the gutters of history. But I kept it short. There was heat here and unless I used it quickly it would grow cold. So I said, "Your way is wrong. It can only end in repression. This parliament you want to take over will take you over, it will swallow you up. Six months in that place and you'll be a new bunch of Coateses and Wards. These men down here know it. They can hear it in your voices. They've got hungry wives and children at home and that has given them an extra sense. They don't want you going to Wellington to take over old institutions. They want new institutions. Or no institutions. They want a movement, a revolution, a people's government. And if you are too cowardly to talk of it up there, why we'll talk of it down here. We'll talk of it. No, by heaven, we'll do more than that. We won't just talk of it, we'll do it." And I cried, "I put a motion to this meeting, this meeting of the unemployed workers of New Zealand. I put the motion that we declare here and now that our country belongs to its working people and that henceforth its government is a people's government, a dictatorship of the proletariat. There's the motion for you. And I see your chairman won't put it to the vote, he's frightened, he's hiding under his chair, so I'll put it. All in favour say Aye."

I saw the cry that went up as much as heard it. For a moment I felt the intoxication demagogues must feel: they drink their followers up and swell with power. But I was no demagogue, no leader. Just an angry man with a good voice and a sense of other people. I had made my speech. Another man, more ambitious or braver, might have led his followers out of the hall: there would have been broken windows and broken heads. But I was not ambitious, not a man of action. Having got my crowd roaring and ready to move, I did not know what to do with it. I was forced to hand it back to the politicians. I said, "There you are, gentlemen. We've changed the shape of the country for you. It has a new government now. The people have voted. Now you know what you're at the helm of. Let's see whether you can steer a straight course."

I walked out, with Bluey and one or two others at my heels. I do not know how Nash and Fraser and Savage (they are interchangeable) pointed the meeting back in their direction. They were clever. They managed it all right. I waited on the windy footpath, stamping my feet to drive out the cold. After another half-hour the men came out. They were still-faced, grey-faced, sour. The fire was out in them. They turned up their collars, put their hands deep in their pockets, and trudged on their broken shoes off home. Only one or two came up to speak with me. But the politicians came out hearty. Semple rushed up and shouted at me—gutter language. It was a performance. He was not angry. In fact I think he was pleased with me, and his attack a tribute from one clever performer to a person he took for another. The others left me alone. Except Dan Peabody. Dan sidled up.

"That was a foolish thing to do, George."

"You wouldn't have thought so twenty years ago, Dan." I looked at him with pity. I could not dislike him. He had abandoned my daughter to avoid upsetting the Grundyites of his party—the bible and purity boys. He was an object of pity not dislike. And as well as Felicity he had put his young self aside and with it all that was honest and simple in him. He was on his way now, after the job at the top. And I saw in his eyes the fear that he was not going to get it. The others were tougher than he was and had more brains. He was starting to understand. He said, "We're going to be the government, George. At the next election. There's no way we can fail."

"You've failed already."

He smiled. "Double talk again. It's always double talk with you. You're too clever, that's your trouble. And you see where it's got you. Way out on the end of a limb. All by yourself."

"I stand with the Reverend," Bluey said, "and proud of it."

Dan looked at him absently. It was a shocking moment. Dan was a politician now, to his core. And that meant people had no essential being. They were fuel to stoke a career with. He looked through Bluey; but spoke to me because I might have uses—political decoy-bird. I turned away from him, shied away almost, as though from a suddenly incarnate dark angel. I walked up the street. Bluey kept at my side. He too had understood. He retained his good practical sense and his nose for moral decay.

We were shaken. We went to Bluey's room and drank several cups of tea before we were better.

89 One night (the 20th August 1934) I read late in my study. The house shuddered in a winter storm. Draughts stirred the curtains in the windows and when I looked into the night I saw blown leaves pasted to the glass in the shape of eyes. I had a sense of foreboding. Pursuing the Light, I had been deep in my books.

> I go to prove my soul!
> I see my way as birds their trackless way.
> I shall arrive! What time, what circuit first
> I ask not: but unless God send the hail
> Or blinding fire-balls, sleet and stifling snow
> In some time, His good time, I shall arrive.
> He guides me and the bird.

But I had no sense of being guided, or of being about to arrive. On that night I felt I might be struck down. I shook myself; I put it down to tiredness, too much print.

Towards midnight I went to bed. I slipped in beside Edie. In the light of the night-lamp I looked at her sleeping face. It was drained and cavernous. Her beauties were gone. But I knew of other beauties. Behind the suffering mask of the sick Edith Plumb was girl, wife, mother, loving heart, courageous spirit. My tiredness, the pushing restless ideas in me, and perhaps the elemental night, perhaps my love for her, opened a door between us, and I had a vivid and terrifying glimpse of her immortal soul. It was Light. It was Love. But it was not for me to look upon. I backed away. This was a forbidden mystery. I had thrown away my right to look on it. I must concern myself with the mortal part of her. So I thought of her sufferings.

Mirabeau dying after many days of pain signalled for pen and paper and wrote down in two words the only desire he had left: *To sleep*. This was the desire Edie had for herself. I understood. I was even able to hope it would come soon.

I woke at 3 a.m. (the 21st) and felt her beside me fighting for breath. She had no wish to struggle. Her body was fighting of its own accord. I turned on the light and saw she was suffering her last attack. I called out to her, "Edie, don't go. Don't go." And I ran to Robert's room and sent him cycling for Wendy and the doctor. When I came back Edie managed to fix her eyes on me and know who I was. "George." She felt for my hand and took it with a strength that had in it all of our life together. "George." She wanted to say something, but had not time. She died. I know she would have told me I must make peace with Alfred and love him as my son. I would have obeyed. Why, knowing her wish, have I failed to carry it out?

I closed her eyes. For a moment I shared her arrival, shared her joy. Where she was gone was deep and lasting peace. For both of us I heard in my skull, *Non omnis moriar*. Horace had been speaking of fame and poetry; but the words had a better meaning. I looked down at my dead wife. Grief descended and struck me its hammer blow. But still I kept my eyes on her face. And I thought in the words of the ancient philosopher, See the shell of the flown bird.

90 Wendy arrived and the doctor. In the grey dawn Meg and Esther came. I went to my study and locked myself in.

But there was nothing in that room to tell me who my wife had been. I put my head on the desk and struggled to find her. Later in the morning I crept through the house to her sewing-room and took from the cabinet there the exercise books in which she wrote her thoughts and memories. I turned the pages over. But I could not get into the times and places she wrote of. I was like an insect on a window. A hard transparent substance lay between me and Edie. She wrote: "That little woman had a *dirty apron* that she wore nearly all the fortnight she was with us. She used to bring in my meals with a *knife sticking* in a jar of jam. One day she said to me, 'Would you like a wee lick of chicken broth?' I said I would, but when the broth arrived I *changed my mind* as it looked so horrid. It looked like hot water with a lot of little bits of *oil and feathers* in it." I knew who that was: Mrs Evershaw the nurse who tended her in her confinement with Rebecca. But I could not hear the woman's Scotch voice, or see the broth, her dirty apron; or hear Edie, even in that word so dear to her, *horrid*. And I read, "He loved his garden and flowers. He used to say nothing compared with a *dark red rose*." Her father. I had always felt I knew him. I did not know him now. I read on, ". . . a trellis with purple grapes . . . a brick footpath . . . the dining-room window wreathed in climbing roses." I had seen and smelt them for myself. The colour, the scent, were gone. I began to feel my life was leaking away. "We had beautiful rata wood fires. The minister used to put on a *big log* and it lasted all evening." Was I that minister? I could not remember. A glass wall stood between me and George Plumb. I put the books back in their drawer and went outside. The wind had dropped and the rain fell straight and heavy. I sat in the summer-house. And there I began to find myself and my wife. I sat on the wet seat. The rain came down in drops as large as bantam eggs and splashed on my head and cheeks. "George, come out of that," I heard her say, "you'll catch your death of cold." I thought, The light of my life has gone and I will miss her as long as I live. There is a pain in my heart which cannot be removed.

Meg found me. Then there was a great commotion. The girls undressed me and rubbed me with towels. They scolded and screeched like parrots and cooed like doves. I stood like a wooden man. They put me to bed with hot bottles about me and blankets six deep on my chest. Later, when Edie's body was taken away, they shifted me to the big bed. I was easier there. I lay shivering with cold and sweating in fever for many days. Someone else said the service for Edie. I did not mind. They buried the shell of her. I sought her shining soul in other realms.

91 I had been home two days without a visit from Bluey. I asked Meg if he was sick but she did not know. Sutton was always busy in the garden, so she supposed everything was all right.

"I'll go down and see him."

"Here." She gave me a sago pudding in a basin. "Take him that."

"Thank you, Meg. He'll be pleased."

"He's the only person I know who can eat the stuff." Meg had come a long way. In the hard modern manner she tried to detract from her kindness. I smiled at her and said again, "He'll be pleased," and went off down the drive with this mess Bluey would look on as a prize. It was Saturday. As I went through the gate Bobby rode past me on his motorcycle. (Like Emerson's it was an Indian.) Rebecca sat on the pillion seat, dressed in her tennis whites and a blue cardigan. She waved her racquet at me. I waved my trumpet back. (It pleased me now that Meg had named her daughter for her drowned sister. At the time I had thought it unhealthy.)

I walked along the footpath and in at Bluey's gate, wondering at the little car parked outside. Bluey had no friends left that I knew of. Excepting Sutton, of course. The man was at the side window of the cottage, in a burglar's crouch. He saw me on the path and came at me in a lopsided run. With his finger on his lips, he drew me after him to the end of the garden. I do not care for mysteries. But I cannot be brusque with Sutton. He knows it. He exaggerates his vulture's hump with me. But now he had a violence about him. I liked it even less than his usual malice. I did not care for his clutching of my arm, or like the unnatural redness of his eyes. Until, with a start, I realized he had been crying.

"What's wrong, Mr Sutton? Is Bluey all right?"

"They've caught him, Mr Plumb. They've hooked him at last."

"What do you mean?"

"He's got a priest in there."

"Ah, that explains the car."

Sutton hissed. The sound came so sharply down my trumpet it hurt. I drew away. Sutton had been crying with rage more than grief. He had owned Bluey as servant and friend for fifteen years. He must have felt safe. Nobody wanted the old man—even I did not want him. But now the Church claimed Bluey; and Sutton had enough sense to know a good part of his friend had escaped him forever. He was lacerated by his rage and pain. I would not have been surprised to see him stamp himself into the ground like Rumpelstiltskin.

"Is this the first time he's come?"

"He's been once before. They took him to confession yesterday."

"Bluey must have had a lot to confess. He'll be saying Hail Marys for the rest of his life."

"You can do something," Sutton cried.

"No, Mr Sutton. Less than you."

"I thought you were his friend."

"I am. I hope I am. I don't like his church, or any church for that matter. But I think he'll be happy for the first time in fifty years."

"What will happen to me?"

"Why nothing, I should think. You'll have to share him, that's all."

"I won't share him."

"You'll have to, Mr Sutton. Now come on," I said, "you're his friend. You know how tormented he's been. They've got him back and that's a sad thing for us. But he'll be able to relax."

Sutton would have none of this. He was in a sense Bluey's lover and Bluey's master—entirely possessive. He must have Bluey whole. I had seen Sutton first in 1934, walking along behind Bluey with a small happy grin on his face. It was Queen Street, Friday night. Bluey sailed through the crowds like a barge, making a path for the cripple. He waved his heavy oak stick to clear the way. People watched them go by like a circus act. Bluey was unaware. But Sutton loved it. And now, after fifteen years, Bluey was getting away. I understood Sutton's pain, but could do nothing to help him. I offered him a bite of sago pudding.

"Aah," Sutton cried, "it's your fault. With your talk of souls. There's no such thing as souls. It's a dirty trick you church b——s play on us."

I left him in the garden and went to the cottage, where I sat on the bench and waited for Bluey and the priest to come out. Poor Sutton. Bluey's care for him would increase, but I saw the cripple would take it as a loss.

I waited on the bench for a good half-hour. The sun warmed my bones. Off to one side Sutton crept along the garden path. He stationed himself at the cottage window again. I got up and peered round at him, but he bared his teeth so I left him crouching there. I did not think Bluey should be warned. He was probably expecting trouble from Sutton.

When he came out he grew red to find me there. We shook hands. He introduced me to the priest, a Father Pearce. I noticed I was Mister not Reverend, and took from this an unexpected pain. I had had my title from Bluey for forty years. But, I told myself, it was not important. What mattered was that Bluey had come to rest. In spite of this he was shifty. He wanted the priest out of there. Pearce seemed to understand. He was a large man, blue-jowled, bushy-browed; comfort-loving, I guessed. He looked at the sunny bench with longing; but allowed Bluey to ease him towards his car. I sat down again. Remembering Robert's advice, I turned my tender palm towards the sun.

Bluey came back and lowered himself on the bench. I gave him the sago pudding.

"What's this? Sago? Is this from Meg? Ah, that's a good girl . . ."

I wondered if his conversation was to be like this: full of clumsy gaps where in the past he would have said Reverend. "Bluey," I said, "you'd better call me George."

But he could not. Our friendship might founder on this rock. "So you've come back to it, Bluey? I'm not surprised."

"Eh? What's that? I can't hear you."

"You've come back to the church?"

"It's me ears. They're getting worse."

"The church. The church."

But he simply grinned and tapped my trumpet. "I'll have to get one of those."

I gave up. "Meg made the pudding specially, Bluey."

"Ah, she's a good girl. I've always liked sago. I'll have it for lunch."

I told him about my trip to Wellington, about Oliver and the Goodlad case (he told me Goodlad had shot himself: it was in the morning paper); about Robert, whom Bluey had always loved; about Felicity. Felicity would come and see him, I said. I reminded him she was a Catholic. (He had an attack of deafness at that point.) Last I told him Esther was arranging for me to see Alfred, my son Alfred Plumb. Bluey's pleasure in that shone on his face. He nearly called me Reverend again. With luck, I thought, we would keep our friendship going.

I said goodbye and left him at his door. Sutton crept round the corner and stood by his side. Bluey showed him the pudding. They went inside. I walked home. The whole business, I thought, was a defeat for good sense. It did not fail to make me angry. The priests who had crippled Bluey Considine in his youth would get no congratulations from me for providing him with a crutch in his old age. Still, he was happy, for the first time in fifty years.

I could not take the debate through to its end. It became too much for me.

92 In any case, I thought, it has no end. Or if it ends it will be with Man. And history closes its pages at that point. There will be a new book, a new reality.

Emerson roused me from that reverie. He came down to the summer-house where I had hidden and threw his arm round my shoulders.

"Lurking in the bushes, dad? Come and have a walk."

I had not seen him for several months. In that time he had, as the newspapers say, brushed shoulders with death. Two hundred miles out over the Tasman Sea his aeroplane had started to sputter and smoke. He switched one engine off and flew back home on the others, whistling a tune, his co-pilot said, with thirty terrified people still as mice in the cabin behind him. His landing on the harbour had been a model of neatness.

I said, "When are you going to give that flying up, son?"

He laughed. "Soon, dad. I'm getting a bit long in the tooth. I think I'll grow grapefruit like Willis."

"What tune was it you whistled?"

"I don't know. Something mum used to play." He whistled it down my trumpet.

"I dreamt I dwelt in marble halls," I said.

"Is that it? Anyway, it was all that kept the old pile of scrap in the air."

I believed him. We strolled down the lawn and over the brick bridge into the orchard. The trees were dying. Nobody had pruned them since Robert had gone. I was not concerned. They and I kept pace. We would end together. Fergus would have the bulldozers in soon after my death. So it seemed a kindness to the trees to let them take the course natural to them. Age and weight split their trunks as cleanly as kindling.

Emerson shook some late apples off a branch. We ate as we

went along. He took off his jacket and slung it over his shoulder. On his wrists I saw the tiny white scars made by an exploding bottle in John Jepson's aerated-water factory. I said, "Do you see anything of Alfred?"

He took it calmly. The others must have warned him. "We haven't got much in common."

"When did you see him last?"

"Oh—" he shrugged. "A couple of years back. At Esther's, I think."

"How was he?"

"Seemed O.K. to me. He'd put on a bit of weight."

"Did he talk about John Willis?"

"No."

"John's dead."

"So I hear."

He was uncomfortable. He felt the same way I did about homosexuality. I changed the subject. But as we walked down to the house he said, "Mum used to meet him here, you know."

"Alfred?"

"Esther told me. He used to come in through the farm at the back."

The way, I thought, he had come to meet John Willis. I felt a tremor in my universe, and thought for a moment things would fall apart. But then felt a settling, and looked with a sharp eye at the new conformations. I did not like them. Edie had walked in the orchard, deceiving me; I had put her to this torment. So, in concealment, she had met the needs of her life. I did not like the part I played in this.

Emerson stopped on the bridge. He threw his apple core into the water. An eel rose from the deep, nosed it, and sank again. Emerson said, "Alfred's started drinking."

"Did Esther tell you that?"

"She wanted you to know. He's on it pretty heavily, she says."

"Because John Willis is dead?"

Emerson frowned. "Evidently." He looked at the sky; wishing he was up there. "Do you think it's a good idea to see him?"

"Yes. I do."

"Esther told me to tell you he mightn't come."

"We'll wait and see."

Emerson flapped his jacket. He wanted to say something more but did not know how. I could not help him. He had extraordinary skills. He could loop the loop and do the falling leaf. He could fly under bridges. And given a single piston or shaft, like an archaeologist the bone of an extinct beast, he would probably manage to put the original machine together around it. But he could not say what he had to say to me. We walked up to the house. There, in the backyard, he managed.

"Dad, look, some of the others are still sore at you. For turning him out, I mean. But I want you to know I understand. I'm not saying you should have. I mean, he's my brother. But I see why you had to do it."

"Thank you, Emerson."

"But what I want to say is, why do you have to go and dig it up now? It's ancient history. Let it lie is what I say. You can't change anything now."

"Don't worry, son. You won't be involved."

"We're all involved."

93 Meg called us in to lunch. I would have liked to have mine in my study but could not with Emerson visiting. So I sat between him and Meg and ate a piece of luncheon sausage and a lettuce leaf.

Emerson's words had set up a trembling in my mind. I was on the point of seeing my family whole. Of course they were all involved. The conversation was about motorbikes, with Bobby and Emerson swapping anecdotes and Raymond and Fergus chipping in now and then. But the real conversation (Meg, Felicity, Emerson) ran like an underground stream beneath all this. I saw its progress in their unnatural ease, in their heartiness and sudden preoccupations, and in the glances they sometimes gave each other, or sent in my direction to see if I had changed my shape again. I remembered Edie's phrase, another shake of the kaleidoscope. I had shaken it, and now my children were jostling at my shoulder to see the new pattern. I had a more intimate sense of them than I'd had in years; since they had been neat-haired Sunday children assembled in the parlour at the Manse to sing to their mother's playing "Saviour, breathe an evening blessing" or "Flow gently, sweet Afton". I even had dead Rebecca in my mind. And banished Alfred. I had Edie.

Felicity shouted, "Wool-gathering, dad?"

I smiled at her but made no answer.

"A penny for them."

"I was thinking of your mother."

This made her frown, and made Meg's eyes grow misty. I said, "And Alfred. I'd better have a rest if I'm seeing him this afternoon." I thanked Meg for the meal and went to my study. Fergus followed and opened the door for me. His tough man's-man face had an anxious look. But he was too proud to say what was on his mind— something, I guessed, about Alfred displacing the Soles at Peacehaven, or in my will.

"It's all right, Fergus. This doesn't change anything."

"It's none of my business. I never knew him."

"Look on it the way Bobby and Raymond do. A sporting event."

He laughed; but was not amused.

94   I had not been in the study long before Meg let herself in. She carried a cup of tea and a plate of biscuits.

"Thank you my dear, but I don't want any."

She put them on the desk and pulled up the stool. She had not come to talk but to sit with me. I would sooner have been alone. But this was the most vulnerable of my children and I could not turn her out.

"Felicity's doing the dishes."

"Good. Good."

I sat and dreamed a while and she sat beside me with her hand on my knee. My past was returning to me in colours unnaturally bright, in smells of cooking and burning and growth, and in sounds that I being deaf could never have heard. I remembered this child, Meg, bringing my tea to the study one night. It was 1917. She was nine. We were just back from America. She put her face against my shoulder and asked me why I was worried. I was worried about many things. I told her the least of them. A man from the insurance company had called to say his firm would not insure our furniture because somebody might burn down our house. Meg stamped her foot. She had that beautiful strong sense of justice that resides in children—a primary sense that too soon becomes muddied. She stamped her foot. She cried out with anger. Was he, she wanted to know, the young man who had come to see me late in the afternoon, the young man with the thick glasses and leather bag? Yes, I said, that was him. "Then I wish he'd fall off his bike," she cried. "I wish he'd fall off his bike and break his neck." I was astonished at this from my gentle Meg. I explained that it was not the young man's fault, that above him were the company managers, and above them the profiteers and warmongers, and they were the evil men, not the clerk with the pebble glasses, who had been ashamed of the job he had to do. Tears ran down Meg's cheeks. "It's not fair," she wept, "it's not fair the way they're cruel to you." We talked for a long time that evening. I told her what Keats had meant when he called the world a vale of soul-making. And I gave her to read that same little poem of Ella Wheeler Wilcox's I had given Felicity: "Let there be many windows to your soul   " The next night she had it by heart.

That had been more than thirty years ago. With a pain like that of bereavement I realized this was not a nine-year-old child sitting with me but a grown woman, and an unhappy one. I said, "Do you remember the insurance man, Meg? The one you wished would fall off his bicycle?"

"Vaguely. Did he have pebble glasses?"

"That's him." And I went on to speak of that night, of our talk about the soul's pilgrimage, and of the poem she had learned.

I should not have. She did not remember. I took her hand. She was suffering, I thought, from a stupor in those bright life-giving cells where the past resides. The blows of the present rained too heavily on her. Unless she could learn to take them, ride with them in Bobby's phrase, she would not recover the lost part of herself and become whole again. It seemed to me the most simple of diagnoses, and I explained it to her. She did not listen.

"Oh dad," she cried, "what am I going to do?" She spoke of her troubles. Fergus was growing away from her. He lived for his work. He had become a stranger. And the children were growing up. They would soon be gone. What would she do then?

"You must look inside yourself, Meg. You still have yourself."

"Some self!"

"It's all you've got, my dear. It's all any of us have. But it's enough. Because the Light is an inner light. And that's where we find God."

"Oh God," she cried. "That old stuff. I thought you gave that up."

"No," I said, shivering a little, for I saw she was bent on self-destruction, I could not see how to save her. I would even have turned her at that moment towards Felicity's church, Bluey's church. But I did not know the way. So I kept on talking—religious waffle Willis calls it. And soon she began to pat my knee absently.

I said, "Why don't you talk to Felicity?"

"About the Catholic Church, you mean? Don't think I haven't thought of it."

"Why don't you then?"

"Because you've ruined that for me. All churches."

"Good," I joked.

"That's all very well for you . . . I've even been to see the doctor."

"What did he say?"

"He thinks I've got too much time on my hands. He told me it's not too late to have another baby."

I laughed.

"It's not funny. I've thought of seeing a psychiatrist."

235

"And what would you tell him, my dear? That you've got an ache in your pineal gland?"

She did not understand.

"That's where Descartes located the soul."

"Who's Descartes?"

95 Felicity said from the door, "What are you two talking about?"

"Who's Descartes?"

"Des Cartes," Felicity said. "He's a cousin of Les Miserables." They laughed. I watched them with astonishment. It made them laugh even louder.

"Dad's trying to talk me into joining your church," Meg said.

"You could do worse. There's a woman out here to see you, dad. She says her name's Wendy Philson. Do you want me to tell her to go away?"

"You remember Wendy."

"Never seen her in my life."

"You met her at Esther's wedding. And she was at your mother's funeral." I knew she remembered—she did not suffer from Meg's disease. She was provoking me. Like Meg she disapproves of Wendy's role in my life.

"Tell her to come in, Felicity. And I hope you'll remember your manners." She grinned and went out. Meg followed with the cup and plate. A moment later Wendy took her place.

"Hello, George. How did the trip go? How's your hand?" She took it and opened it out. "It's healing."

"Yes," I said. I told her about Robert. She had never been close to him. She thought him dull. And, I could see, thought my account of his present life sentimental. She gave a faint smile when I said he had healed my palm.

"You don't have to believe it, Wendy. I'm not trying to set him up as a faith healer."

"It would have got better by itself."

"Perhaps." It was not that she disbelieved in supernatural forces. But they worked, she believed, through superfine souls. Robert, lumpish Robert, was not equipped. I was not going to argue with her. I knew him. I put down my trumpet and handed her a writing pad and pencil. This is an intimate act. It makes her blush, especially in the privacy of my study. "Now my dear, tell me what you've been up to. Last time you came you said you'd been doing some reading."

She put her head down like a child and wrote. (I'm not sure she doesn't put her tongue out.) *I'm reading Jung. All about the interpretation of dreams.* She wrote on at length about the dream as the key to the world of one's psyche, the dream as empirical data. She claimed that all the evidence pointed towards the truth of reincarnation. When she paused I said, "Is this in Jung? I haven't read him."

Jung stops short, she wrote. *He didn't dream his other lives. But I do.*

"Tell me one of them."

She wrote (and I read over her shoulder): *I was a young girl. I was fourteen. I found myself descending stairs which were of stone, and narrow and low. As I descended they become so low I had to crawl. They were fearsome, and ended in a large underground cavern out of which I came to a labyrinth of narrow dark passages. These led to a small room with no doors or windows. I was simply in it and did not know how to get out. I tried the walls for an opening. After what seemed an eternity I was walking along a wide light passage. I noticed a door on the right-hand side, and put my hand on the handle. As I did so I heard myself exclaiming joyously, "And this is the room of light."*

"But Wendy," I said, "isn't this the initiation ceremony of the Eleusinian mysteries?"

"Exactly," she cried. And wrote: *It's the ceremony that confers the long memory. It symbolizes a journey, an inner evolution. But don't you see, it's more than that? This was a dream of one of my past lives. I must have been an Eleusinian initiate. Otherwise how would I know all that? The dream is data. I had one about the Egyptian mysteries too.*

"Perhaps you'd better teach me, Wendy."

No, you are the teacher. You've always been my master in our past lives. I'm your pupil. You're ahead of me in the evolutionary scale.

I did not take this lightly. Wendy was in earnest. She was no intellectual butterfly, like Merle and Graydon (two wings of the same creature). She would have tested her new belief for faults. I said, "If you'll lend me the books I'll try to read them."

You don't need to. You knew it when you had to know it. You're close to the Light now. You don't need dreams any more. The Light blinds you. And she wrote: *George, I think this is your last reincarnation. You're a long way ahead of me. I'll have to go on alone.*

She smiled at me from a very great distance. There was nothing I could do but pat her hand.

96 She was born in the year of *Peter Pan*. She hated her name. But could not use her second. It was Ouida. Her parents came to New Zealand when she was four. She grew up in a country town, attended university, trained as a teacher; and rented the cottage from me when Willis moved out. She was Alfred's friend; my friendly acquaintance. She withdrew from me in horror when I sent him away. She was inward looking. She learned to look even deeper. She had believed me a good man. I showed her a gross imperfection that led her on to views of human nature that almost cost her her reason. Evil was a force that battered on the doors of her sanity. (The words are hers.) Once she tried to drown herself in the creek. But the black water took on the nature of a hellish fluid and the life in her, the good, refused it entry. Finally she tried to save herself by refusing the world. She hid in the cottage. Robert told me he thought she was "off her rocker". I went down. I knocked at the door. But she would not let me in. I saw the curtains breathing, that was all. So I got in touch with her parents. They took her away.

When Edie and I entered the little cottage to tidy it up we saw the pathetic childishness of her retreat. Everything was pasted over with brown paper. All surfaces: walls, floors, table tops. All objects: chairs, sideboards, pots and pans. Brown paper covered everything. She had used flour and water paste. When that ran out she had made do with condensed milk. It took Edie weeks of work to scrape everything clean. We decided not to let the cottage again but keep it as an overflow house for visitors. Then after more than two years we had a letter from Wendy saying she was well again and asking if she might have the cottage back. We did not hesitate. She had made it hers with that brown paper.

When she came back she was slower, older, and gave the impression of being less fully alive. She had closed off a part of herself. Spiritually, I thought, she would never be whole. (I was wrong in that.) But socially she was whole. She and Edie became friends. As Edie's illness worsened, Wendy was with us more, as nurse and companion to her; as pupil to me. And teacher. I will never forget her kindness to my wife. Or the part she played in my recovery.

I was deep in the pit of my own evil nature. This was my dark night of the soul. I had been close to the Light; and blind to the flaws in my nature. I had believed I was Chosen. And at the point of victory I fell. "The radiance of Paradise alternates with deep and dreadful night." I was in that deep and dreadful night; and believed there was no way out. Paradise was no more than a pinprick of light at the end of a tunnel I would never pass through. How could I move in any direction but down while my black hatred of my son Alfred endured? This is no rhetorical question. It fixes me in my location at that time.

The economic depression came. I wrote. I lectured. I left my small mark on events. Then Edie died. And her death moved me a painful step on my journey. I began to pass along the tunnel, for I knew that in the light beyond its end she had her new being. I worked towards it.

Wendy was my companion on the way. One evening she read me Whitman's *Song of Myself*. It was well known to me. But it had been growing on both of us that Whitman was a key figure, and the *Song* a key text. It was a winter night. A fire was burning in the study grate. In another part of the house Robert was sleeping, worn out by his day's labour. Wendy had put on her coat to go home, and come to my side to say goodnight to me. I was depressed. Our talk that night had led nowhere. And yet I had in my mind the Persian text: *Whatever road I take joins the highway that leads to Thee.* She picked up *Leaves of Grass.* She began to read. From habit more than interest I turned my trumpet towards her.

". . . What I assume you shall assume, For every atom belonging to me as good belongs to you."

I accepted that, and I began to listen. And for the first time began to see a pattern. Wendy read the *Song* from beginning to end. It took an hour. And then, as if she understood her part ended there, went home. I sat and worked on it. I understood for the first time that in the mystical state all was not joy, that dark and light were complementary parts.

My *Commentary on "The Song of Myself"* was the last of my publications. It came out as a pamphlet in 1939. I paid its way. And to my knowledge, not a soul noticed it. There are two copies in the General Assembly Library and two in the Turnbull Library. And three hundred more in a cardboard box under the house. It is not important. I wrote the piece for Wendy and myself. Its twenty pages are the fruit of three years' thought and conversation. Briefly, the *Song* is the record of Whitman's entry into, journey through, and emergence from the mystical state. I broke the poem into five parts: Awakening to self; Purification of self; Illumination; Dark night of the soul; Union. And these into smaller parts. Union for example is twofold, made up of faith/love on the one hand and perception on the other. I will not go into it. As I have said, the pamphlets are in the libraries and can be consulted there. And I have three hundred copies under the house. They are only sixpence each. What I must say is that the lessons of those dreadful sections 33–37 were the hardest to learn. Many a time, beaten, I cried with the poet, "Enough! enough! enough!" But I learned. In the end I was able to say along with him, "Do you see O my brothers and sisters? It is not chaos or death—it is form, union, plan—it is eternal life—it is Happiness."

As I sent my *Commentary* off to the printer I knew that I would not re-enter the Light. I was too old, my imperfections lay heavily upon me. But I had gained three things: a knowledge and acceptance of my nature; a knowledge of the Cosmic order; and a fixed memory of my glimpse of God. Like Bucke's memory of the full experience, it would stay with me even in times of depression. It was, to use Wendy's later phrase, empirical data. And grasping it, and grasping my self, I had made the next-to-last of my journeys. Death remained.

Wendy was forty years younger. Wendy went on.

97 When the Second War started I wrote to Dan Peabody, and to Semple and Webb, reminding them of their stand against conscription in the first. I hoped they would make that stand again now they were in power. But it was just because of their power my hope was not real. Power had moved them beyond idealism. Sadly I watched the old men bury the young.

And the Hitler-Stalin pact? It did not surprise me. The Bolsheviks were men. Because I knew the way to super-humanity was spiritual I could not believe they had changed their essential natures. Many believed it. The last letter I had from Andrew Collie was full of bitterness at my defection. I had said to him that the stories coming out of Russia—of labour camps and blood purges and secret police—had the ring of truth about them. A human sound. Andrew damned me for a traitor. He had religion. It was complete not only with doctrine and prophecy but with revelation. "I have seen the future and it works." Faith carried him over inconsistencies. I wrote to him again, several times. I told him I still believed in communism, that it was the only just system, but that men being men it would be corrupted where it appeared; that man's salvation lay in another direction. I did not deny that we must keep on trying to improve our social organization—we must try for justice and equality. Unless we had a passion for justice we were less than men. But until we were more—until we achieved a higher consciousness—we would never inhabit Jerusalem. I should have known better than to use that language to Andrew. He never replied.

I was losing Wendy too. She wanted to marry me. I had overlooked a whole side of her nature. She wanted to bear my child. When she had taken us to the point of speaking of it, and I had told her why it could not be, there was nothing for her to do but pass out of my life.

She owned a little car and into it she packed her few belongings—her clothes, her books. She was going back to the town she had grown up in. When she had locked the cottage she brought me the key.

I was in the summer-house. Meg's children played on the lawn—a game full of shooting and falling down dead. (The kaleidoscope had been given another shake. Fergus had shocked us all by enlisting; and Meg and her children had come to live at Peacehaven.) Lifting my trumpet, I heard their agonized cries. Wendy walked by them with a middle-aged tread. She put the key on the tea-tree table in front of me.

"There you are, George. I've given the place a scrub. There's no brown paper this time."

"Thank you, my dear."

"Do you know yet who's going in?"

"Bluey and his friend."

"That'll be a change. Is he still scared of hell?"

"You're not interested in Bluey. Talk about yourself."

"I've finished with myself. That self, anyway. I'll make another." She grimaced. "Spinster living with her widowed mother. Not an original role."

"It's one you'll play well, my dear."

She narrowed her eyes angrily. But these days she was not able to keep her feelings going. "You'll write to me?"

"Of course."

"And if you want me to come back I'll come back."

"I'd like you to visit me, Wendy."

"No. Not for a long while anyway."

"My dear—"

"I'll come back as your wife, George, no other way. Or as your mistress." The word made her blush. She took my notebook and wrote: *We have been part of each other in many lives.* She looked at it. It seemed to surprise her. She wrote: *I love you. Our place is together.*

"My dear, I love you too. You are my child."

She looked at me as if she meant to strike me.

"The time has gone by when anything more would be proper."

"Proper!"

It did seem a mean little word. But I had meant it in a larger sense. Marriage would return me to a world I had left, would re-open rooms that were closed. Besides, I did not love her in that way. I loved only Edie. Wendy I loved as my child.

I tried to explain. (I had explained before.) She did not listen. She sank again into that half-alive state that enabled her to keep going. Now and then she looked at what she had written. It still seemed to surprise her.

After we had been silent for a time I gave her the present I had chosen for her: my copy of *Leaves of Grass*. She thanked me. She kissed me on the forehead and went away. Through the trees I saw her little car flickering off down the road.

I did not see her again for many years. She was a sexless being when she came back. Her body had thickened, a dropsical complaint had swollen her legs. And her beliefs had changed. She was reading books, following gurus, I had never heard of. It all seemed proper (again in a special sense). For the world had changed: mine and everyone's. Millions of people had died: been burned and blown up and bayoneted and gassed in specially constructed chambers. More than one sort of bomb had fallen, more than one sort of mushroom cloud hung over man.

I no longer knew all my children. Oliver was a judge, had sentenced men to life imprisonment. Felicity was Catholic. Esther, in her own words, had grown "hard as nails" (while Fred swelled with money like a toad). And Robert had gone to live on Parminter's farm.

98 Meg was the only one I knew. Fergus, puzzled by his motives, had gone off to camp; to Crete, Egypt, Italy. He was guilty as he left and so he blustered, "Somebody's got to stop him," etc. I believe he saw his chance to step out of a role—husband, father, workman—that had him turning like a zoo animal in a cage. The war finished that, remade him. He came back tough, diminished, free—a freed carnivore.

Meg and her children lived out the years of his absence with me. For Meg coming back to Peacehaven was coming home. The pain of Fergus's desertion never left her. But the old house, her old room, the creek, the orchard, acted as a balm. And caring for Robert pleased her. She added him to her children; almost, I think, loved him equally. When he was sent to an objectors' camp she behaved as though he had died. I tried to tell her he was well off—told her how in the First War objectors had been sent to the front and tied to posts in no-man's land. Tortured, in fact. But she continued to mourn him. She knew better than I the effect imprisonment would have on him. At the end of it he went to Parminter's farm, he left the world; and Meg was not surprised. Nor did she grieve again. She had got over that.

We lived at Peacehaven as though on an island. Few people came to see us. Willis and Mirth and their children came. Esther came (Fred was busy). Sometimes she brought Emerson with her, sometimes an American marine or soldier. Bluey puffed up almost every day, tormented by his fear of hell. (Sutton peered through the trees.) And the Butterses walked over in the weekends. But they were remote. Their son had joined the Air Force and died in a training crash. They were practising spiritualism and had succeeded in speaking with him. Their visits were charitable.

I spent much of my time with Meg's son Raymond. He was the quietest, the most thoughtful of the three. Rebecca was a tomboy, a noisy affectionate child, who would not let herself be loved. Robert, or Bobby as he came to be called, was a ruffian, an intelligent oaf; he was gang-leader, girl-chaser, jaw-puncher, eel-catcher—a manly fellow who knew the high value placed on his qualities, but knew he could not fool me. He kept out of my way. And he tortured his brother with the Chinese burn for, as he put it, "sliming round the old geezer all the time". But Raymond was not after anything Bobby would value. He was after my talk. For him being entertained meant having his understanding increased and his emotions stirred. So I told him about his grandmother and of our days on the Coast, of the Gardners and Joseph Sullivan and Johnny Potter. I told him about my friends Edward Cryer and John Jepson; about my trial for heresy, my street corner preaching, the Plumb family in California, my days in Lyttelton jail. In this way my history became part of his; and history slid into myth. He will carry it with him forever, an extra chamber in his mind. I did a good job there. It was though more than a job. I loved the boy. And though he has put himself at a distance now—girl-chaser himself—and chooses to play draughts with me more often than talk, I love him still. I am pleased to have given him something that increases him.

But I began with Meg. The child I loved best. Poor Meg. As her children grew she decreased. She put herself into them and got little back, and though she claimed to see this as natural she began to look on herself as nearing the end of her effective life. She tried to discover resources in herself, invent selfish roles. She tried to write, tried to paint; but found that cooking and sewing were all she was good for. She did not pity herself. But she came to pity her children, and love them desperately. She took her unhappiness as general evidence.

I disappointed her. She looked on my concerns as an elaborate game. She could not see their connection with her life, and I could not show her. Hers is the artist's type of mind, not the philosopher's or mystic's. She sees particular things, the simplest and hardest seeing to accomplish. (I have never managed it.) And I think takes the next step, transforms them imaginatively. But this is not the whole creative act. There is a final connection she never makes. She fails to find language. Poet *manqué*. She was close to being great—the closest of my children. As it is her life is a series of poems that never get written.

She survives. She cries on my shoulder from time to time, but accepts her condition; the fact that she and Fergus are strangers to each other, that her children are "beings from Mars". And that she and I fail to meet. These things wound her, make her cry inwardly. But this she accepts as part of the natural order; believes it the same for everyone.

I have not given up hope for her. She comes very close, close to expressing it. One day the wall may go down.

99 Felicity put her head round the study door. "Time we were off, dad." Wendy said goodbye. I wished her pleasant dreams. But she's a serious girl. She does not understand jokes. I kissed her cheek. She has the look of a person setting off on a long journey.

When she had gone I picked up my walking stick and trumpet. The stick is a present from Bluey. Its handle is made in the form of a swan's head with two black beads for eyes. I don't know why I took it. I'm steady on my feet. When I got out to the yard I found I was to travel in Emerson's car. Meg was going with Felicity. I made the Sundowner of the Skies promise to drive slowly. No aerobatics, I said. But the drive was a nightmare. We left the girls far behind. The winding road up the valley was a challenge to Emerson: he was incapable of not responding. Dust sprang up like a smoke-screen behind us. We whistled over bridges, slid round corners sideways, clipped bracken fronds that hung down from the banks. If I'd known which of the knobs to push to stop the car I'd have pushed it. Instead I closed my eyes, even though it made me feel sick. I have claimed to understand Emerson. On that ride I lost my understanding. He pulled up at Willis's gate. "There you are, dad. A nice steady drive." At least that's what I think he said. I was too busy getting out of the car to take much notice.

"I'll walk up," I said.

"It's a quarter of a mile."

"I'll walk up." I was grateful for my stick. (If he'd tried to make me get back in I'd have attacked him with it.)

He grinned. "O.K., dad." He opened the gate and sped away up the drive.

To avoid his dust I retreated into the trees. How grateful I was for their stillness. Orchards are part of the world I understand. I struck in deeper. The leaves lost their coating of dust and became glossy green. Weeds lapped about my knees. The internal combustion engine seemed centuries away. I sat down beneath a tree whose fruit had been left to ripen. The golden orbs hung like suns above my head. I put my stick and trumpet in the grass and lay back on a natural springy pillow. Shortly we would be driving to Esther's house, and there I would meet Alfred. In the meantime how pleasant just to loaf in the grass—"loafe and invite my Soul". Well, that was Whitman, and I a lesser being. And Alfred's path curved towards mine with a geometrical, a terrifying beauty. But I took this moment like a gift. A moment lying outside time and care. I closed my eyes. I folded my hands on my chest. The old are great improvisers. I went to sleep.

When I woke Willis was sitting beside me. He was smoking his pipe and smiling to himself. On his naked arm I saw the tattoo of a heart transfixed by an arrow. Underneath was printed *Rosy*.

He saw me looking at it and said a name I think was Liverpool. He knocked his pipe out (on his wooden leg) and stuck it in his belt like a cowboy's six-shooter.

"Come on, dad. The girls are getting stroppy."

He helped me up. We walked through the trees to the house, which is no more than a collection of railway huts joined to an old tramcar. It grew as Willis's family grew. Mirth has painted sunflowers on the doors. Mirth herself was sitting on the lawn with Emerson, Felicity and Meg. My girls were ladies beside her. I make no judgement. But Mirth was an extraordinary figure: straw-hatted, straw-haired, roly-poly and brown as boot polish, clad in the briefest of shorts (a man's shorts with their top button burst open) and a ragged blouse fixed with a pin in the middle.

The pin was a concession to my coming. Indeed the blouse might have been. I could count myself lucky not to have found her naked. Meg and Felicity cried out together, "There you are, dad. Where have you been?" They claim to like Mirth but I thought their behaviour strained.

I sat down. Mirth took my hand. "I'll get some tea in a minute, George. Unless you'd like something stronger?"

"Tea will be fine." I had wanted as wives for my sons women who were beautiful, intelligent, fine-souled, spirited—rather like the young Felicity. But only Oliver and Willis had married (I could not count Robert as married), and I had as daughters-in-law Beatrice and Mirth. Mirth I would not swap for one of those imaginary creatures. She had the gift of making people happy. I had left that quality out of the ideal wives.

She made tea and brought it out on a tray. We talked for half an hour. Willis told us yarns—Rosy, Ingrid, Sue—while Mirth smiled resignedly. Felicity kept glancing at her watch, but Meg began to relax. Perhaps it was the sun, perhaps the air of contentment Mirth and Willis gave off. She lay down and closed her eyes; opened them again only when Willis said, "Well, dad, so you're going to see our brother?"

"I am," I said. "Everybody seems to disapprove."

"I think it's a good idea."

"I don't disapprove," Felicity cried. "What I don't like is the casual way you're doing it."

They debated that. I took no part. I put my trumpet down and enjoyed the sun. Mirth took no part either. Whenever I caught her eye she smiled at me. Willis was lucky to find this woman, I thought. She had left behind two grown-up children, an important husband, money; and built a home with sunflowers on the door. Her second family (she had borne sons and daughters until she was fifty) ran in the trees like dryads, fauns. She did not worry how they would fit into the world. She was not clever. My daughters have pointed out to her the damage she may do. But Mirth has knowledge from another source. She has instinctive wisdom. Her children are happier than Meg's and Felicity's.

I drank my tea; and looked at my watch; and saw it was time

to go. Mirth helped me to my feet. The others had reached no
agreement. Emerson was looking embarrassed and Meg distressed.
Felicity had a steely gleam in her eye. Only Willis could muster up
a smile. He put me into Felicity's car, lifting in my feet as though
they were a separate item.

"There you are, dad. Comfortable?"

"Thank you Willis. Is there any message I can give Alfred for
you?"

"No. No need. I see him all the time. He comes up here."

"He does?"

"Sure, dad. He's my brother. Pansy or not."

I have seen myself as the centre of the universe, around which
everything revolves. My children surprise me with their
independent lives. I held Willis's hand for a moment. I remembered
I had told him nothing of Robert.

Emerson came to say goodbye. He was staying for tea.
"Emerson," I said, "tell Felicity to drive slowly, will you?"

"Sure, dad," he grinned.

We drove away. I looked at Willis and Mirth out the back
window: the peg-legged sailor and his fat old wife. One at least of
my children has built his Jerusalem.

100 "He hasn't come yet," Esther said. "In fact I'm not
sure he will."

She took us into a sitting-room. "Who'd like
something to drink? Dally plonk."

"Me," Felicity said; and Meg nodded too.

"How about you, dad? You can't be a wowser all your life."

"No thank you, Esther. I'll just sit here and rest." And to
make sure I would not be talked at I put my trumpet on the floor.
The girls walked about. They could not be still. I watched them
with sadness and love and amusement. Each had a glass of purple
drink in her fist. They traversed the room as if in a dance. Esther
turned. So did Felicity. And Meg. Felicity took out a cigarette.

Esther lit up too. And Meg. One swallowed. They all swallowed. And puffed. They blew out clouds of blue smoke. Life had taught them no tranquillity.

I was calm. I did not congratulate myself. I was old and tired. I had learned not to waste emotion.

When they rushed to the window I guessed they had heard Alfred's car.

101 "Hello, Alfred," I said.
He made no reply. He did not even look towards my chair. With a smile he closed on Felicity and kissed her cheek. "You're looking well. How's Max?" More coolly he kissed Meg. He did not ask after Fergus. Fergus, I knew, had always refused to meet him.

Then he sat down on the sofa. Still he did not look at me. "Well Sis, I'll have a glass of that purple death."

I took this in through my trumpet. He had a clear reedy voice; a voice I remembered; but ragged now and with a damaged edge. I put it down to alcohol more than the years. Alcohol was the fuel that kept him going—alcohol, memories, hatred. In spite of his friendliness to the girls that emotion radiated from him. I felt it in my chair across the room. I watched his ruined Shelleyan head turn slowly in my direction. His red-brown curls were gone: he was bald. He had a wet lower lip the colour of raspberries, and baggy cheeks, and red eyelids. His eyes were the yellow of a healing bruise, and whitish-blue, and blind with water not made up of tears. They stopped short of me, went back to Esther, who brought him a glass of wine and said something I did not hear. Alfred did not hear either. He cupped his hand behind his ear. At this I felt a shock of pain at our common blood, and terror at the blind progressions of life. I had given Alfred my deafness.

I said, "I'd like to talk to Alfred alone."

The girls began to move. But he stopped them with a lifting of his hand; then looked at me for the first time. "Who are you?

I don't know you. Have we got anything to say? Esther—" he turned to her—"who is this man? Introduce us please."

"Go on, Esther," I said.

"Oh, Alfred . . ."

"Well, he looks familiar."

"Go on," I said. "He's got the right to this."

But Esther could not play the game. She splashed more wine in her glass.

Alfred smiled. "It seems we'll have to introduce ourselves. I'm Alfred Hamer. I lost my parents when I was quite young." I saw he would not be able to keep it up. He was trembling. Twenty years of pain and hatred found no expression in elaborate games.

"Alfred," I said, "I don't know why I wanted to see you. If it's a mistake forgive me please. But I saw your brother Robert a few weeks ago. And when I'd seen him I knew I had to see you. He healed my hand." I held it up. The connections were clear to me. I did not expect him to see them. Like Wendy he had looked on Robert as an inferior being. And now he cried, "Robert. My half-wit brother. How is he? Still shovelling dung?"

"He could help you, Alfred. You should go and see him."

He turned to his sisters. "Who is this man? Who is he? Telling me what to do?"

"Dad, you can see it's no good going on with this," Felicity said.

"Do you still write poetry, Alfred?"

"Poetry! My God! My God! Do you hear him?"

"Alfred—"

"He thinks he can turn this into a social chat."

"It's more than that. I'm trying to find out who you are."

"Why? Why should you care?"

"I don't know. I behaved very badly to you. If there's any way I can help you now—"

"My God! The stupidity. The blind arrogance. Help me! The only way you can help me is by jumping off a cliff."

"Alfred," Meg cried loudly.

"Help me! You heard him. After treating me as though I was some sort of maggot or slug. And pretending I was dead for

251

twenty years. And John Willis too. John used to be his friend and he treated him like filth."

"Alfred, I'm sorry," I said. "I can't do anything about that now—"

"John was a good man."

"I know—"

"You don't know anything. You have the nerve to offer help to me. After what you've done. Well I don't need your help. I've got plenty of money. More money than you've ever seen. And more friends too. No shortage of friends, thank you."

He told me then that Edie had hated me. That was a lie. I watched him invent it. When he saw it fail he told me in gutter language what he and John Willis had done together, under my roof, and in the orchard at Peacehaven. I had seen some of it. The rest seemed to follow. But it upset me only to hear his rage, his rage to crush me. I would not hold myself responsible for it, but neither could I say I was not responsible.

When it was over he sat trembling. Meg had gone out with her hand over her face. Felicity stood white-faced in a corner. Esther poured him another glass of wine. She opened his hand and put it in. She said, "Don't talk like that in my house again."

"I'm sorry. I'm sorry."

"And dad, you go home."

"All right." I stood up.

"No," Alfred cried, "he's not getting away as easy as that."

"Alfred," I said, "I'm sorry I've brought on this. I didn't want to go back into the past. That's done with. I just wanted to tell you about Robert. He touched my hand and now it's healed up. Why don't you go and see Robert?"

"To stop me being a homosexual?"

"I didn't say that."

"What then?" And suddenly he cried out in a frenzy, "Stop pointing that thing at me," and he came at me three steps and smacked his open hand against my trumpet. It flew out of my grasp and sailed across the room. He ran after it, grabbed it like a club and battered it on the wall. Chips of black horn flew about the room. Esther tried to hold his arm. Deaf now, I could not hear their cries. But Meg rushed in again and ran to me. Felicity helped Esther. They wrestled Alfred's arm down to his side. They made him drop the ruined trumpet. Then they got him out of the room into Esther's bedroom. Esther stayed with him. Felicity came back. She bullied Meg and me out to the car, knocking us along with thrusts of her arms. On the drive home she raged at me. Her eyes were rarely on the road. I heard nothing. Being without my trumpet was an advantage. I knew I would not buy another one.

Halfway home Meg had her sister stop the car. She came into the back and held my hand.

102 Edward Cryer said to me, "When morality triumphs nasty things happen." He was quoting from somewhere. I thought of Alfred, the clever boy, the happy youth. Morality triumphed. But also something more. I can only call it evil. It was not all mine. John Willis was our guest, he corrupted our son. But then I slew my son. Yes, evil worked in me. I had thought of him as mine, as my achievement. His glory belonged to me. So when he showed his nature I destroyed him. This brings the event too much into the open. It took place in deep shadow. But I saw it clearly as I rode in Felicity's car. And did not judge myself. The time for judgements had gone.

Meg's hand lay in mind. I thanked her for its warmth. And closing my eyes found myself saying Edwin Markham's line: *Sorrows come To stretch out spaces in the heart for joy.* I had taken comfort from it many times. But no, not now—now it would not do. Alfred's ruined life, his ruined unhappy face: that was more than a sorrow.

Felicity brought the car to a halt in the yard—a skidding halt. I got out and walked away from the house. I told the girls I was going into the orchard. Meg made a move to follow me, but I waved her away with my swan-stick. I walked over the bridge and into the trees. Beyond the fence, shining in the sun, was the Butters's mansion. Merle and Graydon were standing in the garden hand in hand. They did not see me go by. Perhaps they were in a state of Wordsworthian—Plumbian they would call it—bliss. They caused me no amusement, no envy. I thanked them for their thirty years of kindness.

When I had climbed the little hill and looked down into the hollow I knew I was near my death. It would not keep me long. The rotting trunk poked up through the bracken. On that evening twenty years ago I had sent Robert out with an axe to chop the quince tree down. He had been unwilling, then defiant; but had gone when I raised my hand. He did not speak to me for several days. Robert, I thought, Robert. I prayed that Alfred would go to him. Robert would cure Alfred of his rage. But I knew they would never meet. Alfred would go down to a bitter death. His hatred of me was so great I did not believe he would survive me long.

I walked back through the trees and on to the bridge. I found a few crumbs of bread in my pocket and scattered them on the water. After a little while an eel floated up. I saw why people found them sinister. Dead mouth, snake's body. And they rose from dark holes in the slime. But I did not pursue it. They were God's creatures. And looking for symbols a game.

I went round the lawn, keeping by the creek, and peered through the trees at Bluey's cottage. Like the Butters's house it glowed in the sun. Bluey was sitting in his cane chair asleep. Something shining dangled from his hand. A rosary? He jerked awake; yawned and scratched himself; and went on with his interrupted penance. The sun shone on his sweating easy face. Sutton, black Sutton, watched from behind a bean row. He saw me, snarled. I moved away.

I could not understand life. I had, I thought, a better understanding of death. *On the earth the broken arcs; in the heaven a perfect round.* Browning: a useful poet. I went into the summer-house. "Edie," I said, "I haven't got my trumpet any more. I can't tell whether your thrush is singing or not."

Presently Raymond came down with the draughts. He set them out on the table. We played a game. I played hard. I saw no reason to let him beat me.

When I looked up Meg was in the door, smiling anxiously

and making eating movements with her hands. I jumped Raymond's last piece. I thought, I'm ready to die, or live, or understand, or love, or whatever it is. I'm glad of the good I've done, and sorry about the bad.

Meg took my hand and led me in to tea.

MEG

1 The priest phoned to tell me Sutton was dead. It was all I could do to stop myself crying, "Goody," and clapping my hands. I managed to say, "Oh, well, I'm sorry." There was a singing in me. After our long marking time we were off. When the priest hung up I telegrammed Robert: *Sutton no more. Will collect you tomorrow.* After that I was a little ashamed. Facing facts was all very well, but rejoicing in someone's death going too far. Even Sutton's.

In twenty-five years I had had only snarls from him. Memory of them brought on a stronger attack—an assault by what my father would have called Sutton's "selfhood" A blunt instrument. I retreated before it: and told myself it would not be right to hurry down to his cottage with mop and "Camfosa", and the man's body not yet trollied to the hospital morgue. An hour seemed little enough to offer one whose life had been no life, through a fault not entirely his own. In that hour I fought back fairly strongly: he was interfering between Robert and me! I was giving in to his spiteful demand! My need to get the cottage ready made me jumpy as a cat.

I gathered my things and made them ready on the back verandah: sandsoap, brush, disinfectant, half a dozen cloths, window-cleaner, all in the bucket; mop at attention by the rail, with its fringe of sun-dried white hair on its brow. No—I must avoid these fancies, Raymond says they spoil me as a writer, he calls them coy and clever and tells me I must be plain or fall into self-regard and falsity. I'll leave this one (I rather like it, that's the puzzle) as an example of what I must steer clear of. So—I sat on the verandah with my mop and watched the housewives over the creek pegging out their washing. Their children rode tricycles on the footpaths, screeching down concrete so white it hurt my eyes and braking with their feet on the sun-dried grass. One came close to the old brick bridge but I had no fear for him,

1

it's gated and padlocked on that side and carries the Council's notice warning of danger. The child urinated at the water, but missed reaching it by a good many yards. The clear rainbow of his urine sparkled in the sun. (Raymond would approve of my recording this, but object to "clear rainbow" as inaccurate. He is right. I must be careful. He would not like my seeing the concrete footpath round the turning bay as a noose, nor as my father's "perfect round" He is right again. It's a concrete path and I am not to spill my emotions over it.)

The children played and cried and fought, their mothers scolded and slapped them, cuddled them too (I must be fair), and took them in to biscuits and fizz in their own or each other's houses. Several of the young women noticed me and one or two waved. I'm not disliked, though considered odd. I waved back. I hoped none would invite me over for tea. I have little to say to them, but they miss their mothers or fathers, or their freedom, poor young things, and they pour out their sadnesses to me—and their happiness too, with a desire to fix it, I suspect, before it washes out of the bright new cloth of their married lives. (Raymond would be cross—with reason, I think.) Some of them I like. Some not. They make me feel useful for a short time.

Robert was to make me useful again. His coming down would turn my role to nurse's. I hoped our love would not suffer from it. I believed my skills of subtlety and quiet and wordless doing would prevent his taking fright and running for cover. I wondered how much of gift there was, to me, in his surrender to his illness—for his move into the cottage, into my care, was that: confession, surrender. And gift? Not in a way open to such plain statement. It was part of a natural movement in our affairs. And possibly it was a relief to him.

Dad's old clock in the hall struck the hour of eleven. It has a brassy, gonging, Eastern sound, bringing to mind eunuchs and Turkish harems, echoing marble courts, fountains, palm trees, Moorish warriors in flowing robes, triremes or asps in the bosom—depends on my mood—and its dark English appearance, antique calling-up of a mythical Home, is the least of its qualities. For me. Always that. Others feel differently. A lesson that took me far too long to learn. I mistook my recognitions for an absolute.

Anyway, eleven struck, Sutton was in the morgue, and I could scrub out his cottage.

I walked through a greasy heat filling the driveway. The hedges and shrubs and the trees by the humming creek were rank with a growth that seemed almost tropical. I have never been at home in the Northern summer, with its thick nights and its moody skies, and the biting insects that breed in its tepid swamps. I long for the clean summers of the South. But I love the spring up here, a green bold tender time before all turns to competition; to a seeking, a strangling, a rankness, a pungency—and I love those acres of ground my mother named Peacehaven; the house and gardens. They had seemed, for a time, outside the laws of this place. It was my doing, it was my seeing and blindness, which set them on the outside; and now they are subject to reality. Have been for many years. My vision was false, and I learned to see with a usual eye, and have learned much more that way, and am happier. So, with bucket clanking and mop in hand, I walked down the drive, at home on my piece of the valley, though it's not the magical home I had once made of it.

I do not want to spend my time looking back. Yet I am forced to turn there. Much has to be looked at with a cold eye, there is much to be stripped of its clothing and seen nakedly. This is a duty, and it is a need. If I am to hold myself steady in my shape, which is a sensible one, a shape that makes me useful, I must look at the person I came from. There was a girl, a sister, a wife, sentimental, tender, green, open, painfully open, closed, darkly closed. I was that woman; brought surely, unknowing, to my doom—which was to see. See life, understand circumstance, know death—to get an eyeful, as my sons would say. I have got more than that. And to understand how, must look at that girl, etc. But not yet, not yet a while. Let me set my feet on these days.

I went out the gate, along the footpath a little way, and let myself into the cottage that had been lived in by my brother Willis, by Wendy Philson, by Bluey Considine and Roger Sutton, and by Sutton alone after Bluey's death. Traces of them all remain. The hearth Willis laid about the fireplace forty years ago is there. And the name he carved in the mantelpiece, *Mirth*, can be traced with a finger under the layers of paint slapped over it. Below is a heart pierced with an arrow. Willis never grew up. Mirth was his lady-love, who became his wife, and made him happy, and gave him children, but he never abandoned with her all the paraphernalia of romantic attachment. He clings to them still, flowers and kisses, although she's a crumpled eighty and he sixty-five. It has been a happy marriage.

Wendy's traces are a few scraps of brown paper pasted in corners and behind the doors. Wendy went mad in the cottage, and pasted over the real world in order to bring an unreal one into being, where she could survive. Which she did, at a cost—and came back with many parts missing, and went on with a life of lesser madnesses. My mother scraped her paper off the walls, but missed a scrap here and there. I am moved to see them; for they bring her strongly back, my mother, who was a woman less clever than Wendy Philson but wiser by far.

Bluey. Now Bluey. The place on that morning seemed to reek of him, in spite of Sutton's long residence there. Forgotten racehorses, polished and impossibly refined, posed in dusty frames about the walls. Bluey had money on all of them, and won a bit and lost a bit. That, he used to say, was the story of his life. I took them down, found a cardboard carton and laid them in. But I could not deal with the smell so easily—the mutton-fatty smell that established itself in the cottage in Bluey's time. It will, I think, never go away. It's the smell of Bluey as much as of his food. Other people are not sensitive to it. But I knew him; better even than my father knew him, who was interested only in his mind, and better than Sutton, blinded by his need. I knew him, and loved him grudgingly; and could not abide the man. I set about the impossible task of scrubbing him out of the place.

I forgot my lunch, and would have forgotten afternoon tea if

4

the priest had not come in. I made him a cup and found a damp biscuit for him. He was the man who had helped Bluey back into his church (or is it their belief that one cannot leave it?), who had been with Sutton lately, helping him die. Father Pearce. He had come about Sutton's few belongings, which he had been told he could take for some Catholic charity or other. If I would help him sort them out he would send a van to pick them up. I was pleased to get rid of the rubbish: a broken sea-grass chair, a low-boy with jamming drawers, a tin trunk stuffed with clothes, Sutton's surgical boots—though how Father Pearce expected to get rid of those I don't know. I put out things that had been Bluey's too: the racehorse pictures, a museum of walking-sticks, his old wind-up gramophone and his collection of comic and sentimental Irish songs. We piled them outside the door.

"Did you know Mr Sutton well?" Father Pearce asked.

"Nobody did. He wouldn't let them."

"I believe I was getting to know him. He was—making progress."

I told him I was not interested in Catholic things; but asked him if the Church would bury Sutton, and what the rites would be for one who had only made progress and not reached the goal. He looked at me patiently, and changed the subject.

"Mr Sutton seemed to think you were going to evict him."

"Nonsense," I said. "He was trying to make trouble. It's typical of him."

"He wasn't an easy man."

"He lived in this place rent-free for ten years. And Bluey Considine I don't know how long before that."

"He told me he paid five pounds a week. And had to mow your lawns."

I laughed. A cripple mowing lawns. Sutton had a real gift for malicious invention. "I fed him and spring-cleaned for him. And for Bluey too. And Robert never charged them a penny rent. They had this place from the time my father died. *I* mowed *Mr Sutton's* lawn."

"Thank you."

"If you found any good in Sutton I'll be surprised."

"Oh, there was good all right. You had to dig for it."

"I'll bet."

"And Mr Considine was a good man."

"Bluey's a different kettle of fish."

The priest went away. I made myself a new cup of tea and drank it hot. My anger was for Robert. He had never had thanks for anything, only blows and sneers and contempt. That is what goodness gets. He made no complaint. But I complained for him. That black little vulture Sutton—to spread lies about him! I was glad he was dead.

I took a third cup of tea into the sun and sat on Bluey's bench by the front wall. I calmed down there. Sutton had not been all bad. That was a proposition, and I looked for something to stand it on, and found after some searching of memories (and that was a walk through dark and smelly rooms—he lived determinedly in such, with a kind of dogged glee, proving a point substantial enough to him; God knows), found before me, in the real world, his ruined garden, his strangled plantings of the spring. Cabbages on knotted legs, collapsed rows of butter beans, split radishes of turnip size, rattling corn: all awash in a sea of convolvulus. Convolvulus is the curse of this section. Willis, Wendy, Bluey-and-Sutton, fought against it over forty years. And Sutton had only given up on the day they had carted him, snarling, off to the Mater for his "man's operation" The thought of Sutton in starched sheets, catheterized, tended by nuns—hump in pillows, club foot naked of its iron boot—forced a squeak of amusement from me. Or was it pain? I could not tell. I turned my mind firmly on to his garden.

Mother held that gardening was a moral act. It's easy to see what she meant. One puts back what one has taken, hands in soil are the medium of life. So—the man who gardens cannot be all bad. But was Sutton aware, if not with his mind, then his heart? I had thought I was moving nicely to my conclusion but suddenly I was trapped in uncertainties. Capitals reared up and hung like clouds over me. I thought of my brothers and sisters in the Dark Wood: following fairy lights, sinking in swamps, lying down and dying. One had been torn apart by wild beasts.   I thought of them on the Black River, floating by; and saw them grey and blind, deaf and tongueless, in the Land of Missing. There is no help for me in this. I have these attacks. They don't come as often as they used to.

I've banished other Capitals altogether: the Plumbs as Chosen Ones, my Father as a Giant Among Men. Drunk on family, I lost all judgement. Well, it's over. I see these happy titles for the false things that they were. I'm grown up now. The Plumbs have a human shape. They're nothing special.

But I've forgotten: the Plumb Zoo. I've taken it over from Felicity, who visits us from Wellington and wanders round the cages, clucking her tongue. I use it from time to time, consciously. Sometimes I simply need to be comfortable. So I fit stylized beings in front of the real ones: a wine-gulping, poker-playing, bookie-ringing Esther; a Willis among his grapefruit, plucking yellow suns from his leafy trees; and Emerson looping the loop in his Gypsy Moth. I can even get Oliver in a cage— wigged and gowned, sitting high above the mass of men; and Felix, flashing with a cold Catholic fire. They are not real. But useful now and then.

So, on that day, I turned aside from the Land of Missing and entered the Plumb Zoo. I strolled there grinning at furry things, coloured things in cages. It's always fun. I don't stay long.

I tipped my lukewarm tea in the roots of Sutton's parsley. No, I don't stay long. Alfred is not there—not since his death. Back in the kitchen, rinsing cups, I took another look at that. I have no rest from it. I carry his death in me as part of my life. I saw him in the flowering onion weed, with his ribs splintered and his jaw broken and his mouth full of blood and urine. I looked at it, in the familiar sickness and the pain. It happened, so I looked. I failed to understand it, but that was neither here nor there, I did not expect to.

Then I dried the cups. I mopped the floor.

2 Two men came in a van and took the furniture and other rubbish away. I threw in several things at the last moment, including Sutton's mattress.

"We don't want this, lady," one of them said. He held his nose.

I asked them to drop it off at the tip for me. They were getting the other stuff free, so it was the least they could do.

When they were gone I saw I would have to bring down a new mattress from the house, and some mats and bedding, and some pictures too. I clanked my way back up the drive; put my cleaning stuff in the wash-house, and went to the kitchen. Fergus was leaning on the bench, with a glass of whisky.

"Pour you one?" he asked.

I told him Sutton was dead and put him to humping the mattress and blankets from the spare room down to the cottage. I got sheets and a pillow case, and the two pictures from Raymond's old room—the Dutch (or are they Flemish?) ones of peasants harvesting wheat and making hay—and carried them down. As I hung the pictures I saw I had made a good choice. Robert would understand them. I put one on each side of the fireplace. Fergus watched and told me when I had them straight. He was anxious to be helpful, but I put off looking at what that might mean. I sent him back to the house for mats, and made the bed while he was gone.

"Where do you want them? No, I'll do it."

He laid one beside Robert's bed—I called it Robert's now, with its fresh linen—and one in front of the hearth.

"Have you heard from him?"

"Not today."

"How do you know he's going to like living here? He hasn't seen it for more than twenty years."

"He'll like it."

"It's pretty run-down."

8

"Robert's used to run-down places."

"Did you tell him what I said?" He spoke in an off-hand way, thinking perhaps it would make me less angry if he seemed not to care.

"I told him. He wasn't interested. He's not selling this place Fergus, so you can stop thinking about it."

He shrugged. "It would have helped me out. Him too, I guess. He must be pretty broke. But O.K.," he said, seeing me move angrily, "if he doesn't want to sell he doesn't want to sell. Suits me."

That was so plainly not so, and so much in line with his other confusion, that I felt sorry for him. "Fergus," I said, "getting Robert's land wouldn't really help. It would put things off, that's all."

"You don't know."

"What would you have? Another half acre? Another two sections?"

"It would let me put a road in and open up the other four.   I'd give him a fair price."

"No, Fergus."

"It's in your interests too."

"The only thing that's in my interests is to get Robert down here so I can look after him."

"If we go broke it doesn't matter?"

"Are we going broke, Fergus?"

"We could." He forgot me. I saw his look go inward, saw him begin to pick again at that giant knot, his entanglement with his brother-in-law, Fred Meggett. I watched him for a while and wished I could help. I had known he was giving away part of himself when he went in with Fred. I had warned him. But he saw the chance of money, real money, and he betrayed himself. He is a loner; alone he knows his shape, he sees what he must do and sets about it. Fergus is a man who believes in duty. But with Fred, as a part of the Meggett empire, he lost his sight of duty, and lost sight of himself. He began to suffer from other temptations than greed.

9

"Can't you get out, Fergus?"

"I'm trying. It's not as easy as you think."

"I don't think it's easy. Not with Fred." And not, I added to myself, with the woman either. I knew she was on Fergus's mind as much as his other trouble. And I knew he both wanted more and wanted less to be out of his entanglement with her. I was less sure he would manage that escape than manage the other. He had come to believe he owed her something—and I was ready to say, if it would help him, that he owed me nothing, all he had ever owed me he had paid. But I knew it would be no help. He had his delusions, poor man, and one was that I needed him. He was quite wrong. I loved him, but did not need him any longer.

I took a last look round the cottage. It would do. The peasants with their scythes and jars of wine brought it alive. I closed and locked the door and walked with my husband up the drive to Peacehaven. I cooked us a meal and we ate it in the kitchen—tycoon and wife, eating off a wooden table among the pots and pans. It was like our meals of thirty years before, and I supposed it said something for us that we were still at home in the kitchen. Fergus had taken off his jacket and tie and rolled up his sleeves. He has the strong forearms of the young man who was able to hit a cricket ball out of the ground, and the hands of a plumber. He has a weathered face, an outdoors face, and good thick hair, nicely pepper-and-salted. It brings to mind the man behind the desk. So he belongs in two worlds, which increases his attractions one hundred percent. You cannot tell his teeth are not his own. I saw how a young woman might come to believe she loved Fergus and could not live without him.

We did not talk of her over the meal. But when we had taken our coffee out to the verandah, I said, "Have you seen Miss Not Quite today?" That was my name for her. (She's Miss Neeley.) It helped Fergus into the subject of his guilty love. He was able to suppose me fighting back, and he soothed me with accounts of how nothing happened; and soon was deep in the pleasures of talking about her—to his wife, which made it legitimate. He had to go through this, and much else, and I saw my part as

10

something I could do. I said *Miss Not Quite* though with some malice.

"Now, Meg."

"Oh, I'm not jealous. I'm interested, that's all. I like to know how office affairs are managed."

"There's no affair, I've told you."

"Just a few kisses."

He reddened. "That was a mistake. We'd both had a few." They had embraced beside her car after the office party. I had a letter from *A Friend* describing it: *Ha, ha Fergus Sole loves Beth Neeley. I saw them in the carpark, feeling each other up.* It had come in the mail between Christmas and New Year, when we had Rebecca and Tom and their children staying. I saved it till mid-January and showed it to Fergus then. He could not speak for several moments. Fergus took a blow. He's a simple man and he believes in goodness. The letter gave him glimpses of things he would rather not see. It also made him look at what he was doing. Until then he had kept it under the headings, "a bit of fun", "a bit of flirting". Those phrases rattled out when he began to talk, but he was simply getting rid of rubbish. He had to say he liked Beth Neeley much more than he should. And she liked him. But he would tell her nothing could come of it. He would tell her she should look for another job.

"You can't do that."

And of course he agreed. He has a sense of honour. If anyone should go, he should. But how could he, when he was boss of the place?

"I'll finish it, that's what I'll do. We'll just be friends."

"Will that work, Fergus?"

"Of course. Nothing's happened, Meg. It's just an infatuation." That was not his sort of word at all. Not a man's word. He kept it in his mind for a good long time as a weapon he could turn on himself.

Now, in March, he let it go. This was the new thing I had sensed in him.

"Fergus, why don't you take her away? Go away for a week.

Maybe you can work it out of your systems."

Again his face went red: this was dirty talk. He was shocked to hear it from his wife. But I had had enough of evasions, and more than enough of his proprieties; I meant to lay it down for him, make my position clear.

"Take her to a hotel. As man and wife. Then at least you'll know if you want to go on."

"You don't know what you're talking about."

"If you don't you'll just explode one day. And think of the poor girl. She must be dying of frustration."

"Stop it, Meg."

I saw I had made a mistake. I had wanted to show him I would not be hurt. I should have known he would take my flippancy for pain. I kept on for a while, but his face had taken a stubborn set and my thirty years experience of him told me I would not get anywhere. So I lit a cigarette and looked at the houses over the creek, with their lights coming on in the dusk and their front rooms turning blue from TV sets, and I wondered what it was that had happened today. More kisses perhaps, in a corridor, behind a door. That was the sort of behaviour Fergus disapproved of. He was a man for the open, for honesty. A week in a hotel really was the answer. I hoped he would see his way to it soon. It was no fun waiting.

"What happened, Fergus? Did your hands brush or something?"

"Meg, I'm sorry. It's not fair to you."

"But I'm finding it funny. Come on, tell me."

"We had a talk, that's all."

"What sort of talk?"

"About ourselves. And you."

"Me? How dare you talk about me?"

"She cares, Meg. She cares about you. She doesn't want to hurt you."

"It's a good line for her to take."

"No, Meg. You're wrong about her. She's not the sort of person you think she is."

"I've no ideas about her at all. She's just a face. A body."

"She's not. She's more than that."

"It's the first thing you see though, isn't it?"

Simply in talking to her Fergus had found himself involved in sex. It unbalanced him, poor man. He had had his diet of me for thirty-five years and I'm thin gruel. Beth Neeley was apples, peaches, she was roast beef and red wine. Fergus had never been at a feast before. Or, I should say, been so near a feast—so far he had not had a bite—well, no more than a nibble. And thinking thus, elaborating a fancy, I wanted that food for him. I wanted him to have it. I almost found my own mouth watering.

"Oh Fergus, for heaven's sake stop all the talk. Take her away. Be a man for once."

I struck him sharply with that. He sees himself above all as a man—tough, decisive, a person who gets things done. He stammered in his anger, but got nothing out. The trouble is that though he is a "man"—no doubt about that—he has pockets in his mind where corrupting influences work. (1) He has a sense of honour—for that *I* admire him. (2) He has a sense of things unclean. It cripples him.

He could not admit he just wanted Beth Neeley in bed.

3 I listened to him ramble about her sentimentally. He was not himself. He believed this sort of talk was realistic, especially as it took place with his wife. It was "bringing things out in the open" I felt like telling him he was indulging in a solitary vice.

We were rescued by the arrival of Bill McBride, Fergus's accountant. Bill and Fergus and Jack Short, his lawyer, had been having meetings at our house all week. They were trying to save some of Fergus's money—my money, too. Meggett Enterprises was collapsing on itself, sucking all its parts in with a convoluted roar. And they were searching for ways of keeping

Fergus out of court. Fred was definitely going. There had been no charges laid, the police were still investigating M.E. (*Truth* had played great games with that acronym.) These things move with a dreadful slow inevitability. But we were close now to the day of arrests. Dippers-in-the-till would have bolted long ago. Not Fred. Fred was a big-time swindler, no petty thief. A police team had taken away his books, the affairs of M.E. had ground to a halt, its glossy prospectuses had been carted off in van loads to the tip, and its staff laid off, except the construction staff (Fergus's side). Fred was ruined. Shortly he would occupy a cell. But it made no difference to the way he lived. His laugh still racketed through the members' bar at Ellerslie. He led a winner back to scale now and then, and was clapped for it. People touched the cloth of his coat, hoping even now to carry some of his greatness away with them.

It was different with Fergus. Fergus was cast as the fool. He had had no idea what Fred and his smart managers were up to. That did not mean he was safe, Jack Short explained. He was head of the M.E. house construction side, and as a director was, at least nominally, a party to the consortium's money-raising activities. The thing Jack Short must demonstrate, he said, was that Fergus in practice was a field man. It would help too that he had been trying to get away from M.E. for years. The police might decide to grab just the inside boys: Fred Meggett and John Gundry, Graham Tarleton and George Sloane.

I hoped that would be the case. I did not want to see Fergus in prison. That sounds cool—but my concern for him was that he should retain his idea of himself as an honest man. He could keep it in the face of a legal judgement, and keep it in prison. But if he judged himself a thief he was lost.

Jack Short drove up and parked in the yard. He sidled by me with an embarrassed nod.

"Don't keep him too late, Jack. He needs a good night's sleep."

"Right, Meg. Right, Mrs Sole." He cannot work out whether or not he knows me socially.

14

"See if you can persuade him to take a holiday."

"He can't do that. There's too much going on."

"What he needs is a few days away with a chorus girl. Or a secretary or something."

"Ha, ha." Not a convincing laugh. In his eyes I'm another burden Fergus carries.

Well, I thought, I try. "I'll bring you a cup of tea later on."

When he had gone I turned the verandah light off and sat in darkness on my sea-grass chair, watching the goings-on in the little tongue of suburbia over the creek. (The orchard had been there. Robert had grazed his sheep under the pear trees.) When I say goings-on I mean the occasional switching off or switching on of a light, or the passing of a figure in front of a window. I mean the blue flicker of TV sets. Once though a man went out, slamming the door behind him. He drove away with a sound of tyres like a screech of pain. A few moments later his wife ran out of the house, carrying her children wrapped in blankets, one on each arm. She went two doors up the street and someone drew her in. Her house was left empty, blazing its lights over the shaven lawn and the ornamental shrubs. I knew her. She had told me only the day before how good her husband was and how the children had drawn them closer together. Perhaps it's true.

On the rise beyond the turning bay the Butters house stood on its acre of ground. A blue porch-light gleamed on the backs of half a dozen cars. Merle was holding a séance. She is the *grande dame* of Auckland spiritualist circles. Messages from the Beyond enter our world through Merle and her favourite medium, Mrs Peet. Naturally some are for me. We played a game of hide and seek. I would see her floating out from her house. She speared a finger in my direction as she bossed the driver. (A taxi for that quarter-mile trip!) It gave me time to lock my doors and curl deep in a chair. She wrote messages on a little pad and pushed them through the windows. I saw them flutter in. *Your father came through last night, Meg dear. He and Alfred are the best of friends now. He says beware of electric stoves and bottles without labels.* At first

15

I tore them up, but later I thought it would do no harm to put them with Dad's papers. (Wendy Philson goes pale when she finds them there.) After all, I owed something to Merle. She had made no complaint about losing a large sum of money in the M.E. collapse. I hoped though that the messages she was receiving tonight would not include any from my father. It disturbed my calm to have his voice, even though spurious, come fluttering like a bird through my living-room window.

At nine o'clock Wendy Philson's car turned in at our gate.

"Bother," I said. I had forgotten she was calling. She clumped up the steps on her swollen legs and sat down in the other sea-grass chair. Fergus put his head out of the study to see who it was, and went in again. He and Wendy make each other nervous. His maleness is a force she cannot ignore. There is in Wendy a deeply buried ember of sexuality and Fergus sets it glowing now and then. She hates it. She is filled with contempt for herself and puts on the hair shirt of her lost ambition—to find the Way and write wise books about it. When she speaks of things like that Fergus finds a reason to leave the room. He is no fool. He has intimations of a world beyond his own. Wendy makes him glimpse it. He does not like that. Questions and discomforts would never stop, and there's more than enough in the world he understands to keep him busy. He gets out. And he knocks Wendy down in his mind by saying that what she had really needed was a husband to look after and some kids.

Wendy, dropsical, diabetic, sighed at the pleasure of sitting down after her struggle with the verandah steps. She took out a bag of nuts and offered me one.

"No thanks." I rolled a cigarette.

"Those things are bad for you, Meg. Your father never smoked."

"It's my only vice. Are you sure you're warm enough? Are the mosquitoes biting you?"—and I went to the bathroom for some insect repellent. Wendy and I do not care for each other and we disguise it by handing small courtesies back and forth.

She rubbed the stuff on her arms and legs and dabbed some

16

on her face. Then we sat in the luminous night, conversing politely. She noticed the cars gleaming in Merle's driveway.

"What? It looks like another table-rapping night at Madame Merle's." She gave the name the full French treatment, but somehow made herself, not Merle, seem foolish. "Who goes to those things? What sort of people are taken in by it?"

"Bankers," I said, "schoolteachers, bricklayers, housewives, old maids, hospital matrons—"

"Yes, yes, you've made your point."

"Have you seen her latest book?"

"That rubbish! It's full of bad grammar. She speaks of Perfection in one sentence and misrelates a participle in the next."

"It all comes from a Japanese man."

Merle's books—there are three so far, all published by herself—are the versified thoughts of a thirteenth-century Japanese court official. He dictates them to her. I have not liked to ask how he comes to know English. Or why he leans so heavily on Kahlil Gibran. Or where he could possibly have seen pohutukawa trees in bloom. Wendy would ask, if she and Merle ever met. She would point out the bad grammar and proofreading errors. And explain Merle's motives to her.

"She's been writing bad verse all her life. She knows it's bad. And now she's found a way of putting it in print without being held responsible."

"It makes her happy."

"That's not a good enough reason."

I think it is, but I did not argue. I asked Wendy how she was getting on with her own work.

"Ah, well," she dug in her bag and brought out half a dozen of Dad's notebooks and a packet of letters. "I've brought these back. I'm ready for the next lot."

"Was there anything useful?"

"Those were his political years. Pretty much a waste of time. It's the twenties and thirties that really interest me. When it was all coming clear for him."

I smiled at that. She was getting ready to write my father's

life. It was not to be the usual sort of thing. "A spiritual biography, Meg." Mundane things would have no place: politics,
orthodox religion, domestic life. She had warned me several
times I would not figure there. I did not mind. It sounded like a
piece of fiction to me.

But Wendy was a methodical worker. Dad had left mountains of notebooks and letters. I sorted them into chronological
order after his death, and fought off Oliver and Felicity, who
wanted to carry parts of them away. If people—and that in-
cluded family—wanted to look at Dad's papers they could do it
in his study. That was my rule. I had relaxed it for Wendy. She
would not want to burn or tear or annotate or hide things away
for fifty years in cupboards. Her concern was for evidence; for
marking in my father's steps on the Way to Illumination, to that
moment of permission received to step off the Wheel and
proceed to Nirvana. (I may have mixed her terminology up, I'm
not all that interested.) But Wendy was methodical, as I've said.
She had started at the beginning and was working through to
the end. Now and then she congratulated me on the way I had
put Dad's papers in order. She regarded it as proper that one
of the great man's children should have become custodian of his
relics.

I took the notebooks and letters and went along to the study.
The three men were in a cloud of tobacco smoke, busy with their
papers on Dad's huge desk. They looked up like conspirators
when I came in. I apologized for disturbing them and told
Fergus I had come to get some notebooks for Wendy. I went at it
quickly: some inhibition prevented them from working while I
was there. The notebooks were in a glass-doored shelf. My
reflection grimaced at me as I approached. I do not like Dad's
notebooks. Filling them was a habit he had, like chewing gum.
They're fat little books, easy to handle. There are seventy-one.
Dad had bought them in dozen lots. And I had done my duty
when he died—numbered them, strengthened their spines with
tape. Today I handle them without care. I banged in Wendy's
six and pulled six out. She was up to twenty-four. I took a

blue-ribboned packet of letters from a hidden drawer in the back of the desk. "Love letters, Jack."

"Ha ha." What a nervous little man.

"Come on, Meg. We're busy," Fergus said.

"Right. I'll bring some tea in soon," and I left them in their tobacco smoke, smiled on by Dad's brass Buddha, who had been a smoker himself (thin sticks of incense). I gave Wendy the notebooks and letters.

"Ah, thank you." She took them with an air of reverence. "This looks more like it. 'He who knows God will need no priest.' That's Emerson."

"Is it?" I took little notice of her as she dipped here and there and read out quotations and gems of Plumbian wisdom. I was tired of all that. Wendy salivated like a cow. I wondered if I should mention again that Dad had written his own life. I had offered her the manuscript more than once, and seen her fingers creep on it greedily, like caterpillars. But no; she stroked and patted it but would not turn a page. He had "composed" it last, she would come to it last. It was the fabulous peak she climbed towards.

"Wendy," I said, "it's not like that. There's nothing spiritual."

She smiled at my ignorance. *She* would take the real meaning from it.

I made tea and brought her a cup and took some to the men. I was glad not to be partner in either quest.

Wendy sweetened her tea and drank it hot. She kissed my brow in a manner I thought Eastern, and drove away, treasures deep in her bag. I hoped the George Plumb she was so busy creating would be one who would keep her satisfied. If he failed her it would be the failure of the main prop of her world. But I had little fear for her. She had great cunning as well as strength of mind.

Jack Short and Bill McBride came out of the study at half past ten. They made toothy goodbyes and purred discreetly off in their fat cars. Fergus sat with me for two or three minutes. He smoked half a cigarette and stubbed it out.

"Did you get anything settled, Fergus?"

"It's a bloody mess. I can't understand how it happened."

"It'll sort itself out."

He sighed. "I suppose so. I'm off to bed. I'm bushed."

"I won't be long."

Merle's séance guests came out of her house and drove away. I watched that dark-clad lady on her porch. She seemed to be peering at me. I wondered if perhaps she had some message to bring over. But after a moment she went inside, the blue light went out, and soon her house was in darkness.

I fetched the men's cups from the study, emptied the ashtrays, opened the windows to clear the room of smoke. Then I went back and sat on the verandah for another hour. I knew I should go to bed. Tomorrow I was driving north for Robert. Getting there and bringing him back and settling him in the cottage would take the whole day. But I was not ready for sleep. The present: I was determined to live in it. But the past was demanding admittance, my deep past. Robert had been with me all through the day; and Robert was *there*. He had a dimension everyone lacked. Wendy and Merle, even poor Fergus too, were like cut-out figures from a book. Robert on that murmuring night was flesh of my flesh, bone of my bone: I sat there living over our childhood together.

Sometime, midnight said my watch, the angry husband from the house over the creek came home in his car. He searched his house, then stood on the front lawn bawling for his wife. Lights went on. Up the street a door opened and the woman came out. She went to him, bravely I thought, and coaxed him inside. The children, it seemed, would stay at the neighbour's that night. Then the lights went out again, one by one. The suburb was quiet. Only the car lights burned outside the garage. I wondered if I should ring the man and tell him. By morning his battery would be flat. But he would not thank me. And I was pleased to see this evidence of disorder, passion, of the primitive thing, burning in the darkened suburb.

I went to bed and listened to Fergus breathing heavily on his side of the room. Tomorrow morning I would go for Robert. I lay in the dark smiling about that.

4   Robert saved me from the sackman. He rode away in the sackman's cart to a dungeon where he would be kept in a cage and fattened up for breakfast. The sackman was old, the sackman was filthy. He wore a coat with the lining poking out. He had whiskers on his chin, grey and white and yellow. He made noises in his throat and spat fat gobs of phlegm into the gutters. His cart was full of lumpy sacks with captured children in them, and his horse had one white eye. His horse never ran, it walked, clump, clump, slow as an elephant, and sometimes it stopped and rested with its head hanging down and the sackman talked to himself while he waited for it to go on.

It was best to hide in a ditch when the sackman came by. The ditches on the long road home were deep and running with slime. But my brother Alfred had told me the sackman liked girls best, they tasted sweeter. If he caught one as fat as me he would eat me on the spot and spit out the bones. So I hid. I hid deep in the ditches. I crouched with my bare feet in the slime, with the hem of my dress bunched in my hand, and watched the hairy feet of the horse go by, and heard the sackman talking to himself and heard him spit and heard him make rude noises from his bottom. Then I ran home crying, and mother gave me bread and jam and told me I was a funny little thing.

One day in autumn I was close to home when I heard the slow sound of hooves and saw the sackman's cart come round the corner. I thought if I ran I would beat him to our gate, and then I knew I could not, my legs would stop moving and he would lift me into his cart and tie me in a sack with the other children. I hid in the ditch. His cart creaked up, clump went the horse and blew shudderingly, and the iron rims on the wheels cracked

21

stones and sent bits of them flying into the grass. I put my forehead on the mud wall of the ditch and closed my eyes. Under my breath I prayed, "Please God, save me." Over and over I prayed—until the sounds stopped. I felt my back go cold, and all the hair moved on my head like ants. Then the horse blew again, right over me, and I opened my eyes and saw his milky eye so close I could have touched it. Through the long grass I saw flies on his skin; and I saw flies sitting on the sackman's coat and on his beard. I saw a piece of meat stuck in his beard. He was right above me, up against the sky. There was the tall wheel, with spokes like a ladder, and the broken boards of the cart, painted green, and the black flies, warm and happy on his coat, and his face, bigger than a moon in the sky, hanging down like his horse's face—but not at me. That stopped me from screaming. Spiders and frogs in the ditch—I did not care. "Oh God save me," I prayed. The sackman laughed. He made noises in his throat, round and round, like scraping a pot, and he spat, and I heard something wet smack on the fence post behind me. "I'll skin 'im alive when I catch 'im," the sackman said. "Aarg," he said, "bustid, I'll skin 'im alive."

He was quiet. His horse swished its tail. I knew they would stay till he saw me. His head would come round like a door. He would bend down from his cart and put his arm in the ditch and lift me out and drop me in a sack and tie it up. (I did not believe he would eat me straight away.) Then he would spit and the horse would clump away. "Oh God, please save me. Oh Mummy, Mummy, please." But it was Robert who came. He came with a sound on the road—feet padding in the dust and clicking stones together like glass marbles. He looked at me in the gutter.

"She's a right 'un, ain't she?" the sackman said.

Robert touched the horse. "She only wants some grass, Meg." He tore a handful from the ditch and fed it past the horse's rubber lips and yellow teeth.

"Climb aboard, young 'un. Up you come."

Robert stepped on the wheel like a ladder. He went up in

three steps, sat down with the sackman. The horse leaned
forward and they clopped away.

I scrambled out of the ditch. I left my books and slate. I ran
home crying, into the kitchen, into Mother's skirts.

"The sackman's got him," I wept.

She wiped my face, she warmed my feet in the oven, she gave
me bread and jam, and said I was a strange little girl and Robert
was all right. Then Robert came in. He grinned at me.

"Went as far as the corner."

"How did you escape?"

"I go with him lots of times. He lets me hold the reins."

"Don't you go bothering him," Mother said.

"He taught me to say whoa."

I believed none of this. I had no need of it. I had need of the
sackman, and his lumpy sacks, and of the children he ate.
Robert had saved me. How he had done it was not something I
wondered about. Mother sent me back to the ditch for my
books. Robert came with me, throwing stones at fence posts all
the way. He jumped into the ditch, tossed up my things, and
stood there a while, letting long-legged spiders run up his arms.

I was six. He was nearly five. He saved me from the sackman
in the year the Great War started.

5 On Belinda Beach we saw a troop of soldiers singing war
songs. One of them was my brother Oliver. He looked as if
he was only moving his mouth and not saying words, but
that was because he hated people looking at him. He believed in
war. My father said so. He believed in slaughtering his fellow
man.

Oliver was in a khaki uniform and a hat with the top squeezed
in. He had come home in those clothes the day before and Father
had ordered him to leave our house, and Mother pulled him
away to change in the boys' bedroom. But Oliver shouted he was

proud to wear his country's uniform and proud to fight her
enemies. Father was a traitor, he said, and the sooner he was
locked up the better. Father rushed to his study for his cane but
Oliver climbed out the bedroom window and ran away. He did
not come back. Mother cried, and she and Felicity talked to
Father a long time in his study. Father caned Emerson that night
for saying "bum" (which was not the worst word he could say,
that would have been Hun or bayonet or Attention, stand up
straight). "Look," Emerson said, pulling his pants down in our
bedroom, "I've got a mark on my bum." Esther told on him,
and Father caned him again. Then he came into the sitting-room
and took down Oliver's photograph from the mantelpiece and
put it on the fire like a piece of wood.

On Belinda Beach we waved to Oliver. He did not wave back.
Soon he went away to camp and before long Mother told us he
had gone to the war. He was a Lieutenant. That was a French
word, Mother said. It meant a man who fills a place for somebody else. It would have been a good word if the military men
had not got hold of it.

Oliver started fighting straight away. He was in the Dar-
danelles. Felicity showed us where that was on the globe. It was
round the other side of the world. She told us secretly; Father
would not have the war talked about in our house, unless he did
it himself with his friends Mr Jepson and Mr Cryer. But I
dreamed about the war, day and night. My Turks were story-
book Turks. They wore turbans and baggy blue pants and black
moustaches and carried swords like sickles curved the wrong
way. I saw one of them hit my brother Oliver and Oliver's head
jumped from his shoulders and rolled along the ground.

My Germans, though, were real. There were no Germans in
the books I read, but pictures of them in the magazines. In an
Illustrated London News Mr Jepson brought to our house I found a
picture of a man with a nose like a snout and fat cheeks and a
bristly chin and ugly eyes. He had an iron hat on his head.
Underneath it said: *The Physiognomy of the Hun.* I asked Mother
what that meant. She told me physiognomy meant the way a

person's face was made: it showed what he was really like. She would not say the other word. But I said it to myself when I was alone, and felt myself grow hot to be using it. It made me frightened and I knew Hun was a real word whatever Father said.

The other word that frightened me was *missing*. The paper had lists of men who were missing. There were killed and wounded too, but I knew where they were, in hospital or in heaven. I wondered and wondered where the missing had gone, and what sort of world was Missing. I thought it would be grey and if you went to it you would not be able to taste anything or hear anything or see any colours, you just walked about waiting for someone to come and let you out, but nobody came.

I had a dream that Robert and I were in the vegetable garden and we heard the Germans coming. We hid under the trellis with the scarlet runner beans on it and we saw the German boots go marching by and then one German stopped and lifted up the runner beans. It was the Hun from the magazine, the one with the physiognomy. He reached down with his hands and if he caught us we would go to Missing. But I screamed and woke up and found myself sleeping on the floor in our empty house. Robert was beside me, sucking his thumb. His head was on the boards. I lifted it up with two hands like a ball and put it on the pillow. It was warm, and heavier than I had expected. I began to feel safe. I knew where all my family were. Father and Mother and Felicity were in the kitchen drinking tea and talking about tomorrow when we were leaving on the train for California. Esther and Rebecca and Alfred were over the room from me, sleeping on cushions. I saw the moonlight shine on Alfred's hair. Emerson was in the shed out the back, where he had made a bed for himself in an old seaman's hammock. Edith and Florence were staying with friends on the other side of town—in proper beds, for they were almost grown up and it would not have been right for them to sleep on the floor. Agnes was outside under the trees, saying goodbye to her sweetheart. She had been crying all day, but Felicity had told me not to be sorry for her because

Agnes was enjoying every minute of it. I did not see how that could be, but I always believed Felicity. And when Agnes came climbing in the window soon afterwards she was smiling. She saw me watching her. "Still awake, Goody two-shoes?" "Did you kiss him, Agnes?" "What do you know about kissing, little dope?" She took off her dress and put on her nightie and wriggled into her blankets. Soon she was fast asleep. So Felicity had been right. I felt very happy about it. We were all safe. I did not even mind going to California. Once or twice I had thought it might be like Missing, but if we were all together, the Plumbs, nothing bad could happen. Our father could preach peace there without being put in prison.

I began to go to sleep. My face was on a wet patch on the pillow where Robert had dribbled but I did not even mind that. I remembered I had left my blue tea-set in the hedge. I hoped somebody nice would find it. I hoped my best friend Madge would find it. I would write her a letter from California telling her where to look. I went to sleep thinking of Madge and the tea-set and kissing and how warm Robert's head had been and Emerson in his hammock, bent like a banana, and trains and boats, and the Plumbs all up on the sunny deck where the sharks could not get them.

When I woke up we all went to the station—"Keep together or you'll get left behind," Felicity cried—and we went to California. We were safe on the deck. The sharks never got us.

6 But I had been wrong about California. California was the Land of Missing. Nothing there looked right. When I talk to people about it now they say I must be making it up. Children are like weeds, they say, they grow anywhere. But in California I did not grow. Mother said I was a tree that would not transplant. Perhaps I make up a physical wasting-away—my cheeks all hollow and my bones sticking out. My skin could

not have been as white as I see it—not in the California sunshine. But inside, there is no doubt, I wasted away. I longed for Thorpe with a longing like that for food. There I was in a land all brightly coloured, a land that became for my brothers and sisters a kind of Arcadia, I saw the leafy suburbs, I saw the golden Fall, my friends at school—for I made friends—put grapes into my mouth. I swam on the warm beaches, swam in the millionaire pools. And all the time I saw Thorpe—saw grey ditches full of frogs, and saw the black pine row where goblin toadstools forced their way through needles, and saw cold willows over narrow streams. I talk of these things in an adult way. They were not cold for me then. They were not uncoloured.

There were other things too. I wrote about them passionately in my language book at school. There was the traction engine, chugging across the paddock, pulling the cookhouse behind it. Its loose belt flapped and thundered and flew round fast enough to tear our arms off. The ground shook, we felt it up to our knees. Chaff filled the air and wheat began to pour into the sacks like yellow water. We sat in the cookhouse talking to the cook. He gave us scones to eat. We asked if we could sleep in the bunk-house with him. But Felicity called us from the far-away fence. The men finished work and stopped the engine and the sun went down behind the pinerow. Our bare feet hurt as we walked home over the stubble. They stung in the tub—Robert and I back to back so we could not see each other—and stung in bed as we went to sleep. But tomorrow the engine would start chugging again and chaff would fill the air like golden rain, and the cook had said he would bake us something nobody had ever tasted before.

I wrote about the traction engine. The teacher called me out to read my story to the class. But I could not. I read a few words and I began to cry. She thought it was shyness. It was not that—it was longing, it was hunger: for the engine and the cookhouse and the cook and the stubble fields, and Felicity waving us home from the far-away fence.

I did not live in this state for the whole of our two-year stay in

California. That would not have been possible. I would not have survived. But I ached from time to time with the kind of ache one feels in a missing limb. Anything could set it off: a leaf, a footfall on a stair, the taste of a vegetable, a colour in the sky, a word in a book, a word spoken in another room that was, suddenly, not a room in Thorpe. I think I remember truly when I say I always felt myself in danger. I felt us all in danger, but Robert especially, for Robert was dearest to me, and Robert was, I knew, the one who would meet my danger and try to save me.

I have a small notebook in which I wrote at that time. I find in it a poem called *A Mother's Love*. It is dated 1917.

Silently it made it's way upon that little bed,
Silently it went to sleep just near that curly head,
A fierce-eyed poisness dreaded snake.
O mercy if that child should wake,
Or if that little arm should bend
It certainly would bring the end,
For a sleeping snake is a dangerous thing
And if wakened makes ready to use its sting.

And so it was a mother came to kiss her little son.
And so it was she crept upstairs to get that awful gun.
Some minutes passed, a rifle shot, a baby's startled cry.
That loving woman's work was done,
Yes saved was her precious son.

The danger is more convincing than the rescue. I was, I think, pleading with our parents to take us home. Robert had stopped me that day on our walk from school. He had made me stand absolutely silent on the sidewalk, listening for something—he would not tell me what. In a moment he handed me his books. I heard a rustle in the dry leaves in the gutter. It moved along and Robert followed it.

"Is it a lizard?" I whispered. There had been lizards in Thorpe.

"Shh," he said. At last he made a dive. He threw handfuls of leaves on the pavement and scattered them with his shoe. I saw a wriggling thing six inches long, earthy brown, with patches of pink on it, like sores. Robert dived after it as it squirmed away, and held it triumphantly in the air. It was a snake. He held it by the tail and it wrapped itself like rubber round his hand and opened its sharp mouth. Robert held it out for me to see. I was making little screaming noises but he told me not to be a sap. This was not a poisonous snake—and he showed me the inside of its mouth, clean as a baby's. But I screamed. I could not help myself. Snakes were from the dark, the dangerous place, they were poisonous, they killed—and I wet my pants. Robert put the snake down in the gutter. He took his books and mine and made me run home with him through the back streets so people would not see my legs were wet. He took me into the garden and made me hold my dress up while he turned the hose on me. What a sap I was, he said. He told me he knew where there were tarantula spiders, but he wouldn't show me in case I did something worse than wet my pants.

I wrote my poem that night, sitting cross-legged on my bed. The child is Robert and me both, and perhaps Alfred too, with his curly hair, but I did not show it to them, for they liked California. I showed it to Mother and she was pleased with it. She took it though as an exercise not a plea, and told me I had spelled poisonous wrong. When she showed it to Dad he wrote *Good girl, Meg* in the margin and corrected poisonous. Neither of them understood. They had their own troubles. The greatest of them was that they too were unhappy in California—but I did not know that. I did not know they were searching for ways of getting back to New Zealand.

7 I had another dream. I dreamed it often. And when I woke crying or calling out one of the others would come into my bed, Esther or Rebecca, and with them lying against me I would drift back to sleep; or Mother or Felicity would hear and come from the kitchen and sit with me, stroking my face or holding my hand and I would tell them I had had my dream, but it faded so fast I could never describe it, I would say just that it was about floating, and sinking in water, and they would stroke me kindly and say, "There Meg, there little one, it's gone now, go back to sleep," and with them sitting on the edge of my bed it was easy, that is what I would do.

Mother thought I dreamed because I was displaced, because I was the tree that would not transplant. "It's a California dream. When we go back to New Zealand it will stop." I believed her. For a wonderful thing had happened. Felicity had been charged with the message and she came to me first, sitting in the shade out in the garden reading my book. I had been sick again and was wrapped in blankets and had on my new red slippers with the blue pom-poms. I loved them so much I was certain they came from Thorpe. "Meg," she said, closing the pages, taking my hands, "what would you wish for most?" I read her as clearly as I had the print on the page, and I laughed and said, "Thorpe. We're going back."

"Not quite, little goose. But very close. We're going to Christchurch. To New Zealand."

"When?"

"Soon. As soon as Father and Mother get the money."

"Will Father be able to preach there?"

"Yes."

"Will he go to prison?"

"Probably. But you mustn't worry about that. Now, shall we tell the others?"

30

"Can I tell Robert?"

I found him and Alfred in their tree hut and I told them. I yelled it to them and their heads poked out and they looked at each other, not knowing whether to be pleased or cross, until Robert said, "Hey, we'll go on the ship again," and they yelled and thumped each other.

Felicity told my sisters and they cried. "I'll be able to go to Thorpe and get my tea-set," I said to Agnes. "Oh shut up, Goody two-shoes." She was leaving another sweetheart in the garden.

So the Plumbs got on their ship and sailed to Christchurch, and I stopped having my dream of standing on the banks of a dark river, while my dead family floated by, Mother first, and then my brothers and sisters, one by one—I reaching out my hands to catch them until I found myself in the water too and sinking down. I had it once on the ship but Mother said that was because the boys had been talking too much about U-boats. She said it would not come back any more, and it never came back.

I was happy in Christchurch. It had not been Thorpe I needed, but something in the air and in the ground. I could list a hundred particulars, I could tell of deep and instant recognitions, of things seen and touched and heard, of faces on which a nose, a mouth, sat rightly—I do not joke—of voices making just the sounds they should. But there's no way of taking the clumsiness off such declarations, so I will leave it. It was delicate and hidden, never clumsy. Mother said I started to grow again. I grew in more ways than one.

Our house in Shirley was larger than the one we had left in Thorpe, almost as large as our California house. I do not know who paid the rent, but think it was our father's friend Mr Jepson, who owned a soft-drink factory, and perhaps some others of Dad's followers, and perhaps even Grandfather Willis. We had an orchard and a rose garden and a creek with willows growing on its banks. The boys swung out on the branches over the water, and I made playhouses under them, sometimes with

31

my nearest sister Rebecca, although she was too old for that sort of thing and joined me out of kindness. For a while I watched for the yellow water snakes that had lived in the California swimming pools and watched for tarantula spiders under the rocks, but I soon got out of that. There was nothing poisonous in New Zealand. I did not feel threatened. I did not even feel threatened when Dad went to prison and people started throwing stones on our roof. They crossed to the other side of the street when they saw us coming. I did not mind. It was part of being a Plumb, and Plumbs were special.

The headmaster at school knew they were special. The day after Dad was sent to prison I saw him watching Robert and Alfred in the playground and I heard him say to the teacher next to him, "We'll have to see the others don't pick on them." When the other teacher, a returned soldier, who coughed a lot and had pains in his chest, muttered that he didn't care too much, the headmaster said, "You'll do what I say, Mr Gibbons. I'll not have any sins visited on the children here."

It was soon after that I stopped saluting the flag. The drum and fife band played, dressed in their belts and Glengarries, and the classes marched into school one by one, saluting the flag as they went. I had made up my mind to stop. It was something I could do for my father in prison, and for Mother. I had found her that morning in his study, hunched up on the footstool like a child. She was crying into her hands. So I went by the flag without saluting. Mr Gibbons's little slug moustache jumped up and down. It looked as if it was trying to get up his nose. He took me by the ear, and caught some of my hair too and gave it a painful tug. He marched me off to the headmaster's office. I waited there like Mother in the study, all alone. I was frightened when I heard the headmaster coming. He sat behind his desk and looked at me. I waited for him to get his strap from the cupboard.

"Tell me why you didn't salute the flag, Margaret."

"I don't know." That was the truth. The reason had gone away. I looked at this man with his big head and big nose and yellow stains on his teeth and knew that I would have to do what he said.

"Did Mr Gibbons hurt you?"

"He twisted my ear," and I began to cry.

The headmaster filled his pipe. "We have to make allowances for Mr Gibbons. He was badly gassed. He's very sick. But I don't want you to tell anyone that."

"All right." I didn't see how being gassed gave him the right to twist my ear and pull my hair.

"The flag means a lot to him."

"Yes."

"Is it because your father's a pacifist that you didn't salute it?"

"He doesn't believe in flags and war and I want to be on his side."

"Yes, I suppose you do.   Will you salute it tomorrow?"

"I still don't want to."

He lit his pipe and puffed a while. The room filled with smoke, like the gas that had got Mr Gibbons. It made me cough.

"Well Margaret, we'll make a bargain. When the first bell rings in the morning you go into your room and start your work. That way you'll miss assembly and you won't have to salute the flag. But you must be very quiet and you must do some work."

"Won't Mr Gibbons be cross?"

"Oh, he'll be cross all right. But you leave him to me." He smiled at me as if we had a secret. And nothing, not even Mr Gibbons, not children punching me and tipping water down my dress and knocking my lunch bag out of my hand and calling "Passifisst" at me as I walked home, could frighten me at that school any more.

Oliver came home from the war a Captain. He came to see us once then stayed away. He had a medal, which he showed us, and a wound in his leg which he would not. He said Father deserved to be where he was, and Mother told him he was in Father's house and he would please have the courtesy not to talk in that way.

"You understand he's ruined my career," Oliver shouted, but Mother said only Oliver could do that.

His visit made me unhappy. But I was inventive enough not to remain in that state. My reading showed me a way Oliver might be expelled from our family. I worked up a story in my mind: Oliver was the child of our father's enemy—one of the "wicked men" who, according to Mother, had been against him from the start of his time as a "crusader" The child was left an orphan, and our parents adopted him and brought him up a Plumb and tried to make him good—but it did not work, Oliver's bad blood was too strong and he became Father's enemy too, and worked against him. It remained for me to declare him no longer a Plumb, which I did, secretly, in my playhouse by the creek, kneeling in an Islamic pose, tinkling a little hand-bell three times and intoning words of banishment: "Out into the Darkness Oliver Plumb, we banish thee from Light." It was done, and I shivered for him, but felt very warm myself, and immensely powerful. I felt strong enough to put the world to rights with a word and make our father king. He and I would see that people were happy, for evermore. Meanwhile Oliver was gone, and although in the months that followed I saw him from time to time, in the streets of the town, even in our house, I knew that was just the wraith of him come to see what mischief it could do, for his real self had gone to the grey land of Missing and could trouble us no more. Alfred told me he had seen the wound in Oliver's leg. It was sucked-in like a mouth without any teeth. But that could not frighten me. Oliver was no more, I had seen to it. Even today Oliver does not seem quite real to me.

So our times went by. Nothing could touch us. Sometimes I was sad, but it was a pleasant sadness, for animals, for birds, like the blackbirds Robert killed and plucked and baked into a pie—which I had a small taste of. I could not swallow it. The birds had looked so sick with their feathers off. And sometimes I wept for no reason at all. It did not bother me, I felt it was special, and the tears were so warm and friendly running down my cheeks. The doctor came to look at me and said I was shooting up too fast, and he and Mother spoke privately about some other thing—I was only mildly curious. After that I had to drink water that had a few drops of iodine put in. Mother kept it in a big jug on the bench, and although I hated the taste I drank it willingly for I made of it a magical brew that only princesses drank.

I knew the 'flu would not touch us. I knew it would touch none of our family. Mother said it was the fault of the war (the dead soldiers, I heard someone say, had not been buried in time and the germs came from there), and as we had been against that it seemed to me we must be immune. Besides, I had tinkled my bell again and driven the germs away. So I watched with a kindly interest as the epidemic worked its way through our town. Two people died in our street. Every day we saw funerals and we stood silently as they went by, and the boys took off their caps, and sometimes I wept and felt the relatives must be pleased to see me weeping for them. Although we were immune we too had to walk through the tram drawn up by the shops and open our mouths for the spray the nurses squirted down your throat. It made our noses tickle and our eyes water. When we came out we pretended to be crying. We kept our S.O.S. stickers in a drawer. Robert pasted one on the lavatory door. We counted stickers in windows, but Robert always counted most because he went furthest from home. Mother could not keep him from wandering. He said he was hunting burglars.

There were a lot of burglaries, especially in the houses of rich people who had gone to stay in the country. Agnes said it wasn't fair that we weren't rich as well. She said our father was a bad man for making us suffer so much. If he really loved us he would not have gone to prison and made people talk, he would have earned us some money so we could go away and be safe from the 'flu; and she rushed away crying to her room and lay sobbing on her bed for a long time. I listened to Mother comforting her. The worst thing, it seemed, was that the girls in the embroidery shop where she worked would not sit with her in the lunch hour. Although I felt sorry for Agnes I began to wonder if she had been

adopted like Oliver, and I hoped I would not have to send her off
to the Land of Missing. But that very night Grandpa Willis
called and told us he had rented a cottage for us at New Brighton
beach. We were to go next morning and could stay until the 'flu
epidemic was over. We all shouted with delight, and Agnes
looked so pleased I knew she was one of us, so she was saved.

We sat in the parlour talking to Grandpa Willis and while we
were there the widow lady from next door ran in and said her boy
had jumped out the window and run away to the creek. He had
gone down with 'flu that day and was too hot in his bed and
wanted to get cool. We all ran out. And there the boy was,
Tommy Bracewell, lying in the creek under the willow
branches, naked and sick as Robert's plucked blackbirds, splashing up and down with his arms and looking like Tom in *The
Water Babies*. Alfred and Grandpa Willis pulled him out.
Robert helped too. They pulled him all the way back to Mrs
Bracewell's house. Tommy bit Robert's finger. He didn't mean
to, Mother explained, putting iodine on it in the kitchen. He
did it because he had fever and didn't know what he was doing.
But it seemed unfair to me, and suddenly we weren't as safe as
we had been, the 'flu had closed in. Grandpa Willis felt it too. It
was just as well we were off tomorrow, he said.

So we went to the country, like rich people. (Felicity stayed
behind to look after things. Oliver would come to be with her,
so there would be a man about the house. Esther winked at me
when Felix said that. It wasn't Oliver who would come, Esther
said, but Dan Peabody, our father's friend and a married man.
Felicity was sweet on him, and he would take the chance with all
of us gone to make her do with him the dirty things that married
people did. At least, I thought they were dirty, and thought
them made up as well, but Esther said they were fun or why
would people do them all the time. I did not listen. Felicity was
a Plumb, and not like that.) We packed our summer clothes in
suitcases and put them on the porch for Grandpa Willis to pick
up. Then we went along the street and caught the tram to New
Brighton. Seven Plumbs together: Mother and me, Agnes and

Esther and Rebecca, Alfred and Robert. The same number, I thought, as the seven little Australians from the book that had made me cry so much when I read it the week before. In the end the big sister, Judy, was crushed under a falling tree, saving the little ones. I had thought her sacrifice beautiful, and the saddest and noblest thing I had ever heard of. I shed a few tears on the tram, thinking about it, but cheered up when New Brighton came into view.

It was lovely there. There was hardly any work to do in the house, and we were able to run on the beach and the sandhills all day long. Grandpa Willis brought our groceries out to us in his trap and sometimes his son John, whom we called uncle, brought them in his motor car and took us for rides on the roads at the back of the sandhills. Grandpa was always cheerful, although he was ill and was still mourning his wife, our grandmother, but John was a gloomy man and did not talk much. I thought perhaps he had been in love and been jilted. He drove our mother out to Paparua prison on visiting days. Sometimes they took Alfred or Esther or Rebecca or picked Felicity up from town. They thought I was too young, and that suited me. I did not want to visit Paparua prison. I knew it would be—I will not say too real, but just *ordinary*. It would not be the prison I had built in my mind, with stone walls and towers and iron doors and dripping passages, and the deep cell where our father languished, chained against the wall, waiting for the day when he would come out and put the world to rights. I stayed at home with Agnes. I modelled castles and dragons in plasticine.

So my waking dream went on. I sat alone in the sandhills with my book, or I followed the shapeless marks of giant feet until they became lost in marram grass. I was lost in there too. Each hill was like the next, and it was easy to think you were in a desert, or that the little bowl you rested in was the whole of the world and outside was nothing but blue with you floating in it. Lying on my back, I watched the sky move. There was no sound, unless you counted the sea rustling away, thumping away, telling the direction home.

I found a grave in there. I thought it was a grave, but I did not dare dig it up to make sure. It was shaped in a mound and had a jam jar with red geraniums at each end. It wasn't long enough to be a grown-up's grave. I sat down by it and felt very sad and queer. Someone's child had died of 'flu, I thought, and there hadn't been enough proper people to bury her, and so her family had carried her quietly into the sandhills at night and buried her there. I was sure she was a girl like me and I wondered what it was like to be dead. I got very frightened. I listened for the sea and ran down to it and ran all the way home. I told my brothers about the grave, but when I tried to take them to it next day I couldn't find the place. Alfred said I was dreaming it because I was a dope and so romantic. He went home. But Robert and I made a new grave. We decorated it with shells and pieces of wood. "Now all you need is someone to put in it," Alfred said, when we told him.

The next day was our last at New Brighton beach. A wind from the plains lifted the sea into sharp little waves that slapped our cheeks and blinded us. We swam all morning, shrieking in the tide that lifted itself up the dry sand like a live thing to swallow the world. It swelled and grew, and frightened me and drew me in, and I saw no reason why it should stop at the sandhills or the houses, or at the city beyond, and the cathedral and the park, or stop at the hills. I would not go as far out as the others. I saw them diving like porpoises in the waves. Alfred spouted water from his mouth. "It tastes like old Meg's iodine," he yelled. I ran in to the beach and wrapped my towel round me and sheltered from the wind in the little group of Mother and Grandpa Willis and Uncle John.

"This child's cold," Mother said. "It's time we all went in." She called my brothers and sisters, and we went single file through the sandhills, like Indians, and dried ourselves in our rooms with our coloured towels, and gathered for lunch. Then I looked round and I saw one of us was missing. The world went grey, like tin. Colour went from the sky outside the window and the flowers on the table in their vase, and the food and the faces, and death came in for the Plumbs. I knew who the grave in the sandhills was for. Agnes took me by the shoulders and pushed me to the table. "Come on, dreamy," she said.

Then Mother knew what I had known. She turned from the bench where she had been cutting bread. "Where's Rebecca?" Her face was like a face in an old broken book.

We ran down to the beach. Uncle John found her in the waves. He ran in up to his waist in his Sunday clothes and carried her out and ran through the sandhills with her to the cottage and we stood and looked at her—Rebecca dead. They laid her on her face on a towel on the floor and turned her head side on and pulled her tongue out. Water ran out of her mouth. Robert gave her artificial respiration. He was the only one who knew how to do it. He knelt beside her and pressed with his thin hands on the ribs of her back, and lifted his hands away, counting one, two, three, one, two, three. More water came from her mouth. But even Robert, I knew, would not bring her back. Robert would not save the Plumbs. Presently a man came in from the cottage next door, and lifted him aside and took over from him.

I walked out of the house into the sandhills. I sat down. I did not look for the grave. I knew it was there. I did not cry. My dream had been a true one, my California dream. It had been sent to show the way things were. The Plumbs were floating by on the Black River. One by one they were sinking. Rebecca was first.

8 We had shared many things. Her dresses and dolls were handed down to me. I came to the books she had read, crossed her neat *Rebecca* from their pages and wrote *Margaret Plumb*. She told me the ones I would like. *Seven Little Australians* had been hers. She had come to me in my bed when I had bad dreams. She saw things I was able to see. Like me she drew wizards and witches, magical doors and sleeping princesses. I

loved her next to Robert. When she died I came to love Robert with a kind of desperation. I knew we were doomed.

That was long ago. Now Robert's turn was coming. I drove north for him on a summer's day. Rebecca had died, and Mother and Father had died, and Alfred had had the life kicked out of him. Agnes was dead in San Francisco, from a stroke that had come at a bridge party, just when she was on the point of slamming, her husband wrote. And now Robert, who once I had thought might save us, was entering the last few months of his life. He was fifty-four.

I hummed a tune as I drove along. I was not unhappy. Robert had taught me this. I drove through vineyards and orchards, and pine forests where the trees were of Christmas-tree size. I drove past sawmills and yellow heaps of sawdust falling into the mud of mangrove creeks. Men in black singlets stood upon the logs. I drove by the muddy harbour and through a little town, and went along a dusty road beyond the furthest houses, and there I came to Robert's iron shack. It stood in the fenced-off corner of a field where cattle grazed in the shade of manuka trees. Its corrugated walls were green and its roof tarred black. Robert's garden came up to the door. Corn stood at shoulder height. Pumpkins and marrows lay on beds of straw. The fields around were baked to a grey colour by the hard summer, but coolness seemed to rise up from the ground on Robert's section. This was no magic. I do not claim any special relationship for him with "the soil." He worked at it, that's all, and knew what it needed; so he could keep it healthy, even when sick himself. He had rain-water tanks and an artesian bore and compost bins. He collected animal manure. He left trees about his property for shade. Looking at all this, I was guilty to be taking him away.

I walked up the path and looked in at his door. "Robert." I went to his bedroom, treading softly in case he was asleep. The bed was neatly made. Folded on it was a patchwork quilt Mother had sewn thirty years before. There were squares in it from the frock I had worn at Esther's twenty-first birthday party— forget-me-nots, blue on blue—and squares of midnight serge from my Epsom Grammar gym frocks. I had given Robert the quilt to bring him back into our family. It made me smile—not convincingly: I am still prone to symbolic acts. The quilt at least kept him warm at nights. But I put aside any meaning from that, and went back to his kitchen—living-room too. I looked about in a sharp housewifely way. Although no larger than our bathroom at home, it did not seem cramped. Nothing was out of its place. On the table was a cloth embroidered with birds. (Mother's work too. Dad liked to see her making pretty things. She put useful tasks aside when he sat with her.) An easy chair stood by the range and a box of kindling wood on the hearth. Clean dishes from Robert's breakfast sparkled in a drying rack on the bench. There were books in a shelf, a calendar over the mantelpiece, with tide times pencilled on it, and on the wall by the door a hand-drawn map of the south side of the harbour, showing the creeks and mangrove swamps and shoals. Fishing grounds were cross-hatched in red pencil. It had been a good many months since he had been well enough to take his boat out fishing.

I went through the lean-to on the back of the house, past his iron bath and copper and tubs, and walked down through the garden to the orchard. Black Orpingtons scratched among the trees. They had blood-red crowns and crazy eyes: Renaissance kings. A beehive hummed, with guards darting at the door. I kept well clear of it; and startled a wild black cat, which ran away to a blackberry patch in a field. A path led to the river. I went along it through ripening fruit that banged me on the arms. He had planted sensibly: apples, peaches, plums. But here was a row of guavas, and there a persimmon tree.

When I came out by the creek I saw him sitting on his jetty. That was of his making too. It had his mark. For me jetties mean rotting piles and sun-warped planks—the romantic view. Robert's was tarred and creosoted. Its thick legs grew out of the mud like trees. A dinghy was tied at the foot of iron steps. It lay tilted on its side, lapped under half its length by rising water. Robert had named it *Susan*. No woman of that name was in his life. It was simply to Robert the sort of name one gave a boat. In the old days at Peacehaven his cow had always been Daisy and his goat Nan.

He turned when he heard my feet on the jetty deck. "Don't get up, Robert." I put my hand on his shoulder. He made a place for me and we sat with our feet dangling towards the mud.

"Good drive?" he asked.

"Not bad. What time's the tide?"

"It's half-way in. Dick'll be bringing his boat up in an hour."

"Is that the man you're letting have this place?"

"That's him. He's a good bloke."

I knew that was all I would get about Dick. It was strange with Robert, he reversed so many things. What would have come as meanness from other people emerged from him as a sign of his fullness.

"I've tidied your place up," I said. "I hope it will be all right."

"Sutton died? I got your telegram."

"Yesterday morning."

He nodded. I watched the warm salt water advance on the mud. Air bubbled out of crab holes and mud-crabs darted here and there with the sun glistening on their backs. The flanks of the river gleamed, the mangrove trees lay yellow-green, crocodile-still. As a rule I did not care for this scenery. Today I thought it beautiful. And Sutton's death seemed right, as Robert's death would be, and mine.

He had lived twelve years on this piece of land. I had been visiting him for ten. Silence was as good as conversation to us. I pulled my cardigan off and enjoyed the sun. Robert took out his handkerchief and knotted it at the corners for a hat. He was bald, as all the Plumb men were. He had the round Plumb face that even in the worldly and selfish ones appears innocent. Suffering had not taken that away. If anything his disease had made him seem stronger. It had given him a barrel chest and thickened him round the shoulders. But I had spoken its name to my doctor in Loomis and he had told me what Robert kept to

42

himself or perhaps did not know. I knew of the broken lung tissues and air rattling in the pleural sac, and of his heart swollen by the pressure and strained to the point where soon it would collapse. On the mudflats I heard a continuous crackle, a salty sound, as the tide advanced; and from Robert's chest a noise like gravel shaken in a sieve.

"Does your doctor say it's all right for you to come?"

"He thinks it's a good idea. He's written me a letter. Who is it down there now? Still Doctor Walker?"

"He died. It's a man called Webley-Brown."

"An Englishman? Is he O.K.?"

"He's not English. I suppose he can't help his name." I was moved by the way he had spoken of Doctor Walker. When Robert became an objector in the war, Walker, a fierce old gun-boat Britisher, had steamed round to Peacehaven with abuse—"worse than a rapist", "shooting would be too good", etc. Yet Robert would have gone to him now. His innocence, his acceptance, made me want to cry.

"If I put the kettle on, Robert, will you come in for some tea?" I wanted to get away by myself for a moment. But he struggled to his feet.

"It's getting hot."

We went slowly along the jetty. The dinghy *Susan* was afloat, rubbing on the piles. The water, pushing a rim of scum, eased into the roots of the mangrove trees. We walked through the orchard, Robert first, no taller than me in the bent-forward stance his illness forced on him. He picked a few late plums and offered them to me.

"Burbanks. They weren't very good this year."

"Can you really leave this, Robert?"

"Dick'll look after it. He's been helping already."

"You'll miss your grapes being ripe."

He shrugged. It meant, I think, they would ripen without him. Again I accepted it; and the guilt that had had me argue for a moment against his leaving lifted from me. The trees that had taken twelve years to grow, the grape vines over the shed and along the trellis, the fowls in their seventh or eighth generation, the sheds, the tanks, the jetty and the boat *Susan*; and the bach—he was leaving these for Sutton's smelly rooms and dusty garden (he knew, I had described them); and he shrugged at it and took it as his next step—so it became acceptable to me.

I put the kettle on and we had tea. Robert drank his in his easy chair. "I'll kill a chook for you before we go."

"Oh no, Robert."

He grinned at me. "You don't have to watch. You'd like a chook for your dinner, wouldn't you?"

I had to admit that was true, but the thought of Robert's hatchet falling on one of those beautiful red-combed birds I had seen in the orchard disturbed me terribly. So did the dreadful accident of selection. Which would it be?—its death already approaching as it scratched happily under some plum or peach tree. The others, I supposed, would squawk a bit, and then carry on with their feeding.

"There's a couple that aren't laying too well. I'll take one of those."

I looked at him sitting there, with his round face and bald head and badly-shaven chin and crooked teeth, and looked at his body, new-shapen by his disease; and told myself what I had known since my girlhood—that he had no intelligence to speak of, and little imagination, but that he was good. I had seen goodness in him, plain as blue eyes and rounded chin. (Raymond snorts at this, and uses words like quietism, passivism. "Was he driven to goodness, did it come from an inner compulsion? Seems to me it might have been the line of least resistance." He claims Alfred was the better man. "Alfred tried to help people, he didn't just take off for the bush like a hermit." He finds the very idea of Robert tiresome. When I took him with me on a visit he enjoyed the fishing, but found his uncle's simpleness a bore. *Robert*, he believes, is my creation. That's not so, but I do not argue. I look for less contentious ground, and say that what was just as impressive about Robert as his goodness was that he had known himself. But Raymond won't allow this any importance. "Oh we all get acquainted. Just by staying alive. It's the self you find that matters. Wouldn't have taken much effort for old Robert to know himself." I get angry—and grow silent. I'll do that now; and not swell Robert up with meaning. He would strut through my story like a pouter pigeon, and that is not him at all. Someone said, "I know what Time is, but I cannot tell you." That is how I am with Robert's goodness.)

Now all of this does not mean I was ready to see him cut the heads off chickens. I told him I was happy to go without. "Don't spoil your last day here by killing things, Robert."

He laughed. "All right. But Dick'll soon have them in the pot."

"Have you sold him everything?"

"I've given my boat to one of the boys down the road. He helps with the garden."

"Have you got the house sale sorted out?"

"We'll stop and see the lawyer on our way through town. Dick's got it arranged."

"What about packing?"

"I haven't got much."

"Whatever it is, we'd better get it together."

So we went about the rooms, he told me things he wanted to take, and I packed them up: his clothes in a suitcase, and mother's patchwork quilt and embroidered cloth in a cardboard box. I made him take blankets and pillows, sheets and towels— but other things (cutlery and plates and pots and pans and his hearth shovel and brush, and tools from his shed) he told me he had promised Dick. It was all in the price. I did not believe him. The real reason was that Robert placed no value on things—no, that is wrong. He felt that things belonged to places, belonged where their use had been. He had, I think, an instinct not to possess. I did not keep on at him. He was in distress from his emphysema and leaned over the table for a few moments to ease his pain. He allowed me to pack his books. That was no pleasure. Wiping the dust from them, placing them neatly in an apple box, I was a prey to emotions as different as sentimental love and bitter hatred. I had thought myself past both, long past, on a sensible ground, but here I had tears on my cheeks and the hardness of rage on my mouth. The books had been Dad's. His own were there: *The Growing Point of Truth*, *New Reasons For the Future Life*, *The World's Disease*. He was good at titles. And each had its tag of Latin, boldly pencilled at poor Robert: *Post tenebras lux* and *Tempori parendum*. They confused me too. I wanted to cry, "Onward!"; yet was saying, "Enough of this stuff, Dad, enough!" I closed the books roughly, packed them in.

"Do you ever read these, Robert?"

"I'm not much of a reader." He pushed himself up painfully from the table. "I never really knew what he was getting at."

"You became a conscientious objector."

"That was for me, not him. I'm glad it made him happy though."

"Was he happy? To see you in that place?"

"Yes. He never thought things were easy."

"Do you?"

He had himself almost straight by now. "I've never worried about it."

I opened another book. A silverfish flashed into the spine. "'To Robert. Yours to right the wrong and wrong nothing that is right.'"

"I wasn't doing that.   I don't know whether I want to take them, Meg."

"I'll have them then. I'm collecting his old stuff. Did I tell you Wendy Philson is writing his life?"

He shook his head.

"And Merle Butters is getting messages from him. From the Great Beyond."

"What does he say?"

"Oh, weed the carrots. And, love makes the world go round. It's him all right." But my bitterness was passing, and my love, and I began to be ashamed of myself. It was a long time since I had suffered an attack of that sort. I came back to normal. What

I had for my father these days was an easy love, a calm respect, an eye that made no distortions.

We carried Robert's belongings out to my car, packed them in the boot and the back seat. Then we walked to the jetty. The mudflats had gone. Green water stretched to the creek mouth. I saw small schools of sprats darting through the piles. Robert sat down, taking the slightly forward-leaning position that eased his chest. It gave him a dejected look, but I knew he was not dejected. I took my place beside him and we sat without speaking, letting the warmth touch our bones—pleasant for a few moments, but soon I had to put on my hat and Robert covered his head with his handkerchief. I heard his breath rattling, endlessly turning.

"What does the doctor say about you, Robert?"

"Just take my pills."

"Do you?"

"Yes. No trouble. I think from the way it's going I'll die about the middle of the year."

"What makes you think that?"

"Just the way it's going. It kind of grows. It's got times—and new stages. And it feels as if it'll all finish in winter."

"So," I said, "you'll have your last few months back at Peacehaven."

He nodded. "Not at the house, Meg. I want to be at the cottage."

"You'll come up for your tea? I thought we agreed."

"Yes, that's all right. But I won't be able to get there. Not always. It's getting worse pretty fast."

"Then I'll come and cook it down at your place."

We left it at that. Presently Robert said, "Here's Dick," and I saw a launch come round the farthest mangroves and head towards us.

"Who is he, Robert?"

"A retired fisherman. He lives in a little shack on the edge of town."

"I hope you're getting a good price from him."

I had my answer when Dick climbed on the jetty. There was something furtive in the way he looked at me. He was like a man who has won a lottery and is afraid it might all be a mistake. He climbed back into his launch—the most down-at-heel boat I had ever seen—and threw a fish on the jetty.

"There you are, Bob. There you are, Mrs Sole. Beauty, ain't she? Caught her out at your spot this morning, Bob."

It was a schnapper, all rosy-coloured and plump and beautiful. It must have weighed ten pounds.

"Scaled her and gutted her. Don't find them that big much more." He was trying to make Robert some return. The fish was all he could manage, and it did not seem inadequate. It made me hungry just to look at it. Robert was pleased too.

"We'll have it tonight. You can bake it, Meg."

"Stuff it with a few onions," Dick said. "She'll feed your whole family." He climbed back on the jetty, picked up the schnapper, and we walked to the house.

"You'll have a good crop off those tree tomatoes, Dick," Robert said.

"Looks like it, looks like it," Dick answered, looking uneasy.

We wrapped the fish in newspaper and stowed it in the car. Then I made lunch. I felt sorry for Dick, and was impatient with him. His smiles and silences were a poor thing for a man who, from the look of him, was used to speaking out. I was glad when the meal was over. I cleared the dishes away and started to wash them. Robert went to his chair and sat there, looking exhausted.

"Are you sure you're up to travelling today?"

"I'll be all right. I'll help you with the dishes in a minute."

"No you won't."

"I've got the thing for you," Dick said. From the window I saw him heading down to his launch. Presently he came back with a bottle of beer. He poured Robert a glass.

"Mrs Sole?"

"No thank you." But I was pleased with Dick. Robert sipped the beer and seemed to grow easy.

"How about some plums?" Dick said. He picked a bag and

48

put them on the table. He was getting lively. "Not finished yet." He winked at Robert and made another sortie down the orchard. I could not see what he was doing. I had the dishes away and was ready to leave by the time he came back. He slapped something on the table with a heavy sound. "There," he said, "a pot-roaster. Feel how heavy she is," and he dug his thumb in. It was a fowl; beheaded, gutted, plucked. "Run like a rabbit, she did. But I got her. She'll make a good couple of meals, eh Bob?"

Robert laughed: a wheezy lurching sound. "I guess his number was up, Meg."

I was furious. "Mr Webster, until Robert signs the papers this place is his. And the livestock. And the fruit. I think you could have the courtesy to ask before you touch things."

"Now, Meg. Now, Meg," Robert said. "She doesn't like killing things, Dick. She thought she'd saved old chooky here."

"I'm sorry," Dick began, but I cut him off.

"Come on, Robert. It's time we were leaving."

"We'll take the chook. Can't waste that. Thanks, Dick. I hope you didn't get one of the layers."

"She was the one you showed me. With the torn comb."

"I won't cook it, Robert."

"Yes you will, Meg. See how fat she is." He had come to the table and, like Dick, he dug his thumb in the fowl. "Get us some paper, Dick, and we'll wrap her up."

So we took it. We put it on the back seat of the car, along with the bag of plums and the hump-backed schnapper. Then Dick went off to his launch and chugged away. He would meet us in half an hour in the lawyer's office in town.

Robert got in the car. I was disturbed at his easy behaviour. I would have wandered round touching things. I started the car and drove away. At the corner he looked back—a painful turning of his misshapen torso. "She wasn't a bad little place."

I was satisfied. I am still satisfied. I have these attacks of sentimentality, and am glad to have them. It would be unnatural, I would be some sort of monster, if I had entirely put off the habit of mind that dominated my life for thirty years. I take these things as a sign of my health.

We drove along the dusty road and through the town to the wharf. Robert got out and sat on a fishing crate in a band of shade tight under a wall. I sat beside him and looked over the harbour at the hills. The water was green, a salty colour, and striped with yellow where the mudbanks lay. Soon Dick's launch came round the nearest headland and turned towards us.

"Dick's not a bad bloke," Robert said.

I did not want to talk about him. With the wide view ahead of me, the sun on the boards, the sound of gulls, I felt very peaceful. I felt my mind expand to take in the past. I thought of the years Robert had vanished from us to a community—I shall have to call it Christian—run by a crazy man called Parminter. Robert was no Christian, no believer in whatever variation Parminter taught. But he was happy on Parminter's farm. Dad had a letter from him, and went to visit him there, and said he was happy. He seemed to believe Robert's mind was healed of the wounds it had taken in his four years in the camps. So I was pleased, moderately pleased, to think of him there, living out his life. But then a letter I wrote him came back to me. Someone had written on it in a neat hand: *Gone to join his Master in the Pit.* I wrote to Parminter, asking what had happened, but had no reply. So Robert was lost again.

Now, on the wharf, I said, "You never told me why you left the farm. Parminter's place."

He shrugged. "Long time ago, Meg."

"What sort of man was Parminter?"

"He was mad."

"Dad said you liked it there."

"It was all right."

"And you had a wife?"

"I just lived with her, that's all."

We had had this conversation before, and got no further. I believed I was going to get no further that day. I sighed, but was not too discouraged. Then Robert surprised me by saying, "They stopped talking to me. Even Betty stopped. They made her move out. So I packed up and got out of there."

"Betty was your wife?"

He nodded.

"Why did they stop talking to you?"

"Money."

I did not understand.

"It was when Dad died. He left me the cottage. When I told Tom Parminter, he wanted me to sell it and put the money in the farm. Everything belonged to us all, he said. But I had a letter from Bluey Considine asking if he could stay on there. I told him he could have it without any rent. And that's what I told Tom." Robert grinned. "He said I was the Anti-Christ."

"So you left?"

"After they stopped talking. More than two weeks Meg, and not one of them said a word to me. I tried to get to Betty to see if she'd come but they locked her up. And then Tom started saying he could see my cloven hoof. So I left that night. It was too crazy for me."

"And you came up here?"

"Wandered around a bit. Then I found this place."

That was his life, these were the places of his life: Peacehaven, then the camps, Parminter's farm, his bach by the creek (Dick's place now), and Peacehaven again, or at least its fringes. Until he died. I had no doubt that would come in the winter. I looked calmly at it all. I did not see that his life should be called a failure, as Oliver and Felicity call it.

On the other hand I did not see why I should be happy with all he did. In the solicitor's office I could not keep quiet. I saw the price he was asking Dick for his property.

"Are you crazy, Robert? It must be worth three times that much."

"It's the price I paid. I told Dick he could have it for what I paid."

"But what about your improvements? You told me yourself it was falling down when you bought it."

"I don't want any profits."

"It's not a question of profits, it's a question of what it's worth. Property values have gone up three or four times. You ask Fergus, he'll tell you."

"Meg—"

"I'm not going to stand here and see you cheated."

The solicitor made an angry sound. Dick said, "Nobody's cheating him, Mrs Sole. I've told him all of this a dozen times."

"I wonder."

He looked miserable, and I understood a future he had dreamed of was slipping away. And suddenly I had had enough of my anger and talk of money. Robert would be dead in the winter. What he was getting would keep him very comfortably till then.

"I'm sorry. I didn't mean that."

"Yes, Meg, you keep out of it. We've got an agreement and that's what I'm going to sign. Now," he said to the lawyer, "where do I do it?" He put his name on the paper and that was that. He grinned at me. He knew I was ashamed of myself.

We said goodbye. Dick got into his launch, and Robert and I in the car. I drove south, through the forests and farms, and came to Peacehaven.

The journey exhausted Robert. I made him lie down while I unpacked. Then I went up to the house and baked the schnapper. Robert was not well enough to come up. I took some to him in a covered dish.

The next day he felt better. He was able to come up. I roasted the fowl.

9 Robert looked at the garden and shook his head. There was little he could do with it. He dug a small patch out the back and put some seeds in. I tried to burn the convolvulus he had weeded out but it made a thick white smoke that set us coughing. I had to walk him up the road to get away from it.

The doctor called and spent half an hour with him. After-wards we talked out by his car.

"He'll need a lot of care. He'd be better staying with you."

"He won't do that."

"It's got to the point where he's in a lot of discomfort. He's finding it difficult to breathe."

"Can't you give him something?"

"I've given him what I can. It's not much help. I'd be happier if someone was in the house."

"I'll shift down."

"Yes. Soon, I think. I suppose we can't talk him into going to hospital?"

"No."

"That's what I thought." He drove away and I went in to see Robert. He was resting on the sofa.

"Seems to know what he's doing," Robert said.

"Did he leave a prescription?"

"Here. I wonder why he calls himself Webley-Brown." He was as near to being offended as I had ever seen him.

Later in the day we walked in the grounds of Peacehaven. We went by the ruins of the summer-house and round the edge of the lawn till we came to the bridge.

"It's not safe, Robert."

"Looks sound enough to me." He went on to it and looked at the water. "I wonder if there are still any eels."

"I think the boys from the houses have caught them all. Sutton used to fish for eels. It's a long time since I saw him catch any though."

"What did he do with them?"

"Bluey used to say he ate them. But I think he just caught them for fun."

Robert walked to the other side of the bridge. He looked past the danger notice at the houses stretching up the line of the creek.

"Nothing left."

"There's an old pear tree in one of the back yards up there."

"Merle's garden looks O.K."

"She pays a man. She's not short of money."

"How is she?"

"Since Graydon died? I thought she'd fold up. They were more like Siamese twins than husband and wife. But of course all she did was get in touch with his spirit. She'd managed that before he was even buried. Now it's mostly Dad she's getting through to. And her Japanese man. Graydon hasn't got much to say any more."

"You sound as if you don't like her."

"She's all right. But I've had her for forty years."

"I'd like to go and see her."

"You won't have to. She's coming to see you."

Merle was floating down through her garden, through the roses, through the hydrangea walks, like the Queen of the Fairies. She had a marvellous air of commanding nature. But when she had opened the gate at the garden bottom and come on to the concrete suburban paths she looked ridiculous. She had always affected a flowing style of dress, taking it from Graydon's mother, Ella Satterthwaite, who had claimed to be a poet—or, as she put it, poetess. But Ella preferred blue or mauve. Merle chose darker colours. Today she was in black, with purple at the cuffs and at her throat. It was easy to see why the children in the houses called her a witch.

She crossed the turning bay and came across the broken ground to the fence. She moved with amazing lightness for a woman of her age. Robert met her. They kissed by the padlocked gate.

"Robert, my dear, my boy. I knew you had come home. Your father told me. You've no idea how pleased he is."

I had told her too, on the telephone, but she did not mention that. She caressed his cheek. "Robert, it's so good you've come. How could you not come? All your dear ones from the Other Side have been making the path, and now at last you've travelled along it. And dear Meg fetched you in her car. What a good girl she is." She is like that, she makes such easy passage between her worlds that she disarms me. She held Robert's hand. She smiled at him. It was an unlikely conjunction: the stately and beautiful—Merle had always been beautiful—eighty-year-old witchwoman, in her black and purple clothes, in her rings and bangles and scarf and cameo brooch, with cheeks of silk, with English voice; and Robert, my slow brother, misshapen Robert, in sleeves rolled up tight under his arms, in waistcoat from somebody's suit, and thick trousers, and thick boots—his ugly clothes of thirty years ago. They held hands. Something was passing between them. Perhaps it was just affection. I was not jealous. Not at all. I was mystified, and envious; and thrown into confusion by something not complicated enough for me to understand.

"And so," Merle said, "you're starting on your passage. What an exciting journey. You are fortunate."

"For heaven's sake, Merle," I cried.

She smiled at me. "Meg doesn't understand. We understand, don't we Robert? Your dear ones are waiting for you. There'll be a great celebration when you arrive."

"You'd better remind them Robert doesn't drink."

For a moment I thought I had managed to offend her. But she smiled at last and said, "Meg dear, death isn't what you think. You mustn't allow it to frighten you. It doesn't frighten Robert."

"I'm not dead yet," he said.

"We never die. There is no such thing as death. The body may decay but our spirit will go on and on until it reaches God."

"In the meantime," I said, "weed the carrots."

"Oh Meg, oh Meg, you don't give yourself a chance."

"What else did Dad say the other night? Did he have a message for me?"

"He said you must be brave. Grief is a part of it all. Now my dears, I must go. Mr Fujikawa always speaks at two twenty-seven. He gets very cross if I keep him waiting. He pinches me, do you know that? I really don't know how he manages it, but I have the bruises on my arms for weeks afterwards. Robert dear, you must come and visit me. You can walk that far? Don't bring Meg. Her aura has a jagged edge and it hurts my friends."

"I can come," Robert said.

"Not between half past two and three. Mr Fujikawa can't bear interruptions. Goodbye, dear." She kissed him again. "It's a pity your illness has made you look so ugly. But never mind. Your spirit is beautiful, isn't it? That's what counts."

She went away up the slope, but stopped on the turning bay and called, "Oh, Meg dear, I almost forgot. Your tomatoes have got borer. You need some arsenate of lead. I can let you have some." And she went on, up the concrete path into her garden, through the hydrangea walks and the roses, into her house—and to the dark drawing-room with the inlaid table, where she entertained her Japanese gentleman.

"She doesn't change," Robert said.

"She changes all the time."

He shrugged. "All that spirit stuff is new, but that's not important."

"Don't let her hear you say so." I had spoken to no one about Robert's death. That meant Merle had seen it for herself. I supposed it was plain. It was plain to me—but I did not want others to see it; and if they saw, did not think it right for them to say so. Not even Merle. I was sure she looked on her own body as more than a parcel of flesh, a sack of bones. She dressed it up as though it had great importance.

Robert said, "We had a spiritualist in Shannon camp. He was the happiest bloke there. He reckoned his spirit used to leave his body every night and spend the time at home."

We strolled along the path by the stream. Fergus kept the section in reasonable trim, and I did my bit. He mowed the lawns, pruned the fruit trees and dug and mulched around them. He planted the heavy crops—potatoes and kumara. I looked after the rest. I did not grow many flowers. After Dad's death I had Mother's rose garden rooted out. There was too much snipping and pruning. And the budding of those fragrant lovely flowers from a stem so arthritic, so dangerously barbed, struck me as a falsification.

Robert noticed they were gone and said it was a pity. "They were too much work," I said. "Mother only played games with them anyhow." I meant that in moving in hat and gloves among her roses, cutting here and there a perfect bloom, she had been playing the lady she might have been. It was her only pretence. I understood her need of it. But roses did not work that way for me. I had made a bonfire of them by the creek.

Robert said, "You kept the fruit trees though." He walked round trees he had planted thirty years before, but was not moved by any great emotion. He was simply happy. We made our tour, he admired my tomatoes (Merle was right, they had borer) and ate half a dozen gooseberries, stripping their paper clothes with his rough hands; and up by the bend in the creek, where pine roots make a ladder down to the pools, he watched three boys building a dam and called advice to them. (They thought he was crackers.) By then he had had enough, his breathing was painful, and I took him inside. He rested for an hour on the sofa. I brought him a cup of tea and played popular tunes on Mother's piano. This was as I had imagined it. I too was simply happy. I thought later if caring for Robert was my pretence there was no reason why I should not have it. I did not believe, though, it was all pretence.

Robert came up to the house for tea that night. I had asked if he would mind meeting Esther and Fred. "Whatever you like, Meg." So I asked them over: not for the meal though. Robert's breathing made an invasion of the dining table. We ate, Fergus and Robert and I, and Fergus was good with Robert. That gravelly rattle did not trouble him. He remains an accepting and a natural man. I saw his worries come swimming to the surface of his eyes—swift and flicking and irritable for M.E., and for Beth Neeley slower, somehow eel-like, with a trace of red. Poor Fergus, I thought, I really must try to help him. He smiled and talked with Robert about fishing and about gardening, and about Bluey Considine and Sutton. He had gone to Sutton's funeral. There had been only the priest and one or two others.

Fergus had been moved by the words of burial. He could not find masculine terms to admit it in, so he did no more than say it made you think.

He came with us after the meal when I showed Robert Dad's study, and I could not resent his air of proprietorship. He worked there nightly. His study was one thing, Dad's another. The desk was his place of activity, and Dad's books, floor to ceiling on every wall, were as distant from him as a ring of mountains. When he saw them at all he took them for scenery.

Robert had no entry to that world either. But he had come to the study as a child and taken his turn on the stool while Dad scratched away above him at essay or lecture or commentary or letter to some fellow-crusader in Sydney, London, Bombay, Thorpe, or Kumara. We had all gone through it. I will not say it had no value. I will not even say there was no pleasure in it. I made many discoveries on that footstool, and Dad's hand on my head was a natural blessing. He was kinder with me than with most of the others. But even I was nervous. We never knew when a question would fall—come rolling down like thunder out of the sky. We learned not to say we had liked a poem or we would have to say why. Our reasons were never good enough. We crept out with the knowledge of having failed him. At least, I had thought it so until that night. But Robert grinned when I spoke of it.

"I told him I didn't like reading. He let me play with his ear trumpet."

I could not believe it. Nobody touched his trumpet. *I* had never laid a hand on it.

"I used to carve heads on his walking sticks. This is one I did," and he took a stick from the stand in the corner and looked at it and grinned. "Pretty good for a kid." It was an ugly goat's head, roughly done. I had often wondered about it. "Later on I used to polish the Buddha." That was on a stand in a corner and he went to it and slapped it softly on its shining head. "We used to grin at each other. Have you got any incense?"

"No," I said.

"He let me light the incense. We always had some when I came in here."

I was thinking, a little bitterly, that it would have been better to be dull. Dull Robert. Slow Robert. Dad had never let me light the incense. He had burned a stick for me when I brought home my school report with every subject marked *Excellent*— but in his canny way had stubbed it out. "We'll save a bit for next time." He had not offered a next time. I was jealous. But I looked at Robert grinning there, patting the Buddha on its head, and the feeling went away.

Later I asked Esther, "Did Dad ever light any incense for you?"

"Never, the old skinflint. He said it cost too much."

"George was one of the good guys," Fred Meggett said. Since his first big success with U.S. Army surplus after the war, Fred had been full of Americanisms. They marked his moments of sincerity. He had always admired my father. They used to spar with each other, play a game: Fred felt the qualities he admired in himself thrown into relief by Dad's semi-comical judgements, while Dad relaxed with him, suspended judgement, and treated Fred like a naughty boy. It was easier for us all than open war.

Esther said, "We're all good guys as long as we help you make a buck." Her Americanisms mock her husband.

Fergus poured Fred a whisky, and Esther helped herself from her jar of port wine. (She carried it in a brown-paper bag everywhere she went.) My sister had grown into what her husband called "a big soft pudding" It was a description full of inaccuracies. She was hard rather than soft, even her fatty swellings (and these, I suppose, are what Fred was talking about) were firm to touch; and as for sweetness, there was not the slightest bit of that in her. Once she'd been able to love, in her noisy way. Not any longer. Love had been treated to doses of what she called "life", and it did not survive. Fred called her Fatso, Guzzleguts, Pisshead, and worse names. That was his response to "life".

I looked at her with affection. I had no other way of seeing her. She wore expensive clothes, and wore them badly. She rolled up the sleeves of her blouses like a man. Her buttons came undone and her seams went crooked. She did not care. Her dresses rucked at her waist (though she had no waist) and rode up her thighs when she sat in a chair. That was a pain to us—her legs were a pain. She would not wear a suspender belt, but secured her stockings with tight garters, just above her knees. Over the years a trench had been cut there. Her thighs were white and lumpy as scone dough. Esther knew she had grown ugly. But she laughed at me when I tried to make her take better care of herself. She saw her ugliness as what she deserved. But greedily she hunted after comforts. She guzzled her sugary wine by the tumblerful, she gobbled cakes, ate mountains of fried food—chips and chicken and sausages done in batter—she smoked without a pause, lighting her new cigarette from the butt of her old. Her talk was all of racehorses and poker schools. But her winnings gave her happiness only briefly. She soon looked on them as a dirty trick—and lost soon enough.

So Esther lived a life turning from her girlhood to this end. She had chased after pleasure ceaselessly, and it left her disappointed, wanting more. Fred had meant parties, kissing, drinking beer—so she married him. Love was not part of it. They never had a special private place.

I cannot go on. Although I have opened my eyes and see things clearly, and accept what had to be and cannot be changed, Esther makes me want to weep. There is nothing for me but to offer her love. But she had wanted love only from Alfred. They were close, as Robert and I were close. A special private place? She had it with Alfred. He kept her human in her Meggett shape. To her children she gave an impatient care, love of a kind, but for Alfred she kept an open door into a self she could not find unless he took her hand and led her there. I am being sentimental. Am I? My son Raymond would certainly say yes. But am I? Is this not the way it happened—charged like this, charged to its brim, with feelings all confused? With Alfred she entered herself. Then Alfred died. And she believed she had killed him.

Enough. I will come to it in its place. On this night in the sitting-room at Peacehaven she grinned at her brother Robert without love. She tried to get him smoking cigarettes and drinking port. He smiled at her, but her loudness knocks one about. He was soon exhausted.

"Leave him alone, Esther. He can't smoke, you can see that. Or drink that stuff of yours."

"What a pair of wet blankets. I thought we came here for a party."

"Nobody mentioned a party. You came to see Robert."

"Well, I've seen him. What happens next?"

"We can talk. Like civilized people."

"You sound like our dear old dad. I'm not civilized. I want a bit of fun."

"Shut up and drink your plonk," Fred Meggett said.

They make me angry. And they make Fergus angry. He wants to take Esther into a corner and give her a good talking to. And he wants to punch Fred on the jaw for speaking to a woman in that way. Fred knows it. He looks at my husband with a contempt that I find even harder to bear than his treatment of Esther.

I said, "I'm going to take Robert home. I think he's had enough of you two."

"Hold on, we came to see him. Let's have a look. You haven't got any prettier looking, Bobby. What's that noise you make?"

"For heaven's sake, it's his lungs. Now behave yourself."

"She can't, can you, Fatso?" Fred said. "But you can shut up while I talk to Robert. I've got a business proposition for him." And he came right out with it in the way that had earned him his reputation for "bull-headedness." He offered Robert three thousand pounds for the cottage.

Robert struggled out of his chair. He shook his head at Fred; and with my help he went behind the chair and bent forward over it, letting the back take his weight. He rested there a moment, then managed to say, through a dry bubbling in his chest, "No, Fred, thanks. I've had an offer from Fergus so he'd have first option. But I'm not selling it. I'm leaving it to Meg. Maybe when I'm dead she'll sell it to you."

Fred's eyes drooped; his sign of displeasure. "Pretty quick off the mark, eh son?" he said to Fergus.

"He's not selling, Fred, so we can both forget it."

"What do you need property for? You've got M.E. looking after you."

"M.E.'s going bust and you know it."

"Everybody have a drink," Esther cried.

"Who said it's going bust? Things don't go bust when I'm running them."

"Come on, Fred. When are you going to admit it?"

"Christ, what a party. Everybody bitching," Esther said.

"I'm taking Robert home now, so you'd better say good-night."

"Goodnight, brother. Take something for that throat. You sound like a blocked plughole."

Robert took my arm and we left. We walked down the drive of Peacehaven and along the footpath to the cottage.

"Is she always like that?"

"More or less."

"And Fred?"

"Him too. He was fairly mild tonight.   I don't know what to do for Esther."

He shook his head. His breathing was horrible.

"I don't think you need to see them again, Robert."

"I suppose not. I've always brought out something funny in Esther."

I took him into the cottage and helped him to bed. I gave him his drugs and sat with him until his breathing settled down. Then I went back to Peacehaven.

Fergus and Fred and Esther were playing poker. They dealt me a hand and I played a while. I even drank a glass of my sister's wine. "To help me sleep."

"Little Goody two-shoes."

At half past ten I went to bed. The wine did help me drift off into sleep. Esther's cries from the sitting-room became a sound from my childhood. I dreamed of her as a happy ten-year-old.

In the morning, Fergus told me they had played poker till one o'clock. Fred won more than fifteen pounds from his wife.

10 My first sight of Fred Meggett was memorable. When I feel at a disadvantage with him I have only to bring it to mind. I have seen his face naked and greedy, I have seen it charged to the vein-ends with gobbling hunger. Today's false-hearty man-breaking tycoon cannot scare me. I have only to think of it and I want to laugh.

We had travelled north from Christchurch to settle in Loomis. A year had turned about. Peacehaven, the house and grounds, were tight around me. I was twelve. I had heard of this sweetheart of Esther's. He was a butcher. My revulsion was aesthetic more than snobbish. But I wanted to see him; I had a curiosity turning about the flesh—ugly, ambiguous, attractive— and my sister's meeting with it in this man. She brought him home one Saturday afternoon. I was reading in the orchard and did not know of his visit until I came down. Mother turned from her cooking and looked at my eyes. She was worried I was straining them and she laid her hands on the lids to cool them down.

"What are you reading, dear?"

I showed her. She was disappointed. "You'd better not let your father see. One shock for him a day is enough."

"What's he shocked about?"

She would not say. She never spoke against people. But when I went to my bedroom I saw Esther disappearing down the bank by the creek in company with a young man, and I knew my father's shock had been his meeting with the butcher.

I did not want to meet him. But I was determined to *see* him. I used my rights of ownership as an excuse. The bank above the creek where she had taken him was my place, Robert's place. Our tracks were over it; and my reading places, soft and warm and peopled from my dreams, were flattened into the grass from the edge of the eely creek up to the rhododendron by the lawn. Esther had no right there, especially with Fred Meggett, a butcher's boy. I worked up my indignation. I combed and plaited my hair, and composed my face. Then I set off to come on them and with my presence drive them from my ground. I saw it more as poetry than drama. Of course, before they went, I would take a good look at Fred. He would have clothes with stains on them (it made me shiver), and meaty hands and a red hot face. Yet with all this, he would have a power—a dark magnetism, turning my sister Esther into his slave. I was familiar with this sort of thing from my reading. It was likely Fred Meggett had it. How else would he get Esther? She was a Plumb. I thought my purity would be a match for him.

I approached, though, with a shrinking confidence. I sensed the closeness of some mystery, and a danger of revelation. I stepped into the dreaming ground of my childhood, but advanced on another level into a place where adult things might happen. Shadows fell across the summer bank. Heavy insects flew up from the grass and went ahead of me with whirring wings. I walked light-footed, straight, imperious; with a frightened crying at the heart of me.

What I came upon was an idyllic scene: lovers resting on a grassy bank. But standing out from it was Fred Meggett's face. It had a colour, a greed, a vulgarity, that drained the life from everything around it—from Esther, who was no more than a black and white figure from a photograph, from the sky and the clouds and the trees and the bank. The sunlight faded. I was dry, with the white dryness of dust. I was a vacuum, I was null. I will not exaggerate the moment—the moment I caught sight of an enemy and was slain by him. It lasted only the space of a heartbeat or two. I came back to life. I came back with a thumping in my heart. Esther saw me. Her face rose up like a shape from under water. It burst into the air, took colour from the light. I saw her grinning at me, winking at me.

Today I am impressed by the comicalness of the scene, and a certain rightness it has. There was my sister Esther, lying on the bank in her blue summer dress, holding Fred Meggett in one arm like a giant baby. She had a look of interest on her face. Fred had his blind face at me. His mouth was open. His nose appeared to be swollen. I could see his tongue. Esther's hand was down in his trousers, through his opened fly, at some work. She stopped it when she saw me. "Don't stop," he whimpered. So she went on. Interest on her face. Yes. And a little boredom. A little contempt. I am probably imagining it. What I do not imagine is the spurt of enjoyment she felt on seeing me there. She grinned at me. She winked at me. Her hand got busy again. Easily she took me into the play and got more from it. Fred began to gasp.

I laugh at it now. On that day I turned and ran. My plaits urged me on with heavy bangs upon my back. I scrambled up the bank and through the branches of the rhododendron tree, and ran past the rockery and through the garden, and burst at last with a hot face into Mother's kitchen, where she stood peeling potatoes at the bench.

"Easy child, easy." She looked at me more closely. "Go and wash your face in cold water and you will feel better." My world jolted back into something like its shape. I ran to her and pressed myself against her. She wiped her hands and took my face in her palms. "What is it, little Meg?"

"Nothing. Nothing."

"Go and wash, there's a dear. Then you can help me put the dates in my pudding."

I did as I was told. We made date-roll, which was my favourite pudding. I helped Mother tidy up the bench, and together we set the dining-room table for dinner. Laying out the serviettes in their rings, making a box with knife and fork and spoon, I gained a balance. I was able to giggle at what I had seen, and feel pleased at my daring. I was worried though about what

Esther would do. She was seventeen. She was big and strong. I kept within a step of Mother, chattering all the time, until she raised her eyes in mock annoyance.

"Stop getting under my feet, child."

"Shall I take Dad a cup of tea?" I would be even safer in the study. But Mother said no. "You might spoil his line of thought."

Esther came in. She was unhurried, she looked cool, and she sat at the kitchen table and gave a wide yawn.

"Put your hand over your mouth," Mother said.

"Too tired."

"A lady covers her mouth when she yawns. A gentleman too. In fact it's better to yawn in your room if you must."

"Ho hum," Esther said. She grinned at me. "You live and learn, dopey."

"Has Mr Meggett gone?" Mother asked.

"Yep. I had enough of him."

"He seems a nice young man," Mother lied.

"I guess he'll do."

"Really Esther, you shouldn't talk like that. You should speak of him with respect if you really like him."

Esther yawned again. She grinned half-way through and covered her mouth. With horror I realized she was using the hand that had been in Fred Meggett's trousers. She had not even washed it.

"What are you looking so goofy for?"

"Nothing," I squeaked.

"You're going cross-eyed. That's the second time today."

"Leave her alone," Mother said. "She's got a nice face. She's got a very kind face."

"Yes, like a cow. Moo-oo. Watch out the bull doesn't catch you."

"Go to your room if you can't speak like a lady."

"I'm going. I hope tea's early. I've got to go to a party."

"Well," Mother said sharply, "I hope you're not putting any of that lipstick on your face."

"Of course I am. That's half the fun."

"You're prettier without it. And you'll meet nicer young men."

"I knew you didn't like him," Esther said happily. "Never mind, Meg likes him, don't you dope?" She winked at me. "You can meet him if you like when he calls tonight."

"I don't want to meet him."

"Of course you do. I've told him all about you."

"You keep your young men away from Meg. She's not ready yet."

"I'm beginning to wonder if she ever will be."

Esther went to our room and laid out her dress. She had a bath. Alfred and Robert hurried in with buckets of hot water from the copper until it was full enough to please her. She put in bath salts and soaked for half an hour, then called me in to scrub her back. I did it with eyes turned away. I could not look at her woman's body. Later she called me to the bedroom to button her dress at the back. I found then I could look at her. In fact, I could not take my eyes off her. She glittered like the bad queen, I could imagine her mirror telling her that she was most beautiful of all. She had eyes like Pola Negri—"dark lagoons wherein men drown"—but had the trick of widening them and darting them about. She laughed with them, she used them. Light seemed to sparkle out, and life sparkle too. Her features were not pretty. She had a mouth too large and a flaring nose. But that was not something you noticed about her, unless to notice that her mouth smiled happily, and her nose seemed to drink up life. I exaggerate. I have worked my way to that, hunted it out. Her young men heard her laughter, saw her beautiful eyes and painted mouth, and asked no more than that. Asked though, perhaps, favours of her hand. Fred was not the only one. But I do not believe she obliged with more than hand. Not at that time.

She let me watch while she put her lipstick on. She dabbed some of her perfume behind my ears. Never once did she mention my spying on her, she did not hint at it. That was past, she was looking ahead to the next thing. I had the beginnings of knowledge that she had gone too far, too carelessly, she was out of her depth; and, like Rebecca, she would drown.

Fred called for her in his father's car. She brought him into the living-room to say hallo. Alfred looked up from his book and gave a nod so small I don't think Fred saw it. The rest of us were polite. But I could not look at him, I could not meet his eye. He shook hands with me, and I pulled my fingers quickly out of his grip—it was a jerking-away I could not help, as though from something unclean. Esther's had been the hand, but I was not in any reasonable state. I had seen his tongue, and the whites of his eyes, and his nose swollen like—I shall not say. I could not stand chatting with him in our father's house and Mother's house, in my clean world.

Dad said, "You have Esther home by half past ten, young man."

"Half past ten?" Esther screeched. But Dad had spoken. He lowered his ear trumpet and took no more part in the argument—which determined that Esther should be home by half past twelve.

Mother said, "I mean it, Esther. You're only seventeen. And don't you smoke. Mr Meggett, you must not offer her cigarettes."

"I can't stop her smoking, Mrs Plumb. She doesn't listen to me."

"You must treat your bodies with respect," Mother said.

"We will, we promise," they chorused. Their hands behind their backs were highly amused; began, in a clump of three, secret ticklings, a dirty game. I felt sick. I wanted to scream at my sister, and beat Fred Meggett out of our house with my fists. Instead, I left the room, I ran to my bed, and there I dived for safety into my book. I bathed in it like a spring of water.

Mother was right, *Bab of the Backwoods* would have shocked Dad. But on that summer night, as the warm air brought a dampness on my skin and the dark made noises, as Esther's laugh by the car and the butcher's red guffaw and the sound of a palm smacking rump, and words like damn and bugger came through the trees, it gave me Monte Baron to set against Fred. Monte. His name still brings a faster beat to my heart. And her name: Bab. It was so like Meg. For the rest of that year I secretly called myself Bab, and even more secretly her other name, Running Water. The only flaw in the book was that it was set in California. California made me cold, it fell like an icy hand on me; and still does that. But the magic world Monte and Bab made for themselves, their world of love, was safe inside and cut off from the California that threatened me so, just as my new world of Peacehaven was safe inside the north. I had no Monte yet, but I waited for him. Fred I saw as Conroy. "Conroy, a gross man, licked his lips." I found the sentence in my mind whenever I thought of Fred. I made him helpless with those words, he was no threat to me. I waited for Monte Baron to come and take me by the hand. I waited for his kiss. I ran my fingers softly over my lips and felt them tingle. "She lifted her eyes to his; her lips were lifted, slightly parted, inviting.   " I practised that. Physical realities throbbed below the surface in that book. But other realities had not the smallest place there.

Fred followed me into the orchard one day. By this time I was fourteen. I had grown breasts, of which I was suspicious. He tried to put his hands on them. He told me how much he liked me. I was not the least bit frightened, but felt very sure of myself and powerful. Fred was lusting after me, in his Conroy way. I said, "I could never be interested in a man who handles raw meat all day." He went the red of steak. He grabbed me and tried to kiss me but I jerked away from him, in a dignified way, still not frightened, and his mouth came down by my ear. "I'll give you something you won't forget." I began to worry then. I could not break out of his arms. Down against my hip he butted at me with a part I had never thought of as so leathery and long. I could not scream. The best I could manage was to say, "You smell of meat."

I must have excited him terribly. He pulled me hard against him, as if his body wanted to take in mine. His face nuzzled and ground into my neck and his loins rolled on the hip bone I still managed to present to him. He groaned and drew in long shuddery breaths. I stood stiff, my face turned up and away from him. I was not part of it. When he had finished I stepped away and began in a bored way to walk into the trees. He followed me, panting, almost crying. "That was your fault," he managed to get out, "so don't blame me." "Go away." I began to be pleased. Whatever he had done, it was inside him and had nothing to do with me. I saw it as a kind of animal tribute, the pathetic groping out of a lower nature. I laughed at it.

He said, "If you tell anyone about this I'll run you over in my car."

He meant that, or thought he did. I said, "Go away, Fred. I'm waiting for somebody." I was waiting for Monte. One day he would come and say, "You precious girl!   Kiss me!" "Yes," I would say, "yes." And he would say, "I want you for mine, for all time. For this life and the next and all through eternity."

Fred was real all right (had left a damp patch on my dress to prove it), but I had weapons against him. He did not scare me.

11 Mother was my life-line. She was always there to bring me back into the world. Most of my memories of her are kitchen memories. It seems to me she passed her life in the kitchen. I came in warm from my bed, came in to the sound of bubbling porridge, the cat's miaow by the meat-safe, Mother's slippered feet as she moved in the triangle, table, stove, bench—endlessly: table, stove, bench—sometimes humming a tune, always with a smile and a word of greeting. She served us all (she served the cat), and the help we were able to give her with washing-up, and cooking, and laying the table, made only a small reduction in her work. At night when I came to kiss her, there she was at the bench, setting our father's tray

with teacup and biscuits, and pouring tea to carry to his study—
not too hot, not too strong, always perfect tea. She would not let
me take in his night-time cup. That was her job. She guarded it
jealously. (Sometimes though, when he tinkled his spoon on his
saucer, she let me fetch the tray for his second cup.)

It may seem contradictory to say that Mother always had
time. But she was always ready to sit down and talk. The
dishwater was left to go cold in the sink, the fire in the range die
down, if I had a trouble. She sat me down at the table and made
me tell it. It was the same for the others. I came in to find Alfred
with his eyes full of tears and his voice grown shrill (soon she
would calm it); or Robert there, grumbling softly, with a grin;
or grown-up Agnes, hoping for California; or Emerson with a
dream that receded from him—new motor bike, or Model T, or
flight into the clouds. Mother heard us all and calmed us down,
and taught us what it was we might properly hope for. (Esther
came there too, sometimes, but Mother never taught her.)
Mother told me I must not hope my brown eyes would turn blue
or my teeth grow straight. "Crooked teeth are no great tragedy.
Now a crooked soul, Meg dear, that would be something to
worry about." I took it from her because she spoke of souls, and
hearts, and God, and love, and truth, as easily as if they were
carrots and potatoes. And Mother was never high and mighty or
censorious. She could be stern. Wrong was as much a part of her
talk as right. But everything came out of a ground of love. She
put a serenity in me, under my troubles. I look for it and find it
there today.

So I came out of Monte's world into the kitchen. I forgot my
name, Running Water. I was Meg Plumb. This was my home.
Mother was mixing a dough-boy for the stew. Dad was in his study,
smiting away at the war-lords with his pen. No more was needed for
my happiness. I must not forget what a happy girl I was.

I was happy on the night of Esther's twenty-first birthday
party. I had helped Mother all through the day with her baking.
I had tidied the house and polished the furniture. Esther did not
help. "Why should I? It's my birthday." Her contribution was

71

to throw open the double doors between the dining-room and the sitting-room. Her eyes shone at the expanse for dancing. Emerson and Alfred had pushed the furniture to the walls and rolled up the mats. She caught Emerson, who was nearest her, and waltzed into the centre of the room, trailing one arm in an extravagant way (one could almost see the gauze scarf floating from it), throwing her head back languorously. Alfred went to the piano and fitted a tune to their rhythms. Robert and I watched, grinning a little with embarrassment, and Mother came from the kitchen with a mixing bowl in her arm and stood in the doorway, turning with her wooden spoon and smiling approval of the stately dance.

She was less happy when Alfred played a Charleston and Esther flung herself into double-jointed motions. Emerson could not keep up with her. She gave us a solo performance. "Like a rag doll having fits," Alfred said later. "Remember how Jehovah looked on his mountain?" That was Dad. He had come from a stroll in the orchard. We did not see him in the doorway until Esther was done. She fell into a posture of exhaustion: loose at the knees, arms hanging loose, and her tongue poking out. Mother said, "Esther, that's vulgar." At the same time we heard Dad's voice: "A Hottentot," he said, "a Hottentot." He had the look of a man who has come upon something not just outside his experience but beyond imagination.

"It's the new dance, Dad. It's all the rage," Esther said.

He was without his trumpet. "A Hottentot." I don't think that word expressed it for him at all. He put his hand on his forehead in a way that meant he must find the peace of his study or go mad. It was a stagy gesture, but usually it made us feel guilty or contrite. On that day, when he had gone, we spluttered with laughter. Even Mother gave a smile.

"I hope you won't be doing that tonight, Esther."

"Of course we will. None of them can do it as fast as me."

"I'll have to keep your father well away."

She handed me the mixing bowl and went to the study to calm him. Alfred, clever Alfred, played their conversation on the piano, thundering with the bass notes for "Jehovah", and soothing, soothing, overcoming his thunder, smoothing his brow, in the treble for Mum. We laughed until we cried. Those fading rolls of thunder, those tinkles at once so gentle and so strong! For me it was wildly funny; and it was sad. My tears fell into the mixing bowl. Emerson had to take it away from me.

"Sorrow cakes," Alfred said. "Or happy cakes. Is it sorrow from the left eye Meg and happy from the right or vice versa?"

"I'm not eating them," Esther cried. "What a sap you are."

That night we had a special tea, just for the family. We had it in the kitchen because the dining-room table was set for the party. It was a crush. Dad sat alone at the head with plenty of room for his arms, and Mother had the other end to herself. The rest of us had our arms pressed to our sides. We girls were in our party frocks and one or other of us was always rushing off to the bathroom to sponge out some gravy spot or custard spot. Dad frowned at this. We had given up saying grace long ago, but he started the meal with a prayer.

"Lord, in your mystery, in your immanence, suffer our voices to find a path to Thee. We ask for Thy blessing on one who has come to adulthood. May she put off the childish ways that cling to her—" Esther bridled. "—and grow into wisdom and maturity, and exercise her mind and discover her heart and come out of selfish strivings—" "Do I really have to listen to this?" "Hush," Mother said. "—and learn modesty and a womanly restraint. And may she find Thee Lord, and know happiness, for at present she is lost on a darkened way." "Really!" "And we ask that our children, our brother and sister, Agnes and Emerson, know Thy comfort on their travels in the world. They have chosen to leave us. We pray that they may grow in wisdom, and that the love that surrounds them now may go out with them into those places where they will pass their lives. " Agnes and Emerson looked uncomfortable. Dad had not meant his disapproval to come so strongly through. But California, where Agnes was booked to go, had always been for him a land where frivolities reigned and vices thrived. (I take the words from his essay on the place.) And Emerson's plan to get to England and somehow learn to fly was one he had no sympathy with.

Willis and Mirth arrived at the end of the meal. "Ah," Willis cried, "just in time for some pudding,"—(which sums up his life). Mother gave them bowls, and the Auckland part of our family was complete, eating peaches and cream. Mirth was in the last months of her pregnancy—her second with her second family. I confined myself to looking at her face. I could not bear to look at her swollen body. (No more could Dad. He insisted on the beauty of women expecting, but when faced with them he turned away.) It made me feel choked and gave me the feeling some great slippery thing was on the point of sliding out of my mouth. When Dad had gone she invited us girls to feel the baby kicking, but Mother reminded her sharply the boys were in the room. She believed in a *purdah* for women in their last months. Mirth apologized, and Willis took out his mouth organ and knelt in front of his wife and played the unborn baby a lullaby, which had us all laughing; even Mother.

When I had helped with the dishes I went to the bedroom to rub some of Esther's cold cream on my hands. She gave it to me grudgingly—a waste on my fat paws. My hands were thin and beautiful, one of the things I was sure of. I smiled at her and scooped out a large fingerful. "Take it easy," she cried.

Alfred grinned at me. He was sitting on my bed, watching Esther put the finishing touches to her hair. He liked to watch this sort of thing and pass comment on it, and usually we listened with respect. He had a flair. As a last touch Esther tucked a red hibiscus in the dark waves of her hair and fastened it with a diamante clasp. I thought it made her even more beautiful, it made her look dramatic, but Alfred said, "That's all wrong."

"Why?"

"You girls always overdo things. You want one or the other, not both."

"Which then?" She turned her head this way and that.

"The flower," I said.

"No one asked you."

"The clasp," Alfred said.

"I could have the flower on one side and the clasp on the other."

"You could not. Not unless you want to look like a *fille de joie*."

I was thrilled by the term, which I understood instantly. But Esther said, "Talk English. Tell me what to do."

"Take out the flower."

She tried but the stem tangled in her hair. "Why didn't you tell me before I pinned it?"

"How did I know it would make you look cheap?" I thought he probably had known. He sometimes played with Esther like a doll.

She redid her hair and repainted her lips.

"Wipe all that off and put on half as much." He was watching with a deep interest, and an emotion that made him irritable. I thought it strange.

"Is mine all right, Alfred?" I had barely touched my lips.

He glanced at me. "Yours is good. You've got taste."

"Angel face," Esther sneered.

"She knows when to stop."

"Her? She doesn't even know when to start."

He watched her coolly. "You've got on too much. It makes you look like a tart."

"What would you know about tarts?"

"As much as I need to. Come on Esther, wipe it off and start again."

"No."

"It'll be over half the men in town by morning."

"You," she cried, "you pig!"

"Who are you laying the net for? I thought you had old Pickled Pork all wrapped up."

She threw the lipstick at him. It struck him on the forehead and fell on the bed. He picked it up and put it in his pocket. "I'll keep it for that."

"Give that back to me."

"It's wasted on you."

"Damn you," she said. "Damn you."

"Language," Alfred said.

"Get out. Get out of my room."

"I'm going." He stood up. His eyes were watering from the blow and a red mark was coming up on his brow. But I saw he was happy; and in a way she was too. I could not understand it.

She rounded on me. "You clear out as well."

"It's my room as much as yours."

"Just for once, on my birthday, can I have it to myself?"

"Come on, Sis," Alfred said. He took me by the hand and pulled me out. Esther slammed the door.

"A real fire-eater, ain't she?" Alfred said. He took the lipstick out of his pocket and tossed it in the air. "Tell you what, you could do with just a touch of this. Come here." He stood me up against the door and painted my lips. "There you are, young Meg. You look like a *femme fatale.*" He was doing it for Esther, on the other side of the door. I knew she was listening. I felt as if I had stepped, not into the adult world—that was serious—but into a world where make-believe was on the point of being real. I liked the strange excited feeling it gave me, but did not like the danger I felt I was in.

That night I had a heightened sense of things. I look on it as the last night of my girlhood. Nothing dramatic happened. But I was in my family, deep in my family, in a blissful, accepting, elegiac way. Everything that happened on that night was confusing yet absolutely right. I was happy, I was taking it all deep into myself, yet I was weeping at the loss of it all. Today I would probably put it down to hormonal imbalance—being a modern woman. I am glad I was not modern on that night. I was outside the party. I understood that perfectly. Esther's guests were glittering apes and birds. Only the Plumbs were human. From time to time I danced with some Alan or Morrie or Murray, with some Tiny or Knuckles or Squidge. They had brought along a gramophone and a stack of records. I even tried the Charleston, and didn't do it badly. Noise and colour tumbled in the room. The dizzy music turned us upside down. But through it all there strolled significant beings: Alfred and Emerson, Agnes and Esther and Robert, Willis, Mother and Dad. Yes, Dad put in an appearance. He made a speech and presented Esther with a key cut out of box-wood and pasted over with silver paper. He talked for too long, too heavily—of youth, and duty, and the tasks of life and its rewards. The Dust of Conflict and the Palm of Victory. People sneaked on to the verandah and came back when it was over. Dad watched Esther blow the candles out with a mystified air. He had not come across that tradition before. He ate a piece of cake. Then he put his hand on his forehead, and went to his study. I loved him for it.

The food quietened everybody down. Willis snored away on his mouth organ, then sang sentimental songs while Mirth played the piano. His voice was naturally tearful. After *Danny Boy* and *Kathleen Mavourneen*, which dampened his eye, he grabbed two spoons from the table and played a tune on his wooden leg. Then he asked some of the girls to carve their initials on it. I shivered at their cutting, I felt sharp pains in my leg; and then came worse, I felt that tearing-off at the knee he had suffered in Copenhagen. I limped outside, and sank down on the lawn and was nearly sick.

"Come here, goof," a voice said from the dark. I saw a cigarette glowing by the peach tree.

"Is that you, Agnes?"

"Of course it's me."

"What are you doing out here?" I hobbled over.

"Sit down and talk to me. What have you done to your leg?"

"It's nothing. It's gone away now."

"How can you stand it in there?"

"Willis singing, do you mean? He's all right."

"What a family. Thank God for California."

That was all right too. That was acceptable—it was, I understood, her role in the family to say this thing and run away from us.

"I love you, Agnes," I said.

"I love you, too. Do you think I don't?" She rubbed her cheek and I knew she had rubbed away a tear. I felt the same one tickling on my cheek.

"What will you do over there?"

"I'll find a man and get married. There's plenty of men. But I won't let him treat me the way *he* treats Mum."

"They're all right, Agnes." I knew they were all right, though I could not explain it.

"They're not. She's just his slave. I'll never be like that for any man." She smoked, and puffed out furiously, and suddenly she began to cry. I put my arm round her and she bored in close to me and soaked the whole of my bodice with her tears.

"Agnes," I screamed, "your dress is on fire." She had dropped her cigarette on a fold of it. We beat the smouldering cloth out with our hands.

Agnes laughed. "It was an ugly dress anyway. I was going to give it to you." She lit another cigarette. "Here, have a puff."

"No, Agnes."

"It'll do you good."

"No, I don't want to."

"Come on, no one's watching. You can't be a goody-goody all your life."

The smoke burned me deep in my chest. I coughed and sagged on the grass and Agnes, laughing, banged me on my back. When I was better she showed me how to smoke. She took the smoke into her mouth and let it trickle out her nostrils. Every time she drew on the cigarette her wet cheeks gleamed.

"Willis and his leg," she said. "Oh, God. And his awful wife. And Esther and that butcher. She's a tramp. And Alfred."

"Alfred's all right."

"He's not all right. Can't you see?" Just for a flash I did. I could not hold it.

"Alfred's going to be a poet."

"Thank God I'm going." She brooded. "And *him*, and *her*. How could he make that awful speech? Telling us to go out and

78

do those things? We can never do them. People on the porch were laughing at him." She puffed. "And you mooning like a cow. What a family."

"Please don't cry again, Agnes."

"I won't cry. Not me.—Tell me Meg, do you know how babies come?"

"I think I do."

"You think? But you're not sure?"

"I can't understand some things."

"I've got a book. I'll give it to you. It will be my going away present. That and a dress with a hole burnt in it."

"Will you come back, Agnes?"

"No. Not ever. It's California for me."

"I didn't like it there."

"You wouldn't. But I'll like it."

Emerson came over the lawn to us. "Which one of you's first for a joyride?"

"On your bike? No fear. You'll break our necks," Agnes said.

"Come on. They all want one—" he waved towards a group of girls coming down the verandah steps, "—but I said I was going to take my sisters first."

"I'll come, Emerson," I said. I had never been on his bike, it terrified me, but tonight I felt I must meet everything my brothers and sisters offered, they were revealing themselves and I would see things I would never see again, and perhaps I would help them; certainly I would take a grip on them that would never be broken. Emerson wheeled his bike out of the shed. With admiring girls about him he kicked it once, twice, three times. It roared like a mountain lion, then sank to a gargle. One of the girls tried to climb on the back but Emerson held her off with a straightened arm. "Come on, Meg."

"Goodbye," I said to Agnes.

"What do you mean? I've got two more weeks here yet."

I meant goodbye. I went across the lawn to Emerson, the girls parted unwillingly to let me through—I was a nobody to them—and I sat on the pillion seat of the Indian and wrapped my arms about my brother's waist.

"Gangway," Emerson yelled. He wriggled the bike through them and suddenly we were free, thundering with an impossible noise, yet sliding as though on oil, down the drive between the bank and Mother's rose garden. The gate was open. We broadsided out. The road leaned up to meet me and fell away, and off we raced through the white dust and spitting metal, chasing the rigid beam of light that shone out of Emerson's face. I was not frightened. I held him with arms tight locked, one on the other, knowing he was all that kept me alive in the tiny dangerous world he created on this pitch-bright road. I knew at last where he lived. I laid my cheek hard against his spine and screamed with joy. And he, poor wordless fellow, yelled back at me, "Fun, eh Meg?" He did not need words. We went to the end of Millbrook Road and crossed the thundering wooden bridge. The wind blew water from my eyes in trickles back into my hair. We raced through the main street of Loomis, where people were coming out of the picture theatre. A boy I had once had a Monte crush on, Fergus Sole, was there, holding his girl by the hand, and as their faces flickered like movie-faces I laughed at them. We roared up the concrete Great North Road past the vineyards until we came to View Road. Skidding and scrambling, we came down, down to the wooden bridge and Millbrook Road, and zoomed back past the giant pines— "Doing fifty," Emerson yelled—leaning over this way, that, my dress hem brushing in the dust, until we came again to Peacehaven's gate; and there Emerson puttered up and stopped us safely on the lawn.

"Thank you Emerson," I whispered into his back.

"O.K. Meg?" He unlocked my hands. I climbed off the bike and ran away into the dark, past those cold girl-faces staring at me. Emerson had showed me where he lived.

"My turn, my turn," cried the girls.

"Esther. I want Esther," Emerson yelled.

Off they rode; and when they came back he went to Agnes, smoking in the dark, and picked her up and put her on the seat—so she went too. Then, though the girls screeched at him and slapped him on his arms and swore at him, he pushed his bike into the shed. "That's enough for one night." He closed and padlocked the door. He had never meant to take more than Agnes and Esther and me. I laughed from my place by the creek. We were a family.

After that I wanted no more of the party. I do not mean I wanted it to be over. I was content to swim on the edges of it—no, I shall change that. I wanted to stroll through the party like a zoo, and feel the pity one feels for caged animals. I wanted no more dancing with Murray and Morrie and no more plates of food delivered by Squidge. I wanted to see how Murray and Morrie and Squidge, and Betty and Rae, behaved in their little cages, and see whether any realization came to them that they were not Plumbs, not strolling free. After a while I found Alfred at what I took to be the same occupation. He was coming down the steps from the top lawn. I waited for him on the path.

"Hello, Moony Meg."

"I'm not mooning, Alfred. I'm watching people."

"A great sport, isn't it? A great sport for those who can't join in."

"Do you want to join in, Alfred?"

"With that lot of Woolworth girls?"

"And butchers and bakers."

"And joystick makers. Sorry Meg, you wouldn't understand."

"Where are you going, Alfred?"

"I thought I might climb a tree. But I'll walk with you instead."

We went across the lower lawn to the summer-house. A glow of cigarettes turned us away.

"I don't think that was Esther."

"Do you envy them?"

"No."

"You mustn't always be alone, Meg. Don't you want a boyfriend sometimes?"

"Now and then I think it would be nice. Not just any boy though."

"Sir Percival, the perfect knight. Me too, but where on earth do we find him?"

"Do they have lady knights?"

"Ah Meg, you do me good."

"Why are you laughing?"

"It's that sort of night. You laugh or cry."

We came to the rhododendron trees. Beyond them on the slope voices murmured, bottles clinked. "The Carcase Cutter and his friends," Alfred said. "They've got little stores of beer all over the section."

"That's Esther's voice."

"She's there. She's where the fun is. Good old Esther."

We went along by the trees, following the curve of the creek. The cottage windows turned into our view, making a framed picture in the dark. Wendy Philson sat at her table, writing. From time to time she raised her head and listened to the cries in the grounds of Peacehaven.

"That's what I should be like," Alfred said. "Cut off from the monkey house. Writing poetry. She's probably copying recipes though."

"She's marking school books, I think."

"Well, she's busy, that's the thing. She's got a meaning."

"You'll write poetry, Alfred."

"Oh, I do, I do. Sentimental odes. Dirty limericks."

"You'll write something good."

"I've got to, Meg. I've got to write something better than good. Or else I've got no meaning. Meg, love is no good for me. Love is out. It's got to be work. Forget Sir Percival. That's a dream. That's for kids. I've got to find the Grail myself. Alone."

"You will, Alfred."

"Will I?" He laughed. "Will I? Perhaps I will. Thank you, Sister." He was quiet for a moment. "Meanwhile, listen to the denizens of the zoo." Beyond the rhododendrons a bottle smashed. Esther's voice rose scolding, Fred guffawed. In the cottage Wendy Philson stopped her writing, sat up straight. After a while she put her pen down. She stretched her arms and yawned. She scratched beneath her breasts.

Alfred said, "That's what happens to the ideal. Suddenly it gets fleas."

"Oh Alfred, that wasn't fleas."

"If we watch long enough we'll see her pick her nose."

"Come with me. It isn't right to watch."

"Most things that are any fun aren't right."

He let me pull him away. We walked back past the summer-house and climbed the steps to the top lawn. A few people were dancing in the sitting-room. We watched through the open French doors. Moths turned into the room and the music flowed out. Mirth was sitting in an easy chair, watching with patient adoration while Willis danced energetically with a lopsided fat girl in a purple frock.

"How does he manage, with his leg?"

"Worth more to him than a thousand golden words. Look at that girl, she's in love with it."

"Mirth doesn't seem to care."

"That's how she keeps him. Shall I tell you something, you won't be shocked?"

"No," I said, believing I probably would be.

"He told me the other day he's had ninety-six women in his life. Do you know what I mean?"

"I know."

"Course some of them he paid for. But ninety-six!"

"Fancy counting."

"He takes it seriously. This girl looks as if she'll be ninety-seven."

"When he gets to a hundred we'll bake him a cake."

Alfred laughed. "Good girl, Meg. You're coming on." We were quiet for a while. Then Alfred said, "There's no such thing as love, you know."

"Yes there is. There's got to be."

"I agree with the second part."

"There is love. Look at Mum and Dad."

He stared at me. "I really think you mean that."

"I do. They love each other. Why can't anybody else see how happy she is? And Dad."

"Oh, *he's* happy all right. But I don't know why you think it's love. It's not much better than Willie in there, cutting another notch in his belt."

"You don't believe that. I know you don't believe it."

"I do, Meg. But I've got a feeling—you might be the one who gets it. Love, I mean." He made a sudden violent cut with his arm. "God, the bilge I talk."

"Why aren't you happy, Alfred?"

"I'm not, that's all."

"You'll find someone."

"Will I? Will I?"

"I know you will."

"Unless I do, unless I find that person Meg, I'll never find out who I am. I—can't—find—out."

"Alfred, you'll find her soon. I know you will."

"Ha!" he cried, "find her! I do like that. What a chump you are, Meg. Well—well—there is some love you know, because I love you. And crazy old Esther down there in the bushes. Here—" he took something out of his pocket, "—give this to her. She needs it more than me." He put her lipstick in my hand.

"Alfred, you've put some on." I saw his face clearly in the light.

He grinned. "I like to try things out. It tastes like cherries."

"Where are you going?"

"I think I'll climb that tree now."

He went down the steps and ran away into the dark. Even that did not make me unhappy. His talk of there being no love, for him, for anyone, of Mum and Dad not being in love—these did not, on that night, make me unhappy. I was drinking my family down. My family made me drunk. I was at that stage of intoxication when even pain is good. Sitting on the stone wall in the garden, I saw Mother come into the sitting-room. She looked startled to find only Willis there. She asked him a question but he shrugged and went on dancing. She came towards the door, with a look on her face I knew well—that look she got when she meant to round up her children. But half-way there she stopped, she gave it up. She said something to Mirth, sprawled in her chair. Mirth smiled and sat up straight and closed her legs. Mother went out of the room. I understood it all, in detail, perfectly. I lived the moment with her. Then I walked down the steps and down to the creek. Agnes was gone from under the peach tree. But on the brick bridge I met Robert. I had not seen him since early in the night.

"Where have you been?"

"Over at the Butterses' You know what Meg, they believe plants have souls and they're trying to talk to us. Merle was kissing a begonia."

"Oh, Robert." I laughed until I was gasping.

"Yeah, it's a lot of hooey. I'm hot. I'm going for a swim." He began to take off his clothes.

"Robert."

"I'll keep my underpants on."

"You can't swim there. It's dark."

"I know where the rocks are."

"What about the eels?"

"They don't hurt you."

I looked down into the water—into the dark, for no gleam showed. It might have been a pit dropping forever. The blackness seemed to suck all the blood from my body and flesh from my bones. It seemed to suck the whole world into it. On the edge of terror, on the edge of Missing, I knew that Robert would turn it into water, make it our creek. He lined himself up carefully.

"If you dive out towards that tree you miss the rocks. It's just deep enough."

"Go on, Robert." Others would fall down the hole into Missing, but Robert, Robert would do it like walking down a wide street. I saw the white blur of his body as he dived, and heard his splash, and another sound. It was flat and deadly, it met nothing in me that understood, and my heart stood for a moment utterly still, I believe I died. For one missed beat of my heart Robert vanished from the world. Then he splashed up and yelled at me, "What was that?"

I could not answer. The swelling beat of my heart left me no room. Robert splashed about down there, a blur, and soon he said, "It's a bottle. Someone must have bished a beer bottle in."

"Are you all right?"

"I hit it with my elbow."

"Come out, Robert."

He swam to the side of the pool and put the bottle on the rocks. It made a musical sound.

I said, "It was probably Fred. He's been drinking."

"Probably was. He's got no sense." He swam across the pool. "This is good. Come on in. Hey, that was an eel. He's swimming up my back. Eee, it's like a snake."

"He might bite you."

"It's just a little one. Hey, that one was big. He's nibbling my toes. Come on, they don't hurt."

If I had gone into that dark water with the eels I might not have been afraid of anything again, for the rest of my life. Robert was down there swimming in the stream, conquering it. Yes, I have worked it up, it is no longer pure, but once it was below my consciousness and it was pure. It would have given me life if I had been able to go down there. I stood on the bridge and did not go, and presently Robert came out and dried himself with his shirt and pulled his trousers on.

"That was great. I wonder if I can tame those eels. We could go in a circus."

We walked up to the house. Music still splashed into the night. Couples sat on the lawn, smoking and kissing. On the verandah steps Emerson sat with a group of young men, talking about motorbikes. He was already a hero. Robert said goodnight. He meant to sleep in the garden shed to get away from the noise. When I had left him I walked along the gravel path by the bedrooms. I put my head in Agnes's window. Her dark head moved on the pillow.

"Agnes?"

"Meg. What do you want?"

"Goodnight."

"Goodnight, Meg."

I went to the sitting-room and found Mirth there, listening to the music dreamily.

"Where's Willis?"

"Outside with some girl. He won't be long."

I blushed.

"He'll give her a few kisses Meg, that's all."

"Don't you mind?"

"No. I don't think anyone's ever kissed her before. Willie's a very kind man."

"Won't he enjoy it too, Mirth?"

"You're a sly little thing. Do you know what men and women do yet?"

"Agnes is going to tell me." I wondered why they made such a fuss about it. It was interesting, no doubt, and disturbing, but there were more interesting things, and much more disturbing. Things, I mean, that men and women did. I knew that already.

I went down the hall to my bedroom, but on the way noticed Dad's study door slightly ajar. I stood there a moment wondering if I should go in. We had set times for visiting. Then I heard Mother cough. I pushed the door a little and put my head in. They were having one of their "paper chats" She handed him a sheet of paper; he read; wrote something and handed it back. Then he saw me and cried, "Ho, it's Meg. Come into my parlour."

Mother did not look pleased. I had interrupted one of her times with him. I said to her, "I'm sorry. I was on my way to bed and I thought I'd say goodnight."

"Goodnight, Meg."

"Sit down, my dear," cried Dad, who had heard none of this. "Pull up a chair and join our paper chat."

Mother put the paper sharply away. "What are they all doing?"

"Oh, talking," I said, "wandering round."

"It's time they all went home. Where's Alfred?"

"Up a tree."

"What's that?" Dad said, "what's that?"

"Alfred's up a tree."

"Is he now? Writing poetry?" That excused all sorts of odd behaviour; and I wondered if it would have excused Robert in the creek with eels and Esther with her butcher down the bank—even Willis off in the orchard with a woman not his wife. I hoped Mother was not going to ask me where they all were. I should have to lie.

"Well," Dad said, "we'll light some incense. It isn't often I get a visit from my wife and my daughter at once."

Mother softened to me. She had to work at hardness, it was not in her. She gave me a chair to sit on, and we stayed there, paper-chatting while midnight passed and the spice-and-sugar of incense filled the room. Buddha smiled on us.

It's been a lovely party, I wrote. *The night's so beautiful.*

Have you all been happy? Mother wrote.

It is a beauteous evening, calm and free, Dad wrote.

"Did you all get enough to eat?"

"We had happy cakes."

The holy time is quiet as a nun, breathless with adoration, Dad went on.

Screams came from the night, and Mother smiled. "It's time we sent them home," she said to me.

I stood up. "Going already?" Dad cried.

"It's half-past twelve." I pointed at his clock.

"Well bless my soul!"

I kissed them. Dad looked at me. "Stand still, Meg." Then he said to Mother, "She's grown up, Edie. When did she do that?" And to me: "You've grown up behind our backs."

"She's still a child and she should be in bed. Off you go, Meg."

I went, and closed the door, and washed, and brushed my teeth, and climbed in my summer nightie into my bed. I sighed with happiness. I heard Mum and Dad calling everyone in, sending them home, and heard Mum clattering dishes, tidying up. Esther slammed into the room and pulled off her dress and threw it on the floor. She got into bed in her underthings.

"Goodnight, Esther."

"Shut up."

I smiled and went happily to sleep. Later I woke and saw her dressing. I kept still but she said, "You can stop pretending."

"Where are you going?"

"It's none of your business.—No one's sending me to bed any more." She went to the window and raised it. "If you tell anyone this I'll murder you."

"I won't tell."

"I'm twenty-one. I can do what I like."

"Why don't you go out the door then?"

"The window's more fun." She grinned at me, and climbed out, and was gone.

After a while I went back to sleep, happily still; and it seems to me now I slept through the rest of that year, through winter, and Esther's wedding in the spring, and woke up only in late spring, in December. That was the time when uncle John Willis stayed with us. John Willis: I thought of him as having a physiognomy—but the physiognomy of what? As I watched him mooning about, it seemed almost of darkness and of death. I did not like him. He was a closed-up man, he seemed to carry about him odours of deception and odours of private delight. I was the only one to see that somehow, secretly, he made Alfred happy. It was not a happiness I liked. Watching them together, I felt myself cramped up, with all my limbs forced tight into my body, as though I had been stuffed into a sack. I waited in a kind of breathlessness for John to go.

His last week came. One Saturday morning Dad found Alfred

and John Willis in the orchard. Doing something unspeakable? Making love? Both are true. Dad cursed Alfred and drove him out from Peacehaven.

Then I had my dream again: a black river, with the Plumbs all sinking. I did not sleep, but lay wide-eyed in bed, watching it happen.

12 On racedays Fred Meggett was away in the pubs taking bets. With Mother I walked across Loomis to visit Esther. Sometimes Alfred called in. He came alone. Mother did not want to see John Willis. Alfred was hurt by that, he told me so. "She thinks he's my bad habit, like gambling or drinking—but a good deal worse." It gave her love for him a desperate edge.

As for me, I did not understand him. "He's a marvellous person, Meg. He's so good to me." I did not understand. "Yes," I said. By this time they were living together. I wondered if they had a double bed.

"Do you remember I told you I couldn't find out who I was? Well now I know."

"That's good," I said. (Who are you?)

"He's introduced me to some marvellous people."

"That's nice."

He had given up his university studies.

"Are you writing poetry, Alfred?"

"Not yet. But I will soon. I'm getting ready."

I did not think he would ever start. The knowledge came to me intuitively. His happiness might give him weight, but rage and pain made him light, unstable. He would never settle down to work.

"You should have seen Jehovah when he found us. His eyes went red. Literally. He nearly fell over. And his hat fell off—"

"Alfred—"

90

"He ran away like this, like a chimpanzee."

"I don't want to hear. Please."

"And then when he met us on the bridge with his handful of money. It was straight out of the Old Testament. 'I curse you, Alfred. You are no longer a Plumb. Here's money to change your name.' Half of it went in the water. You'd better tell Robert to fish it out. Sovereigns, after all."

"Alfred, please don't hate him."

"I don't hate him, Meg. I laugh at him. My God though, when I think of his face in that orchard. He was like Moses coming down with his tablets and finding us worshipping the golden calf." He laughed. "That's what John calls me. It's his name for me. The Golden Calf. He's marvellous with words."

"Alfred—"

"Heee, when his hat fell off."

"He loves you, Alfred."

"You're joking. He loves himself."

"We all love you."

"And I love John. No need to look like that. I do."

"You told me there was no love."

"I was wrong."

"You can't love him. Not the way people love."

"Meg, Meg—how can I explain it? You'll understand one day."

I wanted to ask him why he didn't see a doctor. I thought he had a disease. But I did not dare. Instead I asked if he was really going to change his name.

"Yes. As soon as I'm twenty-one. I'm going to be Alfred Hamer. It's got a good sound, don't you think?"

"Have you told Mum?"

"It's best not to tell her anything, Meg. Just let her keep boxing on."

Mother and Esther came in from the kitchen with cups of tea and a plate of the pikelets mother had brought. (Esther did no baking.)

"Mm, I've been missing these," Alfred said.

"Which one of you does the cooking?" Esther said.

"We take it in turns."

"I've had a letter from Agnes," Mother said.

"Whose turn is it tonight?"

"Oh, I do Saturdays. We've got some people coming in. I'm a better cook than John."

"She says she's met a nice young man called Jerry. I suppose that's Gerald. He's an engineer."

"He even burns the toast, John does."

"I hope she doesn't rush into things too fast."

Oh help her, Alfred, I wanted to cry out. Mother sat very pale.

"Mirth is expecting again."

"He's a phenomenon, that man." This time he meant Willie.

"Children are a blessing," Mother said. "Life is nothing without children," she said. I could no longer tell whom she was talking to. When she and Esther took the tea things out I hissed at him, "You said it was best not to tell her anything. And you spend all your time talking about John."

"That's a fact, Meg. John's a fact. You've all got to get used to that."

"Can't you help her?"

"I've got to live my life. If people can't fit in they've got to stay out."

"Mother isn't people."

"I suppose she's not. But what can I do? I can't pretend to be something I'm not."

"Pretend to her. Forget the rest of us."

He tried, but it did not work. Her ear was impossibly refined.

"I planted some spring onions this morning." With John.

"Can I take some of these pikelets home?" For John.

"It's getting late. I suppose I'd better be going." Home to John.

So it went on, through those Saturday afternoons. Alfred turned twenty-one. He changed his name to Hamer, Mother's name. I do not know what she thought of that. Esther became busier. She was always running out of the room to answer the door. Fred was a land agent now, but his more profitable line was bookmaking. People slunk up to the back door with bets, and Esther came back scribbling in a notebook. "What a lot of callers you have," Mother said. She never discovered the source of their new wealth.

"I'll have ten bob each way on Prester John," Alfred said. Prester John? Mother looked at him with agonized love. He saw the love, he was used to it, lapped it up. Only I saw the pain.

At home Dad had locked himself away. He was like a man in sickness, half-way recovered, and one did not know whether he would slip back, and die perhaps, or whether he would slowly, day by day, get well and be his old self. He was in that condition for the rest of his life. I tried very hard to make him well; and coming from an hour spent in his study (holding his hand, and he there scratching a sentence or two in his notebook) I likened myself to Abishag, the Shunammite maiden, sent to warm King David in his old age. But I could not warm Dad. Something had gone cold at his centre, far beyond my touch. There was a little damp closed room in there. I caught a musty smell. He smelt it himself, and for a while he tried to wash it away—bathing and soaping—but then gave up and lived with it. Bodily cleanliness had always been one of his moral aims. After banishing Alfred he gave up cleanliness.

He came out of his study in the end. He and Mother were very kind to each other. After several years they resumed their paper chats. I watched them study each other, puzzling at the way to happiness. They had taken it so easily before. Now they had to think out every step. She would take his arm on Sundays and they would do their round of the garden—but they kept clear of the orchard. They strolled about the lawns, through the rose garden and the flower beds, and they spent a long time in the vegetable garden, admiring Robert's work and praising him for it. They strolled along Millbrook Road arm in arm, she showed him secret places—perhaps in one a bird had made its nest and was hatching eggs, perhaps weeds flowered in one, beautifully as roses in a garden—and he spoke of some political matter, some new cause, some injustice, or in his orator's voice boomed out a poem. It was unreal. I sat at my books in the evenings and heard their laughter coming from the study. It was unreal. It was our new reality.

"I hope we can be like that," Fergus Sole said.

Fergus Sole? Yes, I had him. In that unhappy time I found my husband. He became my lifeline, replacing Mother.

"For God's sake Meg, get yourself a boy," Esther had said. She was kinder to me now that she was married.

"How?" I said, "how?" I wanted a boy, I wanted Monte— Monte/Fergus, Monte/Simon, Monte/David, Monte/Doug.

"Let them kiss you. Let them get their hand up your dress. That's all they want."

"No."

"You're not bad looking. Even Fred says so. You know about precautions, don't you?"

I let them kiss me. But Simon did it in a way I did not like, and David picked his ears and rolled the wax in little balls, which he smeared under his chair, and Doug used bad language to make me think he was a man of the world.

I had gone off Fergus too. He was two years older than me. When I began taking the train from Loomis station on my way to the Girls' Grammar School, Fergus was in the fourth form at Seddon Tech. He wore the green and yellow Seddon cap, which I thought more attractive than the Mt Albert Grammar one— though the Grammar boys were the ones I should be interested in. (Agnes had told me, but I did not need telling. They would be doctors and lawyers, some of them, while the Seddon boys would only be butchers and bricklayers.) I thought none of the Grammar boys would ever be interested in me. It did not make me sad, for they were a rowdy lot, cheeking the guard, smoking cigarettes, throwing water-bombs at our carriage windows when we came into Mt Albert station. One or two made verbal lunges at me, but found me "stuck-up" So they mimicked my vowel sounds and my way of saying, "Oh dear," and they named me Plumb Jam because of my straw cady with the broken top that opened like the lid of a can. They lifted it as they went by and put apple cores in. I thought very few of them would be doctors and lawyers. The world was a complicated place. The most gentlemanly boy on the train was Fergus Sole, from Seddon Tech. He stood back at the train steps to let the girls down. "Watch it," he said, "there's girls here," when his friends said bugger or damn. Once he lifted my bag down from the rack when its handle was caught in the netting. "Thank you," I said, blushing. But then he was gone from the train, apprenticed to a plumber, and I forgot him. For three years I never gave him a thought.

I left the Epsom Grammar School—the gym frocks and ties and starched collars and cady I had sewn up a hundred times—and began to train as a teacher. Simon and David and Doug were fellow students. I found their shortcomings out. I clung to impossible Monte—against the evidence I clung to him. "You precious girl!   kiss me!" Simon tried to put his tongue in my mouth, and David had more than one bad habit. Doug used words that seemed to me to give him a bad smell. I think I should have gone on believing in Monte and drifting further and further out of the world, if one Saturday afternoon my walk had not taken me past the Loomis cricket ground. I had no interest in sport. But I saw men in white clothes strolling on the grass beyond the trees, and I heard the crack of bat on ball, and on that afternoon, filled as all my afternoons were with Alfred and Mother and Dad, it seemed beautifully simple and cool and pure. It was part of our mythology that Mother and Dad had met at a cricket match. It crossed my mind, obscurely, that I might find their primal place for them, and bring them to it, and start them on their proper way again.

I went under the trees and walked along the whitewashed circle that marked the boundary of the field. I came towards a small grandstand holding a dozen people. On the grass in front of it players were lounging, waiting their turn at bat. I did not go close. I chose an empty bench in front of a paling fence and sat

there in the sun, watching the leisurely game. I circled in a lazy
contented way a mystery that would not be penetrated. The
rules of the game were strange to me; and the white-clad figures,
flicking into time, and out of it, had a meaning I could not
understand. It did not matter. Soon it did not matter. The sun
warmed my skin and made me want to sprawl and open my
limbs and catch it in my mouth and throat, and to my puzzle-
ment and shame, further down. I mean, it made me sexy. That
was not a word I knew. But I felt I was damaging my vision of
the game—formal and pure—and made it my business to sit up
straight and keep my knees together and keep my hands tight
folded in my lap.

I heard a smack as the bat struck the ball, and saw the red orb
fly into the air and make an arc and fall with a papery sound into
a bamboo clump at the far end of the ground. Sparrows flew
out in droves. In the stand people clapped. "Sixer. Good old
Fergie," someone yelled.

So I knew Fergus Sole. I saw him again. I had been half an
hour at the ground, sunning and dreaming in my ladylike pose,
watching, half-watching, a man with a bat hitting a ball with it,
before I suddenly saw Fergus Sole. He invaded me then, he filled
my mind, and somehow seemed to fill my body too. I took into
myself his shining hair (that was Vaseline putting light on it)
and his widow's peak that made his face so stern, and his eyes of
blue (blue of water and sky), and his arms and bony wrists and
plumber's hands. He struck the ball and it sped like a weasel at
me, deadly, true. It struck the palings and bounced back to my
feet and lay there throbbing. A fieldsman picked it up and
lobbed it back. But Fergus had sent me a message. On the paling
fence was a red bruise. There was a bruise in me—in my heart,
on my mind—somewhere in there. I had fallen in love. That is
how I saw it. I don't see why I should choose other ways of
describing it now. He swung his bat again. The ball clacked on
the palings further along. People cheered, and Fergus raised his
bat in a small salute. "Century!" Such a cut-and-dried word to
take on magic for me. His bat was a sword. I thought of Alfred's

Percival, and Monte Baron of the West, and they faded away and Fergus Sole stood there. Or someone like Fergus, a Fergus-shape filled with their virtues.

He struck. The ball sped away. High in the air it curved, and down by the bamboo clump a man got under it and juggled it once or twice and fell down on his knees, and Fergus was out. It did not matter. He had made his century. I was only cross that the man on the fence had made such a clumsy catch. A perfect catch was the end for Fergus. He came back to the stand. His bat was under his arm. He walked by me. He saw me. I knew he did. He made no sign.

And made no sign on the next Saturday. I came there again, I sat in the sun, I watched Fergus Sole fielding, watched him bowl. When he walked out with his bat I could not help it: I felt pure and soulful and sexy. Being there was my declaration. The whole of Loomis saw it. Fergus saw it, though he made no sign. The ball bruised the fence again. It came between my feet, increasing the bruise in me. But Fergus was quickly out. His stumps crashed over—perfect end for him. He walked back grinning ruefully, and wiped his hand on his brow so our eyes should not meet. I smiled at that.

Through the summer, whenever the Loomis side played at the park, I was there. I seldom went with Mother to see Alfred. I became expert in the rules of cricket. Other players sat on the seat by the palings and talked with me. I was a puzzle to them. Once Fergus Sole came with three others and sat by my feet and rubbed oil on his bat and looked at me. "Are you at the Training College?" he asked gruffly. "Yes," I said. It worried him. He snapped dry stalks of grass with his plumber's hands. The time was coming, I knew, when I would say, "I love your hands."

I went with my friend Lorna to a party. Lorna was a girl I had been at school with. She worked in the baker's shop in Loomis, selling cakes by the dozen and loaves of bread. She was an unhappy girl. She could not stop eating and at eighteen her flesh was swelling out on her thighs and arms. She wailed at it, and wept at it, and went on eating Lamingtons and cream buns and chocolate eclairs. Her boyfriend at this time was Jimmy Jessop, a member of the Loomis cricket team. The party was at his place. I went along. I painted myself very lightly and put some perfume on my wrists and throat and put my best dress on (a simple thing Alfred had once passed as "not too bad") and I went along for my meeting with Fergus Sole.

I did not stay long. Jimmy Jessop pestered me. Fergus stood in a corner and pretended not to see. Lorna watched from the supper table, gobbling cakes. This could not be the place. "Leave me alone, Jimmy Jessop. I don't like you." I made sure Fergus heard. I went out into the night and walked down the path and sought the concealing shade of a big macrocarpa tree by the gate. There in the cool dark, with aromatic branches about my head, I waited for Fergus Sole to come and find me. But it was Jimmy Jessop who came in the moonlight, and called my name and sensed me breathing there. He lifted the branches and came inside.

"Meg? Let me kiss you, Meg."

"Please don't, Jimmy. I don't like you like that."

"What's wrong with me? Lorna thinks I'm O.K." He was a stupid boy. He told me Lorna thought he was good at kissing. He was like a weak Fred Meggett, a weak Conroy.

"Don't touch me, Jimmy. I'll kick your shins."

He tried to grab me. I struck him with my fist high on his chest.

"Ow! That hurt."

"Go away. I'm waiting for someone."

"Who? Old Fergie Sole? You've got a crush on him, but he doesn't like you."

"That's all you know."

He grabbed me then and pushed his mouth at me. It was like being licked by a dog.

"Let me go. I hate being kissed like that."

"Hallo," a voice said from outside the tree. Fergus lifted the branches and came along, and stood up straight by Jimmy, half a head taller. Jimmy let me go.

"Who asked you in, Fergie?"

"Asked myself."

"I got here first."

"You can leave first then."

"Yeah?"

Fergus jerked his thumb. "Clear out, Jimmy."

"You going to make me?"

"Yep." It was almost as if Fergus too had read about Monte and Bab. "I'll count to three. One, two—"

Jimmy cleared out. "You're welcome to her. She doesn't even know what it's for." From further up the path he yelled, "And don't come back to my party."

"I'm sorry if he upset you," Fergus said.

"I'm all right now." I took out my handkerchief and rubbed my cheek where Jimmy had licked me.

"I'll walk you home."

"My shawl's up there," I said.

"I'll get it. I saw where you put it."

I waited in the aromatic dark. It was perfect. Our meeting was as romantic as I had hoped it would be. Even Jimmy Jessop added to it. Fergus came back with my shawl and wrapped it round my shoulders. We walked through Loomis and along Millbrook Road. The creek shone in the moonlight.

"I used to fish for eels in there," Fergus said.

"My brother swims with them."

"Bob? He's a funny kid, Bob." He took my hand. "Your father's a parson, isn't he?"

"Not any more. He gave it up. He doesn't believe in churches." I was confident that would not worry Fergus, although I had no idea what he believed. Nothing could go wrong, this was our meeting.

"Do you believe in them?" he asked.

"No. I think there's a God somewhere though."

"I don't know what I think."

"My father says God is in our minds."

"I don't know whether it's important."

"You're a funny plumber's apprentice," I said.

He was quiet at that, his hand went still.

"I love your hands," I said. "All the boys at Training College have got soft hands."

"Never done any work." He was unsure still.

"I love it when you hit sixers. I saw you hit one into the bamboo."

"We lost the ball.   Do you like it at Training College?"

"No. I don't want to be a teacher."

"Why do you go there, then?"

"There's nothing else to do. I don't want to work in a cake shop either." I want to be your wife, I almost said. "How long does your apprenticeship last?"

"Two more years."

"You'll be a plumber then?"

"Yes. There's nothing wrong with plumbers, Meg."

"I know. I know. They're better than schoolteachers."

"Teachers don't scare me."

He put his arms around me at the gate. He did not say, "You precious girl!   Kiss me!" I said it for him, in my mind. I held up my mouth as I had practised, in a way perfectly natural. We kissed softly.

"I'd like to see you again," he said.

"Yes."

"When?"

"Tomorrow?"

"I'd like you to meet my parents."

He did not realize what he had said, or that when I answered, "Yes," I was saying I would marry him.

Mother was waiting up for me in the kitchen. She looked at my flushed cheeks and said, "You'd better splash some cold water on your face."

"I've met the most wonderful boy."

"Cold water's the thing for wonderful boys."

"He wants me to meet his parents."

That worried her. "Who is he, Meg? What does he do?"

"His name is Fergus Sole. He's a plumber's apprentice. You're not to say a word, Mum. Plumbers are all right."

"Yes, Meg."

"He's much better than a plumber."

"But plumbers are all right."

"He's better than Simon and Doug."

"Of course. Whoever they are."

"Don't laugh at me, Mum."

"I'm not laughing. Go and wash your face and I'll make some tea."

I told her all about Fergus. She became very worried. She had not realized how far I had moved away from the real world.

"Don't make him something he's not, Meg dear."

"You did. Remember the cricket match."

"I always saw your father very clearly." But did not know, I saw her add, that he would ever turn out one of his sons. Seeing her pain, I came as close to seeing a real Fergus as I was to come for several years.

The next day he called for me in a small car and drove me into a street of railway houses. They had numbers stencilled high under their eaves. Fergus lived in A27. His father was a big slow heavy man, with grime in his scalp and hair sprouting from his ears. He was a railway blacksmith. He never spoke more than half a dozen words to me on a visit—no more than a hundred or so in his life. Mrs Sole made up for him: a skinny woman, with her skull all plain to see, and scaly clothes-peg hands, and her joints standing out of her skin. She had sinews in her arms, thin as wire, terribly strong, and sinews in her throat; and in her tongue. She was a worker. She told me so. All her life she had worked, she had known nothing else. To make sense of it, she placed all virtue there. I was a soft and useless thing to her. "Look at those hands. Never seen a scrubbing board, they haven't. You'll have to learn to scrub if you're going to have my boy." I was not good enough, she made no bones about it.

They appalled me. I felt a little sick. But they changed my view of Fergus only for the better. I described him in a poem I wrote: "growing to perfection in the mud"

On our second Sunday he took me on the train to Redwood Park. At Swanson station he held up his arms to help me from the carriage, and I, absurdly overdressed, and trying for "a gay insouciance", jumped instead of stepping down, and caught him unready. I had no lightness. The heel of my shoe caught in his fly and all the buttons sprang off and ping-ed on the carriage wheels. We should have laughed. If I had been Esther I suppose I would have gone into the bushes with him and made love. But it ruined our day. We took the next train back to Loomis. He was not even able to walk me home from the station. He ran off in the other direction, waving one-handed, pink in his face as a baby (that pink had been coming and going all of our silent ride home); and told his mother some tale, and she sewed his buttons on.

We recovered. After some months we made love. I will not go into that. It was not much fun, but was a business highly charged with feeling for both of us. We were in love. And as we went on with what I termed, rather oddly, "having a good time", I came to like it fairly well. I mean the physical doings and responses. I always loved the emotional side of it (always in those days), especially the sacrificial part, and I loved his pleasure, and loved to watch while he lost himself, taking that for his finding of me. He said my name.

Well, enough of that. We became engaged. Mother liked him, up to a point. She would have wished him cleverer, and less of the physical man. But she recognized his honesty and goodness. Dad had a much sterner disapproval. And his absurdities led him into a sensible judgement. He was full of ambitions for Man, and full of plans for Eugenic Betterment (that nonsense that became so dangerous). Even his Socialism required an élite, though he never found a way of saying so. What it boiled down to was that Fergus was not good enough. That was not the sensible part of his judgement. Fergus and I were not suited— that was it. I would have loved to hear him talking about it with Mrs Sole.

But I saw Fergus slowly break him down. He did it by laughing, nervously at first, at Dad's innocent jokes and his foolish remarks about women. "Trout, like women, Fergus, are taken by a bit of coloured feather or rag. They jump, my boy, they jump readily." Fergus laughed—a nervous laugh, that one. And Dad told him about the Irish woman coming through customs. "'What's in the bottle?' the customs man said. 'Lourdes water.' 'It smells like gin to me.' 'I knew a blessed miracle would happen before I got home.'" (Bluey Considine had told it to him.) Fergus laughed again, more happily. And before very long Dad began to tell him tales about me as a child. "I came across her once drawing a picture—it was a sort of cloudy presence. 'What's that?' I said. 'God, said Meg. 'But nobody knows what God looks like.' 'Well, they will when I'm finished.'"

Fergus fixed the spouting on our house and put new washers in our dripping taps. Robert was annoyed about that, but he liked Fergus too. The two of them spent four summer Sundays digging out and re-laying the Peacehaven drains. Dad offered Fergus a pound, which he would not take. So he gave him a book of Emerson's essays instead.

"I can't read it, Meg."

"Never mind, never mind, tell him you haven't got time."

"What does *Mens agitat molem* mean? He wrote it in the front. Is it something to do with teeth?"

We sneaked into Dad's study and looked it up in Webster. "I found out what *Mens agitat molem* means, Mr Plumb," Fergus shouted that afternoon into Dad's trumpet. "Mind moves matter."

"Ah, you're coming on. You're learning, Fergus." He still thought ours a bad match; but he liked Fergus. They went off together to cricket matches.

It made me happy to see them. I thought of myself as possessing (and wrote it too) a gently welling cup of happiness. The books I read, and the language they taught me! *A gently welling cup of happiness.* But Alfred was still banished; and that darkness lay between Mother and Dad. So I wrote that my cup "was held in the Dark Hand of Life" But there was hope. I wept over *Precious Bane*, and rejoiced in its ending, indeed I almost cried out with belief. Kester Woodseaves kissed Prue Sarn on her hare-shotten lip. That for me was realism. A hare-shotten lip came from the Dark Hand of Life. And Kester Woodseaves lowered his mouth and kissed her. I lived in hope. And I had Fergus Sole.

I taught school for a year. He finished his apprenticeship. We married then, and settled down to be happy.

13 To be happy? Our expectations were not impossibly high. But my mother-in-law. The depression. And childbirth. Moony Meg. I cannot blame our fall on one of these; or all of them. There was something else. We tumbled down. But I shall say a word or two first on how for a time we found our rosy future almost coming true.

There was, to begin with, his coming home. How my day lit up. We had rented a house too expensive for us in one of the better streets of Loomis not far from Esther's place. I could not believe it was mine (and was just coming to believe when the depression put us into a three-roomed shack down by the creek—but that comes later). I played in the kitchen nervously. I made the double bed in something between disbelief and guilt. Was it true I had grown up? As the day went on I came to believe it. And Fergus, coming home, stamped on me the mark of womanhood. I do not mean he took me off to bed, though once or twice he did, and we found that "love" did not *have* to be done at night. I mean he kissed me, told me of his day; took off his boots, washed his feet in the bath; I served his meal, and we sat through the evening as man and wife. That lit me up with what I shall have to call *meaning*.

I walked out with my shopping kit and filled it with meat

from Porky Meggett's butcher shop. I gossiped in the baker's with Lorna Tilley—Ten-ton Lorna they called her—and she slipped an extra fruit square in with my dozen. ("Fly cemeteries," Lorna giggled, shocking me.) At the grocer's I bought cheese and butter and flour and a new scrubbing brush. And at Doctor Walker's I learned I was expecting. I went to the draper's and bought some wool to start knitting. Meaning! I wore it like a crown upon my head.

"Who have you told?" Fergus asked.

"Just Mum. I went round this afternoon."

"Did you tell my mum?"

"Not yet."

That was a small shadow. We celebrated with an extra chop and a glass of beer.

Childbirth that first time was not easy, nor too hard. The pain came in waves, and sank away. I could hear it rustling with a shingly sound, leaving a beautiful calm, all light and peace; and feel it building, building to a new wave that might wash me out of life—but always it stopped, just at the point when I knew I should have to cry out and give way and start screaming. It wasn't too bad. They wheeled me into the delivery room and Robert was born. *Meaning* went away and left me holding my baby, feeling him suck. I felt very peaceful, happy down into my bones, and grown up at last.

Fergus brought me flowers and fruit and chocolates. The spring scent of stock filled the room. He knew my favourites. His happiness was different from mine. There was a crowing in him, and a masculine increase, a pushing out. I said, "You won't go chasing anyone while I'm in here?"

"Hey, you're crackers Meg, it's you I love."

"You won't get in any fights?"

He came along the ward the next night with his eyes burning and hurt and his face white as paper. He held his handkerchief to his mouth. "I can't kiss you, Meg."

"Fergus," I cried, "you've been fighting."

"No. I've had my teeth out."

I made a sound like fingernails on silk. Fergus, bending close to me, an anxious giant, suddenly shrank to a goblin size. For me his nature changed. He was Fergus no longer—and he has never grown back, though he grew into other shapes I could admire. But in that moment, as he withered and shrank beside my bed, I felt his loss as deeply as Rebecca's drowning and Alfred's banishment, and I felt a bitter dislike of this strange man bending dumbly over me, bleeding into his crumpled handkerchief. His mouth would grow like the sucked-in wound on my brother Oliver's leg.

"Why? Why did you do that?"

"I thought it would be a good idea. Mum thought so."

"Your mother?"

"I won't have to go to the dentist, Meg. No trouble with fillings and things."

"She's a stupid bitch." I had never spoken that word before.

"Meg!"

"Did you have gas?"

"No."

"Just like you. Proving you're a man."

"You can't blame Mum."

"Who can I blame? No, don't talk if it hurts. Go home, Fergus. I want to sleep." I turned to the wall. After a while he went away.

I lay in my bed wanting nothing except to be back home at Peacehaven with Mother. Home, that was my knowledge. Peacehaven was home. Out in the world was danger and ugliness and pain; and what seemed worse, stupidity. To pull out teeth that were not too bad just so that he need not worry about fillings any more! I made the screeching noise again, and a passing nurse stopped to ask if I had a pain. "Yes, yes," I said, but would not tell her where. I told her I wanted to go home.

"Oh, it's too soon yet. And here comes your mother-in-law."

The woman sat in the straight chair by my bed and held her hard purse on her scrawny knees. I let her have it. She grinned with pleasure in fighting, and answered back, better than I could give. Mr Sole, grimy old blacksmith Sole, winked at me sadly from his post at her back, trying to let me see he cared for me. "Let there be harmony." There would never be that between Mrs Sole and me. We screamed at each other. The sister came running and joined in the shouting too. Mrs Sole stood up, she mounted on her toes like a little brightly coloured crowing bird. "I told my boy he should never have married you."

I cried my new word, bitch, and my certainty, stupid; put them together, shrieked them at her. "Stupid bitch!" It was all I could say.

"Please. Please. Out you go," cried the sister, pushing Mrs Sole. Mrs Sole turned on her, I thought for a moment she was going to scratch her. But Mr Sole put his arms round her waist from behind, lifted her up, said, "Enough's enough, Mother," and walked down the ward with her. She kicked like a child. Bang, bang went her heels on his shins. She struck back-handed with her long leather purse, but he kept on, past Fergus bleeding in the door, and out of the hospital.

"Now, Mrs Sole!" the sister said, exploding out her breath. I turned to the wall again. I did not listen. "I want to go home."

I went home not to Peacehaven, but to our rented house. I began the job of learning Fergus again. I soon grew to like him, and make declarations of love. I would not examine what I meant by that. Well, who does? I remember the time as being happy enough. I got used to his false teeth, and his sucked-in mouth when he took them out at night. For several months I would not visit his mother. Fergus walked there on Sundays, with Bobby in his pram. When I went at last we stood at arms length and were formal, and that's the way we went on. She learned to pour out words about nothing at all, and I to say, "Yes, that's true," and "You may be right." No real word passed between us again. Poor Ted Sole sat in his chair, breathing and smoking his pipe. Now and then he winked at me heavily.

Down in Wellington Felicity had her baby. Her long affair with the politician Dan Peabody came to an end and she married

Max Waring, a civil servant. My brilliant sister, Felicity, the one who would follow Dad: she married a shy ugly little man who was not very clever. It did not bother me that her baby was well on the way—that was part of her "freedom" But Max! It was many years before I understood Felicity, not her husband, was the lucky one.

But all was changing, all was unexpected and strange. There were babies everywhere: Mirth's and Esther's and mine and Felicity's. Agnes and Edith had babies in California. Sometimes when I remembered that I, the youngest sister, had had my child in the same year as Felicity, the oldest, I would be caught in a fear that everything had happened too suddenly, too fast, that there were things I should have known, and should have done, before I married. I thought again of the Black River and the Land of Missing, or I sat at the kitchen table drinking tea and feeling a yearning in me for Peacehaven and the Plumbs, and sometimes for the world, which came before my eyes in story-book shapes and story-book colours. Would I ever know it?

Then Fergus came home and said he had lost his job. For months he was about the house, fretting, and turning suddenly, and kicking things, and digging fiercely in the garden. I had two children. Bobby was the easy one. Fergus made me ache with pity for him.

We left our expensive house and moved to a little shack down by the creek. I was more at home there. I met the discomforts of the place—the tin bath in a lean-to out with the cooper and tubs, the cooking-place dug into a bank and sheltered by a beaten-out piece of roofing iron—I met them with a kind of recognition. In Beavis Street, up by Esther Meggett, I had only been playing at house.

Rebecca was born. I boiled napkins in the copper and wrung them out by hand and pegged them up to dry on a line held clear of the potato patch by a tea-tree prop. At last I began to feel I was grown up, a married woman.

I named our first two children so it was only fair that Fergus should name our third. He came up with Nelson, and was proud of himself, but I took violently against it: a military name. "Nelson was a sailor." "You know very well what I mean." So he left it to me. I chose Raymond.

He was born at St Helen's hospital in Auckland. Whenever I come across the word workhouse I think of St Helen's. That is being unfair to it. Without a place like that we depression wives might have had our babies in ditches. But in that grey city building birth somehow became grey. Again I am being unfair. But that is common with women in childbirth, and I am concerned with how it struck me then.

I travelled in by train for my pre-natal examinations. The tutor sister used us to teach her students. "Nurse Cooper, find me the head. No! Warm your hands, you ninny." And Nurse Cooper, with a tear running down her nose, felt about with her fat hands and found my baby's buttocks and head and feet. "Now, Nurse Todd. Open your legs, Mrs Sole, you don't have to be shy with us. Warm hands, Nurse Todd?" It was not kindness made her insist on that. The textbook insisted. She made them find the place, and had poor Nurse Cooper read it aloud.

When my labour pains started Fergus called in a neighbour. He rode off on his bicycle for a taxi. Two weeks the money had lain on my dressing-table, and though we had had no meat in the house in that time we had not touched it. We rode into Auckland in an Essex Super Six. "Don't have it in my car, lady," the driver said. Fergus held my hand. He has held it many times since, but that, in a way, was the last time.

Raymond's was a hard birth: for him too, I believe, although there is no way of knowing. Once the midwife slapped me on my buttocks. "Come on Mrs Sole, you're not trying." I am not an unforgiving person, but I have hated that woman ever since. When it was over I was numb and drained and torn and deeply bruised, and my certainty was not that I had given birth but that I was violated. I made a vow—it was more than that, I made a change in myself, in the chemistry of myself, in my body's cells, and if the feelings have cells, in those cells too: there would be no more doctors and nurses, no babies—no husband bringing this violation on me. I cannot alter it. I have tried.

Fergus came in. They showed him the baby. He kissed me and held my hand—but my holding was different from that in the taxi. He peered at me anxiously. "What is it, Meg? What's wrong?"

"No more babies, Fergus. I don't want any more babies."

"No, no, three's enough."

"Come on, Mr Sole, she needs to sleep."

"I'm sorry, Fergus." I knew what I was withdrawing from him. Not my body. It was more than that. He would have me no more. I would not have him.

But there was Raymond. We are not supposed to have favourites, and I said whenever it came up that I loved my children equally. But deep in me I knew I loved Raymond best. I was hurt for the other two. There had been nothing special in the pain of their births. They were unlucky—maybe lucky. I loved them with a placid protecting love, full of good feeling. It would have grown fierce if it needed to. But when the nurse brought Raymond to me in St Helen's and I put him on my breast and felt him suck, and knew us safe from that violation we had undergone, then all my bad emotions flowed across into the balancing cup, and down I came on the side of love. Overbrimming love. I can use that language.

From the next bed Mirth laughed at my face. Yes, she was there. She too had a baby on her breast: Douglas, her last. (He was Sebastian Douglas, but the boy made up his mind for the second name—and the politician he has become finds the choice a smart one.) Mirth was forty-eight. When I mentioned that recently to my daughter-in-law, Bobby's wife, who's a nurse, she said, "Good God, she really was an elderly multi-gravida." I don't think they used that term in St Helen's. But the tutors brought their classes to look at her. They were amazed at her flow of milk. Mirth took it in good part. And Willis, stumping in whenever it pleased him, made hay of those snapping sisters. "You watch me blarney the starch out of them."

Mirth thrust her baby at me one morning. "Swap you. Give them a change of diet. Mine's flavoured with grapefruit." She laughed at my horrified face (she really meant to swap), and said, "You're a soft little thing. You're all marshmallows. That's what I like about you."

She became ward mother, padding about barefooted in an old army greatcoat. We confessed our troubles to her. Even the nurses confessed. Mirth wiped Nurse Cooper's tear-wet nose on the edge of her bed sheet. She waved an advancing sister away. "Don't you try and boss me, dear. I'm old enough to be your mother. You give this girl a moment. Off you go. Do your work." The sister went.

I told Mirth I was not having any more babies. She said that was all right, the woman should decide. She wasn't having any more babies either. She'd enjoyed the lot of them, but three in her first marriage and five in her second was enough. "The trouble is," she said, "Willie's such an eager little devil. I often think all the energy that should have gone into that leg he lost is being sent somewhere else. Don't worry, he's the only man for me. But this time he's going to give me time to get my menopause started." I think Willis wanted to climb in with her in the home. He probably would have tried if his sister had not been watching from the next bed.

Fergus came to see me every night. Dad came, bringing roses. "A mother, Meg. A mother for the third time. I can hardly believe it. It seems only yesterday you were born." Mother came only once. She was not well. The noise and the crowding in the ward upset her. She had had her babies at home and she thought of birth as a private business. She was driven away by the women in beds, by husbands in their boots and mothers in print dresses, and by the smell of milk and the monkey-house chatter. She kissed me and hurried down the ward, dark in her clothes, cut off from it all, and in that moment I understood she was dying. Dad had not brought his trumpet. I wrote on a scrap of paper,

How is she, Dad? He said, "Not well, Meg. I'm worried about her. But we mustn't talk about that here." He did not like the forced intimacies of the place either, but still he managed to see it as a kind of temple. Especially, he liked seeing the babies in the nursery. They blasted him with their urgency and greed. I believe he almost heard them through his deafness. "The Life Force is in that room. You can feel it, Meg." I found him rather tiresome in St Helen's.

I asked Fergus about Mother, but he had noticed nothing. "She seems all right to me. When can you come home, Meg? The kids are missing you."

"Two more days. They'll survive." I was getting tough. But a moment later my eyes filled with tears at the thought of Rebecca and Bobby. "I wish I could see them."

"Not long now, Meg." He went a little pink, but made himself say what he thought was owing to both of us. "We'll have to be careful. We'll have to take precautions." I said nothing to that. I must have looked stony. He said, "I'd better go and see Ray. It's nearly closing time."

"Raymond."

"Esther says Raymong."

"She would."

"They've all got the same initial. She jokes about that too."

"I think it's nice. I don't see any joke."

"The way R goes with Sole."

I did not see it and he would not tell me. (For more than thirty years I did not understand. Bobby told me last Christmas—a little drunk. In a perverse way, he's pleased with his name these days.) Fergus went off to the nursery and looked at his son. He came back grinning and held my hand until the bell drove him out. I gave him a letter to drop in Mr Tilley's box on his ride home. And through this act discovered the sort of love I wanted from Fergus.

Mirth had gone home. Lorna Tilley had taken her bed— Jimmy Jessop's Lorna. She came to St Helen's off the street, walked in, cramped in two, far gone in labour. They got her on the table, where she gave birth to a girl. When the ward came to life in the morning Lorna found me in the bed next to hers. She turned her face away, but I got her talking, and weeping too, in no time. She would not tell me who her baby's father was. It was not Jimmy Jessop, it was no one I knew. "It happened after a party, Meg. I didn't like him much. But no one looked at me any more. I'd got so fat." She was fat enough to conceal her condition into her seventh month. Then her mother, a glass-sharp, glittering, poisonous, Christian lady, turned her out. She lived with friends, with men. They turned her out too. That was her story. St Helen's accepted her. The nurses came round that morning when Lorna was bathing and took donations for her: a nightie here, bonnets and booties and napkins. She cried when she saw them. "Nobody's been nice to me for so long."

Lorna wanted to see her father. He had been kind, away from his wife's view. But she could not write and tell him where she was. She was ashamed. In my letter I told him. I told him she and the baby were well, but that she had nothing and nowhere to go.

The next day a huge booted man creaked along the ward. He wore a Sunday suit and a collar with pointed wings. I had not seen that sort of thing for fifteen years. He had dressed for his daughter. He had dressed to offer himself. He carried his hat. He carried violets. His red ears, thick as hands, stood out from his head. Some of the girls laughed, but he was not a comic figure. Lorna cried hugely; and tears ran down Mr Tilley's face. "There, there," he said, "there, there." He patted her. They rocked in each other's arms.

It was a love that placed her in no danger. She could relax in it—grow fatter if she pleased. I did not ask what return she made, or what it was I would be giving Fergus if I took from him the sort of love Lorna Tilley had. I simply knew *that* was what I wanted—and knew as Fergus walked up the ward, clumsy and shy and red as Mr Tilley, but with a man-light in his eye, it was something I could not have. Momentarily, I hated him. He saw it on my face, and paused, and then came bravely on, frowning a little.

"What is it, Meg?"

"I'm sore." I did not see how a man could desire a woman who was torn and stitched, whose nightie was damp with milk leaking from her breasts. It seemed unnatural. It seemed a thing for beasts.

He brought me home to Loomis in Fred Meggett's car. For three more years we lived in our rusty shack. I boiled my wash and hung the nappies out over the bean rows. With the wind blowing smoke about my face and rain drumming on the iron, I boiled our meals of neck chops and spuds and turnips and corn and beans. I showed Fergus's mother I could work. I grew thin and strong as her, stringy muscles stood out in my arms. Still she would not like me. I did not care. Nothing about the Soles was of interest to me. My children were Plumbs, I said, and Fergus in his good parts was a Plumb. It was the Sole in him that moved us apart—what Alfred would have called the peasant. I called it that, in my snobbish moments, when I was attacked in my "understandings", but more often I thought of it as the animal. We got along, we gave each other a good deal of kindness, but where we had come together once in love we came now only in duty on my part, and in a dumb rage and resentment and greed—and sometimes in guilt—on his. There were times when I loved him like a child, my tenderness for him overflowed and I wanted to stroke him and hold him and cure all his troubles. He hated that.

"Meg," he said as we lay in bed one night. His hand came cautiously on to my hip. I had been nearly asleep.

"Oh, Fergus," I whispered, "I'm so tired. The children have been so naughty today," and I rolled away from him on to my side—acting sleepiness, for such things always brought me wide awake. "Tomorrow night," I murmured, and I breathed as though I had sunk into sleep.

Fergus lay still for a moment. I felt his rage. It filled the bed and filled the room and drummed under the roof. It seemed to me it would wake the children and set them screaming. I shrank under it. I became small and withered, like a dried-up fruit.

Fergus climbed out of bed. He was quick, he was full of ugliness.

"Where are you going?"

"Shut up."

He went out into the night. I ran after him as far as the door, and saw him in the moonlight dragging his axe out from the old rain tank we used as a wood store. It was only for a moment I believed he would come back into the house and butcher us all: the barest moment, a blink of pure terror. Even before he turned away from me I knew it was not possible, and a kind of gratitude came on me, and a kind of contentment, that I would be troubled no more, that he was working out his rage in some final way. He turned into the garden, and there by the silver-beet patch he attacked the trunk of our huge old wattle tree.

He chopped as white moths flew about his head. The gleaming axe and flying chips; his wide-legged stance; Fergus in pyjamas, altering us: I will never forget. The tree rang like a bell. Soon it creaked and shuddered in its head. It leaned towards the garden, and crashed at last over the bean frames, over the pumpkin patch. Its branches crushed my wash-house into the ground. Pollen smoked up into the silver night. I felt like clapping.

Fergus drove his axe into the stump. He went to the rain-water tank and turned on the tap and splashed water on his face. I got him a towel. "Thanks." He walked past me into the house and into the bedroom. When I came in he was dressing. He put in his teeth.

"Where are you going?" I asked.

"I need a walk. Don't worry, I'm coming back."

"Fergus, I'm sorry."

"Go to bed, Meg. Go to sleep." He was very calm, very slow. He smiled at me. "It's late. Raymong will be coming in soon."

I heard the gate creak and I heard him whistling as he walked up the road. I went to bed, and I went to sleep. Soon Raymond snuggled in beside me. He did not seem surprised to find his father gone.

When I woke, Fergus was cooking breakfast. He brought me a cup of tea. That day he did not ride out looking for work, but chopped the branches off the wattle tree and sawed its trunk into lengths and dragged them away. I took out a bucket and picked the beans from the crushed bean-row.

"I'll have to get that wash-house fixed," Fergus said.

So we lived together and grew apart. There was little drama in it after that night. I loaned him my body now and then, enough to keep a kind of contentment in him. It was a shallow thing, but he had, I think, another sort, much deeper. I robbed him of manhood, but he went out with his axe and proved to himself he was a man. He saved himself—in a way, he saved us all.

He took up cricket again and played in friendly matches. Sometimes we all went along. Rebecca sat on the bar of his bike and Bobby on the back mudguard. I wheeled Raymond in his pushchair. Now and then Dad came along and we sat on the grass and watched Fergus hitting sixers. Mother came only once. She had been at Esther's for lunch and Esther drove her down to the ground in the middle of the afternoon. No one in the teams could afford white trousers (Fergus, though, had his old Loomis cap) but I think Mother saw enough in the bowling and batting to take her back those forty years to the time of her meeting with Dad. "Your father used to play cricket," she said to me. And Dad, reading her lips, aware of her in this setting, and troubled by their lives, said, "Your mother and I met at a cricket match. Didn't we, Edie? They used to call me the steady little trundler." He tried to push away the shadow by bringing up a thing not essential to them. Fergus hit a boundary and he clapped. Mother led me off to the next-door paddock to pick blackberries. We picked into her hat, lining it first with her handkerchief. "He was very good at cricket. I'll make the children a blackberry pie." A little later she said, "Meg dear, you're not happy. I can tell."

"I'm all right, Mum. If only Fergus could find a job. That's what the trouble is." I don't think she believed me. I did not lie well.

"Open your mouth. Open. Open wide." She put a fat black-berry into Raymond's mouth.

"Greedy boy," I said.

"They should be greedy at this age."

"He looks as if he's been sucking blood. Little vampire."

"Meg, what a dreadful thing to say."

I thought so too. I hugged Raymond in apology. Mother smiled. "You're a soft-hearted girl."

"Not any more. I'm hard."

"Nonsense, Meg."

"Yes, it is nonsense. Sometimes I wish I could be."

"And not have any love left? That would be the worst thing." She was a practical woman. She spoke of love and courage and honesty as though of things in her kitchen. And when she said, "We must love one another, Meg," she was telling me some-thing she had learned as a fact. As we picked blackberries, and fed the children the juiciest ones, she told me we must love, and we must struggle, and in the end we must accept. She told me acceptance is hardest. All this is true. But the fact is that if she managed to accept, and I'm not sure she did, it was because she believed in an after-life. Everything would be made right in that place. But I would not allow her to speak of God as she spoke of love and courage. I would have none of God, and none in this existence of an after-life. I was committed to a life of feeling, the life of now. Love I could manage, and I could struggle too. But acceptance?—accept that pain?—no. Look for an understanding of it all in the hereafter? Never! Never! I could see very clearly that it would have been something to drop into the hole left in me by the withering away of my romantic and sentimental view. But I felt too strongly the injustice of things. I felt that joys we could imagine we also had a right to.

I worried Mother, and hurt her too, that day. I told her she was foolish. But of course, soft-hearted, said that I was sorry: and I was, although I believed that in this thing (belief in God) Mother was foolish. (So was Dad, but I never found the courage to tell him.) Her hat was overflowing with blackberries. The sun beating on her head was making her dizzy, so I gave her my head-scarf, and took the hat from her, and we went back to the cricket ground. Fergus was out. He helped us through the fence. "I'll make you a blackberry pie, Fergus," Mother said. She flirted with him. They were easy with each other. Soon Esther arrived to drive her home. We sat on the warm grass for a while and picked at the blackberries like sweets until Mother covered the hat with her hands. We joked about her hardness. She saved enough to make a pie and when I went round to see her the following day she gave it to me to take home for our pudding.

We drank a cup of tea in the summer-house. Bobby and Rebecca played on the slope above the creek where I had spied on Esther and Fred Meggett. Robert kept an eye on them to see they did not fall in. We had called him from the garden behind the house. He washed his hands in the creek. "Scones, eh Mum? You'll be making us fat." We did not eat many though, we fed the children. I calculated how much less they would need for tea if they filled up now.

Mother's illness had aged her. She was sixty-four and looked ten years older. But she gave the impression of being tired rather than ill. Bone-tired: that term might have been invented for Mother. On that day in the summer-house, feeding scones into the mouths of greedy children (hungry at first, but greedy in the end), I was able to grasp her life and examine it as though it had been an object. I had not been able to do that before, though I had seen parts of it clearly enough. I had seen a surface play—those endless kitchen tasks, that seasonal activity of planting and pruning, and seen her care of Dad and her keeping of the world's life out of his study. I had known her love. But that was not all. I had known there must be more, and had never seen it. She did not speak differently that day. She told the stories she had always told. But I saw her bone-tiredness, saw death approaching, and I had a half-hour's sight of who she was. She was Edith Hamer, she was Edie Plumb—and below the surface workings of her life was a rich fullness, love and joy and contentment, and an endless sacrificing of self and a finding of self. And disappointment and pain. But above all, love.

I write as though of a saint. She was close to that. Dad had hurt her. Dad had struck her to the heart. The others—Oliver, Felicity, Esther—carry on about his selfishness. It obsesses them. Oliver, in his pedantic way, writes to me of "Dad's retreat from the quotidian" And Felicity says that when he got off to his study with his books he was "making one little room an everywhere—but, poor old thing, in human terms he was nowhere" And even I find myself recalling his way of putting his hand to his forehead when family got too much for him and running away to Browning or Emerson. Mother stayed and coped. But this is off to one side in their life. It is not at the centre, where the others would have it. "The quotidian" was her part of the contract. She understood that with the utmost clarity. His was to seek after truth, to stand and fight. He martyred himself to his conscience, and she to him. She of course had a better understanding of it all. (That's by the way, though it makes her the wiser person.) As long as the whole thing stood upon love, she saw it as their bargain. And he failed her there. He failed in love; and Mother was struck to the heart.

Well, I grasped all this as I listened to her talk that afternoon, telling stories I had heard as a child. She gave me the blackberry pie. "We used to have blackberry picnics in Kumara, altogether, all the churches together. It was such a funny sight to see us all setting out, twenty or thirty women in their oldest clothes, carrying buckets, and a tribe of children running by their sides with billies and cans. Dressed in rags, some of them. We didn't care. They were special days. We took lemon drinks and sandwiches and plenty of cake for the children, and we enjoyed it so much, the outing, Meg, and the sun, and the *abandon* of it. We came home with our dresses torn and the children with their faces stained all purple. We looked like a tribe of gypsies (begging their pardon), and our buckets all overflowing. The next day we made jam. For the most delicious jam give me sunripe blackberries."

"There's still a few up the paddock. I'll pick them," Robert said.

"You know," Mother said, "the chimneys in Kumura were all tin ones and after a windy night they would all be pointing in different directions." And she said, "There was a boy brought the milk to the back door in the evening. He was a bit simple. One night I thought I'd talk to him a bit. I thought, Poor fellow, no one bothers to talk to him. So I asked him where he was working and things like that. And after a minute he said, 'Well, I can't waste any more time with you, I must be going.' George, your father, used to tease me about it. He'd say, 'If Joe Kent can't waste time talking to you I can't, I'm sure.'" I had heard that story many times—and laughed at it because she thought it funny. Then she told us one I had not heard. "When we were in Emslie the Church of England minister's wife died, and the Wesleyan minister's wife died. One of our elders said to me, 'Don't you die, Mrs Plumb, or folks might think the ministers are killing off their wives.'"

What made her remember that? Knowing her as I did that day, I felt it piercing me. "Oh, Mother," I said.

"What is it, Meg?"

"If only   "

But she was not as deep down in her life as I had been. She smiled at me. "If only, Meg? If only fisherman Jack loved Kate, and fisherman John loved me. It won't do, dear."

Soon I gathered my children and took my blackberry pie and went off home.

Winter. A cold that made our bones ache. Frost crackling like glass on the sunless bank below our house. Robert banging our window in the dawn. Mother was having an attack. I put on Fergus's oilskin and took his bike and rode through the icy rain and yellow puddles to Peacehaven. I pushed through Wendy Philson's embrace and came to Mother's bed. She lay there waxen, amber, tidied up.

"Meg, it was very quick," Wendy sobbed.

"Go away."

I kissed Mother on her brow. "Mother," I said, "I loved you so much. I'm glad you're happy now."

Of course, I only believed that for a moment. But the moment is what's important, not its shortness. I know. I felt it.

14 Felicity telephoned from Wellington and asked to speak to Robert. I told her it would cost her a fortune to hold on while I fetched him from the cottage. Besides, he was not well enough to be running up all that way. She got big-sisterish, but I laughed at her. "That won't work, Felicity. If you want to talk to Robert you'll have to come to Auckland."

"All right, I will. I'll come up next week. You can meet me off the plane. I'll telegram you."

In fact, she phoned again. "Oliver's coming too. I couldn't put him off. He wants to look at Dad's papers."

"It's a bit inconvenient. Robert really isn't very well."

"He won't want to see Robert. It doesn't suit me, either. But what could I do? Can you meet the plane?"

I drove them home in time for lunch on a mild summer day. Oliver was offended by my car.

"What did you expect? A Rolls Royce?" Felicity asked.

"I would just as soon have taken a taxi." He got in quickly in case someone should see him.

"Sir Oliver Plumb in a Hillman Imp. It'll make a good chapter for your autobiography."

"Fergus uses the big car," I said. "Tuck your knees up, Oliver. You would have been better in the front."

"Knights of the realm don't sit next to the driver," Felicity said.

"I trust you're not going to keep this up."

"Off we go." I drove home fast.

After lunch Felicity walked down to see Robert. I had warned him she was coming. They had not met for twenty-five years. I

sat in the living-room with Oliver. He had climbed down a lot.
Peacehaven relaxed him.

"You've kept the place up well. I approve of that. I wouldn't
mind living here myself."

I must have shown my alarm for he said, a little stiffly, "Oh,
don't worry. The capital's the place for me. I still exercise some
influence. They need the sort of attention I bring to things.
You'd be surprised, Meg, the people who call on me." He
named a couple. I was surprised. I was a good deal impressed.
He smiled at me. "And of course I go to Government House.
We have much in common."

"I'm glad you're not lonely, Oliver."

"I could never be that."

"Are you really writing your autobiography?"

"Memoirs, Meg, they're memoirs. I'll suppress a lot. It serves
no purpose to bring up certain things. I'll deal mainly with my
career in the law. That is what will interest people. But you
understand, when the Chief Justice—the former Chief Justice—
writes of his life, he has to be discreet. He's a public figure. An
elevated one, I grant you that. But there's no point in dwelling
on—what shall we say, unedifying matters? I'll go through
Dad's papers though. I may come across one or two things that
will throw some light."

"Will you write about him?"

"No. I shall say he trained for the law. But did not practice.
That has some interest."

"His trials would have some interest."

"None, Meg. They're forgotten. Let's keep them so."

I showed him into the study and showed him where the
notebooks and letters were kept.

"Wendy Philson has some. But I don't think there's anything
in them to interest you."

"That woman who wanted to marry him?" He must have had
that from Felicity. "What's she doing with them?"

"She's writing his life."

"Good heavens! You're not letting her?"

"Don't worry, it's a spiritual life. Like your legal one. There won't be any trials. Not in earthly courts anyway."

"But our early days? When we had no money?"

"She's not interested in that. Basically, she's concerned with her influence on him. She doesn't know that, of course."

"It sounds unhealthy to me. Don't you let her in when I'm here. You'll vet what she writes, of course?"

To calm him I said I would.

"Another thing, Meg. I don't want to meet Fred Meggett. I'm not even sure I should see Esther Meggett."

"Ever again?"

"At least till this thing's over. I know a bit about it. I can't tell you, of course. But it's most unfair, the things I've had to put up with from my relations."

"We'll try to be good."

I left him leafing fastidiously through Dad's letters. When I took him a cup of tea he was deep in them, and into the notebooks. I was surprised. I had expected him to be systematic. But he was here and there—he did not know where he was.

"He really was a most dreadful man. And yet.   "

"What, Oliver?"

"All that intelligence. What led him astray?"

"Conscience."

"I've got that. It hasn't led me astray. He could have been someone. We could have been proud of him."

"I'm proud of him."

He looked at me. "You're just a woman."

"Thank you, Oliver."

I went back to the sitting-room. He made me laugh. I really enjoyed that laugh. I rolled in my chair. Felicity came in while I was wiping my eyes.

"What's the matter with you? I heard you on the path."

"Something Oliver said."

"What?"

"He said I was just a woman."

"You think that's funny?"

"From Oliver. I'd hate to have his approval."

She agreed with that. She laughed a bit too. Then she said, "Tell me what the doctor says about Robert."

"How did you find him?"

"Dreadful. Shouldn't he have a nurse?"

"I'm going down. When it's time. The doctor's going to tell me."

"I'll take some of the load off you. For as long as I'm here."

"It's no load. But thank you. How did you get on?"

"Very well. He's a lot more sensible than I remember. He's not exactly talkative though, is he?"

"Did you try to convert him?"

She pointed her finger. "Keep off my religion."

"I thought you had to. When you met someone dying."

"My God, the idea people have got of Catholics."

"Well, did you ask about his soul? Surely Catholics do that?"

"You're making fun of me, Meg. I won't have that."

"I'm not. I'm interested. Tell me about it, Felix."

So she did, cautiously at first, then with passion. I was not much interested in her beliefs, but she, my sister, fascinated me. The passion, the strength, the purpose—she is Dad. Of course, with her, conscience is mixed up with the doctrines of her church—she is less pure. But he is there. She has, though, something that was not in him—I never saw it—an appetite for power. She is the terror of her parish: I have it from Max, her husband, in admiring letters. Once she had wanted to alter the world; today she confines it to the Catholic world. She is full of impatience with "soft religion"—novenas and penances and rosaries. That, she says, is for Irish peasants. She wants a larger place for mind. She wants "intellectual muscle" in the teaching. *The Tablet* and *Zealandia* are full of letters from her: programmes and prescriptions and reading lists. Her priests damp her down as much as they are able. They marvel at her, admire her, and run for cover when they see her coming. (Father Pearce, shifting furniture, had asked me how "my sister" was getting on. He did not need to say which one. And he had glanced nervously over his shoulder, as though mention of her might bring her through the door.)

When she wound down at last to the matter of faith, I said, "It all seems so medieval."

"Nonsense. It's eternal."

"I don't see it."

"You can. You can. I'll give you some books to read."

"Oh Felix, you are like Dad."

"Keep that old phoney out of it. He didn't know a thing."

"Alfred used to call him Jehovah."

"My God, Meg, you've got a frivolous mind. Keep to the point."

"If you'll tell me what it is."

"I've spent the last hour telling you. Listen. Listen." She started again. I could not get away till Oliver came. (Calvinist and papist, they talk determinedly of other matters.) He sat down on the sofa and put his hands primly on his knees. "There's a smell of tobacco in the study, Meg." I went off to prepare our evening meal. Fergus drove his car into the yard. He came in through the kitchen.

"They in there?"

"Yes. Go and see them."

"I suppose I have to." Felicity talks down to him like a teacher and Oliver like a judge. When I went back he was slumped forward in his chair, arms on knees, staring at his shoes. I was not going to see him ill at ease in his own house.

"Have your whisky, Fergus. Oliver won't mind."

Oliver turned his upright head at me. "Is it too much to ask you to give up that indulgence while I'm here?"

"Far too much. Felix, would you like something?"

"Sherry?"

"Yes. Esther keeps us supplied. You get them, Fergus. I'll have a small gin and tonic. We've got fruit juice, Oliver."

"No thank you. I'll go to my room."

"Don't be silly. If you keep over there you won't even smell it. Anyway, purity's in the mind. You're O.K."

125

His family reduce him to a boy. In Wellington he might hobnob with ambassadors and statesmen. At Peacehaven he grows shrill, he trembles with that impotent rage families generate so easily in their members. "One of our finest legal minds," a fellow jurist says in his dusty memoirs. That is hard to believe when Oliver mounts his high horse in my kitchen. I would like to see the other side of him, if only to be fair. But I would tremble in his court the way he trembles among his brothers and sisters. I would grow thin as glass, you would see right through me. "What was he like?" "A stone god, an eagle," Felicity says—his rulings came like bolts from Mt Olympus. He might try for that at Peacehaven, but was soft and crêpey, like a balloon with most of its air leaked out.

"Would it be too much to ask for my meal in my room?"

"It would. We saw enough of that with Dad. If you want your food in this house you come to the table."

He went off in a huff. Felicity grinned at me. "You're a bit of a tiger."

"I wonder what he did at state banquets."

"That was different."

"I dare say."

"You shouldn't talk to him like that," Fergus said.

"Because he's Sir Oliver? Nobody takes that seriously."

Fergus cannot be sure. He had tried to laugh at the new Oliver, but could not manage. He was brought up short by a kind of magic—all that power in word and ceremony. He poured our drinks, shaking his head at not being able to say what it was he felt.

"Thank you. How was your day?"

"Not bad."

"Did you see Fred?"

"Nobody sees him. He's locked up on the top floor with his lawyers."

"Will they take him to court? Is he really a crook?" Felicity asked.

"I wish I knew."

"Come on Fergus, you must know. Maybe they'll take you to court as well."

"That's not funny," I said.

"Aren't all the directors equally culpable? Is that the word?"

"I've resigned."

"It's hard to believe you don't know what's going on."

I began to be angry. Fergus had gone pale.

"Leave it, Felicity. It's none of your business. Help me take Robert's dinner down."

"I've just started my drink."

"You can have that later."

"You *are* tough."

I served the meal and put it on a tray. "There, you carry it." But I took it from her half-way down the path. I saw she was a woman of seventy. Her breathing was not good. I had always looked on her as Felicity Plumb, twenty years old, light and quick and sparkling with cleverness. She was three score and ten. It took my breath away.

"Here Felix, give it to me. You go back. Have your drink."

"Thank you. I am a bit tired."

I watched her trudge thick-bodied up the path. What's happened to us? I thought.

It was a question I asked again on the Sunday they all came to Peacehaven: Willis and Mirth, Esther and Fred, Emerson, Robert. But of course by then it was simply a question—no revelation in it. The afternoon was cool. We met indoors. Felicity was at her best, strolling through the Zoo looking at Plumbs. They seemed to amuse more than annoy her that day. Especially withered old sagging old Mirth and her peg-legged lover. (Willis, though, has a new pink leg and wears a shoe on his plastic foot. I miss his old peg and its carved lady-names.) Mirth is doddery, and not quite right in her mind these last few years—but that does not cause us pain. She is brimming with her fulfilments. Willis squires her with untiring devotion. He has given up other women. He looks on Mirth as a wonder and sees his role as that of custodian. Perhaps in private he dusts and

127

polishes her. He conducts tours. "Felicity, come and see Mirth. She's over here. This is her. See how happy she is. Look at the glow in her cheeks. *Roses in your cheeks, love. Roses, I say.* I'll have to get her one of those trumpets Dad used to have. She's eighty now, Felix. Eighty-one next birthday. Isn't she phenomenal? Look at her eyes. There's a real sparkle there."

"Willie," Mirth said, "stand aside so I can see this lady."

"Hello, Mirth," Felicity said.

"Are you the Catholic one? What made you take up that nonsense?"

"She's got a sharp mind," Willis said.

"Terrible nonsense, religion. All you need is a man like Willie."

"She can't see past me," Willis grinned.

"Wine is for drinking, dear, not mumbo-jumbo."

Felicity laughed, there was nothing else to do. Willis took Oliver's sleeve and led him over.

"Here's the knight, lovey. Sir Oliver."

Mirth wagged her finger at him. "Why do you need medals? Monkeys don't pin medals on themselves."

"I see your point."

"They tell me you were a judge. How many men have you hanged?"

"Really—" he was shocked, "—I can't answer that."

"A terrible thing to do. I don't want to talk to him any more, Willis."

"She's got your number, Ollie. She's not done for. *Still got something left, eh love?* Course," he said, "she's not right up here—" tapping his head "—some of the time. She gets things a bit mixed up. Gets up in the night to feed the babies. *No babies left. All gone, out in the world.* And then there are times she doesn't make it to the dunny in time. She sort of forgets. But that's the way things go. She's happy as Larry."

"Hanging's a terrible thing," Mirth said.

"It's not as if I put the rope round their necks."

"Who did if it wasn't you? Putting on your black cap."

"Hee hee," Willis said.

"Look here," Oliver stammered; but I led him away. I saw an old man with a trembling lip and trembling hands. Dad had been breaking him down all week. He would come from the study icy and precise, but soon would turn with a fussed look on his face, as if aware of something behind him he must take notice of. "Do you know what he says?—here, I've written it down. 'By deafness you learn to hear the inaudible, see the invisible, and touch the incomprehensible.' Now what sort of nonsense is that? Of course, it all comes from denying authority." So Dad drove him back on his certainties. He needed his wife to direct them at—found me evasive—but she was dead many years. And soon he would fish another scrap of paper from his pocket and his fussed look would return. Now even Mirth, daft and doddery, could make him forget he was after all who he was.

"What a dreadful woman. How dare she say those things?"

"Never mind. Never mind." A brother he approved of was standing by the door. "Come and say hallo to Emerson."

"Yes, indeed. (Abominable woman!) How good of him to come."

Emerson has made money. He bought a glass-house when he gave up flying, and now has a city of glass, and patents on spray delivery and trickle irrigation systems that have made him the most successful tomato grower in Auckland. It is hard to remember he has flown crazy flights, that he has been the Sundowner of the Skies, and looped the loop, and walked on aeroplane wings.

He and Oliver shook hands.

"Congratulations, Oliver. I don't have to call you Sir, do I?"

"Not in the family. Although I must say I can't understand those people who say they intend to go on being Tom or Jack. What is the point?"

"Yes, yes, I agree," Emerson said. "Well, you've had a great career. We're all very proud of you." He is good at saying the right thing. He noticed once when looking at the world—a rare event—that the trick was useful, so he learned it; but listens with surprise to hear himself.

"Thank you, Emerson. That's more than some of the others have managed to say."

"You've done the family credit."

Oliver inclined his head. "It's good of you to say so. I've often thought that *you* deserved an honour. Not for that flight, of course. That was foolishness. But for all the flying you did for TEAL. I think an M.B.E. would have fitted the bill."

Emerson looked alarmed. "That's not my sort of thing."

"You're too modest."

"Someone has to be with you around." It was Esther. She had come through the door ("Essie," I hissed, "Essie") and barged her way past me and banged him on the shoulder. He ducked his head, a movement I had seen last—how it fastened on me over the years—when Dad had raised his arm to order him out of our house in his uniform. For a moment he was shorter than Esther. Then he recovered himself.

"I had no idea you were coming."

"Couldn't keep away. The Order of St Michael and St George, eh? You'll be fighting dragons. Beats me what you'll do with the maidens, though."

"Now just you listen to me—"

"No chance. What's it going to be next, the jolly old garter? How about gentleman of the bed chamber? You'll be carrying out the royal piss pot, Ollie. They say it's blue."

"How dare you!"

"I dare anything. Hasn't Meg Muggins told you?"

"Has she been drinking?" Felicity said at my shoulder.

"I'm afraid so."

"Poor Oliver. No, leave them. It's family after all. Oliver has got to look after himself."

"Fred, Fred," Esther called, "come and shake hands with Sir Oliver. Where'd you leave your horse, Ollie? Got it parked outside?"

"I can't meet your husband. Surely you understand that."

"Why not? He was good enough to meet the queen last time

she was out. They talked about racehorses and he gave her a tip. Come on, Fred. Get away from Fergus, he's got no gong. No offence, Fergie, you have to stand in line."

Fred came over. Whatever he felt, he covered it with a grin. "Gidday, Oliver."

"This is improper."

"Don't see why. You've retired, haven't you?"

"If you hadn't it could have been you who puts him in prison. Fergus too. What a laugh that would have been."

"She's been drinking," Fred said. "Do I have to tell you?"

"Since I got out of bed," Esther cried.

"Since yesterday morning, if you want to know. Found her out on the patio, sucking it up. I guess you all know why."

It dropped into my mind like dye in water. I felt that cloudy roiling out; and must have swayed or staggered. Felicity took my arm.

"What is it?"

"I forgot."

"Meg?"

"It was yesterday Alfred died."

"Thirteen years. Everybody have a drink," Esther cried.

Felicity tried to make me sit down.

"No, I've got to get Robert," and I left the room, and the house, and ran down to his cottage. At Alfred's funeral service I had thought I was going mad. Then Robert walked in, from nowhere. He sat behind me and put his hand on my shoulder and we listened to Alfred's friends say words of farewell. I found I was able to bear it, I should not go mad. I needed Robert now, not in anything like that desperation, but as one needs holding after some dreadful fright.

"Robert," I said, coming to his chair, "they're all up there. Are you ready?" I gave his arm a tug. It was only then I saw how bad he was.

"Help me up, Meg."

"What is it? Shall I call the doctor?"

"Help me to the table."

When I had him there he leaned over it and rested on his forearms. His breathing kept its gravelly sound of stones shaken in a tin. I fetched a glass of water and his pills and put them on the table. His head was on his fists, but he saw the bottles, with their coloured bits of useless magic inside, and he seemed to grin. Soon he pushed himself up. "Better keep old double-barrel happy." He took two pills and washed them down.

"I'll get your bed ready."

"I'm coming up. Got to see all my brothers and sisters."

"Oh Robert, no. You're not well enough."

"I'll be all right."

"They can come down. I'll send them one by one."

"I think I'd head for the bush. I'm all right. It's kind of like a wheel. It won't be bad again till next time round."

We walked along the road arm in arm. A little car was drawn up at our gate. The woman in it turned her head to watch us. She had been there when I ran down but I had scarcely seen her, and I took little notice now. I was too conscious of Robert at my side. His illness was galloping forward: it was time I moved to the cottage. I made up my mind to tell him when we got back.

Oliver had come into the garden. He was walking about in an agitated way. "Meg," he cried when he saw me, "you never told me you were inviting those two."

"It was supposed to be a family gathering."

"Yes, but Meggett! The fellow's a criminal. I can't be seen talking to him."

"Sit in the summer-house, then. Before you go, say hallo to Robert."

"Imagine if anyone got hold of this. Do you realize I'm taking the chairmanship of a Royal Commission next month? On property development! And here you've brought Meggett into the house."

"This is Robert."

"I'll talk to him in a minute. But what I'm going to do is sit down there and I want nobody to come near me until Meggett's gone."

"I'll hang a tea-towel out the window."

"This is no joke, Meg."

"It seems like one. Do say hallo to your brother."

"You've behaved very badly in this."

"Can it really affect you? I thought you were above such things. Where you couldn't be touched."

"In a sense I am.   I won't be laughed at."

"I want you to say a proper hallo to Robert."

"Very well. Robert, I'm pleased to see you."

"Hello, Oliver," Robert said. "Congratulations on your knighthood."

"Thank you.—We were at different ends of the family, Meg." It was his way of saying that the meeting was pointless. He looked at Robert severely. "But you were a victim too. We were all victims. If it hadn't been for him you wouldn't have got in that appalling mess in the war. And after. Well, it's water under the bridge. No one connected our names." He looked Robert up and down—a bumpkin, Robert, even in his best clothes—and managed a smile. "It's good to see you looking so well. Meg, I'll be in that ruin. Not till he's gone, remember."

He went away to the summer-house.

"I might leave him there all night."

"Sir Oliver," Robert said. "I don't think he liked me."

"He doesn't like anyone." But I had a last look at him, hiding behind the rambler roses in his Wellington suit. I had not known him. None of us had taken the trouble. Well, we had our own lives.

I helped Robert over the patio and into the living-room and left him with Willis and Emerson. Esther was on the other side of the room, as far away as she could get from Mirth, whom she thought of as "gaga" She was slumped in her chair—almost it seemed she ingested it like an amoeba—and was staring about her angrily. Her jar of wine in its brown-paper bag was sitting between her feet. I took a chair beside her.

"I thought I might get a phone call. At the very least."

"I'm sorry. With Felix and Oliver here, I just forgot. And Robert to look after."

"Too busy with the living, eh, to worry about the dead?"

"I haven't forgotten him. I'll never forget."

"But you won't go out of your way to remember him either."

"That's not fair."

"Nothing's fair. How about getting me a glass?"

I fetched one from the kitchen and she poured herself a drink.

"Don't you think you've had enough of that, Essie? I'll be making tea in a minute."

"Leave me out. Last one who drank with me was Alf." Felicity joined us and sat in a chair on her other side. "You won't drink with me, will you? Didn't think so. I'm stuck in a family of wowsers."

"I'm sorry I forgot. It's fifteen years."

"Thirteen. That's not long."

"I've grown into an old woman in that time."

"Haven't we all? Alf wouldn't be sixty."

"He's still alive, Essie. If you'll only believe it."

"Souls, eh? I thought you'd try that on. Well, you can save your breath. When you're dead you're dead. The lights go out. O.K.? Alf isn't floating around anywhere."

"We all have immortal souls."

"Grow up, Felix. Meg here doesn't believe it, do you, Meg?"

"I don't suppose I do. But while we remember Alfred he's still alive."

"Jesus! Fairy-tale time. For God's sake where's some grown-ups I can talk to?" She took a large swallow of her wine. Her face went pale. "I think I'm going to be sick."

"I'll look after her," Felicity said. She helped Esther out of the room. I went to the kitchen and put the kettle on. The afternoon was proving a great strain. Robert ill and Esther drunk and Oliver sulking in the summer-house. I was grateful that Mirth was asleep and that Fergus had taken Fred to the study. I went along the hall and looked at them. They were drinking whisky. Fred had his feet up on Dad's desk.

134

"Esther's lying down."

"Thank God for that."

I went back to the kitchen. Something was pressing softly on the edges of my mind. I made the tea, trying hard to let it in, but it would not come. Something to do with Fergus.

Then I had it. The woman in the car down by the road was Beth Neeley. "Oh, no," I said. I had enough to put up with. For a moment I thought I would run to the study and ask Fergus to go down and send her away. But then I saw it would be simpler to pretend she wasn't there.

Felicity came in. "I put her on my bed. I think she's asleep."

"Was she sick?"

"Got her to the toilet in time. Rather nasty. Isn't there anything we can do for her?"

"You can pray."

"Don't start that. You know what I mean."

"There's nothing you can do from Wellington. Write to her if you like. All I can do is keep on visiting her. It's going to be hard with Robert. I'm moving down tonight."

"To Robert's?"

"I thought he was dying when I went to get him."

"Who'll look after Fergus?"

I wish he'd let Beth Neeley, I thought, it would take a load off me. "I'll only be down there at nights. I'll spend a good part of the day up here."

"It would help if Robert shifted up."

"He doesn't want to."

"I'd stay and help, Meg. But I've got Max."

"I know. It's my job."

We carried the tea on trays to the sitting-room. Only Mirth was there, sleeping open-mouthed in Dad's winged chair. Voices came from the patio. Willis and Robert and Emerson were sitting in a row on the garden seat.

"Hear no evil, see no evil, speak no evil," Felicity said. We laughed. Willis looked up.

"Here's the girls with tea. How's my old Mirth?"

"Sleeping."

"Sleeps all day. She's a wonder."

We poured them tea and gave them cake and left them there, still talking. Felicity went to look at Esther and I took a cup to Oliver in the summer-house. He thanked me and I went back. Climbing the steps, seeing my brothers like the three monkeys, I felt they had done well: better than Sir Oliver, alone in the summer-house. They had done better than Fergus and Fred.

I poured myself a cup and sat with them. Willis began to flatter me shamelessly. It's the only style he has with women, and it has bowled them over all his life.

"Willis," I said, "do stop it. I've got better things to worry about than my appearance."

"Our sisters have always been beautiful. Every one of them. Better than film stars."

Emerson looked startled at the idea. Robert smiled, but it was an effort for him. I thought perhaps the wheel was coming round and I touched his arm and asked him in a whisper if he wanted to go home.

"Not yet. In a minute."

"Mirth's eighty-one next week," Willis said. "I'm writing a poem for her. Listen, Meg. You were good at poetry.

> "My wife is eighty-one,
> Her life is nearly done,
> But roses bloom in her cheeks so fair
> And violet scent is in her hair.

"That's as far as I've got. What do you think?"

"She'll be pleased with it. Any woman would be."

"Alf liked poetry. He'd be able to help. I've got to say something about her eyes. And her mouth. About her kisses."

Emerson looked embarrassed.

"Her kisses are what I misses," I said.

"No, Meg. Seriously. I want to please her. Here's Duggie. I'll ask him."

Duggie is their son, Sebastian Douglas, the National Party politician. I cannot be fair to him. I look on him as a traitor, like

Oliver, but he's not my brother and I make no allowances for him. Plumbs should not be Tories. About that I cannot be reasonable. Every time I read in the newspaper, *Douglas Plumb, the National member for Epsom*, I feel sick. When I saw him drive up that day in his flash car (no flasher than Fergus's, I admit) I gathered the tea things quickly on their trays and took them inside. I did not want to offer him a cup. I think he noticed. He does not miss much.

"She still asleep?" I asked Felicity, who was in the kitchen.

"Yes. I don't like her colour. Who's arrived?"

"Douglas Plumb. The member for Epsom."

"I must see him. The poor man's Holyoake. That's what Max calls him."

"He wouldn't like that. He wants to be the rich man's Plumb."

"Let's have a look."

Douglas was squatting cow-cocky style—one of his tricks— in front of his father and uncles. He could not place Robert and that worried him. He prides himself on his encyclopaedic mind.

"I've got it," he said, "you were the conscientious objector."

"Yes," Robert said.

"I knew I'd get you." He looked pleased with himself. "Which camps were you in?"

"Hautu. Strathmore. Shannon."

"We must have a talk some time." But he filed Robert at once in a dead file. He would be of no use.

"Douglas," I said, "here's your Aunt Felicity."

"Ah, Felicity. Of course, of course." He kissed her cheek. Douglas is thirty-two. He has his father's good looks and his mother's liveliness. Raymond, who seems to detest him, although I'm not sure, says he's very clever, he means to be Prime Minister one day and he'll probably make it. I cannot believe it. Everyone, when you see them close, even Duggie, seems too human for that. Could a Prime Minister survive with Douglas's mouth and his red Plumb hair? And especially his eyes? They are not evasive, but they're never still, they're always looking out for the place he should be. They're handsome eyes, they twinkle with geniality, but they look past you obsessively for someone more important. He'll have to learn. Of course, when they've found that most important person they become still.

But enough of Duggie. He's not worth anyone's time. I don't think he is. He talked to Felicity a while, wanted to know what was amusing her (it was his resemblance to Dan Peabody), recalled her friendship with Peabody, "a clever chap", and then he spotted Oliver in the summer-house and he hared off there— proving, I suppose, that Oliver still is important. Willis had not had a chance to ask him about his poem. He looked glum. His son, it almost seems, has stolen his vitality. I've heard it said (Raymond) that Duggie has an appetite for women that would put Willis's in the shade. The old man would seem like a piker. I can't believe it. I remember his carved leg and his one hundred women.

Presently I took Robert back to the cottage. Beth Neeley watched us boldly from her car. I ignored her. I got Robert on to his bed and took off his shoes. He stopped me from undressing him.

"This'll be over in a minute. Let me do it as long as I can."

"Robert, I'm shifting down. You need someone here at night."

"Tell Fergus I'm sorry."

"He'll understand."

I waited until the attack was over. He changed into his pyjamas and got into bed. "Glad I went. Good to see Willie and Emo. Pair of clowns."

I went back along the road and got in Beth Neeley's car.

"Hello, Miss Neeley. You've been here a long time."

"Nobody asked you in. Get out of my car."

"I'm here now. What shall we talk about?"

"This is a public road. I've got every right to park here."

"Come on, dear, don't play games. Is it my husband you want to see?"

"He's not your husband. Why don't you let him go? I'd let a man go if I knew he didn't love me any more."

"My dear, if it was just love everything would be simple. But there's more to it than that. Fergus loves you, all right. But he's not a simple man. I wish he were."

"I don't know what you're talking about."

She was a handsome girl—twenty-five, I guess. Big and ripe, I've said it before. A meal for any man. There was more to her than that, but I was not concerned to see it. I did notice she was suffering.

"Would you like to talk to him? Shall I send him down?"

She decided I was trying to devalue him, and declared that she would take no favours from me—she wanted me simply to "get my hooks out of Fergus" She actually said it. If I had not still been full of Robert I would have been furious.

"I'm trying to get my hooks out. I've told him to go to you. Take you to a hotel if he wants."

"That's a horrible thing to say."

"Isn't it what you both want? I'm trying to help."

"We don't want anything from you."

"Except for me to let him go. I'm trying."

We were going in circles and I became impatient. I wanted to shift my things down to the cottage.

"You're a pretty girl. You don't need help from me."

She widened her eyes: Esther's trick. She had some of Esther's sparkle—but darker eyes, and a beakier nose, and a greedy mouth. Physiognomy! That was no science. She was just a stranger; a mystery I had no wish to solve.

"I'm leaving Fergus. I'm shifting out tonight. I don't care if you move in, although you'd better leave it a few more days because my brother and sister are there. But after that he's all yours. If you want him." I shook my head. I had to tell her the truth. "But it won't have a happy ending. I wish you could see."

"You're playing some trick."

"No. Fergus is free. Move in if you want."

"I'll never go into your house."

"Then take him away. Now I've got things to do. I'll tell him you're here. Goodbye."

"Don't tell him. You're an evil woman."

The word shook me. For a moment I wondered if I *were* playing some game, working this woman subtly to her ruin. As if she recognized it, she cried, "You're trying to destroy us." But that was melodrama.

"I'm trying to help you."

It was true. And I saw it was useless. My best course was to do nothing, simply be quiet.

"I hope it works out." And I went away. I got rid of my guests. Duggie drove his parents home. Felicity and I wrestled Esther into Fred's Mercedes and he drove her off. I fetched her jar of wine from the sitting-room and poured it down the sink. It almost fumed. It was like some acid substitute for blood. Oliver came up from the summer-house. He sat in Dad's chair and wanted to praise Douglas Plumb. I left him with Felicity and went to talk with Fergus in the study.

He poured me a drink.

"Fred thinks the police will arrest him soon. It's the first time he's said it to me."

"Is he very worried?"

Fergus shrugged. "There's nothing he can do. He thinks they'll leave me alone."

"You haven't done anything wrong."

"I don't think I have."

I sipped my drink. I found it easy to be honest with him. "Robert's a lot worse. I'm moving down tonight."

"I thought he looked bad. Have you had the doctor?"

"He's coming tomorrow. But someone should be there. He needs a nurse."

"Are you sure you can manage? I'll help all I can."

"I know you will. But there's someone else I think you should worry about."

"Who?" He knew at once. That, I suppose, is infatuation.

"Miss Neeley. She's been parked down on the road all afternoon. No, she's gone." I had heard her car drive away as I walked up the path. "Fergus, she's in a bad way. You got her in and you've got to get her out. She's your responsibility."

"She had no right to come here. Was she upset?" He was confused. I hated to see it. He's so impressive to watch when he knows where he's going, he goes full bore; but now he was like a lost child.

"Help her, Fergus. Take her away somewhere. You won't be doing any wrong to me."

"Is this why you're moving down to Robert's?"

"No, no, Robert's a different matter."

"Did you talk to her?"

"For a moment or two."

"What did she say?"

"Only that she loves you. Fergus, she does. Or thinks she does. Let her find out." I hoped to give him a goal. But as I'd said to Beth Neeley, it wasn't that simple. In this Fergus was not a simple man. Nor was the end of it plain. I saw the possibility of Beth Neeley unmanning him, as I had done, and saw that at fifty-eight he might not have the strength to re-make himself. My talk might be dangerous. On the other hand it might be the saving of him. I grew confused as he. It was better, yes it really was better, if I simply stayed quiet. And I thought of Robert waiting in the cottage. That was where I wanted to be.

I put my drink down and kissed Fergus on his cheek.

"How long was she there?"

"An hour or so."

"I'd better go and see her."

"I think you should."

Presently he drove away. Felicity helped me carry my few things down.

15 Fergus volunteered for overseas service in the first week of the war. He sailed away with the Second Echelon in May 1940. His ship was a luxury liner, *The Empress of Japan*. There was nothing luxurious in his attitude. He was cutting down another wattle tree.

For five years we had rented a railway house in his parents' street. Twice he had tried to set himself up in business, and twice gone back on wages. He seized the war when it came. He made himself a man. I had thought there was some life in our marriage. We were doing all right. He grinned at me when he walked in that night. "I've enlisted." The life all drained away.

We argued late, shouting at each other, but he gave no explanation, and I could not make it for him, knowing private ground when I came on it. He would turn destruction on me—no axe, no, but words not expungeable. I saved what I could.

He has not told me much about the war. As far as I can make out his group—battalion or brigade or echelon—trained at a place called Aldershot and was stationed in Kent in the Battle of Britain, ready to turn back a German invasion. Then he went to Greece, and missed the evacuation but came out in a small boat with six others. He has not said much about it, but is neither laconic nor secretive. He added a part to himself in the war, necessary as an arm or leg, but as it grew it lost its definition. He has it, but does not know.

When he came home on furlough in '44 I pleaded with him not to go back. Hundreds of men were refusing. They went absent without leave. They demanded furlough extensions. Some were tried as mutineers. Not Fergus. "I'm going back. I made a bargain, Meg."

"You made a bargain with me."

He had no answer to that. His face took points of colour, but I

142

saw how tough he was and how removed. I gave up arguing. But if anything, he was more aware of me and gentler with me. He could not give me what I asked, but felt he had payments to make. We were almost lovers on that furlough. I kept back only a small part. I had given up the rented house and gone with my children to Peacehaven. When Fergus came home from his trips to camp I met him on Millbrook Road with a bag of clothes. He would not wear his uniform in front of Dad, but changed into civvies by the creek. Sometimes he went swimming. He shinned up willow trees like a boy and ran along the branches and dived in the leaf-strewn water, holding his underpants on with one hand. Once, in a hollow in the grass, he persuaded me to make love. I would not undress. I felt foolish and girlish and pleased, but spent the next weeks in terror that I had conceived. Soon he sailed away a second time: Italy. Cassino. He was made sergeant. He did not come home again for another year.

Robert never came home. Well, he came home after twenty-five years. When the war started he said to me, "I'm not going." He never said more than that, even to Dad. His decision was not so much conscientious as intuitive. So it could not be argued. His call-up notice came in 1940. By that time Fergus was at Aldershot and the children and I had moved to Peacehaven. I brought the letter to Robert in the garden. He read it and handed it to me. "I'm not going."

Dad could get no sense from him and had to content himself with saying, "By a divine instinct, men's minds mistrust Ensuing dangers"—dangers, he made clear, not to Robert's body but to his soul. He would have liked him to be a political and a religious objector in equal parts, and the statement he prepared for him spoke with his usual eloquence of the "necessity of a New Way of Love beyond the old religions", and of "the pagan barbarities of the imperialist war" Robert went off to face the Tribunal with its sixteen pages in his pocket, but I don't believe he had read them, and he did not read them there.

We sat on benches in a small room above Queen Street. The King, that clerkish little man, looked down on proceedings that had about them nothing of the majesty of justice. We sat through the rustle of papers and the scratch of pens. Even that dreadful question, "What would you do if you saw a German bayonetting your wife and children?"—even that took a dusty sound. Robert said he would do his best to stop him.

"How?" the chairman asked, "with a bayonet or gun?"

"I don't have a bayonet or gun," Robert said.

"If we gave you one would you use it? Your wife and children, remember."

Robert could not answer. It was plain to him that he would do anything, use any weapon, to stop a German—anyone—from bayonetting children. But he saw he had been taken off his ground and he struggled to find a way back. Dad had his trumpet pointed at him, but had heard very little. He said loudly, "Read your statement, Robert."

"Quiet," the chairman said. He asked Robert if he had a statement.

"No," Robert answered.

"And you have no argument for appealing?"

"I'm just not going, that's all. I'm not going to kill anyone."

"You must do better than this. Have you any objection to serving as a non-combatant?"

"That's the army, isn't it?" Robert said.

"It is."

"I'm not going in the army."

They stood him down. Plainly they thought him half-witted.

Robert and I rode home in the train, leaving Dad in the city browsing in bookshops. He would buy heavily to cure his disappointment.

"I can't answer questions," Robert said.

"They're not fair questions."

"Yes they are."

"Do you want to go then?"

"I can't go."

He hung on to a knowledge that came from—where? A divine source? Came as spiritual perception? Burned as revelation in the sky? Or was it in his being, was it coursing with his blood, the knowledge of this not that, of here not there, of yes and no? He was never able to make it clear.

John Willis (as lawyer) gave Alfred a message for Robert. Alfred passed it on through me: When your final papers come report to the army and tell them you're an objector. Then you'll go to an objector's camp. If you don't do that you're a military defaulter, you go up in front of a magistrate and you'll get a sentence of hard labour in prison. I wrote it all down and told Robert.

"I'm staying here, Meg. They can come and get me."

And they came: a sergeant and a constable. I sent them to Willis's place, where Robert was doing a season in the orchard. It all happened as John had foretold. Robert spent the night in the Loomis lock-up, and the next day in town the magistrate sentenced him to two months hard labour. He did his time in Mt Eden jail and then went off to a detention camp for the rest of the war.

Twenty-five years later, we sat in the cottage and talked about those times. On fine afternoons we took chairs into the garden (the wilderness), to the spot where Bluey had told his beads and Dad had sat turning philosophies over with Wendy Philson; and I drank cups of tea while Robert washed his pills down with swallows of water and talked of Strathmore, Whitenui, Terrill's Farm, Hautu. He spoke of them in a bare way, yet I was fascinated, for here were years of his life that were lost to me, and as I listened I re-created them, I breathed a life into the dry-as-dust Robert he held up to me.

He began in Strathmore, out in the pumice lands from Rotorua. The barbed-wire fences bothered him. They stood eight feet tall and were elbowed in at the top. Their strands were less than a body's width apart, meant to tear a man. As he lay in his hut at night he felt the fences in his mind. Five hundred men were at Strathmore. He felt them too, like bees in a hive, and he felt a choking in the mess hall, in the social hall, as if he were in the middle of the swarm and could not get out. The one-man huts were no hardship. And scrub-cutting, scrub-burning, was work he understood. He went out daily into the pumice lands with no complaint. But in this camp, and in Whitenui, where he was shifted, his simplicity was under heavy strain. Robert knew a lot, had seen a lot, but had not thought at all.

The camp at Whitenui was on the banks of the Manawatu River. It was smaller than Strathmore. Robert was one of only two hundred men. The main work was grubbing weeds in the flax plantations owned by the Woolpack and Textile Company. Robert was soon in a gang building a railway into the swamps. The work was useful enough, yet Robert's greatest burden was a feeling of uselessness. That was because of the fence that cut the camp off from the world; and of the men detained, so it seemed to Robert, outside time. Whitenui was no place, time made no movement there. (It was, I supplied, listening, the Land of Missing.)

Men did not go mad there, or die there, but their lives closed down. They worked in the laundries, the cookhouse, and the camp garden, they played tennis and cricket and football, read books from the library van, played records in their huts, put on a play, talked about religion and politics; but they were shadows of men. They were sentenced to a compound outside time and outside place. This is Robert's view. There must have been many who did not share it. The religious objectors, I think he tried to say, lived in another world, a parallel world, where the laws were different—the Jehovah's Witnesses, the Pentecostals, the men of the Christian Assembly. Robert found he could not speak to them. Words would not make the journey between those worlds, but rattled like gravel thrown against a pane.

In the spring of 1943 Robert stood up from his bed. He had no watch but guessed it was after nine. Soon the screw Black-tracker would be round to lock the huts. Robert put on his warmest clothes. He turned out the light and stepped outside and closed his door. He walked down the line of huts to the back of the camp. It was easy enough to squeeze under the wire. All you did was find a place where the ground was uneven. As soon as he was outside he was greeted by tiny noises, tiny movements: a sound of water trickling, the touch of a leaf on his cheek and of cold air moving off the river. It was as if his senses had come alive after being held in a stupor for two years; as if the world had begun to roll on its axis and time to move again. He said simply that he felt alive for the first time since stepping into the police car at Willis's orchard.

He struck out up the river in the direction of Palmerston North. He walked on country roads while all around the fields grew sharp with frost and the ditches iced over. When the moon came up he climbed a fence and set off over the fields. Dogs barked at him from the backs of houses. The moon told him north and east and west and he kept heading north, not in the hope of reaching any place but because he was cold, had been cold for years, and north had the warmest sound and seemed to mean beaches and orchards and somehow summer. He did not mind being lost, he was lost somewhere, not locked outside.

Morning was clear, the grass was spiky with frost. A polar chill filled the sunless land west of the mountains. Robert walked into a farm. Beyond a row of macrocarpa trees men were yelling cows into a yard. He waited till the machines began to thump. Then he knocked at the farmhouse door and asked the woman who came if she could let him have some food.

"You'd better come in."

He warmed himself at the kitchen range while she fried him bread and eggs. When he was eating, she said, "Are you the man who ran away from the conchy camp?"

"Yes," Robert said.

"You've come to a dangerous place. My husband would shoot you. I think my son would too."

"I'll go when I've finished," Robert said.

She asked him if he had become a conchy because he was scared. Robert said no. She poured him a cup of tea. "You should be scared." She told him her husband had won a medal in the first war and her sons, Jack and Peter, had enlisted in the second as soon as it started. Jack had been wounded in Crete—

that was him down in the shed milking with his father. He was
very quick, but he had a plate in his skull and was not always
sure where he was any more. Peter had been killed in the desert.

"I'm sorry," Robert said.

"You're not the one who should be sorry."

She asked him where he was going. North, he told her. But
first he was going to find a hayshed and sleep, he had walked all
night.

"Come here. I'll give you a bed. They only come in for
lunch." She showed him into a small bedroom, with a bed made
up and photos of football teams pinned on the walls. "This was
Peter's room. No, I don't mind. Keep quiet at lunch time, that's
all you need to worry about."

He did not feel safe, but saw using the room as a return he
could make her. He slept in his underclothes, and woke only
once, when boots clumped in the yard and men's voices
grumbled through the wall. The woman came back later. She
gave him sandwiches and told him where to find the lavatory.
He slept again, and woke in the late afternoon. Sunlight slanted
through the shelter-belt and came under the half-drawn blinds.
The faces of the young men in the football teams were lit up.
Some grinned happily. Others tried to be tough. He wondered
which ones were Peter and Jack.

He thanked the woman. She gave him a packet of sandwiches
and a bottle of tea. "There's mutton and chutney and some
gooseberry jam. I hope you get where you're going."

He went down to the road, hearing the noise of milking
again, and turned towards the low hills on his left and started
walking. He hid when cars came by, but soon the sun went
down and he felt safer. The night was clear and starry and very
cold, but after his day in bed he felt warm and strong. The bottle
of tea was hot inside his jacket. He hid from three cars, but later
in the hills nothing came, and he strode along in the moonlight
whistling tunes Mother had played when we were young.
Something heavy—a truck he thought or tractor—grinding up
behind him had a friendly sound. Its lights slanted over the

hillsides into scrub and bracken. He had plenty of time to hide, but decided to try for a lift. It came up at last, an old Dodge truck with cracked headlights and high rattling sides. Two men were in it.

"Want a lift, mate?"

"Thanks," Robert said.

"Where you heading?"

"Anywhere up there."

"Hop on the back."

He climbed up and sat with his back to the cab. A dog lying there thumped its tail on the tray. Robert patted its head. Later he gave it the meat from one of his sandwiches. He drank some tea, only warm by now but very sweet, and wondered if he should offer some to the men in the cab.

It was then he noticed the moon had turned round, they were driving away from it, out of the hills. In a moment they turned on to a sealed road. He banged on the cab and peered into it. A moonlit face grinned at him. Slick in the yellow light, a scar showed, long and wide in the close-cut hair.

Robert sat down again. He wondered if he was being taken to Whitenui or to some quiet patch of ground to be shot. Soon he recognized the road to the camp. He ate all his sandwiches and drank the last of his tea and threw the bottle as far as he could into a paddock. It might save the woman trouble. That made him wonder if he could jump off. He went to the end of the tray but the scarred boy banged the window with his fist. He showed Robert a gun. So Robert sat with the dog and patted it and hugged himself against the frozen wind, and was reasonably content. He had had a day and a night. He knew the world outside was there and he could live in it if he had the chance.

They came up to the main gates of the camp. The driver reversed hard against the wire, trapping Robert in a cage. He put his head out the window. "Hey, yer bloody twits in there, we brung one of yer yeller-bellies back."

Black-tracker came, and The Screaming Skull. Robert

149

climbed the side of the truck and jumped to the ground. They took his arms and marched him to a security hut and locked him in.

"The next day," Robert said, "they sent me to the bad boys camp at Hautu."

"What happened there?"

"Nothing much."

That was a pattern for his answers. It seems to me what happened was something like this: he learned in Hautu things that shone a light back down his life and changed the way he saw a part of it. Hautu was cold and beautiful—the country at least was beautiful, bush and birds and mountains and a stream running by the camp. The working parties went out grubbing gorse and manuka. If you watched and were quiet the land began to stir with thousands of rabbits. Trout hung in streams as clear as glass. Far away, black bush on the mountains, snow along the tops, and a line as fine as a cotton thread marking the sky. That was all right. Robert was happy with that. But at night he came back to the compounds. He woke to them in the morning. And he took from them a feeling of betrayal he had known once before in his life and forgotten about.

If Hautu had a centre it was the place known as the Red Compound. It never left Robert's mind all the six months he was there. Everything turned around it. They broke the resisters, the real "bad boys", in there. In Robert's time there were only a dozen or so. Twenty years later, in the sun of our wilderness, in the ease of our sea-grass chairs, Hautu for Robert was: ten-foot high barbed fences, two of them, a patrol track in between, a verandah right round the camp for the guards to walk on; it was the cold mad glare of floodlights through the night, and search-lights tracking lazily over the huts; it was the bush beyond the lights—lights watching the men, bush watching over all, the black still bush; and at the centre it was the Red Compound, the huts with their barred windows and frames that opened five inches at the bottom, enough for white hands in the light and white faces of men who knelt to see what the world was like.

Robert understood that Hautu was mad. It was a madness he had seen before. He never brought this into the open for me, I understood from his silences, and sentences begun but not gone on with. He said, "Dad and Alfred   " He said, "I knew I could never go back to Peacehaven."

"Did Dad ever know this?"

"I never told him. I couldn't tell him that. I loved him, Meg."

Dad visited him when he was in Hautu, and again when he was at Terrill's Farm. They sat in the visitors' hut and talked, and Robert told Dad he was well, he was warm enough and had enough to eat and books to read, and he got on with the men, and he told Dad about the Jehovah's Witnesses and the Pentecostals and the couple of men from the Radiant Living Church and the Christadelphians, and Dad laughed at them and wanted to know how the politicals got on. Robert asked nothing about Peacehaven but Dad did not seem to notice. He came home and told me Robert was doing all right, and the next day posted him a parcel of books.

Hautu had Robert sick with 'flus and fevers. Back in Whitenui, he went down with pneumonia and had to be taken to Palmerston North hospital. I set out to visit him there. It was early spring, 1944. Fergus was in Italy. We had begun to see an end to the war. I caught the Limited on Friday night, and sat dozing and waking through the country and the towns, through Te Kuiti and Taumarunui, through the Spiral and National Park and past the mountains, and came to Palmerston North at four in the morning. I sat huddled in my coat in the waiting room. At nine o'clock I walked to the hospital, ready with my story of having come all the way from Auckland, and please could I see my brother without having to wait for the visiting hour. They told me he had been discharged the previous day and was back in Whitenui. I cried in a chair, I was tired and cold and I needed a wash and somewhere to lie down. A nurse brought me a cup of tea. She told me there was a local train to Shannon. From there I could catch a taxi to Whitenui.

So I got on the train and I paid for a taxi, ten miles through green farms with early lambs, and I came to the barbed-wire gates at two o'clock, and the guard would not let me in. I had not made arrangements for my visit. I pleaded with him but he kept an official face and said if I liked I could put my name down for a visit tomorrow, but today it was not possible, the rules were the rules. He would not even let me leave my parcel. (I had brought honey and a cake and a bag of grapefruit from Willis.) I looked at him with hatred—a weathered man with blue eyes and a handsome face. He had a strange lilt in his voice. Now I see it must have been Rhodesian, and he the one Robert called Black-tracker. I turned away so I would not hit him, and walked up the road, and turned round and came back and made proper arrangements for my visit the next day.

A farmer gave me a lift into Palmerston North. I changed my train ticket, and ate a pie and drank a cup of tea. In a cheap boarding-house I listened to the war news. New Zealand troops were fighting on the Adriatic coast near Rimini. I did not know if Fergus would be among them, but I lay sleepless in a broken bed and prayed (not to God, I did not know to whom) that he would be unharmed. I prayed for Robert to be well and happy. The next day I got myself to Shannon and shared a taxi with three other women to the camp, and a familiar Robert, a strange Robert, stood inside the wire and smiled at me.

He was weak from pneumonia. That did not cause his strangeness. Something inside him was strange. A part of his mind I had known almost as well as my own had gone away from me and could not be touched.

"Robert," I said, "the war is finishing. They'll let you out."

"Not till the troops are home."

"But that'll be soon. The Russians are nearly in Germany."

"The Japanese war has to finish too."

"That won't be long. You'll be at Peacehaven, Robert."

"I've got to go where there's no barbed wire." It was perhaps the completest statement he had ever made, and I did not understand it.

"There's no barbed wire at Peacehaven. It's your place, Robert."

He said nothing. He began to talk to me about his friends in camp. Bert Chambers had a gramophone in his hut and a collection of classical records. Bert was an orchardist from Loomis, Willis had helped him when he planted his trees. It was funny, Robert said, how many of the men in the camp came off farms and orchards. And Dick Jacobs—Dick had gone under the wire a month ago and they hadn't caught him yet. He had been sailing a yacht in the Pacific Islands when the war broke out, and he just kept on sailing. The French picked him up and handed him over to the Australians who passed him on to the New Zealanders. Now he was gone and it looked as if he'd made it. (Robert grinned at me from his sea-grass chair. "Remember I told you once about Dick Jacobs? He was Dick Webster, the bloke who bought my bach. He sailed his launch up the creek one day and I was building my jetty. He just about run his boat in the mangroves. Reckoned I brought it all back, the wire and all. He'd been up there ever since, changed his name. He was a good bloke, Dick.") And there were two brothers he'd got to know. Parminter was their name. They came off a farm in the Wairarapa, and they thought it was the Ark. Everything was damned outside the Ark. That was why they would not fight. The war was the start of the wrath of God.

"Crackers," Robert said. "But they reckon it's a good farm."

"Don't go there, Robert. Come back to us." But I saw he was gone. For the rest of my visit I sniffled in my hankie and dabbed my eyes, and Robert patted my shoulder, and I said things like, "Please don't, I'm all right," and "I know you'll do what you have to," and "We love you, Robert." I badly needed to sleep; and second class seat or no, I slept all night on the Express going home. I put Robert from my mind—or rather, I let the strangeness in him become Robert, and that was something I could not understand or soon be bothered with. I loved him as though he were dead.

When the European war ended the government allowed the

C.O.s a weekend leave. Robert went with the Parminter brothers to their farm. He liked it there and went back in March 1946, when he was finally released, and lived there five years, pushing the craziness of it to one side. According to Dad, who went to see him once, the Noah on that Ark, Tom Parminter, decided Robert was a sort of Christ. (That did not make him boss though.) I asked Robert about it, but he just grinned.

"They were all screw-loose. Nothing wrong with the farm though. That was all right."

16 My children ran wild at Peacehaven. I never knew where they were on those fifteen acres. I had grown into it, now they had their turn. Watching them, I imagined a pathway for myself into their lives: I knew places they believed were known only to them. There were dangers: shadows fell on me. From my bedroom window I saw Becky, fourteen that year, leading her boyfriend by the hand through the rhododendron trees above my bank. For a while I said, no, no, I won't interfere, but I could not stop myself and I crept down. There was a hideous creaking in my mind, time strained its joints. But there was nothing going on, no Fred-and-Esther work. Rebecca and the boy were eating apples and talking about tennis. She went red when she saw me.

"Come on, Mum, stop spying on us."

"I'm sorry dear, I just.   "

She seemed to understand I was caught on some barb from another time and she smiled at me with pity and laid it clearly down that things had changed.

"Buzz off, Mum. This is our place now."

She was a physical girl, tough and quick. Back in the house, I smiled with pleasure at her understanding. Because of her forehand drive and her somersaults and handsprings and her burping at the table I always underestimated her mind. Her affections too; perhaps her needs. Others filled them. She has been the happiest of my children. After her infant and her growing-up times, I can remember her hugging me only once. She was nineteen. She burst into my kitchen like a wind, the door smacked the wall and bounded back and crockery rattled in my cupboards. "I'm in, Mum, I'm in." She hugged the breath out of me and danced me round the kitchen. A better mother would have known at once: she had been chosen for the New Zealand basketball team to tour Australia.

I am getting ahead of my story. And I do not mean to write about my children. They had no path to that centre my generation of Plumbs turned about. I would not have wanted them there. Raymond saw more than the others, but knew enough to follow them into the world. He has lived his life as a Sole, not as Raymond Plumb, which I heard him once wishing for as his name.

Dad saw him as a Plumb. But then, he saw a number of people as that, Wendy Philson especially. Wendy though was not happy to be just an honorary Plumb. I shall be fair to her and say she loved Dad. In her way. And being already his companion, his disciple, his lover (in a narrow sense, though she would have said it was broad as the sky), she saw no reason why she should not be Mrs Plumb. I have said already sexual feeling is in her nature. She would have enjoyed loving Dad and becoming mother to new Plumbs.

I saw it all when I came to Peacehaven. I knew what was gone from Dad. I knew he had no strength now to take up life with a woman. Wendy should have known it, but she could not get properly rid of self (though that had been the goal of most of her strivings). So I worried. I had no need to.

"Meg, come in a moment. I've got something I need your advice on."

That was enough to make me put down my broom. I went into his study and sat on the stool.

"Life is funny, Meg." He did not hear my reply—"There's

not much in it makes me want to laugh"—but wagged his head and tapped his desk with his fingers. "Misunderstandings arise. The human mind is so imperfect. We can make it a clear stream if we try hard enough, but there are all these tributaries coming in. Muddy streams. It's most annoying."

I agreed it must be.

"The spirit, Meg. How to free the spirit from the flesh."

"Is this what you want my advice on?"

"Women's business, Meg. What do you think of Miss Philson? What's your opinion?"

"She's all right."

"Come my dear, you can do better than that."

"Why do you want to know?"

"I find myself in a difficult position. Wendy has been useful to me. No, no, it's more than that. I've grown very fond of her. As a daughter, mind. You don't object if I see her as one of my daughters?"

"Not in the least."

"It never crossed my mind she would want to be more. You know how good she's been. She's helped me in more ways than I can name. But Meg .   "

"Go on."

"I don't understand women. Your mother was the only woman I understood."

"Go on about Wendy."

"It seems she wants to be my wife."

"I've known that for a long time. She's not going to be happy as secretary when she thinks she can be more."

"Well, she is more than secretary."

"But less than wife?"

"Oh yes. Oh yes.—Meg, she *will* look at me."

I was sorry for him. A seventy-year-old man should not have to put up with being sexual prey. I told him he must make Wendy's position clear to her.

"I have, Meg."

"That she's a muddy stream?"

156

He smiled—the nearest thing to a grin he was able to manage. "You mustn't take my flights too seriously. No. She is, of course, a very gifted woman. She has a good mind—very clear. If she could only keep the other thing out."

"Do you want me to talk to her."

"No, no, it's my duty. But Meg, you see—I can only love your mother. That's the truth of it."

I returned to my sweeping. I hummed as I went along and grinned to myself. I should have known Dad better. The man who had met his church head on and the state head on was not going to cave in to Wendy Philson—though she was a tricky proposition. She came to me in the kitchen. I thought she was going to hit me, but I kept my ground. I had got to the point in my life where I wasn't going to run.

"You're my enemy, Meg. And your father's enemy."

"Not in the least."

"You've interfered in something you don't understand."

"Some meeting of souls, you mean? I'm afraid it was one-sided."

We went on like that for a while. She had become a big woman, broad in her body, and physically she frightened me a little. But I grew sorry for her. She was a woman going after love and missing her clutch. She was in pain, she kept on turning, looking for a way, but could not find it. She stepped back all the time on her special ground.

"You can't destroy what we have. We are man and wife already. We are soul-mates."

"I'm happy for you to be that."

"We don't need blessings from people of your sort. We're above you, so far above you'll never understand."

"I'll make you a cup of tea, Wendy."

"We don't need bodies. We're on another plane."

"Then stay on it, don't pester him. He's an old man. Talk your ideas with him. He's happy with ideas."

"You don't understand happiness."

She stung me with that. "Perhaps I don't. But I know the sort of happiness you want. You want to be in bed with him."

She came at me. "We could have wonderful children, don't you see?"

"Soul-babies?" I laughed. "You're a stupid girl, Wendy. They fill their napkins too."

She sat down at my table and wept. She made a puddle of tears on the polished wood. I served her tea, and she blew her nose and thanked me. I had not meant to beat her so finally.

I was cross with Dad for several days. I went down to the empty cottage, and thought of Wendy packing up her love, carting it away, carting away her years of devotion to him, going off with uselessness at the centre of her life. I got myself in a state and I sat at the table and wept as Wendy had done. I told myself this was what men did with women, used them in one way or another and tossed them aside. I was angry at the part he had made me play. Yet thinking of them married, I saw how impossible it would be.

"Meg, my child," boomed a voice from the door.

"Who is she? What's she doing here?" another voice said.

"She is our landlord's daughter. What's this I see? Tears? Let me dry your eyes, child. You're too pretty for this." Bluey Considine advanced on me with a glued-up handkerchief in his hand. Behind him came a little black-dressed hunchback, stumping on a surgical boot, grinning—or was he snarling?—with a pink mouth like the mouth of the snake Robert had held up to me in California.

"I don't like women in the house, Bluey."

"Meg is special. She is the Reverend's daughter."

I had managed to put the table between me and the dreadful rag he offered; and I managed to say, "What are you doing here? Dad's at the house."

"We'll be going up to see the Reverend. But when I noticed the door open I thought I'd show Roger our new abode. This is Roger Sutton, my good friend."

"Will she come here often, Bluey? You know how women interfere."

"Now, Roger. She'll make us puddings, won't you Meg? I can taste them already."

"Has Dad rented you this place? He never told me."

"He has his mind on higher things. Painful descents, Meg. We mustn't ask a man like the Reverend to bother himself with the world. But yes, it's ours, Roger's and mine. Just down the road from you, my dear. The dinners we'll have, eh Roger?"

"I do the cooking, Bluey. No visitors. Remember our agreement."

"Ah Roger, relax boyo. You're in the Reverend's country. Life is different here." Bluey was nervous though. He knew my dislike of him, as he had known Mother's, and he wanted to be settled in before I could upset things.

"Which bedroom will you have, Roger? You can choose."

"When did Dad arrange this?"

"Why Meg, he wrote me a letter. I had it yesterday. It came like a benediction. No, we mustn't use that language in the Reverend's country. Meg, it came like the offer of a five-course meal to me. If you could have seen the place we had you'd understand. A tin shack in Freeman's Bay. Stairs like an engine-room ladder, and Roger with his boot. And the lavatory—I won't offend you, Meg. Now listen, listen." He bent close to me (Sutton was inspecting the bedrooms), and in his Irish beery eye was a toughness I had never seen before. "You can see how it is with Roger. You can guess the care he needs."

But Sutton, club-footed, hump-backed, never moved me to compassion in the twenty-five years I knew him. Bluey now and then did, and this was a time. I said, "Oh, bring your stuff, but don't expect any puddings," and I walked out of the cottage, promising myself I would never go back. If Dad wanted Bluey as neighbour, Dad could pay with his time. But I knew it would be no pleasure to him. Bluey was a burden he had carried half his life. It was no act of selfishness having him there.

So Bluey's voice sounded in the study on afternoons, and Sutton fought his battle against convolvulus and did very well. He enjoyed hating me. He needed a woman around. Now and then I took a pudding down.

One day Esther walked into my kitchen. She sat down and asked for a cup of tea. Fred had driven her round, she said. He'd come to squeeze some money out of Bluey Considine.

"What money? What are you talking about?"

"Not in the world, are you Meg?"

"Yes I am. Further than you think. Has Bluey been betting?"

"He backs slow horses, the silly old bugger. And then he doesn't pay up. Fred's gunner have to twist his arm."

I was excitable in those days, I was turning all ways, in a rage I could not fasten on any object. But Fred!—here was something. It seemed I had a sight of all that was wrong. I ran down there. I came into the kitchen at a run. I had taken Esther literally and expected to find Fred torturing Bluey in some gangster way, and Bluey crying for mercy, and I was prepared to jump on Fred and beat him with my fists. I was not prepared for anything so casual as Fred sitting on the table swinging his foot or Bluey in the sofa, spooning up mouthfuls of rice pudding and plums. Only Sutton was right. He faced Fred like a terrier. He shook Bluey's shillelagh in the air. Fred was calling him a tough little rooster. When he saw me, he said, "Not another one."

"Get out of here, Fred," I said.

"Meg, Meg," Bluey boomed, "Mr Meggett and I are talking some business. I'm thinking of putting money into his firm."

"Get out before I call the police."

"Police?"

"Don't mention those people. They're terrible people, Meg."

"You be quiet. How dare you bring bookmakers into my house?" I meant on to Peacehaven, into our lives; and meant bring ugliness into the world. They could not follow me, and who can blame them? Fred, shocked as much as Bluey by my mention of police, tried to say he was only collecting a debt, but I would not be stopped. I grabbed Sutton's shillelagh and waved it at Fred. I told him to get out before I hit him.

"You're off your rocker, Meg."

"Go on. And take your wife with you. I don't want to see her."

"I'll tell her that."

"You do. Tell her she can come back when she learns to behave decently."

Fred left, and I rounded on Bluey and Sutton, I stamped my foot. "You too. Go on, both of you get out."

Sutton looked as if he would fight and Bluey huffed a little, but they went when I banged my stick on the table.

"She's mad, Bluey."

"She's upset. Come on, Roger. The poor girl wants a little time to cry."

They left me in the room, with its mutton smell and its framed racehorses, and I did not know where I was. I gripped the table edge and closed my eyes. I thought I was fainting, and I knew I was lost. Always I had found that serenity Mother had made in me, and rested there, but now it was gone, I turned but could not find it. For many years I had kept the image—kept it as a kind of explanation—of a small room at the top of stairs. I went in and bolted the door and was in *my* place, where no one could come—a white room with a clean bed and a ewer set and fresh water and outside a sunny garden with birds singing. I washed my face with water, I was new. But now I could not even find the stairs or see the door, I ran for them but they were gone, there was nothing there, and I fell, down, down, becoming thin as air—and Bluey was right in a way: I wanted time to cry—I wanted all the rest of time to cry. I sat on the sofa, let my tears run out, and felt they were blood running down my cheeks and my life was running away. I let it go.

Esther came for me. She took me to Peacehaven and put me to bed, and she and Mirth nursed me through the half year of my breakdown—an easy name, it annoyed me as I got better. And "got better" is wrong too. I simply gathered up pieces I could find of myself and started on a way they allowed me to go. I behaved acceptably; was, as one of Esther's Americans said, "an O.K. gal" But I knew I was robbed, and damaged by my loss. I waited to be whole for many years. People liked me better. I learned to smoke and drink. Dad was the only one who saw that

I was less than I had been.

Esther was determined that what I really needed was "a good time." She dragged me off to parties with Bob and Al and Spike and Tony Cucchiella. I had to be dragged, their voices reminded me of California; but once there I smoked my Lucky Strikes and drank my wine. An O.K. gal, in the words of Spike O'Dowd. I was sorry for Spike, loud and very young and always a step or two behind the others, but could not get Mother out of my head. Vulgar! Bob would just have got by. He did not chew gum.

Bob fell in love with me. He was a pleasant boy and I had come back far enough into life to be mildly flattered. That was all. I tried to be good to him. He was full of experience he could not digest, and saw me as the older woman, "wise in living" (the Americans are like that), who would help him come to terms with it. That is a way of being loved few women can cope with. But as I said, I was good to him and let him kiss me—nothing more. He said he would be killed when he got back to the war. Looking at his face (I had told him it was handsome and he said it was "kinda Boston"), I believed him. I saw how something as fragile as this, made of stuff like bone and flesh, must fall to pieces, war or no war, and I had no reason to doubt his foreknowledge of the time. I put my own face in my hands as though I were holding it together and I felt tears running into my palms. I had these minor relapses, small "breakdowns." I turned and got away from Bob, not wanting him to see.

I think it was that night Esther got him to her bed. She had always liked him best and had only been filling in time with Tony Cucchiella. Soon he was telling her she was "wise in living" (Good God!). His face, he admitted, was "kinda Hollywood." Her son Adrian, born in 1944, is Bob's, I'm sure. So Pittsburgh Irish genes got left in Loomis. When Spike wrote to say Bob had died on a beach landing in Iwo Jima, Esther sat still for a long time with the letter in her hand. Then she said, "What the hell did I expect? It was just a fling. Get me a glass of plonk, Meg." She would not let me kiss her.

Esther's Americans were privates and corporals. Fred mixed

with captains and majors: crooks in uniform. He called them "smart cookies", and that's what they called him. Everyone made a buck, the American way. Fred saw the war as machines, not men. He asked himself what would happen to all those trucks and jeeps when it was over. He asked his majors and they grinned and wanted to know what he thought.

There's a story that Fred leased a ship and sent it round the Pacific Islands buying G.M.C. trucks. He got them at a few pounds each and brought them back to New Zealand, where he sold them to farmers, mostly returned servicemen, at profits of two and three thousand per cent. Nobody seems to know whether it's true, and Fred just grins when he hears it. What is true—the newspapers made a huge story of it—is that he bought war-surplus trucks and jeeps from the government for twenty pounds each and sold them a few months later for four hundred pounds. Fergus clipped the reports of the Royal Commission hearing into the scandal. Looking at them, I see that Fred bought fifteen hundred trucks. The tyres and tubes alone were worth more than the whole price he paid. He stripped the power winches off some and sold them back to the government for eighty pounds each. "Scrap" he bought for eight hundred pounds was full of ball races and starter motors and generators. Fred claimed he took a great risk. He had no idea the demand would be so great. When it was pointed out he had made a gross profit of eighty-six thousand pounds and a net profit of at least fifty thousand, and acquired twenty-five thousand pounds worth of new capital assets, and that he still had sixty percent of the trucks to get rid of, Fred replied that he had the right, in the ordinary way, to get what the public was prepared to pay. Nobody quarrelled with that—not in the courtroom; and most of the people I spoke to had made a sort of swashbuckling hero of Fred. The politicians, the public servants, were the ones to blame: idiots they were, and maybe crooks.

Trade in surplus kept Fred busy for several years. Then he turned his eye on Loomis. Loomis was ripe for plucking—or, as he puts it, ripe for development. Don't ask me why no one else had tried it. These things wait for men like Fred, and others spend the rest of their lives talking about the chances they missed. They saw Loomis waiting there, but something held them back. Nothing held Fred back. Half a chance was all he ever needed. "Vision, gents," he says (uneasy with the word). I call it nerve. He's the boy who sticks his hand in the jar and steals the lollies. To hell with the risk! It's plain why people admire him and will keep on admiring him even when he's locked up. He does a lot of damage and some good, but they're not interested in that. He's not much interested himself.

Fergus watched him enviously. Back from the war, Fergus had changed, but other things were the same. He was working as a plumber, and trying to get enough together to start out on his own. He circled round Fred, sensing his chance lay there. He was too proud to ask favours, but when Fred set up his own construction company and started putting up blocks of shops on the Great North Road between the Loomis bridges, Fergus went to him with a plumbing tender Fred couldn't turn down. All Fred had to do in return was put up the money to get him started. I did not like it. I did not like any connection with Fred. But Fergus argued it was a plain business deal and once it was over he'd go his own way. That was how it turned out. I saw Fergus happy, growing in the post-war boom into *Fergus Sole, Plumber*, employer of three tradesmen and an apprentice. He spoke of overheads and tax. I thought it a game he played. He still went off each day in his working clothes and when I called at his jobs there he was on his back under a sink. He spoke to his men in their Middle East slang: *shufti* and *maleesh* and *bint*. I did not think he would grow into a boss.

Meanwhile, Dad grew old, he grew very old. He said about old age, "It's hard work, Meg. After this dying will be a treat."

His favourite place was the summer-house. He sat there writing in his shiny-covered red or black notebooks. He wrote nothing long. He had twitted me once for having nothing but "thoughts" In his old age thoughts were all he could manage. He always had a book with him, and many times what he scribbled down belonged to others: chiefly his favourites, Whitman and Emerson and Browning. He wrote a funeral service for himself. Even that was made up of quotations. He handed it to me in a notebook of its own. *Funeral Service of George Plumb.* It began: I have light; nor fear of the dark at all. I recognized that: Browning. Further down was a piece I did not know:

> Thy thoughts and feelings shall not die
> Or leave thee, when grey hairs are nigh,
> A melancholy clave;
> But an old age serene and bright
> And lovely as a Lapland night
> Shall lead thee to thy grave.

Dad had put a question mark beside it.

"But it's lovely," I said. "I'm going to leave it in."

"Still sentimental, Meg?"

"But Dad—"

"I want the truth."

"It is the truth. You're happy now, aren't you?"

"Oh, happy enough."

"And anyway, you've put in stuff from the Bible."

"There's a lot that's good there, Meg. All right, keep it if you must. There's another one further down."

He asked me to have it typed out. "No parsons reading it, mind. I want one of my sons."

"Which one?" Not Oliver. Not Robert. Certainly not Alfred.

"You choose. Don't bother me with that."

In his last year he wrote the story of his life. He put thoughts aside, and book-dipping aside, and looked at himself, with a fair amount of knowledge and not too many evasions—perhaps none, perhaps he came to places and was genuinely blind. Yes, that is it. He wanted the truth. I do not know where he found strength to begin, but strength to carry on came from his visit to Robert on "the Ark" He told of that visit; and of his disastrous meeting with Alfred. He said in the end he was ready to die; and he signalled his readiness by taking up a new notebook and scribbling borrowed thoughts again.

"What's he copying?"

"Whitman," Raymond said. "It seems a bit unfair on Uncle Alf."

"How do you mean?"

"Well, Whitman was—you know. It sticks out a mile."

"Raymond!"

"He liked women but he liked men too. All that stuff about beard and brawn and fibre of manly wheat. I don't think Grandpa sees it, though."

Everybody was wanting to criticize him. Alfred had smashed his trumpet. He seemed almost naked without it, he had lost some of his strength. Felicity mentioned Samson shorn, with his eyes put out. She had no sympathy. "Serves him right. You can't switch the world on and off when it pleases you. Alfred saw that."

Dad sat in his chair by the winter fire. The only way to talk with him was paper-chat. Everybody had that privilege now. Bluey came up and wrote in his copperplate hand, and sometimes forgot himself and blarneyed away. I heard him from the kitchen. Dad did not mind. I think he even picked up a bit of it. Most of their talk was about the old days—John Jepson, Edward Cryer, the wharfies' strike in Thorpe and Dad's trial for seditious utterance. They kept off religion. Once, when Dad was dying, I came in and found Bluey sitting by his bed holding his hand. I wished Raymond could have seen it.

At the end Bluey, who had been such a burden always, was Dad's most welcome visitor. I turned Merle and Graydon away and made Wendy wait if Bluey had called. Wendy tapped her foot and looked dangerous. "He can't like that old soak. You're a weakling, Meg. I'd soon throw him out."

"He goes much further back in Dad's life than you."

"What does that matter? The future is all that counts."

"Dad hasn't any future."

"You deliberately misunderstand. Well, never mind, I'll see he's not forgotten."

The Butterses took their disappointment better. They had

each other. They came to their mentor hand in hand with a new report on Oneness, and if he was not available went away to take a little more of it. Sometimes I let them in with Wendy. That annoyed her too, but it gave me the opportunity for telling all of them that time was up. Dad found them a strain. He would sometimes close his eyes and pretend to sleep.

Oneness, George, soon you will know, Merle wrote.

"He'll know," Graydon said.

"Not if you two don't give him some peace," Wendy said.

Oh the joy of it!

"Melting into God."

"They sound like a pair of ice creams."

Indeed we must believe that we have seen, when light suddenly dawns on the soul.

"Plotinus," Wendy said contemptuously.

"We've known it. He's known it too."

"He has. I give you that. He's known it in several lives."

"The future life is what counts."

"Agreed, agreed. But what would you know about it?"

"What we have seen."

Merle wrote, *George, now you are close, what can you tell us of the future life?*

Dad roused himself. "One world at a time."

Wendy pounced on the paper and scrawled, *Thoreau!* and Dad looked annoyed.

"Wisdom is transferable, Wendy. It belongs to no one man." He closed his eyes.

"He's tired," I said. "Everybody out."

"He's pretending," Wendy said. "He just wants to get rid of these two."

"He's communing. We know, don't we?" Graydon said.

"Everybody out."

I got them out of the house and went back to Dad.

"Please, one at a time Meg, not three."

I can keep the lot out if you like.

"No, no, they've been kind to me. But don't mix them

together. I don't know where I am."

They all believe in Oneness, don't they?

"They don't know what they believe. None of them. And Oneness is all very well—but Meg, I want to see your mother."

Willis and Emerson came to visit him. Esther came now and then. As a young woman, she had entertained him. He had seen her grabbing at pleasures, but knew that she was happy and generous. Now he saw her standing soul-less in the human world, turned into stone like a troll. I told him he was wrong, but did not press it. His extravagance came from sensibilities a little out of control in his last days. Good and evil pressed on him. He told me that all his life his knowledge of the evil in man had made him tremble with fear and loathing, just as his knowledge of the good had uplifted him. Orthodox theologies, he said, have a place for evil—that is one of the greatest of their attractions. We must resist that easy way. But that leaves us facing evil alone. He had never discovered how to fight it except to fight, in himself and in the world. He believed good was stronger. Faith in the end was his strongest weapon.

His dying though was not a time of battle but, for most of it, a tranquil running-down. He enjoyed Willis and Emerson. He laughed with them. Felicity paid a visit and was good. She kept her impatience down. I saw the way she must have been with him as a girl. She found pleasure in returning to it. And Dad lifted himself in his pillows, laying down Man's destiny to this strongest child. I was a little jealous.

Emerson came one Saturday morning in spring and took me for a ride in his Gypsy Moth. It was the aeroplane he had flown from England to Australia twenty years before. He was a well-known pilot now, a captain with TEAL, flying four-engined seaplanes across the Tasman; but real flying, he said, could only be done in small planes. He had tracked his Gypsy Moth down, found it mouldering in a barn in the Waikato, and bought it for a few pounds. He worked on it and now it flew again.

"Come on, Meg. I want to see how she goes with a passenger."

"You can get plenty of passengers."

"I want one of my sisters."

"Take Felix."

"Not me," Felicity said, "I'm too old for joyriding."

"Aeroplanes crash," I said.

"Not when I'm flying them."

"The Sundowner of the Skies," I joked. I wanted to go. I would be terrified, but I felt something might lie on the other side of that. And I could not turn Emerson down when he looked at me in his eager way.

"Come on, Sis."

"Yes, go on," Felicity said. "You need a break. I'll look after Dad."

We drove to Ardmore aerodrome. I put on a flying helmet and goggles. "No stunts, promise me."

"Bank left, bank right, land and take off." He crossed his heart.

He helped me into the front cockpit. A mechanic swung the propellor, and it was a wonder to me how something as solid as that could dissolve in a blur. I had never flown, but as we raced shuddering over the grass, and lost our weight, and the earth slipped into a wrong dimension, wonder kept me turning my head and crying back at Emerson. There was no place for fear. Thin streets and tiny cars and houses with cardboard roofs, lead cows and a tin sea, hills patted smooth by hand: all wrong, and recognizable to my special sight. Human kind seemed impossibly brave, inhabiting a crust of fields and streets through which they might fall at any moment into space. It seemed Emerson would be able to fly his aeroplane to the edge of the world and dive under it and we would find brown earth and the roots of trees.

Slowly as we droned along I lost this sense; miraculous perspectives shivered into ordinary. Emerson leaned the plane over to the left and right and I saw fields and hedges and milking sheds and small towns. Suburbs went by, racecourses, volcanic cones with houses up their sides. We flew over Mt Eden and looked in the crater. Emerson pointed ahead.

"Loomis?" his mouth seemed to say.

"Yes," I yelled.

We flew over the mangrove swamps at the mouth of the Whau creek and over the farms of Te Atatu. Emerson wheeled the plane and we followed another creek into the land. Children in coloured canoes waved their paddles at us. I saw a waterfall splashing into a pool. The brown salt water changed to green. "Moa Park," I cried. There were the diving board and the swings and the roundabouts and the pirate ship rocking on its axle. We had had our school picnics there. On that green strip by the creek I had come second-to-last in the egg and spoon race.

"Esther's place," I pointed. Shining-new, shining with glass and clinker-brick, it stood in the trees above Moa Park, pointing its glossy face at the town of Loomis. Emerson took the plane across the hill and swooped down waggling his wings. He banked at the bottom, almost touching the tree tops, and again we beat our way round. I saw birds flitting in the branches like sprats in water. Esther ran out on to her patio. She waved; a square foreshortened figure. The next time we came round she was back with a tea-towel in her hand, and a man with her. I saw the sun gleaming on his bald head. "Alfred," I screamed. His arms went up and down like railway signals. Emerson took the plane up high until we saw the sea again. He dived at Alfred and Esther. We went straight down at them. I did not scream, for I trusted him, but the world narrowed, shrinking like the pupil in an eye: park lost, then trees, then lawns, then the roof of the house, until the patio was left; and Esther and Alfred, faces white, dish-flat, on bodies short as tree stumps. They scuttled one each way. We zoomed past the chimney, we rocketed over the trees, and Emerson climbed, grinning, his joke over. He waved lazily at the two on the patio—they were clutching each other—and turned the plane along the line of the creek and our visit was done. I watched them, Esther and Alfred, I waved at them until a hill swung round and hid them from sight.

We followed the creek. I saw Loomis, the golden mile—

Meggettsville—and the railway settlement, where widowed Mrs Sole lived in her numbered house, still working herself to the bone, and saw the bridge by Millbrook Road, and then we were following the road. The white dust shone, the pools of the creek flashed yellow. Emerson leaned the plane this way and that, as he had leaned his motor bike on our night ride.

We made a wide circle round Peacehaven. Like Esther's house it stood on the side of a hill, but it seemed more to have grown out of it than to have been put down there. The terraces of lawn and garden made shallow steps up from the creek and the house under its hedge of trees carried on that natural-seeming rise and levelling-out. Over the creek was Merle and Graydon's castle, and Bluey's cottage in the wattle trees. Sutton shook his spade at us from the garden. He was angry at our noise. Bluey filled the door and put up his hand to shade his eyes as we crossed the sun. We ambled past Peacehaven, close and low. Dad sat wrapped in blankets in a chair by the French doors. Fergus must have carried him out before going to the cricket. Tea things stood on a table at his side. Felicity was pointing. I'm not sure Dad saw us.

Emerson climbed. I turned and made a fierce no with my mouth. He must not dive at Dad. He shook his head, pretending he hadn't meant to, and he took the plane across the orchard and the lawns. We came almost on eye level over the summer-house. Dad was ready and he waved at us. He was wrapped in blankets like a doll and had a blue woollen cap on his head, pulled over his ears. As we climbed away and turned for a last look I kept that little patch of blue in my sight. It was bright as a flower. We went up and I lost it. Loomis was under our wings. The creek and Millbrook Road ran side by side. As we droned over shrinking houses, I had again a moment of special sight. I was aware of Dad at Peacehaven and of Alfred on that patio two miles away. I saw their closeness and their pain. I saw like a bow in the sky the joining of them that would never break; and felt, like the sky we floated in, their distance from each other. I felt it like a distance between us all.

Emerson took us high. We coasted down to Ardmore aerodrome like a car down a hill.

"Come again one day, Meg."

"Once is enough. But I wouldn't have missed it. Thank you, Emerson."

By the time I got home Bobby and Raymond had lifted Dad back to bed.

"You were like a bird, Meg. It was miraculous."

"The noise," Felicity complained.

"He couldn't hear it."

"The story of his life. He just looks up and sees a great white bird."

"That's not fair."

"What are you girls talking about?"

"Tea," Felicity yelled; and wrote, *Tea. What would you like?* on his pad.

"An egg, I think. Boiled four minutes. Only your mother boiled my egg properly."

"Orders, Meg. Into the kitchen, girl. I'll hold his hand."

When I came back Dad was propped high in his pillows. His eyes were bright. Felicity smiled at him, nodding sharply and keeping quiet. He told her about Woman's Task in the Coming World. I put his tray in front of him and he said, "I've got good girls."

He lived into the new year. Labour was out; Fraser and Nash were out. Dan Peabody had lost his seat in Thorpe. Sid Holland was Prime Minister. New Zealand had what Dad called "a ruling party of cannibals" That was not one of his better shots. Since Labour had brought in conscription in the war he had lost all interest in politics and looked on parliament as a monkey-show.

January, 1950. I came into his bedroom and found him dead. He looked as if he had died peacefully. His face was more friendly than stern. It was faintly querulous. He did not look dead. His hands on the turned-down sheet had the look of resting. I covered them up. I went out and phoned my brothers Emerson and Willis. I phoned Esther and sent a wire to Felicity.

She and Oliver came up for the funeral. I showed Oliver the service Dad had composed. He said it was a disgrace. Felicity sniffed and said it was about what she had expected. But Willis, pleased to be chosen, read it in a bold and musical voice. He read it better than he sang *Danny Boy*.

> So be my passing!
> My task accomplished and the long day done,
> My wages taken, and in my heart
> Some late lark singing,
> Let me be gathered to the quiet West,
> The sundown splendid and serene,
> Death.

Yes, I thought, that's close enough. It wasn't quite like that, but it will do.

17 He had said Alfred would not survive him long. Is four years long? In Alfred's life that time was full of turnings this way and that, yet in another way it was just a breath.

John Willis was dead. No one took his place. That does not mean Alfred lived alone. He was seldom without a young man. Sometimes he had two or three in tow. They were not all his lovers. His house in Herne Bay became a centre for homo-sexuals. Alfred, at forty-five, was an elder of his tribe. He gave a roof, he dispensed wisdom; he took, I suppose, love when he could find it. Once he told Esther he had saved half a dozen lives at the very least, and saved the sanity of more young men than he could count, and one or two women. Saving his own was more difficult. Loneliness, in the midst of those young men, and drink, and hatred, were his troubles.

After Dad's death I went through the books in his study. Felicity and Oliver had taken some—Oliver the rare and valuable ones, Felicity said—and I chose others I thought Willis and Emerson might like. Esther refused books but took a painting. I posted Robert Dad's copy of *Walden*. One day I pulled from the top shelf a little selection of Shelley's poems. Bobby had left home to teach in the country and I was choosing books I thought he might like. As I climbed down the steps to put it on the desk I noticed several brown spikes poking from the pages at the top. They snapped when I touched them. I opened the book and found half a dozen pine needles inside. At first I thought Dad had tried to press them like wild flowers. Then it came to me that here, half-way through *Prometheus Unbound*, Alfred had stopped his reading one day, and marked his place, and climbed down from his tree; and that day or the next Dad had discovered him and turned him out.

I opened the book at the front. *To Alfred Plumb from his father. April 1922. Poets are the unacknowledged legislators of the world.* Alfred had scrawled his name at the top of the page. I put the book on the desk beside Bobby's pile and went on with my work, glancing at it from time to time. Mother must have found it in his room and put it on Dad's shelves, where it had stayed for twenty-five years.

The next day was Saturday. I wrapped the book in brown paper and walked into Loomis, where I caught the bus to town. Esther had told me Alfred's address. I took a taxi from the terminus. It drove through Freeman's Bay and Ponsonby and I thought this was just the place for Alfred—it was seedy, beaten-down. But Herne Bay was a surprise. Houses like Peacehaven, flowering trees everywhere. The gardens seemed tropical. I asked the driver to put me down at the end of Alfred's street. I meant to come up gradually on his world. I had the idea that the whole of a homosexual's life was sex. When they were not actually "at it" (Rebecca's phrase) they were getting ready, or recovering from it, or circling round each other, passing signals and intriguing. So I banged the gate at number 9

174

and walked slowly up the path, sniffing flowers, talking to the birds.

The house would have delighted me if I had been able to see it properly. It was like a wedding cake covered with fancy icing—fretwork, finials—yet it had a simple look, almost an austere look. On later visits I saw that Alfred had managed this by having the walls painted white and the roof stone-grey. The house was solid but light, frivolous but pure. I approached it along a red scoria path, sure it was a deception. John had left Alfred "rolling in it", Esther said; but here was a lack of ostentation, a signalling of wealth, I thought of as aristocratic. There had to be a mistake. Alfred could not be here.

Someone was playing the piano in a room along the hall. The music had the purity of birdsong. I waited for it to finish, but it kept on. At last I knocked. The player cut off with an angry chord. A young man came to the door. "If you're from some church we're Catholics here."

"No," I said, "I'm looking for Mr Hamer. Alfred Hamer."

"Is it business? He doesn't like being disturbed."

"No, no, it's a friendly call."

"Oh. Well. What name shall I say?"

"Mrs Sole. I'm his sister."

"Ah, one of the sisters." He looked at me with a friendly alertness. "I'm not sure he'll want to see you but I'll ask. Don't go away."

Alfred came cautiously down the hall. "Well, well," he said, "well, well." They were Dad's words, spoken with Dad's intonation. The small bald man was a Plumb through and through. "Meg, this is a surprise. I'd given up all hope of getting you to visit me."

"You've never invited me, Alfred."

"I thought you'd run a mile."

"Well   here I am."

"So I see. You'd better come in. It's lovely to see you, Meg." He kissed my cheek and took my hand, and pulled me over the doorstep. And seeing my fright, he gave a quack of laughter.

"No one will hurt you. There are no monsters in the thickets here. Only poor Bruce. You probably heard him playing. Bruce will make us a cup of tea, won't you Bruce? Or perhaps you'd rather have wine?"

"Tea will be nice."

"Tea will be naice. Try the wine, Meg. Burgundy from Burgundy, not Loomis creek. Come on, come on." He led me up the hall and into a room so bright and airy I felt I would float away. I looked around for something to hang on to.

"Sit down. Grab a chair."

"What a lovely room."

"You like it?" He smiled at me. I think he almost blushed. "This is my work. This is what I do instead of poetry. Come on, I'll show you. I'll show you my whole house."

We went back to the verandah and started from there. He had reason to be proud of it. If he had not had money he could have made a living as a decorator. Where I had expected darkness there was light—there was light even in his bedroom, even though the coverlet on his bed was midnight blue. I took that as a touch of defiance. There were mirrors everywhere, flashing light, opening into worlds from which my own meek face suddenly blinked out. There were paintings and photographs, beautiful and cruel young men, with their faces naked. The kitchen settled me—"clashing" colours stood side by side in harmony. I was learning something. But in the end—after bathroom, sun-room, guest-room, lounge again ("don't use that word")—I was not happy. There were signs of grubbiness, and a museum stillness, and I saw the house as something he had done and finished with. He seemed a little bored by the time we sat down. He was more enthusiastic about his wine.

"How do you like that, Meg? New Zealanders don't know what wine is. I don't waste this on Esther, you know. You're privileged."

"I love those curtains, Alfred. I just love them."

"Those? Swedish. I've got a friend who imports stuff. He gets my wine for me too. 'Tisn't easy."

176

"Could you get me some?"

"I don't know, Meg.   "

"I mean the curtain material. You can keep the wine. It's too sour for me."

He was shocked. "I give up. I give up hope for all New Zealanders. Here, give that to me, I'll drink it. Make her a cup of tea, Bruce."

Bruce ("I'm giving him a roof, Meg. Don't be nervous.") made me lemon tea and then sat at the piano, picking out notes softly and smiling at us with a sly goodwill.

"He wants to play. He's got a passion for music, haven't you Bruce? Apart from that he's a nosey little devil. All right, give us a tune. Show us how good you are."

While the boy played, Alfred sipped his wine (sip sip, sip sip) and topped it up and studied me. He suffered moments of love and hostility. Time had damaged his face, but expressions stay the same. He had loved me once and his love kept on, but I came out of Dad's world and he hated that.

I clapped when Bruce finished playing. He gave a professional nod. Alfred said, "You've showed off long enough. Leave us alone now. Go and mow the lawns. Earn your keep."

The boy showed no resentment. Cool in his blue shirt and belted slacks, insulated in his youth and skill, he was not touched by Alfred, who suddenly seemed petulant and seedy.

"I'll tinkle here. Don't mind me." Bruce smiled. "I'll play you something else later on."

"Bloody little skite." Alfred hauled himself into the other corner of his chair, turning his back on Bruce and facing me. "Well, what did you come for? What have you got in your little parcel?"

"Something of yours."

"Be careful, Meg."

"I thought you'd like to have it. It's something you left behind."

"I left nothing behind."

"Here." I offered the parcel. "It won't bite." But I had made a mistake. His mind went rushing somewhere. I saw a burning on his skin and a pushing behind his eye.

"It's just a book. Please? For me?" I tried to charm him. What else could I do?

He forced his breath out with a tearing sound. "You're a stupid bitch."

"Don't swear at me, Alfred." I began to be frightened. "I'm sorry. I'd better go home."

He came out of his chair, springing frog-like. "Give that to me. Give it to me now."

He snatched the book and tore the paper off. The little green Shelley, gold embossed, fluttered in his hands like a bird.

"See the pine needles? You must have been reading it in your tree." Against his rage it was nothing. He shivered for a moment. His eyes took an oily sheen. I tried to see where he was going. But he was quick as water. His feelings slid about like butter in a pan. I thought he might tear the book to pieces. But a gloating satisfaction came on him at last. "Meg, ha ha, we'll see. Bruce, where's my fountain pen?"

The boy fetched it from the mantel-piece.

"Alfred, Dad was proud of you," I said.

"Ha! Thank you, Bruce. No, don't go away. This is for you, my dear." He wrote on the fly-leaf, under Dad's inscription. "There you are. Show Meg."

Bruce made a face. He handed me the book. *To my dear young friend Bruce Barnhill, from his fellow twilight dweller Alfred Hamer, born Alfred Plumb. April, 1950.*

"Tells an interesting story, that page. Here, I'll put some wisdom in. A gem. He was good at gems. Bring it here, Bruce."

He wrote: *On the other side of the river is a boy with a bum like a ripe peach, and Alas! I have no boat.* "There. A good bit of life in that, don't you think? I'd like to see how poets would legislate for that."

"I don't want to have it, Alf. This is your game, not mine."

"You'll keep it if you want to stay here. Go and tinkle on your piano. A bit of crying music, please. Meg wants to cry."

"I do not. I'm going home."

"Go then. Go on. No, wait. Tell me what you thought you were doing."

"I was trying to stop you being unhappy."

"By bringing me a book from my sainted dad?"

"You can't hate him all your life."

"Can't I? You watch me. She's got a Jesus complex, Bruce. She wants to heal the world."

"Leave her alone. Have another drink."

"A Jesus complex, Meg. No, that's a bit on the firm side. What you've got is a female thing. All these emotions you pour out, it's as if you're bleeding all the time. So undifferentiated. It's almost biological, Bruce. I suppose it's got something to do with menstruation."

"Shut up, Alf. You make me sick sometimes."

"I make him sick! Go and tinkle, you little pansy bludger. That's why I keep you here. And don't you lose that book."

Bruce went to his room and closed the door. Alfred sighed. He poured more wine in his glass. After a while he took out his handkerchief and wiped his face. "You've had me sweating, Meg."

"I'm sorry I made you quarrel with your friend."

"That? That was no quarrel. You should hear us sometimes."

"I think I'll go now, Alfred."

"Good idea. The day's a bit of a wreck."

I telephoned for a taxi. While I was waiting in the hall Bruce put his head out of his room and whispered, "He's drinking himself to death."

"But only on the best Burgundy," Alfred shouted.

Bruce looked startled. "He's half deaf, you know. He's psychic." He shot back and closed his door. A moment later he was out again. "He drinks whisky too."

"Betrayal, Meg," Alfred called. "But I don't mind. He does it out of affection."

When the taxi sounded its horn he came into the hall. "Goodbye, Sis. Come again. But don't bring any books."

"Do you really want me to come?"

"Oh yes. Apart from John there's only been Esther and you. Bring me a rose from Mother's garden."

"We're pulling them out. And the orchard too. We're selling that."

"Bring me one before they go. But no emotions. O.K.?"

"Yes. O.K."

"I'm sorry about my shouting. It wasn't for you."

I became a regular visitor at his house. Fergus did not like my going there but I explained it was a family duty. That was a lie. Unless Alfred was too far gone in drink I enjoyed my visits. I never lost my nervousness of homosexuals. Touching between them, words of affection, made me uncomfortable. I was afraid they might start enjoying their sex lives in front of me, like dogs. Alfred was amused by my discomfort. Only once or twice it made him angry.

"We're people, Meg. There are other things in our lives."

I did see that. Music was more important to Bruce than sex. I grew fond of him and missed him when he went to study in London. I did not like any of the others so much, and they did not care for me. My nervousness did not amuse them. There were men there like estate agents and bank managers, and young men like rugby footballers—young men who were rugby footballers. None were as beautiful as Bruce and none, as far as I knew, were talented. I could not understand them desiring each other.

I understood the girls better—Ailsa and Pauline and Kay. Alfred explained there were no sexual connections amongst those three. That made me a little more easy with them. But when Ailsa came in one day with Joan, her lover ("butch", Alfred said; the meaning was plain at once), I almost had to leave the room. Later I came to like her very well. She was an artist. I went to one of her exhibitions and bought a painting of two little girls, one with Ailsa's face and one with hers, building a castle in a sandpit while their mothers gossiped, drinking tea. It troubled me a little, but the girls had faces smoothly white, one plain, one beautiful. I saw that they were living by some inner rule or logic. I saw they were themselves. But while I tried to explain that to Joan, I found myself caught on her difference; I imagined her and Ailsa doing things to each other, and I looked at her as though she were an animal in a zoo. She saw. I'm not sure why she bothered with me after that.

My usual day for visiting was Saturday. I never stayed to the parties. Tea remained my drink. Once it fell to me to answer the door and explain to a pair of Jehovah's Witnesses that we were all good Catholics in this house.

"You did that very well."

"I've no patience with them. How can they believe that stuff?"

"Easy. Belief is easy. Look at Felix."

"More nonsense," I said.

"At least the tikes have got some style. They please the senses. Shall I nail a crucifix on the door? One with lots of blood?"

Once when Felicity was up I took her with me to Herne Bay. It was a dangerous thing. I took the precaution of telephoning first. Alfred was pleased, and apprehensive. As our taxi took us through Ponsonby, I reflected on the complex of feelings in him. I saw how their strain against each other must stretch him almost to a breaking point.

"Don't talk about Dad."

"I'm not daft."

In fact, she was cleverer with him than I could be. She praised his wine. She got him talking about mother, and growing up, and his university days; and, at last, about his discovery of his nature. I was on edge. I expected Dad to rear up at any moment. But they trod around him without seeming to know that he was there.

"Didn't you ever like girls?"

"Oh yes, you bet I did. I liked anything beautiful. When one of Meg's little friends took down her knickers and showed me what she had—I'm not making it up, Madge something,

Meg—anyway, I thought it was a lovely little place. But boys
were lovelier. There was never any question in my mind. I could
look at myself, Felix. Living proof."

"What about now?"

"Now? If a woman made a pass at me I'd run to the ends of the
earth."

"So you really are one?"

"The genuine article."

He was flippant about his agonies. He had us laughing with
talk of his "runaway organ"—even I laughed—and his lusting
after boys on tennis courts. "They were so pure in their whites.
That was part of it. God, I was confused." He had known he was
real but thought he was possessed. Later he had thought he was a
freak. Then he discovered from books there were others like
him. But where? Where?

"They must have been in my class at school. They must have
been thick on the ground at university. I know for a fact they
were. But I never found them. I can't work out now why they
never found me."

John came along. Alfred did not like the look of him. But
John knew Alfred. One day he took him by the hand and said,
"Isn't it time you found out who you are?"

"What are you grinning at, Meg?"

"He sounds as if he'd been reading *Bab of the Backwoods*."

"What?"

"Never mind. What about that lipstick you wore?"

"Ha! My transvestite phase. Lasted half an hour. I was never
one of those. John showed me who I was."

John was his great love. He never found another. It was bad
luck for him that he came on it first and came to promiscuity
second. The other way round would have been better. He lived
with John for twenty years and when John died Alfred had only
the experience of love to carry with him into his twilight world.
He kept his loneliness to himself. He became an elder of his
tribe.

While we talked a woman came in and sat down on the squab

by Alfred's chair. She was dressed in scarves and bangles and bright bits of cloth. Dresses were down to mid-calf that year, with waists of elastic. There was nothing of that for her. Her dress came to her ankles. It was belted with a piece of plaited leather hung with Pisces, Taurus, Scorpio etc., in brass and zinc. I thought she was probably trying to look like a gypsy, though her high-bred English face gave her little chance of that.

Alfred introduced her as Sybil.

"We're in for an oracle," Felicity whispered.

It was less than that. Sybil read handwriting. "She's done me," Alfred said. "Tell them what you found, Syb."

Her voice was rich and trembling—her most attractive part. "He is seeking a great love, but it eludes him. In his past there is great love and bitter sorrow—"

"Keep off that. Stick to what's up front."

"He is destroying himself. Unless he finds a love that cures him—"

"She doesn't mean earthly love, she means divine."

"Time is short unless he discovers that."

"She thinks I'm for the chopper." Alfred drew his hand across his throat.

"I see violence, Alfred. Take my warning."

"She won't say what sort."

"Because I don't see what sort. But it's there. Not far away."

"Good, isn't she? She's a real performer."

"He doesn't take me seriously. That's one of the penalties of my gift. And the pain of seeing too much."

"What do you think, Felix?"

"What should I think?"

"Let her try you. Come on."

"I will not."

"It's not a sin. You wouldn't have to confess it."

"It's got nothing to do with that. I won't be a party to confidence tricks, that's all."

"How about you then, Meg? I'll pay."

"Oh no." The woman made me nervous. She had hit on some truth about Alfred, and that showed insight, whether it came from handwriting or not. I was disturbed by her prophecy and wanted to be left alone with it. Alfred brought a pencil and pad. He put them on my knee.

"Come on. Give it a birl. There's no dirt she can dig up about you."

Sybil pushed her squab close to my chair. "Just write what comes into your head."

"I don't believe in it," I complained. I wrote my name and address.

"Oh come on," Alfred said. "Something with a bit of meaning in it. She's not just reading your character you know, she's telling your future."

"If I write something with meaning it'll give her a clue."

"This will do," Sybil said. "In fact, this is perfect. I need some quiet now."

Alfred shifted her squab into the corner by the piano. "She goes into a trance," he whispered. "The handwriting starts to tremble and then it speaks to her. Course we can't hear," he grinned.

"You don't believe this nonsense?" Felicity said.

"She's a pro. This'll cost me a quid. So we'll play along. You've got to admit it's a pretty good performance. Look at her."

Sybil, in the shadows, in what might very well have been a trance, black and red and green and gypsyish, did appear to me a person who might possess some occult power. Felicity snorted. "Let's go outside." Sybil gave a small sigh. I thought it had a gloating sound. I was not happy leaving her with my name and address.

We sat on the lawn underneath a flowering cherry tree. Petals fell on our shoulders. Soon Joan and Ailsa joined us, and one of the managers came in with his boyfriend. I wondered if spring and flowers and singing birds worked a magic for that kind of lover Joan winked at me.

Later a starved-looking boy came up the path. He turned
when he saw us and made back for the gate. I saw a grey bandage
on his wrist. Alfred called his name and ran after him. For
several moments they talked in the shade of trees by the garden
fence.

"He cut his wrists," the manager said. "Alfie's good with
these kids. If anyone can put the poor little blighter right he can.
It's dangerous though. Alfie takes too many risks."

I did not understand. Joan explained, "They're so unstable,
these boys. They're like quicksilver. It would be easy for one of
them to turn against him."

"Attack him, you mean?"

"No, no. Tell someone. It could end up with the police."

The boy came back with Alfred. He sat down awkwardly and
kept his silence. He had warts on his neck. It was always a puzzle
to me to discover homosexuals could be ugly.

I wandered in the garden, picking flowers. Down at the end of
the road a white railing marked the edge of a cliff. Yachts lay
becalmed on a pearly sea. Nature was indifferent, I thought.
Coming back, I found Joan waiting for me. "I know what you're
thinking, Meg. He helps these people but nobody helps him."

"He's so lonely. And he's drinking so much."

"We try, Meg. We do try. But there's this thing he won't let
us talk about."

"Come on, Meg," Alfred called. "It's time we saw what
Sybil's dreamed up about you."

The woman had come out of her trance and was enthroned in
Alfred's chair. She spoke in a voice that seemed to come out of
caverns, but what she said was ordinary enough. She told me I
had been a happy child. Family was my emotional ground. She
told me I was lucky in my husband. Heart ruled me, not head,
suffering therefore could not be escaped, but happiness for me
would be intense. Sentiment though was a danger to me. I had
let it cloud my love and distort my view of the real world.
Sentiment, she said, was an illness I suffered. Even those ruled
by the heart must strive to achieve clear sight.

"That's pretty good," Alfred said, "that's not bad at all."

"Anyone could tell that just by looking at her," Felicity said.

"Ah wait, give her a chance, you haven't heard the prognostications yet. Come on Syb, give us a bit of gloom."

Sybil lowered her eyelids. There was something reptilian about her. She seemed to sleep.

"Now don't play hard to get."

"The future is not clear."

"That doesn't surprise me," Felicity said.

"I was working in a fog." Her eyes flicked open and fixed on Felicity, making it plain who was to blame for that. Then they came to me, changing on that quarter turn from spite to melancholy. "But I saw a great tragedy. And then I saw one come and teach you to see."

"Do you mean one with a capital O?" Alfred asked. He grinned at me. "You don't feel religion coming on by any chance?"

"What sort of tragedy?" I had strongly at that time a knowledge of the body's fragility, and with it precise visions of dreadful events. I saw my children crushed and burned and torn.

Sybil turned her eyes on Felicity. "I could not see. Unbelief brings a darkness down."

"Mumbo-jumbo," Felicity said. "Come on, Meg. I've had enough of this woman. We'll go home."

"You didn't see any of my children in danger?"

"Oh Meg, she's a fake, can't you see?"

"Relax, Felicity," Alfred said. "Give old Sybil a chance. She's just an honest working girl, aren't you Syb? Don't spoil her act."

Sybil said, "I know when I'm not wanted."

"Oh stay. Have a glass of wine. You can do some of the others. Do Joan. I'll pay."

So Joan wrote down her name, and we trooped out to the lawn again and sat under the cherry tree drinking wine and lemon tea. Soon our taxi came. Felicity hugged Alfred. She told him to be good, and he crossed his fingers, grinning, and promised he'd try.

In the bus going home she lamented the waste of so much good feeling and good sense. I did not think it wasted. I had seen how useful Alfred was and how well loved. I talked about his loneliness and his drinking. Neither of us could think of a way to help him.

Esther was the only one who could help. He loved her far above me.

18 Esther, in her palace above Moa Park, was going through a bad time. She did not love Fred, but it had little to do with that. They had given each other licence to "play around". He had simply shrugged his shoulders at her Yanks. If he knew the boy Adrian was not his he gave no sign. Esther and he were "buddies"—she said "mates"—in a confidence trick they played upon the world. At least, for Esther it was a confidence trick. She never understood where the money came from, and seemed to believe that as long as she kept on grinning and "whooping it up" things would get better all the time. She did not know she had an emotional life.

Fred passed out of that world while her back was turned. Fun drained out of him. He settled down to make money seriously. His experience in building and letting shops in Loomis convinced him there was a fortune to be made in commercial properties. He saw what he had done small he could do large. Meggett Enterprises became his life. I do not mean that business was all of it. He found a kind of propriety in letting his appetites go.

It was some time before Esther discovered she was alone. Her "good times" kept on for several years. Then she began to see that good was gone, they were no more than noise. Fred was somewhere else, her buddy no longer. His girls did not worry her even then. But to be outside the trick he played on the world, that money-gathering trick, was to be without her habits of twenty years; her certainties, her resting place, her home and hearth; things that she had never known she had.

She turned to Adrian, to Alfred, and to drink. Her care of her children had been rough at the best, and very much off and on. Now, for the younger, it became obsessive. Fred had no part in Adrian. Her retreat into love for the child—I'll call it love— punished him; although I doubt he noticed. His focus could no longer be shortened to take in domestic events. He had his own construction company putting up buildings large and small, not only in Auckland but all over the North Island. And he was involved in mortgage gearing—borrowing huge sums of money, shifting them here and there, and coming up in the end with returns for himself of twenty and twenty-five percent. It was legal, but it was risky. Fred took the risks. People began to say he was a millionaire. Once the word would have made Esther squeal and throw a party. Now she said, "What the hell, it's his not mine." Fred too made a sour face: trying to make out there was something special about a million was just a way of tying a man down. He didn't know how much he had, he paid an accountant to look after that sort of thing.

Fergus's career had been going well too. He waited for what he thought a decent interval after Dad's death and then suggested we pull the orchard out and subdivide the land as building sections. "I know how you feel about the place, Meg, but no one's looking after the trees—it's not worth even picking the fruit. The land's going back. We could really make a packet out of it. The way I see it is, we bring a road in from the back, right down to the creek, and make a turning bay there.   "

I thought about it for several weeks. Bobby had gone to do his country service, Rebecca was shifting to a flat in town, and Raymond, after less than a term, was talking about giving up university and training as a journalist. He had an attachment to the orchard, but it was romantic rather than practical. No one had given the trees proper care since Robert's time.

I went walking there in the dawn. I had to decide. Fergus had waited long enough for his answer. I looked at the bearded trees, with bare branches and sweet apples high up. Dew gleamed in spider webs. The little stream coming down to the creek oozed through patches of swampy ground where tea-red water lapped about my gumboots. Brambles stood in banks as tall as houses. This had been elf country once. Now it was nothing special.

I walked in the hollow where Alfred and John Willis had made love. I felt no fear, though always before I had approached with a shiver, half-expecting to find something hideous there. It was an unattractive place. Gorse and bracken stood in clotted lumps. On the far side pear trees rose clear of the undergrowth. They were hung with brown withered-looking pears. I waded into the bracken and found the rotting quince stump with my feet. I stood on it. Dad had forced Robert to chop down the tree. I thought of his behaviour with impatience, nothing more. It was as if I had held my nerve: figures haunting the place were only fence posts; moans and cries of passion were the wind. I saw the orchard in Fergus's way: land "going back" It gave me a lonely feeling. But then I thought sensibly that if my life at Peacehaven was locked in me the orchard as it had been was there too. So let the bulldozers come, let houses go up and new people move in. The place might just as well be used. I walked down to the house and announced it to Fergus. He was pleased with me. I was glad to have made him happy. Later in the morning I wondered if I had shrunk or grown.

The bulldozers came the following summer. We let the trees dry out, then made a huge bonfire. It looked as if a building was on fire. I walked up with Fergus after work and stood by the embers. All around, the land was scraped to its clay. A tar-sealed road and concrete footpaths ran down to the creek and surveyor's pegs marked quarter-acre sections.

"Forty-three new houses, Meg. That's something."

"You can do the plumbing."

"I'll do more than that. I'm going to build them."

"Won't that take a long time?"

He laughed louder than was necessary "Not with my own

hands. I'll set up a company. We'll go in for house construction in a big way."

"That'll take money, Fergus."

"Sure, sure. I've got that all worked out. .   "

He had talked to Fred. The new company would be part of Meggett Enterprises. Fred would have the controlling interest in it. "But I'll be the manager. I'll have the say," Fergus said.

"So what you'll do is use these sections to buy yourself in with Fred?"

"He's going places, Meg. I don't see why we shouldn't tag along." I tried to break in but he shushed me. "I know what he's like, you don't have to tell me. But I'm the one who knows about house construction. As long as we're making money he won't stick his nose in. We'll have our shares in it Meg, and my salary too."

"You were happy as a plumber."

"That was small stuff. This is my chance to get in with the big boys."

"Is that what you want?"

"I can't stand still. You'd like some real money, wouldn't you? You'd like a better house?"

"I'm not leaving Peacehaven."

"It's getting pretty crummy, Meg."

"Spend some of your real money on it. I'm not leaving."

The argument shifted its ground. I gave way on the construction company but would not give an inch about the house. Fergus nodded and grinned. "O.K. It's a deal."

So Fred Meggett sucked my husband in. The new houses went up and Fergus was happy. He drove around in a flash new car with *Sole Construction* painted on the door. He was off to Hamilton, to Wellington, to Christchurch, even to Sydney. When Meggett House went up in town Sole Construction had a whole floor and Fergus an office as big as our sitting-room, with a secretary posted at the door. He never tried to live Fred's sort of life. He liked to dig in our garden and go to the cricket. His idea of a real break was a weekend fishing trip with friends; and letting his hair down—he had nothing against it—a party, a few beers, jokes in the kitchen. Fred sucked him in but did not spoil him. I admired Fergus. Sometimes I wished we could be more than friends.

Esther declared him too good to be true. She was sure he had a secret life and she joked with me about office girls and dives of sin. Alfred found it easier to believe in him. He had named Fred's world The Sties and Fred King Porker. Fergus became The Pig Immaculate. The name made me angry. I reminded Alfred of his own wealth, which he had done not a hand's turn for. "True," he said, "but I pretend to no virtues. Fergus does. Well, he doesn't pretend. But you do, don't you Meg? And you're just a fat little piglet, really. You've got your snout in the trough."

"None of us would please Dad any more." That shut him up. He poured himself another whisky. We were at Esther's place, at the patio table, on a summer afternoon. At the bottom of the hill Moa Park vibrated with children. The wooden moa nodded at the gate and the pirate ship showed its Jolly Roger in the trees. We could see a stretch of river, with coloured canoes paddling back and forth. Fergus was in Sydney, setting up a deal in prefab houses. Fred was "away" The three of us, three Plumbs, well fed, discontented, self-pitying, sat at the brick table making ourselves silly with strong drink. Now and then Esther jumped up and ran inside to see Adrian, who was in bed with the mumps.

"She fusses over him too much," I complained.

Alfred shrugged. "He's all she's got."

"She's spoiling him. He's unbearable enough as it is."

"Are you scared she'll turn him into another queer?"

"Nonsense. I never said that."

"You're thinking it though. You really can't stand us, can you? You come among us as though you're kissing lepers."

"That's not fair."

"What you'd like is a little magic pill you could slip in my drink. Make me normal, eh? I'll tell you Meg, you'd be killing me."

"You've had too much to drink. We all have."

"What have we got but drink, you and I? And that poor old wash-tub in there. We might as well enjoy life while we can."

"That's not true. I've got a lot more." And I meant it. "I don't even like this stuff. I'm only trying to keep you company. But why should I bother?" I pushed my glass away.

Alfred laughed. "Good old Meg. A drunkard through compassion. You're a real original."

"I'm not a drunkard. Please Alfred, do we have to talk like this?"

"My little sister wants me to be nice. O.K., I'll be nice. I really do love you, Meg. But I hate you too. You look like him."

"So do you."

"I know. Look. Look,"—touching his round Plumb forehead and his cheeks. "And look, I'm bald. Look at these, I'm going deaf. What a revenge he's having. But I've got one trick left. I'm alive, he's dead."

"You're so nasty, Alfred. Sometimes you make me want to vomit."

He put his head down. I thought he was going to cry. He stayed like that a long time. I saw how far he had let himself go—black fingernails, grime in his scalp. I began to think I smelled him: a smell of clothes worn too long, and a dunny smell. I saw him purely, as my brother, whom I loved, and I began to get up and go round the table to him.

"Don't talk to me like that. I've got nothing left."

"I know. I know."

"Don't touch me." He pulled away. "You don't have to touch me, Meg. I know you and I are all right." He stood up and went to the French doors. "Pour me another whisky while I'm gone."

Soon, through the house, I heard him piddling in the toilet. He had never learned to close the door. Mother had followed him there and pulled it shut, averting her eyes. I wondered what he would say if I did that.

Esther came back. "Where's Alfie?"

"In the dunny."

"Dunny, Meg? You are getting crude."

"How's Adrian?"

"Suffering, the poor little bugger. He wants to get up."

"And you'll let him, I suppose."

"I will not. What's the matter with you? Have you and Alf been quarreling?"

"He's drinking too much."

"You can't stop that."

"I can't stop anything. Nor can you. I thought you could once, he's always been closest to you, but it's too late."

"You are getting morbid. Alfie's all right. I don't know what he sees in those boys, but that's his worry. Where is he? Where are you, Alf? I'm trying to keep him away from Adrian."

"What?"

"Well, you know, he's a good-looking kid. It must be a temptation."

"That's ridiculous."

"You can't be too careful, Meg. I wouldn't want Adrian—you know?"

"But Alfred's his uncle. Adrian's a child."

"And Alf's a pansy. I've got to be realistic."

"But Esther—" She was gone into the house and I followed her. I could not believe this. But there she was at Adrian's bedroom door, hooking her finger at Alfred and saying in a merry voice, "Come on out of there."

Alfred was sitting on the bed. He did not understand. "Hold on, I'm telling him something."

"Out, Alf." She took his arm and pulled him to the door. "You go to sleep, Adrian."

"I'm talking to him. He's not sleepy, Esther."

She took no notice, but got him into the hall. Then she closed the door. She turned the key. "That room's out of bounds."

Alfred understood. His high-coloured face took a yellow tinge. Water came from his eyes. He whispered to me, "She's not serious, Meg?"

"She's not. She's just being crazy."

Esther said, "You can look Alf, but you mustn't touch.
Them's the rules."

His nose began to run. "I'm a homosexual, not a paederast.
Meg, Meg—" he turned to me—"I wouldn't touch him."

"Come on, we need some more hooch," Esther said briskly.

"Adrian's my nephew."

"She's crazy, Alfred. She's not well. She doesn't know what
she's saying."

"I know, all right. I've said my piece. And now we know
where we stand. Come on Alf, wipe your silly face. You look a
sight."

Alfred ran out of the house. I followed him and caught him at
his car.

"Alfred, she didn't mean it. Please come back."

I pulled him by his arm but he jerked free. "I've got to get out
of here."

"Come back with me. I'll make her apologize."

He got into his car and closed the door. "How?
How?   " I don't know what he was asking. I tried to tell him
I would see him tomorrow, phone him tonight. But he looked at
me in a way that held no recognition. He was gone out of my
world.

"She loves you, Alfred. She really does."

He drove away. When the car had turned behind the trees I
went a dozen steps back and screeched at Esther on the patio,
"You bloody fool." I could not bear to be near her. I got in my
own car and drove home. When she rang me later I banged the
phone down. I could not bear her—stupid and destructive and
self-indulgent. I thought that very likely she had killed Alfred.

That night I rattled around in my big house. It seemed to be
full of ghosts. From the verandah I looked at the Sole houses over
the creek. I had grown snooty about them—raw and ugly on
their scraped-down sections. Tonight they were huddled in a
cosy way, in company. I tried phoning Alfred. Ailsa told me he
had not come in. They were waiting for him. Bruce was home on
a visit but the party could not start till Alfred came. Parties were

never the same without old Alf. I spoke to Bruce. He told me
not to worry. Alfred had all sorts of haunts. He'd be home before
long with his tail between his legs. "Come in tomorrow Meg
and I'll play you a concert. This piano's got cobwebs in it
though. It's a real mess."

"Bruce, he was upset. And he'd been drinking."

"Don't worry. Alfie doesn't do silly things."

I rang Esther. Adrian answered the phone. He said his mother
had gone to bed. That meant she was drunk. I asked if he was all
right and he said he was great, his mumps had gone down and he
was making a feast. Uncle Alf hadn't turned up again.

I sat on the verandah, drinking tea. The lights went out in
Merle and Graydon's house. Down in the trees Bluey's cottage
was dark. In one of the new houses people were playing cards at
the kitchen table. Loud music came from further up the street.
The singer was Johnny Ray, Rebecca's favourite. His howls rang
along the creek and tightened like a lassoo round the houses. In a
back garden a man was digging a hole.

At midnight I made my last call to Herne Bay. The party was
subdued. They had rung around and no one knew where Alfred
was. Everyone was going home, Bruce said. He would leave the
light on for Alfred. The silly old dear had probably found the
hairy beast somewhere.

I lay in bed and tried to read a book, but could not make one
sentence follow another. I played over accidents he might have. I
saw fire and deep water and high cliffs and a plunging car. I
cancelled Alfred's deaths by calling them up.

I was wakened by the sun shining on my face. A thrush was
singing. The fears and dreams of my night pushed to come back,
but met the sun, the day, the singing of the bird. I got up busily
and made tea and toast and boiled an egg.

I was spooning up the last of it when the telephone rang.
"Bother," I said.

"Is that you, Meg? This is Bruce. Meg, something's wrong.
The police have been. They wanted the names of Alfie's next of
kin. Meg, are you there?"

195

"Yes."

"They asked all sorts of questions. What was he doing last night? When did I see him last? Meg?"

"Yes?"

"Next of kin? Why would they want that?"

"It means he's dead."

I took it like a knife driving into me, but took it calmly. When the detectives arrived I was waiting at the door. I told them I had seen my brother last at four o'clock yesterday afternoon. I told them he had been drinking and was in an emotional state. In return they told me he was dead. They tried to say it kindly and would not tell me what his injuries were or put a name to the way he died. A man walking his dog had found the body at six o'clock that morning in the trees at Moa Park. Alfred had been assaulted: that was all they would say. They asked me if there was someone here, my husband perhaps, who could make a formal identification. I told them Fergus was in Sydney. "Well—" they said.

"No. Oh no. I couldn't. Did they hurt his face?"

"His face was damaged, Mrs Sole."

"You'll have to try Willis. Or Fred. Fred Meggett will do it."

And Fred, in fact, made the identification. He had come home to find police in his house and Esther hysterical. The doctor was trying to get a sedative into her. He rang me when he came back from the morgue. Although he tried to sound mournful I heard the cheerfulness in his voice. He was always happy when he was up and doing. The way it looked to him, he said, was that Alfred had gone into Moa Park and tried to pick someone up and whoever it was didn't like it and kicked him to death.

"Kicked?"

" 'Fraid so, Meg. Kicked him all over, really. Not very nice. His face—"

"Stop. Please. I don't want to hear."

"Sorry. You've got to know some time. Do you want me to ring the others?"

"I'll do it. They're my family."

I rang Willis and Emerson and Felicity. I rang Bruce; Bobby; Rebecca; Raymond. When the conversations were done I wrote to Agnes in San Francisco and asked her to get in touch with the others. (I could not remember some of my sisters. Edith, Florence: who were they?)

Willis came late in the afternoon. He cried, and drank Fergus's beer His grief washed round the house in salty waves. Emerson arrived. He chewed his lips and sat dejectedly in a chair I sent them home.

I was alone at Peacehaven. It grew dark. I did practical things but the house grew haunted and I had to leave. I went down to Bluey's cottage. Sutton put on his boots and went for a walk. I told Bluey what had happened. I sat there for an hour while he patted me, made me tea. He rumbled his distress and wiped his eyes and blew his nose. I confessed I had never been able to get used to Alfred's homosexuality and I cried that his life had been wasted.

"Ah Meg, dear girl, where's your charity? Alfred was a good boy He was all right. Love him, let the rest go." He told me Sutton was a homosexual. "For twenty years he's wanted to be my wife. I would have obliged him. Roger loves me, that's the truth of it. But I just can't get my pecker up with a man."

Sutton passed me crabwise in the gate. He gave a grin of contempt. "Bluey's mine."

I hurried back to Peacehaven. The night was black and the stars sparkled like glass. I stopped on the drive. The soft noises of the creek made me think of Dad: streams symbolized the spiritual quest, and stars that Perfection we should one day attain. Alfred though, for all his verse-making, had seen streams as streams and stars as stars. I could not bring them together. Between them was only grieving and hatred and pain. Yet their lives had depended on each other.

I went on up the drive and across the yard. Light from the open door fell on the steps. How was I to take my brother's death into my life? It seemed that it might kill me. I did not want to die and I did not want to live. I ran up the steps into my kitchen. I looked around for something that might save me. There was nothing. I walked across the room and I walked back. I plucked at myself with my fingers. Were they part of me? I laid them on the wood of Mother's table and tried to find a way of going on. Alfred was dead, gone through a pain and horror that might just as well have been inflicted with knives. How could I take that into myself?

Peacehaven creaked and shivered. The tap dripped into the sink. Cats raised their dead howls in the night. I sat down. My fingers slid on the table—the polished wood. I found a way to run, and I ran there. That smoothness grew on me like a skin. I hooked my legs childishly in my chair. I anchored myself and placed my cheek on my hands. In a grizzling voice, I complained of my sorrows.

Presently Mother came and touched my cheek and stroked my brow.

19 Fergus flew home in time for the funeral. I rang Bruce and told him he could come if he wanted to.

"Have you worked the music out, Meg? Can I choose it?"

I had no idea what form the service would take. I asked him if he had any suggestions, thinking that homosexuals, like rationalists and humanists, might have a service of their own.

"Maybe if some of us say how we felt about him?"

We agreed that he should work things out, leaving a place for Willis and Emerson.

On the morning of the funeral I read in the *Herald* that four youths had appeared in the magistrate's court charged with Alfred's manslaughter. "Fergus, look how old they are."

"Manslaughter," Fergus said. "I thought it was murder."

"Fifteen. Sixteen. They're not grown up."

All the way to the crematorium I could not get the picture out of my mind of boys killing Alfred. I saw them as fat and happy, dressed in navy-blue shorts and grammar school caps. I had been calm since my night at the kitchen table, but those sweet-sucking boys unbalanced me. I had seen only their ages and failed to notice one was a steam-presser and one an electrical apprentice and two were unemployed. They grinned at me from the cold air in the crematorium chapel. There was a hideous dislocation between their faces and the solemn music. I sat in the front pew with Fergus and Willis and Emerson. Fred had not come and Esther was under sedation. Bruce and Joan and Ailsa and two of the managers and the boy who had slashed his wrists sat opposite. Bruce spoke. More music played. One of the managers spoke. I thought I should go mad. Did none of them see there were things that could not be borne? Life must stop. The moment was coming when I would stand and scream.

Then Robert walked into the chapel. I felt him in the door, and in the aisle, and heard him breathe as he entered the pew behind me. His hand came to rest on my shoulder, and I sighed, and in the space of a second remade myself and accepted life. I do not wish to play the moment up. It was quick. It was, I suppose, ordinary. But I know I was on the point of going mad; and because Robert came and put his hand on my shoulder I did not go mad. I have lived fairly easily since. I have toughened myself and let a good deal go.

It was not so easy for others. The boy who had slashed his wrists stood up. His cheeks were wet with tears. Light from the stained glass windows coloured his warts red and yellow. "Alfie saved my life. He showed me who I was. I'll never forget him." Fergus moved uneasily. I patted him on his thigh. The boy sat down and Bruce put music on. Then Willis stood up, clumping his leg on the floor. He had wet cheeks too. He spoke about Alfred as a boy. A good deal of it was invention. Willis had been away at sea. I think he believed it though. He spoke of tree huts and building mud dams in creeks, and evenings round the piano while Mother played, and a church picnic where Alfred tried the lucky dip and won a kewpie doll, which he gave to his sister

Meg. Like me Willis was a sentimentalist, but it was fitting in him. I was pleased someone was speaking for us and that Alfred's friends could see we loved him. Nobody seemed to mind when he said it was a great tragedy that Alfred had never known the love of a woman.

The coffin slid away on rollers. We filed outside and stood on the slope of the hill, with headstones and crosses stretching away to the pine forest over the valley. "Come home for a drink," Fergus said. But the homosexuals said no and said goodbye. They drove away in a large red car—"Bentley," Emerson said—belonging to one of the managers. I have not met any of them again. Fergus relaxed a little. He repeated his invitation, but we decided to go to Willis's. Fergus, his duty done, went off to work.

Mirth made us lunch. My brothers talked, lying in the sun. We made a fuss of Robert and asked where he had come from. He said he had read about Alfred's death in the paper, and watched for the funeral notice and caught the train down to Glen Eden that morning.

"Down from where?"

"North. I've got a little place."

His brothers did not press him. They had never pressed each other. We girls had always been the demanding ones.

In the middle of the afternoon Emerson ran me to Peacehaven for my car. I left a note for Fergus and I picked Robert up and drove him home. I saw the creeks and sawmills for the first time. Robert led me into his house in a diffident way. "It's not much, Meg." He had been there for two years and was just starting to get things the way he wanted them. It all looked scruffy to me, but I did not say so. When I had been there a little longer I began to see how things might be. He was going to renew the roof. When that was done he would throw a lean-to out the back for a bathroom and wash-house. We walked down to the river. An old dinghy was lying bottom-up on the bank.

"I'm caulking her. She'll be as good as new. There's plenty of fish out there."

"The jetty doesn't look safe."

"I'm putting a new one in. That's my job for next summer."

We had not talked about Alfred; but I began to speak of him as we walked up the section. I told Robert about my visits to Herne Bay—about Bruce and Joan and Ailsa and the boy who had cut his wrists.

"They all loved him. His life wasn't wasted."

"Of course not."

"Did you see how old they were—those ones who killed him?"

"Yes."

"Will you come with me to the trial?"

"Do you want to go, Meg?"

"I have to. I'm trying to understand it." I did not tell him he had saved my life. But I knew I must do something for myself. If I left the thing unended it might come back one day and take some shape that would destroy me. I had to see the boys and take them with Alfred, Dad, with Bruce and all the others, into my life. I did not try to explain it to Robert—had not explained it properly to myself—but said to him, "Come with me, Robert. There should be someone from our family."

When I drove home that night I had his promise.

The case came up in June. I met Robert off the train in Loomis and we drove into Auckland and parked by the university. We walked along to the court past Government House. The trees and the paths settled Robert down after the dangers of our drive through the traffic. I felt my tension reduced too, and though I was going in a few moments to hear the story of Alfred's death I felt the danger to me recede. We joined the crowd outside the Supreme Court. I heard one man—I took him for a lawyer—lay a ten shilling bet with his friend that Alfred's killers would get off. "I'd have those boys spruced up and looking clean. I'd have them like a bunch of wing three-quarters."

That was just the way they were. They were scrubbed and innocent. The electrical apprentice had an impish look, and the steam-presser—Peter Parker, six months out of school—was blue-eyed, pink-and-white, cow-licked by his mother. They sat in the dock through the trial, shoulders back, while the facts came out, and it was plain that other forces must have been at work. I knew as soon as I looked at them guilt would come down on Alfred. Even Reeves, the prosecutor, could not leave him alone.

He spoke with affectations of care and precision. I did not care for him. He was like an amateur actor playing the lawyer, and his interest went only as far as his role. I thought how absurd wigs and gowns were, a prop to vanity. The judge was Mr Justice Stavely. A harmless little cocoa-drinking man blinked out from underneath his wig. Alfred, I said to myself, none of this has anything to do with you. But that changed. Through the medium of Reeves's voice Alfred's last hours began to thicken and stand up before me.

Witnesses had noticed him in Moa Park from four o'clock onwards. He had watched children playing in the pirate ship. He had hired a canoe and paddled about inexpertly. People using the diving-board had had to shout at him to get out of the way. There was evidence to show, Reeves said, that the deceased was in an emotional state and that he had been consuming liquor. He was seen in the trees drinking from a bottle. In this condition, with his judgement impaired, he had fallen prey to four young men who had gone to Moa Park with the express intention of hunting down a homosexual and assaulting him. The statements of the accused, Reeves said, would make it plain that they had found a person they thought to be a homosexual—"they refer to such a person as 'a queer'"—that they did assault him, and he died.

I held Robert's hand. This was not just two hours of time Reeves was describing, this was a whole life coming to its end. A part of us was contained in it, of Dad and me and Esther, and Robert too. Esther had done to Alfred what Dad had done thirty years before—pushed him out of his family into the dark. This time he had found no John to save him. At some point—after how long in *his* time?—he had noticed someone moving on the edges of the dark: a boy with grinning mouth and crooked teeth. He had swum to that human shape through an element as empty to him as water, and stood by him, and said his name was Plumb. Yes, Plumb. He was trying to get back into our family.

The boy, the decoy, thought he was saying Plum. (The name had an unpleasant sound. The judge wrote it down.) They met in the lavatory at the back of the pirate ship. Alfred gave the boy a drink from his bottle. He made indecent remarks to him. That is true. But Alfred was crying for help. He spoke whatever words he thought were expected.

Reeves called a woman who had seen the two walking—"sky-larking a bit"—through the park towards the place where Alfred's body had been found. After that no one saw him, except the four who killed him in a clearing in the trees.

Late in the day Reeves called a pathologist, Carmichael. This man described his work much as Fergus would have done. He was flat and practical. He had examined Hamer at 7.45 a.m. on March 16 and formed the opinion that death had occurred between 5 p.m. and 9 p.m. the previous day. Hamer had two broken ribs and contusions on his chest and abdomen. In addition he had a fractured jaw and a fractured nose and a fracture to the base of the skull—the bony plates above his eye sockets. There had been considerable bleeding. There was a pool of blood over the right eye and a pool of blood and urine in the fold of the cheek and gums. In Carmichael's opinion the cause of death was haemorrhaging of the brain associated with a minor fracture of the skull and a severe fracture of the nose.

"What could cause such fractures?"

"A heavy blow or blows."

"With the fist?"

"That is certainly possible."

The defence lawyers were up then, one by one, and it seemed to me they were blaming Alfred for having a thin skull. Parker's lawyer in particular kept after Carmichael. Wasn't it true, he asked, that the bony plates above Hamer's eye sockets were very much thinner than in a normal skull? (He was a clever man, his

"normal" made it plain that Alfred's was a homosexual skull.)
Carmichael said yes, they were thinner. Paper thin? the lawyer
asked. That, Carmichael said, was an exaggeration. But he
agreed it was possible the haemorrhage would have been less
severe had the bones been thicker. The lawyer gave an angry
smile. Having a thin skull, he seemed to say, was the sort of
trick one would expect from a queer.

He was the only lawyer to ask Carmichael about the urine in
Alfred's mouth. His concern was to show that Alfred had not
drowned in urine. The rest of the body, his clothing (though
clothing was a matter for the police), gave evidence of having
been splashed with that substance. It was likely then, the lawyer
asked, that some of it had arrived in the deceased's mouth by
accident, misdirection? Carmichael said he could not answer
that, but the lawyer had made his point; and the judge, with the
air of a man who has heard enough unpleasantness for one day,
called a halt to proceedings.

As I drove Robert back to Loomis I asked him if Dad had ever
spoken with him about the way he had been troubled by a
knowledge of evil. It came down on him like a physical thing,
like a black fog, cutting out light and warmth, and he was aware
that powers hating life sat watching him. They could see in that
element. "There's a place in us Meg that belongs to them and all
our lives they're trying to get in. A room in our hearts. But we
control the door. We are the ones who open it and close it." That
empty place, he told me, is man's hatred of himself. He told me
of his meeting with Sullivan, a murderer, on the West Coast.
Sullivan had killed many men, most by strangling and stabbing.
In him that space had been filled. And evil, Dad went on, had
got into him, into George Plumb. It got in on the day he drove
his son Alfred Plumb away. "I held open the door. They
came in. There was a dreadful shrieking. I heard it all through
me."

I don't suppose he meant it literally. He was standing evil up
to look at it, and standing up responsibility too.

"No," Robert said, "he never told me. Poor old Dad."

"Robert, I think I can go by myself tomorrow. I can manage."

"Are you sure?"

"Yes. Yes." I stumbled on for a bit, saying that Alfred's life had ended before the blows were struck. We were a part of that. What happened in Moa Park was a part of those who killed him. I could face that perfectly well by myself.

For its final three days I sat at the trial alone. I did not take all the arguments in—what was the point?—but watched Parker and his friends for a sign that they understood what had happened to them. I knew I was expecting too much of boys. It had taken Dad twenty years to understand. I heard Parker's lawyer call them "lads", and saw them sit up straight and look like lads. I watched in hope that they would understand they were not that.

A few days ago I went to the Public Library in Auckland and looked up the newspaper reports of the trial. I found that a good deal happened while I sat there lost in my hope for those boys. Policemen came to the stand. They read statements they had taken and the lawyers questioned them. One boy, Fredericks, the electrical apprentice, admitted punching Alfred's face while his friend, Tucker, held him by the arms. Alfred fell on his hands and knees, making a gasping noise. Fredericks kicked him in the chest and this made some money fall out of his pocket. Tucker picked it up and shared it with the fourth boy, Moore. And Parker—"I needed to go. I just got the idea." Tucker pulled him away before he had finished. When they left, Alfred was lying on the ground grunting. They ran to their car and drove away.

I remembered the part about Parker. I remembered Alfred's grunting. It took his humanity away. He was an object lying on the grass, making animal noises, splashed with urine that might just as well have been his own. There was no pity in the room, but a trembling of disgust and a shrinking away. Parker's lawyer felt it: he said nothing. Later he seemed to suggest that Parker's urinating was in the nature of a prank. Boys had always done that sort of thing—piddling up walls to see who could go highest.

They made their final speeches. That was on the third day. I heard very little. The prosecutor said that Alfred, "the unfortunate man", had a right to live in spite of his shortcomings. He spoke of the four boys as "a pack" But it seemed to me the jury preferred the defence view—they were "lads" No one saw what they really were. No one told them they were lost, and yet might save themselves.

Fergus had made a fire in the sitting-room. We sat up late talking about the trial. He could not believe the boys would be acquitted.

"They will be, Fergus. Their lawyers had all sorts of arguments. No one knows who made the punch that killed him. It was like a dance."

Fergus was shocked. But I meant a puppet dance, a sort of wooden turning into the event and out of it. I could not explain it to him.

"What happens tomorrow?"

"The judge sums up. And then the jury goes out."

"Do you have to go, Meg? You can read it in the paper." He believed I was punishing myself, and was afraid I would have another breakdown.

The court was crowded next morning. I managed to get a seat at the back. I caught only glimpses of Parker and his friends. They were as well brushed as ever. The judge was cross and tired. He must have worked late on his summing-up. One of the curls on his wig had lost its stiffness and hung half-open. To me he looked like a woman at her washing, quite worn out. He went over the arguments on both sides and showed the jury all their parts again. Aiding and abetting kept him a long while. It was impossible to tell whether he believed the boys were guilty or not. His voice had a lifeless fall. I wondered if he had come to understand nothing that he said was relevant.

The jury went out before lunch. I bought myself some sandwiches and went into Albert Park. The sun was shining after rain. I dried a seat with my handkerchief and sat looking down Victoria Street into the city. The sky had a pearly glow that reflected off the streets. It seemed to me I was in a clean and windy place, looking down the long trough of my life. I apologized to Alfred. None of my activities, and none of my thoughts, of the last few days had been in any way a memorial to him. Alfred was gone. All that could be said now was that we were brother and sister, and that I had loved him, but not enough. I watched the people hurry through the streets. It's common at such time to look down on them in a god-like way and see them as ant creatures, scurrying about their bits of business; or to take a sense of their pain, and suffer the illusion of carrying it and of saving them. One is Jove or Jesus. I've been both in my time. But on that day I had a better sight and did not take shapes blurred with my feelings for real things. People bent into the cold wind in the street. Trams ground through the intersection. A pattering of rain came over the trees. I sat there taking it in. Horns blew crazily. Students ran up the steps, turning their winter faces to the sky. I did not want to make something of it. Man's love? Man's hatred of himself? I ate my sandwiches.

I went back to the court several times. The jury had come out of their room for direction on some point, but I missed that. From four o'clock I waited on the court steps. They were ready to come back at a quarter to five. Parker and Fredericks and Moore and Tucker climbed up from somewhere in the depths of the building. They had washed their faces and combed their hair. A drop of water gleamed in Parker's cow-lick. The jury filed in and found their seats with a gritty shuffling. Their foreman was a bald rosy man with a gold watch-chain on his belly. Four times, in a round convincing voice, he answered the clerk's question: "Not guilty."

A rumble of content sounded in the room. Parker gave Fredericks a dig with his elbow. The judge discharged those two. He remanded Moore and Tucker to face another charge. That puzzled me until I remembered they had shared the money that fell from Alfred's pocket. That was theft, and so they would be charged. It struck me as mad and I gave a little laugh.

"Good, eh?" said a man beside me. "I knew they'd get off."

I drove down to the Post Office and telephoned Fergus. I told him I was neither surprised nor angry, but he thought I was simply being brave. He told me to hurry home. He would race me out to Loomis and have a drink ready for me, and then he'd fry a steak.

"Thank you, but I've got to tell Esther. And I want to see Robert."

"Meg, you've done enough. Come home. You'll make yourself ill. I'll go and tell Esther."

"No. I'll be all right dear. I might be late, so don't wait up."

"You're sure you're not upset? I can't understand that verdict. It's a bloody disgrace. Even a homosexual   "

"Yes, Fergus. I'll see you later. Don't worry about me."

He had looked forward to propping me up, but then was relieved not to have the trouble. I thought about our life together as I drove to Loomis. Although the things that had filled it had drained away, through my fault as much as his—was it anyone's fault though, was not some law at work?—there was, it seemed to me, enough left to make it worth going on with. We would never make each other happy. He lived so much in the regard of men, and so much in his own private regard that took in notions of manliness and honesty and courage, inexpressible though they were by him, that little room was left for a third place in his life, a place for me. We took from each other the comforts of proximity and habit, and in extraordinary times supported each other more out of affection than from duty. If asked we would have said we loved each other, and believed it true, though neither would have been able to say what we meant by love. So we had a marriage. I say that in no cynical way. All the same, I did not want Fergus on that night.

I went the back way down to Moa Park. It was dark by the time I turned off the road opposite the blue-eyed wooden moa and drove up the scoria drive to Esther's door. I was not looking forward to seeing her and for once hoped Fred Meggett would be home.

Adrian let me in. He said his father had not come in for tea. The woman who did the housework was washing the dishes. Esther, wrapped in an eiderdown, reclined on a sofa pulled up to the fire.

"Meg," she cried when she saw me, "Get my wine, will you? That bitch in the kitchen won't let me have any. That's not her job. I'm going to make Fred fire her."

"I want to talk to you first."

"Not about Alfie. I don't want to talk about him."

"The trial's over, Esther. It's all finished, dear."

"I can't face talking about it without my wine. Get it for me, please. Come on, Sis."

I went to the kitchen and asked the woman where she had hidden it.

"She's not supposed to have any. That's Mr Meggett's orders."

"I'll take responsibility."

I took the wine back to the sitting-room and Esther poured herself a tumblerful.

"They were let off, Esther. The jury found them not guilty."

"Fred said they would. Anyhow Meg, we both know who killed him."

"Nonsense. If I thought you'd done it I'd tell you. All you did was behave like a silly fool."

The wine helped her speak with clarity. "I know what I did. So shut up, little sister. You always were a do-goody little thing."

"Listen—"

"I will not. Who needs your guff any more? What I need is my vino. And I need Alfie. The only way I can have him is by knowing what I did."

I let her go over it. Adrian came in. She caressed him absently. She had switched off her love for the boy at Alfred's death. She patted his hair and allowed him every bit of food he

209

asked for, and gave him no other care than that.

"Can I have that chicken leg in the fridge, Mum?"

"You've just had tea."

"I'm still hungry."

"All right. All right. Go and get it."

"Esther," I said, "I'm going up to see Robert."

"Who? Oh, him. Fred told me he'd turned up. You always liked him. I'll tell you Meg, Alfie was in love with me once. We used to kiss. His sister! He never said, but he wanted to go to bed with me. I always knew when some boy wanted that, and he wanted it. God, I wish we'd done it. God, I wish we had."

"He still would have been a homosexual, Esther."

"I'm not talking about that. You're such a stupid bitch. Let me fill my glass. I'm sick of everyone. Of everyone. All I want is Alfie."

I stayed with her until Fred came home. He frowned at the wine. "Did you give her that?"

"Yes."

"Well,"—he shrugged—"what the hell? I hear they got off. I suppose you're sore about that?"

"Not particularly."

"I can't work you Plumb sheilas out. Jesus, will you look at her! She was good-looking once."

"So were you. At least I suppose she thought so."

"I've got something better. Don't you forget it."

"Money, Fred? It's never worked with me."

"You're too bloody dumb. Both of you are dumb."

I laughed at him. His cheeks went red and swelled up. "I'm glad those kids got off. I used to do some queer-bashing myself."

"I'm sure you did. Goodbye, Esther. I'll come and see you soon."

Driving north in my little car, I considered the waste of her life. She had made a greedy demand on it, but there were certain immutable things that would not be turned to her satisfaction. Now she had come to grief on one of them, and because in all things she had been immoderate there was no controlling the event and her life was a waste. I did not see a way for her to restore any part of it. Fred would be no help. He was a devourer too, more ruthless than greedy. I saw a long future for Esther. She would hang on to life, not in any hope, but for its bodily gratifications. I supposed I would take her on, up to a point; take her like a retarded child; but I would not let her spoil my life.

Robert's bach was dark. I let myself in and felt for a light switch, then remembered he used a Tilley lamp. I felt in my bag for matches and struck a light. The little room came into view, velvety in the dimness. Here, I thought, was the home of a man who made only proper demands. For a moment I was righteous on his behalf. Then I told myself to stop pushing at things. I tried to light the lamp but it was too complicated for me. I lit a candle and looked in Robert's bedroom. His bed lay white and simple, neatly made. Pyjamas striped like a peppermint stick were folded on a chair. I opened the back door. "Robert."

Not since I was a child, listening in the dark, had I been so aware of silence. There was no human sound, no animal or insect sound, no rustle of leaf or sound from the earth or river. There was only a winter stillness, winter silence. It made me almost faint with happiness. The cold, and the black night, and the huge stars were a benediction. I set off down the garden. The flame of my candle fluttered, so I cupped it in my hand. Wax ran on to my fingers, hot as blood. I saw a moving shadow that might have been a cat. Trees with great depths in them moved by. A clucking and a flutter came from the fowl house.

I went along Robert's jetty and stood on the end. Foam patches moved on the water, floating up-river. The old dinghy was gone. Robert was out fishing and would row in on the tide. I sat down, blew my candle out, and pulled my coat around me. I waited there. Every now and then I closed my eyes and rocked in a kind of unthinking contentment.

Presently I heard the sound of whistling. It was *The Vale of Tralee*, one of Willis's songs. After a while it stopped. I heard only the sounds of the boat: rowlocks, water splashing. A dome of light moved along the top of the mangrove bank. Soon the dinghy nosed out and turned towards me. Robert had fastened a lantern to a pole fixed on its prow. The night enclosed the boat on a disc of water. It seemed to mould a yellow ball about the figure bending at the oars.

Ten yards away he turned. "Is that you, Meg?"

"Yes. Hallo. Isn't it late for fishing?"

"I went out about five to look at my nets. Had to wait while the tide turned."

He brought the dinghy in at the side of the jetty and hauled it half-way on to land.

"What have you got?"

"Flounder. Have you had tea, Meg?"

"No."

"We'll cook some." He shifted a sack from a wooden box in the boat and showed me his catch.

"Lovely. You're out of breath."

"She's a long row."

"It didn't stop you whistling."

"You heard that? Sound carries in the dark. You take the lamp."

We walked up through the garden. I told him the trial was over.

"What happened to them?"

"They're not guilty. Incredible, isn't it?"

"They'll have to live with it, Meg."

"Oh, they'll manage that. No trouble."

"You can't say that."

He lit the Tilley lamp and stoked up the range. "Put the kettle on, Meg. I'll do the fish."

We sat down to our meal, and we talked into the night. We remembered things about our childhood that we had never spoken of, and I think it was the same for him as me: we gave them shape and put them safely away.

He wrapped me two flounder in newspaper and brought the lamp to show me to my car. I drove home down the road to

Loomis. Drawn along by my yellow lights, I too seemed to be in a world moulded by the night.

Fergus was asleep. I kissed him on his forehead and slipped into bed.

20 Through the spring and summer I have been possessed by what Dad would have called a *furor scribendi*. I am not the only one suffering in this way. Up in her witch's castle Merle Butters scribbles in blank verse to the dictation of her Japanese lover. And over the creek in Peacehaven Wendy Philson labours day-long at the story of George Plumb. She's still in the note-taking stage, but soon (in several years) she will be ready to take her place at his side, recording selected adventures in the Odyssey of his soul. So we go on.

Mine has been a tale of deaths. Rebecca, Mother, Dad, Agnes (in spite of the attentions of a San Francisco Fire Department resuscitator squad). And of course Alfred. Sutton has died. (Outside of my pages Bluey has died. Fergus's parents have, as he puts it, passed on.) And now I come to the death of Robert. Yet I go on thinking of mine as a happy tale. It seems to me to have more of life in it than of death.

I will take it up from the night I became Robert's nurse. He woke several times.

"You've shifted in have you, Meg? Does Fergus mind?"

"No. I think he'll be going away for a while."

"Business?"

"Something like that." But I told myself to stop playing the nurse. Washing him and seeing to him physically was enough. For the rest of it I must be his sister. "He's got a girl-friend and I think he's going away with her."

"I'm sorry, Meg."

"I haven't been a very good wife to him."

213

"Will he come back?"

"I've no idea."

"Will you take him?"

"I think I will. But I'm not sure. I don't want him *creeping* back."

"That doesn't sound like Fergus."

"Beth Neeley's just a young woman. I don't think she's twenty-five. I'm frightened of what she'll do when she finds out Fergus is sixty."

"She must know that."

"In some ways. And then of course Fergus is a puritan. I don't think she's one of those."

In the morning I went to Peacehaven and helped Felicity and Oliver get ready to catch their plane. Fergus had not come back. I hoped his night had been a happy one and that morning would not waken his conscience. I worried about him sleeping without pyjamas.

"Where's Fergus?" Felicity asked. "We should say goodbye."

"Gone to work. He starts early on Mondays." I did not want to go into explanations, or have Oliver score another failure to a Plumb. "You'll have to ring a taxi. I want to be with Robert when the doctor comes."

"Good. Good," Oliver said. He was spared another ride in my Hillman Imp.

When they had driven away I went back to the cottage and did my housework. Robert had dressed himself. He felt a little better, but something had altered in his mind. He seemed smaller this morning. A new look of quiet was on his face.

The doctor came at mid-day and spent a long time with him in his room. When he came out I told him I had moved down and would be nursing Robert from now on.

"I was going to say it was time."

"He was bad last night."

"Yes, well—" he looked at me cautiously, "the disease can accelerate you know, and I think it's doing that to some degree. But there are steps in the mind sickness can take."

"He's getting ready to die."

"If you can persuade him that he needn't give up   "

"Robert accepts things. He'll fight as much as he has to. And die when it's time."

"Well, well, I don't have an opinion about that. At this stage he needs a bronchodilator. I'll arrange that. There'll be more sputum, I'm afraid. But what I'm frightened of is congestive heart failure."

"Heart failure?"

"No, it's not an attack, it's just a condition. If that comes he has to have complete bed rest. He can't lift a finger. You might need to hire a professional nurse. But of course, we may avoid it. Now I want you to look out for—cyanosis. Do you know what that is?"

"Blue fingernails?"

"Any bluish discoloration. Skin. Fingernails. Watch out for headaches. Watch out for fevers. If you see anything you don't like give me a ring. I'll come as often as I can anyway."

"Can I take him visiting?"

"Not too much. We don't want any strain."

I called at his surgery in the afternoon and picked up the bronchodilator. It gave Robert a lot of relief. The doctor also tried him on mist inhalations. He seemed to enjoy those. "We used to do this in the kitchen. What was that stuff?"

"Friar's balsam."

Fergus called and took away his things. I heard his car go up the drive, but decided not to interrupt him. He knew where I was if he needed me. I went up when he was gone and found a letter on the table. He hates writing letters. He cannot reveal himself. Even when he wrote from Italy he kept to stiff accounts of his health and the weather. In this letter he had tried very hard:

"Dear Meg, You were right about Beth being my responsibility. But if I go to her I've got to stay. It can't be just an affair—that's not my sort of thing. It's got to be divorce and then a remarriage. {"Good God," I said, "he's going to keep her waiting."} I've promised her that. But naturally she doesn't want to wait. So we're going to start sharing a place straight away. ["Thank God for that."] I can't see you again. No matter what you say I've treated you badly.

Well, chin up Meg.

Yours sincerely,

Fergus.

P.S. I'll be the guilty one in the divorce. Beth doesn't like it, but I owe you that."

I laughed and put it away. I hoped that whatever happened would not be too painful for him.

He made arrangements to have his mail picked up, and for the lawns to be mowed so that I should not have that expense. I kept our separation from everyone but Robert. Others found out soon enough. Esther was angry with me. She would have excused my letting Fergus "take off for a dirty weekend", but losing him altogether was another thing. She wanted me to put detectives on him, show some fight. "He's got troubles enough," I said.

The children sent me letters. Fergus had written to them, saying he was to blame. None of them accepted that. Raymond, in some pain, blamed Life—but did not go so far as to mention its Dark Hand. Bobby said we were a pair of silly bloody fools, he'd always known it. All the same, "splitting up" was probably for the best. The wonder was we hadn't done it before. Rebecca offered to come if I needed her. I answered that I was all right, and Fergus was all right as far as I knew, and I told them they should get on with their lives.

Winter came and Robert seemed to be holding his own. It was important he should pick up no infection in his lungs. The doctor was not keen on my taking him out. But Robert fretted in our little house. He tried to make a start on painting the kitchen but the fumes were bad for him and the exertion too much. I turned over some garden to put winter vegetables in. The most Robert could manage was to push a few seeds in the ground—broad beans and carrots—and the sound of his breathing after that frightened even him. So I took him on visits

216

to Willis and Emerson, and talking to his brothers he was happy.

One day we picked Willis up and drove out to Mangere, where Emerson had his tomato farm. We saw glass roofs shining in the sun as we approached. Willis said, "There's more than last time." I think he disapproved. Emerson's glass metropolis was too far from nature. It probably struck Robert that way too, but he said nothing. I thought the place entirely right for Emerson. It had an airy quality, the whiteness and the space of upper air.

Every time we called on him he showed us everything. So we made the tour again, and saw the irrigation controls and the spray controls and the boiler room and the packing room, and last we stood at the door of each of the ten vast glittering sheds where the crops were grown. Some were empty, with only pipes like plumbing on the brown earth, others had young plants, and three or four grew pieces of tropical jungle, love apples. I felt the hot wet air, and smelled the peppery smell of spray and the smell of crushed tomato leaves, and would not let Robert put his foot inside the door.

"She looks after me, Emo. But it's quite a place. Quite a place."

Emerson blushed. There is something of lover in him where his brothers are concerned. He took us up to his house for a cup of tea. It's a pink stucco cottage, Spanish style, with two black vertical lines over the door. They make the narrow porch frown. Inside, the rooms are small and dark. It's not an adequate stopping-place for a man who has flown over jungles. He should build himself a house of glass.

Emerson lives in his kitchen but he opened the lounge for us and we sat on wooden-armed chairs with their seats puffed up like balloons. Framed photos of Mum and Dad stood on the mantelpiece. Robert went close to look at them. They were photographs taken in Thorpe about 1905. Emerson was a boy then and Robert and I not born. Dad was safe inside his church, though making noises, and Mum in the St Andrews manse, that house she had loved in her life second only to Peacehaven. The

Reverend looked stern, a little angry, a little as though he had just smelled something bad, but his wife was smiling gently and had that look of faint surprise turning into delight that came on her face when she had found some perfect rose in her garden.

The sentimentalist in me will not die. Once it had the shape of my whole life, but now it's a dried-up thing, light as a bat, hanging upside down with its feet clawed tight on my ribs. Occasionally it gives a flutter and squeak. I watched Robert with the photographs. He took them to the window to see them better. Willis came to his side: two men with the round Plumb face and the Plumb bald head.

"She was a good-looking woman."

"She was a beauty. Look at this old so-and-so, ready to take on the world."

"Bugger," I said, and took out my handkerchief.

"What did you say?" asked Emerson, coming in with tea.

"Nothing. Here, let me pour."

He put down the tray. "I'll show you jokers something." He went to his bedroom and came back with a piece of cardboard the size of an exercise book. "Take a look at that." He laid it on the coffee table and we crowded round. It was a photograph from the *San Francisco Chronicle*, dated July 18, 1915. Emerson had pasted it on cardboard.

Pastor, 10 Children Seek Home In California. Denied Free Speech In New Zealand.

And we all smiled out.

This is not a convention of children. It is merely the family of the Rev. George Plumb, a Unitarian Minister from New Zealand. The happy group came from that country because the clergyman denounced war and was denied free speech. Here is the family, snapped by a Chronicle photographer upon arrival here by the liner Marama.

My smile was uneasy. California was not my land. But Esther sparkled, Agnes, Edith, Florence had looks of delight. Rebecca had a thoughtful smile. The boys all grinned. They had been told to say cheese. Only Mum and Dad and Felicity made no show of pleasure. Dad had a sharp eye, a speculative look. In other photos I have seen he manages the appearance of a visionary. But arrival in this new land had him worried. Felicity was worn out. She had spent two weeks chasing lively children over three decks of an ocean liner. No wonder she could not sparkle. And Mother, in lace choker and cameo brooch and feathered hat, Mother was at her most ladylike. She looked slightly down, as though at something very small in stature, and her coolness survived fifty years and the furry paper. Newsmen were an intrusion on our life, she found them vulgar. In her hand she carried a posy of violets.

So the Plumbs came to California, and I looked at them with long sight and what cameramen call, I believe, a wide lens. There was Rebecca, who would drown in three years time at New Brighton beach, thousands of miles away in the other hemisphere. And there was Alfred, a beautiful child, curly haired, wide-eyed, with pictures, one would say, alive in his head, and his future simple, crystal clear, like a cup of water to be drunk. He would die at a place called Moa Park, cast out from his family, beaten and kicked by a boy in the grip of evil. And there was Esther, practising her eyes on the cameraman and drinking up life. I saw her broken. And Robert, freckle-faced, more stolid than his brothers. A solitary life waited him, four years behind barbed wire, and death at fifty-four from a disease that destroyed his lungs. Mother, Dad, Agnes, Felicity. And me. Me. Me! Pain grew in my chest, tears flooded my eyes.

"Weepies, Sis? Come on," Emerson said.

"Damn it. Damn it. I thought I was over this."

"I'm not there," Willis cried. "It isn't fair. Why did I get left out?" He was trying to clown me out of my grief, but with a preternatural understanding I was aware of the disappointment in his cry. Life had not given Willis all he had wanted.

Robert slapped his hand on Willis's pate and moved it as though ruffling curls. "Poor old Willie, he always did want to be everywhere. You should have been ten men. Don't you remember, you were away at sea loving all those ladies?"

"I'd sooner have been with you lot. Hey Meg, wipe your eyes

and I'll tell you about Carmelita from Rio."

"I've heard that one. She stole your underpants."

"No," he cried in delight, "that was Bonita in Port of Spain. Carmelita was a great big girl—"

"You take milk and sugar, don't you Willie? Emerson, put that photo away, it'll get tea on it. Do you want something, Robert?"

We recovered. We passed the rest of the afternoon in a jokey manner. Emerson told us flying stories and Willis, signalling his conquests with rude mouth-organ chords, told us about his ladies and the sea. "But you mustn't think there was anyone like old Mirth. She's still my best girl." He blew a sweet enduring middle C.

Loaded down with tomatoes, we drove home. Willis got out at his gate and limped away. I put Robert to bed and heated some soup. He could take only a few mouthfuls. I was up to him half a dozen times in the night. "Too much laughing, Meg."

That did not stop us going again. We picked Willis up and drove there the following Sunday.

When Wendy Philson heard Peacehaven was empty she asked if she could stay one or two nights instead of driving all the way back home. That way too she need not take Dad's papers out of the house. I was pleased to have someone there. I told her she could stay as long as she liked. When Robert and I strolled in the grounds on fine afternoons we saw her through the study window, head down at Dad's desk, her pencil going nineteen to the dozen. At other times she just sat with an ecstatic look on her face.

"She's communing with him. Do you feel him in the air?"

Robert grinned. He could not manage walking and speech together.

"I feel him. I feel Mother too. Wendy wouldn't like it if she knew she was about. Not up to the spiritual mark, I'm afraid.

Poor Mum." I laughed. "Well," I said, "it's actually got nothing to do with Wendy, that's her game. I've had them like a buzzing in my head ever since they died. I don't need Wendy for that. Or old Merle either."

Robert paid his visit to Merle on a wet July afternoon. We had to fit it in between three and four o'clock. "I don't have much time," Merle said on the phone. "Mr Fujikawa is very demanding these days. He's suffering from the cold."

"You mean," I said, "there are seasons where he is?"

"I've told you my dear, when he visits me our weather takes over. Mr Fujikawa wants me to book on a Pacific cruise. I think I should go. I hate to hear him coughing."

She tried to turn me away at the door but I pushed my way in, saying Robert was not well enough to be left alone. The truth is I was curious. Mrs Peet, the medium, had promised to call and if she found the occasion right would try to make contact with Dad. Merle took us to her drawing-room—she's the only person I know to use that word now—and we sat down and waited for Mrs Peet to arrive. Robert's breathing was louder even than the crackling fire. I half expected it to dislodge the china Pans and shepherdesses, the Venetian glass vases, from their ledges and shelves about the room. Merle seemed a little dismayed.

"Mr Fujikawa doesn't care for loud noises."

"We'll go before he comes," I said.

"In a sense he's always here. He's always just a short way round the corner. You needn't look Meg, that's not funny. I believe, Robert, that one day Mr Fujikawa will come right through. He will join us on this side. That will be the most important event in man's history. And I of course will be his wife. Ah, here's Mrs Peet." She went to answer the door.

"Are you all right?" I asked Robert. "We can go soon."

"I'll make it. Old Merle's a dag."

Mrs Peet had brought her sister, Mrs Thomas. They were stick-thin tall gaunt women with long jaws and long noses and beautiful liquid eyes. Mrs Thomas did the talking for them. The other, Mrs Peet, simply inclined her head on its too-thin neck, and gave a far-away smile that had in it so much of artifice I felt like applauding. But when she spoke—and she spoke to say, Yes she would love some sherry ("If it's dry")—I looked at her more sharply. I knew that ginny plum-cake tremolo—and in a flash had Sybil, belted Sybil, in her flowing robes and zodiacal signs, reaching out her hand for Alfred's pound note. She had obviously prospered. Rings on her fingers now, with genuine stones, and, unless I was mistaken, a hand-tailored frock and hand-tailored coat. The gypsy was gone. I felt delighted, almost as if she had declared some part of my own life a success; and in that mood was prepared to let her have her way with Dad.

"Do you still read handwriting?" I asked.

"You must be mistaken. I've never read handwriting."

"But when we met—"

"We have never met. Merle, this isn't dry sherry. I can't drink this."

"You should have medium dry," I laughed.

They looked at me blankly—even Robert, who usually understood my jokes. I let it go. I was still pleased with Mrs Peet. Merle asked anxiously if she felt the signs were right for—you know?—was she receptive? "I'm not sure that all of us here will give you quite the right sort of ambience."

"Oh," I said, "I believe in Mrs Peet. I really do. And Robert's got an open mind, haven't you Robert?"

"I hope so," Robert said.

Mrs Thomas gave us a fastidious sidelong look. "She can't work if anyone breaks the circle. She'll get a migraine. I'm not sure I should let her take the risk."

"Oh please, we'll really try hard."

Mrs Peet gave her far-away smile, but made a languid sign with her hand, and Mrs Thomas said to me, "There is of course the wee matter of fee."

"I'll pay. I'll pay. How much?"

"After, please," said Mrs Peet, frowning for the first time. I said I was sorry.

Merle blacked out the room. She lit a lamp and placed it on

222

the sideboard. The air became heavy with shadows.

"Why the gloom? I thought it was all light on the other side."

"And we are in darkness," Merle said. "The weather is ours."

"I hope they'll be wearing their woollies."

"Meg," she warned severely.

"I'm sorry. Do let's go on."

We sat at a round mahogany table inlaid with a sun and crescent moons, and laid our hands on its surface with our little fingers touching. I was thrilled and a little afraid. This was just as I had found it described in so many novels. We waited a long time as Sybil (I'll call her that) prepared herself. Her face became more horsey, more refined. The room, the shadows, the sinking fire in the grate, Robert's breathing, the faces of the women, the delay that went on and on, all worked on me and put me into a state of light hypnosis. I was ready for Dad. Without warning, Sybil's head slumped on her chest. Her heavy ear-rings dangled by her nose. Shudders ran through her body and penetrated to our fingertips. Her breathing became almost as ugly as Robert's. Then she raised her head. Her face had taken an unearthly glow. Her beautiful smooth eyelids gleamed like pats of butter. I felt a stab that Alfred was not here to join me in admiring her. She grinned secretly, clicked her bony teeth.

"Who wishes to speak with me?" Sybil asked in Dad's voice—Dad asked in Sybil's voice? I cannot decide which it was.

Merle must have signalled to Robert for I saw him shake his head. She pressed her little finger on mine.

"Is that you, Dad?"

"Meg. I have been waiting."

I wanted to ask him what he was doing in such company. I also wanted to ask had he met God. In the end I said, "I hope you're well."

"I cannot stay long, Meg. Ask what you want to know."

"Is Mother with you?"

"Your mother is happy."

"Have you met God?"

Sybil gave a little jerk and through the gloom I saw Mrs Thomas frowning. Robert had a grin on his face.

"You must not ask about the great mysteries. Knowledge would destroy you. But I say, have faith."

"I can't."

"Is the leap too great? The world is flimsy. It has not sufficient substance to hold you back."

But I thought of flesh and thought of blood. I thought of love. Substance was there.

"Will Fergus come back to me?"

"Ah." Sybil/Dad sounded pleased. "If you love him sufficiently he will come."

That was nonsense, and I almost said so. "Can you explain?"

"You must not ask for explanations, child."

"Why not?"

"Because I do not wish to give them." That was in his style.

"What did you think about all the time when you were in your study and Mum was in the kitchen with twelve kids?" But I thought, Good God, I'm giving ammunition to this woman, and I said, "I'm sorry, I take that back. How's Alfred getting on?" I threw it lightly in; but my heart gave a terrible lurch and my knowledge of where I was, and even who, fell off balance. Whatever it might be for others, this could never be a game for me.

"He is well," Sybil said. "He has seen his errors. Here what was crooked is made straight."

I gasped at that—her impudence. It cured me of distress and I flashed with anger. Robert came to my help. He coughed and fished for his handkerchief. The circle broke. Sybil clacked her mouth shut. I thought she might have bitten through her tongue. She made an empty sound, a grieving moo, from deep in her. Mrs Thomas pulled her like a child into her arms.

"Don't you know that's like a punch on the face?"

"I had to get my handkerchief out. Meg, I'll have to go."

"You'll all have to go. Mr Fujikawa wants to come through," Merle cried. "Yes darling, yes, too many people. I'll get rid of them."

"How much?" I asked. "It used to be a pound."

Sybil groaned on her sister's chest.

"Ten," Mrs Thomas snapped. "Guineas, please."

"Good heavens." I had to write a cheque. "Merle, thank you. It's been interesting."

Then we were out on the porch, with rain beating over our heads, and Peacehaven ghostly in a mist.

"What did you think of that?" I said to Robert.

"They were a pair of twisters. Merle's all right, though. Mr Fujikawa's real."

I drove him home and got the range fire blazing, and we sat in the warm kitchen drinking cocoa. At five o'clock we heard on the radio news that Fred Meggett had been arrested and charged with fraud. "Now there's a message from another world." I worried about Fergus and thought of running up to Peacehaven to use the phone. But I waited till after tea. I got Robert to bed, and said I would be gone for half an hour. I drove around to Moa Park to see Esther.

She was by her fire, glass in hand and wine jar at her feet. She welcomed me with a screech. "Adrian, get her a glass. We'll drink the bastard down, Meg. I knew we'd get him in the end."

"No thank you, Adrian," I said.

I looked at him to see how he was taking it, but all I could see was an extra watchfulness in his eyes. Old eyes, boardroom eyes. I've heard it said Adrian is on his way to becoming richer than Fred. He buys old houses in Mt Eden and Newton Gully and crams them up to the eaves with tenants; and, they say, collects his rents himself, every Thursday, in his Jaguar. A fat young man in a yellow waistcoat and gold watch chain. "Not bad for twenty-one," Esther crows. Adrian has never had anything to do with his father's business. "Too many risks." Fred calls his son, contemptuously, a percentage man.

"Have they locked him up?"

"Out on bail. But that's not for long," Esther cried. "We're all sitting here gloating. Even Porky's gloating, aren't you love?"

I looked at the old man on the other side of the fire. He was
huge and loose in his chair, all folds of skin. He was like a giant
sack half-emptied. His ancient sunken face was shaking with
mirth.

"You remember Porky?" Esther said.

"Oh yes." Fred's father, Porky Meggett, had been our
butcher when Loomis was a country town. I had not seen him
since his shop became a Mighty Meatery. "How are you, Mr
Meggett?"

The old man rumbled and shook. "You've heard about my
boy? He's gone and done the biggest fraud of 'em all. He'll go
down in all the history books."

I asked Esther what had happened to Fergus. She gave a snort.
"He's small fry. They're not going to worry about him. It's the
big boys they're after. All Fred's mates. They're going to lock
'em up and throw away the key."

"Who did they arrest?"

"Fergus is all right," Adrian said. "They got Dad and
Tarleton and Gundry and Sloane. That's all. But I think Fergus
is going to have to close up. The bottom's falling out."

"You know where Fred was when they arrested him?" Esther
cried. "He was with his floosie. Ha ha ha. In the middle of the
afternoon. In the sack. They had to wait while he put his
underpants on."

"Who told you that?"

"Adie. Fat boy here."

Adrian went pink. "They did arrest him at her place."

"He upped a girl when he was only twelve," Porky Meggett
said. "I took the skin off him but it didn't do no good."

Esther filled her glass. "Come on Meg, don't make me drink
alone. Not on a night like this. Let's all drink. We'll drink to the
great man's downfall. Downfall! Hee hee, that's good."

I let Adrian bring me a glass and I sat on a squab pretending to
sip, watching Esther gulp down glass after glass. She pulled the
most hideous faces. She hated the stuff but could not live
without it. I thought it a pity her pleasure in Fred's arrest could

226

not take the place of wine. It was hard to say which was making her drunker.

"I've been salting cash away, you know that Meg? I've got plenty. I'll stay up when he goes down. This house is mine. In my name. That was his idea—a tax dodge. But it's mine. Ha ha. He thought he could walk on water but he's sunk."

"Fred'll come back. You watch," Porky Meggett said.

"He's sunk. He's bloody sunk. Down with his ship. Toot toot. Gurgle gurgle. Ha ha ha."

I stayed until she fell sideways and began to snore. Adrian helped me get her to her bedroom.

"I'll manage. You go away."

I pulled off her dress and rolled her stockings down her pudgy legs. Anger made me rough. I had to get out of there. I rolled her into bed and covered her up. I kissed her forehead. "Hi, Sis," she moaned, "where did you come from?" I ran out of her bedroom and out of her house and sat in my car and smoked a cigarette. Then I drove home to Robert. He was sitting up in bed, using his bronchodilator.

"Not you too?"

"Is she bad?"

"Yes. Yes. She's a mess."

"What about Fergus?"

"He's all right. They left him alone."

I sat with him a while. He tried to talk about Esther and Fergus, but all the time he could not help looking at his disease. He was wondering when it would kill him. After a while he said he felt like sleeping. I turned out his light and went to my room. I got into bed and lay awake for a long time thinking about my life and all our lives. I did not try to make any sense of them, I simply turned them over. Robert's breathing sounded in the cottage. Esther, Robert, Alfred, Fergus, me, Mum and Dad: then again, in a different order, with old faces, younger faces: they rolled as though on a drum, came up foreshortened, smiled fat-cheeked at me, and rolled away. It seemed to go on all night. They seemed to go on turning in my sleep. I had a headache

227

when I woke in the morning. I took three Disprins with my cup of tea. Forty, fifty years ago, I had gulped my family down, grown drunk on them. I supposed I had been drunk on them all my life. Now I wished I could vomit them up.

In the afternoon I had a visit from Jack Short. He hung about the door, unwilling to come in.

"How's Fergus, Jack?"

"He's well, Mrs Sole. As far as I know he's well."

"He's not staying up too late at nights?"

"I don't know what he does at nights. I don't think—I can—really discuss that with you."

"Come in, man. I won't bite." I sat him at the table. "Now, I suppose you've come about a divorce?"

"I know nothing about that, Mrs Sole."

"Call me Meg. Have a drink, Jack. No? Well, a cup of tea?" He turned that down as well. The mention of divorce had unsettled him. He saw himself in an improper relationship with me. He spoke fast.

"The truth is that Fergus—you've heard about yesterday? Meggett being arrested? Fergus is all right, they're not going to proceed against him. Well, that's only proper. He hasn't done anything wrong. But the truth is—everything's gone down a hole. We're fighting to save what we can. And Fergus—well, Fergus is short of cash."

"Does he want a loan?"

"No, no, nothing like that. What he asked me to suggest to you—well, the house is your joint property, you see?"

"He wants to sell Peacehaven? The cheeky blighter."

"He knows how you feel about the place, Mrs Sole. He truly does. "

"You bet he truly does. Well. Well. Sell Peacehaven, eh?" It appealed to me. I pursed my lips and nodded my head and walked about the room. Jack Short sat there, watching anxiously. I put the kettle on. The sun was going down behind the trees and Robert came in from his chair in the garden.

"How would you feel if I sold Peacehaven? I'd have to live

here for the rest of my life."

"It's your place, Meg. You know that."

"You don't think I should hang on to it? For sentimental reasons?"

Robert had turned inwards to his disease. He seemed to be having long conversations with it. His eyes looked deep as wells. I saw him struggle to come back, and suddenly I was distressed for him, and I put my arms around him. "It's all right, don't worry, I'll make up my own mind. You just go to bed."

Jack Short had watched all this with horror. "I think I'll just go—"

"Sit down. I'll get to you."

I took Robert into his bedroom and helped him to bed.

"Sell it if you want to," he said in a vague way.

"Don't you worry about it. Shall I get the doctor?"

"Not yet. Not yet."

I went back to the kitchen and made tea. "There you are, Jack. How much does Fergus think we could get for it?"

He named a price.

"That's low. I suppose he wants a quick sale?"

"I don't think you'd get any more, Mrs Sole."

"I can get a thousand on top of that. Fred Meggett told me what it was worth one day."

"Yes? Well—actually, we do have a buyer. He can settle tomorrow if we say yes. He just needs to have a quick inspection."

"I can sell the place in half an hour."

"You can?" I had said something improper again.

"Do you want to wait or shall I give you a call?"

"Look, Mrs Sole—"

"I'm not interested, Jack. We sell at my price, to my buyer. Otherwise it's no deal."

When I had got rid of him I looked at Robert again. He was lying on his bed with his inward look. I said I would be out for a short while but he did not hear. I put on my coat and went up to Peacehaven.

"Wendy, how would you like to buy this place?"

"Me? You'd never sell. Not your father's house."

"It's too big for me. And I need the money."

"Money," she cried. "But this is Peacehaven, Meg. George Plumb's house." I was betraying him. Then joy took over. "I've dreamed of it. I dream of it every night. Oh Meg, thank you, thank you. I'll look after it. You can come whenever you want."

"There are some conditions." I wanted her to buy the furniture too. I would own Dad's books and papers, but they would stay in the study. She would let in any Plumb who wanted to use them. And she would let me visit the house when I chose, and walk in the grounds. But I wanted that, I told myself, for pleasure, not to come home. All that was left to me of home was myself.

"I want the Buddha."

"Oh, I wanted that."

"Well, you can't have it. I'm sorry."

"I hope you won't disturb me when I'm working." But joy still dazzled her. She did not argue at my price.

So I set things moving and stood aside, and Wendy became the new owner. Fergus wrote a note thanking me. He said he was well and hoped I was the same. Winter went on and Robert sank deeper into his illness. He had, most times, the look of hearing whispers in his mind. On sunny days I got him into the garden and once or twice took him walking as far as the summer-house. "This needs repairing," he said. He did not seem to remember building it.

In August I began to notice an increasing ruddiness in his face and a blue coloration in his lips.

"Heart, Mrs Sole. It's what I warned you of," the doctor said. He mentioned hospital and again I said Robert would not go.

"He may need oxygen."

"Can't we get that here?"

"If you don't mind the expense."

"I don't mind. I've sold my house."

He suggested a professional nurse. Robert would have to stay in bed. He must be fed and bathed and clothed as though he could not lift a finger to help himself.

"I can do all that."

"A nurse would do it better."

In the end we agreed I should have someone in each afternoon to bed-wash him. He recommended a woman called Mrs Petley, who looked jolly and smiled a lot but rarely spoke a word. She always seemed to be rushing off and I learned she had seven or eight other patients to wash in her afternoon. But she did her job well. Robert liked her. Sometimes I heard the murmur of her voice coming from his room. I arranged for her to come in for an hour two mornings a week so I could do my shopping.

One day I stopped at the Post Office and telephoned Fergus. The phone rang and rang but no one came. I tried Jack Short and he told me Sole Construction Co. was closed. He gave me a number where I might find Fergus. I half expected to hear Beth Neeley's voice, but Fergus answered.

"Fergus," I said, "it's Meg. I'd like you to do something for me."

"If I can." After his surprise he was very formal.

I told him about Robert. Nervousness made me tumble things out. I spoke about enlargement of the ventricle, and right heart failure, and dyspnea and cyanosis, and respiratory failure—all the words the doctor had used to me. I told him Robert was dying and would not get out of his bed again.

"He should be in hospital, shouldn't he?"

"No. He doesn't want to."

"That's not the point—"

"It is the point. He'll die wherever he goes. He's got a right to choose."

He was silent. "I see what you mean. But it's hard on you."

"Maybe. I knew what I was getting into, though."

He asked me what I wanted him to do. I said that Robert needed a hospital bed, one with a head that jacked up. I thought Fergus might know where to pick up a second-hand one. And I had thought he might be able to make an over-bed table in one of his workshops—but Jack had told me they were closed up now.

"I can do it. Leave it to me."

"I can pay, Fergus."

"You don't need to pay. I think I know where I can get a bed."

"Thank you."

"I'll get started on the table right away."

"Thank you."

"I'll send them out by carrier."

"All right.—Goodbye."

"Goodbye, Meg."

"Oh Fergus, the table will have to be on wheels."

"Yes, I know."

"He can lie across it, you see. I can pad it up with pillows for when he gets tired sitting up."

"That's good."

"Goodbye then, Fergus."

"Goodbye, Meg."

I hung up. I was trembling. I did not know whether it was from need of him or love. I had said I did not need him long ago; and told myself love was just a word. But if it was not these, why did I tremble? Why did I lean on my elbows over the phone with my thumbs pressed in my eyes to keep back the tears? Soon I managed to think of other reasons. I had not slept properly for months, and tiredness always made one emotional. Fergus was in another country, another life. I took my handkerchief out and dried my eyes; I promised myself I would hold to that view.

The bed and table arrived later that week. I had to get Willis and Emerson to help me move them into Robert's room. After that he was more comfortable. He slept a lot. He no longer seemed to look in at his illness. He and it had made a kind of marriage, but somehow Robert had come out on top, the one who earned the money and paid the rent. He looked out now at the world with an interest almost childlike.

The world, though, had shrunk to his little room—twelve feet by nine. I left the curtains open so he could see the peach tree and the lemon tree by the creek. The peach tree was breaking into blossom—blossom on its red new twigs and close on its ash-grey trunk. Each unbroken bud was like a pink lolly. Deep in the lemon tree yellow lemons gleamed with a waxy look. I had picked the outside ones, and as I leaned into the tree, bending my way round the prickly branches, I saw Robert propped up high in his bed, smiling at me. "All those colours, Meg." I put a branch of peach blossom in his room. "I didn't think I'd make it into spring."

Bad weather came again. I had to keep his curtains closed for warmth. He asked me to bring the wheat-field and the hay-field prints to his room. I propped one on a chair and one on his bed.

"Who painted those?"

"Someone called—I can't pronounce it."

"I wouldn't mind being there. You can almost taste the water in that jar."

"It might be wine."

"Whatever it is you can taste it."

He kept them all day. "I like those girls." "Look at those quail go up." "You can tell how sharp that scythe is."

He wanted them back next day so I hung them in his room and often when I went in I found him watching them as though they were fields outside his window.

The doctor had said he should not talk, but I did not see the sense in that. I sat with him many hours, sometimes at night when he could not sleep. We talked about our childhood, pulling things out of the past as though from a penny bag of broken biscuits. Neither of us knew what we would find. It almost became a game. Sometimes Robert even tried to laugh.

When Emerson and Willis called the game became an orgy. I did not enjoy that so much. I could feel us straining. Robert seemed to be humouring us. I had the feeling that he was in the room but also at a distance. His illness and his knowledge of his death worked in him like an extra sense, putting him beyond us. I was not aware of it when we were alone, but when Willis sat there rocking his pink foot and snoring tunes on his mouth organ, and Emerson, a little flushed with emotion, leaned forward and recalled another event—one I would have thought him far too wrapped up in his motor bike to have noticed—then Robert began to flicker in my consciousness, in and out of reality, and I strained like a man lifting weights after recollection and sent my girl's laugh pealing round the room. When they had gone I always gave Robert an hour alone.

October came. The rains stopped. A real spring began. I kept his windows open. The scented breeze came in and played round his face. I do not think he could smell it, any more than he could smell the rot from his lungs. The doctor put him on cortico steroids and they gave him relief. But there were times when I thought his struggle to breathe (not to get air into his lungs but to force it out) would kill him. I thought it would burst his heart. He spent hours lying over his table. That was the only position that gave him comfort. He lay so still that several times I thought he was dead. Now and then he fell into a state of semi-consciousness. It seemed to serve him in place of sleep. I put my face down by his glassy eyes. They seemed to presage annihilation. I could not believe in that. "Robert," I whispered, "can you hear me?" Usually he came back and said my name and held my hand.

He died one morning when I was out shopping. Mrs Petley met me at the door. She had a greedy look.

"Come in, dear. Let me take those groceries." She put them on the table. "Sit down. Take the weight off your feet."

"I don't want to sit down."

"I think you should. I've got something to tell you."

"Robert," I said; and at once felt incredibly stupid. I seemed to regress to a childhood state. Giant shapes I could not understand came pressing in. It was only for a moment. In that time Mrs Petley forced me into a chair. I jumped up.

"There was no pain, Mrs Sole. He died very peacefully. A model death."

I walked without hurry into Robert's room. She had lowered the head of his bed and pulled a sheet over his face. I was not

ready for it and I said loudly, "Robert?" I folded the sheet back
to see his face. She had closed his eyes and combed the tufts of
hair above his ears, and bound his jaw up with a cloth. She had
no right. I wanted to undo that knot and take the cloth away.
Instead I looked at him. I sagged against his ridiculous bed. Mrs
Petley leaned past me and twitched the sheet neatly over his face.
She turned me round and walked me into the kitchen.

"I'll make you a cup of tea. Then I'll have to rush."

"I don't want tea."

"You should, Mrs Sole. Death is always a shock."

"I've been expecting it." I smiled at her. It forced her back a
step.

"Is there someone you can get to sit with you?"

"I don't need anyone."

"In that case I'll get about my business. I laid him out. At
times like this I don't like to talk about money.   ."

"I'll see you get paid."

"Thank you. I'll call in at the doctor's as I go through town.
He'll want to get down for a death certificate."

"Yes."

"He shouldn't be long." For a moment I thought she was
going to overcome her dislike and kiss me. But she nodded and
said, "Sympathies," and took herself off.

I waited till the sound of her car died away. Then I went to
Robert's room. I looked at his mummy shape lying on the bed. I
had meant to fold the sheet back. I had half-intended taking the
cloth from his jaw and ruffling his tufts of hair. I had thought I
might open his eyes and close them for myself. I did none of
that. I looked at the sheet marking the points of his face—
forehead, nose, chin. He had slipped beyond any act of possession I might make, or act of love. He had lost all definition and
had gone out of my time. I did not touch him.

I went back to the kitchen and put the kettle on. After a few
minutes it started to sing. I left it there. I went to my room and
closed the door. I sat on my bed and wept for Robert, and for all
of us.

21 Emerson was fretting to overtake the hearse. We followed it at forty miles an hour, past the mangrove creeks and busy sawmills. The morning was sunny and blue. Willis sat in the front with Emerson. Felicity and I were in the back.

"Calm down, Emerson. It's a funeral procession."

I had brought a bunch of stock to put on the grave. They were tumbling from their paper in my lap—milky white and a dozen shades of lilac. Their perfume was spicy and light, rubbing on our skins and enlivening us.

"Have you got the service, Willis?" It was the third time I had asked. He grinned and patted his pocket.

"I think it's right there'll be just us," Felicity said. "Just his brothers and sisters. No one else."

"There might be one other. I dropped a note to the man who bought his bach."

"Oh. That's a pity isn't it? The notice said private interment."

"He was in camp with Robert."

Emerson twitched his shoulders nervously. "I was meaning to say, I had a phone call too. From a bloke who said he and his brother were in Shannon camp. He said they'd like to bring their father along. I didn't feel I could say no."

"So much for a quiet family service," Felicity said.

"It can't do any harm. Robert might have liked it," I said.

"And he might not."

"Don't quarrel, girls. Not on this day," Willis said.

We followed the hearse along the thin sealed road by brown drainage canals and hedges of toi-toi and fields of fat spring grass. The little red-roofed town came into view, with the harbour beyond.

"What made him choose this place?"

"He found it when he was drifting round."

We drove through the town and wound up a metalled road to the cemetery. It lay above an arm of the harbour, cut off from the fields by a paling fence. Trees had been left to grow in it. Here and there roots broke up through the ground and pushed the old headstones askew.

The hearse was at the gate, while a man dressed in a sports coat and tie struggled to unchain it.

"That's Dick Webster. Robert's friend."

The hearse drove through and stopped in the shade of a tree. Emerson parked in the grass at the side of the road. Dick Webster came over. He told us he was sorry about Robert and thanked me for inviting him. He had come to town in his launch and walked up from the wharf. "The bach is in good shape, Mrs Sole. I'm looking after it." He was still uneasy.

While we talked an old Ford car red-spotted with primer paint rattled by and pulled up in the grass. A notice on the rear window said: *God Speaks*. Three men and a woman got out and made a circle by the gaping doors: thick granite-seeming men, and a woman bony as a starving child. They stood dark-grey, aloof, still as broken columns, stone angels. I realized they were praying. Dick Webster stared at them. "Bloody Parminters." He went red. "Pardon my language. I'll go and help with the coffin." He went down to the hearse, where the undertaker's man was waiting by the raised back door. Emerson and Willis followed him. They started to roll out the coffin.

"Did he say Parminter?" Felicity asked.

"I think so."

"Robert lived with them in the Wairarapa. Religious cranks. They've got a nerve."

The prayer finished with a slow raising of heads. The Parminters seemed to come out of a trance. The old man, the patriarch, felt his way into the car. I saw he was blind. The woman helped him nervously, moving her skinny limbs like a stick insect. She took a humble seat, dimly alert. The two younger men tramped down the verge to us, raising dust from the seeding grass. Their awkward suits and ties were ridged with fold-marks.

"Is this Bob Plumb's funeral?"

"Yes," I said. "Are you the ones who rang my brother up?"

"I'm Ralph Parminter. This is my brother Wallace. Bob used to live with us on the farm."

"On the Ark. Are you still there?"

"The police drove us out. Them and the reporters. We live at Warkworth now."

"How many? Just the four of you?"

"We're all that's left. And our wives."

"Believers still?" I asked. "Still on the Ark?"

They did not answer that. "Bob was one of the Chosen Ones. He was the Vehicle. My father would like to say the words over him."

I looked at his countryman's face and his great hands poking like snapped-off roots out of the narrow sleeves of his black suit. He and his father and brother had turned Robert out from a home he loved and set him wandering, but I could feel no hostility to him. I smiled and said, "That's not possible. But if you want to share our service that will be all right."

"Bob belongs to us."

"Rubbish," Felicity said. "You're a bunch of loonies. Go away. You're not wanted here."

"Quiet, Felicity. I'm sorry, Mr Parminter, but we are the next of kin. You can join us if you like."

Ralph Parminter shook his head. Breath whistled in his nose. "No, you're mistaken. We've got Betty here. She was his wife."

"That woman in the car?" Dimly through the glass I saw her skinny shoulders and thin hair, and face with its bulbous forehead and mongoloid eyes. "Who married them?"

"My father."

"Is he licensed? Do you have a certificate with you?"

"He's licensed before God."

"That's not good enough, I'm sorry to say. I'll tell you what. We'll have our service first. After that if your father wants to say some words he can.—Be quiet, Felicity.—How does that seem? We'll be gone and you can say what you like."

The brothers looked at each other. Ralph went to the car. He leaned in and talked with his father. The old man's blind white eyes were luminous in the shadows. Ralph came back. "As long as we go last."

"Oh, yes."

"We'll come down when you've finished."

"I hope you're not going to say any mumbo-jumbo," Felicity said.

"Felicity, please. Whatever they say, it can do no harm."

"They'll insult his memory."

"Robert can't be hurt. Now come on, please. I'm sorry, Mr Parminter."

Emerson and Willis, with Dick Webster and the undertaker's man, were carrying the coffin down through the trees. We followed them. Willis had taken off his hat and put it on the coffin. When he came into sunlight his bald head shone.

"Look where he's put his hat," Felicity said.

"Do stop complaining. Isn't this beautiful? I think I'd like to be buried here."

Red cattle were grazing in fields sloping down to the shore. Seagulls screamed and squabbled over the crablands. Out in the river mouth two men in a dinghy were checking set-lines fixed to a buoy. On the other shore, behind drab-green mangroves, Robert's bach, Dick Webster's bach, stood in its garden and orchard.

I showed it to Felicity. She was more interested in Willis's hat. "For heaven's sake take it off there. Here, I'll carry it." She frowned at me. "They're like the Marx brothers."

"Robert wouldn't mind."

"Stop being sentimental."

The accusation startled me. I had thought I was simply pointing something out.

Willis turned his head. "Don't quarrel, girls." Tears had started running down his cheeks.

"That's all we need," Felicity muttered.

The men put the coffin down by the grave. They looked at me.

"You'd better lower it in. Then Willis can read the service."

The undertaker brought some tapes from his pocket and showed the others what to do. A gravedigger, resting on his shovel by the fence, walked over to help. It was just as well. Willis looked unsteady.

When the coffin was in the ground the undertaker left. The gravedigger went off to a far corner and rolled a cigarette.

"Willis, can you manage?"

He took out Dad's service and started to read.

"Lord, Thou hast been our dwelling-place in all generations. Before the mountains were brought forth, or ever Thou hadst formed the earth and the world, even from everlasting to everlasting Thou art God. Thou turnest man to destruction, and sayest, Return, ye children of men. For a thousand years in Thy sight are but as yesterday when it is past, and as a watch in the night. "

His voice grew stronger. He read through to the end. Some of it did not fit. Dad had prepared it late and Robert had not lived into old age. It did not seem to matter. And God? And immortality? That did not matter either. Who can tell?

When Willis had finished he took out his mouth organ and played *Danny Boy*. Felicity grew stiff with indignation. I patted her arm. The last wail of the tune died away. Emerson scattered a handful of earth on the coffin. He had probably seen it done in the movies. The sun-dried granules of clay pattered down like rain.

"Is that all?" Felicity asked.

"Unless you want to say anything."

"Not me. Not here. I'll have a mass said for him."

"What about you, Mr Webster?"

He shook his head.

"Thank you for coming." I put my flowers at the head of the grave.

We walked back to the trees. The Parminters passed us, coming down. The two sons, in their black suits (as ancient as Robert's clothes had been), walked on either side of their father, holding his arms. Betty came behind, with her eyes looking about. Her green head-scarf had yellow horseshoes on it. She smiled at us in a scared way. Willis stepped across to speak with her but the old man heard. He freed himself and swung round. His white eyes glared through us. "Betty, come!"

We watched them go down to the head of the grave. The gravedigger was approaching but Ralph Parminter waved him off. The old man stopped. His voice boomed in the air, the same Old Testament voice my father had been able to turn on. "Lord! Lord, hear me!"

"Or else," Felicity said. She looked as if she might march down and drive them all away. I held her arm.

"Lord, we come before you to intercede for the soul of one who strayed from the paths of righteousness. Hear us, Lord. We are your Chosen Ones.   "

"Bunkum! Bunkum! How can you allow it?"

I led her through the trees, wondering why she could not accept whatever happened on this day. I felt again the extra-ordinary happiness I had felt in the garden in San Francisco when Felicity had come out and told me we were going home to New Zealand.

At the car I shook hands with Dick Webster. He turned down Emerson's offer of a ride and trudged off down the hill. Emerson drove us home to Loomis, banking the car like a Gypsy Moth on the corners. He dropped Willis at his gate and me at the cottage. Felicity was going with him and flying home to Wellington later in the day. I kissed them goodbye and went into the cottage.

Well, I thought, I'm alone here now. I'll have to make the best of it.

But I have not been alone, in my *furor scribendi*. I have had more company than I have known what to do with. They are leaving me. I wonder if it's true I am acquainted with myself. In

241

a curious way I am both empty and full. The figure I see is an hour-glass. With Robert's burial the last of the sand trickled through. By an act of will (but an irresistible act) I up-ended myself. I let it all trickle back. The story ends.

I want very much to be quit of that metaphor. So—I'll put down one more thing. Rebecca and her husband drove up yesterday from Napier. He has applied for a job in Auckland. While he was being interviewed she came out to visit me. We talked about her brothers. She is not, it seems, satisfied with them. They've both "fluffed about" and wasted their chances. We talked about Fred Meggett's appeal against his sentence. But as far as she's concerned four years is not enough. I smiled at her and tried to make it seem that I agreed. This loud stranger was my daughter. That was more than I could understand.

We walked up to look at Peacehaven. She is not sentimental about the place. "It's a good job you got out. It was a bloody millstone round your neck. That was a good price you got from old Tinkerbell."

We stood on the verandah looking over the little piece of new Loomis at Merle's house. I said, "How do you know how much I got?"

"Well . . ." Some of her confidence slipped away. She got on to the business that had really brought her out. "I went to see Dad last night. He told me."

"How is your father?"

"He's getting by.   I won't beat about the bush. He wants to see you."

"Did he tell you that?"

"He's too proud. But I know."

"And what will Miss Neeley say?"

"Miss Neeley? Where have you been, Mum? Hasn't anyone told you?"

"Told me what?"

"For God's sake, that only lasted a week. She walked out on him."

"I see." And I did see. I saw it all.

"He's quite funny about it. Like, when she found out he had false teeth." But he had found out things about her too. "You know that letter you got, saying Dad and her were having it off? Well, she wrote it. Just to get things moving. She told him. Poor old Dad, he couldn't get over it."

"What's he doing?"

"Plumbing again. He's a plumbing repairman. He's got this little van. *F. Sole. Plumbing Repairs.* It's a bit of a come down."

I smiled. I smiled in praise of him. He had re-made himself a second time. It had taken longer than chopping down a tree.

Rebecca and I walked back to the cottage. She said, "I'm not your bloody keeper. All I know is that he'd like to see you." She grinned at me anxiously. She has always loved him more than she loves me. "Think about it, eh?" She drove away.

I have thought about it. She left me his address. I'll visit him tonight. There's room for him here if he wants to come. We'll have to get rid of the hospital bed. I am trying to be realistic. He can carry on with his plumbing repairs. I shall work in the garden. I'll paint the kitchen. For the rest of our days we'll treat each other kindly.

Well, that's what I've come to hope for in the last few hours. Not a large hope, surely; and one that has no undue sentiment in it.

SOLE
SURVIVOR

1 This morning I watched my niece and her cousin making love in the river. I was walking on a track by the Aorere in Golden Bay and they were in the shallows of a pool that plunged down in mid-river thirty feet, drowning blocks of stone as large as houses. It was getting on for noon. I was sweating from my walk and needed a breather. But I would have stopped even if I'd been running to catch a train. That is not a confession to be ashamed of. I can't imagine anyone walking on. I'm careful with the word but I say without hesitation that Jilly and Hank were beautiful.

And I had come from my talk with John Jolly, Jolly John. I needed something to take my mind off that. John had found me with a telegram. My face throbbed as I read it, I swelled with anger. *Ha gotcher. Ring me soonest. Clink clink. J. J.* Clink clink meant there was money in it for me. I did not need money. I did not need work or Wellington or telegrams that threatened while pretending cheeriness. Soonest! I let him stew two days. Then I took Sharon's shopping list and a sack of returnable tonic water bottles and set off for Collingwood. I turned into the loop path and stopped at the Gypsy Trailer to see if Jilly and Hank wanted anything. Jilly, as usual, ignored me. "No thanks, Uncle Ray," Hank sang in his Yankee falsetto. He was tacking opened-out plastic bags over the windows of their saucer. *Golden Grain Fibre Bread* said the sheet he was fixing. I wondered what the Venusians would make of that. Jilly painted *Gilgamesh* on the prow. Neat little letters. She was a neat little girl.

"Would you like me to bring a bottle of fizz for the launching?"

She must have murmured her opinion of me to Hank for he patted her and gave his squeaky laugh. They were, I thought, marvellous to look at; in their surfaces and joints; but a disappointment in most other ways. They had, though, purpose and certainty. One can only laugh at them for a while. I went off defeated down the track.

1

In Collingwood the tide was in. I drove up the narrow road by the fishing boats and rickety jetties and stood outside the pub admiring the town. It has a hick-town seediness, the kind of distillation of minimized aims—and, I imagined, crooked desires. It belongs more to its rednecks than the commune and craft and simple-life folk who have come in lately. I feel threatened in its main street and listen for rumours of incest and of lynchings.

Talking to Jolly John blew that away: city air. He demanded a profile of Douglas Plumb. "One of your clever pieces. Bography-cum-hatchet job. In a velvet glove. In view of what's happening."

"What's happening?"

"Come on Raymie, don't play games. All that country air has made you dull."

"I like dull. I haven't read a paper in three weeks. Or heard a radio."

"Stop being boastful. The TV news—"

"We don't have TV So what's with Duggie? Someone assassinated him?"

"Would that they had. No, he's making his move. He's let it be known etcetera. Willing to serve. In the interests of the party. No personal ambitions, mind."

"Did he talk about the fall of the Roman Empire?"

"The fall of Singapore."

"Ha!"

"Is that all you can say?"

"That and no. I'm out of the bography business. And the Duggie Plumb business. How did you find me?"

"No one knows him like you, Raymie."

"Don't call me that."

"Sorry. Raymong."

"Or Raymong."

"If you do this for me R. Sole I'll call you Ray for ever."

Jolly John going down with his guns all firing. We argued away, and I had the last word: no.

"How did you find me?"

2

"Your cretin brother phoned. I told him Raymond Sole doesn't work here any more. His guess was you'd be at your daughter's place."

"What did he want?"

"His runaway little girl. His good-kid-really-in-spite-of-everything. Thought you might put your ear to the ground. He's coming to see you."

I drove ten miles down the Aorere, sweated across the paddocks with my sack of groceries, and came on Bobby's little girl making love with her cousin in the river. Her second cousin, let me get that straight. But I'm an old ex-puritan and ex-family-freak. I caught a brimstone whiff and mounted on my toes to thunderbolt them. Then I saw that what they made was beautiful. My aesthetic sense is not always in good order. On this occasion it saved me from foolishness. I watched, admiring, breathless. They were like figures on a vase. Behind them pool, translucent; blocks of stone tumbled in green water. He stood thigh-deep and she was locked on him. She was slick as a seal, seal-head gleaming. Her sodden hair lay spade-shaped on her back. Their bodies glistened. His bony Pilgrim-father hands were cupped under her buttocks, pulling her in. He rocked a little, bounced with a water-supported finesse, providing their motion. Soon it was not enough. Jilly unlocked her arms. They joined hands, hooked their bones, and began a good old-fashioned in and out, working with tensed arms and elbows concertina'd. Jilly arched her back. Her hair went splash splash splash in leaden lumps. The crown of her head dipped in the water. Hank was solid, a post. She worked against him. Still I did not feel like a voyeur. She gave a cry when she came, like a child at the top of a Ferris wheel.

He let her float a moment, then drew her up and hugged her. They kissed long. Then she backed off him with a school-gymnasium jump and knelt up to her armpits in the water. To me his penis seemed out of proportion, not unnatural so much as extravagant. I was surprised to see Jilly so familiar with it. She changed its angle to suit her and took it in her mouth.

Now I was more than admiring, so it was time to go. I did not

3

want to but I was ashamed. My vision, if I can call it that, was over. This was what Duggie Plumb called going down town for lunch. Hank had his hands on Jilly's head, making her go faster. Greedy devil, I thought, full of envy. But when he saw me I winked encouragement. I swung my sack on my shoulders and trudged on up the path.

Sharon was digging in her garden, bare to the waist. She put her T-shirt on when she saw me coming. Carlo had made a road for his truck up the side of a tomato row. "Brmm, brmm," he said.

I put down the groceries and pulled my fingers straight. "I'm not fit."

"Grab a spade," Sharon said.

"I'll take these up. I got everything."

"Did you see Hank and Jilly? They were heading for town."

"They're in the river."

"What doing?" She looked at me sharply. "They'd do it up trees if they could."

I crossed the garden—"Grandpa, you trod on my bridge," Carlo wailed—let myself through the possum fence and climbed the bush path to the house. Sharon worries me. She claims to be happy but she is not happy. She claims to have got her life all sorted out, but is full of badly-hidden discontents. Hostilities make her tongue an iron spike. She whacks her tomahawk into a pumpkin, splits it like a head. But later her face seems to bloom, she breathes in deeply, slows all her movements down—and though she does not say so I know that *now* she's happy. It's almost as if she has taken a shot of some drug; but it isn't that, she leaves that to Hank and Jilly. She knows some secret but cannot always find it when she wants. I do not try to help. That's not my role. A parent can only keep on loving; be around when he's wanted, make himself scarce when he's not.

Instead of going back to help her I set the table for lunch. She meant to pass the rest of her life in this place, drawing her benefit, growing food in her garden. Desi, her man, was booted out. "I couldn't stand him any longer. Boohooing round the place. One kid's enough." She let him get the compost privy

4

finished, then sent him down the road. "He's not Carlo's father anyway." She doesn't only worry me, she scares me. She's one of this new breed of women that cuts the balls off rapists; or rapes men. And I bred her, with a little help from Glenda. Sharon, the pre-schooler who had wanted to marry Daddy: now she would let me stay a while, as long as I didn't get under her feet.

I went outside and sat in the sun. Knuckles of hill stood behind me, bushed up to the skyline. South were Mount Olympus and Lead Hills, reddish-brown. The Heaphy Track started round to the right: three days walking to the Tasman Sea. I had sunned myself like this for several weeks, through Jan. into Feb. and my hairy paunch had a yellow patina. Lovely sun, I thought, lovely silence; and wondered why I was half-hearted about them. Not just those children in the river, those golden ninnies. I grew randy thinking of them, and told myself, Come on, you're fifty. And fifty was the age of Douglas Plumb.

Yes, Douglas Plumb. In spite of my claim to be finished with him Duggie sat squarely in my mind—always had, always will. Cousin Duggie. How could I hope to ignore his "move"? He was like a wart on my palm or flea in my crotch.

So I drank two cans of beer and made myself sleepy. A helicopter flew by with a policeman hanging out of the door looking for marijuana gardens. I waved at him. Soon I fell into a doze. "You lazy old bugger," Sharon said, clunking down her spade. I jumped up guiltily. An empty can rolled off my chest and she belted it, killed it stone dead. That seemed to make her happy.

"Get my tonic water?"

"Yes. I set the table."

"Good for you. Your phone call go all right?"

"He wants me to write a profile on Douglas Plumb."

"That pig."

"He's trying for Muldoon's job."

"Another pig. Are you going to do it?"

"No."

"What are you going to do?"

"Stay here a while. Dig in your garden."

"Huh!"

"John told me Bobby's coming down. Your uncle Bob."

"Pig number three. What does he want?"

"He thinks I might know where to find Jilly."

"In the river. Did that upset you?"

"It made me envious. We didn't do things like that when I was young. 'Sexual intercourse began in nineteen sixty-three.' That's a quote."

"Don't you start. Desi kept on Hesseing me and this lot keeps Von Daniking away and God knows what. Think some thoughts of your own."

This lot, Hank and Jilly, joined us for lunch. Jilly's hair was plastered on her skull, bunned on her neck. She was like a weasel and would have loved a free bite at my throat. Beautiful in the river, ugly now. I turned that about and found no answer.

"Speak up, Jilly."

She tore a crust instead. Her nose was white with anger, a little icy peak in her brown face.

"I was on a public path."

"You didn't have to stop." Her teeth made an ugly wound in a tomato and I heard her mutter, "Dirty old pervert."

"Wrong three times, my dear. I wash a lot. I'm very clean. And I'm only middle-aged. I don't expect young people to know the difference. And what I am is curious not perverted. I thought you were beautiful in the river. I went away when it got too interesting."

Sharon giggled. I make these locutions to amuse her and am pleased that I can still succeed with them. But our exchange made Jilly angrier. "I'm not going to be old. I'll kill myself when I'm twenty-five."

"It used to be twenty. But of course, you're getting close. And Hank's twenty-two." I smiled at her. "Things will be better on Venus."

"Everyone over twenty-five is dead."

"I'm over twenty-five," Sharon said.

"Jilly's a bit spaced out," Hank said.

We exchanged sly grins. Masculine stuff. But what a child he is, this New England boy. There's puppy fat on his face; and an incredible innocence in his voice, though he's as amoral as a rabbit and foxy in his dealings with his elders. He's the grandson of my mother's sister Agnes, who fled the crazy Plumbs to San Francisco and married an engineer, Gerry Lerhke. Their son went east, lost himself on the teeming seaboard, and thirty years later Hank Lerhke stood on my brother's doorstep: bare feet and beads, rucksack and guitar. Bobby asked him in, there was no way round it.

Jilly's tomato squirted on my wrist. That pleased her. She's no child, though young enough to be at school. Sharon, in one of those intimacies that break me up by the ease with which they subsume our past, took my hand and licked off the seeds.

"You two are in trouble."

"Why?"

"Your father's on his way. He's probably got his shotgun in the car."

Jilly went pale with fright. Then she was beautiful, with eyes gone mad and tilted chin. She was my mother. "How did he find out? You rang him, Ray. By God—by God—"

"Jilly," Hank cried. He was too late. She threw her tomato at me. It struck me on the cheek. Modern times are too much for me. I felt like crying. Associations are too much. I had seen my mother, saw her still.

Sharon handed me a cloth. "You two can clear out of the trailer. I need it for Dad."

"Ah, Sharon," Hank began.

"Stuff it, Hank. Don't crawl to them. We're going anyway. And not coming back. So fuck my father." She ran out.

"Jilly cross," Carlo said.

"I'll say." Sharon stroked his hair.

"We were going to leave," Hank said. He made a little bow in his New World way and thanked Sharon for having them so long.

"Flying out in your saucer?" I asked.

His clear-eyed look made me feel ashamed. "It's been swell

7

knowing you, Uncle Ray." I thought his whistling sad as he went to the trailer, but soon the bush made it indifferent.

Sharon washed the dishes and I dried. "I'll be pleased to see the back of them," she said.

"Are they really going to fly? In that thing?"

"They're on a grid intersection. It makes a force field. That's what they fly in."

"Are we allowed to watch?"

"Might as well. It's something to do." She was sour again. She put Carlo down for his nap and lay on her bed. "Close that door."

"Yes, dear." It was like being married. I pottered round the kitchen and the shed. I had not been lonely here but now I was lonely. Sharon and Carlo were sleeping. Hank and Jilly were in the trailer, smoking pot and sniffing amyl nitrite. And here I was, Raymong Sole, wondering how to fill the afternoon.

After a while I fetched my exercise book: the one I'd bought in Collingwood after talking to Jolly John.

2 Sharon and I crept out in the dusk to watch Hank and Jilly fly away. We each had a glass of her boysenberry wine, made drinkable with tonic water, and we sat in the bush by the saucer, whispering back and forth. She was happy again; slowed down, rounded out. She leaned on my shoulder. I put my arm around her.

"What do you do when you lock yourself in the bedroom?"

"Meditate."

"Ah. Here's to the Maharishi."

"I don't need him."

"It does more for you than pot does for Hank and Jilly."

"I don't need that either. I'm glad they're going."

"Did you mean it when you said I could have the trailer?"

"If you want it."

"I do."

"I might have someone coming into the house."

"A new man?"

I felt her smiling on my shoulder. "Good old Dad. Interested. Do you think you'll ever get yourself a new woman?"

"One day. One day I might."

She yawned and dozed a while until wine spilled on her leg. "I'd better get back. Carlo wakes sometimes."

"Here they come."

Hank and Jilly walked hand in hand out from the trailer. They had not dressed for travel. As far as I could make out Hank was in his overalls and Jilly in one of her wrap-around "ethnic" skirts. She had plaited her hair. He helped her into *Gilgamesh* in a gentlemanly way. Its timbers creaked.

"Fuck," Jilly said. "I've torn my dress."

Hank pulled the cardboard hatches down. Then a bush silence fell. Insect hummings grew in it and faded out of hearing. Sharon went to sleep. I heard my stomach rumble. I was feeling foolish and wanted to shout derisively; but remembered that I'd been around and nothing got me worked up any more. A match flared behind the plastic bags. They were smoking Golden Bay green in there, waiting for power to concentrate and lift them away.

Sharon woke and gave a sigh. "I dreamed they were floating like one of Mum's mobiles." She pecked my cheek. "Come in quietly."

I sat in the bush and sipped my wine; felt my blood coursing silkily; and felt a dread grow on me until I had an arterial thump in my joints and a prickling in my fingertips. I seemed to hear a humming from deep space. The night was velvety and the stars were bright. Mount Haidinger, up north, crouched like a cat. Forces were in the air, invisible. I felt them lapping round my face like water. And surely in the clearing was a dreadful hole in nature—Hank and Jilly sucked up into nothing.

The bush can make a man believe anything. I got to my feet and crashed around like a boar. "Jilly. Hank. Are you in there?"

The hatch sprang up against the sky. Jilly arched out and spat at me. Hank squeezed up in front of her. His voice seemed to

come from her belly. "Uncle Ray, they won't come while you're
here."

"Oh," I said, "I'll get to bed then. Bon voyage." I trudged
back to the house and got into my sleeping bag. I stayed awake
for a while, my heart knocking, but heard no humming, saw no
brilliant lights. In the morning Hank and Jilly were gone. A
stubbed-out joint lay on the nursery stool that served as a pilot's
seat in *Gilgamesh*. Jilly's clothes, Hank's guitar and book or two
were missing from the trailer. I walked down to the river and
looked over the paddocks. Their van was gone.

"Good riddance," Sharon said.

We worked among her beans and gooseberries. In the afternoon I cleaned out the trailer. It has yellow wheels and green
sides and an overhanging roof with an iron chimney. There's a
double bunk inside, a Tilley lamp, a small pot-bellied stove, a
table and chair, crockery, cutlery, a pot, a pan, an enamel basin
for washing up. I saw I would be happy there. No water. But I
would fetch that in a bucket from Sharon's tank. I would grow a
beard, bathe in the river, and be a little dirty in the winter. As
for calls of nature, I had peed in preserving jars before. And Desi
had dug a long-drop in the bush.

I swept the floor. I cleaned the stove. I carried Jilly's love-
stained sheets round to Sharon's for washing. There Bobby
found us; panting up from his rental car, with a king-sized
bottle of *Wilson's* held like a club.

"Ah, Bobby. John told me you'd be coming."

"Stuffed. Rooted. 'Scuse, Sharon. Let me get my breath." He
collapsed on the divan. "Places people live. Jilly here? I'm
looking for my girl." Beetroot red. I thought he might have a
stroke.

"Beer?" I got him a can from the fridge.

"Thanks." He guzzled it. "Saved my life. Is Jilly here?"

"She was, Uncle Bobby, but she's gone," Sharon said.

I told him all about it and Bobby began to cry. He made deep
gulping noises, oop, oop; then said, "Sorry, sorry. I'm like a
bloody girl."

Sharon got a cloth and washed his face. Bobby is a tough guy but when he gives in to things he really gives in. I went outside while she helped him get together. I carried Carlo round the paths on my shoulders. Bobby and I are opposites. Where I'm inclined to be mild he's all bull's-roar. I'm likely to feel quickly, soften up, but soon I have to fight against cynicism. Bobby will sneer, he'll wisecrack, talk about bleeding hearts, say the only thing that counts is money and the only friend you've got is number one; but in the end tears start in his eyes. You never know where you are with Bobby. The children at his school must love and hate him.

He came out and joined me, thrusting out his chin like Mussolini. I put Carlo down and he ran in to his mother.

"Well, Bobby—"

"I'm going after that Yankee prick. I'll have him in the courts for carnal knowledge."

"Jilly's over sixteen."

"She wasn't when they met. He was into her the day he got in my house."

"Can you prove it?"

"I'll prove it. Walk down to the car with me."

"Relax, Bobby. They're through the Lewis Pass. Or down the Coast. Come and see where they lived."

He cried again when he saw the double bunk. "He'll be teaching her that ninety-six. Oop, oop. The day he came my little girl was in her school uniform." And she looked round her father's shoulder, saw this barefoot freak, and turned her nose up. Bobby didn't understand. It wasn't Hank's beads and guitar that did for Jilly, it was his saucers. His faith was what seduced her. Jilly wanted above everything else to fly away. From all sorts of things, not least of them Bobby.

I looked at the roll of fat on his neck. He had been a beefy boy and I had spent half the day trailing along with him in an armbar. When I cried he felt a rush of love. It was terrifying. Now his meat and muscles had turned to lard. And I felt something like love for him.

"She'll get sick of him. Give her time."

"Maybe. I went to see Duggie Plumb last night."

11

"Why Duggie?"

"He's my M.P He's Minister of Police. Do you know what he said?"

"I can guess."

"Screwing never did a girl any harm. To me. Her father. Doesn't he know I vote for him? Not any bloody more."

"Duggie chucks a vote away now and then. It makes him feel good."

"He kicked me out. Said he was busy. He'll need to be. Muldoon will eat the prick."

"I wouldn't be too sure."

I took him outside to look at the saucer. He kicked holes in its sides. "What's happened to kids? They've gone all soft. This Zing stuff. Zang. Whatever it is. I liked them better when they were screaming murder."

"She'll come home."

"Sharon too, with a tarpot kid."

For what was left of the afternoon we drank his whisky. At tea we got sentimental and talked about our mother.

"'That's not a table topic.'"

"'Who made an odour?'"

Sharon put Carlo to bed. She stayed in her room to meditate, while Bobby and I played our family like cards. We trumped each other: Grandpa in his study, while the world rolled by: Auntie Esther, with her purple plonk: Willis chasing ladies in his orchard: Emerson, the Sundowner of the Skies, beating up Peacehaven in his Gypsy Moth. There were others too: mad old Wendy weeping as she packed her car with books: mad old Merle and Graydon, naked as skinned rabbits on their lawn. We grew drunk on memories as much as whisky.

I helped Bobby into the sleeping bag and wrapped myself in blankets in the trailer. I could not sleep but that did not bother me. Possums coughed in the night. I believed I would be happy.

In the morning I took him swimming to cure his hangover. We porpoised in the river, yelling like boys. "Ow, Googie Withers." He dived and came up purple. "Touched the bottom. Your turn."

12

"I get scared down there."

"Yeller-belly." Down he went again. I saw him in the green water, breaking into cubes.

"You'll kill yourself."

"Still a bit of a pansy, ain't yer? I thought old Uncle Alf was going to get you for a while. He fancied me."

"Did he?"

"Liked me muscles. Jesus, I scared the little bugger. I went into one of those underground dunnies in town. And there he was in a corner, chatting up some kid. 'Gidday, Uncle Alf,' I yelled. You should've seen the little sod. He almost went through the roof. Then he was up those stairs like a rat up a drain pipe. Last time I ever saw him."

We towelled ourselves on Hank and Jilly's sand. I came on schoolgirl footprints in a corner and trod them out.

"How long are you going to stay here, Ray?"

"Through the winter."

"Doing what?"

"I thought I might get on to my book on Mickey Savage."

"Go back to the *Sunday Post*. That's where you belong, boy. Reckon you'll ever get married again?"

"Who knows? If I meet the right woman." I do not believe in right woman. Or right anything much. Right beginnings, right ends. Even right circumstances.

"That Glenda really sucked you dry. Bit of the old knuckle needed there."

"Come on Bobby, save the act for someone you can impress."

"No act. It proves you love 'em. Oh my God, look, look. That's Jilly's footprint. And that one must be his. *In between*. Oh Jesus, my little girl."

So I took him to the house and fed him beer. After lunch I put him in his car. He smiled at me and blinked his eyes, ready to work up some feeling.

"You'll miss your plane, Bobby." He had worn me out. I watched him as far as the corner, then walked across the paddocks to Barlow's cow-shed and dipped a billy of milk from one of the vats. I whistled as I walked back to the river. The Bobby

13

thing, the Jilly thing, was over. I swung the billy in a giant wheel without spilling a drop. Then I saw Bobby's car coming back up the road. It was slewing in the metal, pouring dust. He skidded a quarter-circle on the grass and burst his door open. The scream of steel guitars came over the paddock. He climbed on to the bottom wire of the fence. "Duggie Plumb's been shot."

I put the billy down and lumbered through the cow pats.

"I got the end of a special bulletin. They've taken him to Auckland hospital."

"Who?" I said. Duggie made a collage: face upright, diagonal, lying on its cheek. Splashes of blood coloured him.

"They don't know how serious it is. You've gone all white."

"Who did it?"

"There's a man in custody. Stand up, son. You don't like the bugger that much."

I let the fence-wire go and started to run.

"They said there'd be more bulletins," Bobby yelled. "Get your radio on. I've got to go or I'll miss my plane."

I picked the billy up and ran slopping milk down to the river. Through the trees I saw dust smoking in the hedges as Bobby drove away. Sharon was in her garden. I yelled the news to her as I went by. She followed me to the house and we tried to thump her radio alive but got only threads of a voice.

"I'll listen in my car." I hurried to the road and sat spinning knobs. Music: pop here, Sunday there. I lay on the seat a moment. Running had made me dizzy. Heart beating away, whacking my ribs. I felt blood running in my wrists and ankles. How comical it would be if Duggie and I, born within a day or two of each other, should die on the same day. The Corsican brothers: I felt his wounds in my chest. Comical because I hated the bastard. "Don't die, Duggie. You're going to be Prime Minister."

Soon I climbed up behind the wheel. I felt old, slack-muscled, full of broken tissues, and felt it unjust that I should be forced into action like a boy. Then my head began to clear, the

14

noises stopped, I was rational and fifty. I drove fast and safe to Collingwood.

"I thought you wouldn't be long," John Jolly said.

"John, can you give me the news? What's the latest?"

"For people who won't write for me, no news."

"I'll write for you."

"Next Sunday? A nice long piece?"

"Anything you want. Just how is he?"

"Hang on. There's someone coming on the other line."

I heard clicks and a distant voice that only grunted.

"Well now, Raymie," John came back. "This isn't timed right for us. Yesterday would've been spot on. We'll have to let the dailies do the news. But what's it matter when we've got Raymond Sole?"

"For Christ's sake, John."

"I want all that dirt you've been sitting on. You can't slander the dead."

"Dead?" I heard my voice smack like a rolled-up newspaper on the walls of the booth, and I kept safe by imagining an existence for myself outside attachments and concerns.

"Dead on arrival. Ray, you there?" John's happy voice was suddenly careful. "Why don't you sleep on it, eh? Then get yourself weaving."

"Who did it?"

"Some old bastard. No names yet. I've got Tom Farquhar fishing. Blew a hole in his chest with a German pistol. War souvenir, Tom thinks."

I saw the old man with his pared-down face, vestigial face; and saw the gun—a Walther P38—lying unused since the war in a strong-box in that little house in Parnell. And I thought, It happens that way. You can't just pretend you're empty in there.

"Ray?"

It comes and gets you. You can't just walk off in another direction.

"You know who this old guy is?"

"No," I said.

"O.K. Now look, you can do this job better in the office."

15

"I'm not coming."

"You're doing this for me. You gave your word."

"I'm sorry, John." I put the phone down and walked out into the main street of Collingwood. Duggie was dead. I tried to imagine that the empty street lay outside time.

3 Duggie said he came from humble beginnings. It's a common boast of public men. They also claim their honours make them humble. Duggie never did that. And he spoke of his beginnings only once. He was helping out in a marginal at election time and hoped that he might sneak a few votes over. He went on to say what hard times his parents had seen, and confessed they voted Labour in the thirties. But those times were gone, good times were here, and his parents—"my old Mum and Dad"—had switched their vote to National before they died. That was a lie but nobody could catch him out in it. Willis Plumb learned to hate Tories at his mother's knee. He was all over the place in his other opinions but never budged an inch in politics. As for Aunt Mirth, nothing mattered to her but "my man", whoever he might be. He was mostly Willis. I heard her say once that she'd never voted.

Duggie did not have humble beginnings either. Mirth and Willis were poor but never meek. They were flamboyant and tricky. They were life-lovers. Everything that pleased them they devoured. Duggie could not be sure of anything. Perhaps, though, he was sure of me.

I lived in the Loomis valley, west of Auckland. Peacehaven was my grandfather's house. Duggie lived four miles up the road on a citrus orchard hacked out of scrub at the foot of the ranges. A mile of Loomis creek "belonged" to us. It started over the road from Peacehaven and ran in a shallow gorge past the back of town and ended at the tidal pool above Moa Park. The Peacehaven orchard also belonged, with the swamp and paddocks at the back. The swamp drained into a stream flowing under a

16

toy-town bridge and through a culvert under Millbrook road. It joined the creek in a small waterfall. Peacehaven stood on a hillside looking over the lawns and summer-house at Wendy Philson's cottage, hidden in wattles, and Merle and Graydon Butters' turretted house. Uncle Robert looked after the garden. He kept a house cow and a dozen sheep. Grandpa Plumb, dressed always in a grey suit and tennis shoes, dozed in the summer-house or scribbled in his study. The Butterses crossed the bridge two or three times a week to visit him. Wendy came up daily. Later Bluey Considine lived in the cottage with a cripple called Sutton. I catalogue these names and map the place to hold them still.

The war was on and walls had ears. For Duggie and me it was the time of Beautiful Olga and Schimmler, the Serpent of Berlin. They might be sitting by you on the bus. They might ask if your father was fighting and where his unit was stationed, and Olga would smile and breathe sexy things in her German voice. We would not be fooled, we would gather evidence and report them to the army. But we never found anyone beautiful or even sinister. No one said "Donner und blitzen" by mistake. So we spied on Wendy Philson and Merle Butters instead.

Wendy was lovesick. She stood on her side of the creek, watching our grandfather on his lawn. Tears ran down her face and she licked them from the corners of her mouth. Down the bank by the water Duggie and I practised our self-increasing art. We heard her groan and saw her work her fingers in her ribs. It was my first acquaintance with adult passion. I was panting with a kind of sickness and greed. I wanted more of Wendy but wanted to run and hide. "She wants to have a go with him," Duggie said. All I could see was that she was in pain. I thought she might be poisoned. She bent almost double, folding her hands inside. Her mouth was black and her eyes were messy. "Oh George, love me," she groaned.

"See," Duggie grinned. He felt around for a stone. I was a better spy than Duggie. All I wanted was to take it down and creep away. That's probably why I'm a journalist. Duggie wanted to be part of the action. He wanted to add his bit. He

17

lobbed the stone at the pool by the culvert, where it plopped like a frog. Wendy jumped to her feet and backed away. Her face was blunted with fright. She tried to push something off with her hands. Then she turned and lumbered through the bean-rows to her cottage.

"Jesus," Duggie breathed. He was delighted.

"That's the pool she tried to drown herself in. It's true," I said. "Uncle Bob had to pull her out."

"Who told you that?"

"Mum." She had also made me promise never to tell. "They had to stick her in the wow." I threw a stone at the pool. "She must have thought something was coming to get her."

It pleased me that Duggie looked alarmed. We went to the bridge and crossed the lawn, which brought us up on Grandpa Plumb. He was deaf and that made him easy. One of Duggie's pleasures was to stand behind him and fart. Grandpa was sleeping in the summer-house. He had his handkerchief on his face. It blew like a flag when he breathed out, then dented in his mouth neat as a spoon. Before long it slid off and settled on his chest.

Duggie said, "My turn." I did not like the way he had made a game of this. Grandpa was a sacred being to me. When I put his handkerchief back I was purified. And when I failed and his eyes sprang open—eyes of a fighter ace—I felt shrunken and unclean. My sitting with him then and my grinning chatter was a kind of prayer for renewal.

Duggie took the handkerchief by the corners. He raised it and let it fall in place. My grandfather's fingers twitched. The handkerchief started fluttering. Duggie grinned. He put his hands together and made a Japanese bow. I pulled him out of the summer-house by his arm. I was confused. Duggie freed me but he put me in danger.

Who came next? My mother in her kitchen. She saw our heads popping up at the window and gave us lumps of *zwieback* —horrible crusts of twice-baked bread—and sent us away. We went down through the garden, where Uncle Bob was digging. He wore a handkerchief too, knotted at the corners, on his head.

Although he was only thirty he was bald. He was adenoidal and breathed through his mouth. I got on well with Uncle Bob, but Duggie had a way of making him not there.

We crossed the bridge and wriggled under a barbed wire fence into the Butterses' place. And this was the greatest of our days, for Merle and Graydon were lying on the lawn without any clothes on. They were worshipping the sun. Bobby had told me about it but this was the first time I had seen. They lay supine, outspread. I'm not sure whether they embraced the sun or were crucified. Merle's face had a look of ecstasy. When I had wondered at her other parts I lay cheek down to see it better. Its purity of line—her forehead, nose and mouth—was startling to me. I knew that Merle and Graydon were in a kind of madness; but not a kind that made me want to laugh. They were untouchable. I do not know even now whether theirs was a triumph of faith or art.

Duggie was wriggling. "Look at the size of. Look at her."

I had seen. It was the first I had known that women had hair between their legs and pink knobs like lollies on their breasts. I had not known men grew penises so big. But it was their faces that intrigued me, especially Merle's. I became outraged. Some trick was being played against everything I knew. My anger made me want to go away.

I started to crawl backwards through the hydrangeas. But seeing was never enough for Duggie. A garden hose ran snaking down the lawn to Merle and Graydon. He crept round to the tap on the wall of the house and turned it on. The end of the hose reared up like a cobra and sent a jet of water over Merle. She screamed. Graydon rose on his arms, his head went round like a periscope. He ran towards the house, where Duggie was slipping into the shrubbery.

"Do go away, you silly little boys," Merle cried in her la-de-da voice. Then Graydon started to laugh. He galloped back down the slope with penis jigging and seized the hose and charged among the hydrangeas, flashing it like a scimitar. I saw him coming, maniacal, bright-eyed. His hairless chest wobbled like a lady's. He wet me from the back of my neck to my heels. Then he made hunting cries and went after Duggie. But the hose had reached its full length and though he put his thumb on it to make it squirt further Duggie scrambled off without a wetting.

We stopped at the curve in the gravel drive. Graydon was hosing Merle and she was squealing. They ran up to the house hand in hand and left the hose writhing on the lawn. Their white rumps flashed as they passed inside.

"Loonies," Duggie said. "Did you see.   ?"

Yes, I had seen. More than he had seen. And taken it all down. And he had made them jump for him. So both of us were happy. I had the worry though of what my mother would do when she found out. As well as being naughty I had sinned against purity. I knew that I should have to pretend that all I had seen was bottoms.

I am distorting him. There was more to Duggie than this. What I cannot get away from is his dominance of me. It came from his ease and knowingness in places where I was guilty, out of my depth, plain ignorant. I should have been boss. I was bigger and stronger. He dominated me through knowledge; but if I had been equal would have managed it through will.

Wendy packed her car with books and drove away to live somewhere else. Bluey and Sutton came to live in the cottage. The police called for Uncle Bob and though Mum insisted he was as brave as any soldier Duggie and I kept quiet about him. No one had to tell us conchies were cowards. Soon we heard of Pearl Harbour and we set about making buck teeth and Japanese fingers in tobacco tins. Auckland filled up with Americans. We collected cigarette packets—Camels and Chesterfields and green Luckies and white—and hung around Auntie Esther's Yanks until they fished gum from their pockets and told us, "Get lost, kid."

They liked Duggie though. His bold talk made their cheeks turn pink and they gave their hee-haw laugh and said to their girls, "You hear that, honey?" The girls looked on Duggie with horror. They nodded with prim satisfaction when Esther came up on him quietly and slapped his behind so hard sparrows scattered from the summer-house roof. "Go home and tell your mother she wants you." Tears of humiliation streamed on his cheeks. "Go on, or you'll get another one." She had no liking and no pity for him. When she looked at him after that he slunk away.

To get his revenge he told stories about her. She stopped her car on Millbrook Road and passed a note to a man. "Heil Hitler," she said, and drove away. She left her kitchen light on for Japanese bombers to see. And once in the drive at Peacehaven with Marine Sergeant Cuchiella—"my Brooklyn boy"—she reached through his legs from behind and grabbed his tool as though she was picking grapes. "Yeah," Duggie told me twenty years later, "that one was true. The poor bugger looked as if he'd swallowed a golf ball."

The Americans enriched our lives in a number of ways. We even saw one die. It was on a Saturday afternoon. We paddled down Loomis creek in canoes made from roofing iron and sealed with pitch. Duggie led. Beak Wyatt, a stringy boy with a blade of a nose, came in the middle. The black pools made him jumpy. He always spoke rapidly on the creek and laughed a lot in a screechy way I came last because I thought the middle place unworthy I gave myself the task of guarding the rear Like Beak Wyatt I was nervous on the creek. We broke into a darkness, we killed quiet. Mum praised me for imagination so trying hard became natural to me. The creek was also Nature. Brought up without religion, I had been told to worship there. Duggie was the only one who was free. He shot his canoe ahead like a busy steamboat.

In mid-afternoon we came to the tidal pool. We pulled our canoes up on the bank and climbed into the open. "This is the place to come if you want to find Frenchies," Duggie said. He went looking but came back empty-handed. The pool, which was simply the Pool, lay brown and salty in the sun. Green water from the creek ran into it down a rock slide overgrown with slime. All around were willow trees and gums. We lay in

21

the grass at the top of the bank and brooded on the water, seeing tribes of sprats and eels in there. Cries came up from Moa Park. Canoes nosed round the corner but could not mount the rapids to the Pool.

When a jeep drove up from the gate we slithered further back. Two marines and their girlfriends carried rugs and beer down to the flat place by the diving board. The girls were permed and had painted nails, which my mother had told me was a sure sign a girl was no lady. Duggie and I slipped into our spying role but Beak half rose and swayed like a praying mantis.

"D-do you think they're going to do it?"

"Get down," Duggie snarled.

The men opened bottles of beer and passed them to the girls, who drank manlike, ladylike. A lump grew in my chest, hard as a cricket ball.

"Yanks always fuck their sheilas," Duggie said.

These ones went to the bathing shed and changed into swimming togs. They came back with their clothes neatly folded. One of them put his cap on his girl. She rubbed his thigh. That was more like it. But again reality let us down. The man walked on to the diving board.

"Hey—hey—" Beak Wyatt squeaked.

"He knows," Duggie said.

"Sure," I said.

The Yank bounced high in the air and seemed to hang there, arms outspread. The old board rattled and chattered. On the bank the girls clapped.

"Bloody skite," Duggie said.

I did not think so. He seemed to touch the sky. Then, bending his knees, he made the board go still. He strutted to the rug and slapped the girls' behinds. They ran away to change while the men lay on their elbows, drinking beer.

"They're not going to do it," Beak Wyatt said. He was relieved.

The girls ran back. Seeing them made the day go brighter. One was in red, the other in yellow. They looked as if they had stepped out of magazines.

"Wow," yelled one of the Yanks. He made curvy shapes in the air with his hands.

"Dirty bugger," Duggie said.

But, like Beak, I was relieved they weren't going to do it. The pressure was gone from my chest. I wished the Yank would go on the board and bounce. And soon he made that strutting walk out there. The board rattled, the big long-legged Yank hung in the air. "Zowie," he yelled.

The other one stood up and took a final swig from his bottle. He was smaller and whiter and had bones standing out in his elbows. "Move over, Joe." The big Yank came back and stood aside. He smoothed his hair and winked at the girls.

"I'll show you how we do it back home, baby," the small one said. He flexed his shoulders in a clowning way. He was skinny but he was strong. His back was shaped like a cobra's hood. Joe grinned and whacked his bum. "Go man," he said.

The small man ran. I see him still. He was Munro Gussey from Bay City, Michigan. I can feel the day break apart. Something broke in me, like snapping rubber. I was half-way to my feet, suspended there. My head was in my shoulders, my mouth hung stupidly, squeaking a word that was never finished.

The board shot Munro Gussey high in the air. I see him grinning as he began to fall. His arms came round and chopped the water. Yellow splashes flew, sharp as glass. His body went down cleanly.

The girls yelled their zowies, but after a little time became uncertain. "He's swimming under water," Joe explained. "You watch the other bank." Munro Gussey floated up. His buttocks surfaced like a jelly fish. Then his white back showed, and his pale head, spilling a fan of blood on the water.

Beak Wyatt had run. I saw him sprinting high-kneed to the gate. Duggie and I started down to the board. We made jerky progress; we believed, and could not believe, and did not know what to do.

Joe ploughed out to his friend. "There's no water here." It came as high as our waists as we went in to help him. He turned his face at the sky. "There's no water."

23

"The tide's out," Duggie said. "We thought you knew."

We wrestled Munro Gussey up the bank and laid him on the rug. The girls hovered. "Gus," they whispered.

"Jesus, Jesus," Joe cried. He was in a rage and he was weeping. The girl in the yellow togs knelt beside Gus and stroked his face. She got a handkerchief from her purse and dabbed the top of his head.

"Don't touch him," Joe yelled. He went down on his knees and looked at the wound. A cut like the split in a melon showed in the crown of Gus's head. Blood oozed in his pale hair. Joe felt the back of his neck. "There's a lump there big as my fist. Jesus," he yelled at the sky, "there was supposed to be water." He walked away and knelt in the grass. Then he jumped up. "We've got to get a saw-bones." He started to run to his jeep.

"I'm coming too, Joe," cried the girl in the red bathing suit. Her bottom wobbled as she ran. Her friend looked round wildly and half rose to her feet. "They're going."

"They're getting a doctor. I think I'd better—"

Duggie beat me to it. There seemed to be space behind his eyes. He took a dozen backward steps from Gus. "I'm not staying here." Grass tangled his feet and made him lurch, but he scrambled four-legged. "I'll show you where."

When the jeep had gone the girl sank on to her knees. She looked at Gus and she looked at me. "I was with Joe." She began to cry, rocking back and forth as though doing exercises. She cried with closed eyes, through a mouth shut tightly, making a steady hum, an insect buzz. Joe's cap was sitting on her hair. I saw she was not pretty—her prettiness was gone. Red spots stood out around her mouth. I wanted to tell her to use her handkerchief but she kept it in her fist, down on her thigh, where it smeared her skin with blood. Once she leaned at Gus and slipped her fingers under his neck. Then she set up her rocking again, and her buzzing grief.

I started to ease away. I did not like being tangled up in this, I thought it unfair; and I was wild with Duggie for leaving me. I felt hollowed out every time I looked at the man on the rug, so I let my eyes go quickly over him, and collected a series of images:

his eyes staring up with a faraway look; the wound in his head, oozing like a boil; and the lump on his neck, white and shiny as an egg. I remember his name tag lying in the damp hair on his chest. His fingers were broken and their nails bleeding. But the little finger on one of his hands was bent back at an angle and the nail there was a lady's, white as milk and beautifully clean.

I soft-footed away. "Don't go," said the girl. Every time I moved she spoke again. "I didn't want to come. My friend made me." So I shuffled up and down. I edged around her, careful not to step on the rug. She was young, I saw with fright, not an adult. She could not have been more than seventeen. But she held me. It was as if every time I moved she reached out and gripped me in my chest. I felt if I ran away she would make me die.

I straightened the edge of the rug. I picked bottle tops up in my toes and lobbed them into the water. The yells of children came from Moa Park. I thought that was wrong. I walked on the diving board and looked at the canoes nosing in the rapids.

When we heard the jeep coming the girl jumped up and collected the beer bottles. She hid them behind the changing sheds. Joe and Doctor Walker ran down to the rug. Duggie was not there. Another car arrived. He was not in that one either. I watched for a while, circling away, and heard Doctor Walker say Gus was dead. The girls walked to the jeep, holding each other. Joe stood with his hands on his hips, staring at The Pool and talking to himself. Gus was covered up. No one took any notice of me.

At the top of the bank I turned and ran. I ran through the main street of Loomis and along Millbrook Road. I came charging into the kitchen. "Where's Duggie?" I yelled at my mother.

"What's the matter, Raymie? You look flushed."

"Where is he?"

"Heavens, I don't know. Go and wash your face."

When I saw him next he looked at me with his eyes distended. "I didn't want to be in the way. There were plenty of people there." He did not know whether he was lying or telling the truth. I saw his face change like that of a person who has

25

picked up something ordinary from the ground, and rubs it, and sees it shine.

4 We told our story to the Loomis constable. He wrote it down on sheets of yellow paper.

"Now, you saw him go on the board?"

"I didn't know he was going to dive. I thought he was going to bounce."

We agreed on that; even Beak Wyatt, with Adam's apple jumping. The constable went tsk, tsk and looked at us sadly. There was nothing he could do so he sent us home.

My mother hovered over me for a while. She thought that seeing a man die might scar me mentally. She worked me into a state of tears about this young American dying so far from home. I felt better after it. I'd done something to please her, passed a test.

Tears marked the stations of our day. She cried in the morning and at night, and at intervals between. My mother was coming to terms. What she felt was less than a cosmic grief but more than private. My father had gone off to the war before his papers came—that was one thing. And mankind had gone mad and killing was everywhere. She had taken my grandfather's faith in man's becoming Man, but in her it was sentimental, it had no under-pinning, it was simply an image of Man and Woman, naked and sexless, walking into the Dawn. She cancelled it and could discover nothing to fill herself with. I find myself wanting to use her language. It was full of cuts and wounds and fractures and dark night.

Before long she had what used to be known as a nervous breakdown. For six months we had to tiptoe round her. She lay in her bed, she drifted about the house. She sat on the floor and tears dripped in her lap. Bobby and Becky and I did our best. We knew she might go mad and that placed a terrible weight on every word we spoke. Grandpa tried hard too. He was impatient of "female matters" but saw that this was more. For the first time in his life he made his own cup of tea. Becky did the cooking. She was twelve. Aunt Esther came as often as she could and Aunt Mirth now and then, or sent one of her older girls to help. And my mother, by some means unknown to me, began to get well.

Bluey Considine lent her his gramophone. In the evenings she sat on the back veranda looking down at the creek and played *Lindy Lou* over and over. Each time it came to an end she felt a little less, a little better.

> Lindy, did you hear dat mockin' bird sing las' night?
> Honey, he was singin' so sweet in de moo-onlight.

Paul Robeson: one of the gods in her pantheon. The flatness in his voice increased its feeling. When the record ended she lit a cigarette—a Camel from Esther—and smoked a while. She rested her hand on mine where I sat in the other seagrass chair. Then she leaned to the little table and wound the gramophone.
"What a wonderful voice, Ray."
Scratch went the needle.

> Lindy, did you hear dat mockin bird.

She had believed in this and was looking as one looks at old photographs.

> I'd lay right down and die
> If I could sing like dat bird sings to you-oo,
> My little Lindy Lou-oo.

Tears trickled on her cheeks. She squashed them matter-of-factly "Well Ray, I think we've had enough of that. What would you like?"
I chose *Phil the Fluter's Ball* and we had a laugh.
"But remember Ray, there's another side. Life is beautiful."
My lesson for the night. "Go to bed now." As I changed into my pyjamas I heard *Lindy Lou* again.
Aunt Esther took my mother to parties. She went as though to the dentist. And when Esther brought Yanks to Peacehaven

27

on Sunday afternoons and they sat on the lawn drinking Dally wine Mum would come up to the house and sit in the kitchen with her put-upon look. "I wish she'd take them home." But when she went back she laughed and smoked and drank and enjoyed herself. Once a Yank who looked like Errol Flynn tried to kiss her. "Please Bob, I don't want that." She tried to get her hand free but he held on hard. I looked at him murderously. If my father were home he would knock him into the middle of next week.

I knew what went on. In spite of her talk about the love of husbands and wives being beautiful and pure and not having a great deal to do with bodies I knew that with her body she had done it with my father. I was proof of that. And with the novels and poetry on her bedroom shelf was *Married Love* done up in brown paper like a recipe book. I had sneaked along by her bed and read it, cover to cover. Marie Stopes had the trick of sliding away from things; but I made out in spite of her exactly what adults did. I was sickened and excited.

So I watched the Yank Duggie and I called Errol. He was not going to get my mother. I thought of writing to Dad but felt if I worried him he might be careless and a German sniper would shoot him. I prowled from my bed in the night, making sure that Errol was out of the house. I crept along to my mother's window and peered at her white bed floating on the night. She was alone. Her hair made a smudge on the pillow. Once I heard her weeping. Once I heard her snore.

And one night she said to me, "Go back to bed, Raymie. Everything's all right now."

After that things were almost all right. She managed to get through her day without those tears that began so deep in her they seemed to come out black. She did some spur-of-the-moment crying of course: for a broken plate, for a kitchen range that would not draw properly. Errol went back to the war. My mother kept on smoking, and drank a glass of wine now and then. I took that hard and dared to mention it. She spoke of moderation and the power of the mind over appetites. But she had made a puritan of me and could not undo it.

When I visited Grandma Sole, which I did once a week—Mum insisted—she asked me how "poor Meg" was getting on. She hammered questions into me like tacks. "Does she have many visitors?" "Do any of them ever stay all night?" I don't know what she wrote to Dad, but if he had been killed I would have blamed her. She never left off working when I called, and made me follow with a bucket as she washed the ceilings—tiny, spindly, at the top of her ladder—and made me turn the wringer while she fed in clothes. If I sat down she was at me with a duster, wiping the arm of my chair, and while I ate a biscuit was kneeling at my feet brushing up crumbs. As a treat she would let me have five minutes in the front room.

It was a box, ten by ten; but for us, Aladdin's cave. It was her treat as much as mine. She softened in there, she blossomed. She never turned the light on and never drew back the curtains. Clack went the door behind us. I heard her breathe. Her eyes shone in the dark, her face opened like a flower. And the room took on a magic for me. The firescreen, the tongs, poker, andiron, gleamed like gold. The knick-knacks on the china cabinet were rich as the crown jewels; and the crockery inside—plates like shells, cups like butterflies—seemed to me the finest in the world. I could not imagine the king and queen having better.

"See, Ray. Here's your great-grandma and pa. And this is Ted and me on our wedding day." Whiskery great-grandpa, great-grandma black and lacy, as stuck-up as Queen Victoria. I thought I was special having them. The wedding photo—well, it was interesting: Grandpa Sole like a forward missing the match and Grandma thin as pea-sticks, neat as a doll. She was the kitchen Grandma Sole, not the front room one.

I touched the "sweet", sat primly, fingers folded, in a chair. She sat in the one next to it—"just for a jiffy"—smiled and wrapped her arms around herself. Then she was up and lifting the lid of her box. I took the other end. We leaned it on the wall and gazed on the treasures—rolls of linen, heavy as folded lead and cold as stone; towels of pink and blue and royal purple; embroidered pillow cases; embroidered table cloths with birds and roses. Lace like spider webs. It seemed right to me they were in the box and never came out.

"I've never showed your mum these."

We went out quietly and closed the door. Ha!—we let our breath out and blinked in the light. Then her face began to close. A sharpness came on her. She saw something that needed doing, and rushed at it, and snapped at me, "Don't get under my feet, boy. Go and see your grandpa in the garden. He wants some weeding done."

I went, with a last glance at the door. I'm glad I never saw that room with the light on.

Grandpa Sole did not want weeding done. Today when people say "your grandfather", it's Grandpa Plumb they mean, but Ted Sole who comes into my mind. He may not stay there long but he comes first. I see his grimy head and porous cheeks and granite chin. His hairy ears. His body clothed in railway black. He was a great block of a man and he stands at one side of my childhood like a wall I could lean against. He had little clear blue eyes. I wonder if I loved him so much because I did not have to share him with Duggie. He was a railway blacksmith. Soot was in his scalp and forehead, in his nose and cheeks. It was deep in his hands like a million black prickles. I longed to take a needle and dig them out.

Grandpa Sole showed me what order might achieve. At the back of his railway house was a patch of garden made with a fierce geometry. Everything was there, space and angle; and last year, next year, in his head. He had less than a quarter acre but no farmer knew the seasons better than Ted Sole. Order, knowledge, patience. He would not have cared for my language. All he did was what his old man did. Deep digging, natural manures, plenty of air round the roots. And squash them snails. And move your plants around son. Cabbages here one year, over there the next. I went out with him, riding in his barrow, and climbed the hilly paddocks around Loomis. I prised up crusted cow-pats from the grass while he scooped up the wet ones in his shovel. We made liquid manure in an oil drum. And squashed butterfly eggs. And staked tomatoes, trained the runner beans. I folded back the sacks where he bred worms and counted them out in dozens and planted them like seeds in the earth.

One day we boiled water in Grandma's copper and washed three dozen bottles till they sparkled in the sun. In the garden shed we bottled his home brew. I used the capper he had made at work: set a silver crown on each brown bottle, gave a press with all my body in it, felt a firm resistance and a beautiful give, and was fulfilled. I could have stayed there working with him forever.

But Grandma Sole came out and sent me home. "What are you doing Ted, letting the boy see that beer?"

"Now mother, it's all right."

"It is not all right. He'll tell those wowsers round there. That Reverend and that Meg."

"Mum drinks wine."

"She does? How much? Who with? Does some man bring it for her?"

"Now mother, don't ask the boy questions. Get off home, Ray. Come and help me next weekend. I know where we can get some horse manure."

I went home to that Meg and that Reverend. Bobby and Becky. Duggie Plumb. They were in a different world from Ted Sole's world, where hidden things, tears and violence, suddenly leaped on you. It was more real in the end. It was where I had to live.

For a spell of several months Duggie stayed with us at Peacehaven. There was, I heard, trouble at the orchard—something Uncle Willis was up to. "More of his shenanigans," Mum said. That did not sound too bad and I could not see why Duggie had to come. But although Mum never cared for him she thought I spent too much time alone. She had become suspicious of solitude. "Things" happened when you were by yourself and company was a kind of medicine.

So Duggie came and shared my room and was like a piece of grit in my eye. He chipped round the edges of our family. When he watched and turned away I knew he was grinning. And some piece of our behaviour that I had never given any thought to was

31

in question. I came to doubt my mother. Was she right? Was she, even, good? While Duggie was with us I began to see she was not pretty. I saw her crooked teeth and skinny throat. I blushed at the little belches she hid behind her hand. And when she said, "That's not a table topic," I had to join Duggie in a smirk.

He did not know he was damaging me. He did not know that in another way he made me free. He had no plan, no programme. Anarchy was as natural to him as affection was to Grandpa Sole.

I asked him what the trouble was at home. "Dad's rooting some sheila in town. Mum beats him up when he comes home."

At school I would have been at him for details. But in our living-room I shied away. It was as if I'd caught him doing his job on the hearthmat. Next day when I was ready he chewed his nails and looked at me dark-eyed and turned away.

He was built like his father: short legs, big behind. (Cartoonists came to label it G.N.P. and stuck a little head and limbs on it.) At school he was Plumbum, a name you pressed like a button: he went berserk and fought with a monkey gabble and spit frothing on his mouth. I ran for his brother Cliff, who saved him and washed his face with water. Then Duggie went away and hid himself. I hunted in the dunnies and slit trenches but he pelted me with clay, he climbed on the seat and punched me when I looked over the wall.

Bluey Considine heard of our fights and tried to teach us how to box. He showed us the English style, straight left, right cross, and the Yankee crouch. Five minutes of it had him purple-faced. He sat in his chair and talked about the fighters he had known. "Say we're in a pub. Now, who was the first New Zealander to win a world boxing title?"

"Bob Fitzsimmons."

"The Freckled Wonder."

"You're a pair of ignoramuses. He was second. The first one was Torpedo Billy Murphy, the Little Tailor. He knocked out Spider Weir in San Francisco, 1890. I knew Ike Weir. He was a Belfast man. And too good for Billy. He made a fool of him.

Turned a somersault, danced a jig, and kicked him in the bum.
Then he'd give him the left and give him the right. Poor Billy
didn't know what town he was in. But he kept on swinging and
in the thirteenth Ike walked into one. He never saw it coming.
Billy put him down five times and in the fourteenth knocked
him out stone cold. I can still see Ike's head banging on the
canvas. So the Little Tailor was featherweight champion of the
world. He was the first. Now if we were in a pub you'd owe me a
beer."

Duggie loved those tales, those fighters Bluey had seen in the
States in the 1890s, and loved their names; and I liked them.
The kids at school never knew what we were talking about as we
sparred around the playground shouting, "Here's Young Griffo.
Here's Little Chocolate. Here's the Nonpareel. Here's George La
Blanche, the pivot puncher." Duggie practised the solar plexus
punch, Bob Fitzsimmons' favourite. "When Fitz knocked out
Jim Corbett he got him with the solar plexus punch," Bluey
said, "and Corbett lay there paralysed while the referee counted
him out. He heard it all. One, two, three. "

'They've just got to lie there watching," Duggie said.

Sutton also drew him to the cottage. Sutton was hump-
backed and club-footed. Bluey had picked him up somewhere
and taken him under his care and Sutton had a pure love for
Bluey and an impure passion. We never knew of that but sensed
something black in him, some cause beyond his hump and foot
for his hatreds and his bitterness. Sutton had a head too large for
him. His legs were jockey's legs and his hands wide as dinner
plates. His mouth and gums were red as rubber. One of his eyes
was tea-coloured and the other baby-blue. Here was a bogeyman
handy to my door but I was never scared of him. Though once or
twice he chased me in my dreams in the daytime he was only a
joke. But Duggie found more than that in him. And something
in Duggie gave Sutton pauses in his bitterness.

"Round the back with Roger," Bluey said. "They're doing
the snails." He looked at me sadly. "I wouldn't go round there."

I crept to the corner. There were Sutton and Duggie, squatting one each side of the chopping block. Duggie had a biscuit

tin in his hand. I had seen Sutton with it in the garden hunting snails but never thought about what happened to them. Duggie took them out one by one and put them on the block, where Sutton hit them with a hammer. "Forty-three," Duggie said. He scraped the remains off with a garden trowel. "This one's a baby." "Doesn't matter what they are, the buggers," Sutton said. Duggie's face and Sutton's shirt were splashed with bits of snail. Their mouths were set in grins. "You said I could do the last one," Duggie said. Sutton gave him the hammer. "That's a granddaddy. That's the boss. You kept him on purpose."

I backed away and sat with Bluey. "He's a strange one, Roger. I think I'll have a chat with the Reverend." We went up together. "Don't tell Meg about the snails."

Uncle Willis "came to his senses" and Duggie went home. It was too soon. Mirth and Willis had been happy, and would be happy again. She had not worried about his women when she knew he liked her best; and when they were old they became infatuated with each other. But Willis was in his mid-forties and jumping out of his skin. Mirth was close to sixty. He explained to her that she should be thinking of other things. He told her how young women affected him; and, kindly, that she had done that to him not long ago. He advised her to enjoy her memories.

I waited for Duggie on Millbrook Road the morning after he left. I knelt among the pine-roots ready to ambush him. He came along barefooted, carrying his books and lunch in a cut-down sugarbag. I shrank into the roots, for Duggie was crying. Tears made slug tracks on his face. He stood in the dust ten feet away and threw stones at the insulators on a power pole. He threw with a quiet ferocity, broken only by sobs and gluey sniffs. Grey heads of snot slid from his nose and he sniffed them back. He was throwing there five minutes. Then one of his stones hit a cup and chips of porcelain rained down. Duggie wiped his nose on his forearm. He picked his sugarbag up and walked on. I did not come out of the roots until he was over the bridge into Loomis. I knew he would kill me.

He told me nothing about his life at home. But one day Mum sent me up to the orchard with a message and I saw. It was four

miles up the road, a walk through yellow cuttings and gorse
fields. The road crossed a railway line and passed a Dally vine-
yard, where the old Dally was out shooting blackbirds with his
shotgun. After that it climbed into the hills. Willis's orchard lay
on a north-facing slope. It *looked* like the Garden of Eden. I went
along a drive through trees so green and glossy they seemed to be
modelled in wax. The house increased my sense of unreality. It
was a railway carriage, blue and red, with lean-tos stuck on it.
Mirth was in the yard with babies.

My mother made a myth of Mirth and Willis. That pair
always made her soft and blind. They had the same effect on
Grandpa Plumb. He elevated the orchard into a temple and
found there natural wisdom, lessons in acceptance and fruitful-
ness. Mirth was priestess/Mother. He thought those naked
children in the trees—"dryads, fauns"—were Mirth's, but they
were grandchildren of her first marriage, and later on of her
second.

As for natural wisdom.

I gave Mum's note to Mirth and went looking for Duggie. I
found him in a shed in the grapefruit trees, sweeping the floor
with a witch's broom. For a moment he looked as if he would
take to me, but I told him about my message and he calmed
down.

"Who sleeps here?"

"Dad." When he had finished the floor he made the bed.
"Mum's kicked him out of the house." He began to fold clothes
heaped on a chair. I saw in his eyes the black fall into emptiness I
had seen when Munro Gussey died. "I tidy it up so Mum'll think
he's done it."

"Ah," I said.

"There's a tap up at the tank-stand. Give that cup a rinse.
Don't let her see you."

I did as I was told. When the shed was tidy we went into the
trees and lay in the grass. "He's got another sheila. She's only
thirty-five."

"That's old."

He gave me a look of contempt. He was years ahead of me in

many things. "He told Mum he can't keep his hands off her
He's in his prime."

That gave me a picture of Willis hanging naked on a hook like
a side of beef. I was still contemplating it when Mirth's shouting
started.

"Jesus," Duggie said, "he's home." He ran through the trees.
When I came to the yard he was hopping round them, making
cries. Willis was on his knees—not easy for him with his
peg-leg. His hands were praying. Mirth knocked his hat off with
a swipe. His head shone bald in the sun and she cracked her
knuckles on it.

"Look at him. What woman would want him?" She was
flopping in her clothes, her breasts and buttocks jumping.

Two of her girls came out of the house. "Come on, Mum.
Don't bother with him," but they looked amused.

"It's in my nature. I can't help myself," Willis whined.

Mirth slapped his face.

"Yes, I deserve it. Hit me again."

"He's got her on his pants," Mirth screamed. "He hasn't even
done his filthy fly up."

"Mirth dear, Mirth. "

"Mum, Dad," Duggie squeaked. His eyes were popping from
his head.

"I'm going to cut it off. She's not having it." She rushed into
the house, scattering babies.

The two girls, Irene, Melva, took Willis's arms and heaved
him up. "She means it, Dad. You'd better start running."

"Dad, Dad, lock yourself in the shed," Duggie wept.

Mirth burst out of the house. She tumbled down the steps and
fell on her knees. The carving knife in her hand glinted in the
sun.

"Dad," Duggie screamed.

Irene gave Willis a push. "Go," she laughed. Willis started
running, hopping, away. He went behind the tank-stand and
came round the other side, but found Mirth crouching there. Her
knife flashed as she swung it like a sickle. He backed away and
tumbled down a slope into the trees, rolling like a boy. Irene was

42   36

shrieking with laughter, and Melva, laughing too, tried half-heartedly to take Mirth's arm. Mirth pushed her away and started down the slope. Duggie got in front of her. Tiny sounds came out of his mouth. Mirth hit him back-handed. She ran into the trees, where Willis was flitting like a satyr. His peg-leg tangled in the grass and down he went and banged his head on a tree-trunk. Mirth stood over him. "Ha!" she cried, ripping at his stained fly with her hand. He wriggled round the trunk like a swollen snake, and was up and off again, making cries and plunging in the leaves. He had forgotten the shed but it came at him and knocked him flat. Mirth tumbled over him. The knife stabbed the wall. She tugged it out two-handed and turned her great balloon face at her husband. But he was gone. He had crawled round the corner and in at the door of the shed and as Mirth came rushing he slammed it in her face and bolted it.

Mirth went berserk. She stabbed the door. She kicked it. She hit it with her side and with her bottom. "Mirth love, Mirth," Willis cried. The shed was rocking. She left her knife embedded in the door and found a length of four by two and smashed the window in. She hurled the wood at Willis, pale on the other side. "Mirth my love, have a snooze and you'll soon feel better."

She ran up to the house. Irene and Melva, Duggie and I, waited by the door. We heard her heaving things around.

"She's going to chop the door down," Melva said.

But Mirth came back with an armful of firewood and some crumpled paper. She stacked it against the door.

"Gee whizz," Irene said.

Duggie fell on his knees. He wept into his hands.

Mirth struck a match and lit the paper and flames climbed up the door.

"What's happening?" Willis cried, putting his head out the window. He sniffed the smoke. "Mirth, you're burning me."

She said nothing. A collapse was starting in her. Air rushed out her mouth with a whistling sound. Irene and Melva took her arms. Melva winked at me. They put their hands on Mirth and seemed to hold her in a piece. Carefully they walked her to the house, where a sound of wailing babies came. "You'd better do some wees on that," Irene said over her shoulder.

But it was Cliff, coming from somewhere, who threw a bucket of water on the fire. He pulled the knife out of the door, going tsk tsk tsk like a policeman.

Duggie went round to the window. His face was streaked with tears. I did not like the look of him. There was Willis, framed. He had a wild look in his eye, but he managed to smile.

"Dad," Duggie croaked.

Still I was the only one to see him.

"My word Duggie, how that woman loves me. She's a princess," Willis said.

5   That was one Duggie story I never told my fellow reporters in the Parliamentary Press Gallery. They often asked me for a Duggie story. I kept them short and I kept them clean. I mean, no sex; though they were keen for sex. I told them how Duggie dared anything. We had a friend at school, I said, who had a nasty habit. One day I dared Duggie to tell the teacher. He looked at me a moment, then put up his hand. "Please Miss Hoyle, Beak Wyatt's stuck a steelie up his bum."

They liked that one. A game grew out of it. "Please Mr Speaker, Keith Holyoake's dropped an aitch." "Please Mr Speaker, Norman Kirk's eating a pie."

And I told them one I called Duggie Plumb Practises Politics. It happened at Loomis school in standard six. Duggie and Beak and I and a couple of others were eating lunch in a corner of the playground when Duggie pulled a matchbox out of his pocket. He opened it and showed us a little heap of yellow flakes and bits of grit in one corner.

"That's just a week's worth," Duggie said.

"What is it?"

"Sleepers from my eyes."

I felt sick. I threw away the sandwich I was eating.

"Ha," Duggie laughed. "Arsehole doesn't feel good."

The others tried to prove they were no sissies. One of them bet he could get more. So Duggie got a competition going. We had a week. And no cheating, no dandruff.

I went in it too. I wasn't being left out. I even asked Becky for her sleepers and she told me what a filthy pig I was.

After a week the four of us got together and went to Duggie. Beak Wyatt had the biggest pile but none of us had done badly.

"What's this?" Duggie said.

"Our sleepers. Let's see yours."

"Sleepers?" Duggie said. "You mean sleepers from your eyes? You filthy buggers." He walked away.

We dropped our matchboxes in the rubbish tin. No one ever mentioned them again.

The gallery boys liked that one too. Some of them loved it. "My God, he'll make Prime Minister one day."

After Loomis school I saw less of Duggie. We went to Rosebank College, half an hour's ride on the train, and there Duggie took a commercial course, book-keeping in place of my French and Latin. I wasn't as "smart" as Duggie but Mum told me I had a better mind. Rosebank College was in its first year. The Americans had built it as a hospital and the Education Department took it over in 1946. Our classrooms had been wards. The gym was made for indoor basketball. There was more light and air about than we had been used to, but no more than the usual amount in the teaching.

By late April the sports grounds were ready and we had a ceremony to open them. Only the day before, Ormiston, our headmaster, had sent the girls out of assembly and spent an hour lashing at us boys for moral filth. Someone had drawn dirty pictures on the lavatory walls. Sex, he glittered at us, leads to madness. These suicides you read about in the newspapers, they're all people who've been obsessed with sex. That's the way you boys will end up. We came out and pretended to swallow poison and jump off bridges. I played along, although it was no joke to me.

On the cold autumn day when the grounds were opened

Ormiston showed he was out to get us. He made us parade
barefooted, wearing shorts and singlets. The wind was blowing
over the new grass and asphalt courts as he introduced the
speaker, the Hon. H. G. R. Mason, Minister of Education. I felt
a little better that he was Labour but as he went on—our
privilege, our splendid grounds, the fine traditions we must
build—I started to hate him. I thought I was going to fall over.
The wind got up my shorts and made my balls shrink. Two rows
down I saw Duggie gritting his teeth. The boy beside me was
crying quietly. Ormiston's glasses caught the pale sun. Blue sky
looked at us, expressionless. The Hon. H. G. R. talked for forty
minutes. Then he smiled kindly and said he thought we were
getting cold and he'd better let us go. But these splendid
grounds, how privileged we were.

"Jesus," Duggie said, "I'm going to be a politician."

He hated Ormiston. He hated most of his teachers. I liked
mine. I even said Ormiston wasn't too bad—if he'd only smile.
He never smiled in the five years I was there. But he came to look
on Duggie with approval. Duggie managed it. We fell under his
notice on the same day. The school went into town to see *The
Way Ahead* at the Roxy Theatre in Queen Street. The war was
being kept alive for us and we approved of that if it meant going
to the pictures. Stanley Holloway and his platoon walked into
the desert smoke with bayonets fixed and faces ready. Comradeship. Heroism. My dad had done that. "They'll get their heads
shot off," Duggie said. We came out into the sun and lined up
for our trams and he talked me into sneaking down an alleyway
and spending the afternoon at the Tepid Baths. We hired togs
and splashed about in the warm salt water and when we looked
up there was Freddie Shanks our Phys. Ed. teacher smiling
down at us with gleaming teeth. Ormiston had sent him out to
round up Rosebank strays.

The suburbs rolled by in reverse. Freddie enjoyed himself.
"Any last messages for your folks?" He thrust us in by our necks
to face the moral glitter of Ormiston.

"Well, I'm disgusted. I'm appalled."

Then Duggie set about saving himself. He opened up his face.

His cheeks grew round and seemed to shine and his eyes grew larger. He stood up straight.

"It was my idea, sir."

"I don't believe that, Plumb."

Ormiston looked at me and I looked at the floor. In those years I was eaten with sexual guilt. Guilt was the big thing in my life. I knew I was filthy and doomed to madness. Meeting anyone's eye was more than I could manage. Glimpses showed me how Ormiston loathed me.

"We shouldn't have done it, sir. Not after that picture," Duggie said.

"I'm glad you understand, Plumb. But I think you were led astray. I don't know what to say to you, Sole. I wish I didn't have you in my school. I hope this punishment will be a lesson. Though I doubt it. Hold out your hand."

He hit me six times with his whippy cane. On the last blow I shrieked.

"Don't blubber, boy. Be a man."

Duggie got one hit.

"I advise you to seek out other company, Plumb. Cousins or not. Now clear out, both of you." He opened his windows.

Duggie and I walked side by side to the lavatories. "My fingers are broken," I wept.

He looked at them. "They'll be all right."

"Why did he give me six?"

"Search me."

We ran our hands under water. "You only got one."

"I told him it was my idea. It's not my fault if he didn't believe me. And you'd better stop crying. Teachers don't like it when you cry."

Nobody seemed to like it when you cried so I learned not to. Even Mum wasn't keen on it any more. Dad thought like Ormiston, men didn't do it. He would not let Mum write to him about my swollen hand. I'd taken a chance and been caught and that was that.

It was good having Dad home. I found that I'd remembered him pretty well and I got used to him being not so big and more

41

bad tempered. I could not talk to him about the thing that worried me—tortured me—but I took his company as a holiday. I went with him to his parents' house and sat on the lawn with him and Grandpa Sole while they drank home brew. Dad let me have half a glass and I seemed to glimpse as I took it that what was happening on the lawn was true and the world outside was full of lies and that I might come out of my pain and find that I was not sick after all. I leaned on my elbow like a man, sipped my beer—finding it sour but not saying so—and listened to Dad and Grandpa talk about plumbing. Dad was trying to start up in business and he wanted to ask his brother-in-law Fred Meggett for a loan. Grandpa was against it. He advised Dad to save his money and do things on his own. In his opinion Meggett was a crook. It was the middle of the war surplus scandal. Surplus made Fred rich—jeeps and G.M. trucks, and piles of "scrap" that turned out to be worth thousands of pounds. Fred bought cheap and sold dear and soon he was swimming in money. It was spectacular, and very fishy, and a Royal Commission had been set up to look into it. "Keep away from him, son. You'll get tarred with the same brush," Grandpa said. Dad frowned and fidgeted. He stood up and practised cricket strokes. His wrists and arms and legs and pale blue eyes and jet-black hair made me think him tough and dangerous. I could not see Fred Meggett ever getting the better of him.

We rode our bicycles home past the shunting yards and the jam factory and freewheeled down to Millbrook Road with our hands dangling at our sides. All along Millbrook Road we competed making skid marks. Becky and Bobby were on the lawn with tennis rackets, practising lobs over the summer-house. Dad rode off the drive at Becky, trying to grab the ball. She gave a shriek and tumbled him into the rhododendrons. We went into a tangle, struggling for the ball. Our yells brought Mum out to the veranda, holding her breast. "Oh Becky, come out of that. You look like.   " Becky, flushed and shrieking, gave Dad a shove that sent him tumbling almost to the creek. She darted off with the ball and Bobby brought her down with an ankle tap. I wrestled him over the top of her and the three of us rolled into the wall of the summer-house, where Grandpa Plumb was sleeping with his handkerchief over his face.

"You'll wake Dad," Mum cried.

"A buzz-bomb wouldn't wake him," Dad said, stealing the ball. He ran over the bridge into the orchard with us at his heels. We ended rolling in the swamp and had to hose each other in the garden, where Mum caught us.

"Fergus, you! I'll never understand you. And Becky, look at you. You're supposed to be a lady."

"Who told you that?"

"Ray, I thought you had more sense."

Dad gave her a squirt with the hose and she fled into the house. He had an instinctive wisdom with her. That wetting made her part of us and though she ran away she was humming a tune when we came into the kitchen.

She sent me down to bring Grandpa in. He had not wakened though his handkerchief lay on his chest like a bib. The lace of one of his sandshoes was undone and I tied it up. His eyes shot open, fierce and lonely. He touched my head. "You're a good boy, Raymond." He seemed to have grown very old lately and his statements of approval and disapproval were mundane. They kept the weight of moral dogma though. I saw even at fourteen that his was a simple view of things.

Lunch. I made the shape with my mouth.

"Mealtimes are a great robber of time. Sleep," he said, seeing my objection, "there's a better nourishment than food. Sleep that knits up the ravell'd sleave of care. *Macbeth.* You know that play? Well, you'll come to it." He took my arm and we went along by the rose garden, where he stopped to sniff a bloom. "Roses are the most beautiful flowers." More dogma. If I had disagreed he would have been outraged.

Mum sat him at the head of the table. Sunday lunch she termed "a family time" and she made him join us. He took all other meals in his study, which never seemed to strike him as unusual. His hatred of tyrannies did not extend into the home. Mum did not have the energy, or even the desire, to make more

43

than small dents in his comfort. But she would not let Becky even rinse a cup for him.

Dad carved the roast. "George?" He put the browned first cut on Grandpa's plate. It happened every Sunday, and still we resented it. Grandpa never ate more than a bite and the rest sat on his plate oozing juice till the end of the meal. Then the cat got it. Mum saw to that. Eating scraps from other people's plates might be all right for Bluey Considine but we were supposed to be civilized beings.

We ate, remembering our manners. Gentility had infected us through Mum and though she struggled to be free, Sunday lunch brought a flush like fever on her cheeks at the "niceness" of her family. We passed the salt and passed the gravy boat. We remembered not to rub our hands and say how good the food looked.

Grandpa was outside this. He ate as much as he wanted, then he stopped. He dabbed his lips with his serviette and drank from his glass of water. He did not bring his ear trumpet to table but now and then dropped some remark into our talk. Sometimes they were to the point. Seeing Mum angrily wiping a gravy spot from the cloth—"A man—or woman, Meg—is as big as the things that annoy him." And to Becky, holding out her bowl: "The hunger of a fresh young heart." It had affection but it had an edge. He said to me, "The sick dog refuses all food." My heart began to thump. I wondered what he knew. "I'm not sick." But he was looking into the distance at some landscape none of us could see. He had this way of coming and going. "World, world, I cannot get thee close enough."

"Jesus," Bobby muttered, turning up his eyes.

"Prithee, let no bird call," Grandpa said. "Meg dear, may I be excused? That was a lovely meal." And off he went to his study to scribble something down, leaving us sniggering; confused; or in a state of wonder.

In the afternoon Esther and Fred Meggett called to see us. We went out to the lawn and sat in the sun. I lay a little way off, brooding on Grandpa's remark. Mum had set Becky to watch the Meggett child, Adrian, but he seemed to like me better and he came and sat on my chest. Esther leaned over and gave him a sip of wine.

"Esther," Mum protested.

"No harm in it. Get off your cousin you little horror."

"He's all right," I said.

"You'd sooner have a girl cuddling up. Tell me about your girls, Raymond."

"I haven't got any."

"You're leaving it a bit late. What do you do, just think about them in bed?"

I looked at her with horror. How had she known?

"Thinking's O.K. But doing's a lot more fun." She breathed wine on me and I found I was getting an erection. I rolled over and lay on my stomach. Adrian went sprawling. Esther stood him up and grinned at me. "Get a girl. I'll bet you're big enough."

"Leave him alone," Mum said. "He's got plenty of time."

"Now's the time," Esther said, but she left off tormenting me and listened to Fred telling Dad about the Royal Commission. It was in recess for a day or two.

"They've got nothing on me. I just knew good business when I saw it. It's the civil servants getting it in the neck."

"What are you going to do with all your loot?" Mum said.

"Wouldn't you like to know."

"Tell her, Fred."

"I'm going to build Loomis."

Mum looked puzzled but Dad sat up straighter.

"Shops," Fred said. "The city's got no place to go except out here. So I've taken an option on the land between the bridges. Two years time you won't know Loomis."

"Who's going to do the building?" Dad asked.

"Me. I'm starting my own construction company."

"You don't know anything about building."

"I'll buy people who do know. Might be some plumbing in it, Fergie."

"Fergus is happy where he is," Mum said.

"Don't miss your chance, boy. You mightn't ever get another one."

"I'd have to.   " Dad said.

"I know what you'd have to do. So come and talk to me. What's a family for?"

"Listen to him!" Esther said. "But if you can show him some way to make money you're in Fergie."

Bluey Considine walked by on his way to visit Grandpa. He raised his hat. "Meg. Esther Becky Gentlemen."

"That old bugger owes me fifty quid," Fred said.

"Slow horses," Esther laughed. "You'll never see it."

"He's under Meg's protection."

"Remember that. I won't have betting."

"I've written it off, Meg. I'm in the big time now. Going places."

"I'm going too," Esther cried. She swallowed wine and winked at me. "Here's a cobber of yours. Tell me what the pair of you talk about."

It was Duggie, coming uncertainly over the lawn. Esther had her usual effect on him. While everybody looked at him I scuttled to the creek, hiding my condition. Duggie came after me when they let him go. I was all right by then.

"What's the matter? What did you clear out for?"

"I can't stand that Esther "

"Me neither Fat bitch. Is anyone in the house?"

"Grandpa and Bluey."

We went into the living-room. Duggie loved getting in there, especially when no one was about. He poked at things and weighed them in his hands. His eyes gleamed with desire but he kept a sneer on his mouth and threatened to smash vases and tear books. We had nothing grand; no treasures, real or supposed. Unlike Grandma Sole's front room ours was for living in. But something in it drove Duggie wild. He called it stuck-up and called it pansy He kicked the chairs and joggled ornaments on the mantel piece.

"Lay off, Duggie."

"I suppose you'll get all this one day."

"Why should I? Bobby'll get it."

"You'll get this house. You'll be rich." He jerked the edge of a picture, setting it askew. I ran to straighten it.

"Lay off."

He went into the hall and listened outside the study. "There's no one in there. You stand guard."

"No. " But he was gone, bent at the waist, tip-toeing. My world began to tremble, then was still. I put my head in at the door and saw Duggie moving round Grandpa's desk trying the drawers.

"Duggie. " I wanted him to go on. I wanted him to defile the study. He flicked things in a drawer and gave a grunt.

"Where does he keep his sovereigns?"

"I don't know."

"Maybe they're in here." He picked up Grandpa's trumpet from the desk and looked in it. "Empty. Hey, I reckon you could piss through this." He stuck it on the front of his trousers. I gave a burst of laughter. Duggie grinned. He put the trumpet to his eye and tried to look at the shelves. "You reckon he's got any hot books here?"

"I don't think so." I was deep in betrayal. "Mum and Dad have got one in their bedroom."

But Duggie was skimming along the titles. "It's all dry stuff." He went to Grandpa's Buddha and looked at it. "This joker eats too much. He's not made of gold is he?"

"Brass."

"Who are these sheilas?" He had come to a row of plaster figurines.

"Goddesses. Minerva. Venus. Diana's the one with the bow."

"Venus has got nice tits." He fingered them.

I had a touch of my trouble and turned away. Duggie looked at the books climbing to the ceiling. He mounted half-way up Grandpa's steps and stood looking round. "All this must be worth thousands of quids."

"I suppose so."

"Yeah," he said bitterly. "Jesus, I'd like to smash this place up."

I saw that he might come down and begin. I might help him.

47

But as I waited he climbed to the top of the steps and sat down. "I'm going to have a place like this one day."

"Let's get out, Duggie."

"I like it here." He put the trumpet to his mouth and blew a fart.

"He'll come back."

It was too late. Grandpa's voice sounded in the hall. I nearly fainted. But Duggie only gave a blink. He climbed down the steps and set the trumpet on the desk. "Get one, quick," he said, snatching a book. I grabbed one, not knowing why. "Read, you stupid bugger."

Grandpa came through the door. It was not Bluey with him but Wendy Philson. "Hallo," Grandpa said, "a visitation." He came in, frowning, then started looking pleased. "You see Wendy, books are a magnet to the young."

Duggie raised his head and blinked his eyes. "Grandpa."

"What are you reading? Ah, Wordsworth. The Child is father of the Man, eh Wendy? And what about Raymond?" He turned to me and took my book. "Ovid? I didn't know your Latin was that good."

"He was reading it upside down too," Wendy said. Grandpa went to his desk and picked up his trumpet.

"You kids get out while the going's good," Wendy said.

We started for the door. "Boys. Whenever you want a book come and see me. But I don't recommend Ovid, Raymond."

"No, Grandpa."

"Thank you, Grandpa." Duggie made oriental bows.

"Scram," Wendy said softly.

"Boys. Ask when you want to come in. Many of these books are valuable."

"Yes. Sorry. Thank you. Goodbye."

We got out and ran up the orchard. Duggie rolled in the grass and laughed his head off. "Jesus, he's a stupid old bugger. Jesus, we fooled him."

I lay in the grass and said nothing. I did not know what I thought, or what I felt, or even who I was. I loved and hated Grandpa. I loved and hated Duggie. I was terrified of myself and fascinated with myself. I wished that I was dead, but soon ate an apple and was happy. I joked with Duggie.

When we came down Aunt Esther asked if we'd taken measurements.

6 Dad and I bicycled round to the Soles with a paper bag of kumaras. Grandpa handled them like pieces of sculpture.

"Yes," he said, "beauties. I'll dig some potatoes for you, Fergus." They played a game of exchanging produce so that they might praise and boast.

We sat on the lawn drinking beer. Grandpa gave me a full glass now and I had learned to like the taste. Dad was happy. He had his own business at last. Fred Meggett had started him and Dad had done the plumbing in the Loomis shops. Then he had paid the loan back and was free. Mum stopped worrying and so did Grandpa Sole. He was proud of Dad. When it was time to go he dug a root of potatoes.

"Beauties," Dad said.

"You pick 'em up, Ray. I've been feeling a bit off colour."

I was putting the last ones in the bag when Grandpa fell down beside me. His face was bulging and his lips flapped like rubber. Dad got down on his knees and tried to hook Grandpa's false teeth out. "It's a heart attack. Get the doctor." Grandpa's heels went drumming in the earth. Then he was dead. It all happened in less than a minute. "Too late, son. Too late," Dad said to me. He crouched there looking at Grandpa's face.

"Help me get him on the lawn."

"Are you sure he's.   "

"I'm sure. You take his legs."

We carried Grandpa to the lawn and laid him down. Dad took out the false teeth and put them in his pocket. He wet his handkerchief at the garden tap and washed Grandpa's face.

"You wait here, Ray. I'm going to tell Mum."

I knelt beside Grandpa, and could make nothing of it. He looked like an old man sleeping. Grains of dirt were in his hair.

Dad came back with Grandma. She stood a little way off and looked at the body. Her face had gone thin but her eyes were dry.

"Bring him into the house."

Dad and I carried him again. He was heavy and loose and I made hard work of it. Grandma held the bedroom door open. She followed us in and turned the coverlet down.

"He's got dirt on him."

"Never mind."

She took off his boots, then sat on a chair by the bed and took his hand. Dad and I watched as she laid her cheek on it.

"Mum.   "

"Thank you, son. I'll be all right now."

"I'm going for the doctor. Ray will stay."

"It's too late for doctors."

"I'll get Meg."

"I don't want Meg."

"Mrs Cooper then."

"Or Mrs Cooper."

"He'll need washing."

"I'll wash him."

"Mum—"

"No one is touching Ted but me."

Dad drew me out of the room. He looked as if he had been struck in the throat and could not breathe. "You go home, Ray. There's nothing you can do."

So I cycled home to Peacehaven. I tried to feel something as I went but it took me two or three days to understand. Then I was faced with a great hole in that part of my life I'd been certain of. I circled round it trying to see in, and then backed off and looked for things to keep my mind off it. I felt shrunken and dry and felt there was a stranger in my skull laughing at me. What I had

50

loved was taken away. Ha, ha! He seemed to have my brain squeezed in his fist.

Mum had not known I cared so much for Grandpa Sole. I think she found it unreasonable; and possibly perverse, with Grandpa Plumb handy to admire. She was kind to me and we discussed death and the possibility of a life beyond, but reached no conclusions. Both of us were concerned with now. Usually she finished by jumping up and saying, "Well, I must do the dishes. Life goes on."

That was more wisdom than I could accept. But something or other, life and death, went on. Bobby was some help. He still gave me the Chinese burn. Now and then we caught a bus and went to a Saturday afternoon movie in town.

One day as we came out a voice murmured at our shoulders, "Enjoy the picture, boys?"

We turned and saw a man with a chest and throat both soft and strong, and a mouth that was my mother's, and the Spitfire-pilot eyes of Grandpa Plumb.

"You remember me, Bobby?"

"Sure," Bobby said, "you're Uncle Alf. I met you at Esther's."

"And this is Ray? Raymong. Has your mother told you about me, Ray?"

She had, and she had not. What I did not know made me blush, and Uncle Alf laughed. "You're charming when you blush. How would you boys like to have a milk shake?"

"Sure," Bobby said. He winked at me. We trooped off to a milk-bar and Bobby and I sat down while Uncle Alf bought our drinks.

"Is he.   ?"

"He's the pansy. The one Grandpa kicked out."

"We shouldn't—"

"Free milk shakes. Just make sure he keeps his hands on the table."

Uncle Alf did not stay with us long. He saw someone beckoning from the window. "I've got to go now, boys. But I'm often at the pictures on Saturday. We'll meet again. My love to your mum."

We met several times, then Bobby started Training College and was off after girls. Duggie and I got into the habit of Saturday movies. We played morning sport for Rosebank College, then took a bus or tram and headed for Queen Street. Duggie was after girls too and sometimes picked up a pair of them and dragged me off to milk bars, where I sat silent and miserable, listening to them giggle as he tried out double meanings.

Twice we met Uncle Alf. "So this is Duggie? What a tribe of nephews I've got. But what's that in your bags? Not muddy gear? You boys are really so masculine. I can see I'll have to take you in hand."

He was not usually like that. Just the sight of Duggie was enough to make him perform. It was, I think, a kind of self-defence. All the time he was with us he acted like a girl; and hurried away when he saw people watching from other tables.

"So that's a homo," Duggie said. "What a laugh."

"I don't think he actually—I don't think—"

"How dumb can you get? They suck each other. They go up each other's bums. Grandpa found him doing it in the orchard."

"No," I said. There was no Marie Stopes to make me believe that.

Next time we met, Duggie asked Alf for a loan.

"Money?"

"Sure. A couple of quid would do. I'm taking a girl out."

"A couple of quid! Well! A couple of shillings."

Duggie smiled at him. His ginger eyelashes made him look sleepy. "I haven't told anyone we've been meeting."

"Meeting?"

"On Saturday afternoons. You know? In milk bars."

"I see." Alf took out his wallet, trembling slightly. "Two 'quid', you say? I hope you have a nice time."

"I will." Duggie rolled the notes and slipped them like a pencil into his pocket. "So long Uncle Alf. Watch yourself, Ray." He whistled a tune as he went into the street.

"He'll go far," Alf said. "He'll be a great man one day."

I began to say I was sorry, but Alf stopped me. "It's not your fault. But that boy makes me shiver. I want to keep well away from him. You take my advice and do the same."

But Duggie, like Bobby, had had enough of my sort of Saturday. There was a natural falling into groups as we grew older and his was made up of boys with knowledge beyond their years. They knew all about sex, and the way the world worked, and knew exactly what they were after. I was in a place for discards; giving my superior grin but turning with bewilderment inside.

I still met Alf. Two or three times I went to his house—keeping it secret from Mum and Dad. We met in town and he drove me to Herne Bay. His friend, his lover, John Willis had died several years before and left his money to Alf—"I can spare two quid." Alf had bought an old villa and spent "far too much" doing it up. I sat in the living-room and talked to him, sipping a glass of wine that made all my secrets tumble out. I felt that Alf was an outcast like me. In the beginning my confessions were loaded down with contempt for us. He saw it and was angry, but kept quiet. And I got on the other side of contempt. I saw he understood me, I could say *everything* and not be judged, and relief made me break down and cry. He patted my back and left me alone for a while.

Then, with his glass topped up (and a shake of his head for me): "This manic organ of yours? Where does it happen?"

"Anywhere. In buses. At school. In my School Cert. maths exam."

"Did you pass?"

"Yes. It happens in the pictures all the time. When people kiss. And when I'm reading books. And when I'm eating. Sometimes I can't leave the table."

Alf laughed. "And Meg doesn't see? No, she wouldn't. What goes on in your head?"

"All sorts of things."

"Like what?"

I told him.

53

"Pretty hot stuff. Ha, saying it's given you a stiffy. Put a cushion over it, that's right. Some of it's not possible, Ray. Not for human beings. Well, we've got to get it out of your head."

"How?"

"This partner of yours—these partners? You're sure they're always girls? Never boys?"

"No. I'm sorry, Uncle Alf."

"Don't call me uncle. And don't be sorry, you're not my type. Do you go to dances?"

"I can't."

"Why not? Oh, you'd have to hold them at arm's length. Has it crossed your mind they might like the feel of it? I'm not joking."

"Am I sick? Has it got a name?"

"Everything's got a name. But some things aren't as bad as the names they've got. Priapism. That's," he raised his forearm, "all the time. A mild case. And sex in the head."

"It sounds terrible." But I laughed.

"Pretty usual with boys. Do you come?"

"What?"

"Do you go off pop?"

"Sometimes."

"Embarrassing, eh? It used to happen to me. I used to get erections on parade in the school cadets."

"What did you do?"

He shrugged. "Do you diddle yourself?"

That was hard for me to admit. He waited until I said yes.

"Well, keep it up. Have fun. But try to be less extravagant here." He tapped his head. "The real cure is real girls. Sit in the back row at the pictures, Ray. Put it in their hands. Girls like it. They really do."

"I know that. I know. But I can't *believe* it."

All the same, because of that talk and several others I came to believe. It put me back in the human race. And though it did not get me close to girls I was a little readier in my mind. It put the girls up there in the human race too. I kept on meeting Alf from time to time. I think he found me fairly heavy going; but

54

kept his patience, kept his smile, enquired how I was getting on.

In most things I was getting on well. I was in the first fifteen at school. I edited the school magazine—and laid a clutch of sonnets there demanding that Nature satisfy me. My English teacher called them sensitive. As for Duggie, he left Rosebank College at the end of his sixth-form year. Grandpa Plumb had helped Willis with money to keep him there and he was not pleased when Duggie went into an accountant's office and started doing Accountancy I at the university. He wasn't pleased either when I became a prefect in 6A. I didn't like it myself but I didn't know how to say no. Ormiston pinned my badge on me but did not smile. For a year I wandered around giving detentions. I never wore my prefect's badge at home. If Grandpa saw it he spoke about "the aristocratic embrace"

Since Grandpa Sole's death I had turned to him. In my confused state it was a natural gravitation. I overlooked his confusions and saw him as a kind of monolith, an Easter Island god frowning at the horizon. He took me out there with him and for a time I was safe. We talked in large terms and never questioned their meaning. Generalities lapped me round and buoyed me up. When we got down to cases they were in another age. I spent much anger on dead villains and was heartened by story-book victories of George Plumb. Grandpa mythologized himself. Later in my life I was cynical; but these days I would not be without him.

He told me how he had battled his church. I saw his resignation as a victory for Man. His voice was modulated beautifully. It rang and boomed and whispered over the lawns. It made my spine prickle and made me catch my breath. I thought of Paul Robeson singing *Lindy Lou*. But this was better. This was heroic. Even when he'd known they were after him he would not stop his lectures against the war. Policemen came and wrote down what he said, and he lectured at *them*. "No ground is too stony, Raymond." In Paparua prison he made converts. These were victories. I believed in them. I even managed to carry them back to the place where I suffered my defeats. So I had something. I came to believe I was descended from a special line. It helped explain my loneliness and helped me fix my superior smile.

A year or so before he died Grandpa met Uncle Alf round at Esther's. I had not known how much Alf hated him. Grandpa came home and sat in the summer-house. There he was, a little withered man in a grey suit and tennis shoes. Peering from the edge of the lawn I saw he was stunned and patient. He was waiting to die.

Mum beckoned me to the veranda. "Alfred smashed his trumpet." I did not let on I knew Alfred. "It was so horrible. He was, he seemed, all wet and red. Dad was like a child."

"Shall I play draughts with him?"

I went to the summer-house and set the board up on the table. I put out my fists and Grandpa tapped one. He did not make his usual remark about the symbolism of black and white. I had beaten him several times lately but that day I made sure he won. He seemed to me childlike. He forgot Alfred, and his trumpet, and set his eyes darting round the board. "Crown me," he said when I was slow.

Soon Mum came and led him in for tea. He had it in his study and that night I saw no more of him. Aunt Felicity, who was up on a visit, sat and smouldered during our meal. She had gone with Mum and Grandpa to see Alf and she was full of rage at "that stupid old man". Now and then she broke out but Mum shushed her angrily.

Felicity had the effect on me that Esther had on Duggie. She set me off balance. She took on a complacent air in talk about religion or "the mind". I felt second-rate. Nothing I managed to say ever surprised her. She looked at me and said, "Well, you'll grow up." It pleased me that Mum wasn't scared of her. Mum got very blunt, almost crude. That day she said, "Don't get all Catholic and sniffy."

"Catholic?—"

"How can you listen to those blue-chinned priests?"

"Now just hold on—"

"If you ask me what they need is a bit of loving from a pretty girl."

We looked at her with astonishment. Felicity laughed. "I do like your way with a *non sequitur*." We relaxed—which might have been the end Mum was looking for. None of us knew what a *non sequitur* was but we were pleased Mum was good at them.

My talks with Grandpa changed. He stopped booming at me about his battles and seemed to recall, with a kind of wonder, that other things had happened in his life. I learned more about my grandmother than I had known before. But he stopped frequently and seemed to listen, and he turned as though someone was creeping up on him. Now that his trumpet was broken he was more eager to hear than he had been before.

"Can you hear the creek, Raymond? I haven't heard a creek for fifty years. What does it sound like?"

"Music," I cried. "Wind. A breeze," mouthing like cheese.

"Like an Aeolean harp. Is the thrush singing?"

"No. There's a skylark over the orchard."

"What?"

"SKY-LARK."

"Ah." He looked up in the wrong direction. "Hail to thee, blithe Spirit! Your uncle Alfred looked like Percy Bysshe Shelley when he was young. Is it still there?"

"Yes."

"Your grandmother loved skylarks. She said their song was snow flakes turned into music."

He was burning a candle to her. She was his personal saint. He did not seem to regret the pain he had caused her, but put it down to the springs of wickedness in him. There was some complacency in his recognition that he was like other men.

He told me of an experience called vastation and found me William James's account of his experience of it. Vastation had come on Grandpa several times. Only recently he had been felled by it—yes, he had actually staggered as though a fist had struck him between the eyes. He had fallen to his knees. It was at the sight of Sutton's face looking at him from the cottage window. Sutton seemed to peer out of a cave; and yet the pane of glass was a mirror. Primitive man, man the brute, squatted in the dark, with nothing learned through the millennia. He picked fleas from his armpits and crushed them in his teeth. With vacant eyes he saw the world, and now and then gibbered with fear and hatred. Grandpa was knocked to his knees. He saw himself and the human race.

I thought he had dressed it up. It was too poetical. "What about the other side of things?"

He watched my lips. "Ah, mystical experience. Illumination. I've had that too. And it was real. I won't deny it. Unforgettable, Raymond. And yet I forget. There's too much there, too much light, we can't hold it; and what we can hold becomes the enemy of life and the human emotions. There's the rub. No, reason is more use to man. That's his weapon, because the irrational is in us—the dark side is here"—he struck his breast—"in the best of us. And so we've got to hold on to reason and good sense."

"Ah," I said, "I see," although I did not. He seemed tired of it too. He sighed and shook his head; and began talking about his wife again.

When he was dying I lost interest in him. Something was going on but it was too far from me. He was a little yellow man in a bed, too weak to lift his hands or talk to me or even look at me. I sat a while, then I went away, worrying about my lack of feeling. I could no longer believe in him as a man, he was something else, some product of his end. What he had been he had put away.

He died. I did not feel the loss I had felt at Ted Sole's death. Today I think of Ted Sole first, and think of George Plumb longer.

7   I was writing a Political Science essay in the university library when Duggie came up to me and said, "Put that stuff back on the shelves. We're going to Wellington."

"What?"

"Do you want to come? We're leaving in half an hour."

"I can't come to Wellington."

"Or Mummy might be cross."

"Lay off, Duggie."

He looked at my books, flicked their covers closed. "All these jokers are dead. I'm offering the real thing, boy."

People were frowning at us so I gathered my notes and we went into the foyer. "What is this, Duggie?"

"There's five of us going down in Tim Gibbons' van. We need one more."

"What for? How long are you going?"

"The weekend. Back on Sunday night."

"I haven't got clothes. Or a toothbrush."

"You'll be worrying about your pyjamas next."

"Who's going?"

"Me and Tim. A couple of sheilas he knows. And Miss Gobbloffski."

"Who?"

"Myra Payne. Myra pain in the arse. Wait till you see her mouth, boy. She's like a vacuum cleaner. You'll find out." As simply as that he reeled me in. "How much money you got, Ray?"

"Just my bus fare home."

"Pity."

"I've got my Post Office book. I can be back here in half an hour."

"You'd better run. Tim's arriving in a minute."

"How much shall I bring?"

"Twenty quid should do it."

Even that did not stop me. I ran all right. I ran all the way to the Post Office and all the way back, stopping only at Milne and Choyce's to send a message home with Becky that I was off to Wellington. Then we waited two hours for Tim Gibbons. It did not bother me that Duggie had lied. With girls on my mind I did not care. He broke one of my fivers on draught beer and after two drinks I felt the world was a fine place. I trusted Duggie. Words like friends, cousins, went running in my mind.

"What about these sheilas? Is one of them for me?"

Duggie shrugged. "Try your luck. You'd better lay off that beer, Ray. You're not used to it."

"One more, eh?"

At six o'clock we walked through Albert Park to the university. Tim Gibbons was waiting in his van, and two girls sitting high with him, straight and pink and white and porcelain. I peered at them and smiled but they kept the inhuman look girls saved for me and my smile sank into my jaws.

"You're late," Tim Gibbons said.

"We're here now. Give us a tenner, Ray."

I handed over two fivers carelessly and Duggie gave them to Tim. "One for him, one for me."

"What about?—" Tim gestured at the back of the van.

"She pays for herself."

"She hasn't yet."

"She will."

"O.K. Hop in."

Duggie opened the rear doors and there was Myra Payne as advertised. She was sitting on a blanket, on a mattress. She smiled at Duggie; and she frowned at me. I had expected a slut, with that gluey lipstick that sluts wore. This girl was elegant and pretty. She wore pale lipstick and no paint on her nails. She had what my mother called a generous mouth. I knew there was no way she would look at me and I made little nervous bobs of my head.

"This is Ray," Duggie said. "Myra."

"You didn't say anyone else was coming."

"Plenty of room. Hop in, Ray. Shift your arse over, Payne."

I put my satchel in the van and clambered up. Tim Gibbons locked the doors and we started out of Auckland.

"Hey Tim," Duggie yelled, "push one of those sheilas back for Ray."

But the cab was a substantive world and had no connection with ours. Down the Great South Road, over the Bombay hill, my sense of unreality grew until I was in a panic. Where was I going? How had I got into this? I was on the point of yelling for the van to stop. I leaned on the doors, thinking it would be a release if they sprang open and threw me on the road, shattered me.

Myra sulked. Duggie winked at me. He felt in her bag and conjured out a bottle with a horse on it. "Presto! Gee up, Payne." She gave a defeated smile and drank from it and gasped and rolled her eyes. It placed her for me as surely as if she had spoken dirty words. The glugging sound marked her equally. But I made no return from my limbo. Drink, women, conversation— everything was beyond me. When she offered me the bottle I shook my head. I watched while she and Duggie started kissing. When it was dark they did other things. I saw them in flashes from the street lights. I saw locking forearm and bald knee and heard soft cries. They sat up smoking cigarettes. Myra offered her packet. "No thank you."

"He's got a mummy," Duggie said. Myra whispered something in his ear "She reckons you must be sublimating, Ray."

In Te Kuiti we bought pies and coffee. Tim Gibbons and his girls ate high in the cab. "You should be doing law. They'd be all over you," Duggie said. We went across to the station lavatory. "Did you see her gobbling me off. Then she wanted to kiss me. Dirty bitch."

Back in the van. Down through the hills to Taumarunui. Down past the mountains. More things were going on. I tried to sleep and managed it in snatches. Somewhere south of Taihape Myra and Duggie hissed a quarrel. She gave a screech of pain. "All right, all right." I saw her crawling at me like a hedgehog. In flashing lights I saw her face was wet. Her hand was at my fly. I got those buttons open with a rip, and had her hand on me as I said kindly, "You don't have to."

"Shut up," she moaned.

"Compliments of the management," Duggie said.

It didn't take long. I censored anger from her hand and shame from me. She crawled away and huddled in a corner.

"Nice?" Duggie asked. His face had an elevated look. He was benevolent and careless. Later Myra shifted back to him and did some more of what he liked. "You like that?" "Sure I like." "I'm the only one who'll do that for you."

We came into Wellington at dawn. Tired, half-sick, tormented by shame, I saw the hills and harbour and felt their shape and stillness cleansing me. I told myself I would live in this town. Duggie and Myra were sleeping. She looked smeared and swollen. Her prettiness, her elegance, were gone. She made little farts and twitched her hands. Duggie looked seedy too, but dangerous in his sleep.

The van climbed into a suburb of tall houses and narrow streets. Tim Gibbons came round and opened the doors.

"Out."

Duggie did not wake up.

"You've had your ride."

"I'm staying here."

"Listen—"

"I paid a tenner. So you piss off."

Tim Gibbons blinked. He shrank. The two girls stared at me.

"Well if that's how you feel," Gibbons said. They went into a house.

"Good on you, Ray. You told him," Duggie said.

We slept in the van for most of the morning. Then Duggie wobbled Myra awake. He had a bag with him and he took out a clean shirt and underpants and a toilet bag. I was not surprised. He had his toothbrush.

"Let's go in and twist old Timothy's arm. Stay here Ray till I get the lay of the land."

He came back in half an hour, clean and shaved. "Get in and wash, you scruffy bugger."

"I'm staying here." I was determined to be dirty. I was going to sit this weekend out, get myself through it by sitting still, and back in Auckland I was going to write Duggie out of my life.

"Suit yourself," Duggie said. He went away.

At midday I walked down into the town. I ate another pie and sat on the wharves watching the black mountains over the harbour. A wind was raising white caps and blowing gulls in curving falls out towards an island with yellow cliffs. That, I

62

guessed, was Somes Island, where they had kept enemy aliens in the war. It looked like a haven more than a prison. In the wind and sunlight I began to feel better. I followed the wharves and the waterfront road and came to Oriental Bay. There I sat in the bandstand, watching yachts, watching hills, until I began to be cold. Wellington, I thought, I'll live here one day. I told myself I would start again.

The rest of the afternoon I sat in the movies. Then I followed my nose back up the hills and found the van still parked by tall thin houses. I opened the doors and there was Myra again, wrapped in her blanket. Her hair was down and she looked like a squaw.

"Where's Duggie?"

"How would I know?"

"When's he coming back?"

"How would I know?" Tears rolled on her cheeks. I offered my handkerchief. She shook her head. "Please go away."

"Have you had tea?"

"I can't eat."

"I'll get some fish and chips."

I walked down town again and found a fish shop and came striding back with my warm packet. It took an hour but Myra was still there. We ate fish and chips.

"He just went away and left me."

"It's the sort of thing he does."

"He's a bastard."

"You don't have to tell me. I grew up with him."

"You're cousins?"

"Yes."

"I love Duggie. I know he's only eighteen. I'm twenty seven."

"Age," I said, "doesn't make any difference. If you're in love."

"That's what I think. I'd do anything for him. Why does he treat me so badly?"

She cried quietly. I knew I should put my arm round her but I could not do it. I sat there being helpless, sentimental. She was pretty again, and pitiable. Not elegant. Grease and tears were round her mouth.

I did not expect to see Duggie again but he came as dark was falling, in a car with a young man and two girls.

"Oh-uh, oh-uh," Myra wept. "Please don't let him see me."

Duggie jumped out of the back seat, leaving a girl who seemed at a distance beautiful, cool, composed. She had blond hair falling on her cheeks.

"Ray." He drew me up the road past the van. "Is Myra there? Look, take care of her eh? I've got this little piece. I don't want Miss Gobbloffski on my back."

"What am I supposed to do?"

"Just look after her. I need a fiver. You still got some money?"

"No."

"Come on, Ray. A fiver and you can have Miss Gobbloffski."

"Listen—"

"Joke, joke. This Glenda's real class, Ray. I've got to have some money."

"She looks about fifteen."

"She's old enough. Come on, I'll pay you back."

I gave him my last note.

"Thanks." He dug me with his elbow and jerked his thumb at the van. "Get in there boy." He ran to the car, the blonde girl drew him in, and they were gone.

I climbed into the van. Myra was a bruised shape in the dark.

"Where's he gone?"

"I don't know."

"Who was the girl with him?"

"I don't know. He took my money."

"She was young."

"He sold you to me for a fiver."

She lay in her corner and sobbed evenly, making a sound like tearing paper.

"Myra."

"Leave me alone."

I sat on the edge of the mattress and listened to her. After a while she said, "Have you got that hankie?"

I gave it to her.

"I wish I could kill him."

"Myra, I'm sorry." I had begun to smell her. She was wet and pungent. I moved close and touched her cheek. A throbbing started in me. I was tumid with lust and pity. "Myra, I'll help you. I really like you." I took her hand and put it on my trousers. The bulge there was the size of a cucumber and I felt her hand take notice of its shape. Then she gave a yelping laugh. She pulled open my fly and got her hand inside my underpants. I was dizzy with excitement and exultation. This was me. This was happening to me. Then I screamed. I had never felt worse pain. She had my balls and was twisting them and digging her fingernails in.

"You creepy little bastard," she yelled; and gave another twist.

I screamed like someone murdered and she let go.

"Get out of here. Get out, you creepy sod."

I got out. Somehow I fell out. I was on my knees at the back of the van, holding myself, whimpering with pain. She put her foot on me and sent me sprawling. I got up and stumbled down the road, running bent and throwing up my hands like a capuchin monkey. I wept as I ran. I was destroyed.

After a while I went out of houses into trees and blundered in the dark, sobbing my name. I smelled pine trees, and lay on needles, curled up in a ball. The pain had a beat in it like drums. Sideways, I saw the moon on water, and I thought of going down to the wharves and tumbling off like a shot man, sinking into the clean cold, not coming up. I saw my body in the harbour mud, crusting with mussels; and played that several ways, increasing its attractions, until I was able to get clear of it and snigger with self-contempt. This was not the night I was going to die. If I killed myself it would be without self-indulgence.

When I was able to walk I went higher up the roads. On the hills over the city I found myself on a country track. Cold air.

65

Pine trees heaving in a wind. Lights burned in Oriental Bay and pricked in suburbs at the back of the island, on the lower rim of huge black hills. The sky was clear, the moon was lemon-shaped. Stars trembled on the edge of going out. The harbour seemed to turn itself on and off. It was two things—flat white plate, porcelain and lovely—then a hole that opened into nothing. I watched it flick back and forth. Pain, humiliation, had me in a mildly visionary state, and this was my vision: people showing glow-worm lights on the edge of nothing. I thought it was a good one—it would do me. I promised I would live in Wellington.

I came down a different way, past houses on wide lawns, down a zig-zag angling twenty times. I looked at names of streets but they meant nothing. When I came to the place where the van should have been I gave a laugh. Of course it was gone. Finding it there would have broken the pattern. I stood under a street lamp and looked at my watch. I counted the silver in my pocket. Eight and sixpence. Then I walked down to the city. It was eleven o'clock. I had been playing at desolation. Even when I ran down the street holding my balls I knew I had relatives in this town. One of the names I had seen high on the hill came back to me: Wadestown Road. I had seen Mum write it on a letter to her brother Oliver. But I grinned with fright at the thought of that icy man. At the station I looked in the telephone book and found the address of M. J. and F. E. Waring. It was in Khandallah. I liked that name. Sitting in the taxi, heading into family, I said it to myself. I tried to keep the night alive. What had happened to me was at least *something*.

I paid and had a shilling left. Then I stood among gnome houses and could not make connections. Where was I? What had brought me here? The moon sailed in the sky as strangely as if it sailed over continents of ice. There was nothing I wanted but to sink into warmth. I ran to a letterbox and found my number. If they were not at home I would curl up on their door mat like a dog. I ran up a path through hump-backed shrubs. Steps sent me sprawling on hands and knees. I saw a light somewhere at the back, in a second-storey room. It shone like the sun on me,

enfolded me, it brought me home. I stood up easy, smoothed
my hair and hoped I did not smell, and I checked my fly that had
come undone so easily; and when I was all right, grubby but
sufficiently a Plumb, I knocked on the door.

Max Waring came. I had met him at Grandpa's funeral. He
peered at me over reading glasses. He was wearing a dressing
gown and pom-pommed slippers.

"Hello, Uncle Max."

He put his tiny woman-hands at me. "Raymond. Raymond
Sole. Well I never."

"I was just in Wellington so I.   "

"Come in Ray, come in." He had black darting eyes that took
me in head to foot. "Is something wrong?"

I stepped into the hall. Aunt Felicity leaned over the rail. She
wore a hairnet and her face glistened with cream. "Who is it,
Max? Good grief, Raymond. How did you get here?"

"I was in Wellington and I ran out of money, so.   I'm
sorry it's so late."

She came down the stairs and kissed me. Brisk. No nonsense.
"Something fishy, Max."

"I think so, dear. But let him have a bath. And a sleep. We
can talk in the morning."

"Yes. A bath." Max scuttled away. "Come under the light,
boy." She turned on the hall lamp and dragged me to it. "Is this
one of those escapades? Girls at the back of it, I shouldn't
wonder. Does your mother know you're here?"

"Not exactly."

"Good grief, you smell. How long since you changed that
shirt?"

"Only two days."

"I'll bet your underclothes are a mess. Is anyone with you?"

"Duggie. I don't know where he's gone."

"Attila the Hun. That explains it."

I was back in my place, nobody; with no desire to argue. I let
myself be turned around and prodded to the bathroom. If she
had undressed me I wouldn't have minded.

Max said, "There, nice and hot. Have a good long soak."

I lowered myself in: sour feet, smelly armpits, tender balls. I washed out fish smell, sex smell, cigarette. I washed my hair. Then I wrapped myself in a towel and pulled the plug. Max must have been waiting at the door.

"You out, Ray? You decent?"

Felicity came galloping up. "Don't worry about that, man. Here, give me those." She burst in with pyjamas. "Put these on. They were Peter's, they should fit. And then to bed." She turned my dirty clothes with her toe. "Leave those. I'll wash them in the morning. Have you got that toothbrush, Max? Listen young fellow, I'll be wanting your story. Lock stock and barrel. And no lies."

"Yes, Felicity." I cleaned my teeth and went to bed. Max had put a hot water bottle in. I lay and sighed and smiled into the dark. My balls throbbed pleasantly. I thought with admiration of Myra Payne. I approved of what she had done and wished that she would do the same to Duggie. There wasn't any malice in the thought. I wondered how he was getting on with the blonde girl, Glenda.

The morning wasn't such a happy time. Mornings seldom are. A weasel had my testicles and would not let them go. The bite turned into aching as I woke. Swellings, yellow bruising, had given me a strange unhealthy fruit between my legs. I examined it with fatalism. If she'd ruined me for life that was that.

I covered myself and lay back. There was another thing, less easy to accept. No matter how I cleared my mind it turned there on the blue; a great black bird. *Creepy*. She'd called me *creepy*.

Max came in with porridge and tea. "Sleep well?"

"Yes. Thank you."

"Felicity's gone to mass. What's the matter? You don't look well."

"It's a headache. Maybe if you've got a couple of Aspros."

He ran off and got them. I saw he enjoyed doctoring and wondered if, after all, I should show him my balls. I could see him compassionate, putting on ice packs; and I had a moment's hope that he would cure creepy.

"Eat your porridge while it's hot. Is the tea how you like it?"

"Just right. Thanks very much."

"I'll lend you a razor when you've finished. It would be an idea to be out of bed when Felix gets back."

"Oh. Sure. O.K."

I ate, and kept my troubles to myself. Max found me some old clothes that had been my cousin Peter's. Shaved and dressed, I went downstairs. My movements all that day were measured, stately. I gave white smiles and enjoyed my pain; and talking humorously, being wise, I managed to believe I was not creepy.

Felicity sat in her chair and let Max fuss around her. She pointed to where she'd like me and I sat there. "Stop fussing, Max. Sit down. Right young man, spill the beans."

I told them most of what had happened, leaving out the sex. I made them laugh. Once when I began to complain I saw they liked me less so I dropped that. I praised Duggie for at least knowing who he was and what he wanted.

Felicity snorted. "He's a little crook. This girl of his—he went off with someone else. What happened to her?"

"She cried. Not much else she could do."

"Why didn't you bring her here?"

"She didn't want me. I tried."

"Tried what? Girls get a bad time, Ray. Remember that."

"We all get a bad time," Max said. "The only thing is to keep bouncing back."

"How's that for a philosophy of life?" Felicity said.

"Now Felix, don't get on at me. I'm a humanist, Ray. She doesn't like it."

So we got past my adventures on to the meaning of life and Max and Felicity scored fondly off each other—Max more fond than Felix and more gentle. Neither was touched by any witticism; by logic or by doctrine; they simply put on their show and I was confused. So much that both of them said seemed right, even when they contradicted each other.

Max cooked lunch. Afterwards we went for a walk in Khandallah. They went along more quickly than I liked but I grinned and kept up and gave them all the family news from

Auckland. Felicity made sharp remarks—she had everyone's number; though, as Max told me, she loved them dearly. Coming back, licking an ice cream, she asked me about myself: what was I doing with my life? what was I looking for apart from a good time? I told her about university, how sadly I was lost there. I had not told my parents. It's easier to confess to someone interested than to those who love you. I described my feelings on climbing the stone steps, entering the stone hall under the wedding-cake tower. I felt I was stepping out of my life into some icy marriage. The riches I'd been promised, those feasts and satisfactions of the mind, were not there. I felt like the ghost at the wedding. People seemed to shy away from me. I had been at varsity two months, I said, and spoken to no one.

Felicity laughed. "You're dressing up your shyness in some pretty fancy clothes."

I was offended and tried to explain it was more than shyness. I had to believe there was something in me too fine for the place I'd found myself in. But Felicity raised her eyes and gave a laugh, and I saw how ridiculous I was; and was filled with envy of those easy boys who sat in the cafeteria, who walked in the cloisters and the park, holding girls by the hand. I had an image of myself wrapped in a sticky membrane.

"I'm going to leave. I want to get a job."

"What as?"

"I'm going to be a journalist."

"Ah," Max said, "that's good. I wanted to be a journalist. You'll meet people that way. You'll have to talk to them."

"It'll bring you down to earth," Felicity said. "But your mother won't be pleased. She wants to see you in a cap and gown."

"I've got to do what I want."

"Yes, you have."

Back at the house Max brought my clothes in from the line. He finished drying them in front of a fire. At half past six I was fed and dressed and ready for the Limited. Felicity patted me and gave me a kiss.

"You've got a lot of growing up to do."

70

"Yes. Goodbye. And thank you." She was a tough old thing and I was lucky to have her.

"Keep clear of Duggie. You don't need him."

"I will."

"And get away from that blessed Peacehaven. It's a big wide world out there."

"Stop bossing him, Felicity. He'll find his own way."

She came out to the steps and watched Max get the car out. No "drive carefullys", no watching us out of sight. She went inside and closed the door. Max drove me to the station. He bought a ticket and a pillow and gave me a pound note—"In case of emergencies."

"Thank you, Max."

"There's something I've got to say." This little man who did not come to my shoulder; bright-eyed, bright-faced, sharp as a pixie. "I've noticed the way you're walking. If you've got anything wrong down there, see a doctor. The minute you get home. Don't delay."

I blushed. "It's not that. I got a kick. From a girl. Well—she twisted them."

"Ha! Ha!" He blushed too. "I'll keep it to myself. Ray, this business with girls, if you'll excuse me, you can't go into it with most parts missing. A doo-dah on its own won't get you far."

"No, I see that."

"One day you'll want a woman like Felicity—with a mind."

"Yes, I suppose so."

"Just thought I'd pass it on. Well, all aboard. I'm glad it's not the other thing."

The train rolled along the harbour front and dived into a tunnel. Towards Paekakariki I saw Tim Gibbons' van running parallel with us and caught a glimpse of Duggie next to him. I wondered what had happened to the girls. They were not the sort to be sold off like Myra. The van drew ahead and flicked away under a bridge. My satchel was in the back with my library books and Pol. Sci. essay inside. I was pleased at the idea of them heading off, and the essay finishing in mid-argument. I

71

did not mind if I never saw them again. I did not mind if I never saw Duggie either.

Then I felt a grief like the passing of innocence. It was as if I had believed in magic and now saw tricks for what they were. I was in a world where things were worked by wires—where people had a single shape and ended at their fingertips.

That was no visionary moment but a flash of conviction. It burned an epidermis off my mind and left me free of its sudden grief, and fresh, and ready.

Through the night I watched the towns go by. There was, as Felicity had said, a big wide world out there. I was going to prove I was not creepy.

8 So I missed seeing Duggie's metamorphosis. I had no clear view of mine. I woke one morning in a rusty bed in a boarding house called Primrose Hall set behind Phoenix palms off the main street of Gerriston on the edge of the Hauraki plains. A man called Don snored and farted in a bed over the room. His teeth grinned in a glass of yellow water. He had shown me his hernia. Twice in the night he had got up and pissed out the window. I hugged myself and grinned at the ceiling. Maps of South America up there. And fleas in the mat. There were fleas all over town. A circus had come through and now we had a plague of them. Don had sat with his bare feet on the mat and caught them with a wet piece of soap as they jumped aboard. That was a trick worth knowing. I felt I was away from home at last.

My job was with the *Gerriston Independent*. I was proof-reader and cub reporter. The *Independent* came out on Mondays, Wednesdays and Fridays. Its old press clanked and slapped in a shed with an iron roof at the back of a stationer's shop. The editor's office was ten by ten. The reporters' room was ten by ten. Fleas were in the mat there too. They had our girl reporter Iris in tears. We tried to help her make a joke of them but she was from a good home and fleas meant dirt and she wasn't laughing at that. Trevor Barley, the editor, wrote his Wednesday leader on the need for better public health measures to combat invasions of this sort. The chief reporter, Morrie Horne, wrote the news report. And I did a humorous piece called *The Democracy of Fleas*—how they bit the highest with the low. Trevor Barley cut out several adjectives and ran it—my first article. I posted a clipping home to Mum.

Trevor Barley was pleased with me. I was willing to do just about anything. I would have made the tea and swept the floor. Although my sense of having begun kept my voice firm and my shoulders straight, I was also very humble and had rushes of gratitude that made me want to open doors for people and wash their cups. "Stop being such a goddam girl," Morrie Horne snarled. That cured me. I was sensitive to how people saw me. Humbleness troubled me no more, and gratitude became too generalized for me to hold. It caught me now and then and made me grin; but soon I was more pleased with myself than with other people.

The pay was forty-five shillings a week. When people asked me why I didn't leave Primrose Hall for private board I replied that I couldn't afford to. But nothing would have made me leave the Hall. I shifted from the double room into a single one. That was as far as I meant to go. I pinned a few prints on the wall and screwed a bookcase up for my Penguins, and bought a strip of Feltex for the floor; and left it at that. I did not want to change Primrose Hall. I was there two years and was nervous all the time that fire or flood or Health Department would take it away from me.

The landlady was Mrs Fitz—Fitzwater,—simmons,—hugh, I never found out. She boiled the flavour out of everything. We ate grey cabbage, grey stew, grey tripe, even grey carrots. On Friday nights she came home from the pub with a giant packet of fish and chips and opened it on the kitchen table, where we helped ourselves. Most of her boarders were back from the pub and did not mind. Mrs Fitz had rolling buttocks and a cupid's-bow mouth. Painted nails were the first thing I saw. They made my heart jump. She was a divorceé, disowned by her sons. She cried about it on Friday nights; and then said, "What the hell, I've still got me," and brought out her gin bottle and drank past midnight with whoever was around. I drank with her now and then and we competed in self-pity and unconcern. She took me up to the front room where she had a bed deep as a basin. It was said you could buy Mrs Fitz for a pound. She never asked any payment from me. She showed me what to do and said I needed lots and lots of practice.

In the mornings I came into a dining-room so genteel I felt I had been jerked out of my time. It was as though nature had gone wrong. Mrs Fitz came in with a tray of porridge bowls and set them out. The porridge steamed in the chilly air. She said, "Good morning, Mr Sole." The room made her formal, it restored her, and though she had found it ready-made when she bought Primrose Hall it was fixed and beautiful among the floating pieces of her life. You paid your respects there to Mrs Fitz. You did not raise your voice. You watched your manners.

"A chilly morning, Mrs Fitz."

"You'll have to buy some gloves, Mr Sole."

I felt a little dizzy from my about-face jerk into the day. I'd spent the dark hours cosy in her bed. Done it—what?—seven times? I'd had her breasts, white and warm and spongy, smothering me, and hands that put porridge down and mouth that said Mr Sole busily making me hard for more and more. It helped me when I smelled the porridge burned, and saw the red on her nails flaking off.

"Or you could find a girl to knit you some." That was better.

"I'll have to do that, Mrs Fitz."

She went back to the kitchen.

"They say you can have her for a pound," wheezed an itinerant plasterer.

"Don't you believe it. Good woman, Mrs Fitz. Very moral. Look around if you don't believe me."

The wallpaper might bubble, even breathe, but it was rich gold and rich maroon. Ornate mouldings curved into the ceiling, where a coloured-glass chandelier turned like the minute hand of a clock. Illuminated verses—*We are nearer God's heart in a garden.   I think that I shall never see.*   hung above oak chairs and rosewood cabinets and a black piano with yellow teeth. Over the fireplace was a huge red painting—*Soldiers of the Queen*: Victorian arrogance, moustachioed and paunchy, and the little queen like a chip of ice in the middle of it. There was a Maxfield Patrish too, glaring back in blue at the red: naked maidens, gelded youths, in Greek columns, by a lake. It made me think of my mother.

"Ah," wheezed the plasterer, "I seen some joker coming out of her room the other night."

"You sure?"

"Wednesday. After the pictures."

It was not me. I did not care.

At Primrose Hall we had "some dodgy types", said Mrs Fitz. She did not seem to like them less for that. Maintenance dodgers, tax evaders, passed through. Some were not sure what name they were using. We had a con man in a Tyrolean hat and a porno king with his suitcase full of cyclostyled yarns. The local police sergeant looked in often. He shook his head at finding me still there. One night detectives from Auckland came barging in and arrested the quiet chap in the room next to mine. It turned out he was a tank man. He had his gear and loot in a laundry bag under his bed.

Iris's mother offered me board. She felt it was her duty. I thanked her and said I liked the freedom at Primrose Hall.

After a while I stopped sending clippings home. I tried to stop using the word, believing that it did not suit my style. I went up to Auckland for Becky's wedding and her sugar-cake dress and pink bridesmaids seemed to come out of a fairy-tale book. I had grown out of her, and Mum, and Bobby, and my love for them had become a burden. I took it back to Gerriston, feeling it under my ribs like indigestion. I saw myself like a dog on a running-wire, getting just so far then finding nowhere to go but back to the kennel. For a while I was violent in my mind, inventing fires and drownings at Peacehaven. But that soon passed, and I was scribbling notes about the weather, and saying

I couldn't come for Easter—because of this, because of that.
Mum wrote that she understood.

Morrie Horne became a drinking mate. Later we worked
together on the *Evening Post*. Trevor Barley taught me how to
write. He was a patient man. But it was the owner of the paper,
Charlie Kittredge, who became my only real friend in Gerriston.
Charlie, a returned soldier, started the *Independent* in 1919. He
kept it alive as a broadsheet in the depression, and used sausage
paper in World War 2. He edited it for twenty-five years, but
when he hired Trevor Barley agreed to limit himself to an article
a week. We called it Charlie's porridge. He wrote on political
economy and the social contract. *The Wealth of Nations* was his
holy book and his weekly article was a hymn of praise to free
enterprise. When I told him I was a Socialist he said I had some
growing up to do. Socialism was a young man's disease, a part of
wild oats and Dad-bashing. He warned me that past a certain
age it grew malignant and held up "poor sick Britain" as an
example. It did not trouble him to see the Empire breaking up.
Empire was a malignancy too. But he insisted on a hierarchy
within the state. His ideas shocked me. I had not done Pol. Sci.
long enough to discover their pedigree and thought at first he
was Sid Holland's man. But Charlie loathed Sid Holland and
"that crew" They muddied his ideal. He saw them as self-
seekers. "There's not an ounce of greed in Adam Smith."

Charlie found no heroes in the waterfront dispute of '51 He
saw corruption and betrayal. His view was almost theological.
Evil had lurched out into the open. The bright god was dying.
In other words, passion conquered order. Trevor Barley was
unhappy too. After the February Emergency Regulations he
decided the *Independent* would run no letters on the strike. "If we
can't have both sides we'll have none." His editorials were
among the few in the country that kept a tone of reason.

As for me, I went out in the night painting slogans. My
favourite was $*id ⌐ olland*. I painted it on the brewery gates and
the town water tower. Up there I felt like a hero of the revolution. I hung over an eighty-foot drop with my paint tin on my
thumb and made a fat dollar sign and a swastika like a running

man. The tin slipped off and crashed into the paddock. No matter—I had done it. In the morning Gerriston would read my message. I took my torch out of my windbreaker pocket and played it on the words. I was swollen with accomplishment. Grandpa Plumb would be proud of me.

I dropped my brush down to join the tin and climbed on to the roof of the tower. It was past midnight and most of the town lights were out. I sat and grinned at Gerriston, feeling it was mine; but soon became disturbed by its smallness on the plain. I felt that I was on the edge of nothing, hanging on with finger-nails and teeth. I was afraid of my tininess. The town was made of cardboard. It was accidental. Raymond Sole, sitting on this tower, was accidental.

Then the picture broke and reassembled. No shortage of significance now. That was a police car turning in at the gate. Its lights came stiffly round and settled on the tower base. Flattened on the roof, I heard tyres rasp on gravel, heard doors thump. Torch beams angled up from the rim of the plate where I lay spread out like frog awaiting dissection.

"Sid Holland. It's that bastard." Sergeant Whittle.

"Shall I go up, Sarge?" Constable Toomey. I sometimes had a drink with him. He thought I was a smart-arse. I looked around but there was nowhere to go. I had the urge to climb into the sky.

"Here's his paint tin, Sarge. The bugger's done a bunk."

Whittle gave it a boot. "I'll do the sod over when I catch him. Get out there Frank and have a look in the bushes."

Toomey went off with his torch and I saw its yellow puddle working along the trees by the cricket field. Whittle prowled round the foot of the tower. I heard him muttering. His boots rang as he climbed a dozen steps up the ladder. He shone his torch up. Toomey came back from the trees. "Nothing, Sarge."

"It's the same bloke. He's got his bloody swastika the wrong way round."

After a while they drove away. I lay on the iron lid watching their car slide into the corners of Gerriston. Sometimes it floated like a fish; then its lights would leap at distant things and I felt the menace of it and its power to break my life. It seemed the car was after me, not men.

At three o'clock I lost it. Suddenly it was gone, and then I saw it parked and empty in the police station yard. I climbed down gripping with numb hands, treading on dead feet, and swam home through the streets, working my mouth. I lay in bed with my hands like ice, my frozen buttocks missing from my body. No more slogans, I said. I dreamed I was dying.

In the morning council workmen scrubbed the tower. I wrote a report on "our phantom slogan-writer" but Trevor Barley would not allow me that or $id ⊔ olland, even when I made the swastika right. "An anti-Government slogan" was as far as he would go.

The following day I took my lunch into the park. The water tower stood up over the trees like a martian machine. The ghost of my message was on its side and I drank my bottle of fizz to it, wishing it a long life. Iris and her girlfriend from the Loan and Mercantile office sunned themselves on a bench along from me. When I had finished my lunch I sat with them. The girl from Loan and Merc. was dumb, pretty, remote, and I had grown sure enough of myself to make a game of getting nowhere with her. I had just seen her glaze over and her goldfish mouth contract when a man on the bandstand steps stood up and shouted, "Brothers! Comrades!"

"My God," I said, "a wharfie."

"Brothers, I want to tell you the true story about what's happening in our country."

"Iris, get your camera. Run."

"What for?"

"This is a story. We can get pictures."

"It's no good getting pictures you can't print."

"We'll print them. Go on. You're supposed to be a reporter."

I was making little runs at the bandstand and running back at Iris. She did not move.

"Someone should get the police," the Loan and Merc. girl said. She stood up suddenly, her face gone red. "Communist," she screamed at the wharfie. "Why don't you go to Russia?"

"Go on, Iris."

"Too late. Here's the cops. Plain clothes, eh?"

They came from a car by the fence, slow as Jersey bulls ambling in a show-ring. One of them was eating a pie and he flicked the crust to seagulls on the cricket pitch.

"They're not local. They must have followed him." I ran across the grass and fell in step. *Gerriston Independent.* Can you tell me who you are?"

"Buzz off, sonny."

The wharfie began a gabbling shout. He was a fat man in a tartan shirt and a red tie. "Here they come. Here they come. The minions of Sid Holland's fascist state. Watch them, brothers. Watch them put the boot in." He remembered his message. "This is not a strike, this is a lock-out. The ship owners have bought Sid Holland and his crew. They've bought the newspapers. Don't believe the papers. They're printing lies. We have been locked out. We are not on strike—"

"Come on, Joe." They mounted into the bandstand without hurry. One took him by the back of his neck, the other bent his arm in a hammerlock. The wharfie's hat fell off. I saw his ridged scalp coming down the steps at me, waist high.

"Ow! Ow! You don't have to.   No need.   "

"Shut up, Joe. Move." They kneed his buttocks.

"Gerriston Independent," I gabbled.

"Out of the way, sonny."

They took the wharfie to their car and pushed him into the back seat. One got in with him and the other behind the wheel. "What's your name, son?"

"Ray Sole. *Independent.*"

"You hear that, Mick? His name's R. Sole."

"Don't go printing any stories, R. Sole."

They drove away. I saw Mick sitting sideways and saw his fist come up and fall like a club.

"Did you see? They're beating him up."

The three or four watchers took a dead look.

"Come on, Ray," Iris said. "You'll get yourself in trouble."

"You saw it."

"Serves him right," the Loan and Merc. girl said. "They should shoot them all."

"It's nice to find you've got a voice, Doreen."

"They should shoot you, too." She ran over the grass to the wharfie's hat and gave it a kick that sent it looping in the air. As it came down she caught it and tried to tear the band off. I thought she would attack it with her teeth. Her face was thick with rage. But she worked her fingers in and the stitches popped like corks.

"Come on," Iris said. "Into the office." She pushed me along.

"They can't do that. Not here. Not in New Zealand."

"They can. They did. They'll do it to you if you make any trouble."

"I'll make trouble. Stop pushing me." I ran ahead and had paper in my typewriter before she came in.

When Trevor Barley arrived my story was on his desk. Trevor had been at the pub for his lunchtime stout. It usually made him grumpy but today he just looked tired. He came to our room and closed the door.

"Anyone else see this?"

"I did," Iris said.

He gave her the story to read. "That how it happened?"

"More or less."

"O.K. Do me one column inch. Police arrested a man under the Emergency Regulations. That sort of thing."

"Just a minute," I said.

"Shut up, Ray." He threw the story on my desk. "Keep that for your memoirs. Have you done the stock sale report?"

"No, but listen—"

"You listen. I'm not running a kindergarten for revolutionaries here. You want to write that sort of stuff join the *People's Voice*."

"Trevor, it happened that way."

"You say. They'll say different. Get on with your sale report."

He went out but I passed him in the corridor and ran through the shop to Charlie Kittredge's office. "Mr Kittredge," I said, bursting in, throwing down my story on his blotter. Charlie blinked at me. He had been drinking stout with Trevor Barley.

"What is it, Ray?"

"I wrote this and Mr Barley won't print it. This is an important story."

Trevor came in. He sat down in a chair and took his glasses off and wiped his eyes. "Better read it, Charlie."

"All right." Charlie read. He hunched his shoulders a little and sighed as he went on. Like Trevor Barley he seemed to grow tired.

"You really think the wharfies are the good guys? There aren't any good guys in this thing."

"That's not the point—"

"The point is Ray, under the Emergency Regulations we can't print it."

"I wouldn't print it anyway," Trevor said, "until you took all the sob stuff out. You're supposed to be a reporter not a novelist."

"But," I said. I got myself together. "A man was giving a speech. In a free country. Policemen came and arrested him."

"Not a free country now."

"That's my point. And they beat him up. And how do we know they were even policemen? They might be some sort of secret police."

"Come on, Ray."

"I'd like to follow this up. I'd like to do a proper investigation."

"And get the paper closed?" Trevor said.

"I'm sorry," Charlie said. They were both sorry. They had a shrunken look and would not meet my eyes. Trevor went back to his office. Charlie sat and talked at me aimlessly—telling me he didn't agree with Trevor, my story was well done. He was dithering in himself, there was a question in him and he could not say yes or no. I was too upset to be sorry for him. I feel sorry now. He knew what he should do and could not do it. He had been proud of the *Independent*.

How did it end? I walked out of the paper. But I went back, and wrote my sale report. I was pleased with myself for walking out; and felt a cold satisfaction in going back. I did not feel diminished. This was how life had to be played. I would play along. But I wouldn't pretend to like it. I would keep my eyes open.

Soon afterwards Iris became my girlfriend. We went to pictures and we went to dances and when those preliminaries were done went to Primrose Hall instead and spent the time from ten to one in bed. Iris learned not to mind dirt too much. She liked sex, but liked it slow and tender.

With Mrs Fitz and Iris I began to have some perception of normal feeling between a man and a woman.

9   I cannot be so definite about Duggie's progress. He kept on at the university and in the accountant's office but in the two years I was in Gerriston worked changes in himself that made him barely recognizable. Who was this fellow in the yellow waistcoat, talking like the lord of the manor in some drama club farce? I asked my mother when it had happened, how? But she had seen very little of him. "He's always been like that. Hasn't he?" Now that she thought about it she wasn't sure. Nobody was sure. Duggie had such belief in himself and engaged you so fully that memories of him would not come clear. I had the advantage of our shared childhood. And I had been away, so the gradations in his change were less fine to me. From this time I was the only one to know him.

"Where did you get the voice, Duggie?"

"How do you mean?"

"That's not Rosebank, that's Kinks College. It's damn near Eton."

"I've always talked like this."

"Have you been taking elocution lessons? The rain in Spain. "

We were in a private bar drinking bottled beer. I watched

Duggie fill his glass. He would never be elegant, but there was a measure in him; he had stopped charging.

"It's a good act, Duggie. Who's it for?"

He looked at me over his glass. "Cheers."

"Come on. I'm not one of your girls."

He gave a little nod. I had shown my limitations. "You know what I've found out, Ray? You don't have to sit and take it. You can make things happen."

"I thought you'd always known that. And where does the voice fit in?"

"The way you talk is important," he said vaguely.

"Are you looking for a wife? Some Remuera dame?"

"Ah, Ray." His mildness was deceptive. He was assessing me; and because he was fond of me could not believe I had any substance. My mistaking of his ambitions was further proof of it. Almost by accident I became indispensable to him. He licensed me to point out his mistakes.

"People will think you're a poof. And listen Duggie, get rid of that Karitane waistcoat. It makes you look like a con man."

"Maybe you're right. I didn't like it when I put it on." He picked at it with his fingers and told me about his girls. They had names like Antoinette and Miranda and they seemed to own little cars and call their fathers Daddy. Some learned ballet or the violin. Nevertheless they "turned it up" As usual this sort of talk made me discontented. I told him about Iris and Mrs Fitz. He was not impressed; and I was not. So I boasted of my slogan-writing and my decorating of the water tower.

"Keep quiet about it," he said.

I drew a dollar sign and a swastika in beer.

"Grow up." He smeared them with his hand. "They could still get you. Listen, I'll tell you some news. Beak Wyatt's married."

"Who to?" I had seen almost nothing of Beak since he left Rosebank College. All I knew was that he had gone through a motor mechanic's apprenticeship in a Loomis garage.

Duggie grinned. "I reckon you could sit here all day and

you'd never guess." He swallowed some beer. "Miss Gobbloffski."

"You're kidding. Myra Payne?"

"Poor old Beak, he'll be quiet now."

"She's ten years older than him." I could not marry them in my mind.

"So he's got a mummy. Maybe she'll stick marbles up his bum."

Duggie had bumped into Myra in John Courts—"there was nowhere to run"—then Beak came along. He pushed them at each other and got out of there—"left them sniffing each other's bums." Now there was this photo in the *Loomis Gazette*—Beak wearing a carnation and Myra dressed in white. "In white!"

"I still can't see it."

"She must have been getting desperate. What do you reckon we tell old Beak the sort of girl his wife is?"

They did not matter to him, he was relaxing. I felt more alarmed than privileged at seeing a part of him hidden from others. Then I had a sense that this Duggie, the old one, Millbrook Road boy, was not real. He put the face on like his yellow waistcoat; and I felt myself thinning out, I became as ghostly as Beak and Myra. He picked me up; put me down; forgot me.

"Well, Ray." He looked away from me at the door.

I guessed he was waiting for a girl, and I made a rush at substance: I would see her, I would get her, I would show him I was real.

"You've got a bus to catch," he said.

"There's a later one."

"I'm waiting for some friends, actually."

"Eckchewlay."

"Don't push it, Ray."

I watched him fidget as I drank my beer. Then he gave a small grin over my shoulder and said to me softly "Buzz off, eh?" I turned and saw two young men coming along the room. They were almost as interesting as a girl. The ferrety one in the suit and Calvinist glasses was Mark Brierly. The pink and white hearty in marmalade tweeds, Tony Smith. I saw where Duggie had copied his waistcoat from.

"Ho ho," Tony Smith said as we shook hands.

"My cousin's a journalist," Duggie said. He spoke as if explaining my awkwardness.

"What paper?" Brierly asked.

"The *Gerriston Independent.*"

"Ho. A two-minute silence," Tony Smith said.

Duggie gave him a cold look. "He's just got a job on the *Dominion.*"

"I'm going down next week."

"First-rate paper," Brierly said. "They did a good job for us in the strike."

"Us?"

"We're the Junior National Party. Ball Committee," Tony Smith said.

"Duggie too?" He must have found a way of making money out of them.

Brierly smiled. "Douglas is co-opted. He's very useful. Does the accounts. It's nice to have someone who can add up."

Duggie took this insult without blinking. He simply looked at Brierly, and then at Tony Smith, who suddenly seemed nervous and gave his plummy laugh. I wanted to get Duggie aside and ask him what his game was.

"Let's get on with it," he said. "Raymond, keep in touch. Now, what have we got?"

I caught my bus; and walking by Loomis creek, hearing the pines sigh, I had a sense of Duggie as the boy who had lived on the citrus orchard, and I found that it connected with him now—I knew by a premonition what he was after. The voice fitted in, the clothes fitted in. It was far bigger than I'd thought; and I grew afraid. He had a long way to go, but he would get there. I restored myself by laughing in advance at his mistakes, then thought of Smith and Brierly and was on Duggie's side.

"When did Sebastian join the National Party?" I asked my mother.

"He's not? Not Duggie?" It could not happen to a Plumb.

"He's on the ball committee."

"They'd better watch out, he'll pinch the takings," Dad said.

"I don't believe it," Mum said. "Not a Tory."

"Duggie was never a Plumb. A wolf suckled him."

Dad coughed. He did not like the "fancy talk" Mum and I indulged in. "I'll tell you one thing about young Duggie. Fred Meggett's got his eye on him. And Fred picks winners." He blushed. "Not that I mean me." Dad was part of Meggett Enterprises. He ran a subsidiary called Sole Construction—a sore point with Mum.

I said, "Duggie'll end up owning Fred. But politics is where he's really going."

"He'll want some money first."

Dad took me into the paddocks where the orchard had been. We walked among partly built Sole/Meggett houses. Dad seemed happy and he seemed unhappy. "Forty houses, Ray. I feel like a bloody magician."

"They all look the same."

"They're pre-cut. We're first in that. Most of it's done in the factory." We walked on the hill at the back and looked over new roofs, blinding in the sun. Up this end one or two families had moved in. "It wouldn't have suited my old man. Did you ever see him work a piece of iron? Still, there we are. Houses for people." It was the Sole Construction Company slogan but Dad could not make it sound convincing. "Your mother says it's like toytown."

"Mum's a bit of a snob."

"I'd have put them up one by one. But I'm not blaming Fred. They're good houses, Ray. They'll last."

"Sure. You drained the swamp, eh?" I looked at the front yards running down to footpaths. "Where's all the topsoil gone?"

"Well, you see, you've got to get a contour."

"Fred sells it, I suppose."

"That's about the strength of it," Dad said.

We met Mum on the brick bridge. That was as far as she cared to come now.

"What do you think, Ray?"

"Houses for people."

"I wonder if I clap my hands will they all fall down."

"Grow up, Meg," Dad said.

He started mowing the lawns, using the old hand machine Uncle Robert had owned. It made a pleasant chatter as he closed on Mum and me in the summer-house. To make up for Duggie's defection I told her how I had painted my slogan on the tower. She was pleased, though the danger of my falling worried her. I gave her a version of my life at Primrose Hall.

"I don't think I'd like Mrs Fitz. You'd better be sure you always wash your hands there."

"I do."

"What about girls? You must have a girl by now."

I had not known my backwardness troubled her. "I'm not like Uncle Alf if that's what you mean."

"I don't mean that. Bobby started so early. Becky too." She talked fast for a moment, getting us by the dangerous place.

I said, "I've got a girl called Iris."

"That's a nice name. Is she.   ? Is it   ?"

"Serious?" I had thought it might be. I had even thought I might marry Iris. There was no chance of that now. I had boasted about her to Duggie. "It helps pass the time."

In the afternoon I went down to see Bluey. He had turned eighty-three the week before. I took him a packet of pipe tobacco and he lit up straight away, puffing out aromatic smoke that overcame the meat smell of his kitchen. He had a priest with him, Father Pearce. Bluey had got free of his Church and stayed free fifty years but now he was back inside, rolling comfortably like a basking shark. I shook hands with the priest, uncertain how to address him. I had that trouble even with Protestant clergymen. But with Catholics I had the fear they sniffed my secrets out. I liked to believe they were jolly Irishmen or starved fanatics; but all were celibate and had an extra sense.

Father Pearce did not look starved. He didn't look jolly either I saw where my mother had got her jibe about blue-chinned priests. He and Bluey had the *Herald* open on the table and were picking horses. Pearce went at it fiercely: fanaticism there.

Sutton put the kettle on. I told him Duggie had joined the National Party.

"What's that?" Bluey boomed.

"Duggie's joined the Junior Nats. He's organizing their ball."

"Ah, he'll be after the girls. He'll plough a furrow there."

"I don't know the young man," Father Pearce said. He was not put out by the talk of sex. I had the impression he wanted more.

"Duggie," Bluey said, "is a walking cock and balls. If you'll pardon me, Father."

"There's something in it for him," Sutton said.

Bluey and Father Pearce went back to their horses. I took a book from Bluey's shelf and browsed in it: *The Growing Point of Truth*, one of my grandfather's. I looked at the chapter on Walt Whitman—Whitman as "new man", as exemplar of Man—and wondered if Grandpa Plumb had known that Whitman was as ready to go to bed with men as women. Perhaps at that point he had put judgment aside; just as he had deafened himself to daily noises. I turned a page and came on Edward Carpenter, new man too. Now Carpenter, I had read, was Whitman's "friend" Would Grandpa have banished them like Alf if someone had forced him to know?

"You'll have tea, Ray? Put another cup out, Roger boyo," Bluey said.

Sutton snarled and did it. I watched him secretly, remembering he had brought on Grandpa's experience of vastation. He was ugly all right—but primitive man in his cave? I could not see it. I found his played-out hatreds rather sad. He put leaves in the teapot and hissed with satisfaction as he poured boiling water in. I watched from behind my book, admiring the way he hopped about and the unlikely deftness of his hands. He threw a sidelong look at us, lifted a cup, and dropped a gob of spit in. I heard the little smack as it hit the bottom.

I guessed at once the cup was for the priest. He was the one who had stolen Bluey. But I watched it carefully, watched every move Sutton made. He had never had any liking for me and could spit in two cups as easily as one. It was only my wish to see the priest drinking that kept me there.

"Milk?" Sutton asked. Then he balanced the tray on his fingers and came to us posing as a waiter and doing a little jig that banged his surgical boot on the floor. He was quick as a boy.

"Ah, tea," Father Pearce said. He put his pencil down and reached for a cup; and Sutton was suddenly Irish, giving a leprechaun grin and brogueing extravagantly. "Now don't be getting off with Bluey's cup, Father. I'll be thanking you to see the shamrock on it."

"Stealing my tea, are you?" Bluey said.

Then I looked at Sutton with fear. I saw the richness of his life. This was his way of having Bluey and of forcing Bluey to have him. Each tea-drinking was a communion. I stood my cup on one side and watched Bluey sucking greedily, "Ah," in his swagman way. "Now that's a brew. You make a lovely cup, Roger boyo. Drink up, Ray."

I got my tea down and said goodbye. Sutton gave me his reddest grin. I wondered if he knew that I had seen. I went out the door sideways. Grandpa had been right: Sutton was in the cave. He was terrifying. But Grandpa was wrong. Sutton was at the other end too. He was a man of subtleties. Along one of the branches he was Man.

The next day I went back to Gerriston. I had three days left on the *Independent*. Love, I thought, took some twisted shapes. The betrayal I was guilty of was not worth noticing alongside Sutton's love.

Iris said, "You're not going to write to me, are you?"

"Well," I said.

"Just tell me, Ray."

"I suppose I'm not."

"I could tell."

"Was it different?"

Rain boomed on the roof of Primrose Hall. We were in the hollow of my bed. Now and then it took my breath away. Look,

I wanted to cry out, I'm in bed with a girl, we've got no clothes on.

"I knew this was going to happen," Iris said. I did not know she was crying until I touched her cheeks. "I don't mind. Really," she said.

"I'm sorry, Iris."

"No you're not." Tears rolled like glycerine. I swung between remorse and delight. Look at me, I'm hurting a girl. Look, she loves me. This paid Myra Payne for twisting my balls.

Iris dried her eyes on the sheet. I began stroking her and nuzzling her. "Iris," I said; and whispered things I would like us to do.

She got out of bed. "It's no use starting that when it's all over." She pulled on her clothes.

"It's early, Iris. It's only eleven o'clock."

"Too bad. Don't get out."

I ran down the hall in my underpants and watched her walk away in a tropical storm. The Phoenix palms thrashed over her. Power lines hissed and swung. She did not look back. It was like being in a movie.

Later I saw how it really was. I betrayed myself as well as Iris. I had stepped a long way back. That was my last time with her and, as Max Waring would have said, I had gone into it with only my doo-dah.

Justice, a true balance, would have had Gerriston end for me there. But the rain kept on all night and blocked the roads. Primrose Hall stood in a puddle six inches deep. I borrowed gumboots and waded out to look at the river. It was bucking like a cable. It swelled greasily and ate the stopbanks. Posts and gates and cabbage trees floated by and tangled in the understructure of the railway bridge. The mayor and the town clerk and the borough engineer were watching it. Morrie Horne was squatting, trying to keep his pad dry as he scribbled. Iris was there with her camera, snapping away.

Soon trucks arrived from the Council depot. Men started sandbagging round the ends of the road bridge. I wished I was still with the *Independent*. I wanted to be with Iris and Morrie

Horne. If the stopbanks broke this would be the biggest story in Gerriston since the gold rush. I wondered if I should be writing it for the *Dominion*. Instead I went back to Primrose Hall and changed into my oldest clothes. I borrowed an oilskin and went back to the bridge and helped with the sandbagging. I hoped Iris would photograph me. But soon she was gone with Morrie in his car. The old bridge south of town was washed away.

I stayed with the sandbagging team all that day and half the night. We filled bags at the depot and later at half a dozen yards and drove out to strengthen weak places in the bank. The rain rattled on our oilskins and the river brimmed at our feet. Trees rose in it lazily and crashed down in slow motion. Drowned cows floated by like lost footballs. At midnight farmers with shotguns stopped the engineer from dynamiting the banks on the side away from town.

I slept three hours and went out in the dawn. The rain was heavier. It struck my coat like bird-shot and dented it like copper on my skin. Stormwater was up to the porch of Primrose Hall. I met Mrs Fitz wading back from town.

"We've got to evacuate. They've run out of sandbags."

I helped her get the boarders out and we trudged up to the higher part of town and stood on verandas watching the river, still inside its banks, lurching past level with the shop roofs. It seemed mindlessly happy, like a monster broken through from an unknown world.

At nine o'clock it pushed the bridge aside and sucked it down. At half past ten it broke the bank, punched through like a fist on a corner west of town. It came down curving like the Huka Falls. We saw a man run out of a house. It swallowed him. Then easily, like water, it ran through all the streets and took charge of the buildings up to their window sills. I saw it pouring into my room at Primrose Hall. It was neat and fairly lazy by that time.

They found the drowned man floating by a door with his fingers tapping. Cats and dogs and guinea pigs and budgerigars were drowned. Out on the farms sheep and cattle died in hundreds. Cars died and carpets and furniture.

91

I stood in her dining-room with Mrs Fitz. Silt lay inches deep on the floor. The naked girls and boys and swollen soldiers hid in corners. The water in Primrose Hall had lapped the door heads. All the happy verses lay in mud.

"I'll never get this back the way it was," said Mrs Fitz. I held her hand but she did not cry.

"I knew I couldn't keep it. Come on, Ray. Let's see what's happened to my gin."

10 "You see," I told the girl over the table, "the way I look at it is that we've got a longing in us for happiness but the world is silent, or else it gives us back this idiot chatter We've got a deep desire, a deep nostalgia really, for unity and the world disappoints us. Now in the face of this, all we can do is struggle. The only weapons we have are strength and pride. The only truth we have is in defiance. Meaning is defiance. If there's any meaning. Ha! Another cup of coffee? Well anyway, that's how I see it."

"It's how Albert Camus sees it too." This was Glenda. She punctured me like a bladder My borrowed air came out in a rush. "Everyone I know is reading *The Myth of Sisyphus.* I wish they'd find another book."

"It's a matter of making what you read your own." I tried to sound Olympian and sounded pompous. Glenda smiled at me. "Perhaps. I won't have another cup. I'll have to go."

"Camus has taught me a lot He's made things clear And Kierkegaard."

"I'm pleased. They're too hard for me."

"They're really quite simple—"

"I mean the way is too hard. I want some fun in my life."

"Well. "

She gave a tiny smile at my comic eyebrows. "Groucho Marx. I really think you should acknowledge your sources."

"Can I ring you? Can I see you?"

"I'm rather busy."

"I've met you before. Nearly met. Four years ago. You were in a car with Douglas Plumb."

"I don't know any Douglas Plumb."

"Early nineteen-fifty. Up in Wadestown."

"You've got a better memory than me. Thanks for the coffee." She walked out of my life—so she thought. I might have let her go if she hadn't forgotten Duggie.

Kierkegaard did not deny happiness was possible. My melancholy was a result of breathing air thick with disappointments and defeats. Naturally I came to generalize. No girls—at least none of the sort I wanted—and not much money. Had it gone on I would have turned to ideology. Thought was too difficult. Action was difficult, but within my means. I went after Glenda and I got her. I caught her like a disease. I had been after happiness, but I became filled with uncomfortable sensations. I planned my getting of her anxiously and spent the nights dreaming of triumphs I could never make quite honourable.

"How did you get here?" she said at the party.

"I told them you invited me."

"The cheek!"

"Are you going to kick me out?"

"A gate-crasher, Di. Shall we kick him out?"

"He looks quite nice."

"You look after him then."

Plump Diana looked after me. She pointed out Glenda's boyfriend, a poet in a beret and red cravat. "He's had poems in *Image*."

"Good poems?"

"They're all about thighs and breasts. That's how he sees the hills." She leaned close to me. "Derivative. *Landfall* turned him down. Over there by the door—" she pointed at a fat little man rolling a cigarette "—that's Alan Webster. He's a real poet. He's after Glenda too. You'll have to stand in line."

"Not me."

"I don't think you can compete with Ron O'Connor." That was the bereted poet. "He's got, well, flair. Besides, he's a renegade Catholic. That thickens up the brew."

I began to like Diana. But over the room Glenda pushed her hair back with a gesture almost monkey-like. She took a neat two fingerfuls of dress and gave her pants a hitch. Her laugh chimed out and I watched her in a way that made Diana give her own laugh.

"I really should go and live in another flat."

"I'm sorry."

"Don't be. I wish you luck. I warn you though, she's Mariana in the moated grange."

"Meaning?"

"There's no quick way. You'll find out. If it's any consolation Ron O'Connor's finding out."

She told me she and Glenda were finishing their B.A.s. Then they were going to Training College.

"Secondary?"

"Of course."

"That means Auckland."

She smiled with malice. "It means you've got six months." But she was a jolly girl—jolliness was a style she'd adopted—and she sat and joked with me about flat life and dieting and randy poets while I watched Glenda. Ron O'Connor lit two cigarettes and gave her one. I was astonished by his cheapness and by the flush of pleasure that came on Glenda's cheeks.

Diana said, "He's been seeing too many movies."

"So bloody obvious. Do girls really fall for that stuff?"

"We've been known to."

"He pinched it from Humphrey Bogart."

"So? She's smoking a ciggie he held in his own two lips."

"No she's not." Glenda stubbed it out in an ashtray. She beckoned Diana and went to the kitchen.

"Saved by the gong," Diana said. She followed Glenda out. The other girls sharing the flat cleared dirty glasses off the table. Glenda and Diana carried in plates of sausage rolls and cheese and pickled onions.

I found myself by the door next to Alan Webster and a young

man with sunken shoulders and limp hair. Except for his air of premature bitterness he reminded me of Beak Wyatt.

"Bourgeois bitches," he said.

"What?"

"They know what we want and they bring in supper. Little bits of pineapple and cheese stuck on toothpicks. Bourgeois bitches."

"Stay with it, John," Alan Webster said.

"Bloody culture snobs. I write stories. That's the only reason I get invited. But I can't compete with Webster, the great poet. He's had the lot of them."

"You're thinking of Ron O'Connor," Webster said.

"The young solicitors get the Karori girls and you and O'Connor get the culture snobs. We should send the pair of you out on grummet-chasing expeditions. You could send the ones you don't want back to base. I wouldn't mind leftovers."

"John suffers," Webster said.

"I suffer from these bitches. They don't want cock they want promises. I can't afford promises. We're running against the hounds boy and we can't take on extra weight."

"Put it in a story," I said.

"Nobody'll print the things. Will you look at those bums. I'm aching. O'Connor will get the lot. The mould of their creativity is the womb so before all the squawling and shitting starts they're determined to experience the prick of the great poet."

"Easy, John."

I had supposed they were doing a comic-and-straight-man act but I saw a look of such misery on John's face I thought something in him must have broken.

"I've got to get out of here. I can't stand it."

He rushed out. Webster gave me his drink. "Hold this."

Diana came over with a tray of sausage rolls. "Jolly John fallen to pieces, has he?"

"It looks like it."

"Alan will put him together. He's good at that. It's what he does instead of having girls."

95

"John says he has them."

"I've heard that. Him and Ron. All of us together and one by one. Do you believe it?"

"I don't think so."

"Just as well." She sent a furtive glance at Glenda. "John tries to kill himself. They had to pump him out last week. He puts it all in stories but nobody publishes them." She wasn't a jolly fat girl. "I know what you're thinking."

"No—"

"I could be 'nice' to him. Oh, brother! Take one of these damn sausage rolls. I spent all afternoon making them."

Glenda came over to us. She had a way of pointing her chin and looking at things sidelong that reminded me of my mother.

"What went wrong with John?"

"The usual thing."

Glenda blushed on her cheeks but her forehead stayed white. "Did you say something to him?" she asked me.

"No."

"John Jolly is disturbed."

"So Diana said."

"We try to help him."

"Not the way he wants."

The blush mounted to her forehead. "I can see the sort of mind you've got."

"What sort?"

"Rather grubby." She went to sit with O'Connor on the sofa. I watched his over-ripe face and soft red mouth and wondered how we'd get on in a fight. He was large round the shoulders but his hands made lifts and gestures that set me wondering about his sex. I said to Diana, "Are you sure it's girls he likes?"

"You're clutching at straws."

"I don't know."

"That hand stuff is part of his style. French or something. Read his poetry if you don't believe me. All his hills have got nipples on top."

I put down Alan Webster's glass and wandered away with my

96

sausage roll. People were dancing in a room across the hall. The air was grey with cigarette smoke and the crush of bodies left me no way through. I went down the hall and found a lavatory with fish painted on the walls. Opposite were bedrooms; piles of rain-coats, varsity scarves. I tried guessing at Glenda's bed and chose the one with a dark blue counterpane and a mobile of blue fishes over it. She must lie in bed and sleep as though under water. On the bedside stand was a photograph of a middle-aged man with the same over-ripe look Ron O'Connor had. I wondered where I had seen him.

"Who's this?" I asked Diana, who came in the door.

"Glenda's father."

"He's got a boozer's face. So this is her bed? Nice mobile."

"Glenda made it. She's got a thing about water. The moving waters at their priestlike task etcetera. Would you like to hold her nightie?"

"I like you, Diana."

"Don't let my mind fool you. The important thing about me is my excess of adipose tissue."

"Don't say that." I stroked her arm.

"Get your hands off me. And get out of my bedroom, I've decided to have a cry. Close the door behind you."

I did as I was told and the man in the photo seemed to wink at me as I had a last look at Glenda's bed.

"Excuse me," I said to one of the flatmates, "is Glenda's father famous for anything?"

"Why don't you go home?"

"Yeah, piss off," her boyfriend said.

"Friendly place." I went into the sitting-room. And there the name I heard was Uncle Alf's. It hit me like a punch. I was trying not to think of Alf. He was beaten to death in Moa Park in Loomis. A bunch of boys hunting queers had got him. The trial was just over and the boys had been acquitted. I had used a lot of anger on that, evading my guilt at dropping Alf. He had helped me when there was no one else. "If you can't get in to see me, drop a line. Let me know how you're getting on." I had not done it. His death troubled me in several ways.

"You're wrong," I said to O'Connor. "Alfred Hamer never chased little boys. You'd be his style."

"Who the hell are you?"

"Alfred Hamer was my uncle."

"Oo la," O'Connor said, "so it runs in the family."

"He was a good man." I wondered how soon I would hit O'Connor.

"Boo hoo," he said. He was not going to stand up though. Glenda watched me with a look of calm I took for superiority.

"He's the one who's been on trial, not those thugs who killed him. I'm buggered if I'm going to stand here and listen to him being run down by half-baked poets and their arty girl-friends."

"Go home then," someone said.

"Yeah, go home."

"You can't deny," O'Connor said, "that he was out there chasing little boys."

My mother had an explanation for that and in her grief had written it to me. I said, "My uncle was committing suicide."

I heard a hiss of outrage. A girl behind the sofa hooked her hands on Glenda's collar bones. Another put her face down and rubbed her cheek on Glenda's. "Glenda, love."

"I'm all right."

"Bastard," someone squeaked.

"Boot him out."

I did not know what I had said but it filled me with delight. Somehow I had broken their rules; and now their boyfriends scrummed me out of their house. O'Connor dug his fingers in my neck and gave the knee that sprawled me on the path. The door slammed but I wasn't having that. I found a stone and threw it at the wall.

"We're calling the police," O'Connor yelled.

I gave their letter-box a kick and ran up the road. I could not understand why I was laughing.

Alan Webster found me leaning on a concrete wall in the Terrace. I was licking blood from my wounded palms. "They kicked me out."

"It happens now and then. The boys don't like too much competition."

"Is O'Connor really a poet?"

"He tries. He'd do better if he didn't have to pretend."

"Yeah, I thought so."

"Glenda feels safe with him. Glenda needs to feel safe. You want my advice?"

"Maybe."

"Diana's the best of them. Go after her."

I wrapped my handkerchief round one of my palms. "What did I say wrong?" I told him about Alf and he laughed.

"You shouldn't have said suicide. You know who Glenda is?"

The face in the picture had a name. "God," I said. "Goodlad."

"Graham Goodlad was her father."

"Someone should have told me."

"Suicide is the dirty word in that flat. But I'm glad you've said it. I'll make a prediction."

"What?"

"You'll have her on your doorstep in the morning. Ray— that's your name, isn't it?"

"Yes."

"Go easy on her, Ray."

11 Graham Goodlad was a racing journalist. He wrote a column called *Goodlad's Hot Tips* and was one of the first tipsters to go on radio. Dad used to listen to him on Saturday mornings. That must have been in 1947 In '48 Goodlad left his paper and started *Horse Talk*, a weekly form guide padded out with stable gossip. *Hot Tips* was part of it and Goodlad's whisky face grinned at New Zealand. That was where I had seen him. Goodlad was in half the houses in the country.

Then a brewer called Mottram brought a divorce action against his wife and named Graham Goodlad as co-respondent.

It was in the days when adultery in the courts became a floor show. The Mottram/Goodlad case sent a delicious shiver up our spines. Famous people. High society. It gave us a licence to talk about sex. Graham Goodlad was our hero/victim. His name passed into the language. I still hear people use it. From the *New Zealand Dictionary*: goodlad *noun* (*informal*), a penis: "I gave her a bit of *goodlad*." It appeared in limericks on lavatory walls. And everywhere were pictures: Goodlad in the saddle, Goodlad's hot tip.

For me the case had an extra dimension: Uncle Oliver was the judge. He was famous for his moral homilies and he did not spare Goodlad. His remarks about "the cancer eating home and family" were as talked-of for a time as the Mazengarb Report.

The trial lasted for two weeks and the papers printed every scrap of it. In the end Mottram got his divorce. Mrs Mottram sailed away to England. Graham Goodlad went out to his woodshed, put his shotgun in his mouth, and blew the top of his head off. That's the story. I knew it well. I could not find a place in it for Glenda.

On Sunday morning I lay in bed waiting for her knock. I thought it better not to be polished up and I ran my hand over my stubbly chin, shivering with lust and pity as I thought of the mark I would leave on her. Every sound in the street had me ready. Her knock. Her timid knock.   It did not come. Webster and I had forgotten she did not know where I lived.

At midday I got up and shaved and tidied my rooms. I hoped they'd have a big effect on Glenda. Today the building is gone. The motorway tunnel comes out where it stood in Ghuznee Street and four lanes of traffic pass over the garden where I grew my radishes. In through a high wooden wall, in through a red door in the iron cladding: there was the kitchen—tiny stove, rag mat from my mother, built-in table with a bamboo screen. Up a ladder through a hole in the ceiling: bedroom, painted red. Bookshelves, desk, hand-basin, built-in bed running the width of the room, six feet. A shower in the corner—cold. No lavatory. That was outside through the yard. At Ghuznee Street I learned to pee in preserving jars.

By two o'clock I had to admit Glenda was not coming. I went out to a phone box and rang the flat.

"Is Glenda in?" I asked one of the flatmates.

"She's gone to visit her aunt."

"Oh."

"Any message?"

"No message. Is she all right?"

The girl gave a hiss. "I thought it was you." She hung up.

That made me happy. I saw how it might push Glenda at me. I walked down Willis Street and Lambton Quay and struck up into the hills. I went through the street where Myra Payne had wrecked me and climbed clear of houses into the pines. The white harbour, the hills like black steam trains: I had not grown used to them. Wellington lifted me and blew me about. It still does that. I came down through a wind that tore my hair and tore my coat, making me flap like a bird. In Wadestown Road I buttoned up. I found a still spot and combed my hair.

"Hallo," I said to the woman—nurse it seemed—who opened the door, "is Mr Plumb at home? I'm his nephew." I had been here only once before, with Felicity and Max. Oliver had asked me to call again but a sniffy elevation in his voice had warned me off. I followed the woman in with the feeling that I was back at Ormiston's door.

"Hallo Uncle Oliver. It's Raymond Sole."

"Raymond. Yes, I see. What brings you here?"

"I was passing. I thought I'd drop in."

Oliver frowned at such casualness. His eye took in my tie-less throat as I shed my raincoat. He had not risen from his chair at the fire.

"Can I sit down?"

"Very well. I can't offer you tea."

"That's all right. How's Aunt Beatrice?"

"Unwell. She's most unwell."

"I'm sorry—"

"My own health is good. In spite of the trials my family bring on me."

I understood he was referring to Alf. "That was bad. An incredible verdict."

"The verdict was quite proper. Your newspapers need not have reported the case so fully. At least we can be thankful he changed his name."

Uncle Oliver took my breath away. I was helpless with him, I could find no place of attack. He was in his professional prime. Judgment was his habit; and moral disgust, a disgust I believe encompassing everything not himself, had thrown him into a mental stance so bent that I came to see him as a kind of brother to Roger Sutton. He was riddled with self and hatred. He was the most freakish man I have known.

I said, "I liked Uncle Alf."

He said, "You're not speaking of anyone I know."

"He was—"

"You will kindly not mention him."

"He was your brother."

"Is this what you came to see me for? What then? I'm a busy man."

"Do you remember a case—the Goodlad case?"

"I do."

"What was Goodlad like?"

"I never knew him. I took no notice of him. I took notice of the facts before me."

"You talked about the moral squalor of it."

"Goodlad was an adulterer. He was a man who drank, a man who gambled. I said as much. Beyond that I said nothing."

"Did you know he shot himself?"

"I heard of it."

"Did you know he had a daughter?"

He looked at me with a coldness, a needle sharpness, that made me prickle.

"I can see that this is the point of your visit. No doubt you have met this daughter. I see you have. I can only advise you, as my sister's son, to have nothing to do with her. I remind you of what her father was. Now Raymond, I'm busy. If you decide to visit me again please give me warning. I'd like it too if you dress suitably." He had me at the door. "Mrs Barrett will see you out. Remember me to your parents. I understand your father's doing well." He closed the door, and there I was in the hall, reeling with disbelief. He had got me out of there like a schoolboy.

Mrs Barrett drew me down the hall. I stuttered at her that I was all right, I was going; but she gave a cheery smile, gave a wink. "Dodge along through the garden. I'll open the French doors. Your aunt wants to see you. Don't worry about old Sourpuss, he won't know." She opened the door and pushed me out. I did as I was told; squelched along the lawn through winter shrubs; let her draw me into another room. She smiled and said, "Easy-peasy. Now take off your shoes. Tippy-toes."

We went into a room looking over the harbour and there was my Aunt Beatrice, monkey woman in a wooden bed. Her face was like crinkled paper. I thought there was some hideous mistake. I had met my aunt but not this woman before.

"There we are Plumduff," Mrs Barrett said, "your nephew's come to visit you. Give him a smoochy-smoo." She pushed me over the bed and the woman kissed me, light and sharp as bird claws.

"Raymond? Raymond Sole? You're Meg's son?" *She* did not know *me*. "The newspaperman?"

"Yes. I'm sorry you're not well."

"I've had the jaundice. I can't seem to get better."

"She's only five stoney-oh," Mrs Barrett said. "She used to be thirteen. That's why I call her Plumduff."

"I'm so very tired," Aunt Beatrice said.

"I'm sorry.   "

"Raymond, listen. I want you to do something for me. You work on a newspaper, so you can find things out."

"Well.   "

"I want you to find my daughter. I want you to send her to me."

"Aunt Beatrice—"

"Call me Trixie. People called me that when I was young. Even Oliver. I called him Ollie."

103

"Aunt. Aunt Trixie. I don't know whether I can trace people."

"I've written it all down. Barry will give it to you. Barry dear ."

Mrs Barrett gave me a paper covered with wispy writing. *Helen Plumb. Born in Palmerston North 1921 Adopted 1921 by Oliver and Beatrice Plumb. . .*

"Her mother was an educated girl. Oliver made sure of that."

"Aunt Beatrice, I wouldn't know where to start."

"He pays her money to stay away. I've written it down. You'll know her by her eye. Help me, dear."

I did not know whether she spoke to me or Mrs Barrett. Mrs Barrett knew. "Righty-ho. Outski. Back in a wee mo, Plumduff." She nudged me at the door. "Tippy-toes."

"Aunt—"

"I saw her last in 1942. I want to say I love her. We must tell people we love them."

"Yes, I see."

"Now let's play little mice," Mrs Barrett whispered, easing me out. Aunt Beatrice, Aunt Trixie, smiled tiredly. Even her teeth were yellow. There were yellow stains on the paper in my hand. Later I sniffed them and found they were orange juice.

"Put that in your pocket, just in case. He'd go right through the roof," Mrs Barrett whispered. She waited while I put on my shoes. "Help her. She's had a dreadful life married to that cactus."

"This daughter ?"

"It's worth a try. To help a poor old lady. She won't last long."

"How long?"

"Oh, she's dying. Of thirst if you ask me."

I went down Wadestown Road with her whispered "Cheery-bye" in my ears. I wondered how I was going to get out of this. All the time I was getting to know Glenda it troubled me like a boil. I was scratching it, worrying it, when Glenda tapped on my door the following night. I opened, said hallo, let her in. My smile was cool but my heart was banging and it came to me that her visit marked out the rest of my life.

Glenda had got my address from the office. She said she had come around to apologize. "For Ron talking like that about your uncle."

"He wasn't to know."

"All the same, he shouldn't have said those things. And I want you to know I'm not arty."

"I didn't think you were. I was trying to hurt you."

"What for?"

"For liking Ron O'Connor more than me."

"I don't. He's company."

"I'm sorry I threw a stone at your house."

We went on for a while in that way. It was a verbal current over still deep waters where we met. (Her words, later on.) I showed her round my bach. She thought it "marvellous", the upstairs room like a magic cave. She said it was too bare though and needed treasures in it and said that she would bring me some polished stones from West Coast rivers. She walked about the room, turning on her heel. "Rude," she said of my Modigliani print. When she looked at my books she found Camus and laughed.

I took her downstairs and made a cup of tea and while we were drinking it she asked about Alf. I told her he had been my wailing wall when I was "mixed up". "No," I said, "not that way. I like girls."

"I never doubted it. Your uncle was crucified in court."

"Yes."

"I'm sorry." She did not go on to talk about her father and I was offended not to be given that. Instead she asked about my job. And as I talked the gloss I had put on her fell away and I began to see her. With Mrs Fitz and Iris I had learned a good deal, but I'd forgotten. When Glenda came I started to remember, I grew up. I had taken backward steps, but I took them forward again, then took another. I *saw* Glenda. I forgot about sex.

We walked up Ghuznee Street and up the Terrace.

"Am I going to see you again?"

"I'll only throw my rotten apple at you."

For a moment I was afraid. "I don't mind."

We went into the flat. "You've jumped the queue," Diana said.

Glenda was round at my bach almost every night. She brought me polished stones. She made a lantern from paper and bamboo and fitted it on the naked bulb in my bedroom. It turned the room purple. I did not tell her the light was now too dim for me to read. Sometimes she brought Diana or Alan Webster. I treated them with condescension, believing them unqualified for happiness of the sort we had.

Webster was there the night Ron O'Connor called. O'Connor banged on my door, howling for Glenda. She was Holy Spirit, Holy Mother. Only she could save him from the Pit. O'Connor's voice rose melodiously. It reminded me of Duggie Plumb's new voice. We pulled him in and let him weep at my table, where his beret fell like a tent on the sugar bowl. Alan Webster washed his face with water. Glenda tried to make him drink some tea. Then Ron O'Connor vomited on my floor. Webster washed him again and took him away, while Glenda got some rags and wiped up the vomit. "No," she said, "don't touch it." When she was finished she went upstairs and used my shower. It was a winter night but she stood in there five minutes and then sat wrapped in towels in front of my heater. I made tea. I rubbed her hands and she put her head on my shoulder.

"I collect lame ducks."

"I'm not one."

"That's why I like you. Alan's a lame duck. He's a lame duck who collects lame ducks. He's trying to get rid of me. I'm graduating."

She took off her towels and I gave her clothes to her piece by piece. Later I was astonished. There had been no sex in it.

Walking home, she said, "That cousin of yours? Duggie Plumb? He had a big behind."

"That's Duggie."

"He tried to maul me in the car. I had to get out and catch a taxi home."

"That's Duggie too. Why did you say you didn't remember?"

"He had the same name as the judge at my father's divorce case."

"Oliver Plumb. He's my uncle."

"Yes, I worked that out."

The next night she brought me a mobile of blue and yellow fishes and hung it on a cup hook over my bed. It turned there dreamily.

"Lovely," I said.

She took off her clothes and slipped into bed. She looked like a fish herself in the purple light. "Come in with me."

So that part of it started. I can't really sort it out from the rest. Later things came apart but in the beginning there were no divisions. Our times in bed were nothing out of the ordinary. There was no "sex-book fucking", in Duggie's phrase. Nor did our talk go anywhere unusual. No Camus or Kierkegaard. We talked about my job and her exams; and laughed about Duggie now and then. She showed me how he had mauled her—savage stuff. I gave her his new voice, and hopped out of bed to fetch a clipping from the *Weekly News*. It was hard to see in the dim light, but there was Duggie, no mistake: bum out, belly in, dancing at this year's National Party Ball with Miss Jennifer Gibbs, who looked rather like Kim Novak and a little bit like Glenda.

"Do you ever see your uncle?" Glenda asked.

"Never again." I told her about Aunt Beatrice and my search for Helen Plumb. "Not much of a search." I had gone through the records at the Registrar's Office and through the Wellington electoral rolls. Apart from that I had written to Mum, who told me the story. Aunt Beatrice had given the girl her name—slipped it past Oliver's guard somehow. The child was pretty, clever. She had her education at Marsden School. But at sixteen she started running away (looking for love, Mum said) and at seventeen ran away with a *Maori*! At that point Oliver stopped fetching her home. She came of her own accord on her twenty-first birthday—"for my present" She was wearing a black eye-patch. One of her eyes was gone after a fight. Oliver gave her a cheque, and probably at that time made his arrangement to keep her away. He saw her only once again, drunk in Lambton Quay, arm in arm with a *black*! American sailor. He put his newspaper over his face. "But do try and find her," Mum wrote. "Felicity says Beatrice is wasting away."

"I feel sorry for your uncle," Glenda said.

"He wouldn't like that."

We put on our coats and I took her down through the yard to pee. I waited barefoot on the gravel, then she waited for me. Upstairs we made love hours on end, with tiny tiny movements, and no movements, simply joined. Then Glenda told me about her father.

Graham Goodlad loved three things in his life—horses, women, Glenda. Four if you counted whisky. He did not love his wife, an Englishwoman he'd met on a trip Home in 1922. He was bowled over by her arrogance. It was as if, he said, he was watching it on a stage. He thought she was from "the upper class" Actually her father was a clerk, but she was a climber. She'd learned some tricks and she played them well. That didn't stop her from making the great mistake. She was pregnant and the cad would not marry her. But along came this young New Zealander, rough but presentable; with, it seemed, a little bit of money. He was too nervous to put his hands on her. But all told he would do, though poles away from what she had expected. By this time she too felt she was on a stage. Things had begun that could not be reversed. Dulcie Titheridge spoke the lines left to her. She quickly got the young man over his fright.

Glenda told it like that. Young Graham Goodlad amused and enchanted her. I held her in my arm and stroked her breast and watched her face staring up at the lazy fishes. I did not think she could keep it up. But she put detachment in place of humour, choosing words.

In Wellington the Goodlads settled down. Graham went into his father's importing business. He bought a house in Karori not far from the old Beauchamp place. The baby was named

Gordon. He grew up looking English, speaking county. Dulcie Goodlad worked very hard at him. She made as much of her own life as she could, near the top among the second best. Then the depression came. New Zealanders over a certain age all say that: the depression came. *Goodlads* went down early. Grandpa, who had not spread his money out, worked for the Council painting white lines on the roads. He was almost cheerful about it. Graham did this and that. He wheeled and dealed. He got by. Somehow he became connected with horses. But the car went, the house in Karori went. Glenda had her infancy in a little house in Tinakori Road—quite near the other Beauchamp place.

Dulcie Goodlad never forgave her husband for the late baby. Glenda remembered her mother in little words: cold, sharp, neat, grey, thin. Her father—he was Daddy. He filled all the cold and empty places. Still, there were quarrels; there were shrunken silences and icy dislike; there was reek of whisky and smashing of chairs. "Why go into it?"

Graham Goodlad became a racing writer. In the war he sank out of sight in a department of government. The Goodlads shifted to Brooklyn. Glenda saw the harbour and the mountains. People called her old-fashioned but she was quiet and still. Quiet and still, she floated over the harbour. Albatross, she was tossed by storms. She sat and watched her mother. News came that Gordon was dead in a battle in Italy. She touched her mother's cheeks and felt hands as cold as ice and sharp as claws push her back and down and out of sight. Her father cried round tears. "Poor little bugger, poor little bugger." "You weren't his father," Dulcie Goodlad said.

Then the war was over. Graham Goodlad went back to his newspaper. That was not all. He had, he said, a finger in several pies. There was money to send Glenda to Queen Margaret College. Soon there was enough to shift to Kelburn. Mrs Goodlad sat there, upper-class. It did not matter that she was the only one to see it.

As for Graham Goodlad: race-courses and stables; whisky; women. And there was his lovely daughter Glenda. She was "Princess"

"He took me on a holiday," Glenda said. "We rented a house in the Marlborough Sounds." Mr and Mrs Mottram had the house round the bay. They came over every day in their launch. "Daddy seemed to know them pretty well."

At nights she heard her father creeping out. At last she followed him. She sat in rocks at the end of the bay and watched him swimming with Mrs Mottram. They ran up from the sea. They were beautiful. She saw Mrs Mottram's long breasts swinging. There was a gleaming in their thighs.

They went by Glenda, blind and close. She heard their feet padding and breath hissing. She saw her father's penis long and white. On a beach robe on the dry sand they knelt down. They were horrible and beautiful, making love in the moonlight. They seemed to fight each other and become each other.

Glenda watched. When it was over they saw her in her nightie. She was sitting with her hands folded in her lap. They pulled on their clothes and her father ran to her.

"Darling, Princess, I wouldn't have had you see that for the world."

She wanted him to touch her. She wanted to tell him that she did not mind.

"Princess. Princess. Try to understand. We love each other."

She understood perfectly. She was perfectly happy. But she could not smile. She could not do it, even though, with still face, she looked like Dulcie Goodlad.

Mrs Mottram put her palm on Glenda's cheek. It was soft and cool and smelled of salt. "I want to tell you this. I love your father." She walked off along the sand in her beach robe, with her towel about her hair. She looked like an Arab in the desert.

"Princess," Goodlad said. He sat by Glenda and put his arm around her.

"Then," Glenda said, "Daddy loved me."

I gave a jerk. Whatever I might have expected, this was not it.

"No, no, no," Glenda cried.

"I'm sorry—"

"It's my fault. I said it the wrong way. He showed me that he loved me. He's the only person who could ever do that. Just by being with me."

I began to dislike this clever man. Glenda felt it.

"Please, Ray. Understand." She heard the echo of her father's word and gave a laugh, not doubting then that I would see. I pulled her close. She was clear—clear to me as water. Goodlad? No. I tried to hide that I could not see him. He was always lost in a cloud of laughter; deep in cleverness and quick emotions. I came to see his death as quick and cheap.

What came next? The Mottrams sailed away in their flash launch. Glenda and her father stayed three more days. They walked and fished and swam. He told his daughter how happy Josie Mottram had made him and said that she had made him twenty again. "But if I was twenty, Princess, I wouldn't look past you." They swam off the end of the Mottrams' jetty. Under water, in the slanting sun, they bubbled and made faces at each other Her father's diamond eyes flashed at her. Silver fishes darted in the piles.

And next? The divorce. Still Glenda chose her words with care. It was as if exactness cancelled pain. Dulcie Goodlad did not wait but put things in her lawyer's hands and left for Home, which turned out to be Exeter, on the first ship she could catch. She went through the forms by "insisting" her daughter go with her but gave a smile, at once relieved and bitter, when Glenda said no. "You were never mine. Stay in this wretched country if you must. With that man." Glenda went to her father's sister in Scorching Bay. They sat there being jolly, being brave, while Graham Goodlad and Mrs Mottram became figures in a comic strip. Glenda watched the sea. She watched ships steaming in and out and read their names and home ports with her father's racing binoculars. Graham Goodlad came for dinner every evening. He had sold his interest in *Horse Talk*. *Hot Tips* had a new name, but *hot tip* was everywhere: scratched on walls, painted on railway bridges. *Goodlad* too. Glenda found it written in the sand at Scorching Bay under a penis squirting pipi shells at a vagina.

"Princess, I'm sorry," Goodlad groaned. He was sorry, he

was groggy, he was hurting. Mrs Mottram sat in court with a smile on her lips. She was cool, inviolate, wrapped in furs, and he knew she was gone. Everything was gone. He had loved being famous and popular; but now, Glenda said, his life was like a photographic negative reversed. What had been dark was light, what had been light was dark. At times his eyes sank deep into his head, at others they strained out, blue and bursting. She pictured hands in there squeezing his brain.

On the day Judge Plumb granted the divorce Glenda sat waiting for her father. Aunt Rose had cooked him a fillet steak—a small one, grilled medium. Blood, he said, made him feel sick. Aunt Rose was a teacher at the Girls' College. She had not been to school all week. It was no fun being Miss Goodlad at a time like this. She thought her brother a fool, but tried to take a larger view and talked a good deal about *hubris* and *nemesis*. She advised Glenda to keep her chin up.

Graham Goodlad did not come. Aunt Rose tapped her foot and began to look dangerous. "He's somewhere with his cronies getting drunk."

What Glenda told me next had a quality of neatness that kept me still for fear that I should break it and break her. It was as if she were taking two-footed jumps, landing her feet in squares marked on the floor. The game was to get to the wall without being eaten by crocodiles—or rolled soundlessly screaming into space.

"When he was five minutes late I knew he was dead."

She took his binoculars and watched a freighter coming in from the broken sea by Barretts Reef. Up in Kelburn Graham Goodlad walked through the yard with his brand new shotgun. Mottram had promised to take him duck shooting. He sat on a pile of coalsacks in a corner of the woodshed and put the barrel of the gun in his mouth. He pressed the trigger with a piece of kindling wood.

The phone rang. "That'll be him," Aunt Rose said. "I'll give him a piece of my mind." Glenda smiled. The freighter went by from Liverpool. Before Aunt Rose came back she locked herself in her room.

"I've never blamed him, Ray. I thought it was the proper thing to do."

12 Another proper thing, considering our love, was to take no precautions. She did not want anything between us. And those things, rubber, were so horrible. And fizzy pills to stick up there—she would sooner use a bottle of coke like those girls at Naenae. I agreed. No precautions. Considering our love.

She sat her exams with morning sickness and was capped *in absentia*. I put a payment on a house in Wadestown, an old villa with rust holes in the roof and weatherboards dry-rotted light as balsa and wallpaper flopping off its scrim. I took her there in January from the registry office and Glenda grew round as I tore tobacco-coloured roses from our walls and nailed up sheets of gib board. We were up towards the pines on the Tinakori Hills. Our bedroom looked over the snooty part of Wadestown—Oliver's house—and over the harbour at the Orongorongos. We lay in bed and watched them browse like herds of elephants.

"I love it up here. I never want to leave." She made new mobiles and hung them round the house: octopuses in the lavatory, a school of silver sprats over our bed. When Sharon was born she hung clouds of butterflies over her cot. I lay in bed with my wife and practised happiness. Our balsa walls kept out the southerlies and our web of affections kept out the world. Love turned back time and fate. These are phrases from the poems she wrote.

Glenda had some money from her father. We spent it on the house: re-roofed, re-piled. I put in a retaining wall where the back of our section was slipping into the neighbour's. There on a new little lawn Glenda and Sharon basked in the sun, watching ladybirds and lizards, watching mountains and the sea. On summer evenings we sat on our veranda drinking home brew made from Ted Sole's recipe, while lights swelled from silver to golden across at Eastbourne and Days Bay. Our visitors were

113

polite about the beer; but our house, our view, our marriage seemed to delight them.

Glenda's Aunt Rose had been less upset by our "mistake" than by Glenda's "tossing away" of her career. The girl should at least have qualified, then if anything went wrong.   Rose was a believer in things going wrong. Experience had taught her. But she came to acknowledge that ours was out of the common run of marriages, and she "saw Glenda's point" that happiness itself was a career. When she came to visit us she brought gifts of food and books and pottery, calling them "a little contribution" It seemed to us that she helped herself to pieces of our contentment in return, but we had plenty so we did not mind. She was a crusading rationalist and watched us for signs of belief that more was in our union than met the eye. Glenda, she observed, had "a tendency"

Rose became dry and exact when she found Felicity calling on us. They were full-rigged ladies and should have fired broadsides at each other. But Rose advanced only her common sense and Felicity brushed it off in a friendly way. It seemed that she too shared in our contentment.

"How's Aunt Beatrice?" I asked. I did not really want to know but she troubled me.

"Oh," Felicity said, "so so."

"Is that Barrett woman still there?"

"She is. I suppose we should be grateful Trixie has someone. But she's like one of those Yankee ra-ra girls. Twirling sticks."

"No news of her daughter?"

"None. That's a hopeless business."

"I tried. I don't know where to go next."

"It worries Ray," Glenda said.

"Don't worry. Life's too short."

That was also Rose's philosophy but she wasn't going to agree with Felicity. "Rather brutish without conscience, wouldn't you say?"

"Is conscience part of the doctrine?"

"She was at Marsden," Glenda said. "You might have taught her, Rose."

"Who?"

"Helen Plumb. She had one eye."

"Not when she was at school," Felicity said.

"I remember Helen Plumb," Rose said. "She was the daughter   yes," looking at Glenda. "A pretty girl. Always in trouble. I hadn't realized.   "

"She's Ray's cousin."

"Yes, I see." She studied us, wondering if this might be a crack in our happiness. In spite of the pleasure she took in us the moment satisfied her

"And you remember her?" Glenda asked.

"She's coming back. She had a kind of—eager quality. Yet even then she was somehow beaten. It was all blunted somehow. Helen was a very troubled girl."

"What happened to her?"

"Oh I don't know. She left. They have a way of leaving. That's the end. They don't come back. And I left Marsden myself. I never enjoyed being in a church school. Visits from the bishop and all that. I wouldn't have minded if there'd been more to it than a kind of fancy dress show. Some intellectual distinction. Instead of all that watery piety. And moral precepts dangling kitchen objects round their necks. Egg beaters and measuring spoons. We had one chappie visit there who was always going on about sponge cakes that failed to rise. Because, you see, something was left out. Love of God, apparently, is a kind of baking powder."

Felicity laughed. "Suitable for girls. Plain-ness without plain thinking. Hard thinking, I mean. Why, I heard a fellow on the air   " and she mimicked him: "Have you ever noticed we have two eyes but only one mouth? I'm sure God made us that way on purpose."

It was Rose's turn to laugh. The two ladies beamed at each other. Glenda made tea and offered biscuits.

"Buy your biscuits Glenda, don't waste time making them."

"Read books instead."

They cleared the plate. And disapproved when Glenda gave Sharon her bottle to stop her crying. It was time, they agreed, that the child faced up to things. Parents must not play the role of *deus ex machina* endlessly. In the last analysis a short sharp smack. .

Glenda said, "What rot!" She picked Sharon up and cuddled her.

"You'll spoil the child."

"Like a sponge cake," Glenda said.

"This is a serious matter."

"It is. It is. Come on, love. It's your mummy you want not that old bottle." She opened her blouse and Sharon latched on. That was a time when breast-feeding was frowned on. Rose and Felicity were enlightened women, so they frowned. The child should be broken of *that* habit.

"You pair of silly old noodles," Glenda said.

I asked Rose more about Helen Plumb but she had told me all she could remember. Well, let's see. The child liked Wordsworth: an unusual taste. Usually it was Keats and Shelley. When it was anything. And—music? She played the piano rather well. I rang the secretary of the Marsden Old Girls Association but Helen Plumb was not a member. There I stopped again. There was nothing else I could do. I left a message with Mrs Barrett that I had reached a dead end. She let me know she was "a wee bit disappointed" Beatrice, it seemed, spoke of little else now but her daughter. It worried me, but I wanted to find Helen less than go down to Oliver's house and give the old bugger a talking to. When I thought of him in his study, by his fire, and all human feeling locked outside, and misery and love and desperation tapping like the drowned man at his door, I was filled with rage, and I wanted to do more than tell him he, not the world, was leprous—I wanted to smash him.

Glenda reasoned with me and calmed me down. I saw her as Oliver's victim too; but she cured me, for I believed I had saved her She saved me. I had a sense of *us* that filled my days. When we sat at the breakfast table, or worked side by side in our garden, or when I pulled her by the hand up the steep hill home, it seemed to me we were making love just as surely as when we

coupled in our bed. Everything was easy, there was no intensity—even in our quarrels, which were noise. She went to
bed early and sometimes was asleep by nine o'clock. When she
brushed her teeth she put paste on my brush—a message for me.
I found it there even after our quarrels. Often she was on my side
of the bed. That was a message too: I was to wake her and make
love. Still no precautions, though while she breast-fed Sharon
we hoped she would not conceive.

One night we heard a knocking at our door and there were
Diana and Alan Webster, come to tell us they were getting
married. We had not seen much of Diana since her year in
Auckland. She was teaching out at Naenae and finding it fun. In
spite of what *Truth* and Mazengarb might say, the kids were not
monsters of depravity. "They're just plain bored, poor little
buggers. I try to keep them laughing."

She called our house "The Nest", which offended us. "Alan
and I will call ours Cosy Nook."

"Waiwurri," Alan said. "And talking of *Truth*, have you
heard about John Jolly? He's got a job there. We'll get some
seedy stories from him now."

"And Ron O'Connor's gone into radio. Producing
plays."

"Don't talk about them. They make me depressed," Glenda
said.

"Ron's writing religious verse," Diana said. "All about
Christ with B.O. and the Virgin Mary missing her period."

"Please."

"Sorry, sorry. Where's the baby. I want to get some practice
holding her."

"She's clucky," Alan said. Later he showed us *Numbers* with
some poems he had written for her. I told him they were
beautiful—controlled, shapely, passionate, eager, strong. I ran
out of adjectives. I was moved. I found it hard to believe they
were written by this fat man for this fat girl. Glenda said
nothing. She told me later that she hadn't liked them.

'They're the best things he's ever done."

"I know. I know. Why does he say it's got to end?"

"Well, death—you can't deny it. But now is what counts. That's what he says."

"Ray, I want another baby."

"On the spot. Come here."

"I'm serious. I want to start one soon. I feel it's time, you know, to turn a page. Things are coming back at me. I can't explain."

"John Jolly? Ron O'Connor?"

"Not just them."

I saw she meant her father, and her mother, and the divorce, and the suicide: all those things I described as "rubbish" and had seen myself as sweeping out of her life. I had the glimpse she must have had of desolation, emptiness, and my response was hers: get out of there on the only path we had, which was forward—more love, more babies, more *us*, more of our marriage. She clung to me and cried.

"How long has this been worrying you?"

"It never worries me. It just comes. And then it goes. I don't remember I know it isn't real. But I go into it like falling down a hole."

"Listen—"

"Please Ray, don't worry I can get out of it easily just by thinking of us."

So Sharon was weaned—complaining—and after a month or two Glenda was pregnant. Everybody claimed it suited her

One day Rose rang me at work. "Ray," she said, "I've seen Helen Plumb."

"When? Where?"

"It's fairly nasty. I don't know if I should tell you."

"Now, Rose—"

"Yes, all right. You know behind the public library? Those seats where the winos drink?"

I knew them. I had done an article on alkies, winos, meths drinkers, sleepers-out; and drawn an affecting if inaccurate picture of Wellington's blue-haired matrons selecting their weekend romances while in the windy corner below whiskery

118

old men in torn overcoats passed the bottle and sang, "There's a long long trail a-winding.   "

"I saw her there," Rose said. "I couldn't believe it She had a patch on her eye. There was an old Maori man with her She was drinking from a bottle."

"When?"

"This morning."

"You're absolutely sure?"

"I'm sure, Ray. Although she looked about sixty. I stopped and had a good look. She can't be more than thirty-five, you know. And filthy clothes. I smelt her Like sour apple juice. And Ray, she said, 'Have a drink, Miss Goodlad' ".

"Did you?"

"It's no joking matter And don't tell Glenda this. It would worry her "

It worried me that she thought so. I wondered what it was she had seen in Glenda.

"Oh nothing, Ray. Pregnancy can be a difficult time."

I found Helen Plumb the following morning. The sun burned down from the Terrace and glared off the concrete walls of the library A smell, an essence, of vomit and wine and dog shit moved in the air Helen was on a wooden seat with, as Rose had promised, an old Maori man. He seemed to be sleeping. She was wearing an overcoat with cloth half an inch thick. It was frayed on all its seams and burst at the elbows. She wore man's shoes and a man's felt hat with a nameless feather in the band. She looked, as Rose had said, about sixty. Her eye-patch was cardboard blacked with ink and held on by a chain of rubber bands.

I sat down on the lawn and looked at her

"Hey senor, you want a good time?" Helen said.

"Can I talk to you?"

"Talking's free. No free drinks though. You want to come in this school you pay. She's a dead marine."

I gave her half a crown and she prodded her companion up and sent him shuffling off for a new bottle.

"Senor Amigo. Come and sit next to me." She was not drunk

so much as brain-fogged. She behaved and spoke by a kind of rote, responding to stimuli muzzily sensed in a world that moved around her like an ocean. She was aggressive, kittenish, afraid, and scarcely knew why. Now and then a moment of clarity startled her.

I sat on the ribbed seat, at a distance. "Are you Helen Plumb?"

This threatened her. Something black, with teeth, had swum up close. Her eye seemed to darken and contract. "Helen Rewiti, that's me. Dunno other Helens."

"You're Helen Plumb. Oliver Plumb's daughter. Beatrice Plumb's."

"Who're you? Bugger off."

"I'm Ray Sole. I'm your cousin."

"If you're my cousin you got some money for me."

I gave her another half crown. "Listen, Helen. Your mother's dying. She wants to see you."

Helen drank the dregs of wine from her bottle. She started to sing. The words had no edge but the tune came clearly: *I dreamt I dwelt in marble halls.* My mother had played it on our piano. She had learned it from her mother. Oliver had learned it. The leap from this burning corner and this woman to a drawing-room in a manse fifty years ago was too much for me. I got up and walked around the flower beds. When I came back Helen looked at me. "Senor. Amigo. How'd you like a good time?"

"Helen, listen." I sat down. "Your mother is Beatrice Plumb. Trixie. She's dying. She'd like to see you." But I wondered about that. Would Beatrice want to see this woman? "If you'll clean yourself up and stay sober, one afternoon I'll take you up."

She moved her head like a boxer. "You're one of those gangsters."

"No, Helen."

"They threw my girlfriend overboard. Don't let them throw me overboard." Her hand slid into my pocket, cold and damp. I pulled mine out but she gripped me by the hip-bone. "Take me away, amigo."

"Let me take you to your mother. I'll give you some money."

"My father gives me money. In my bank book."

"How much, Helen?"

"A pound a week. He won't pay me if I go up there."

"He'll never know. We won't tell him."

The old man came back with a bottle of sherry. He opened it with a corkscrew from his pocket and gave it to Helen. She hugged it on her chest and seemed to sleep.

"Mr Rewiti?"

"No son, I'm John Peihana. Rewiti was the one who knocked her eye out."

"Mr Peihana—"

"I don't touch that stuff, son. I've never been a drinking man."

"Helen's mother wants to see her. Is there any way I can talk her into it?"

He shook his head. "Her father doesn't want to see her."

"He doesn't need to know."

"He's a big man, her father. Big pakeha. He's a judge."

"He's Chief Justice. But look—"

"He'll put the kibosh on her money."

"Not if he doesn't find out. If we can get her sober—"

"You'll never do that, son. Stop Helen's sherry, she'll konk out. I'll look after her. You trust me. She doesn't need her mother."

"I'd like to see my mother," Helen said. She began to rock back and forth. Wine spilled down her coat. "I'd like to see my mother."

It took two more meetings to arrange. Helen kept forgetting who I was. I picked them up from their back-yard bach in Upper Cuba Street. John Peihana had Helen in a blue dress spotted with daisies. She had on a knitted cardigan and shoes that were a woman's, although broken. Her eye-patch was cut from purple felt.

We drove into the green suburb of Wadestown, where a scent of gorse and roses filled the air. John Peihana rocked his head. He did not seem impressed with what he saw. At Oliver's house he sat down on the steps and folded his hands on the knob of his stick. I led Helen to the door. Her eye was darting about, she trembled like a child—this woman of thirty-five who was so badly damaged there was no recognizable part of her left.

I had warned Mrs Barrett what to expect but her professional cheeriness became a little jerky at the sight of Helen Plumb.

"Ah, oh, come in. Wipe your tootsies." (Although it was summer.) "I'll just get Plumduff ready. She's not quite with it yet. She's been snoozing."

We waited in the room with the French windows. Helen made unhappy sounds like a dog. "It's all right, Helen. Nothing's going to happen." I patted her arm.

"Don't let him get me."

"He's at work."

"I need a drink. Where's my drink?"

"As soon as this is over. I promise."

"Senor?"

"I'm Ray, Helen."

"I've got to spend a penny. Quick, quick."

"Mrs Barrett," I called. Helen's smell was making me desperate. I thought that she might squat and pee on the floor. "Mrs Barrett, she needs the toilet."

"Ah," Mrs Barrett said, "ah, the wee house. This way, dear." She put out her hand but stopped it short and led Helen without touching down the hall. I went to Aunt Beatrice's door and peered through the crack. Her yellowness had turned to sepia. Hollows deep as spoons lay on her temples. I creaked as I leaned on the doorpost and she cried, "Who's that? Is that you, Helen?"

"No, Auntie, it's me." I showed my face.

"I don't know you."

"Raymond Sole, Aunt Trixie."

"Go away, young man. I'm expecting my daughter."

I waited out of sight. After what seemed a long time, and bumps and grunts and scratching on a wall, Mrs Barrett led Helen back. This time she had her by the elbow. "She tried to lock herself in. I soon fixed that."

"Amigo," Helen cried, grabbing my jacket. Mrs Barrett squeezed her elbow and made her yelp. She pulled her into the bedroom. "Plumduff dear, here's your very own daughter come to visit. What a wonderful day."

Beatrice held her arms out. She was like a jointed puppet, moving stiffly. I seemed to hear her bones click and hear an oily whirring as she turned. Her body, I thought, was barely alive; and the rest of her existed for this moment and would go out when Helen left. Tears made a crooked trickling on her cheeks.

"Helen, let me kiss you. We must put all the wrongs we have done behind."

Helen made nothing of this. She was looking about in a panic. Beatrice was no one she recognized.

"Come closer dear so I can see you."

Mrs Barrett gave Helen a nudge. Helen was throwing wild looks at me and making little steps in my direction. Mrs Barrett moved in time with her as though dancing. She jerked her head at me to get up the hall, then made a dab and closed the door.

I waited by Oliver's study. It was locked; and I glimpsed the attractions of being moral. But I had no time to think about it, or gain any clear sight of a seductiveness that made me dizzy, for Beatrice's door sprang open, cries came out, and Mrs Barrett dragged Helen into the hall like a pile of bedding and dumped her there. "Oh!" she cried, "oh! I knew you didn't do it in the lav. You filthy thing."

I ran to them. "What is it? What's happened?"

"She peed on the floor. All down her legs."

I saw Aunt Beatrice struggling from her bed. "You couldn't help it. I'll wipe it up."

"Get back in, Plumduff," Mrs Barrett shouted. She ran at Beatrice and threw her legs on the bed. Then she came back at me. "Take that woman away. Don't ever bring her back." She slammed the door.

Helen lay where Mrs Barrett had dropped her. She was curled into a ball and making little dog whimpers at the carpet. I tried to lift her but she flopped like a corpse, so I ran down the hall and called John Peihana. He came in slowly, leaning on his stick.

"Helen. Get up, girl."

Together we helped her up. Her patch had ridden up her forehead and her eye socket had the same spoon-hollow as her mother's temples. Through it ran the glued joint of her lids, with eyelashes criss-crossed like stitching. John Peihana lifted the patch and made it straight.

"She wet herself."

"Get me a towel, son."

I fetched one from the bathroom and watched while John Peihana helped Helen get her pants off and went down on his knees and dried her legs. He took a clean pair from his pocket and helped her put them on.

Mrs Barrett came rushing from the bedroom. "Haven't you got her out yet? It smells like tomcat in there."

I took Helen out and down the path. John Peihana followed with her wet pants on the end of his walking stick. He pushed them into a hydrangea bush. In the car he gave her a medicine bottle of sherry.

"You leave us alone now, eh?"

"Yes, all right."

I dropped them in Cuba Street and watched them walk away, Helen holding his hand like a child, John Peihana tapping with his stick. Then I drove to Rose's and had a bath. I did not want Glenda knowing this.

13 I wondered where the money had come from for his glossy handbill. Not from Fred Meggett, I was sure. Duggie had cut that connection. *Career: Financial consultant, Meggett Enterprises, 1954–57*

Financial consultant sounded grand. Surely he had been no more than second or third in the accountant's office. One-line speeches. He would make up for that tonight. I watched him as the mayor plugged on through one of those introductions that wobble away from neutrality and wobble jokily back. He was a

National man and had run Duggie close for the nomination.

Duggie kept an interested face. He practised looking mild, then looking sharp. Honest, thoughtful, resolute, amused. He impressed as quick among the half-dead. The mayor, globbing out phrases, was his zombie. I scribbled that in my pad, then scratched it out. I was not here to glob out phrases myself—or let my special knowledge lead me off on side-tracks from my job; which was to report this meeting of Douglas Plumb, National Party candidate for Loomis, held in the Loomis Town Hall, November 17, 1960. My paper would not thank me for clever phrases, or cynicism about this coming man.

Financial consultant, Meggett Enterprises, 1954–57. B. Com. 1955. Currently Director, Thornley and Plumb, Consultants, Property Developers: Thornley and Webb, Estate Agents: Thomas Tax Consultants. Age, I added, twenty-eight. Young man in a hurry. He had the credentials and the cash, now he was after the real thing. I made a mental scratching out of that. Duggie was never simple. What he'd come to here was a stage in his growth. I had a knowledge of it better than his, but I could not untangle it from will and ambition. Organic Duggie. Duggie as Superman. I was going to have to worry at them alone and present him to our readers simply as Douglas Plumb, one of the party's bright new men, who just might snatch the Loomis seat from Labour. He was running a campaign that had his opponent flapping around like a headless rooster.

"Duggie," I had said, "what's your philosophy in politics?"

"I don't have one of those. I leave the airy-fairy stuff to Latham. He's got a philosophy. Ask him. It's about all he has got. And it comes from Russia. With love. Lift Jack Latham up you'll find Made in Moscow stamped on his bum."

"You don't want me to print that?"

"Say behind."

"Right. Good stuff. It's a dirty fight."

"He started it."

"He says you did."

"You've talked to him, eh?"

"This morning. You've got him hopping. But he's no mug."

125

"He's got a lot of bloody words. You take out the bloodies, Ray."

"Sure."

"I'll do you if you make me look bad."

"Take it easy. My paper doesn't print bloodies anyway. Tell me more about Latham."

"University egghead. Nothing in there but a kind of yolk. He belongs to a party that gives us all this shit—nonsense, Ray—about the common man but he wouldn't know one if he tripped over him. Talks about people in multiples. 'The masses.' What the hell's masses? That's not kiwi talk. That's from Moscow."

I quoted from Duggie's handbill: " 'The class war has no place in New Zealand.' 'The individual does not exist for the State.' He says you didn't write that. Says it came out of the sausage machine."

"I wrote it."

"It's word for word Muldoon's."

"We think alike."

"This playboy label he's pinned on you. Any comment?"

"I live a moral and an honest life."

"Come on, Duggie."

"I live a moral and an honest life. I hope Mr Latham can say the same."

"He makes bachelor sound like a dirty word."

"That's his problem."

"How do you feel about the outcome of this?"

"Loomis? I'll win it. No question."

"Mr Plumb exudes confidence."

"Sounds like shitting. That's enough, Ray. I'm switching you off." He reached out and flicked a switch on my temple. "Have a drink."

"The Playboy Bachelor. You've probably got inflatable girls in there."

"I'll tell you, Ray—" Duggie came back with a bottle and two glasses. "—I'm going to get Latham one day. I'll wait for him. Nobody's saying that stuff about me."

"You'll get him on election day."

"No. He'll win. He'd better win."

I blinked at him. He pushed a drink at me. "You're a bloody innocent. You think I want to spend the rest of my life in a marginal seat?"

"Does the party know this?"

"They know I can't win it. What they don't know is how close I'll get. They'll know I'm here."

"And next time round.   ?"

"A safe seat." He drank. "I'm not the only one. Silly bloody Brierly's doing it in Avondale. He doesn't think I know."

"So what you want is to lose by one vote."

"One hundred. That'd do nicely. Brierly won't get close to that."

"You'll look sick if you win. You might, you know. People seem to like you for some reason. You should have kept your Kings College voice and your yellow waistcoat."

"You'd better forget that, Ray."

"It's a good voice now. Just right of centre. You've got your clothes right too. You might win."

"I won't."

"I know a few people who won't be voting for you."

He did not like that. "Who?"

"My mother."

"Your old man will."

"I wouldn't be too sure. Beak might. Myra won't."

"She won't vote for Latham either."

"Why not?"

"She's dead. Cancer. In here." He dug his thumb at his crotch. "Probably used the bloody thing too much."

"When did she die?"

"Week or two back. She'd had it for years. Probably had it when she married Beak. She should've had cancer of the mouth."

"You're unbelievable, Duggie."

"Why? Here I am."

"She was your girlfriend."

"You want me to cry some tears? Myra was a big girl. She knew what she was into. And she liked it. You couldn't stop her, you'd have needed a football team. As for the cancer, it's like a car accident. It could get you any time. It could get me."

"Cancer won't get you."

"Meaning what?"

I did not know. I had the sense of something looming over Duggie but it would not take shape.

"Meaning you? Listen Ray, I talk to you. I don't talk to anyone else. But if you ever say anything   if you print anything in your paper.   "

"I want you to carry on. I want to watch."

"So watch. But keep your mouth shut. You coming to my meeting?"

"I'll be there. God knows why. I should be watching Muldoon. He's getting a start on you, Duggie. He'll get in."

"So? He's ten years older. He's not going anywhere. He's too damn pushy. This party doesn't like it when you push—not when they notice. Now piss off, Ray. I need some sleep. Big night tomorrow."

He came with me as far as the door of his flat. I stood on the porch a moment looking across the slope of Mt Hobson at One Tree Hill. "This is the one you want. Epsom. Holyoake country. Old Snyder's bound to retire next time round."

"You're saying it, not me."

"I'm right, aren't I?"

"Don't make me fight two elections at once." He closed the door.

I drove home to Loomis, where I was staying. "I talk to you. I don't talk to anyone else." There was something pathetic in it. I wondered if I was all that kept Duggie human. Was that the reason he took the appalling risk for a politician of standing naked before a journalist? There was more to it than self-display. Perhaps he did not know the reason himself: just grabbed me instinctively. But I laughed at that—gave it Duggie's laugh. "All this bullshit about the mind. I've got better things to think about, Ray."

Mum said, "How's Duggie?"

"Sparking on all six. I told him you weren't going to vote for him."

"Good. What did he say?"

"He didn't like it. He reckoned he might get your vote, Dad."

"I'm not saying. I don't go much on this Latham joker though. He's too high-falutin."

"There's nothing wrong with intelligence," Mum said.

"I don't like the stuff he's saying about Meggett Enterprises."

"It's aimed at Duggie," I said.

"I don't like it."

"Fred's getting a bit too big too fast."

"You think so?"

"I know I'd get out if I was you."

The next day I was round the campaign headquarters, talking with candidates and managers. My paper—the *Evening Post*—had me in Auckland for a look at three or four key marginals. It seemed to me this was going to be National's election. Labour, with its majority of one, had no ground it could lose, but bits were crumbling away all along the line. I predicted a National landslide, a majority for them of twenty or so. There were going to be plenty of new faces in Wellington. New careers. Clever grabbing. I admired Duggie's patience in waiting for next time.

Back in Loomis, late in the afternoon, I called on Beak Wyatt. He lived in a house on Dean Street, a blind road running along the creek opposite Millbrook Road.

"Hello, Beak." I offered him my hand. He held it for a moment without pressure. His bony head seemed dented on one side, shaped like a sickle. He did not smile or make any movement of his face, but gave the impression of being set a short way back in time and of having to bring himself forward to see and understand.

"I thought that was your car. I didn't reckon you'd come in here."

"Can I talk to you a minute?"

Again that pause while he understood. Then he walked ahead of me into the kitchen and went on peeling carrots at the sink.

"I heard about your wife. I'm sorry."

He rinsed a carrot under the tap. "Thanks."

"I brought a couple of bottles. Maybe we can have a drink?"

"The opener's in the drawer. I don't drink much."

I filled two glasses and took him one. He was peeling a potato and the skin curled away from his knife and bobbed like a ringlet. He nodded at me to put his drink beside him.

"Sit down, Ray."

I pulled out a chair and sat at the table. A woman had run this kitchen once. It had floral curtains and pretty crockery and pot-mitts run up on a sewing machine. Beak had let it go. Dust balls stirred on the lino and long-legged spiders hung on the walls. A Mighty Meatery calendar, torn off at July, lay where it had fallen on the sideboard. The ceiling, tongue and groove, greasy with cooking moisture and furred with dust, sloped towards the stove, where Beak's head almost touched it as he put on the pot of vegetables. He was six foot four, skinny as a high jumper

He brought his glass to the table. "What are you doing in Auckland?"

I told him. "Duggie thinks he might get your vote."

"Does he?"

"How'd you like him for your M.P.?"

Beak drank some beer. His Adam's apple went up and down. "No," he said.

I finished my glass and poured another one. "How are you getting on, Beak? Are you all right here?"

"I'm all right."

"What do you do? All alone?"

He turned his eyes slowly on to me. "I think about things."

"What things?"

"Remember the Yank who broke his neck at the Pool?"

"Munro Gussey?"

"I think about him. I didn't yell out. I could have saved his life. But I was scared of what Duggie would say." He swallowed more beer. "Duggie knew he was going to dive."

"I don't think so—"

130

"I told Myra about it. She said he would know." He got up and poured the rest of his beer down the sink. "I don't like this stuff." He put a pan on the stove and laid in a chop. "Myra had cancer of the cervix. She was in hospital six times. The last time was July. It took four months."

"I'm sorry, Beak."

"She wanted to die properly. Die well. She read it in a book."

"And did she?"

"No." He turned from the stove and looked at me. "She wanted me to kill her. Pills or something. Smother her with her pillow. I couldn't do it."

"Beak, it's like getting hit by a car. No sense."

"Myra didn't love me."

"I don't know—"

"She told me. It didn't matter. She's the only one who ever talked to me." The lid of the potato pot started jumping. He turned down the element.

I said, "I knew Myra. I liked her."

Beak came back and sat at the table. "She said you and Duggie raped her in a van."

I wondered if he was going to attack me. But he gave a smile, took out his handkerchief and wiped his nose—his famous nose. His Adam's apple bobbed as he swallowed. That was famous too.

I said, "It was rape. In a way. I think about it the way you think about the Yank."

"Do you?"

"Now and then." The pause he made, that lag in time, forced the truth from me. "Not very often."

"It wasn't you she blamed. She reckoned he was raping you too." The chop was burning. He got up and turned it with a knife. "I think about it. I wonder why any of us are alive when Myra's dead."

"Beak—"

"I'm not going to kill anyone.   My tea's about ready, Ray."

"All right."

"Take the beer. I don't like it."

I took the unopened bottle and went to the door. But I could not leave him like that: turning his chop, eating at the bare table.

"Does anyone come and see you?"

He looked surprised. "I don't need anybody."

"What about Myra's friends? Do they keep in touch?"

"She didn't have friends. We were friends to each other."

"You can't stay here alone, Beak."

He prodded his potatoes with a fork. Steam broke past his face and curled on the ceiling. He carried a plate to the table and put it down. "Duggie came once. After we got married."

"What happened?"

"We saw his car so we hid in the bedroom. He went around the house yelling out. He knew we were there. Myra—she hid her face in the pillow so he wouldn't hear her laughing."

"What did he do?"

"Yelled out some name." He gave a little smile in my direction. "That name you used to call her. Then he went away."

"I never called her that."

"It doesn't matter." He took his potatoes to the sink and poured off the water.

While he was busy I let myself out and drove away. That evening I sat in the Loomis Town Hall reading Duggie's career and his credo yet again. Watching Duggie. I could not see him either as simple or complicated. From time to time I lost sight of him altogether, he seemed to float away in a fog like Merlin. He changed all the time for me, the way Grandpa Plumb had changed. I worried at him but he would not come clear. As for Beak, he stood unmoving, rather like Ted Sole.

The mayor finished and sat down, settling his chin on his chest. Duggie walked to the microphone and lifted it aside. He took a little bundle of cards from his pocket, slipped them out of their rubber band and laid them on the lectern. So far he had looked at no one. He watched the cards a moment and scratched his jaw. It was a good attempt at "presence" for a beginner but he kept it up just a shade too long. A couple of feet shuffled, a cough broke out. He raised his eyes and made them flash down the hall. "Friends," he cried. "Ladies and gentlemen. People of Loomis. My friendly rival, my colleague, your mayor, has been generous to me in his introduction.   "

It was a big meeting for Loomis. I made a rough count of two hundred and fifty people. Dad was there. Roger Sutton was there; chalky face, red mouth, scowling in an aisle seat near the back. A dozen old Dalmatians and their sons were in the front row. Duggie was going to have to say something on government aid for the wine industry. And Father Pearce, in an open shirt, would no doubt have a question on state aid for church schools. That was going to be a hard one for Duggie. "Religion is shit," he had told me; and when he had to say, as on radio earlier in the week, "We live in a Christian society," or some such thing, he sounded as if he did not quite know what he meant. The words came out too quickly. Latham hadn't got on to it. Possibly Latham didn't want to. Was he a Christian himself? I thought there might be an article in the religious beliefs of candidates.

"I," Duggie said, "am a Loomis boy. I grew up here. This place is in my blood. I went through Loomis school. I sailed tin canoes on Loomis creek. I had a paper run up Millbrook Road. I raided orchards there. Yes, my friends, Matty Barbarich, Tony Sumich, your orchards. And you put a couple of pellets in my behind. My father was an orchardist—still is. When I was a schoolboy I helped in the grape harvest. I washed bottles for you, Waddy Corban. And I came down to this hall—Loomis Town Hall—on Saturday afternoons, with sixpence in my pocket, to watch the Buck Rogers serial and cheer Johnny Weismuller playing Tarzan—and whistle at Jane. This is my ground, this is my home—"

"Why do you live in Epsom, then?"

"—and over in Epsom I feel like an alien, I'm cut off from my roots, and I can tell you this my friends, if I'm elected in Loomis, *when* I'm elected in Loomis, the first thing I'll do, the very first thing, is go out hunting for a house to buy. Vote for me in Loomis and I'll come home to Loomis."

He did that well. He got them. I had to swallow and pretend there was no prickling in my eye.

"Now," Duggie said, "let's get down to brass tacks—and I don't mean Walter Nash." He spent half an hour on National's policies; they were "solid and sensible"; and he too was solid and sensible. He had a long look at Nordmeyer's "black budget", throwing in figures, prescriptions, with assurance. There was hardly an emotive word in it. "Oh Duggie," I thought, "you're good. Don't try too hard or you'll win this seat." He presented a surface hecklers could only chip at, and with his voice that was round and sharp he rolled right over them or cut straight through. A voice, I thought, like a beaten-copper shield, phoney but antique-looking, and when he wanted to he turned it edge on and chopped with it.

So far he had not mentioned Latham. But at the end he gave a sigh. "A pity we can't stay on this level." He took a sip of water and put the glass back on the table with a bang. "But this after all is an election campaign. So I'm forced to muddy my hands. Excuse me for the word I'm about to say   Latham."

That got a laugh. And some angry yells.

"He's got all his nephews and nieces here. He probably sent them out by bus because none of them live in Loomis. He doesn't live here himself. I've heard he drove through once and bought a pound of apples. On the strength of that he's set himself up as an expert on the fruit industry.

"Now, I've been the subject of some nasty attacks from this man. He seems to think if he can't win your votes through reason he can win them with a sort of vaudeville act—a mixture of muck throwing and cheap wisecracks. He makes a great song and dance over the fact that he wears an R.S.A. badge and I haven't got one. Well, I haven't got one because I was only thirteen when the war ended. He wasn't much older. He's not much older now. But he got into uniform just at the end. They sent him away to guard a few bombed-out buildings when all the shooting was over. On the strength of that he got his badge. Well, I want to announce tonight that I fought in a war too. I'm still fighting in it. And that war, my friends, is the war against

134

communism. I'm even going to pin a badge on my own lapel. I made it myself. Now. " He took something silver out of his pocket and fixed it on his jacket. "You can't see it so I'll tell you what it is. It's a kiwi. It means I was made in this country, not in Russia. And I've even got some battle honours. Do you know what this says, here? It says, *C-Force. 1951* Yes, my friends, I was one of the thousands of New Zealanders who enrolled in the Civil Emergency Organization back in those days when the communists tried to wreck our country. I fought in the war of fifty-one. And where was Mr Latham then? I'll tell you. He was giving comfort to the enemy. He was scribbling pamphlets. He was taking part in illegal marches. As I said to a journalist friend last night, turn Jack Latham over, you'll find Made in Moscow stamped on his behind.

"And I see we have some of his friends here tonight. Listen to them yapping their commie slogans. There's a few card carriers in this hall. Well I've got news for you, you don't scare me. "

He kept on like that for some time and had the hall in an uproar The constable at the door moved uneasily. I thought if Duggie was trying to lose a few votes he had done it. His performance with the badge would have gone down well in Epsom but the ground in Loomis had a way of shifting. Duggie knew it. He drank some water while the shouts fell away. He smiled and dabbed his brow with a handkerchief.

"Now, let's get on to something less unpleasant. Let's have a bit of comedy We'll look at some of the Labour Party prom-ises." He had a small gift for ridicule; he made one or two clever phrases. Nothing was new at this stage of the election, but Duggie worked hard and gave his performance some freshness.

Towards the end he said, "Let me tell you a story It's a sad story, and a foolish story, but then Labour's policies are sad and foolish. This took place in Loomis, when I was a boy. Most of you will know the Pool, down on the creek just above Moa Park. When we were kids that was our swimming hole. It had a diving board and changing sheds. They're probably gone today. They are? That's progress although it makes me a little sad. Anyway, the war was on. And one day two American marines arrived at the Pool with their girlfriends. Pretty girls. I know. I was there. I saw it all. The Yanks got away with the pretty ones. Not that these Yanks were much to look at. The one I want to tell you about was a skinny little bloke. His cobber went out on the end of the board and bounced around a bit—you know, impressing his girlfriend. And then the skinny bloke got up and he ran out on the board—and he did a swallow dive. Beautiful! But my friends, let me remind you—the tide goes out down at the Pool. There wasn't any water there. He broke his neck. He died. Yes, one dead American. Oh, I'm not making fun of him. It was tragic. But that's not the point of my story—although doing a swallow dive into shallow water reminds me of the Labour Party too. No, the point is this: the next day, Monday morning, the Council had workmen down at the Pool putting in a post by the diving board marking off in feet just how deep the water was. So everyone could read it. Even Yanks. And that's the point of my story—that's what reminds me of the Labour Party—putting up their post after someone has dived in and broken his neck. "

It went down well. This was real life, and this was Loomis. Maybe politics was real as well. The *Herald* and the *Star* men wrote it down. I wrote: The Pool—Munro Gussey—Danger post—L.P policy. But I felt that Duggie had told my secrets.

He got tough at question time—"That's a stupid question and I'm not going to answer it. Has anybody got a sensible question?" Sutton asked about pensions and Father Pearce about state aid. Both seemed satisfied with what Duggie told them, though Sutton snarled and left the hall. Duggie wound himself up about the future for the wine industry—"I see the day when we, when Loomis, will be making table wines to rival those of France and Germany." The old Dalmatians did not look sure about that but the young ones nodded their heads. Nobody asked about Meggett Enterprises.

Dad and I drove back to Peacehaven. On Millbrook Road we picked up Roger Sutton. Bluey had died but Sutton was still in the cottage, an ogre or a joke to a new generation of Millbrook children. "He lives in there," Mum said, "like a crab in a mud hole."

"What did you think of Duggie, Mr Sutton?"

"He's not going to win this seat."

"Why not?"

"He's too clever."

I explained to Dad, "Some people reckon Duggie really wants a safe seat next time."

"Will he get one?"

"He'll get what he wants," Sutton said.

"Are you going to vote for him, Mr Sutton?"

"I'm voting for Latham. I like a parliament that's full of fools."

"Is that what he is?"

"I went to one of his meetings. He talked about fair shares for everyone."

Dad went to bed and I sat scratching out my articles. When I heard a car in the drive I guessed it was Duggie and I had a drink ready when he came in.

"What I need now is a woman."

"What you need is for me to tell you how great you were."

"All right. Tell me."

"You were great. You belong in politics."

"Seriously."

"I'm serious." I had power over him. "You speak well, you're quick on your feet, you can make a joke, and wring a tear. You don't believe a word of it. And you love it. It's meat and drink to you. You're a politician. And I nearly forgot, you're not too bright."

"You're a cheeky bugger."

"I tell you what you've got to know."

"So I was O.K.?"

I loved this. "You were O.K. Your party bosses are going to hear about you. Sutton thought you were good."

"Sutton, eh?"

"He's not going to vote for you. He reckons you don't want to win."

"It didn't show?"

"Only to people like Sutton. Duggie, leave out the fall of the Roman Empire. It didn't happen like that."

"Who cares how it happened? It happened any way I like to say."

"Suit yourself. I wouldn't do too much red-bashing with those old Dallies though. They don't like Khrushchev any but most of them have got a photo of Tito in the kitchen."

"Yeah. You're right. Those eyes."

"Stick to Munro Gussey."

"Who's Munro Gussey?"

"The Yank who broke his neck."

"Was that his name?"

"I was round at Beak's today. He talked about him."

"What did you go there for?"

"To say I was sorry about his wife."

"Ha! How is Beak?"

"He remembers things. Like Munro Gussey. He says he knew he was going to dive. He didn't yell out because he was scared of what you'd say."

"Silly bugger."

"He told Myra about it. She said you would have known."

"Did she? It beats me why you people get so worked up about the past."

"You used it in your speech."

He shrugged. "I don't let it screw me up."

"Was she right?"

He drank his whisky, put out his glass for more. When I had filled it and he had sipped again, he lay back in his chair and sighed. "I'll tell you something, Ray. I can't remember. Sometimes I think I knew. And I didn't care. I wanted to see what would happen. But mostly I'm not interested. It was what? Twenty years ago?"

"Seventeen."

"So? It's the bloody dark ages. What else did Beak have to say for himself?"

"He told me how you walked round his house yelling out Miss Gobbloffski."

"Shit!" He pushed his glass away. "What do you think you are, my bloody conscience?"

"I have a hard enough time being my own."

"What's your game then?"

"No game. I'm interested in how you feel about things."

"I don't feel about them. Not Myra. Or Beak. That's finished. I don't see what it's got to do with me now."

"You re-invent yourself every morning? Handy in politics. But you'll have to be careful. Things have got a way of coming back."

He gave a petulant lift of his hands. "I was feeling good when I came round here." I had a moment's pity and could find no basis for it but affection. It troubled me that Duggie and I were bound.

When I let him out I said, "Duggie, you were great up there tonight. No bullshit, Duggie."

14 Peacehaven at new year was scented, lovely. I walked on the lawns and through the gardens with Sharon's hand in mine and Gregory on my shoulders. We played hide-and-seek up and down the terraces and in the summerhouse. Memories pricked at me, I laughed loudly with my children, and had to turn my face away from adults so they should not see my eyes were wet. I was wounded and renewed, and welcomed it, and hated it at times, seeing it as a kind of self-abuse. I was the Wellington journalist not the weepy boy. But if I had wanted to avoid descents I should not have had children, and not have brought them home.

"Why do you call this place home?" Glenda said.

"Do I? I didn't know. That just shows.   "

"What?"

"The way it hangs on. Wadestown is home."

139

"Don't you forget it. I wish your mother wouldn't call you Raymie."

"So do I."

Things were easier when Becky came. Her loudness invaded me and left little space for memories. "Quit that moping about," she yelled. "Come and have a beer. Come and talk to Tom. He wants to know who's putting the boot in down in Wellington." Tom was her husband, a "young executive" with a tobacco company. It was the first time I had heard that term. Becky used it without irony, though it brought a flush on her husband's cheeks.

Tom and I got on well as long as we talked about sport. On everything else we disagreed; and settled into grinning at each other shiftily. We thought each other bloody idiots and left it at that. Becky, thick as a tractor tyre, called us "great old buddies"

She had three sons, the youngest Sharon's age. When Bobby and his wife came up from Pukekohe there were eight children on the lawn. They surrounded Mum, grizzling for biscuits. She enjoyed them—and taught them please and thank you—but wanted to get away after a time. Her own children concerned her more and she tested our happiness with looks and questions.

"Lay off, Mum."

"I'm not prying, Ray. I do like Glenda."

"She keeps to herself. She's not used to this."

"I wish she'd talk to me."

"What about?"

"Oh, things. You."

"No chance. Glenda keeps it here—" I tapped my head. "It won't come out for you or anyone."

"But you are happy?"

"Sure. We're happy."

She took me to visit her brother Robert. We drove north to the Kaipara harbour and found him in his shack on a half-acre section out beyond Helensville. Robert's history is a curious one. He lived at Peacehaven until the war—never a friend, never a girl—then spent four years in conchie camps. When he came

140

out he turned away from his family for some reason—Mum hints at some unspoken disagreement with his father—and lived on a farm with a bunch of religious cranks who practised free love and communal sharing. He had a "wife"—not wives. They turned him out finally for sins against the ethic of the place: his father had left him the cottage and instead of selling it and giving the money to the commune he let Bluey and Sutton stay on there. When they expelled him he wandered north and found his shack on the Kaipara harbour. He had been there ten years but seemed unchanged to me from the Robert who had worked in the gardens at Peacehaven. Slow and adenoidal. Shirt tucked in his underpants. It astonished me that Mum had romanticized him. She set him up as a kind of saint.

It was a frustrating day. I never managed to match my pace with it. We sat on the jetty in the tidal creek and watched the yellow water creep in the mangroves. We talked in sentences that would not have been out of place in an infant reader. "See the crab on the mud." "Listen to the blackbird." "I like to hear the blackbird singing."

After lunch Robert took me out to look at his set lines. We rowed down the creek on to the harbour. I told him about Duggie—"Ah."—and my wife and children. "You're lucky, Ray." There were snapper on his lines and flounder in his net. I got quite excited hauling them in. Robert scaled and gutted them and threw the entrails to the screaming gulls. Rowing back, and making a hash of it, I asked him about his days in the camps. I told him I wanted to do two articles, one about the first war—Archibald Baxter, the crucifixion posts, all that stuff—and one about the second.

"Ah," he said.

"So how about it? I'd only need an hour. We could do it this afternoon."

"No."

"Why not?"

"I don't talk about it. There's plenty of blokes who'll tell you."

"Well, how about that place you went to live in? Parminter's?

141

Truth did a job on it but it might be worth a look."

"I don't talk about that either "

"What do you talk about?" He didn't answer "Why did you go there? Why didn't you come back to Peacehaven?"

"You ask a lot of questions, Ray I suppose—" I noticed his breathing: bronchitic I thought, but I found out later he had emphysema. "—I suppose it's hard for a newspaperman to learn there aren't any answers."

Cleverness? I looked at him with a new interest But he said no more and the work of rowing silenced me—it blistered me—and I watched with a sour admiration the ease with which he sent the dinghy along when he took my place.

Mum and I quarrelled about him on the drive home. I told her his way of life was a cop-out Goodness, I said, was an active thing. Had she heard of the tree crashing down in the forest? If no one was in earshot then there was no sound. And goodness only exists where people are. Nonsense, Mum said. What about saints and hermits, living by themselves in caves and deserts? Was I telling her they were wasting their time? Too right, I said. The only good they did was feeding the lice in their beards. She told me that I disappointed her.

I disappointed my brother and sister too. Like Tom they wanted tales from Wellington but it wasn't power struggles that interested them—I had embroidered a few for Tom, before I found my virtue was his vice—it was what Becky called "the bedroom stuff" "Who's up who?" Bobby said. "Come on, Ray You newspaper blokes are supposed to know everything." I'd heard a rumour or two but I wasn't saying. And if I had, Bobby and Becky would still have been disappointed. Both had an eager belief in orgies involving diplomats and cabinet ministers' wives. It seemed that our mother's lessons in purity had left them unaffected—or had they gone through struggles like my own and come out dirty-minded as a pair of gossip-column journalists?

"If you could see cabinet ministers' wives.   "

"Well, what about those parliamentary typists? You can't tell me" etc. etc.

Glenda gave little smiles, trying to join my family. Becky bossed her like the netball captain she had been, and patted her condescendingly, and made remarks about people who went around head in the clouds. Bobby winked at her, making sure she got his double meanings, and joked about "a certain party's" prowess in the sack. "For a while there he thought all you could poke with it was the fire."

I extricated Glenda and we walked about the section. "I'm sorry They're pretty horrible."

"It's not your fault. I like your father "

"Dad's O.K. So's Mum."

"The children like her Who's that man over the creek? In the garden?"

"Roger Sutton."

"He's the hunchback? I thought he looked odd." She shifted to get a clear look through the trees. "Poor man."

"We've tried to help him, but he won't take help."

"I see why not."

I showed her the eel pools, dirty now with rubbish from the houses. I shifted rocks but could find no lobsters. A smell of rot came from the water Glenda took my hand. "You shouldn't have come."

"I knew how it would be. Let's look at the culvert." Its barrel pointed at us. We looked through the shrinking tube at a world impossibly green; the magic world children in books step through mirrors to, through waterfalls and doors in the trunks of trees. "Let's go there," Glenda said.

"The water's dirty."

"We can have a bath."

We took our sandals off and waded in. Slime and silt came over our ankles. It had a creamy thickness not unpleasant if you forgot the smell. "Vichyssoise," I joked, but Glenda did not laugh. I made her face out dimly, glimmering at the faery world ahead. Then I found she saw it differently. "It's like floating up from under water "

We came out to a little waterfall, a moss-green pool, stones patched with silver lichen. Ferns grew in crevices round the sides of the basin. The trees bent down from the banks as though watching something in the pool but all we saw there was the shape of them and a lightening from the summer sky. Looking up, we saw it flat and pure. To reach the day we would need to rise again from under water.

"This is more spooky than I remember."

"I like it here." She leaned on the culvert, looking happy. Behind her dusty blackberry vines rose in frothing waves to Millbrook Road. A car went by. She did not seem to hear.

"Look back where we came from." I pointed at the same magic world. "They're interchangeable."

"So where do we belong?"

"Not with Bobby and Becky. Still, we'd better get back to the kids."

"You go. Let me stay a while."

"You O.K.?"

"I'm fine. I just want to be by myself for a bit. I'm not very good at families."

So I went back and endured more of my brother and sister. I told them Glenda was resting and Bobby made jokes about nipping in to see if she wanted anything. He was impressed with her good looks. I got him away from that by opening the *Star*. "Any news of Beak Wyatt?"

"He's run away with some sheila if you ask me."

"Who'd have Beak?" Becky said.

"He had a wife. She was a pretty girl."

"If it isn't a woman someone's done him in," Bobby said. "His house is locked up. Car in the garage. He wouldn't leave his car."

"I think he's wandered off," I said. "His wife's death hit him pretty hard." But I believed Beak had killed himself. I remembered him asking why we should be alive when Myra was dead.

The next day we had a party at Peacehaven. The food and drink were in the summer-house and we helped ourselves through the afternoon. Glenda had the chance to meet some more of my family. She met Mirth and Willis, and Willis too

liked the look of her. She met my uncle Emerson, the tomato
grower, the Sundowner of the Skies. He was a shy man, but
crazy in an aeroplane. She met Esther and Fred Meggett and
their younger son Adrian. They rolled up late in Fred's royal-
blue Mercedes with the custom-built upholstery and the built-
in cocktail bar. Esther stepped out holding her flagon of port in
its brown-paper bag. Duggie came late too. I hadn't expected to
see him but his new girl, Tania, wanted to meet his parents. He
found that amusing. "She wants to marry me."

"What are her chances?"

"Doesn't hurt to let them keep on hoping. Makes them
willing."

"And she is?" We were standing on the brick bridge looking
at the party. As usual Duggie had me: I felt all my boyish sexual
unease. He made a tweaking motion in the air. "Give them a
quarter turn they poke out like sticks of chalk."

I watched Tania—black-haired, sun-tanned, in a linen skirt
and schoolgirl blouse—sitting on the lawn with Glenda, while
Duggie told me what he did to her. She was an art teacher at a
girls' high school and had made his C-force badge for him.
"Bloody good painter. So they tell me. Hey, you know those
things they paint on the edge of books? You spread the pages and
you get a picture?"

Yes, I knew. I knew what was coming as well.

"She painted one of those on my cock. We had it going on and
off like TV all afternoon. You don't believe me? I'll make her
come and tell you."

"No, no. I believe you."

"Yeah.   Your little lady's quite a looker. Goodlad's
daughter. How does that affect her?"

"She's over it." He had no memory of her and that made me
easier and marked a victory I made more complete by keeping
from him. I told him I believed Beak had killed himself.

"He wouldn't have the guts," Duggie said. "Myra broke him
in I reckon and he's gone looking for more. He's shacked up
somewhere with his boss's wife. Well, someone's wife. Beak's a
bloody dull subject. How'd you like the result?"

"I said National would win. I can't say I like it."

"In Loomis, I mean. Two hundred and ninety votes. I've made it look like a marginal. Some poor sod's going to get a shock."

"Are they pleased with you?"

"Like I said, they know I'm here."

We strolled back down the lawn and Duggie gave me a nudge. "Who does Adrian remind you of?"

"Only his mother. He goes after food like her."

"Scrape off a couple of layers of fat." I looked and shook my head. "Remember that Yank called Errol?"

"I thought you weren't interested in the past."

"Maybe not. But I wouldn't mind something on old Esther. On Fred either. He's going too bloody fast. Too damn greedy. I want to put a lot of ground between him and me."

"You shouldn't have said you worked for him in your glossy."

"No, I shouldn't. Tell your old man to get away from him. Easy though. I want old Fred to stand up as long as he can."

We sat down with Glenda and Tania and I saw how the girl lit up when Duggie came close. He was good-looking all right, with his auburn hair and pale-lashed eyes and the comic-strip jut of his chin. His bottom and short legs spoiled the effect. It was better when he sat down. Tania put her hand on his. She laid her head for a moment on his shoulder, then shook back her hair and smiled at him. I saw nothing ahead for her but bad times with Duggie—apart from good times in bed and, as he had told me, in the bath, in the lounge, on the kitchen table. I looked at her breasts and thighs and hips shaped like an apple, and with my wife's fingers twined in mine and my children playing on the lawn, I wanted to be with Tania, I wanted her fore-edge painting me. She felt my lust and gave a startled look and gripped Duggie by his knee.

"Douglas and I went to a party last week and I met Mr Holyoake. I liked him. I really did. I mean, I'm Labour. I'm not changing that for anyone."

"I like it," Duggie said. "It gives her something. Like having a girlfriend who's Chinese or cross-eyed."

Tania blushed. She gave Glenda a look of apology.

"You paint?" I said.

"Yes. I do."

"What sort of things?"

"Landscapes mostly."

Duggie was grinning. She looked at him; and I saw her understand. Her face went white and her eyes seemed to darken and turn in. In a tiny voice, from far away: "Hills. I like hills."

Duggie patted her. "You should show Ray and Glenda. They'll buy one."

"Have you had an exhibition?" Glenda said.

Bobby and Becky arrived, bringing Esther.

"That's what we need. An exhibition," Bobby said.

"You boys did all right for yourselves," Esther said. "Pretty girl for a wife, Ray. I didn't think you were going to make it."

"He followed my example," Bobby said. "You can learn all sorts of things from your big brother."

Esther put her wine down next to Glenda and lowered herself heavily on to the grass. She pulled her dress back from her pudgy thighs, "Top me up, Ray." She thrust her glass at me and I filled it from her flagon. "Nice looking kids you've got. Glenda, that's your name. I'll tell you something Glenda, your old man gave me the best tips I've ever had. He was my bible. *Goodlad's Hot Tips.* I stopped winning when he died."

"Yes?" Glenda said. Her face took a marbled appearance, pink and white.

"I wish he was still alive," Esther said. "I need some luck. He should have married Josie Mottram instead of killing himself."

"She went to England," Glenda said.

"She lost a good man. I always felt sorry for Graham Goodlad. It's no crime to go to bed with a woman. Not that dumb old Oliver would know."

"My father loved Mrs Mottram," Glenda said.

"That stuck out a mile."

"But the trial was really too much for both of them."

"Oliver was too much. I always said it was Oliver who killed him."

147

"No. It wasn't."

"Maybe. Well, he knew his horses. Here's to *Goodlad's Hot Tips.*" She drank some wine.

I pulled Glenda up. "Come on. Let's talk to Emerson." I led her over to the summer-house. Her face had pink blotches on the cheeks. I could not tell whether she was trembling with anger or distress. "Why did you do that?"

"I thought it had gone on long enough."

"No, no, no. That's the first time anyone's ever said his name." She freed her hand and ran to Sharon and Gregory and knelt on the lawn with them. I saw Duggie and Tania watching us so I went on and talked with Emerson. He told me about his days in the flying circus and on the mail run from London to Paris in the thirties. I stayed half an hour with him and when I came round the summer-house Glenda was gone. Duggie strolled over.

"She seems to be a jumpy lady, your wife."

"Did you see where she went?"

"Down by the creek somewhere."

I found her sandals by the mouth of the culvert, and looking in saw the dish-flat world at the end of the tunnel. I waded through and found her by the pool.

"Come back to the party, Glenda."

"I just wanted a few minutes by myself."

"I'm sorry I made a mistake."

"It's not your fault."

I led her back and kept close to her while we talked with Fred and Adrian. Fred was paunchy, triple-jowled, he had a blue boiled eye and had still his red rough butcher hands. Jovial, his voice like wooden clappers, he praised my wife's good looks and me for getting her, while Adrian ate mince pies, a little greedy for the neutered Tom, but sleek and fat and shiny, with hair thoroughly oiled and eyes that had an inward look of boredom. A description that, as they say, tells more about the writer than the subject. It comes from a mental twitch there's no getting rid of. I could, with a little effort, have written: Fred, successful, jolly, bending from his affairs just a trace absently, made friendly attempts at flattery, while Adrian ate mince pies, turning his mind on a boy's concerns. But I don't know. I'll never know. It's all approximations and all choices. I do not know what Glenda meant when she said, "What a creepy boy." *Creepy* sets me hunting but I rarely catch anything. She said nothing about Fred. I suspect he reminded her of her father.

As for Mirth and Willis—these were their happiest days. They had sailed home to port and were cosily moored. They groaned and creaked with devotion, rubbing flanks. If you liked that sort of thing they were fun to be with. Tania—had she forgiven Duggie? did his betrayals only make his women love him more?—Tania was enchanted, fascinated. A little of it was enough for me. I don't disapprove; but as much as Grandpa Plumb and Oliver these two locked out the world. I remembered Mirth, with inhuman face, with hair like Strewelpeter, running through the grapefruit trees clutching her butcher's knife while Willis, with grotty crotch and popping eyes, peg-legged madly for the orchard shed. And Duggie howled. They did no damage these days. They were charming in a slightly gruesome way. Our comic turn. Duggie stayed on the other side of the summer-house.

"Everyone has foreign names today," Mirth said. "Willis probably knew a Tania somewhere, didn't you Willie? In one of your ports."

"They let you call them any name you liked if you had the money."

"Now Willie, don't be naughty. Tania goes very nicely with Plumb."

Tania blushed and looked to see if Duggie had heard.

"My dear, I'll give you some advice. Duggie's like his father. He has strong passions. You can't say no to Duggie for very long. So let him, you know, let him.   You modern girls do, I know. And Duggie is not a man you can keep waiting. Nor was his father. Were you, Willie? It's bad for a man if he has to wait. They should teach that in the schools. Then there wouldn't be so many of these boys standing on street corners only thinking. Really, we should have summer camps where young people

149

could go and just make love. Like those health camps we sent
Melva and Irene to, Willie."

"I could be headmaster "

"Now Willie. Ray could have done with something like that
when he was a boy "

I went round the summer-house and found Duggie grinning.
"Now you see why I don't go home."

Merle and Graydon Butters also came. She pushed him along
Millbrook Road in his wheelchair, rolled him on to the lawn,
and I put them here for the effect they had on Glenda. It was
this: when Merle bullied Graydon to talk, and he unloaded
words from his tongue with an agony that made us sweat; and
she pretended they came beautifully and told him that we all, his
dear old friends, understood him, and held his face in her hands
and looked in his eyes, "I know you're in there"; and we laughed;
then Glenda took the handles of his chair and said, cool and
English as her mother, "Do you mind Mrs Butters, I'll just take
your husband for a walk," and pushed him across the lawn and
up the drive and vanished with him in the guava trees.

"Well.   " Merle said. "Who is that woman?"

"She's my wife. I think I'll have a word if you'll excuse
me.

"What are you playing at, Glenda?"

Graydon was in the shade of a tree, with his head slumped on
his chest. I could not tell whether he was resting, weeping,
dead. Glenda stood behind him. She came at me and pulled me
along to the back of the house.

"Couldn't any of you hear what he was saying?"

"No one can understand him. He'll never speak again. Merle
just tries to keep him going."

"I understood. It was plain as day."

"All right. What then?"

"He said, Make her stop."

"Yes—even so—"

"And you all just laughed. You let her go on treating him like
a baby "

150

"Glenda, she's his wife. They've been married for fifty years."

"He said, Make her stop."

"So you made her. Here she comes. Are you going to make her again?"

Merle wheeled Graydon away.

"I want," Glenda said, "I want you to take me to the station. I'm going home."

"Glenda, we can't go."

"By myself. You stay here. It's your family."

"Glenda—"

"I'm not used to it. I can't handle families. I don't know who they all are. I don't know who you are any more."

"We've only got three days. Please, Glenda."

"If you won't drive me I'll take a taxi."

"What about the children?"

"They've got to learn. You bring them back."

"If they've got to.   "

"It's too late for me."

I borrowed Dad's car and drove her to the station. She was in time for the Express. I put her on, rented pillows for her, said goodbye. She was clear-eyed, pink and pretty. She laughed and kissed my cheek. I did not know who she was.

15 I worried about my maturity and quickly seemed to come to the end of myself. My spasm of lust for Tania seems comic now, but I took it to mean there was little to me. I chased after substance recklessly. I became as headlong as a boy. My fantasies took a weird simplicity. No fore-edge painting, no kitchen tables. I wanted to unbutton my wife and lie my hand on her breast. No more than that.

But it had not been simple for some time. Complications broke from us in tangles, like the innards from a broken clock. I look at our conversations and see blind forays, retreats. The words we used had no common meaning. We looked at each

151

other from distances and found no way of coming close—
though we tried, with chat about Sharon and Gregory, with
buying things for the house and holding hands in the pictures.

I did not know what was wrong with her. I asked her to see a
doctor and tried to send her off on holidays. But no—no
doctors; they would only give her tranquillizers or advise her to
find a hobby or a job. She did not need things to do. The
problem was of a different sort. That was as far as she would
define it. As for holidays—Wellington and Wadestown were
her places. She was happy there. She asked me please not to send
her away.

I still found toothpaste on my brush. When I went to bed
Glenda was lying awake. She took cat-naps in the day she said,
so I was not to worry. But what did she think about, I asked,
lying in bed in the darkened room? Please tell me, Glenda. Oh,
she said, things. Everything. We made love. That was still all
right, she enjoyed it; though she made few movements and was
quiet. Our old house shuddered in the wind. A drizzle of dust
fell from the silver sprats.

Out in the world I was busy. I had turned myself into a
political journalist and my editor had promised me the job in the
Press Gallery when Morrie Horne grew tired of it. Morrie said he
would be tired of it soon. He liked a quieter life and had his eye
on Special Features. Meanwhile, I thought about my Uncle
Emerson. Talking with him had given me ideas. *The Sundowner
of the Skies. Emerson Plumb's story, as told to Raymond Sole.* First a
chapter on his boyhood and youth—his motorbikes not his
father. Nobody would want to know about the Reverend
Plumb. Then learning to fly in England; and the crazy flight,
Croydon to Australia in the same year as Kingsford Smith and
Amy Johnson. Then the flying circus, the wing walking. And
mail-run flying in Europe. And the Solent flying boats, seven
hours chugging over the Tasman Sea, with landings on the two
beautiful harbours. I saw it all, I had it written in my mind. In
the last chapter I would tell how he tracked down his old Gypsy
Moth and spent a year rebuilding it and made it fly again. I
roughed out the plan. I made a summary. Then I rang Emerson

and told him the favour I meant to do him. When could I come up with my tape recorder?

Five minutes later the whole thing was gone. I put the phone down shaking. I was hollow with disbelief, and grieving for my book, and blind with anger at these idiot Plumbs, these bloody drongos. What right had Emerson to kill my book?

In revenge I wrote an article on him. What I did not know I invented. Nobody took me up on anything. But it was not enough. I still had my notion of a book, and my torments were not so different from those of a real writer. My problem was I had lost my subject and could not find another. I never saw a book as other than someone's account of his life—and the process I imagined never varied: the famous person talking, Ray Sole taking it down. I asked Alan Webster what I should do. He seemed to think ghosting respectable and he told me to see a publisher: most of them had lists of people anxious to have someone put them on paper. So I went to Reeds and within a week was talking with Albie Marsick. Not the sort of famous person I'd wanted, but a start. His memory was good; he told me what he'd eaten for breakfast at every hotel on tour. He remembered every line-out jump he'd made. So *Play the Man* was born, *The Albie Marsick Story, as told to Raymond Sole*. It seemed to me as rich in incident as *War and Peace*. And Albie himself was a tragic hero. That match where he was ordered off at Cardiff Arms Park.

(Let me get my career in literature out of the way. I did another rugby book, *Boom! Boom!* I did *Sweet Millie*, the story of Millicent Bean, the musical comedy star. I did Frank Murphy's story (the union boss): *Nor Shall My Sword* (his title). I helped Jim Horrocks with *Tough Cop*. Horrocks made my footballers seem like marshmallows. "Just off the record Ray, I'll tell you what we did to that cunt.   " Stomp! Thud! Aargh! I hated Horrocks. Sitting with him, listening to his hatreds, I felt stirrings of nausea; but I got the book finished. And that was enough. I made plans for a different sort of book, *M. J. Savage*: started research, did some interviews. I've still got the stuff in an old suitcase. One day I'll give it to the Turnbull Library.)

Glenda was kind about *Play the Man*. She said it was well done and agreed it was a good way of making extra money. Diana had a lot of fun with it but I told her we'd sold thirty thousand copies. Alan sold five hundred of his books. "Oh well," she said, "if it's money you're after. But Ray, I'm worried about Glenda. What's gone wrong with her?"

Everyone was worried about Glenda. "What's the matter with Mummy?" "She's all right, dear. She's just having a think." "Why does she have to think all the time?" Cute? Not at the time. Not now. I told Gregory that she would stop thinking before long and he was not to worry because Daddy was here; and always to remember that Mummy loved him very much. I told him how special Mummy was; but I was beginning to think of her in terms like those she had used of her mother: pale, cold, lost, sad. Sad was the word I used most. I did not know exactly what it meant. It banged around in my skull, setting up reverberations, then it started wailing like bagpipes.

"Glenda. Glenda."

"Hallo, Ray."

"Have you looked at the children, Glenda?"

"I've given them a kiss."

"Sharon's got earache."

"I know. I took her to the doctor." She did those things. She played with them and read to them and smiled and listened; but it was as if she had learned how from a book. At times I saw her stop as though seeing it, and her hands gave a little jerk and she looked at the children with desperation as though she had remembered there was something she must do, some way to save them.

"Glenda, do you have to go to bed?"

"I'll be awake when you come."

"I want to talk to you, Glenda."

"What about?"

I know you're in there somewhere. Please come out.

I was not always gentle. After a while I found it hard to be even interested. I looked for easy cures. Her father was the trouble, I believed—the bastard who had shot himself and left her to carry on. She had been angry with me for pulling her away from talk of him. O.K., I would talk. She wanted to hear his name? I would say it. I'd drag him from his hiding place and hold him in an armbar for her to see.

"You've got to get him out of your head. He's like a bloody maggot, eating away. Now tell me, you're grown up now, you're not a girl, tell me how you really feel about him. How do you feel about a man who can't face a bit of pain and shoots himself and leaves his daughter to face it for him and carry on?"

That was the way it went. I believed it was practical. Shock tactics.

She looked at me with her turned-in look, eyes out of line; and went out of the room and closed the door.

"Glenda," I yelled, "Glenda," ripping it open, "don't you see he's ruining all our lives. He might just as well have shot us all."

But I was alone in the hall—children behind their doors, Glenda behind her door. I heard her clothing rustle as she changed and heard the bed creak as she got in. She gave a little sigh, neither happy nor sad, expressing something—contentment? dissatisfaction?—whose referents were unknown to me. It was like a sound from outside the house, out in the night. I turned away in fear, as though from a door into nothing; and went back to the lounge and flicked the play button on my recorder and heard a slurp of beer and a voice say, "First tackle of the match Ray, he tries this pansy side-step, thinks he's goin' past me, and I hit that little bugger under his ribs, bowled him arse over kite, heard the air come fartin' out both ends, and I swear to you Ray, no bullshit, he lies on the ground and he says 'Mam', like a lamb bleatin' Talk about laugh. After that he drops every ball he gets. I had him shittin' himself." That was Boom Casey, hero of *Boom! Boom!* I thanked God for him.

When I went to bed after midnight she was awake. And yes, we made love. That happened almost nightly. It was the way we touched. But it seemed to me she felt pleasure on her skin and underneath was not open to me. I penetrated into emptiness.

Meanwhile—I like that word—Duggie prospered. I don't mean he made money, though he made it. Jack Latham called

Muldoon "the monstrous fart of a flatulent party". Duggie's arrival had that quality. From '60 to '63 he was into everything. And when he came forward in his duck waddle with some "grassroots" remit—some plan for hanging or birching or for the outlawing of the communist party—there was a buzz in the conference hall that in political terms was a shout of welcome. But Duggie was too smart to be just the "backwoodsman" party liberals called him. Being a character had its dangers too. He learned how to be quiet, he learned to give the appearance of following. That was not an easy thing for him. But he made it serve, he used endorsement as a substitute for thought. He took things over and made them his. "Other men laboured and he entered into their labours." That was his way—the classic way for a politician.

He put his name forward for Epsom in 1963. Snyder had retired and sixteen people joined the chase for that blue-ribbon seat. Mark Brierly was one. While Duggie had been splashing around Brierly had crept in. Duggie was noticed, Duggie gave an impression of strength—but Brierly, ah, he was a gentle-man. That counted for a great deal in Epsom. He and Duggie and a bank economist and the regional division vice-chairman were the ones with a chance. They nudged each other about in a civilized way. Duggie learned to give a little smile. And he made a lot of ground when he began to escort Sally Carpenter about. Sally was the daughter of a Cabinet Minister; a beautiful girl in her enamelled way; a kind of princess in the social world of the National Party. "Professional virgin," Duggie winked at me. "She's for the duration."

My paper sent me up for a look at Epsom. That was an unusual expense but interest was high. If Brierly or Duggie won the nomination he was safe in parliament for thirty years. It was, my editor said, the perfect springboard for a career—take that line, have a look at them in depth.

I had no time for that. The day I arrived in Auckland Cyril Butts came on the scene. I had rung Duggie and arranged to see him in the morning. Then I sat by the fire talking with Mum and Dad; listening to Dad's worries about M.E., and Mum's about Robert, who was dying. She wanted to bring him down to live in the cottage but Roger Sutton would not get out and Robert, who owned the place, would not evict him. I told them about Glenda, not too much, and saw Mum puzzle for answers, and complain inwardly about the unfairness of things. She knew as well as I there could be no happy ending.

When they had gone to bed I wandered about the house, looked in the study, looked at Grandpa's books—Ovid, Wordsworth, *The History of Pantheism*. Patted the Buddha, gross and spiritual; played some golf shots with a walking stick. Then I walked in the wet grass down to the bridge and heard the water running. Well, I thought, this is where I came in. Time's gone by, the rest of it is atoms knocking about. But I saw the thought as marking my limitations. I did not believe it, but had nothing else. So where was I? Other people got further than that; what was the matter with me that all I had after thirty years was a set of Pavlovian mental tics? Where in them was I? Raymond Sole? There was no answer. Was it possible there was no Raymond Sole? I—or something called I—made my doggy way from feed to feed. I kept my belly full and a number of mental appetites satisfied. I read books—a bit. I listened to music—a bit. I did my best for my wife and children. But if there was no more than that—I might as well join Duggie Plumb in the National Party.

I laughed. That was the answer: wisecrack your way out of trouble. Then I went up to the garage and looked at Grandma Sole's glory box, her china cabinet, her "sweet" etc., left to me when she died. They were piled against the back wall. I should have to tell Dad what to do with them. I shifted the fire set and opened the box. There were the towels and embroidered cloths, the slabs of linen and antimacassars. The sight of them was— moving?—touching?—sad? I felt threatened with speculations about "meaning", and I closed the lid and shrugged and said, "What am I going to do with the bloody things?" The sensible thing was sell them to a junk shop—choose the odd bit for Glenda though, so Dad would not be hurt. I would get on to it.

I locked the garage and was caught against the door by car

157

lights in the drive. They came at me, blinded me, and I thought I was going to be crushed. But Duggie braked, skidded, left his lights glaring, his door wide. He punched the hood and kicked the garage door. Rage frothed out of him.

"Shut up, Duggie." I jerked him, pulled him after me, got him into the house and put a glass of Dad's whisky in his hand. "Now, what's the matter? And keep your voice down. You'll wake Mum."

His face was white and his eyes had a thickening in their blue that made them seem to plunge down and down.

"Ray," he said, "they reopened nominations tonight."

"So, who are they letting in?"

"Cyril Butts."

"Ah, Sir Cyril. Someone to carry on the Snyder tradition."

"The old bastard's been dithering. Last week he said no. He'd made his decision. Tonight he's reconsidered. He wants in. He's had people coming to him—'people whose opinion I respect' The old cunt. He wants it on a plate. I'm not going to give it to him."

"What are the others doing?"

"They've pulled out."

"Brierly?"

"Him too. He's coming out to make a grab for Loomis. Latham'll eat him."

"But you're staying in?"

"I told them straight off. Hignett was the one who came and told us. Said Sir Cyril had changed his mind and the electorate committee was reopening nominations. I told him he couldn't do that but he said they already had. And they wanted us all out—Sir Cyril didn't want all the hurly-burly and so on. I asked him how he'd get on in parliament if he couldn't take a nominations fight. Hignett didn't like that. But the bastards all pulled out. Graceful, you know. Wouldn't dream of standing in Sir Cyril's way. Even Brierly. He went green though. Stupid cunt. I stayed in."

"They won't like that."

"They'll have to like it. Hignett took me off for a little talk.

Told me to wait—'Sir Cyril only wants one term, well maybe two. In six years you can have it.' Thinks I'm buying that. They'll have another Sir Cyril by that time. And I'm not waiting six years for anyone. That's my seat. I've worked for it. They think I'm standing down for some old cunt who's so pickled in gin he can't stand up straight. I told Hignett. I'll tell bloody Holyoake too. There are people in Epsom who want me. They nominated me. You want a story Ray, I'll give you one."

"You want me to say Butts is pickled in gin?"

He said quickly, "I'm not saying that. Here's what I'm giving you." He could not even hint that Butts drank too much. He could not say that at sixty he was too old. Keith Holyoake was fifty-nine. He simply said how much he admired Sir Cyril's career—an M.P. at thirty-one (a good touch: Duggie was thirty-two), a minister in Sid Holland's government; his courage and dignity when he lost his seat (another good touch— Butts should never have lost that seat); the skill with which he'd handled his new job as High Commissioner in London, a job calling for talents of quite a different order from those he had exercised in his parliamentary career. And the scandal of his recall by Nash's Labour government; the honourable retirement, the knighthood putting a seal on his career. No man had done more etc., etc. Duggie organized it beautifully, he turned Butts into a dodo and two-time loser. And those "talents of quite a different order"—that meant boozing if you were in the know.

"Nice work, Duggie. Now what about you?"

"I'm carrying on because I believe in myself and the National Party. Much as I respect Sir Cyril I believe the voters of Epsom want a new face. An energetic member. We're in the sixties now.   ." and so on. At the end of it he'd got his colour back.

I said, "He's still going to beat you. You'd stand a better chance out here in Loomis."

"That's what Hignett said. Brierly wouldn't have a look in. But it's no deal. I'm having Epsom."

"What do you know that I don't know? Have you got some dirt on Butts?"

159

"He drinks himself paralytic every night. I'll make sure one or two people know that."

"They know already. It's one of the things that makes him a character. You're allowed to be a boozer when you've made it."

"Ray, I'm having Epsom. O.K.? It's mine." He laid the words down like coins on a counter. I saw he had nothing left but belief in himself. He had lost belief in the orderly sequence of events. That was the night on which his life in politics really started. Chance became his principle of action.

I interviewed Cyril Butts the following day. He quivered his plum-red jowls at me, boomed his famous laugh, sprayed me with spit that was pure gin, and told me how much he looked forward to the hurly-burly of the house again—how he'd missed it—and serving with his old colleagues Keith and Jack and Ralph, and serving this great little nation once more. I asked him if he hoped for a cabinet appointment. He got cagey and talked about what he had to offer in terms of sheer experience— did I realize he'd been in parliament with Gordon Coates before the National Party took that name? This could surely not be overlooked. But basically, well, he was happy to play whatever role was asked of him.

"How do you feel about keeping younger men out?"

"Ah, Mark Brierly you mean? He's a fine young man. A credit to the party. What a future we've got when young men like that are coming along. And the other chap—what's his name?— Douglas Plumb. I understand their disappointment. But they will have their day. And politics is a battlefield after all."

He had a coughing fit and his face turned purple. I went round the desk to pat his back but he knocked me aside with his tree-trunk arm and grabbed his drink. A swallow put him right. His colour remained alarming and I wondered if somewhere more blood vessels had broken. Duggie might have his hopes on a by-election.

Sir Cyril Butts was chosen as candidate. People who were at the selection meeting say Duggie smiled. He stood up and said that he wished Sir Cyril well, naturally, but more than that, he gave him his whole-hearted support, and what he would like to do now was make himself useful, he would like to turn his knowledge of the electorate to account. People had told him he should try for Loomis. But no, no, he'd made his home in Epsom and that was where his heart was. So   he offered to serve on Sir Cyril's campaign committee. With this Duggie won back the ground he'd lost in opposing Butts. He showed himself a man of "moderation" and "good judgment"

Sir Cyril could only respond by being delighted. Someone told me that although he smiled he was afraid. I don't think that can be true. There's a photograph of him shaking hands with Duggie on that night. He's leaning back a little, the pupils of his eyes seem dilated. He was noticing Duggie for the first time. Duggie looks like a little boy.

He ran Sir Cyril's campaign. Sir Cyril of course did nothing. He burbled. He went through the motions. Duggie shuffled him about. Drove him here, drove him there, held doors open for him. He called for the cheers and led the singing of *For he's* etc. I wondered what it was all about. Duggie as puppet master? That was not what he wanted. Was he just demonstrating the mistake the Nats had made? There he was pouring out energy while Sir Cyril got slower and slower, forgot his speeches, burped on radio.

"What's your game, Duggie?"

"I've got no game."

"You think they might replace him?"

"He's knocking back a quart of gin a day."

"Is that it? You're feeding him the stuff?"

"No, Ray. I'm the one who tries to stop him drinking."

Duggie was first to Sir Cyril when he had his stroke. It happened at a meeting in the Teachers College hall. I was there. I should have been somewhere else but Duggie and Sir Cyril fascinated me. I was at a press table set up at the side of the stage almost in the curtains. I could watch them both: Sir Cyril ripe and dewed with sweat; pumped up, bulging here and there as though he were a bladder with weak places; and Duggie on the other side, in folds of curtains like the trunks of trees. He watched Sir Cyril Butts with the openness of a child. Face white against the curtain, eyes deep black. Where did he keep his rage when he was good-fellowing through the day?

"Look at Plumb," the reporter by me whispered. "Look at his face."

We looked at him. He looked at Cyril Butts. And Butts lost his place; he lost himself; half turned, eyes mad and blind; and shuffled round in a three-quarter circle, facing Duggie. He dragged the podium down. His notes went looping, diving, off the stage. He sat down with a slap on his behind, lay down hard, with a wooden thumping of his head. Air came out of him horribly and spread across the stage.

Duggie was first there. He pulled Sir Cyril's bow-tie off and ripped his collar open. Then he tried to give him mouth to mouth resuscitation. There must have been six doctors in the hall. They lifted Duggie away. They got busy: poked Sir Cyril, thumped his chest, rearranged and listened. Then they squatted on their haunches like boys around a dog that's been run over.

We waited in the auditorium. Hignett came through the curtains, dabbing his eyes and mouth with a handkerchief. "Friends, I have a very painful duty. . ."

Duggie, I said to myself, how did you do it?

We found him at the back of the stage with tears in his eyes. "Mr Plumb. A statement, Mr Plumb."

"The loss—the loss to the National Party. It's immeasurable. I can't say any more."

"Mr Plumb?"

"I had only known Sir Cyril for a few weeks. But in that time. I take this as a personal loss. I can't say any more."

"What will your plans be now?"

"Please. Please. Give me some time. I can't have any plans. I've got to come to terms with what's happened tonight. The loss. "

Later on I rang his flat. There was no answer. I drove around and waited outside for an hour. I tried the electorate office. He wasn't there. I tried Sally Carpenter. What a tinkling voice she had. No, Douglas hadn't called tonight. She really couldn't say where he might be. This dreadful news must be a shock to him.

My next guess, my best guess, was Tania, or some other. That was a way he might celebrate. But I couldn't remember any second names. So I gave up.

He announced his candidacy after Sir Cyril's funeral. Brierly had already been chosen for Loomis. Duggie had no difficulty in beating the economist and the vice-chairman. On election night he took Epsom by more than three thousand votes. Brierly went down by fifteen hundred.

So Duggie Plumb came to Wellington. He was thirty-two. Already the road behind him was strewn with beaten foes. "Watch him," I said. "He's going to be boss." No one took me seriously. McIntyre and Gordon, Talboys, Muldoon, Walker, were up ahead. "Well," I said, "at least he's going to make them know he's there."

He came up to see me after the post-election caucus meeting. "How did it go?"

"I'm the new boy. I kept quiet."

"There's a lot to learn."

"Sure. I'll learn it. Where's your little lady?"

"Gone to bed. It's time you got married, Duggie. Latham's going to trot out this playboy stuff."

"Let him. You got anything to drink?"

I gave him beer, which was all I had. He drank it thirstily. Being new boy had him edgy. He showed no signs of being satisfied, but was looking ahead, looking for ways of shortening the steps he had to take. They made him angry. He was ready *now*.

"Tell me Duggie, how did you know Butts was going to die?"

"I didn't. I saw there was a chance he'd crack up though."

"So you stayed close?"

"I made sure every time he looked over his shoulder he saw me. It got so he was looking all the time. The poor old sod thought I was putting poison in his booze."

"What did you do?"

"How do you mean, Ray?"

"The night he died. You looked as if you were sticking pins in him."

"Did I?"

"I was watching you, Duggie."

"Well," he said; he drank more beer, "like I told you, Epsom was mine. I couldn't listen to the old bugger snuffling on any more."

"So?"

"I stuck my hand in the back of his head and gave his brain a squeeze."

16 For a second or two I took him literally. When Bobby's wrestling holds had made me cry I was terrified he would open me up and put his hands inside to work a cure. I saw Duggie's hatred as giving him the power to open Butts. It held me blind, in an unnatural light; then he laughed.

"You know what I mean."

I shrank still. He had willed Butts dead. I could only see it as a physical act.

So it brought things back into a natural light when his career went suddenly wrong. The cartoonist Sharples drew him climbing a rope and leaning down with scissors to snip it off beneath him. That was Duggie repudiating his past. But the piece of severed rope turned into a snake and fixed its teeth in his behind. It was labelled Meggett Enterprises.

The M.E. collapse and Fred Meggett's imprisonment for fraud were heavy blows for Duggie. He issued statements defending himself, spoke on radio and TV, but it did no good. He had been with Meggett once and Meggett was a crook. It's a toyshop world in politics. Mistakes are not measured by right and wrong.

Latham called for Duggie to resign. There was never any chance of that; but Duggie found himself locked in a cupboard. He had hoped to move the Address in Reply when the session opened. Muldoon had made his maiden speech that way. *Here I am.* Now Duggie was going to say it. But he never even got to

164

second the motion. Up there at the back, alongside the dimmest Labour men, he was in a corner like the dunce. I lounged in the Gallery and watched him—felt for him, but also wanted to laugh. *Hubris, nemesis.* I wanted to fly down paper darts explaining what had happened. He kept his face still. He never smiled. He never blinked. And watching him, I began to be frightened. I understood Duggie was at work, he was making himself. When he got through this he would be Man.

It is time for me to say where I stood in politics. Easy. I stood nówhere. I rationalized it by saying that I followed my sense of right whichever way it led me. It was, I said, the honest thing to do. My socialism was gone—it had never had any real existence. I grew up breathing haunted air. But Grandpa Plumb's socialism was sentimental; and mine was insubstantial as a shadow. I read nothing, thought nothing, but did a lot of "feeling" I joined no organization or party. What I managed was to idealize a class. Joe the wharfie, yelling slogans, made no dent in my idea of him. When I thought of working men I saw myself. What a lot of people there were with my face and my sensibilities.

As for journalism, one reason I chose it was my belief that the press stood for enlightenment. The old machine in Charlie Kittredge's shed was a sacred object, even though Charlie had been on the wrong side himself. When I left Gerriston I still believed journalism might be truth-telling. And I worked for the *Dominion* and later the *Evening Post*! It would be easy to make fun of myself, but that would be to overlook the waste. My stupidities are not the point. The point is that I withered and grew old. I was old at thirty. I passed through no cleansing fire; no fire of thought, experience, language. Daily I rubbed against the mediocre; the clever; the vain. And soon I could not discern, I had no idea of, things that were hard and bright and clean. Nevertheless, I told myself I followed my sense of right. That was how I justified the dislike of everyone that showed in my writing. I was thought of as "hard-hitting". Politicians started hitting back. I enjoyed that.

I treated Duggie just like all the others. When I moved to the

Sunday Post and started my column he became a regular in it:
Duggie Prune. He was in Keith Holysmoke's gang, with Jack
Marshmallow and Rob Mudloon. Norman Berk and You What?
led the other gang. That was the level. But it helped make Jolly
John's the best-selling Sunday yellow in the country.

This takes me ahead, and I must come back. There's no
getting away from the private life. All the rest is only clothes
we wear. I went to a party. Glenda did not come but stayed at
home in our double bed. A girl watched me. I drank a few more
drinks and ambled over. "Do we know each other?" She had
crinkly hair that looked electric. I thought if you pushed in your
fingers you'd get a shock.

"You're Raymond Sole, aren't you?" She gave me a close look,
measured me. "I wondered if I'd meet you down here."

"Down here?"

"I'm from Auckland. I used to know your father." She gave a
little smile, mocking, sour.

"Ah," I said, "Beth Neeley. Well, well, well." My father's
"mistress." She had been his office girl and he had run away with
her, leaving Mum at Peacehaven nursing Robert. Their cohabi-
tation had lasted a week.

"Thanks for what you did for him. It should happen to every
man at sixty." I had never been able to imagine them together—
my picture had been of Dad holding her hand and grinning
shyly. Once or twice I sat him on her knee.

"He went back to your mother, didn't he?"

"Yep. And lost his money. How would you have handled
that?"

"I'd have stayed with him. I just couldn't stand his guilt."

"So it wasn't only his false teeth and his baggy underpants?"

"Are you always so nasty?"

"I'm a journalist. We tell the truth."

All this was moody, edged, and during it we passed into a
kind of erotomania. It was as impure as anything I've
known—and I mean impure in no moral way. Desire came
mixed up with idea.

"I'll drive you home."

"I've got my own car."

"O.K. I'll follow."

Her pubic hair was electric as her head hair. It prickled through her slip like copper wire. And when I hooked my fingers in her crotch a grey flash in the dark part of my brain illuminated caves where inhuman eyes looked out. There was no affection in our coupling. There was more excitement than I had ever known, and through the night an interest that was frantic and hostile. We had a good deal more than Duggie's sex-book fucking.

"I suppose you'll think I'm lying if I say I've never done it that way before."

"Does it matter what I think?"

"Not really."

"Were you pretending I was Dad?"

"No. Oh no. You're you. Not that I'm very sure what that is."

"Are you going to want to know?"

"I don't think so."

I did not want to know either. But that was not in my control. At the end a sleepy fondness grew on us. Our bodies seemed to want to know, and warm down the length of us, casually twined, we found ourselves able to talk in an ordinary way.

We did not spend very long with Dad. Revenge had been a part of her motive, but it seemed a small thing now, she wondered that resentment had troubled her so much. But she had had a sense of being wasted, she had seemed to take no part of herself away. Now it was over, she was back. Not exactly thanks to me, but thanks anyway.

My revenge had been more complicated. It was an act of violence to restore my balance. (To bring a bit of justice back was what I wanted to say; but that would have had the sound of complaint and I thought she might accuse me of self-pity.) Now, like her, I could carry on. Even, I said, if I didn't see her again.

"I'd like to see you. I don't want to hurt your marriage though."

"You won't."

"I'd forgotten how good it was. Just sex."

"You want more?"

"Yes, I do."

"There must have been other men since Dad."

"One or two. Like little dogs. With their tongues hanging out. Telling me how nice I am. 'I love you, Beth.' You won't do that, will you?"

"Not me."

"I might need it one day but I sure don't need it now."

I went home in the dawn. Glenda was sleeping. She stirred and opened her eyes and smiled at me. "Is that the dawn?"

"The party went on late."

"I was lonely. Mm, you feel warm. You've been with a woman, haven't you?"

"No.   "

"She smells nice. Please don't pretend, Ray. I've been waiting for it to happen. I don't mind." She put her hand on my chest. "Bumpity bump. It gives you away."

"I'm sorry, Glenda."

"No. It's my fault. Was she nice?"

"She was all right."

"I hope it was better than that. Oh, you want to have me too. I think you should wash first."

So I washed and I had my wife. Again desire was mixed up with idea. Afterwards she stroked my chest. "It's bursting out of there. Who was she, Ray?"

"A girl. That's all."

"Are you going to see her again?"

"I don't know."

"I think you should. I'm no good to you any more."

I denied that, of course. But she told me it was not for me to say; and she told me not to worry, she didn't worry, not any more, she had a place to go and nothing could touch her when she was there.

"Do the children touch you?"

"I'm no good to them either."

We slept a while, my front cupped round her back, and were woken by Sharon bringing us cups of tea. She was used to seeing us naked and she weighed Glenda's breasts in her hands. "I wish mine would get a move on."

"They're doing very nicely." Glenda put her top on. "Mm, good tea, love." But she was an illusion. Bed, warmth, family; she was no part of it. And I saw her as a kind of perfect robot. She had no life as we had life. Sharon felt it too. She went to the living-room and practised on her flute.

I stayed away from Beth for half a week. When I called on her again we came at each other greedily. That was her mouth on me, a human mouth. I licked her sweat and that was human sweat. Glenda was no good to me any more—now that she had said it I said it too, feeling no guilt. I hungered after all Beth's imperfections, everything she offered I could taste, it nourished me. Yet Glenda, back in Wadestown, immeasurably distant, kept one human attribute that made everything I took from Beth illusory in the end. That was her grave acceptance of her death. I saw clearly where she was, but could not keep my eyes on it and, turning away, quickly forgot. I could not bear to look; but the residual memory—no more than a fleeting image, Glenda's face—troubled me through the day, through my work, in the office, out of the office, when I was with Beth.

Glenda, I said, for God's sake, whatever you're going to do, do it soon.

At night she played the piano, music that was watery and pure. "I must play more often." She stood and looked at the harbour. Then she smiled and kissed me. She kissed Sharon. "Don't stay up too late, love." She sat on Gregory's bed a moment; and Sharon and I lolled and watched TV or read our books. Then Sharon went and I was alone in the room, looking at what was happening and wondering what to do. When I went to bed she was still awake. But I did not touch her and she made no sign she missed me in that way. One of us, and both of us, drifted off to sleep.

What was she? How can I answer? I had no way, and have no way, of getting close to her. Her death was *her* death. I fight not to cheapen it with my emotions.

Her note read: *Dear Ray, I've taken the car. I'm not sure whether I'll be back tonight. I kissed the children. They look beautiful. Love, G.*

She had put toothpaste on my brush.

The wind howled round the house and rattled the windows. On the garage roof iron squealed. I ran out to check that the doors were locked. My dressing gown flapped about my ears and wind gusts had me lurching like a drunk. I saw my neighbour's greenhouse burst. Slates from his roof came looping down at me. I ran inside and slammed the door. What a day for her to take the car. How was I going to get the kids to school and myself to work? Trees would be coming down all over Wadestown.

"Sharon," I yelled, and she came out in her pyjamas. "Get the breakfast will you. Your mother's gone out."

"Where?"

"How would I know? Get Gregory up. On second thoughts, leave him. The pair of you better stay home. There'll be wires coming down."

"Will Mum be all right?"

"I hope so. She shouldn't have gone out."

Sharp little draughts played through the hall and bedroom. Puffs of dust sprang out of the wainscots. Over the bed the sprats turned with more animation than they had shown since the day Glenda had hung them up. I dressed, shivering, and pulled the blankets straight. I thought about Beth and worried about Glenda. She was not a good driver. Then the phone rang and I forgot about her until night.

Morrie Horne, chief reporter now: "Ray, I've sent a car for you. The *Wahine's* on Barretts Reef. She's taking a hell of a pounding. You team up with Colin. He's out at Palmer Head. Stay on this side. I'll send someone else round the harbour."

I heard a horn blowing at my gate, and yelled at Sharon and Gregory not to go out. Then I was at Breaker Bay, watching the black ship, free of the reef, drifting up harbour, with waves bursting on her and spray like hands reaching over her decks.

There is nothing so helpless as a sinking ship. She lumbers, sighs, and seems to want her death.

At midday she was off Steeple Rock. Passengers swarmed on the decks. They wore orange life jackets and moved in clumps, like bees. The ship had too much black on her, she showed her hidden parts. The sea was more alive, all broken points and angled planes—and the *Wahine* was dead. People came sliding down her decks. Some climbed into boats, which started lazily, like fish, and slipped down into troughs. They seemed to stay and stay, it did not seem there could be valleys deep enough to keep them there so long. When they came up they were heavy as logs of wood.

I stayed at Seatoun wharf till late afternoon, watching boats and life rafts ride through the surf and people stagger on the beach. I found survivors to interview. I watched the ship go down under the waves. In the evening I was back at my desk. I rang Sharon and told her I would be late. She and Gregory had been watching the news. More than thirty people were missing, she said, and others had been washed ashore dead. "Yes, I know." It seemed impossible that in the slow sinking I had seen people had died.

When I got home the children were asleep. Sharon had left a note on the table. *I'm sorry about the* Wahine. *I've put some dinner in the oven. I'm a lousy cook. I hope Mum gets home soon. Sharon.*

By that time Glenda was dead. No one saw her die and I can only guess at the details. In fourteen years I have played many versions over but they do not differ in their essential facts. She was at Makara in the morning, watching the sea smashing itself on the shingle beach. She bought a bread roll and ate it in the car. Then she drove back down the road towards Wellington. At Makara South she turned out to Oteranga Bay and drove along the hilltops in a wind that must have threatened to lift the car off the road. She stopped and opened farm gates and drove through, and shut the gates again, while the gale whipped her face and legs and sent her hair streaming out. When the road dropped down to the bay she saw the white wave-broken strait, and Terawhiti Hill, dragon-backed, immense, in all that wild water and wild air. She drove down to the stream and left the car and waded over. In her yellow parka and corduroy skirt she followed the path down to the cliffs at the west side of the bay and started round towards the cape. The air boomed. Spray rattled on her. But I suppose in her a stillness and a cold weight. She felt a gravitational pull towards death. But it was *her* death, *her* death. I must not suppose.

Along towards the cape, an hour's walk, she stopped. There was nothing left of the island. It ran out in the sea. Over the strait South Island hills made a blur on the air. Glenda took off her shoes, her parka, took off all her clothes; she took off her rings and took the wooden hair clip from her hair, and she walked into the sea and was drowned. Or perhaps she died smashing on the rocks. Nobody knows. Her body was never found.

The police drove me out to see the car. I walked along the coast with them and saw where she had left her shoes wedged under a rock with her wedding ring and engagement ring and hair clip in one of them. They showed me the half mile of shore where the wind had blown her clothes.

Yes, I told them, she had been depressed. I offered them the word because they had to have something. It was the word I offered the children too. And once I tried to persuade them it might have been an accident. She had gone there to be free, had taken off her clothes to feel the rain. People did that. Then a wave had come. I told them about the seventh wave.

Sharon smiled and patted me. "Thanks, Dad. But we can take it. Don't try that."

17 This part of Golden Bay has one of the highest rainfalls in New Zealand. Water comes off my roof in curved sheets. I look at the world through water. It presses on me, thunders. I cannot hear my dishes as I wash up. I cannot hear the flames in my iron stove.

In my parka and gumboots I slosh up and down the paths. The Aorere runs black, runs amber, then runs clear again. Ché and Carlo, in yellow slickers, walk down from the house with a thermos flask of soup for me. They flash their smiles but won't come in. They have built a lake in the garden and squelch off there to break a wall and let some water out. Ché belongs to Bella Ross. Sharon's new man turns out to be a lady.

Time passes in the trailer. How it passes. Mornings rush away, decades vanish. I eat cold breakfasts. I don't want fug until my work is done. I sit with my sleeping bag drawn up to my waist and wear two jerseys. At lunch-time I light the stove and eat beans on toast or a can of stew. The air gets thick and I part it with my hands. It fogs my brain, which is nice sometimes and other times nasty. I feel a part of me die: nice, nasty. So I go out walking, or drive into Collingwood and try to find out what the world has been up to. The usual things. I grin with admiration and disgust. And driving back, the pain in my chest starts up. I don't want to crash and kill anybody, but on these roads, in this weather, there are not many cars. I have looked in Sharon's *Pears Encyclopaedia* and diagnosed angina. Soon I'll go over to Nelson and see what can be done about it. In the meantime Sharon watches me—doesn't bully me to go. She walks round to the trailer to see if I'm O.K. Bella doesn't like that. She wishes I would clear out, one way or the other. With heavy irony, she calls me "the necessary male" Sharon grins and doesn't stop calling me Dad. We're secure with each other. They too seem secure. They bicker fondly, at times they're openly carnal— strokings and soft kisses and fingers intertwined. I don't mind. I can understand Sharon wanting Bella. She's a good-looking woman. I wouldn't mind her myself, which she's aware of, and narrow-eyed about.

But I don't need her, or any woman. I have Glenda and Beth. Glenda is dead, twice dead. I've read it over. And see that my life has made me adjectival. I don't like that. The truth is in nouns and pronouns. Adjectives blur things, adverbs too; and verbs can falsify. Glenda. That's the truth. Glenda died—less true. Glenda drowned herself. That can't be said in three words. I haven't enough words for it. Only Glenda.

This leaves aside the question of responsibility. I have, of course, blamed everybody involved, and absolved them. I do that daily. I absolve Graham Goodlad. I ask myself if I have the right, and don't care too much about the answer. It's the same when I absolve myself. I loved Glenda and she loved me. Love is said to be enough. It isn't. Perfect love? Another adjective. In fact, we're fallen. Let's keep that "f" lower-case.

The rain makes the sound of a train in a tunnel. The sheet of water turns silver on its edge where the wind blows it. My chest is hurting me. I'll lie down.

Sharon has had a letter from Gregory.

"Hi Sis, Here we are in the North. Our Work goes well. Last week we brought the Good News to Helensville. Tonight it's Warkworth. The rain comes down but the joy of doing the Lord's work never ceases.   "

That work has taught him full stops and capital letters. Happiness too. Reborn among the reborn, indelible LOVE and HATE etched on his hands, he travels about the country with the Good News; strums his guitar, sings in his creaky voice words simple enough to be true; and confesses that once he hated his Dad, confesses to drugs and drink and theft and to being second in line at the gang-bang. Tells how he heard the Word, how Christ saved him. Gregory Sole, great-grandson of a man who heard something similar in his youth.

"Thank you, Sharon. He seems all right."

"Many are the pathways."

"It was never his fault."

"Or yours. Remember that."

She absolves me. We're a presumptuous lot, but it's hard to carry on without some cheek.

"The curve of tragic action is a curve of self-discovery. On the other hand, the comic curve is one of self-exposure.   " Where does that leave me? Is my life experience or spectacle?

After four years and seven months Beth showed me the door. She pointed to it and said, "The door's right there." She said, "You and your wife are so bloody boring." "I never talk about her " "You don't have to talk. She's in there behind your eyes Ray, swimming like a fish. Anyway, I'm getting married." "Who to?" "Are you really interested? No, I didn't think so." She married a high school teacher and went to live in New Plymouth. "You were always second best of the Soles." There was no malice in that; she was putting her memories in order.

I was glad to see her go, although I loved her. She overlapped with Glenda; and when she went took Glenda too. She took the Glenda swimming like a fish, and left me Glenda of the student flat, and Ghuznee Street, and Wadestown. Not a person that I understand; but my wife, a girl I love. She escapes me continually and goes into her dark. But I'm no longer guilty, no longer obsessed, and because I don't wait for her to come out she comes before long.

I've had other women, but not to speak of. The ones I've had would not speak of me. The only fantasy I allow is that one day I'll meet Tania, whose second name I never knew. With her I'm unreserved. It's love that I imagine and not sex. It can't happen. I asked Duggie about her once and he told me she was married to a farmer and had turned herself into a breeding sow.

The sky was clear today. Lead Hills and Mount Olympus stood out pure and cold. I asked Sharon how they compared with the Himalayas and whether she found it possible to think of them as Cerebrum of the Earth.

"You don't remember that?" she cried.

"I do. I've got your letters." It pleased me to see her blushing. I'm eager to find simplicities in her.

"Burn them."

"I won't do that."

When she was gone I took the letters from their old cigar box. On the flap of the envelopes she had written: Sender: Archana, Himalayan Peaks, Cerebrum of the Earth.

Beloved Father (she wrote), I pray that you are well and in peace. Please do not write to me. I have left the ashram, at least for some months. I shall let you know my whereabouts in due course. There will be no post-box in the deep, secret, sacred regions I shall be roaming before the monsoons come. .

And she wrote: I have been in an ashram at Uttarkashi, halfway to the source. The walls are lapped by Ganga. Her waters are thunderous, louder even than the ocean surf. It is hard to express what Ganga means to me. She has given me so much stillness, so much faith and understanding. Near her mighty flow I feel protected. There is no fear, even of death. One can be so open that prana can replace the need for food.   Never do I need to think of returning to the world.

And: May you soon reach that Peace within. Love, Archana.

I had loved her toughness and her honesty. Flesh and bone had not been more real. Now it seemed she was floating away on a cloud. As I read her letters I made exclamations of distress. At the end I cried, "Your name's Sharon, not Archana." I took out the photo box and looked at her in her school uniform, with silly hat and duffel bag and cocky smile. In those days she had learned French not Hindi. Wisdom came from a best friend Jo and a boyfriend Selwyn. She quoted their opinions relentlessly, and that was in order. Late at night she often saw through them and would announce it with a shrug. She Jekyll-and-Hyded through her teens from silliness to good sense—all O.K. with me, and fascinating. I was spectator at the making of an adult: said as much to Rose when she nagged me about the freedom I allowed "the child"

"You didn't let her go away with them? Three boys and one girl?"

"Stop worrying, Rose. Sharon knows what she's doing."

"But one tent. How are they going to sleep?"

"In sleeping bags." I could not tell her I did not think Sharon was a virgin, even though for Rose virginity was a state of mind and morality less important than Self. I could have argued that Sharon's Self was intact; but left it with the opinion that she had more good sense than both of us.

And in three days Sharon was home. "I didn't go to the Sounds to lie in a tent and smoke pot." That was the last I heard of Selwyn. But late at night (Gregory still out and likely not to come home) she said, "There was an old man in a house round the bay. He was like a little monkey in a chair. He had a male nurse who brought him drinks. And a big flash launch he never went out in. I watched him through the hedge. He sent his nurse to tell me to clear out."

"Ha!" I thought this was a tale about privilege.

"He was K. D. Mottram, the brewer. The nurse told me he was eighty-four. And lived on Complan."

"Mottram, eh?"

"I know who Mottram was, Dad. Mum told me that old stuff."

"When?"

"Right through. It was instead of fairy tales. She sat on the bed and talked. I'd go to sleep and dream about her father—eyes like glass. And Mrs Mottram in a turban, like an oil sheik. When I saw Mr Mottram's launch and jetty it was like walking through a door into fairyland. I went swimming off the jetty the way she did. The water was so clear you could see your skin, all the pores and hairs, all golden, you know, magnified, transformed. There were little fish with transparent flesh, the light came through and you could see their backbones."

"No," I said.

"It's all right, Dad. I'm all right. Mum was mad but I'm not."

"She wasn't mad."

"In a way she was. I suppose Grandpa was just a sort of con-man. A lady-killer. But Mum got kind of fixated on him. She had a kind of vision. Peace, perfection, light. Purity. And nothing was any good after that. Not you or me, or Gregory. Even though she tried."

"Sharon—"

"She had to die, Dad. But I won't, don't you worry. I did a poop on Mottram's jetty before I left. A real biggie. I suppose poor old Selwyn will get the blame."

177

"Did she tell you about watching them?"

"Yes. Grandpa and Mrs Mottram making love. The whole bit. It was interesting. I found the place they did it. Somewhere there. There was no magic spring or anything. I'm glad I went. It's kind of finished." She laughed. "Pooping was juvenile. But it seemed the thing at the time. For K. D. Mottram. Underwater though, what Mum saw.   " She had a little frown of interest, a Glenda inclination of her head, and I saw her suddenly as not reachable by love, not knowable by me, not to be saved or understood.

She said, "We're so proud and selfish. Me. And you. And Greg. And Rose. And K. D. Mottram. Even though it's the same light shining through us all."

"I don't know any light." I was frightened.

She grinned at me. "Maybe my language isn't right. But you know what I mean."

"I don't."

"You don't want to."

"I want to know what *you* mean. I don't suppose I ever will."

"No." She patted me. "Mum loved you, Dad. She kept on telling me. But I guess you were too human. You couldn't compete with old Graham Goodlad and his diamond eyes. I'm off to bed."

She kissed me and was gone. And the next year went to Auckland to study in an ashram; and at nineteen to Holy Ganga, where she meant to conquer Self. Rose and Felicity, for their separate reasons, were appalled.

"Here," I said, "listen. 'I feel a new, a Real birth. A wonderful change has occurred in my life. So much joy, so much unity. The cerebrum of the earth; so close to Heaven.'"

"Oh!" they said, "uh!" They grunted with pain. Listening to them, I felt almost cheerful about Sharon. They were not women you could laugh at though.

Felicity said, "Those so-called holy men are charlatans. They feed off girls like Sharon."

Rose said, "What she'll end up with is hepatitis."

I don't know that her holy man fed off Sharon, but he did

178

some other nasty things. And she got hepatitis.

When she came home she was light as an elf. Her skin was golden white and dry as crêpe paper. Hollows lay on her face where her girl-fat had been. "Sharon, is that you?"

"I think so, Dad."

Her holy man had set out to destroy her—through overwork, humiliation, insult. "The idea was to break me up in pieces until I really didn't exist any more. And then put me together in a way that, well, satisfied him. I had too much pride and selfishness. It's a technique he's got. I think he's mad."

"You won't go back?"

"Not to that ashram. But I'll go back. I'm not finished yet." She told me of a village in the Kumaon Hills, and a cave where she had lived in a temple complex: of gathering wood and washing clothes and learning Hindi songs   of temple bells and mantras and the conch shell sounded to drive out evil spirits and evil thoughts. That is what she was going back to—and the deodar trees and mountains and icy rivers.

"Sharon," I said, "if you get hepatitis again you'll die over there." I told her about Alf's friend John Willis who had been killed by a second attack of hepatitis.

"I got it on purpose," she said. "That was how I escaped. I had just enough me left to get sick."

She sat on the veranda playing her flute. Rose and Felicity came visiting and a war of doctrines raged. Every time I went out to break it up they started laughing. I felt superfluous and I went off and clipped the hedge. Although they could not agree, they shared a biology, and had a knowledge I could not have, and an ease together that made me aware of clumsy limbs and clumsy tongue and a lack of fineness like the lack of a sense. There are circuits in the female brain that astonish me. There are times when I know that men are rudimentary beings.

Gregory rode up on his motorbike. I heard his engine surging and fading in the hilly streets.

"Sharon's home?"

"She's round on the veranda with Felicity and Rose."

179

He scowled and clomped his boots and kneaded his greasy leathers.

"You've got some more tattoos."

"Yeah. Had 'em done." A swastika on his left cheekbone and something like the star of David on his right.

"That swastika's the wrong way round."

"Yeah?" He shrugged. "S'pose I better go and see her."

"Greg. Where are you living? What are you doing?"

"I shift around."

"Any job?"

"Don't need a job."

He had accused me of letting his mother die. "No, Greg. I loved your mother. But she was gone somewhere else."

"I would've saved her. You didn't try."

"I did—"

"You were too busy fucking Beth."

That was at fourteen. Now he did not seem to know who I was. Life among the *Skullmen* had blotted out his past. I took it as a good sign that he remembered Sharon. We walked round to the veranda and she ran at him and hugged him. "Oh, Greg. Oh you look tremendous." She patted his tattoos. "Hey, they're wild." Her peastick arms encircled him, her wrists crossed like crossbones under the skull emblem on his back. "I thought you mightn't come." She pulled him into the hall and closed the door.

"Well!" Rose said.

"Was that Gregory?"

"A swastika! If he comes out here I won't trust myself."

"What a mess you've made of them, Ray. An unholy mess."

"Maybe."

"No maybes about it. They're drifting like bits of flotsam. You know what they've got inside their heads? Chaos. Temple bells and swastikas! It can only end in lunacy."

"It's lunacy already. Your children, Glenda's children, are lost, Ray. If man is in any way a superior being it's through his mind. Through his power of thought. And Gregory comes in here with *Love* and *Hate* written on his hands. And a skull on his

180

back. And Sharon! Sharon! Temple bells indeed! There's bats in her belfry."

"I blame you, Ray."

"And I blame you."

I left them frothing and fizzing and clipped my hedge. They walked out past me—no goodbyes—and drove away in Rose's car. I did not blame them for their anger. Sharon and Gregory were nothing to please rationalist and Catholic. Yet I understood what Rose and Felicity could not: that they were at a beginning not an end. It struck me as an interesting start. The danger to their bodies troubled me more: hepatitis and dysentery and motorbike accidents.

Gregory said, "So long, mate," and rumbled away on his Norton. Sharon raked up my hedge clippings. "Don't worry about the *Skullmen*, Dad. He's just passing through."

"And you're just passing through Eastern religion."

"Ah no. That's different."

In six months she was off, not to mountains and deodar trees after all, but to Poona, to the ashram of a swami called Ragneesh. I helped with money. "Don't get sick."

Gregory was at the airport too. He had scars on his cheekbones in place of tattoos, and a van with donut tyres and paintings of Satan and his angels on its sides. It was called *Van Demon*. He had a girl in skin-tight leather and a see-through blouse. He introduced her to Sharon but not to me. The Boeing climbed over Evans Bay.

"So long, mate," Greg said, and drove away.

18 At about that time I had the first of my letters from Alaric Gibbs. He started by telling me I didn't know him. In spite of its being obvious that seemed to carry a threat.

"I think we might meet to our mutual advantage. I have written a book. " I relaxed and yawned. Then said,

"Damn": the manuscript was on its way "under separate cover"
That meant I should have the trouble of returning it. "I have had
an interesting life. Before the war I worked as an engineer in
Malaya and East Africa, building roads and bridges. In the war I
was attached to the New Zealand Engineers and saw service in
the Middle East and Italy. When I returned to New Zealand I
joined the Ministry of Works and worked on hydro installa-
tions. My life falls into three parts and so does my book.
However, the publisher to whom I submitted it.   "

The manuscript arrived the following day. I took it into the
lounge with my coffee and started reading; and thought perhaps
the publisher had been hasty. With pruning and livening
up.   The war parts were well done. But no, I wasn't going
to be drawn in. *M. J. Savage* was my book. Late that night I
pulled it from the drawer of my writing desk and spread it on the
carpet. I felt a tingling in my fingers. It was seven years since I
had done more than open the drawer and look in. Now I
had Savage on the floor, all his parts. "St Michael", "the
brewer's pimp from Sydney" All I had to do was put him
together

I was up till dawn fiddling with tapes and letters. I shifted
them about like a jigsaw puzzle. Gaps showed up but that didn't
worry me. "Now then. Now then." Mickey—Joe—Savage
belonged to me. Before I went to bed I put Alaric Gibbs'
manuscript on the kitchen table so I wouldn't forget to post it in
the morning.

As things turned out, I delivered it. John Jolly sent me to
Auckland to interview an American Country and Western
singer who was on a secret visit to fish for trout. I finished with
him early and sat in my hotel room while the city squealed and
mumbled and the harbour bridge gleamed like a smile. Bridges
made me think of Alaric Gibbs. I took his manuscript out and
looked at part three. It had none of the life of the early parts. He
mentioned his wife and daughter frequently. "And so I came
home from that mighty structure, that river tamed, to the
cottage and garden that was my own 'little bit of heaven', and
found my ministering angels waiting for me. A man can know

no greater joy than this: a job well done, and dear ones to welcome him back to his hearth." The sentimentality was a new note. He had scarcely mentioned wife and daughter in the first two parts.

I walked up Parnell Rise in the summer twilight and found Gibbs' house at the back of the chocolate factory. He was watching television and I had to tap on a window to get his attention. He switched the set off with a dab of his finger. "It's meant for imbeciles. Nevertheless I watch. Well Mr Sole I didn't expect a visit. Tell me what you thought. Wait though, we'll have a Scotch."

I told him his book needed hard work. If he was interested I would give him the names of a couple of people who might take it on. I mentioned the cost and he said, "I'm not surprised. I'm no writer." The first two parts had been "put down" with his wife's help after the war. She had curbed his flights of fancy—his references to her. Then he had left the thing for twenty-five years, and taken it up again recently, just for something to do. The best part had been typing it with two fingers: that filled up the days admirably.

His wife was dead? I asked.

"Yes. Oh yes. She passed on fifteen years ago. Your verdict doesn't surprise me, Mr Sole. Here, keep it as a souvenir. It might have some value one day." He gave a smile that showed more gleam of teeth than I had expected; and when I demurred put the manuscript firmly in my lap. "You're the only public it will have. Another drink?"

His room gave little of him away. It was neither this nor that: neat nor untidy, dark nor light. The book by his chair came from a library. It was one of Ross Macdonald's Lew Archer stories. The pictures on the walls were photographs of bridges and viaducts, all beautiful and, it seemed, defying nature. On a piano with empty candle arms and a closed lid studio portraits of Gibbs' wife and daughter faced the room and seemed to smile gravely at the point where their eyes would meet. That would be where Alaric Gibbs was placed, completing the figure. The girl was beautiful. In her eyes and brow she resembled Glenda. But

183

the memory that stirred was of some other. Just as I'd missed knowing Graham Goodlad I missed the girl.

"I noticed you looking at my Ross Macdonald. Do you like him?"

"Very much. He's better than Chandler."

"Do you think so? Chandler comes first. Do you know that essay of his on the art of murder? Where he says—"

"'Down these mean streets goes a man who is not himself mean.'"

"Yes. 'Who is neither tarnished nor afraid.' Now that's superb. He gets nothing but his fee for which—remember?— 'he will protect the innocent, guard the helpless and destroy the wicked'"

"It's a bit sentimental."

"Nonsense. Nonsense. It's romantic, yes. It's valorous. Chivalric. My God, it's human in the only sense I care to give the word." His nod of emphasis set his white hair stirring. He was a wispy man and almost seemed to rustle as he moved. Dehydrated face: it looked as if it would soak up water. Pointed cheekbones, pointed mouth, ears from which the lobe and curl had melted. Yellow wax. I wondered if disease had eaten him. But he was stiff, immovable as iron. There was a frame in him that would not bend. Some ideology possessed him; some belief or doctrine. I thought of his letter—"you don't know me"— and the threat returned. Perhaps there was no doctrine. Perhaps just—just?—a bitter love or hatred. He looked as if a wind would blow him away; yet inside, his mass. The star that collapses on itself? White dwarf?

He said, "I enjoy your column in the *Sunday Post*."

"That? It's here today and gone tomorrow."

"No, it's good. Of its kind. One mustn't be fair with politicians."

"Definitely not."

"Mudloon. I like that. And Duggie Prune."

"Believe it or not, he's my cousin."

"Yes, I know. There's not much I don't know about Plumb. You don't let him off lightly, cousins or not. I knew him once."

184

"Oh?"

"Yes, my daughter. " He aimed his finger at the photographs.

"Miss Jennifer Gibbs," I said. "He took her to the National Party ball in '54. I saw the photo in the *Weekly News*. She looks like Kim Novak. An actress," I explained. "And my wife."

"Jenny and Plumb were engaged. Not officially. I've followed his career. Let me show you."

He left the room and came back with three scrapbooks bound in imitation leather. "Jenny started this one. I've kept them going. Here." He opened one of the books and showed me a newspaper photograph. "That's her with Plumb." It was the photo I remembered: Duggie and Miss Jennifer Gibbs dancing at the ball. The girl on the furry newsprint looked like a war bride. She looked like a piece of cloth Duggie was waving. With short-back-and-sides, he was as smooth as a bullet.

The next entry, dated four years later, was a piece about Duggie's joining Thomas Tax Consultants. Then the entries came thick and fast. Divisional conferences. Party conferences. The Loomis campaign. Epsom campaign. The Meggett affair. Duggie in Epsom again, '66. Duggie as Junior Whip, as Under Secretary for Trade and Industries. Minhinnick cartoons. Tom Scott articles. And Duggie married. Half a book on that.

"You've even got Duggie Prune."

"I don't think there's anything I've missed."

"But why?"

"He interests me. That's a good one." He tapped an entry damp with paste. It showed Duggie yesterday, facing the Hell's Angels and Black Power. Their leaders had sleeves ripped off at the shoulder and arms that bulged and shone like Christmas hams. They hung over Duggie, who had his chest out and finger up. "The Minister of Police, Douglas Plumb, at his meeting this morning with leaders of" etc. He looked valiant and decent. He looked clean.

"The sort of photo that makes Prime Ministers."

"Is that where he's going?"

185

"It's where he wants to go. Why have you really got this stuff, Mr Gibbs?"

"It's a hobby." But he could not keep his smile. He was obsessed. "What I need to know is what goes on underneath."

"So you sent me your book?"

"I hoped it might be a way of meeting. I have to give him a chance. You know all the things that are not in here." He laid his hand on the books. "He was a child. What happened then? You see, I'm fair."

"What did he do to your daughter?"

"Ah no—"

"Something bad?"

"No, Mr Sole. That's what I've got already. You tell me the rest. You defend him."

His eyes were dry and small, like the rest of him. They held no power that I could see. Perhaps he compelled me with his obsession, fished memories out of me on the hook of it. I talked for hours. I told Alaric Gibbs things I had not told Glenda, or Beth, or Rose, or my children or parents. Before that night Duggie had had no shape, and there were parts of me unknown. I have a shifting memory of the night, it's never still; but we—Duggie and I—were flesh and bone at the end of it, and our workings clear. It was Duggie who mattered. I was a by-product.

I've already "put down" a part of his life. If I've done it at all clearly it's because of Alaric Gibbs. If it's true then I found the truth that night. I saw a lightening in the sky and heard birds singing in his garden. I was dry and spent; lethargic, happy, dull; as though I had been all night with a woman.

Gibbs asked what Duggie had taken from his childhood. I was not sure. That was the darkest part. A knowledge of how people feed on each other? A sense of the viciousness in life? I did not know. Wasn't it just another case of innocence betrayed? We all went through that. But Duggie, somehow, was rounded off by it, made neat and clean. He never developed a sense of other people.

"Gave his brain a squeeze," Gibbs said. "What did he mean by that?"

"Exactly what he said. He'd set the conditions up. I won't say it was out in the open like that. But somehow he knew the time was right, if he pressed, if he went in there and let Butts feel him Butts was dead."

I did not betray Duggie exactly. At times I exaggerated my delinquencies, my viciousness, to make his less: but Alaric Gibbs only smiled at that. There was a Grand Guignol quality to him and I was close to laughing at the melodrama of this trial in absentia; but could not bring that croak of amusement out. I drank a lot of whisky. He drank none.

"Latham?"

"Ah. He had ways of getting under Duggie's skin. But Duggie waited and he got him. It wasn't so long ago."

"Tell me."

"Well   Latham found out Duggie's first name was Sebastian. Sebastian Douglas. And he never let it alone. He made it seem as if he was only evening things up for Muldoon calling Bill Rowling Wallace. Every time Muldoon said Wallace Rowling, Latham would come back with Sebastian Plumb. He made it sound effeminate. It used to twist Duggie inside. It made him homicidal. Anything else he could take, but not that."

And Latham called Duggie "the crocodile", and though the Speaker made him apologize Latham played endless variations: "tears" and so on, "the Honourable member with the friendly grin"

Latham was one of the few politicians who stood up for Ron O'Connor when Duggie as minister forced him out of Broadcasting. After years of silence O'Connor published a little volume openly homosexual—his first real poetry, Alan Webster said. O'Connor was controller of children's programmes. He knew what he risked but told me he had hidden long enough. "Plumb'll get me fired, Ray. I won't quit. I'll make him do it."

Because Duggie did not care he was forced to act. He was, he said, concerned for the safety of our children—"our most valuable investment in the future"—and he let himself be

187

photographed with a delegation of "parents" and "morals campaigners" Then Latham jumped in, identifying a witch-hunt, and calling Duggie Sebastian, with that intonation, and a lisp added. He made it seem Duggie had something to hide. And Duggie lost his temper. It was hard to tell who he was after, O'Connor or Latham. He got O'Connor fired without much trouble; but he seemed to be a little tack-spitting man, vindictive, hypocritical. He frothed against permissiveness and liberalism and "long-haired trendies" and "so-called artists"; and knew at the end that Latham had made him perform. "Ray," he said, "I'm going to get that prick. If I wait twenty years I'm going to get him."

He waited five. Labour had come and gone. Norman Kirk was dead. Rowling seemed unlikely to lead the party for long. To most of us in the Gallery Latham seemed likeliest to take over. In Muldoon's National government Douglas Plumb was Minister of Police.

I was in the house that night. The debate was on the gangs and what should be done to stop them terrorizing folk and fighting their battles in the streets. A government bill, Duggie's bill, would give the police wider powers of arrest. It would set up squads of what Duggie called "shock troops" and give a specially appointed government tribunal the power to order unemployed gang members into work camps. All over the country people cried "fascist" I cried it myself. But Labour's attack was tired. They still seemed dazed by what had happened to them in November. Latham was tired, half-hearted in his argument. The problem, he said, was a social one, not "law and order" The government should address itself to that. Then his habit of attack overcame him.

"Mr Speaker." His face turned cruel. He pumped with his arms like a distance runner. "Mr Speaker, let me tell the House some simple scientific facts about the human brain. I'll keep it simple, not to tax the understanding of my friends over there. The brain. The human brain. That miraculous organ, that wonderful machine. Did you know, my friends," he swung to the government benches, "that it's in two parts? We have the cerebral cortex, the part that makes us human, the part that differentiates us from the beasts. We all have that, though sometimes it's hard to believe. And then we have the other part—the medulla oblongata, also known as the reptile brain. It's the part we share with the beasts. It's the seat of all those emotions we've been hearing so much about—hatred, anger—the violent emotions that we are led to believe exist only in Black Power and Headhunters and Hell's Angels and Skullmen. What rubbish, Mr Speaker, what rubbish! The reptile brain has much wider dominion than that. I've only to look opposite at all those friendly grins, and one in particular—"

The house was boiling over by that time: a dozen government members on their feet, the Speaker rapping with his gavel, Duggie standing, making pushing movements with his hand for a chance to speak.

Latham stabbed with his finger. "If the Minister, if the Minister would only come out of those swamps and jungles where he spends his time—"

"I do not," Duggie shouted—and his voice climbed over Latham's, it rasped and bit like a saw—"I do not spend my time in motel bedrooms with schoolgirls only fourteen years of age."

I felt as if the blow had been made at me. I felt hollowed out, as if half my being was ripped away. I think everyone in the room felt that, even the government members. In the silence Latham curled slowly over, he brought his hands up to cover his face and sank into his chair. Duggie sat down too, with a jerky movement, like a bad actor.

An isolated shout came from someone on the Labour benches. It was a sound of grief. Latham sat hiding in his chair. That was enough. At last he took his hands down and looked at Duggie. He was like someone waiting to die. Duggie, casual, arm jacked on his seat, legs crossed, watched him with an interested expression. Duggie, I thought, you got him with the solar plexus punch.

In the end, in a silence that was never going to end, Latham stood up and walked out of the chamber like an old man. We ran from the Gallery and met him in the corridors and followed, yapping questions, to his office, where he nodded to us once and closed the door He wrote out his resignation and pushed it out a moment before a Labour squad arrived to guard him from us.

When we got back to the chamber Duggie was gone. I hunted round town for him half the night. He told me later he had driven to Mt Victoria and had sat there watching the city, enjoying himself.

That was Latham.

"But I don't know. Duggie's got a hole in him. His triumphs leak away." It was past three o'clock. Gibbs poured whisky in my glass. "He doesn't believe in the past. So none of his enjoyments stay alive. What he really gets is that he can't be guilty of anything."

"Convenient," Gibbs said.

"Oh yes. But he's a cripple. When we were boys we knew a cripple called Sutton. Club foot Hump back. He and Duggie recognized each other "

At some other time I said, "My grandfather knew the powers of evil. They were demonic You could front up to them like a wrestler And you fought them with reason and right behaviour In the cause of Man. It isn't like that with Duggie. Evil's nihilistic. A vast emptiness. You fight that with a raging in the ego."

Gibbs drove me to my hotel. "There's no pity in consequences. He can't get away," I said. "Can he?"

Gibbs gave a shrug. He was casual, almost contemptuous, and he stopped my babble of words by leaning across and opening my door "There you are. I think you can make it to bed all right."

I stood swaying on the footpath. "Don't blame him too much. He's thirsty. He's empty. He can never find what he wants."

"I don't think I can take that view. Here." He put his manuscript in my hands. "You keep it I know you haven't read it all. Don't bother." He drove away. That was an end. The detail of it all floated away. I found myself in a state of happy collapse. But sleeping in what was left of the night, with Alaric

Gibbs' story on my chest, I dreamed of a page and cried out at the meaning held in it.

When I woke I looked but could not find it. It had been only a line or two in the second part. It told how Gibbs had bought an automatic pistol, a Walther P38, from a Canadian sergeant in Ravenna. "A lovely gun," Gibbs wrote, "beautifully balanced, and because of its double action very safe." He had brought it home with him, but kept it in his strong-box because his wife told him it made her nervous.

I could not remember why I had cried out. The night receded and Gibbs became squeaky and eccentric. I was sick from whisky and lack of sleep, and angry at the wasted time. I threw the manuscript into my bag and forgot it.

19 Becky picked me up from the hotel and drove me to Loomis. We went down the back way, past Moa Park and the Meggett house. An old man was chipping weeds in the drive.

"That looked like Fred."

"It was. Adrian brought him here when Esther died. He works in the garden. Potters round. Talks about how big he was. Ha! He runs a book. Tries to, anyway. Adrian gets his cobbers to ring up with bets. He keeps the old man like a sort of pet. You've heard what they say about Adrian?"

"It's probably true."

"Mr Big. About what you'd expect with his old man a Yank."

"You know that?"

"It's no secret. Fred seems to think it's a hell of a joke. I'll tell you this, if one of my kids goes on drugs I'll come out here with a gun and shoot Adrian."

We drove through the Loomis Fred had built—all supermarkets and boutiques—and along by the scummy ditch of Loomis creek.

"All the best murders happen in Loomis."

191

"They've never found old Beak."

"Never will. It's time they pulled this down and built a new one." The bridge gave its machine-gun rattle. It was only then I felt I was back in Loomis. Millbrook Road was sealed but had no footpaths. The pines stood on the bank with scarred roots leaking gum. A hedge of feijoa trees cut the cottage off from the road. *Journey's End*, the name said on the gate. Mum could never resist that sort of thing. The cottage itself was glossy with paint and hatched with trellises and the lawn was as perfect as a putting green.

We found Mum and Dad walking in the garden. "Ray," Mum said, "look at this," pointing at a leaf breaking through the soil. "Convolvulus. I thought I'd got rid of it but still it comes."

"You'll never get rid of it," Dad said. "It's like.   "

"Dandruff," Becky said.

"Maybe. You're looking well, Ray."

"He's looking tired."

"Boozing all night," Becky said. "Serves him right." She stayed for a cup of tea, then kissed Mum and Dad and drove away.

"She's a loud girl," Mum complained.

"Her heart's in the right place," Dad said. He had aged in the year since I'd seen him. His face was puffy and badly shaved. When he put his fingers on his cheeks they left grey dents.

"I thought you'd be down at bowls, Dad."

"I don't play any more. Do you see that girl—?" he fluttered his hand by his temple, waiting for the name.

"Beth Neeley."

"I know, Meg. I'm not senile."

"She's married," I said. "Lives in New Plymouth. Got three kids."

"I'm glad. I've been off colour, Ray. I'm going to lie down." He went to the bedroom and I heard his heavy sigh as he lowered himself on the bed.

"What's the matter with him?"

"You won't tell the others? He had a heart attack. Just a little

192

one. But it's more than that. I think he's had a stroke. He can't remember. He can't find the words he wants."

She told me how it had happened. "He was in town and he went into one of those underground lavatories. You know the way he dreams. It wasn't till he was down there that he realized it was a Women's."

"Ha!"

"Don't laugh. He's so conventional. He should have raised his hat. But he panicked. He started to run. And that made some silly woman scream."

I could see it: Dad running up the stairs, through the streets, and the woman screaming; and the eager clerk from the mens-wear store charging like Boom Casey and bringing him down with a flying tackle.

"They put him in a doorway and kept on holding him and calling him names and it wasn't until a policeman came they realized he was having a heart attack. It wasn't a bad one. They let him come home next day. But he has to take pills now. The doctor says he should be all right."

"What about the stroke?"

"I don't know whether it's a stroke or he's lost his grip somehow and he can't get it back."

She told me that he'd gone to the opening of the bowls season and played in a four and when it was his turn—"What is it when the balls go crooked, Ray?"

"Bias."

"He chose the wrong bias. The ball—"

"Bowl."

"—bowl went curving in the wrong direction and ended up in another game. So they brought it back and gave it to him, and he did it again. The third time—everyone was embarrassed, Ray, they just put it in his hand and looked away, and he said for a million pounds he couldn't tell which was the proper side. So he put it down and he came home and I don't think he'll ever go back again."

In the afternoon I went with them to have a look at Peace-haven. The drive had narrowed to a foot-track in the weeds and the terraces were overgrown with biddy-bid and foxglove and Scotch thistle. On a patch of lawn the summer-house, never more than a frame of manuka boughs, had fallen into a mouldering pile, held in a net of roses.

"Fergus used to mow the lawns but he can't now. And she can't afford a man. We always thought Wendy was rich, but with inflation   Merle's wealthy of course, but she doesn't help."

"Merle?"

"Wendy took her in. Didn't you know? To save her going into a home. They can't stand each other "

"Merle's leaving all her money to.   "

"The Spiritualist Church. It drives poor Wendy wild."

The two ladies were on the back veranda in seagrass chairs ravelled like old knitting. Wendy had grown huge; blubber-armed, tyres on her throat. Merle was a scrawny hen. She hopped down the steps to welcome us. "I told you he was coming."

"Meg told you," Wendy said.

"Raymond. Ah, dear boy." She pricked me with her nails.

I went up the steps and kissed Wendy on her cheek, which was cold, dry-cold, and soft. My nose sank in.

"She thinks she got a message you were coming. She's a noodle." She put her finger by her head and drew a spiral.

"The Reverend told me," Merle cried.

"The Reverend is far beyond your reach. Meg, do you want to show him over the house? Call me when you get as far as the study. I'll put the kettle on."

The house was tumbling down. "It wants thousands spent on it," Dad said. "Look at that. That's your piles. Watch." He took a tumbler from the bench and laid it on the floor It rolled in a half circle into a corner.

"It'll see me out," Wendy said, wheezing across to the kettle.

"Roof's rusted through," Dad said. "Gutters are gone. Borer the size of huhu grubs, Ray. You can hear 'em chewing."

"Spiders. Mice. I don't draw the line," Wendy said.

"Spiders can pass through," Merle said. "They are messengers."

194

In the bathroom Dad showed me a bar screwed on the wall. "That's so Wendy can get out. She was in the bath all night once."

"She couldn't lift herself up," Mum said, "and she wouldn't let Merle telephone for help. I don't think any man's ever seen her naked. She kept on running hot water in so she wouldn't freeze. But then she had to—you know. So she let Merle ring. Fergus had to do it. She was too heavy for me."

"She made me tie a.   "

"Scarf."

"—over my face. It was like.   "

"Blind man's buff."

"Slippery," Dad said. "I couldn't hold her."

When we reached the study Mum called Wendy, who came with a key. "It's out of bounds for Merle. She thinks I keep George here in a bottle." She locked the door behind her. For a moment we were in a cave, then she crossed to the window and pulled the curtains back and the desk and chairs and ghostly ranks of books took on substance. Some things coming out of the past make one shake apart and reassemble. But in that room, where I had not been in fourteen years, I was curious, no more. Walking sticks. Desk that would have seated ten for dinner. I remembered. *Ars Amatoria*. I found the book and pulled it out and Wendy, sharp in the study, with, it seemed, most of her bulk melted off, grinned at me. I grinned back, but was uneasy. The present not the past made me shiver: this woman, now, guarding what was dead; happy and cruel, circling the artefact of her life; with Merle Butters scratching at the door. Later, on the veranda, drinking tea, I managed a view that troubled me less: listened to Merle and Wendy squabbling over George Plumb, and agreed with Mum that they were like two seagulls having a tug-of-war with a scrap of bread.

Merle beckoned me and led me away. She took me to her bedroom, flitting ahead, and showed me her electric blanket.

"Wendy doesn't know. She'd put my rent up. Raymond, why I brought you here—I saw your wife last night. Glenda, isn't it? She was beautiful. And she's so happy. She was floating like a fish. Like Ophelia. I asked her if she had a message for you but she just smiled and swam away. I must say that was disappointing. What's the use of coming through if you've got no message?"

This was the past that broke me into pieces; and when I came together I had Glenda. And that part, the Glenda part, of myself. I do not mean I understood it, or that I don't puzzle at it still. But it was in me, she was whole. I no longer knew the fear of not having her.

"Raymond, are you all right?"

"Thank you for telling me."

"Your grandfather had some messages. He doesn't come for nothing. But they're for Wendy. He wants her to let me in the study. And he wants her to burn that book she wrote about his life. He says it's idolatry. It's going to burn anyway. She's going to have it cremated with her when she dies. It's in her will. She doesn't know I know that."

"Come on, Merle."

"You were naughty spying on me. And that Duggie. You won't tell her about my electric blanket?"

In the night I walked along Millbrook Road to the boundary post where the seal ended. A dust road ran into the hills, and far away, over the valley, I saw lights shining in the house where Willis and Mirth had lived. Coming back, I listened to the fall of water from the culvert. I walked up the drive at Peacehaven, looked in the windows, and saw Merle in bed, reading through steel spectacles a Mills and Boon romance; and Wendy at her study desk, sorting papers. She stretched her huge arms and yawned on her breast, looking for a moment crucified, then scratched her ribs. I went round the back and climbed on to the veranda. I sat in a seagrass chair and watched the Sole houses beyond the fallen bridge. Trees had grown up round them. They looked as if they belonged there.

On Sunday we drove to Bobby's for lunch. He lived in Epsom and had just been appointed headmaster of a school in Otahuhu. He had wanted something in a better district, but at least he had his house among "the nobs" He lived there with Melody his wife and their daughter Jilly.

He welcomed me by rattling the *Sunday Post*. "What's all this garbage about the gangs? You're soft in the head, Ray. Duggie's on the right track. Except he doesn't go far enough. I'd flog 'em. I'd volunteer myself. And enjoy it. And chop their hands off if they beat up people. Hang the skeletons round their necks." He mimed it.

"Bobby!" Mum said.

"And castrate the buggers if they rape girls. If one of them touched Jilly here, I'd do it. With hedge clippers."

"Bobby!"

He grinned at her. "There's too many bleeding hearts, Mum."

Jilly was no more complimentary about my Country and Western singer. His poor lined face offended her. But I thought she was old herself, older than Bobby. He played at being hard, but she was hard, a tough little dame, and she was smart. It was written on her face that she wouldn't be around this dump much longer.

Melody served the lunch I had forgotten—Sunday dinner. Lamb and roasted pumpkin with peas and new potatoes; mint sauce and gravy; and a trifle with so much sherry in it I drank it from my spoon. Then Jilly went out. "Out," she answered Bobby from the door.

"What a kid, eh?"

"Shouldn't she tell you where? She's only thirteen."

"Modern times, Mum. They've got to have their freedom."

"Is that what you say at school?" I asked.

"There's no Jillys there. Otahuhu kids need discipline. She's got it—" he tapped his skull "—up here."

Dad slept in a chair and the rest of us played Monopoly. "This is like· Peacehaven, eh?" said Bobby, sentimental. But we had never played Monopoly there. I didn't tell him, Mum told him.

At three o'clock Jilly came in with a boy. They went to her room and played records. That woke Dad and he drank a glass of beer and was more lively. Driving home he said, "Let's call in and see Duggie Plumb."

"Why not?" Mum said. "Before he's too puffed up to recognize."

They had not seen him since Willis died, and then, Mum said, he'd been "too busy" to go back to the orchard with his brothers and sisters and uncles and aunts for a drink. They had remembered "dear old Willie" without him, and Melva sang *Danny Boy* while Cliff played the comb.

"He might have been too upset," I said.

"Nonsense. He's a Tory."

We walked up his path of crazy-paving and rang a bell that chimed four happy notes. Sally answered the door. I had to remind her who I was.

"Oh, Ray. You're a Wellington face. I have these faces, Auckland and Wellington. It's the only way I keep track. Douglas is busy."

"We won't keep him. Mum and Dad would like to say hallo."

She showed us into the lounge and went to fetch him. He came in stretching himself, flexing his shoulders. "Gets you, sitting. Hello, Meg. Gidday, Fergus. Long time no see." He shook hands with them.

Mum had decided to play the visit as a comedy. That saved her from moral outrage. She gave a little curtsey as she took his hand.

"Now, Meg," Dad said.

Duggie grinned. "You're like my old man. He used to play *The Donkey's Serenade* on his mouth organ."

"I would have played *The Green-eyed Dragon*." She smiled at Sally. "He feeds with greed on little boys and puppy dogs and big fat snails."

"I've never gone for little boys," Duggie said. "Can I get you a drink, Fergus?"

"I wouldn't say no to a whisky."

Duggie made us drinks.

"We won't keep you if you're busy," Dad said.

"Just finished. I try not to work on Sundays but some-times. " He shrugged.

"You're planning your concentration camps," Mum said.

"Meg."

"Let her go, Fergus. The lunatic left interests me."

Sally laughed. The sound had a disembodied beauty, a clarity that startled. She used it as a command and we fell silent.

"Politics just won't leave us alone."

Mum said, "I'm sorry." She gave the artificial smile that was her expression of dislike. She had met Sally once, years before, and found her "quite empty", "a kewpie doll" "It must be hard being married to a Cabinet Minister."

"My father was one and now my husband's one. I should have known better. It's like being married to a chameleon."

"Duggie would always be royal blue."

"Sally's making a point," I said. It was the first real thing I had heard her say. Duggie married her shortly after he went into parliament. I had not been able to decide whether he had extended "the duration" to his career or whether her indifference challenged him. Sally was indifferent to most things; but that, by a paradox in her nature, made her lively. She played her smallest actions to impress. Lightly once, "Oh," she said, "marrying him was a calculated risk." There was calculation but no risk. I used to feel that if you picked her up she'd be as light as balsa. Unsinkable. She bobbed around, gay and sweet and perfect, surviving through an indifference that lifted her out of the way of all shocks. Once when drunk I said to her, "I suppose when Duggie gets you home he stands you in a corner and switches you off."

"You funny man. I won't tell Douglas you said that."

Now: "They don't know they're changing. They do it just like breathing."

"Dry up," Duggie said in a pleasant way. "She does it too. Look at her. A little bit of feeling because we're family. Come on Sal, sit on my knee."

But she took a chair beside him, put her hand on his. She bent her mouth in a perfect smile, and was quiet.

Duggie said, "More garbage in your column, Ray."

"That's what Bobby said."

"When are you going to give up this smart-arse stuff?"

"I can go on as long as you can."

"You're starting to repeat yourself. You need some new jokes."

"Tell your boss to shuffle his cabinet."

He smiled at Mum. "What do you think of him, Meg?"

"He'll do better work one day."

"See?" Duggie grinned at me.

"He's writing a biography of Michael Joseph Savage."

"If that isn't an admission of failure I don't know what is."

Duggie had worn no better or worse than me. We had both put on weight. We had padded cheeks and incipient jowls: the steak-fed look. His colour was high, mine low. I wasn't sure which was healthier but wondered if the broken veins in his cheeks were a sign he was starting on Cyril Butts' way. A politician had only to limp or hesitate over a word for rumours to begin about his health. There had been none about Duggie's. He worked hard, and relaxed too hard (so we heard), and liked his drop; but played squash when he had the time; and once in a get-fit week he had put on shorts and jogged on the beach at Worser Bay. The photo showed him comically short in the leg.

He went out to the kitchen for some ice. I followed him. "Do you remember a man called Alaric Gibbs?"

"Alaric?"

"The Fall of Rome. He was king of the Visigoths."

"I don't know any Alarics."

"This one's an expert on Douglas Plumb. He keeps a scrapbook."

"There's quite a few people do that. Mostly female."

"Sally's right. You do change colour."

"I give you what you want from me, R. Sole. Who's this Alaric?"

"A retired engineer. He told me you were engaged to his daughter once."

"He'd be lying then." But he turned on me suddenly, with an

200

almost frightened grin. It was not from memory so much as from the shock of going back. There must have been a rushing in his mind, a flashing past of things he had no time to focus on. "Jenny Gibbs."

"Were you engaged?"

"She thought so. Why did you have to spring this on me, Ray?"

I had not seen him so off balance since the night Cyril Butts had put his name up for Epsom. "What happened to her?"

"I don't know." He looked at the tray of ice cubes in his hand and did not seem to know what to do with it. Then he put it on the bench and broke some out. "Give me that jug." When he had it full he grinned at me. The pink was back in his cheeks. "Jenny, eh? That's a lot of girls ago. Can't say I remember her old man."

"Go and see him. He'll give you her address."

"I don't play around in the past."

"You could play around now."

"With some old bag of forty-five. I've got something better in the next room."

"And the rest."

"And all the rest. What do you want, Ray? Some dirty stories? Why don't you go in the dunny and toss yourself off?"

Mum put her head in. "What are you two talking about?"

"He's playing Jiminy Cricket. Take him home, Meg."

"Still quarrelling? When you were boys you never stopped."

"We've stopped now. I don't need him any more."

In the car, I said, "Duggie's tired."

"His wife's under a strain," Mum said. "I felt quite sorry for her."

"She'll be around when Duggie's gone."

"I wouldn't like to see him Prime Minister," Dad said. "Whatsisname. ?"

"Muldoon?"

"He's bad enough. But I think Douglas Plumb would be dangerous."

20 My father died in the winter. He felt a bitter impatience with mind and body and his contempt for them hastened his end. He died without tranquillity or acceptance, with an inner jerkiness and a disgust with death. Sour recollections cast shadows on his life, making it seem of small account. All this surprised me. I had looked for him to make an end having lessons for us. I had not expected him to be impatient. The fear that I should do no better complicated my grief.

Merle Butters was dead too and Wendy proposed that Mum should join her at Peacehaven. "Never," Mum said. "I can't think of a worse fate than being locked up with Wendy. You haven't heard how poor old Merle went have you?"

She had been unwell and, it seems, died peacefully in the night. When she did not come for breakfast Wendy "peeped in" and saw her "sleeping like a baby" It was the same at lunchtime and late in the afternoon. "It must be doing her the world of good." On the second night Wendy began to worry, but she felt in the blankets and Merle was cosy and warm. "It was her electric blanket," Mum said. "Merle had been dead two days before Wendy woke up." She gave a little laugh, then started to cry. She was crying for Dad. "Don't worry about me, Ray. I'll be happy here till my turn comes."

A third death that winter was Helen Plumb's. I had not seen her since her visit to her mother. I went round to her bach after several months and found two old men living there. The woman in the house told me John Peihana had started falling over all the time. Some Maoris came and took him away. She wasn't sure about Helen but someone said the Sallys came for her. "Maybe they put her on the island." That seemed likely. I paid the rent owing and forgot her.

Now I saw Helen dead on Oliver's lawn. It had rained all night, with storms of hail. The clouds had blown away when I came off the zig-zag and saw three men guarding something in the hydrangea bushes. Their breath made grey speech balloons on the air. I walked over and saw Helen's shoes crossed like an X. "Everything's under control." "Press." I went across the lawn and looked at her: the same sort of coat with broken buttons, the same empty bottle on her chest.

"The woman in the house gave us a tea-towel."

I lifted it and looked at Helen's face. Her patch had slid into her hair and a pool of water filled her eye socket. Lashes made their stitching on the bottom. Her other eye, unhuman and alone, seemed like a specimen on a plate. I covered her face and turning saw Mrs Barrett watching me from the door. She closed it when I approached but I knocked softly and said, "Mrs Barrett, it's Ray Sole. Sir Oliver's nephew."

She pulled me in. "This is dreadful."

"You know who that is out there?"

"I know. She came last night. She wanted to see Sir Oliver. I wouldn't let her in."

"So she lay down on the lawn and died."

"That's not my fault. I didn't know."

I asked if I could see Oliver. She made me promise not to mention "that thing", and led me to the room where I had visited Beatrice.

"Here we are Ollie, here's Ray come to pay a little call."

"Ray who? Who is he, Barry?"

"I'm Raymond Sole. Meg's son."

Oliver sat in a bed with polished knobs. He gave the impression of having long dry bones that might be used one day for blowing tunes on. "You're my nephew?"

"I called to see you once a long time ago."

"You married that girl. Goodlad's daughter."

"Against your advice."

"Young men seldom take advice. What do you want this time?"

I thought, To hell with "Barry" "Your daughter Helen died last night on your lawn. She came to see you but she couldn't get in."

Mrs Barrett came at me hissing but I put out my arm and kept her off.

"What's this? What is this, Barry?"

"I told him not to tell you."

"People don't die on lawns."

"Helen did. You'd better think of something to tell the police."

"I'll tell them it's none of my concern. On my lawn! You should have got rid of her, Barry."

"I sent her away. Vamoos, I said. She must have come back."

"I paid money into that woman's account for forty years. I've done my duty."

"You have, Ollie. He has. She came up here and peed on the floor."

"What? What's that?"

"She peed on the floor. In this very room."

"Watch your language, Barry."

"With a Maori."

"I loved that child. And my Trixie loved her. We gave her a home. And look how she thanked us. Running round with black men. Dying on my lawn. All my life, all my life, I've tried to live according to some standards. But people, people.   "

"There there, Ollie." She sat by him and held him in her arms.

"I've done my best."

"He has. You have." She dried his face with the sheet. "Go away, please."

I let myself out and waited till the police came. The soles of Helen's shoes stared at me.

In the afternoon I caught a unit out to Simla Crescent. I sat by a fire of pine logs and talked with Felicity while Nicola her daughter-in-law brought us cups of tea and plates of cake.

"I live off cake," Felicity said. "I'm sure it's bad for me. But I'm eighty-four. This is only made of rags and sticks."

"Oliver must be.   ?"

"Eighty-five. He'll be a hundred. First in, last out. He'll leave all his money to Mrs Barrett."

"I think she loves him."

"She loves the idea of him. I'd go and see poor Ollie but the only thing he knows about me now is that I'm Catholic. He quivers when he sees me."

Our talk of Helen was mainly anecdotal. There was little to say. Her life was impenetrable and every time I worked a little way in, back I was sent reeling by a sense of waste and pain. There must be more, I thought—*some* other thing. Felicity?

"Of course."

"Don't give me that."

Impenetrable too. She told me how she had come to her church. Through waste and pain. Then had come a time when, safe inside, she had sought out danger. "I had Him here," she said, touching her breast, "now I had to have Him here." She tapped her brow. "I had to know Him in my mind. That kept me busy for forty years. It wasn't exactly a waste of time. I was always in good company, you see."

I asked about now.

"Now? I sit here drinking tea. And waiting for Him. It's all so plain, and yet at the heart of it it's mystery. A loving God and Jesus Christ, His Son. *Mysterium tremendum et fascinans.* Go on, pull a face. You're like Max, Ray. Always wanting to know."

"So did you."

"Yes. Forty years. That was my life's work. Hard work too. But, *laborare est orare.* Ha! I'm like my father, dropping bits of Latin everywhere."

When I left she gave me some notes Max had been working on when he died.

"They're for your book. Max's father was a Fabian. Savage used to come to pick his brains. There's a lovely story there about Savage sitting on Max's glass slate and breaking it. A big one, eighteeen inches. Savage said he'd buy a new one for him, but he didn't. Max had to remind him. Then Savage turned up with a little one, six by six."

"That's pretty good for a political promise."

"How is the book?"

I told her I had put it aside again. "Everything's there. The work's all done. But I can't bring it together." I could not make a whole round life. I lacked the stillness and the breadth; I lacked the measure. I had the energy for it but found that I needed tranquillity too. "I guess it's just too hard for me. But I'll keep this. Thank you."

"Don't stop trying, Ray."

"No," I said.

I went home and put Max's notes in my writing desk. Four years of my life went by. There's no way I can give them any measure. All I can do is put down notes. I stayed in my house in Wadestown. I repapered my bedroom and painted the window sills. One day I took Glenda's mobile down from over the bed. The fish were coated with dust, it grew on them like fur. I took them out and burned them in the garden incinerator.

At night I sat in my chair and watched TV. I became addicted to *Coronation Street* and *Close to Home*. I never missed any sporting event. I even watched grid-iron. My friends called me a hermit or a slob. On the other hand, women seemed to find me mysterious. That was in the beginning. As our affairs went on they began to find that what they had thought deep was only empty. Several of them said as much, and more. Clever girls. They complained that I wasn't there, or that only part of me was there, and part was fun for a while, but they started feeling used and feeling dirty. Our terminations were noisy. Once I joined a girl—it's not their fault I can't think of them as women—joined her in crying, and that gave us a couple of extra weeks. When she left she called me creepy.

I looked after myself. Ate well. Drank expensive booze. My clothes were sharp. I wore a leather coat and Italian shoes. But my friends were not friends, they were people I drank with. And my girls were not women. In spite of that, I was not unhappy; only not happy.

Towards the end of that time I heard a voice. Softly in my ear it said, "R. Sole." It came from narrow windows, thin as a bat call. It came in the noise of traffic, and wagons crashing in the railway yards. In trees, in lifts, in doors that closed with a well-bred huff. Sometimes it came shouting from high scaffolds, where men in hard-hats perched against the sky, "Gidday, Arsehole." I thought at first someone was out to get me— Duggie Plumb? Then I thought I was going mad. There was no one I could talk to. I talked to my doctor. He told me I needed a holiday, a Pacific cruise, or maybe something harder, a walk on the Milford Track. "Ha!" I said. Going out, I thought a man in his waiting room said, "R. Sole."

So I talked to John Jolly. I sat in a quiet bar with him and told it like a joke. He was a bitter man who lived with cats. Ash and cat hair drifted from his clothes. Nicotine stained a sore patch on his mouth. He started rolling cigarettes to hide his disbelief at the gift of power I made him.

"R. Sole? It could be me."

"Come on, John."

"Head noises?"

"No."

"What would you be hearing if your parents had called you John?"

"You tell me."

He lit a cigarette. "It's a judgment, maybe?"

"Why?"

"You know what you've done, I don't. Or what you haven't." He gave me a quick half-angry grin. "She's a life problem, boy. See a shrink. Join a church. Jump off a bridge. In that order."

"I'm serious, John."

"I thought you were. You want me to say you've got tangles in there. Then you can take a pill or hire a doc to unpick it all. Nice and easy." He shook his head. "Sorry."

"Is that all? That's a big help."

"Like I said, she's a life problem."

"What's that mean?"

"You got it handed to you. Gift from God. O.K., leave that out. But you got handed this nice shiny thing and look at it now."

"Look at yours."

"Sure. No touché though."

"When did you get religion?"

"I haven't got it, Ray. I can look but I can't touch."

I left him there, dropping ash in his lap, and walked up the hill to Wadestown. I was so contemptuous of him that I did not hear my voice for several days. When it came it had a tone of sadness. It seemed to suggest I had failed again. I found I was afraid of John Jolly. He remained sour and dirty, his usual self, but I had surprised him into speech, he was changed for me.

In 1981 I went to Canberra to cover the Commonwealth Heads of Government Meeting. When it was over I visited Sharon in Sydney. She was living with Desi, a Scot who had "rescued" her in Poona. I was not surprised to find her with a man. Carlo was a surprise.

"Who's his father?"

"You don't need to know."

"An Indian?"

"That's obvious. You're shocked, Dad."

"I'm not. I'm not. I like all this mixing up."

"What do you think of him?"

"He's beautiful."

Sharon wanted to come back to New Zealand. She wanted a little house, a bit of land in the Coromandel or Golden Bay where she could mind her own business.

"Will Desi come?"

"If he wants to."

"Are you going to get married?"

"Good God, no. Do I have to get married before I get your help?"

I could not imagine any future for her. Desi and she did not approach each other. They had no words, they had no looks or glances. He loved her, that was plain, but usefulness was all he had to offer. He had been useful in Poona, and was useful here. Would be, for a while, in Golden Bay. For all his muscles and beard and male smell he had no gender. In the bathroom I found contraceptive pills in a cupboard. But sex, I knew, was another thing.

"How will you live?"

"I'll grow stuff. I'll share. Desi can work."

"Aye," Desi said, and held up his arm for me to admire.

I walked through Kings Cross to my hotel, trying to discover where Sharon was. The "peace" she had found by Holy Ganga? That was gone. She had sniffed when I mentioned it, and had laughed at "understanding" Nothing I could admire was in their place. She worked too hard at toughness and honesty.

But that night I had no time to sort Sharon out—and have never done it—for a message under my door asked me to telephone my brother urgently. He was gulping and sniffing and his sounds hollowed me out. "Where have you been? I've been trying all night."

"What is it, Bobby?"

"Bad news. Are you ready?"

"Yes. Tell me."

"It's Mum. I'm sorry, Ray. She's dead. She's burned. The house caught fire. Becky pulled her out. She's got some burns too. But Mum—she died of shock. She didn't feel anything, Ray. Ray, come home. As quick as you can."

I managed to get a seat on a plane that left in the morning. Sharon came with me to the airport, carrying my bag as though I had grown old. "She was in her seventies. She had to die."

"For God's sake don't tell me things I know. She didn't have to burn."

"No. I'm sorry. I hardly knew her."

"Then just keep quiet."

"Kiss Carlo goodbye."

I kissed them both and left them. Over the Tasman I tried to think of my mother but could not hold her. She vanished behind a figure in a burning shroud. Felicity had told me, "There are so many ways of dying, but only one death." I had felt wise in agreeing, but I could not make the statement fit my mother. I could not get past the horror of her dying.

Bobby met me at the airport and drove me to visit Becky. We sat by her bed and looked at her burns. She would have scars on her arms and face. She spoke in a thick whisper, painfully.

"She would light that bloody stove. I tried to talk her out of it. But no, it warmed the house." And Mum loved wood fires, and loved her range. She had painted it every summer with aluminium paint; reminding herself of her mother, she said.

"The kettle wouldn't boil. The wood was green."

Mum fetched a bottle from the shed. "What's that?" "Kerosene. Your father's trick." She poured into the stove; and fire ran like a weasel up her arm; exploded in the bottle, wrapped her round.

"It was petrol," Becky said. "There was no label on the bottle. All I could see is it was pink. But I didn't have time."

She threw a mat over Mum and put out the flames. Then she pulled her outside and laid her on the lawn and ran to Peace-haven to telephone for help, while the cottage burned. When she came back the flames were spinning like a whirlpool. She felt them sucking at her. Mum was unconscious by the hedge. Becky ran water on her from the hose. "She never woke up. I don't think it hurt her, Ray. It was so quick. She just sort of gave a gasp and died."

Bobby and I drove out to Loomis to look at the cottage. Only the chimney was standing. The stove had collapsed in an even heap. The totara piles had burned and the dirt in between was brown as cocoa. Bed springs and iron frames, Mum's bicycle with the tyres burned off, lay in mounds of charcoal. Pink and blue tears of melted glass gleamed in the ashes.

I turned Grandpa's Buddha with my toe. His smiling cheek lay in a puddle of brass. "Bronze," Bobby said. "The old man had it wrong. Do you want to see Wendy? She's got the Rev all to herself at last."

"No," I said. I left the Buddha lying. Wendy would fossick here and come on it as a treasure. But Mum was dead. The Plumbs were dead. And Peacehaven, Wendy Philson, had no meaning.

After the funeral I rented a car and drove to Wellington. I did not want to be in my house so I crept back. South of the Bombay hills I turned off the main highway and drove across the plains to

Gerriston. I drove up and down the main street but saw no one I knew. Sausage flats with frosted doors and wrought-iron fences stood in the place of Primrose Hall. The stumps of the Phoenix palms were carved into garden seats. I stood on the stop-banks by the bridge and found them unconvincing. They looked as if children had patted them into shape.

The stationer's shop was still called *Kittredges* although Charlie was dead. I walked through to the *Independent*, knocked on the editor's door, and found Iris. We shook hands and said, "Well, Ray," "Well, Iris," "You haven't changed." She poured us drinks from a bottle she kept in a bottom drawer. She was thin and quick and stringy, with shaped and lacquered hair and diamante glasses. (I was square-built, with weak eyes and thinning hair.) We chatted amiably, and now and then caught each other in glances. Here we were. But once we had been a boy and a girl, eyes gleaming in the dark, amazed by what we were doing to each other. I told her about my slogan-writing.

"I knew. You had paint in your fingernails. Come with me." She led me into the yard behind the building. The water tower stood behind the trees, with a swastika and a dollar sign ghostly on its side.

"The only lasting piece of work I've done."

"It's coming down. We've got a new one."

"Well. . ."

"You've done all right. You're a name. Why don't you publish a book of those profiles you do?"

"Because," I said, "they're jokes. That's all they are. Funny for as long as it takes you to read them. Do you know," I said, seeing what to do, "I'm leaving the *Post*. I've been making a fool of myself. I'm irrelevant."

"What to?"

"I don't know. I wish I knew."

She gave me another drink and I took her to lunch. Then I kissed her cheek, she patted me, and I drove south. I was looking for Greg. Sharon had told me his itinerary.

I tried Cambridge and Putaruru but nobody had heard of him. In Tokoroa I found a minister who said a group of evangelists had been in town yesterday. As far as he knew they were heading down the island. Frankly he'd been pleased to see them go. One of them had tattoos on his hands.

In Taupo I strolled out from my motel and down by the lake I heard a voice singing. It was as creaky as an unoiled door. Greg had wanted to be a pop star once and I had told him sourly that he had the voice for it. I walked down and watched him from the dark.

> "Come to Jesus.
> He won't let you down.
> Come to Jesus.
> He never wears a frown."

I guessed he had written the words himself. He strummed his guitar while a girl at his side played a squeeze box and a middle-aged couple whose daughter she plainly was hummed the tune. When it was over Greg put down his guitar. "Friends," he said to the seven listeners, "Jesus is real. He is here now. He is waiting to enter your hearts just as surely as he entered mine." Religion had rounded his vowels. His clothes were clean, his hair was neat, and his eyes held a burning innocence. I was not going to question the quality of his happiness. I was pleased to see him happy and travelling a road.

"Once," he said, "I belonged to Satan. I served him." He told his tale of drugs and theft and sex, while the girl made gasping sounds on her concertina. "I hated my father once but I don't hate him now. Jesus won't let me hate. He makes me love. I hated everybody. Now I love. Friends, I pray to you, learn to love. Open up your hearts.   "

I knew if I stayed I should begin to be disappointed in him. I moved back in the dark and walked along the lake shore, wondering if Greg and the girl were in love. She had a look of contentment but there might be other reasons for that.

When I went back they were packing up.

"Hallo, Greg."

"Gidday, Dad. I thought I saw you there."

The others sat politely in the van while we talked. He told me how he had stood at the back of a crowd and a hand had pushed him forward and when he looked round no one was there. He got to the front and tears were streaming down his face. I was shocked by the banality of it, but saw he was moved in remembering.

"That girl?" I said. "The one with the concertina. Is she. . . ?"

"We share the Lord's work, Dad. We're both happy. Are you happy?"

"Me? Sure. Well.   " I told him about his grandmother. He said the same as Sharon—"I never knew her."

"Is that all you can say?"

"Jesus has her, Dad. She's all right now."

"She was all right alive. Let's not quarrel. It's good to see you looking so well, Greg." I gave him news of Sharon and asked where he was heading. Then we shook hands and I went back to my motel and to bed. I had hoped that Greg would be a scientist—or one of many things, all distinguished. Sharon too. But that seemed impudent now, imperialistic; and hope itself a magnet to danger. I dreamed of them happy, but found their faces simple, out of focus.

Wellington. I told John Jolly I would stay with the *Post* until the election, then finish up. I put my house on the market, sold it well, but kept possession till December. Sharon and Carlo and Desi came over from Sydney and stayed with me a week before moving on to a property I had found in Golden Bay. Sharon was pleased I'd sold the house. She claimed it gave her morbid thoughts.

I wrote my column, packed up lazily. I looked at the fracture in my life and was pleased with it although I could not understand exactly how it had happened. More quickly than I liked I came to accept my mother's death. I even came to think it suited her and once or twice I wished Dad could have had something similar.

The election had me running. I was in Nelson and Palmerston North and Invercargill. But I was home in Wellington one night when Duggie called. We sat among cartons of books and vases wrapped in paper.

"Sorry about your old lady."

"That's all right. You're looking tired."

"I've been up in Kapiti. We're losing that. What I don't like is wasting time."

"You're going to lose more than Kapiti."

"Yeah."

"It doesn't worry you, does it? That's the only way you'll get rid of your boss."

"That's right."

"What makes you think it'll be your turn? He's a confrontation specialist. They don't want another one."

"Is that what you think I am? I can be anything you like."

Expediency moved every thought he had, so nothing really was impossible. He could use the masonic grip while crossing himself and not be diminished. It was all in the service of Duggie Plumb. But lately he had reached a difficult place. The National Party had always been a party of fence menders. Now it was filling up with ideologues. Duggie, by design a populist, achieved the feat of having two styles. He moved carefully, making little signs, dropping hints; and slowly he moved out on to the right wing of the party. He was never the first to move, or second, or third; but he would be left standing when the others were knocked down.

Standing for what? I had watched him raking influence, people, power in front of him. He almost had more than anyone else, almost enough. What was he going to do with it? I filled his glass. He said, "Parliament's for playing games in, Ray. The real thing happens somewhere else."

"I know that."

"Parliament is going to fall to bits. I don't know what happens then. But I'm going to be around." He saw my nervousness and grinned at me. "Nobody's doing it. It's inevitable. Then we'll be in the age of power. Manipulation."

"And you'll be the man on top?"

"If I'm not, somebody will. There's no shortage."

"What if I tell people?"

"Go ahead. Write your stuff. They'll only laugh."

"That's right. There wouldn't be any point anyway. You're too soon, Duggie."

"So what are you worried about?"

"The one who comes after you. And you right now." He would destroy himself not us. "You see it all out there. Outside yourself. You don't seem to have an idea of *you* and *other people*."

He watched me; laughed at me.

"There's privacy. And relationships. You've got to go there, Duggie. You've got to find out what it's all about."

"Do you know?"

"Not very well. But listen, what I'm talking about is being human. Knowing there are real people out there. And *back* there. *In* there."

He was laughing again, but stopped as if I had struck him.

"Nobody owns any part of me. Not you. Or Beak. Or Sally. Nobody." He came to his feet and held his hand up with the fingers spread. "This is where I am. Here! Now!"

"Who's talking about Beak?"

His hand seemed to fascinate him. He closed his fingers, opened them, worked his wrist like a hinge. "That's where I start and where I end."

I took his glass from the chair and filled it with whisky. The sound made him blink and contract his face. With an old man's slowness he sat down. "I always talk bullshit when I'm with you."

"What about Beak?"

He wiped his hand down his cheeks. "I'm tired. I need some sleep."

"Sleep here if you like. There's a bed."

"Can't disappear."

"You came up here to tell me about Beak."

"Yeah."

"What about him?"

"They found him, Ray. All that was left of him. A pile of bones."

215

"Where?"

"In the creek at Millbrook Road. They're putting a new bridge in. When they started excavating they found Beak wedged under the bank. What was left of him. Skull's gone somewhere. Washed away, I guess. Lot of bones gone."

"How do they know it's Beak?"

"They don't. They're guessing. But I know. All the other stuff was there. Axle. Engine block. It's O.K., Ray. I didn't kill him."

He told me the story of that night. He had been out to visit Mirth and Willis—a rare event—and when he came back down Millbrook Road and saw the light in Beak's house over the creek he decided to call on him. He was half full of Dally wine and Beak made a danger signal, a light flashing. He had said that Duggie and I raped Myra. That was a story Duggie must stop.

He left his car at the end of Dean Street and walked along in the shadows. The street runs on a ledge with a row of houses above and one below. No one saw Duggie going along. He came to Beak's house and found it dark. The light he had seen was in a shed. "I heard him in there, Ray. It sounded like a panel beater's shop. When I looked in, he was dressing himself up in bits of iron. He had an axle tied on his back. He had some of those counter weights from windows round his neck. And he had this engine block. God knows how he carried it. He had a rope round it and he tied it round his waist. There must have been a couple of hundredweight of iron on him."

Duggie watched. He crept back from the door when Beak came out, and stood behind a corner of the house. Beak turned out the light and closed the door. That was a struggle. But he was leaving everything locked up. He walked down to the bottom of his section into a path leading to the creek. Duggie followed. There was no light. He heard Beak crashing around in the dark. "He even tried to whistle," Duggie said. "It was that thing—you know, from *The Wizard of Oz*. We're off to see the Wizard. It sounded off key, as if he couldn't work his mouth properly. . I didn't try to stop him, Ray. If he wanted to kill himself it was O.K. with me."

216

Beak came to the pool above the bridge. Duggie saw it glimmering in the light of the street lamp. He squatted on the path and watched Beak wade into the water. He went in steadily, shaped like a hunchback. "There wasn't any sound, just some splashing," Duggie said. Beak stood still while a car passed on the bridge. Then he went on. His head seemed to float on the surface for a moment. That was all. It slid under. There was a bubbling in the water. It must have been, Duggie said, the air from Beak's lungs and from his clothes.

"What happened then?"

"I went home."

"And forgot it?"

"After a while. I could have stopped him, Ray. But he wanted to die."

"And it suited you."

"It suited me. But it wasn't that bloody important."

We drank some more and looked at each other. "What do you want me to do?"

"I don't know. . . . I'm used to trouble. I can handle it. Mostly I see it coming so I'm ready. But this—I'd forgotten it."

"It's like the fall of Singapore. They had the guns pointing out to sea but the Japs came out of the jungle."

"For Christ's sake!" He gave me a naked look. "I'm scared."

"They can never connect it with you."

"That's not what I mean."

"You're scared because it opens you up. You don't like that."

"Why do you get at me? I came for help."

I told him that I could not give him any. That was true. I could not think of anything to say that would be of use. All I could do was pour whisky in his glass. I tried to persuade him to stay the night. We talked about Beak. He told me the story several times and though he was drunker each time he was more in control of it.

I drove him home, out towards the strait. Sally was in Auckland. I took him into the house and put him on his bed and pulled his shoes off.

"Ray," he said.

I stopped at the door.

"You forget all this. You wipe it out—this whole night."

"I'll forget it."

"I mean it, Ray. Else I'll do you. I did Latham."

"Go to sleep, Duggie."

"Yeah. Go to sleep. Ray! Ray!" He reared up, blind. He was like a seal looking round. He looked dark and slippery on the white expanse of his king-sized bed. "Where are you, Ray?"

"I'm here."

"We had some good times when we were kids."

I turned out the light and went downstairs and did not see Duggie Plumb again.

21 The wild apple trees are in blossom by the roadsides. Sharon has cut the last of her winter cabbages and is planting leeks and celery and green peppers. Bella comes along behind and puts frost covers on the peppers. She made them out of plastic bags and slivers of bamboo. Bella is good with her hands. She is going to make sandals and belts in the trailer when I'm gone.

Although the sun spreads a watery light in the understoreys of the bush the cold stays on. The bottoms where I pad along will not warm up until high summer. The paths sink spongily and water drips and trickles in banks of moss. I increase the length of my walks gradually. The doctor said not to overdo things. I don't have angina but my blood pressure is up—nothing to worry about, "You're not to worry." I told him I was pretty relaxed these days. Out in the bush, in the huge silence, I hear no voice, no whisper, no R. Sole.

Yesterday I went up to the mine. The tailing mounds are grown with weeds and trees, but they had a roundness, a plumpness, that reminded me of thighs, and that of course made me see the shaft as a vagina. These images come unbidden and I can't see that they're ugly or that I'm to be condemned for them.

But the darkness that surrounds sex in my mind would take some explaining. I remembered Hank and Jilly in the river—how they stood there in the light—and wondered if I was moved by them because they had no guilt. I went into the shaft a little way but the dripping walls and the darkness frightened me, so I came out.

A mile or so on I came to the forks. There was another chance for images but I kept them out. I climbed down to the water and hung my feet in it where it lay motionless in a little cove. I was not alone. What I took at first for a water-logged branch was a black eel lying half out from under a ledge. He was the biggest eel I had ever seen. He had scars on his body and a battered mouth. He took no notice of my feet above him. I left them there out of trust as much as bravado—but pulled them out soon because the cold made them ache.

Sharon had given me a Marmite jar of peanuts and sultanas. I ate them and drank from the river. On the other side the ridge was almost a cliff. Ferns and trees grew in clefts and hollows and supple jack hung like hair from ledge to ledge. I saw a goat picking his way down. He was tan and black and had a yellow beard and yellow eyes. His horns lay like plating on his skull. He came out neatly on the shingle bank. I heard his hooves clicking on the stones. He drank from the river, more easily than I, then stood in the sun, looking up the left fork and the right. Soon five more goats appeared. They climbed down, stopping and start-ing, and joined the old billy on the shingle. He watched them drink. Three were so fat I guessed they must be close to giving birth. When I moved they all jumped back and ran a dozen steps towards the bush. Then they stopped and looked at me. Their yellow eyes watched without curiosity. There seemed to be millions of years between us. They went up through the trees and clefts, jumping nimbly, stopping to look down, and when they were gone the bush went back another million years. It seemed to watch me with an uncaring eye and want all my memories and obsessions out of it. But I said no. I said no. I did not see why I should not stay. I belonged there as much as anything else.

I have given Sharon her Indian letters. She says they're hers and she has the right to burn them if she wants.

"Carlo will be interested one day."

"Not if I can help it." She promised to tear the stamps off the envelopes for him. "When are you going, Dad?"

"Monday. I'll go through the Lewis Pass."

"Are you sure you've got this job?"

"Morrie Horne thinks it will be all right." Morrie is editor of the *Thorpe Evening Star*. He has offered me the job of assistant editor—subject to my "not saying anything bloody stupid in the interview" I'll have to pull my horns in, Morrie says. So I move south, against the population drift. Thorpe is the town where my grandfather fought his religious battles long ago. I don't think it's grown much since his day.

When Sharon had gone I looked in the cigar box to see what was left. Nothing much. Some letters from my mother, some from Glenda, including her note on the morning of the storm, and two from Alaric Gibbs.

Gibbs' second letter came in a packet redirected from my Wadestown address. When I had read it I wondered what I should do. Duggie was a week dead, and Gibbs in hospital dying of his disease—and, I was sure, not saying a word. My duty was to hand the letter over to the police, but I knew at once I would not do that. I could keep it; or burn it and forget it. Once or twice I was tempted to sell it to Jolly John. In the end I decided to do what Gibbs had asked.

I'll put the letter here in the pages of this book, where it can stay until I need it.

Dear Mr Sole,

Further to our conversation, I have decided not to grant Douglas Plumb a reprieve. Nothing he has done since we spoke together has caused me to change my view of him. Once or twice in our talk I was swayed, I have to admit, and as a result I am leaving the completion of my task open to chance in one particular. But it's my belief he'll die. You must not blame yourself. You defended him most ably.

If you have read my memoirs with any care—I'm sorry to have given you that task—you will know that I own a pistol from the war. That is to be the execution weapon. Notice that I don't say murder weapon. Douglas Plumb is tried and found guilty and the penalty is death. I have studied him over a period of twenty-five years and my great achievement in that time is that I have put hatred aside. I will not claim that my act is impersonal. Somebody must pull the lever, pull the trigger, wield the axe. I am not without pride in being the one.

You will no doubt object that I should not be judge and executioner both. But there is no one else. Do you remember "the man who is not himself mean", who is "neither tarnished nor afraid"? I carry out the task he set himself. And nobody else knows the facts of the case. When I die—very soon—they will be lost. That is why I am writing to you. When my daughter passes on make this letter public in some way. Put the record straight. I know you are his cousin. I think you love him, and hate him too. It is more than likely you will hate me. But I ask you to carry out this task in the name of justice.

Let me tell you about my daughter, Jennifer Gibbs. She had no other name, just Jenny, Jennifer. My wife nearly lost her life giving birth and we had no more children after Jenny. She was six when I went to the war and eleven when I came home. The photograph enclosed shows her at fifteen. She was beautiful, you will agree. She was intelligent, she was happy—joyous is the word I often use. She drank up life. You will see there too a spiritual quality. She was pure. I used to think her incorruptible. I understand why Douglas Plumb would not let her be.

I could afford "good" schools for Jenny. They did not spoil her. Such places often teach nasty lessons—they are chock-full of vulgarities and lies, I see that now. But Jenny came out unscathed. She had a simpleness that protected her. She believed in love and with her it was a practical thing. If I can put it so, love was as real to her as a bodily function. I do not mean man/woman love, I mean loving kindness.

I am not sentimentalizing her, Mr Sole. This was *her*. This was Jenny at nineteen, when she met Douglas Plumb. I don't remember how they met. Perhaps it was at the Shelly Beach baths, where she went swimming on Saturday afternoons. In that summer he was with us, suddenly there, about the house. It was Douglas this and Douglas that. He smiled a lot and deferred to me and I thought him a pleasant foolish boy. It was plain to both my wife and me that he was not good enough for Jenny. We admired her spirit in being "in love"—everything that Jenny did was special—but soon it began to worry us. We began to wonder if she might be foolish.

That was the surface of things. In our worst nightmares we could not have seen what was going on. The business was carnal from the first—*the very first day*. I must believe he had watched her for some time, and she watched him, that he made a kind of poisoned air about them. Then he moved at her and she was gone. It must be that. In some way he turned her love against her. I see now she was pure but *corruptible*.

I watched her happiness, I saw in her a kind of nervous wonder. She was open in so many of her ways. I saw her doubts begin. Do you remember the ball? She was never happy again after that night.

Douglas Plumb grew tired of her. I've gone over this with the greatest of care. Perhaps she was tiresome. Perhaps her simplicities got on his nerves. I've weighed up these things—and much more—but I find them wanting in the balance. He destroyed her, either deliberately or out of boredom. Neither way seems worse than the other. It seems likely though that in the end he played a game with her.

I'll put it simply. Douglas Plumb made Jenny practise intimacies that twisted her life upon its base—worse than that— they twisted her in her soul. I won't say what they were. You will find them in all the modern books. It seems they're not horrifying now. He let her think she held him in this way. Pleasure and disgust were bound inextricably in her mind. Then, when he was thoroughly tired of her, Plumb told her that her appetites filled him with disgust. And, to keep it simple, Jenny went mad. He doesn't know that. I've thought I should tell him before he dies but I don't think I'll have time.

222

My daughter is in Carrington hospital. She was forty-six in January. I took her a bar of chocolate but she doesn't see out any more, she just sees in—we suppose she sees in—and I let another patient snatch it from me. She went inside in 1955 and she's never been out. They have given her all the treatments available. Nothing works. For some years she was aware of me and my wife but she did not seem to notice when Milly died. She doesn't see me any more, though I sit in front of her and say—this and that. I've tried saying Douglas Plumb but she doesn't hear. She's a woman with a smooth face and grey hair cut like a boy's. When they touch her on the shoulder she stands up. She walks when they give her a push. They turn her at the corners. *Where is she? Where has she gone?* I sometimes think that deep inside her head she's curled up tightly. She's warm in there, she's happy and smiles at herself. But perhaps she's screaming. That's a possibility, isn't it?

I don't believe I'll meet her when I die. Or my wife. It's not that I disbelieve in God. I have no belief one way or the other. It's possible He exists, but if He does then He's contemptible. He deserves Douglas Plumb.

There's not a great deal more I need to say. You need not worry about being implicated. I have destroyed everything that might lead the police to you. I've burned the scrapbooks. There is nothing to show I'm not a mad old man who hates the Minister of Police. I suppose someone will find out I had a daughter. They might even remember that she knew Douglas Plumb. But *she'll* say nothing. And I'll say nothing. All I have to say I've said in this letter. It's a matter of propriety not to have it known until Jenny dies—although she's dead. Please let no one see it till that time.

I will die in hospital not in prison, and die soon. I have cancer—riddled with it, as they say. It's beside the point although it determines the time of Douglas Plumb's death. I have waited until the last moment so that I can keep on seeing Jenny. Now I can go no more. The doctors have given me up and put me on cortisone, which makes me eat like a horse and makes me fat. It will be effective for a short time, then the end will come. So I must go tomorrow. I telephoned his house a while ago—I have his unlisted number, I have everything. I heard him say Douglas Plumb before I put the phone down. With any luck he'll be home tomorrow.

I'll end this now and post it in the box on the corner. Then I'll have a good night's sleep and take a taxi round there in the morning.

I'm doing right. I hope that you'll agree. He deserves to die. There's just a chance I've overstepped the bounds. But if it's not my part to judge him then whose is it? I know the answer most people will give, and I don't believe it. I'm prepared to give him a chance though. I haven't fired the pistol since I bought it in Italy. The Canadian I got it from said it was in good condition. That was thirty-five years ago. I've kept the parts oiled but I haven't tested it. Tomorrow I'll point it at him and pull the trigger. I'm reasonably certain it will go off.

Yours sincerely,
Alaric Gibbs

He pulled the trigger and the gun went off. Those large bullets make a nasty hole. Duggie was thrown back into the umbrella stand in the hall. He lay there dying. Alaric Gibbs put the pistol on the doormat. He had not mentioned Sally in his letter and I think perhaps he had forgotten about her. She came running from the lounge and screamed when she saw Duggie, then tried to stop his bleeding with her hands. Gibbs walked down the path and sat on the garden wall waiting for the police. He said to one of the neighbours, "I'm sorry about his wife." He said nothing after that. Everything went much as he had expected.

22 The forks are the limit of my travels. Strictly speaking it's a confluence. Two rivers, creeks, rattle from their gorges and make one. I don't know which is the tributary and which the main river. After rain one may flow darker

than the other. I have seen the left creek black with silt while the other runs clear as lemonade.

I sit on my rock munching peanuts. I have not seen the eel again but the old billy goat comes daily and looks at me. I wonder if he was tame once. Where are his wives drinking? Sometimes I think I smell him—a smell of age and nature—but it's probably my imagination. I smell the river: eels and scouring and decomposition. It smells clean.

There are mysteries. There are connections I cannot make. For half of Duggie's life Alaric Gibbs was ticking like a bomb. And Gibbs' life? Each was the centre of a universe.

Today I heard the rainbird—that urgent little song. It's beautifully exact. There's a knowledge there millions of years old. Before long rain hung in the gorges. The sun made a piece of rainbow in the curve of cliff down-river from me. Here is a place human will does not contaminate. I am gone from it but it's there, lying in the night. I can't imagine it. Imagination cannot touch it either.

I walked home in the rain—heavy rain rattling through the leaves and on my parka. I looked up and saw blue sky. And when I came out by the garden the clouds were black on the mountains and the sky was clear. The raked earth began to steam.

Sharon called me into the house and made me a cup of tea. She scolded me for getting wet. I must look after myself, she said, I'm not a boy any longer. I don't feel like a boy, but I don't feel like a man with high blood pressure either. I feel like a survivor. I feel like Ray, Ray Sole, Raymong, R. Sole. All of those. I've got some life in me. That's what I think. So I'll get to sleep, and in the morning put my things in the car and head for Thorpe.

Through the bush I hear Bella singing. Sharon plays her flute, an ancient sound, but a sound contrived. Carlo and Ché are yelling on the paths. Their mothers let them make their own bed-time. It's part of their programme in being free. I hope things work out for Sharon here.

Tomorrow I'll kiss her goodbye. And offer a man's handshake to her friend. And to Ché. And kiss my Indian grandson if he'll let me. Then I'll go. Get on with it.

225

BLINDSIGHT

Maurice Gee

Blindsight is the story of a good though damaged man and his less than virtuous sister. As their childhood closeness unravels, Alice moves into her career in science (she's a mycologist), while Gordon descends into vagrancy and silence. For more than thirty years they do not meet. Then a young man appears at Alice's door, claiming a relationship she never knew she had. As he becomes part of her carefully guarded world, she cautiously begins to reveal the past. But is she telling him everything?

Jealousy, ambition and love shape the fates of Alice and Gordon in this compelling story of loyalty and family ties.

THE SCORNFUL MOON

Maurice Gee

'Suffice to say that this is vintage Gee.'

Gavin McLean, *Otago Daily Times*

'As you'd expect from our finest novelist, the story-telling and characterisation . . . are superb.'

John McCrystal, *North and South*

'A tense, entertaining and well-plotted crime story. What elevates his work, however, is his genre-bending approach to writing . . . Gee is particularly skilled in peppering his prose with psychological insight and chillingly astute observations of human behaviour.'

Scotland on Sunday

Wellington, 1935. James Tinling, a former Cabinet Minister, plans a political comeback, although a brash newcomer stands in his way. James has methods of dealing with upstarts, but is handicapped by secrets in his life. Eric Clifton, world-renowned moon scientist, has secrets too. He lives hot-bloodedly and is at war with the patrician James.

Sam Holloway, literary man and moralist, records their year – its sexual intrigues and sudden violence and its overturning of political norms.

Election day. Labour wins, crushing James's party. His secrets are shockingly revealed.

SALT

Maurice Gee

Deep Salt strikes terror in the heart.

Hari lives in Blood Burrow, deep in the ruined city of Belong, where he survives by courage and savagery. He is scarred from fighting, but he has a secret gift: he can speak with animals.

Pearl is from Company, the ruling families, which has conquered and enslaved Hari's people. Pampered and beautiful, she is destined for a marriage that will unite her family with that of the powerful and ambitious Ottmar. But Pearl has learned forbidden things from Tealeaf, her maid, and so the two must run.

Hari and Pearl forge an unusual alliance and become reluctant travelling companions. As the two come to grips with their strengthening powers, their quest evolves into a desperate pilgrimage to save the world from a terror beyond their greatest imaginings.